Book of Josiah: A Novel of the Apocalypse

Book of Josiah: A Novel of the Apocalypse

Richard Law

Fine Tooth Press

This is a work of fiction. Names, characters, places, and incidents either are the product of the author's imagination or are used fictitiously. Any resemblence to actual events, locales, organizations, or persons, living or dead, is entirely coincidental and beyond the intent of either the author or the publisher.

© 2008 by Richard Law. All rights reserved.

No part of this book may be reproduced, stored in a retrieval system, or transmitted by any means, electronic or otherwise, without written permission from the author except in the case of brief quotations embodied in critical articles and reviews. For information address Fine Tooth Press, PO Box 11512, Waterbury, CT 06703.

First Trade Paperback edition published 2008.

ISBN 10: 0-9794770-7-7
ISBN 13: 978-0-9794770-7-2

Library of Congress Catalog Card Number: 2008934952

Cover art © 2008 Weatherstock. Used by Permission. All Rights Reserved.

Author photo © 2008 by Richard Law. Used by Permission. All rights reserved.

Additional Editing and Design by JJ Sargent

This book is printed on acid-free paper.

This has been a bit of a long, hard slog. A small group of close friends and family have loyally supported me at every step of the way, reading and commenting on the manuscript, providing insights and encouragement and sound advice, and expressing their love and good will in a thousand ways. Without them, there would have been no more than a few notes and scribbles and a frustrated dream. I am wholly certain, moreover, that these kind and generous people will understand why this book must be dedicated to my brother Larry, who was, for so many years and so vitally, a figure in the front row of my imagined audience. He still is.

THIS BOOK IS DEDICATED

TO

LARRY L. LAW

November 23, 1939—May 27, 2007

The Third Coming

"In Ancient days," the priest declared, "the Lamb returned in glory and gathered the faithful into His Kingdom. On Judgment Day, the Son of Man and His Angels had combat with the Prince of Evil here, *on this very spot. I saw an angel, ascending from the east, having the seal of the living God; and he cried with a loud voice to the four angels, to whom it was given to hurt the earth and the sea, saying, Hurt not the earth, neither the sea, nor the trees, till we have sealed the servants of our God in their foreheads. And He split the earth and imprisoned the great dragon, Beli-az, in the Bottomless Pit beneath—beneath us here, in this very place."*

"The evil-doers," he continued fiercely, "were dealt with on the Day of Wrath. The Lamb gathered them here in the Desolation—you can see it across the Jordan yonder, in daylight, from where we sit. There the wicked were utterly destroyed in a great cataclysm, the effects of which are still plain to behold."

"After gathering the faithful into Paradise, the Lamb turned His face away from the earth. The land and rivers and oceans, all originally created clean and wholesome for man's use, He cursed eternally because of the evil that men had done. He cursed the earth and the sea and the trees and the rivers forever more."

No one stirred. The effects of the conflagration were only too visible around them.

"With the faithful in Paradise and the evil-doers destroyed, there was left on Earth only a pitiful remnant of the Unsealed: those who were neither good nor evil—those who, because they did not choose, were not chosen! Their destiny was to survive and replenish themselves endlessly—to endure miserably among the ruins of creation. Here!" the priest exclaimed, in a voice suddenly powerful, "in the midst of the Desolation. Abandoned by the Creator, living in a world ruined and accursed, we thus play out our desperate lives after the end of time!"

"Amen," the pilgrims cried in unison. "Amen!"

"What remains for us?" the old man demanded, taking up a handful of soil. "What shall be our daily bread? What shall sustain us who live on after Judgment Day? Shall we merely survive?" he demanded, opening his hand. "Shall we live on merely as a handful of dust? Or shall we preserve our deathless hope?"

" Come, Lord Jesus!" he cried, his voice a fiery spark whirling upwards in the darkness. "Come quickly again! And put your foot on the neck of your enemies!"

The Millennial War Begins

"Surely, Excellency, it was God's grace that permitted my undeserving self to survive as witness to the terrible events of May 20th. Be not deceived, your worship, to think that the malice of the infidels awaited their Declaration of Grievances. No, be assured rather that on the night previous, they sent an armed intruder, an assassin of uncanny skill and cunning, into the very citadel of Esdralon, to strike the first treacherous blow at our clergy, aiming, as the evidence clearly shows, at your worship's life. It was your door that the assassin targeted first, finding instead—thanks be to God—our colleague Brother Benedict and the novice Amarante, whose cries roused the others in the dormer, including myself.

"Likewise, it was my good fortune, and the hand of a watchful God, that led me to step into the hall, roused from sleep as I prepared for the nocturnal vigil. By chance, then, I stumbled in the darkness upon the body of our elderly Brother Barnabas, the pain of whose urethral plug and the incontinence of age had driven from his bed for the relief of nature. Brother Barnabas, I am convinced, was by this accident the first victim of the assassin, and he died of a single blow of a sword. Finding him thus, sundered almost in two, I had meant to flee downstairs, to alert the Tabernacle Guard, but tripped, as I say, on Brother his body. I thus lay motionless in the shadows as the intruder dashed past me and entered the dormer. So close was I that I heard the torturer's labored breath and the rustle of his clothing.

"In a moment, eleven of our Order died, pitilessly slain by this monster out of the darkness. I heard their cries for help. I testify that Brother Gaspar recited the prayer for elevation in a strong, undaunted voice, though cut off in mid-phrase. In the silence that followed, I regained my wits and bolted downstairs. Alerted by the sounds of distress and tumult, two of the Tabernacle guards met me on the stairs as they hurried to our aid. I hastened on to inform the Captain of the Guard, while these two rushed upstairs to what I must conjecture were their instant deaths. I cannot speak as a witness of their fates, though I heard their cries. I saw, shortly after, a troop of guards charge up the stairs. Their fates, too, one may surmise from the general disaster, but I saw with my own eyes the flammables stored on the floor above our quarters—barrels of pitch and turpentine and sulfur—come tumbling down the stairs, and afterwards a great explosion and fire that wreaked havoc throughout the Citadel.

"I made my way out of the inferno blindly, led by a Divine hand to a breach in the wall left from the siege, and to the workmen's scaffolding beyond it. I clambered down and escaped, using for exit what must surely have been the assassin's mode of entry into our midst, and who had by this means escaped the notice of the guards outside. I found the Citadel in flames, and the city roused against us. I made my way to the Jordan and stole a boat, happy to make an escape from this unprovoked slaughter. And thus I only am escaped alone to tell you."

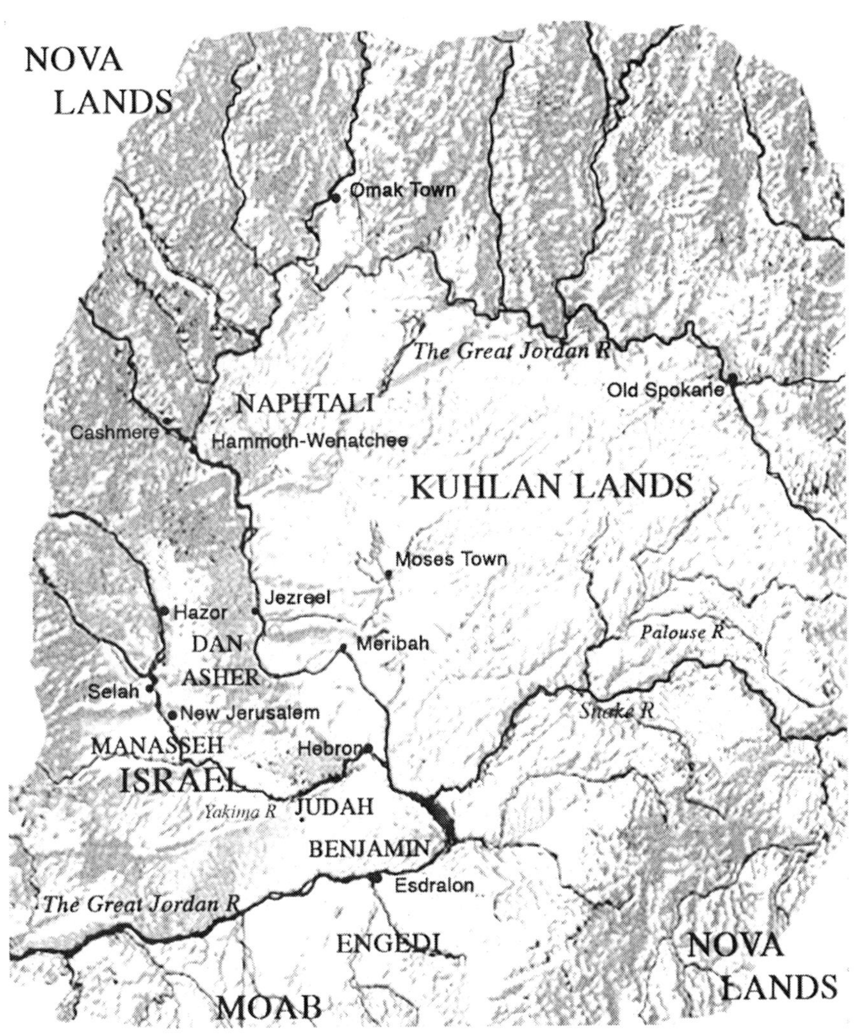
NOVA
LANDS
Omak Town
The Great Jordan R
Old Spokane
NAPHTALI
Cashmere
Hammoth-Wenatchee
KUHLAN LANDS
Moses Town
Jezreel
Hazor
DAN
Meribah
Palouse R
ASHER
Selah
New Jerusalem
Snake R
MANASSEH
Hebron
ISRAEL
Yakima R
JUDAH
BENJAMIN
Esdralon
The Great Jordan R
ENGEDI
NOVA
LANDS
MOAB

Book One:
Wars and Rumors of Wars

Chapter 1: Esdralon

I

There is a jest in Israel that goes, *"How does Tephlin Glanz buy and sell the Apostles?"* The answer is: *"By the dozen."*

Another jest – for Israel is nothing if not famous for its humor – claims that there are three things that Tephlin Glanz does not know: the sum of his wealth, the names of the women he has taken, and the number of his enemies. I maintain, however, that there are three things further that Tephlin Glanz does not know and that his spies cannot tell him: the heart of his first son, Hanford, and that of his second, Justin, and least of all my own. I am Josiah Glanz ben Haggadah, the third acknowledged son of Tephlin Glanz.

Of my eldest brother, Hanford, it is said that he is the child of Glanz's youth, which was brutal and reckless, Hanford's character bears the stamp of it. His mother was a Shimeah, daughter of the great merchant family of Judah, and upon her dowry Tephlin Glanz is said to have built his own vast fortune.

Justin Glanz Apollo, the next eldest, and born of Glanz's second wife, is on the public tongue the seed of Tephlin Glanz's only redeeming quality. Though a woman of obscure family, Justin's mother was a famous beauty. To those willing to condone sexual excess as a natural passion, Justin is the child of Glanz's single human trait. A hint of scandal still attends the death of this second wife, Adrianne Apollo. Whether she took her own life or, as rumor persists, was murdered by our father in a fit of jealous rage, I cannot tell, these events having transpired before my birth. In any case, my brother Justin Apollo, tragically brave and handsome and inastute, as my story shall show, also wears the mark of his conception.

Of my own birth, I know that six years after the death of his second wife, Tephlin Glanz came north to Selah and New Jerusalem. And there, among the impoverished salt-land barons of Asher, he found a third bride – this one of noble birth: my mother. How a match came to be made, I cannot imagine. But it came about that my mother Rachel, a woman of sense and full of spirit, as befits a daughter of the Haggadah, was wed to Tephlin Glanz, reputedly the richest and most detested man in the nation. Born of no distinguished lineage, Glanz could not even aspire to be a Name in Israel. Indeed, as my great uncle, Brandon ben Elath, once remarked of him: Glanz had, by marrying a daughter of Asher, hoped to purchase himself noble ancestors.

A brief and most unhappy union it must have been, though a son was born of it. I try to picture her as she was then: beautiful and headstrong and still expecting much of the world – but, mercifully, knowing little of it. I saw her last in my seventh year, and every year that passes leaves her features a little dimmer. Difficult as it is to retain the image I carry of her, carry it I still do.

Through me, perhaps it could be said, Tephlin Glanz purchased an option on the future. I am, on my mother's side, of Apostle's blood and therefore eligible to hold the Office outright, as blood rights descend in Israel through the mother.

As for myself – concerning the common report of me – I remain for the most part mercifully ignorant, for Israel is a nation of judges. Except for this dubious heritage, I am as yet unknown to my countrymen. Moreover, still untried in this, my twentieth year, I am as yet unknown to myself. Whether I shall prove the son of Tephlin Glanz's disillusioned middle age and unbridled ambition or of my mother's disgrace remains to be told.

Of my earliest life, I possess only a few images—objects preserved in memory like strange creatures trapped in ice. My grandfather had flocks and herds and lived in the old manner, as patriarchs of our family have always lived. Tirzah, our family seat, was ruled by the daily round of chores and the turning of the seasons, as it had been from time out of memory. I recall most vividly the seasonal festivals – the Feast of the In-Gathering in late summer and the Festival of the Three Kings in the mid-winter darkness, when we received gifts and all the servants came to the great house to pay Grandfather reverence. On such occasions, the women raised up their infants for his blessing and the men touched their foreheads to the back of his hand. I remember my terror at one such event, standing beneath my grandfather's gaze after some act of disobedience on my part. I hear my grandfather saying sternly, "Learn the Law and obey it." But I see now that his was a threadbare, down-at-heel grandeur. The Haggadah had had a proud history, but our recent past was an isolated rural life in which money played little part.

Tirzah, stronghold of the Haggadah, was a rambling stone structure with an ancient tower, surrounded by outbuildings and enclosed within a low wall. My first pony, a pinto gelding, threw me in front of the stable door at the feet of my grandfather's gigantic red-haired slave, Lukash. I lit on my head on the hard-packed earth, and for a few days my life was despaired of. But weeks later, I was spurring after Grandfather as he inspected his prized herds of sheep and horses under the holy mountain Rainier. Though I was oblivious as only a landed heir can be, changes in my life were already in motion. That summer Rainier emitted a plume of smoke, which impressed everyone as a fearful omen. On the same day, as we were clearing a spring in the remotest sheep pasture, my uncle and I came upon a death fetish of the forest people. I remember the tiny black infant's hand and the snakeskin, the sight of which plunged my heart into ice water. Soon after, I came down with the mountain fever, and I was given up as lost because I had seen the fetish.

But it is a winter's eve that most teases my recollection. There must have been a storm, with sleet pelting against the roof tiles and bolted shutters, since only in the worst weather did the children of my grandfather's household spend willing time in-doors. I sit at my grandmother's knee, bored and out of sorts, watching her shell beans. If the wind was howling in the eves, as seems likely, my memory has retained no whisper of it. Yet the scene has a vividness now that transcends my memory of my sensations within it. Something else is preserved in it that I cannot quite recall. My mother sits nearby emanating a warmth and aroma in which, in a sense, I still bask. The two women are talking in low voices, but the words are indistinct, uninteresting to the child. I gaze at the cloth that my mother is weaving, but in the moment my memory has preserved, my mother does not work the loom. As I watch, her fingers intertwine and clench. Her eyes are downcast, and I see tears in her dark lashes. She shakes her head in response to something my grandmother has said. "No," she says firmly and repeatedly. *"Never!"*

My mother's presence pervades all these early scenes, but to my child's mind, she seems hardly separate from myself, so I am seldom able to see her clearly. What I recall most vividly from my childhood—what still burns like a live coal in my brain—is her absence. One moment she was the center and circumference of my world, and then she was gone. The day I stumbled upon the fetish of the forest people, she disappeared from my life. "Your mother is dead," my uncle said. "Say nothing, and bear yourself like a Haggadah." Like smoke into a clear sky she vanished utterly.

Yet sometimes, it seems that I hear her voice singing to me in my delirium, at what must have been the crisis of the mountain fever:

O come, o come, Emanuel
And ransom captive Israel,
That mourns in lonely exile
Here until the Son of God appear.
Rejoice! Rejoice!
Emanuel shall come to thee,
O Israel.

But this cannot be, as my illness followed hard upon my mother's disappearance. It is said that one imagines much in a high fever, and yet the imprint of this false memory is greater than that of many true ones. But whether true or imagined, this memory of my mother's lullaby remains infinitely comforting to me.

After I had recovered from the fever, I was taken, still in my seventh year, to the Wayfarers Refuge of the Old Believers, the seat of the Brothers of St. Supplicee in the wilderness of Zoar. There I received my education. In my twelfth year, I returned home for my confirmation rites and to attend my grandfather's funeral. This event, which was my last visit to Tirzah, also nags at me for the memory it holds. Our domestic servant, Abigail, who had been kind to me as a child, and kinder still after the loss of my mother, approached me before the rites and placed the shawl of consecration in my hands. "Treasure this," she whispered, and I saw immediately that the cloth, my shawl of Haggadah colors, was the same cloth *she* had been weaving. *My mother!* I beheld her soft, graceful hands before me, and my heart leapt and melted in that same instant. *She lives*, I thought, and tears, the first tears I had shed since early boyhood, coursed down my cheeks.

"She is dead," Abigail explained in a low voice, "and you must think of her as dead. But the cloth is from her hand and loom, just as the labor is from her heart. I saved it out for you and kept it these many years."

So I knew for the first time, though in a boy's way, what had happened. Israel is very strict about the marriage bond, even in a vile, unsuitable marriage such as my mother had had to endure. And I knew that whatever else she had been guilty of, she had finished weaving the shawl for my confirmation.

When I returned to the Refuge, Brother Josephus saw my distress and said quietly, "I will tell you what I know." In this way, I came into knowledge of my inheritance. But with this shameful legacy, I also possessed one precious piece of knowledge: she *lived.* My mother Rachel remained alive in my heart for she had lived *for* me! And that knowledge glowed like a beacon fire in the lonely, shapeless period after my childhood. Whatever happened, wherever I went, or whomever I was thrown among, I was not utterly alone. And though less than an orphan in the eyes of many, I knew I was not quite orphan either. *She lives!* And that knowledge burned in me, and still burns in me. Even though I may go for days without thinking of her, this knowledge lies near the center of my being. Yet again, at other times, the thought of her disgrace comes like a sudden sword thrust through my heart and I gasp for breath.

II

As selfhood is the first illusion, so it is the last burden. So we are taught concerning the mystery of being, and so my own experience thus far confirms. Experience, our Teacher says, presents us with a show of shapes and light and shadows that play upon our senses, forming patterns that never quite complete themselves in our vision. How then, with my life's tapestry barely begun, can I hope to trace its threads? For I do not mean to speak of past bitterness, but of beginnings. On the day of which I speak, my life as a man began.

Thus far in my life, I had played only apprentice roles, practice for that which was to come. One long apprenticeship I served in my years at the Wayfarers Refuge, acquiring there an education like no other in Israel. I served a second in St. Anthony's Academy, the seedbed of Israel's officer corps, that ended when I was nineteen in disappointment and disgrace. A third apprenticeship, of four months duration, I had just spent in the winter campaign of the present war, serving as an uncommissioned aide to General Abner Mac Dogol of the Second Apostles Legion. This was my introduction to war – which, I confess, I preferred to my time at the Academy. At twenty, I longed to be free of all such apprenticeships and to draw breath and to act as a man.

I count myself a man, however, not from my last miserable day at the Academy nor from my first taste of battle, but from the moment I found myself, at last, an officer of the Army of Israel. On the dawn of March 4, in the nine hundred ninety-seventh year of the World's Third Tribulation, I was commissioned under-lieutenant. And with my commission, I began to see a future take shape before me. At last a new life seemed to be dawning. It would serve my purpose now to act my part well, whatever part was allotted, and await what came to pass.

Daybreak, 5 March 997-III: I paced the landing under the walls of the fortress Techsaymun, the citadel of Hebron, full of the knowledge that my life was bursting from its chrysalis. Fires burned on the docks. A raw wind blew out of the west, sending smoke and sparks in every direction. I chafed at the delay, knowing we must wait until the weather abated. *The young man hates nothing more than necessity*, St. Supplicee says. As a passenger in a convoy to the fighting fronts, I had no duties, no role to perform. I waited, stamping my feet to keep circulation alive, and watched the sailors fuss with the cargo and re-tie the wrappings, securing and rechecking every piece of rigging, every knot, every item of gear.

As a desert-bred northerner, I had never seen the Great Jordan, let alone set foot in a sailing craft. Still, I knew that the winter passage from the Yakima into the Jordan is difficult. The mouth, sailors say, is full of sandbars, snags, and treacherous currents, and the superstitious claim that Beli-az lurks in the depths there. I felt no anxiety, no dread of death, but rather a burning to get on.

Cleave the wood, break the stone; I am there.
Seek me in the heart of the flame.

A novice in the disciplines, I was unable to rise above my senses. Instead, I could only feign composure and allow my consciousness to flow out into the very edges of my being, into my chapped hands and skin, and into the wind-driven moisture in my eyes. As the drizzle turned to sleet, I felt the lash of the cold across my cheeks – all at that moment were delicious sensations to me, to be savored and remembered.

"Come," the Captain said at last, motioning to me. "We'll take the wind as it is." He had seven cargo vessels and three fast patrol boats in his command, the latter the sleek, sixteen-oared water striders that protect Israel's borders. The Captain invited me into the first boat, his own, which would lead the convoy down the channel. We donned the waterproof oilcloth of those who sail the Jordan, and the Captain performed the ceremony of purification. As we descended the river, I was strangely content, pleased merely to be in motion and warm enough that the cold on my face seemed a delight.

As we approached the channels of the mouth, the captain perched in the bow with a mate on either side of him, probing the river with long poles. By hand signals, he communicated adjustments in our course to the sailor at the tiller. The river was running with some force with the winter melt, and our captain took care to seek out the safest possible route through the ever-shifting sand and currents. The trick of navigating the passage was to find a true channel and avoid running upon a gravel bar.

We were making excellent time and approaching the junction when a murmur ran through the boat. Ahead, just where the channel opened up, was a low-lying bank of fog opaque as a wall. In a moment we slipped into it, and our boat was instantly isolated from the others – and seemingly from all else. It was my first such experience in a moving vessel, and I felt a moment of stomach-churning vertigo. Our captain and the mate remained poised at the bow, leaning intently into their poles and seeming to feel our way forward. Suddenly the captain barked a sharp command to back oars. "Back oars!" the sailor at the tiller repeated, shouting over his shoulder – mindful, as I suddenly was, of the loaded cargo vessel behind us.

We continued to move with the current, enveloped in fog. Then, as if in a dream, ahead and to the right, the mist thinned, distilled itself into form, and a dark silhouette emerged, balancing on thin legs above the water. "Hard left," I shouted, as if awakened from a doze. The captain's voice boomed almost simultaneously: "Hard a-port! Back oars!"

"Hard a-port; back oars!" the vessels behind us echoed in order, the sound diminishing swiftly behind us.

The bird had revealed, almost too late, the presence of a bar. As we passed by, breathing deeply, the fog seemed to dissolve in the morning light, and the thin silhouette took on color and substance. The heron regarded us serenely for a moment, and just as we came abreast, it stretched its wings and gracefully lifted itself with sure, strong wing beats into the air.

I clasped my right hand over my heart, accepting the omen. I do not believe in omens ordinarily. But there are, I believe, true ones. The presence of this noble bird had saved us from running blindly upon the bar, perhaps fatally. I decided at that moment that, should I ever achieve fame or significance in Israel, the great blue heron should be my emblem: the body of the great bird mounting upward, wings just opening for flight.

Israel has the custom of scattering the ashes of its dead at the junction where the River of Life, our Mother Yakima, unites with the Great Jordan, River of Death, whose waters are forever unclean. The merging of the two at the mouth of the Yakima is one of the holiest sites in Israel, and we paused, as customary, to contemplate the mystery of that conjunction. Perhaps mistaking me for a Devotee, the captain asked me to perform the rites. I took up the urns in turn, spoke the words of the requiem, which I had by heart and which anyone may properly speak, and then scattered the ashes on the water. The crew rested quietly on their oars, and our tight cluster of crafts floated lightly as feathers:

Let the remnants of these lives return
unto the source of all things, stream
without beginning, ocean without a shore.

Thus, we committed our fellow beings to the restless depths and darkness from which we all emerge. After a silence, the captain gave the order to proceed. The river was vast as an empty sea and the farther shore only a dark line on the horizon. We dipped our oars into unfathomable depths, and the force of a great invisible current bore us onward.

At noon the convoy split up, four of the cargo vessels and two of the water striders entering the mouth of the Snake to carry supplies for our army fighting in the east. The other three vessels stayed on course with us, bound for Engedi. By late afternoon, we hauled in sight of the white towers of Ziklag, the only surviving Israelite settlement on the east, or Kuhlan, side of the Jordan. The fortress had been captured early in the war, by surprise, and so had suffered little damage. We tied up to its moorings and found quarters for the night. The Israelite garrison was from Gad, Home Guards longing for their bare tribal hills. Looking for any excuse for a carouse, they made a night of it with our crews. I slept little, but being young, awoke fresh and eager to get on.

That day, we sailed through the Walula gorge, where the Jordan makes its great bend toward the west. Dark channeled cliffs towered above us, where gulls circled and made shrill cries. The canyon rim was honeycombed with the tombs of the Governors, the entrances to which we could sometimes glimpse from below. I expressed an interest in examining them, but the captain replied that he had climbed the cliffs with the same motive and had been disappointed. The tombs had been desecrated ages ago, he said; the inscriptions were defaced or chipped away. I thought of the great power and wisdom that the Governors had once possessed, and my heart sank a little. I watched the gulls sweep low overhead and saw a feather on the water.

After we made the great westward bend in the Jordan, the wind began to blow in our faces. The water grew choppy and then bucked like a horse. I was astonished that the crew took no precautions to avoid contact with the water. “If you sail the Jordan,” one of the sailors taunted me, “you touch the Jordan. Death can jump up and smack you in the face, so get used to it.” Soon I, too, began to be drenched by the white-capped waves that splashed over our hull. I began to feel sick and then I was sick. Leaning toward the hull in order to vomit discretely overboard, I was smashed full in the face by an icy wave. I spewed on my clothes, and, immediately after, another violent lurch of the boat rammed my face into the hull.

In the midst of my own misery, I heard one of the crew cry out in terror: “Lord, preserve me from the belly of Beli-az! Let me not drown in these unclean waters!” We Old Believers do not share the Messiahists’ superstitious dread of death, only the animal fear that is instinct in all of us. Nevertheless, I almost envied him his faith, if only for the outcry it permitted. But the Way does not alter for us. Chance and law rule, indifferent to our beseeching. For myself, I lay wet and miserable in the bottom of the boat, encompassed in the sour smell of my own stomach.

After an hour, the wind abated, and I was able to shake off the worst of my nausea. The consequences of the contamination, however, were better not to think of. We made the portage in late afternoon, and as another rain squall had come up, we decided to seek shelter, and make the portage to the lower reach in the morning. I never performed the purification rites with better heart. Thus, it was noon of the third day before we hauled into the great port of Esdralon.

III

There was a mystery about my orders, in that I had both an official and a covert assignment. Publicly, I was assigned to the Commissary, the branch that tended to all mundane but essential tasks of the army. In that role, I reported to a Major Israel Cohn-el, a Reubenite and Quartermaster of the Third Army, and it was understood that I was vaguely at the disposal of General of the Host Solomon Boseth of Simeon, commander of the Third Army. I resigned myself – for the time being, at least – to a support rather than line position. I was curious to learn whatever there was to know about supplying an army. I had spent the winter campaigning and had had my fill of fighting. I welcomed a time to rest and recover harmony, for I was no zealot against Benjamin. As a son of the Haggadah, I might have considered such an assignment demeaning, but Israel does not recognize the old warrior castes anymore – officially, at least.

Unofficially, I was also assigned to the Eyes of Israel, the intelligence arm of the service. About the latter, I knew little except that the Eyes are dreaded in many quarters. Mind war is central to Israel's military doctrine, though deception seems at times more a national obsession than a strategy. However, I attributed my assignment to my high marks at the Academy and assumed that my role would involve interpreting information rather than secret missions and intrigues. Oddly, I had been given no briefing on this part of my assignment – no instructions at all – and was assigned no superior to whom I was to report.

On the fourth day of March, during the middle of the night, I had been summoned without explanation to the Palace of Ingots, where I was handed sealed orders by General Simon ben Gurion, after which he casually pinned my under-lieutenant's silver bar on the breast of my tunic.

"That should do it," he said in a disinterested way.

The Palace of Ingots was the unofficial residence of Tephlin Glanz, and I had thought the summons I received had been from my father himself. "Is this all?" I heard myself asking, looking around the room. Ben Gurion's quarters were simply furnished: a soldier's cot, a desk and table, and two chairs. The room was bare of decoration except for a painted screen that divided and hid one portion of the room. There were no windows and only one visible entrance, and the room smelled overpoweringly of the oil lamps that illuminated it almost as bright as day. It occurred to me that in this chamber one could easily forget whether it was day or night, winter or summer.

"All?" Ben Gurion asked. "You have not even looked at your orders. Your commission is contained there. It's all quite official," he added, as if I might be inclined to regard it as bogus.

"I had thought – I had expected a message or an interview. With my father," I was bold enough to add.

"Another time, perhaps." Ben Gurion showed me out without either discourtesy or a hint of kindly interest.

A mysterious business indeed, had I chosen to look at it. But for all I knew, this was routine procedure. One of the most powerful men in Israel, Simon ben Gurion was legendary both for his keen mind and absence of human qualities. Had I been wiser, I would have shrunk from this contact with him. One of the most powerful men in Israel, Ben Gurion was nearly as feared as my father, and for good reason. Yet in my ignorance, I flattered myself that this assignment and my new rank were designed for some good purpose – and betokened higher and more demanding offices to come.

I was given lodging in a barracks converted from a warehouse near the harbor, a small, cell-like room not unlike my quarters at the Refuge and the Academy. I was soon settled in, and my living space soon became familiar and thus invisible. Headquarters, where I worked, was located in what had been the Hall of Government, favorably situated on the bench above the Jordan and only a short walk from the citadel. Our building was fashioned of hewn stone, three stories in height, with an open portico on the second floor. The Commissary Office occupied the second floor, Army Headquarters the top. A few steps from my worktable, I had an unobstructed view of the Jordan and the brown hills of Judah beyond.

The Commissary was staffed by young men of the merchant families; there were no Israelite Names among them. They were aloof at first, but respectful – or wary – of the name I carried. But I had not expected to be embraced by them. After overhearing a remark, I took myself to the barber and had my hair and beard trimmed in the latest fashion, and I bought myself a new uniform. Fairly soon, however, I was largely ignored, and my comrades ceased to fall silent when I approached. As I was attentive to business, I gradually became accepted, as a new piece of furniture is accepted. And through my assignments, I began to assemble some notion of the scale of the army's operations.

Regarding my intelligence role, I assumed that I was to keep my eyes and ears open and gain an overview of the war. This was, I inferred, yet another apprentice task, and more challenging ones would follow once I had proven more than a fool.

Fresh as I was from my studies, I was eager to examine the war and everything pertaining to Benjamin and the power and wealth of our enemies. Above all, I determined to be alert to the implications of my work. Israel's greatest success had come early in the war, here on the plain of Engedi. Since the capture of the fortress city of Esdralon in October, most of Israel's forces had been re-deployed, many dispatched eastward up the Snake River to strengthen the expedition under Admiral Montevideo. I wanted to understand it all and reconstruct it in my mind. At Headquarters I found maps and geographies and some of the older and more reliable chronicles. So with these and my own meager resources, I began my study, jotting down notes in a leather-bound journal that I kept in my quarters. Gradually these notes turned into sentences and paragraphs as I grappled with my elusive subject. Much of the city archives was still intact, and I petitioned General Boseth to grant me access to them. His Chief of Staff informed me that His Excellency had referred the matter to the Messiahist clergy who advised him. I found this highly irregular, even alarming, but I counseled myself to have patience and kept silent. Fed by the approach of the millennium, Messiahist superstition was burgeoning everywhere. While I waited for General Boseth's consent, however, there were a dozen things to occupy my time and satisfy my curiosity. There were veterans of the siege to talk to, and the countryside as well as the conquered city to explore.

Above all, I was eager to seek out my famous half-brother, Justin Glanz Apollo. Though only a captain of engineers, Justin Apollo had distinguished himself at the siege of Esdralon and played an important role in its capture. Unfortunately, he had been wounded severely in the final assault. Hearing that he was recuperating in Judah, I had called at his estate outside Hebron in February, intending to pay my respects. But he had, his wife informed me rather abruptly, already returned to the army. Arriving at Esdralon, my first inquiries confirmed Major Apollo's re-assignment to Engedi, also on the staff of General Boseth. In the interim, my brother had been promoted brevet major. By all accounts, he had become an icon among Israel's younger officers; his style of dress and even his manner of speaking were widely imitated. While on leave, I had heard his praises sung, quite literally, by the ballad singers in Hebron.

Naturally, I was eager to make his acquaintance. I felt a mixture of pleasure at my brother's fame and astonishment that he enjoyed such a reputation. A son of Tephlin Glanz and, on his mother's side, a descendant of merchants, a hero of Israel? But I rebuked myself for such prejudices. Rather than follow his family's trade, Justin Apollo had sought a career in the army, winning admittance to St. Anthony's Academy as a fellowship student, the same as I. After receiving his commission, he had been assigned to the newly formed First Apostles Legion. Establishment of the two "Apostles Legions" unrelated to tribal affiliations was a new thing in Israel, and it occurred to me that their existence had created opportunities for men like him, who were not of the old castes. No doubt he had overcome many obstacles in pursuing a military career, and his success in transcending his origins constituted yet another ground for admiration.

Caste warriors, sons of the noble landed families, had ruled the land for centuries. In former times, on the principle that those who are privileged must carry the heaviest burdens, the landed families had provided Israel's soldiers as well as its leaders. In times of need, others outside the noble clans might be conscripted and set to fight alongside the warriors, but those who might enlist in an emergency were never classified as fighters; they were not *hereditary* warriors. Israel has always lived by such distinctions.

Officially, at least, the warrior caste had been abolished after the religious wars of a century ago. Nowadays, in fact, many disparaged the noble class and mocked their pretensions. Nevertheless, most of the leadership in Israel was still drawn from the ranks of these ancient families, bred to war and nourished on a soldierly ethic.

I encountered many admirers of my brother in Esdralon. Their accounts painted him as a handsome man in his late twenties, full of wit and humor and yet a lion in action. Falling on the ramp in the last assault, Justin Apollo had won glory unheard of for a commoner. In addition to the courage which ordinary soldiers extolled, my brother was credited with planning the siege of Esdralon. It was widely claimed that he had already earned himself a place among the small group of officers destined for high command. Occasionally, I found myself treated with deference because of my connection to him – as if our shared blood alone entitled me to some consideration. To contemplate my Glanz blood as a source of honor was, to say the least, a new experience for me.

It happened that when I arrived in Esdralon, my famous half-brother was away on assignment – on a not very secret reconnaissance down the Jordan toward Lagash and the Dall fortresses. Concerning this mission, highly placed officers explained to me confidentially that it signaled Israel's next move in the war. I made a mental note to be alert for other information that pointed to an impending invasion of Lagash.

In pursuit of more clues, I listened carefully to the views of those around me. The war described in the officer's mess was a merchant's gambit to break the Benjamite monopolies. The war was a nuisance and a swindle, but with luck it would do something for the price of grain and wool in Judah. Views of the progress of the war ranged from cheerful to indifferent. There was only the vaguest interest in what the Second Army was doing 150 miles to the east, at the confluence of the Snake and the Clearwater. In the meantime, there were cockfights nightly, and soon there would be horse races featuring the finest thoroughbreds in Israel. And had I heard of the Ephraimite captain who had gambled away his estate and hanged himself outside the barracks? Pass the wine!

Conversations with merchants in brandy shops along the docks were more informative. The merchants tended to be closed-mouth, shrewd fellows with outlandish names that they pretended were ancient lineages. They dressed in fine linen and robes of lamb's wool and liked to wear heavy chains of metal around their necks. They talked continually in low, intense voices of "conditions" that affected trade. I thought at first that they spoke a private, coded language, but I soon realized that information was a commodity to them, and they were frugal with it. The war interested them only as it related to the rise and fall of prices. Most of them seemed surprised that a young officer showed even a casual interest in their business. When I introduced myself, they became silent at the first mention of the name Glanz. Nevertheless, I managed to extract a few pieces of information.

In particular, I often heard gossip of Hanford Glanz, the eldest acknowledged son of Tephlin Glanz and my other half-brother. Hanford controlled the family operations in northern Israel, in Naphtali and Lebanon, and its far-flung trading operations beyond Israel. Still in his early thirties, Hanford Glanz had acquired a name for close dealing, avarice, and cruelty, and he dominated Naphtali more in his own right than as an agent of the Glanz enterprises. I heard much speculation about a possible rift between father and son. Though Hanford virtually ruled Naphtali, the region had contributed neither a soldier nor a single kanz to the war. What would come of that? There was always a clearing of throats and wise nodding, but no answers.

IV

Two weeks after I had requested access to the archives, I was granted an interview with the highest-ranking Messiahist clergyman in Esdralon. I armed myself mentally for the encounter. While most Messiahist sects were harmless, quarreling groups who cherished beliefs they claimed were handed down from the Ancients, the "Third Comer" Messiahists were an aggressive sect who claimed knowledge of—and proprietary interest in—the imminent destruction of the world. The approaching end times were central to their beliefs. Prior to that event, they demanded—and apparently expected to achieve – conversion of all Israel to their peculiar views. Rather than conceal their willingness to use force to achieve this end, they proclaimed it openly, even proudly. These Messiahists regarded Old Believers like myself – who, of course, dismissed their pretensions – as their special enemies.

A much younger man than I had expected stood leaning over a desk as I approached. I presented myself and waited for him to speak. He continued to examine the documents for a time, studiously ignoring me. Then, without a word of greeting, he demanded to know my purpose in examining the archives. Against both my training and better judgment, I replied crossly: "To fulfill my duties, obviously."

"And what exactly is the nature of those duties, Under-Lieutenant?" he asked. His voice had the high-pitched and broken quality of the castrati. *So, they caught you young, did they*? I thought to myself. My blood rose, and I determined not to give him any information even if it cost me the use of the archives.

"Sorry," I replied. "I am not able to reveal my purposes to you."

He seemed more surprised than indignant at my response. "All those who wish to use the archives must reveal their purpose," he chided. *"All.* Those are the rules."

"Those may be your rules," I retorted, "but I answer to General Boseth. If you doubt my right to be here, you may speak with the General. *He* may be willing to explain my task here, but I am not. In the meantime, I intend to begin my work."

My dislike of Messiahist priests and my disdain of Third Comer claims to authority had overcome my better judgment. Meanwhile, the young priest looked at me as if he had never beheld such impertinence in his life. "Impossible!" he exclaimed. "Absolutely impossible."

"On the contrary, Brother Bulavar," for so I believed him to be, Bulavar being the name of the cleric I had been instructed to see, "I intend to examine these archives. I am Under-Lieutenant Josiah *Glanz* ben Haggadah. Do not pretend that General Boseth has failed to approve my request." I leaned forward over his desk and repeated, "I intend to examine these archives." I thrust my face close to his, and it felt as if I had actually seized him by the throat, so vividly had I imagined myself doing so. He seemed a little taken aback. He paused, leaning discernibly backwards, and stared at me. My behavior, of course, was all bluff and charade; I had no means of making good on any demand whatsoever. I realized in the small corner of my mind capable of self-judgment that this was the first time in my life I had used the family connection, the name of Glanz, to obtain something I wanted. Such a name, I reasoned, should be useful for something, if one must endure the burden of wearing it.

I heard a chair creak behind me. I turned to see a middle-aged man with a massive bald head rising from a table; he was dressed in priestly garb of the finest quality. I had not noticed him as I entered. "I am Bulavar," he said in a fine, deep voice. "I believe I heard my name."

So the underling had been set before me, the better for the real authority to observe me. I should have been embarrassed by this charade and by the ease with which I had been deceived. Instead I was furious. Having fallen deftly into his little trap, I felt myself superior to such shallow devices – and contemptuous of all priestly meddling. "I don't care which of you is Bulavar," I retorted. "You are wasting my time and interfering with the business of the Army of Israel."

The elder man regarded me with a bemused and superior look and then dismissed me, as if the affair were no longer of interest to him: "Brother Rodrig, inform our young colleague that he has my permission to use the archives. Provided, of course, he obeys our rules."

The younger man shrugged and began reciting a list of regulations. Out of sheer unwisdom, I interrupted him to say: "I am aware of the provisions of the Secrecy Act and will abide by them. Any other restrictions I will abide by *if* they do not interfere with my work. In the meantime, I want to see the tax ledgers of the city of Esdralon. And I want them *now*. I have been delayed two weeks already."

He looked past me, over my shoulder, at Bulavar, who must have nodded or winked, because I got what I wanted. At the time, I was elated to have behaved so outrageously and gotten my way. Had I attended to my training at the Refuge, I would have been more alert to the motives of those who would put obstacles in my way. I should have asked *who was testing me and why?* I should have recalled, too, the perverse doubleness of experience and should have sensed – *known*, rather, in every fiber of my being – that what looks like a small victory may in reality be a great disaster. *Victory and defeat are equally illusions*, our Teacher warns us.

Foolish as I was in many ways, I was diligent in my study. Gradually, with the resources of the archive, I began to perceive the shape of the Benjamite trade network. The heart of Benjamin is Engedi, which lies outside of Israel proper, south and on the far side of the Great Jordan after the river makes its sweeping turn from south-flowing to west-flowing. Engedi fronts the Jordan and looks toward Israel; the towns, ports, and settlements of the region lie in a narrow strip along the river. The plain of Engedi is fertile and well watered. The backcountry, which rolls gently toward the Blue Mountains, is suited for grazing, and the pastoral uplands gradually give way to wilderness, which Israel calls Moab.

Engedi is also the gateway to the unknown south country of the Gentiles from which a trickle of strange goods and stranger news comes to us. Two hundred years ago, the plain was one of the wealthiest regions of Israel. During the Wars of Investiture, Engedi was devastated – as, indeed, was much of Israel itself—and many places were sacked and abandoned. Afterwards, the territory was ceded to the Harlech, the chief clan of Benjamin, as part of the general settlement of the Religious Wars. Subsequently, the Harlech, as famous for their energy as for their apostasy, resettled the land, drove out the savages who had filtered in, and restored their fortunes upon the abundant fertility of the land. Thereafter, by means not obvious to outsiders, the Benjamites built their great and overweening wealth, the envy of all Israel. The question I posed to myself, as the novice analyst of war that I now imagined myself to be, was *how*? How did Benjamin wax in power and wealth in a period of general turbulence and decline in the rest of Israel? What was the secret of their success?

The answer eluded me. Esdralon, the chief city of Engedi, lies at the center of a far-flung trading network. Grain and leather and wine, cloth, salt beef, flax and lentils came to market from Engedi. Fine ceramics, linen cloth, and brandy came upstream from Lagash, the isolated stronghold of the Harlech nestled under the Cascade Mountains. Cedar, resin, and a variety of timber products came up the Jordan from unknown western sources. Gold and silver and reclaimed metals came upstream, too, but in all these commodities, the Harlech were merely another group of sellers in Israel. Benjamin dominated the market in one commodity only: they sold enormous quantities of wool.

Interesting information, perhaps, but not an explanation of the causes of the war nor of Israel's aims in it. Nor, as I thought about it, of the power of Benjamite resistance. Their commerce could support a diverse and solid prosperity, but not the riches that had sparked the present conflict. There must be, I deduced, another and fabulous source of wealth in trade, conducted by the Harlech largely outside the sight and knowledge of Israel – though *not,* apparently, outside of the sight and knowledge of those who made decisions in Israel.

So I was puzzled – until I overheard a conversation in a brandy shop. A young Judean, an apprentice in a shipping firm by the look of him, complained that the Harlech had a virtual monopoly on salt, drawn from the western reaches of the Great Jordan and purchased from God knows what sorts of subhumans outside the Law who live in those forbidden parts. His companions affirmed and devoutly believed that Harlech traders themselves went beyond the permitted zones and crossed the borders into Nova lands. More of their cursed apostasy – *or was it shrewd business practice?* Opinion on the latter seemed to vary around the table, but they all agreed that Israel's merchants should get as much of this trade into their hands as possible, and they railed against the monopolies carelessly granted by the Council a hundred years or more ago, when they had meant nothing. For those privileges had, as my informants saw it, grown from acorns into mighty oaks, shading and stunting Israel's own rightful commerce. I joined the conversation at that point, but they grew silent at my questions.

But again, a little checking with members of the Commissary staff revealed that if this alleged Harlech monopoly of salt existed, as claimed, they were not exploiting their position in this precious resource. What the Harlech were selling was wool. Bales of it. Cheap, good quality raw wool and woolen products. So after all my patient digging, I was in possession of knowledge that every child in Israel knew as well as I: if one wants to buy the cheapest woolen stuff, one seeks out the Harlech merchant at the market. With this realization, it began to dawn on me that I was, in all likelihood, cut out for a cavalryman, and that mind war was not for me after all.

I spent that afternoon watching the First Apostles Cavalry go through their mounted drills, admiring the wheeling columns and reveling in the familiar smell of leather and sweat and horses and the harsh cries of the officers.

V

"Never underestimate the Harlech, I tell you! They *see*—they comprehend our situation—which we refuse to do! They discern and plan and wait for the opportune moment. Say what you will, Benjamin is not done with this war. In fact, if they had half our resources, they would be in New Jerusalem by now."

I had just emerged from the pool at the officers' bath. A small group of distinguished-looking men had gathered on the wooden benches around the sauna; a servant was pouring water over the heated stones. In a moment the group was enveloped in steam and I could not hear the response. Whoever they were, they were bold enough not to care who overheard them. Wrapping a towel around my waist, I sat down on a bench opposite them, curious to hear more.

It was the eldest of the group who replied, and he spoke with the air of one who is used to being listened to. "The churchmen be damned," he said complacently. "And Benjamin too. Manasseh and Judah have *always* been supreme. That's the way it will always be."

"I urge you to reconsider," the younger man said. "And to acknowledge that we face a new situation—a new danger." The speaker was the handsomest man I had ever seen. He was of medium height, wiry and quick-motioned, his distinctive features were set off by a small mustache. He spoke in an intense, animated way, his teeth and eyes gleaming even in the poor light of the baths. "I repeat: the Council's alliance with the Messiahists will prove a snare to us," he said, "and we are far from having done with Benjamin."

"But the alliance has obviously worked to our advantage, and Benjamin is routed out of Engedi."

"Perhaps," the younger man said, "the Council would do well to re-examine its policy nonetheless." In the blended voices of the conversation I heard the name "Apollo." *Could this confident young man actually be my brother?* The young man leaned forward to speak and then his eyes met mine and held them. They were bold and curious and not quite friendly, and he held his gaze locked with my own to the point of discourtesy. What he was saying made very good sense to me. When Israel had had serious internal strife in the past, it came either from Manasseh or Judah. Now, however, it was churchmen and merchants who struggled for dominance. This new rivalry, he implied, had altered the politics of the Confederation. "The Council thinks only of balancing the interests of the tribes to keep the peace," he continued. "They live in the past; they do not see the changes. Conflict has shifted away from the rivalry of north and south, away from tribal politics in general. That's what has to be understood."

I found this argument interesting, even provocative, and I examined the others to see if they agreed.

"Israel now divides," the young man added, "along the axis of religious difference – religious fanaticism, to speak plainly. And those differences overshadow the old tribal allegiances. The Religious Settlement, after all, only settled the terms on which the present conflict would ensue." He paused to gauge his reception. His chief auditor seemed to me either stubborn or obtuse.

"My dear Apollo," the man said, "you admitted yourself that the main problem of the war is persuading Manasseh to cooperate with Judah. So what has changed?"

"Not nearly enough!" the young man declared. "But more of this later. I see we have a visitor." His eyes swung back, appraising me.

"Forgive me," I said rising as gracefully as I could, clad only in a towel. "Your conversation did not seem private, and I thought I heard the name of one whose acquaintance I have long sought. I am Josiah Glanz ben Haggadah of Asher; under-lieutenant, Commissary." I bowed slightly. "Can this be brevet-Major Justin Glanz Apollo?"

"I am indeed," he replied. "So this is Josiah Glanz ben Haggadah of Asher; under-lieutenant, Commissary." He gazed impartially at me, not offering his hand.

Was he mocking me in repeating my words? But why? Had I been excessively formal? Perhaps this conversation I had interrupted was other than it seemed – or perhaps Judeans scorned the old courtesies. But as I pondered possible causes of his hostility, he introduced me, with equal formality, to the others, beginning with Asad Shevren of Simeon, Colonel and commander of the detached cavalry of the First Apostle's Legion. Colonel Shevren was a lean, muscular man in his thirties with a stylish mustache and pointed beard. I had seen him several times on the parade ground. He sat stiffly on the wooden bench with his fist resting on his naked hip, elbow extended to the side, as if he were reviewing troops. The other young men were his officers.

When we had seated ourselves there was an awkward pause. I tried to fill it: "A few weeks ago," I said, speaking to Major Apollo, "I happened to visit your estate when my unit was in the vicinity. Your wife was – your wife said that you were absent."

"Charming. And my son?"

"I. . . I did not have the privilege of meeting him. It was a very brief meeting. I called unannounced." *I hoped he did not imagine how brief.* "I'm afraid I may have come at an inconvenient time."

"My household is well acquainted with inconvenience," he said in a tone I could not fathom.

I saw that I had gotten off on the wrong foot. "So," I said, looking for some neutral topic, "what is the news? How do the armies of Israel fare?"

"I hoped you would tell us, Under-Lieutenant," Major Apollo said. "They seem to know so much more in Hebron than we here in Esdralon."

I felt my heart sink as he continued to hold me outside the group rather than draw me into it. I felt I had blundered badly – was continuing to blunder. I resolved to pay my respects and take myself out of their conversation as quickly as possible. "No news, really," I replied, hoping to sound casual. "I passed through Hebron briefly on my way here. I had little time to catch the gossip." I started to rise; another and better start at some other time, I thought. "Pardon me for interrupting, but I have long wanted to make your acquaintance." I felt devastated by his failure to acknowledge our kinship.

"I hear you served with the Second Apostles," Apollo continued, ignoring my attempt to exit. It was his first invitation into the conversation, and I was cautiously pleased to think that my famous brother had been aware of me.

"Yes," I said, "I served on the staff of General Abner Mac Dogol."

"Tell us about the war in Judah," he said, regarding me carefully over his cupped hands. I sensed that I was being invited to stay in order to be probed rather than for friendly reasons or for the sake of kinship. I felt keenly the absence of the etiquette of kinship. *Perhaps, I thought with some resentment, he is ignorant of it.*

"The war in Judah is a standoff, as near as I can tell," I replied, seating myself. "However, as the newest under-lieutenant in the service, I am scarcely qualified to judge."

"I know very well who you are," he said sharply. His eyes narrowed and he seemed about to speak some rebuke or accusation, but instead said mildly, "It is well known you are one the most promising of the younger officers in the service." Hearing his compliment, I hoped that the ice between us might be breaking, but then he added, "A commission is a commission, after all."

He referred to my assignment in the Commissary rather than in a line position. His and his companions' perfunctory congratulations did not elicit any warmth from me. I wondered suddenly if they were aware of the incident at the Academy. The subject of my commission touched a nerve that I had not believed to be so raw. So little healed was it that I blurted out: "You may also have heard that my commission was delayed." Instantly, I would have given anything to recall the words, but my fear of seeming to solicit their understanding made me compound my foolishness. "And you may have heard why," I added sharply, flushing angrily – angry with myself. It was foolish to bring up shame. Doubly foolish to speak of it in a context where Major Apollo or his companions might interpret it as a threat. Fatal quarrels were ignited with less kindling.

He regarded me watchfully, but chose to address my present circumstances: "You hereditary warriors can stand some instruction in the practical side of war, I dare say. But let us hear a little about yourself."

I acquiesced, still hoping to find a path through the barriers between us. I found myself making small talk, as if this were an ordinary conversation and not the wretched disappointment that it was. Justin Apollo continued polite but distant. The gamut of emotions I felt in those moments astonished me. I had been prepared to be in awe of him, a man already a legend in his late twenties, and I expected some reserve in his manner due to his high standing and seniority in the family. And yet in a moment, I had attributed his lack of manners to his low birth. For the first time, I truly valued my discipline, my long training in self-control. Except for one other occasion, I had never felt the need of it so sorely.

Seeing that Major Apollo intended to speak with me further, Colonel Shevren and his chief aid excused themselves and departed. Three officers who looked to be Justin's peers in age stayed. Major Apollo motioned me to sit beside him and asked to hear more about my service with Mac Dogol and the Second Apostles.

"A wise and courageous officer," I said, eager to turn the topic away from myself. "I believe he is underestimated in the higher ranks of the army – though not by his soldiers; certainly not by me. I regard him as one of the most capable officers in the service." I felt suddenly like a fool, as if I had the experience to compare Israel's officer corps. Major Apollo, however, did not seem inclined to dispute this judgment, but rather to approve it, which greatly pleased me.

"General Mac Dogol was a friend to me when others were not," I continued, wishing I had not. I described my service in the Second Apostles briefly, speaking generally of some of the actions in which the unit had engaged but without reference to my own part in them. It was easy to praise General Mac Dogol, and my listeners appeared to follow what I had to say with at least mild interest. I mentioned the enemy's raids into Judean territory and the difficulty of defending the scattered settlements. Major Apollo, who obviously knew all of Judah intimately, probed me about the destruction wrought by them.

As we spoke, an elderly serving woman brought a basin of water and dashed it on the rocks at our feet. Only a little steam rose; it was her way of saying we had overstayed our time. "I am told," Major Apollo said when she had shuffled off, "that the Benjamite cavalry are highly selective in their choice of targets in Judah. Rather than lay waste the entire countryside, they pick and choose."

"It seems so, yes. They may ravage two estates and spare one lying in between."

"My own estate – or, to speak more precisely, my esteemed wife's family estates – are in Judah, and in a particularly exposed part of Judah. They are untouched. What do you make of that?"

I must have looked at him strangely, and suddenly I felt we were on awkward ground again. "I don't know," I replied. "I hadn't thought about it. I would expect the enemy to go out of their way to injure you, assuming that they knew which estates pertained to you."

"They know all right!" he retorted, his eyes probing me. "So what do you make of my lands being spared?"

The question struck me as so dangerous that I said nothing.

"Please do not act as if you hadn't thought about it," he said sharply. "Isn't it precisely our duty to ask that kind of question? Isn't that why you are assigned here, my brother officer? To inquire about those whose property in Judah is still intact, while the estates of patriots burn? And to sound out an erring brother on the side?" He made the last part sound almost a jest, and his companions laughed, but none of his comments seemed humorous to me. It was the first time he had used the word "brother" in addressing me, but in a mocking rather than kindly way. Given the nature of the rumors I had heard, I wondered if he had indeed wandered into dangerous territory in his loyalties. I recalled a wisp of gossip that Justin Apollo had taken a Harlech mistress.

"Your commission," he said, continuing to press me, "is in the Commissary, isn't that right? But you serve, it is well known, with the Eyes of Israel." His voice was soft and mild, and yet I knew from his eyes that a deep and widening gulf was opening between us. For a moment, I was reminded of the calculated hostility of Senesh Velco and his followers at the Academy.

I sat in stunned silence for a moment. Another fatal breach in the making, and this with my own brother? It required my utmost effort to control myself and to prevent my whole frame from shaking. As it was, I felt my palms sweating and a chill passed through my body. I replied slowly, restraining my voice. "Brother, if you err in your behavior, may you find the appropriate ritual to clear your mind and set you on the right path." He met my gaze for a moment and looked away. "The question of why your wife's estates are intact, "I added, "while your neighbors' estates have been destroyed, is an interesting one. Before this moment, no one had brought your good fortune to my attention. However, the sparing of your estates does not seem remarkable to me. I expect many in Judah and elsewhere might be hard pressed to explain why their barns and outbuildings are still standing within sight of the ruins of their neighbors. Such apparent good fortune may seem strange only to someone who has had no part in the war." *Nevertheless, I reflected, few who had been spared would discuss their good fortune in public.* "I can imagine many reasons why the Harlech have not plundered your villa. For one thing, they still may. For another, they are clever; too clever to be predictable. A random pattern of destruction is harder for us to defend against, because we cannot anticipate their targets."

Justin stared at me, his eyes unchanged. "Some in Judah complain about the inactivity of the Second Apostles," he said. "They say Mac Dogol's horsemen languish timidly in their tents." His companions seemed to enjoy his barb, but they also knew we were circling each other mentally – or rather Major Apollo was circling me. Sometimes it happens that, because of the smallest nuance of voice or inflection, such postures of combat become fixed forever, implacable as stars in the firmament.

I shrugged, feigning nonchalance, as though the record of the Second Apostles Cavalry was secure to any knowledgeable person, and nothing else was at stake in this verbal fencing. "The Second Apostles can't be everywhere at the same time," I said. "And you Judeans, as the world knows, had ample opportunity to prove your own zeal in the last campaign." My retort sounded a little more challenging than I intended, so I added: "I say that without seeking to excuse the Second Apostles Cavalry. General Mac Dogol finds it necessary to keep a good portion of the legion concentrated, on the principle that if you try to defend everything, you defend nothing."

"Quite right," one of the officers said. "If Mac Dogol spreads the Legion and pursues every band of raiders, then he creates a greater danger. It would serve the Harlech's purpose." I felt relieved, hearing at last a conciliatory voice.

"Of course," Major Apollo said. One of the other officers remarked that the First Apostles should have been deployed back on Judean soil long ago, that their service here in Esdralon was a waste of time. "But you haven't told me," Major Apollo interrupted, "why *you* think my estates have been spared." It seemed to me that the officers exchanged brief glances; perhaps they were reluctant to try the ice with him.

I wanted fervently to be done with the whole conversation, which had become very dangerous, but I complied. "It may be that the Harlech raiders are saving your estates for later. Perhaps they think they can influence you by sparing your property while retaining the power to take it from you. Or they may intend to strike when you are present so as to include you in the flames." I recounted the possibilities like a lesson at the Academy. Strangely, this recital seemed to draw some of the poison from his mood, just as it began to inflame mine. "But I consider it most likely," I finished with some heat, "that the Harlech are trying to sow dissension among us, to make Israelites suspicious of one another and divide us. If so, it would appear they have succeeded. You are suspicious of me because the enemy's cavalry have not burned down your house and barns. Really, this is a triumph of policy, now that I think about it."

"Well said," one of the officers remarked. "Well said!" The other officers seemed content to end the conversation on that note. Major Apollo gazed at the pool, and I noticed for the first time that he had a fresh, jagged scar from his collarbone part way down his breast, and that his chest was heaving. I waved away a servant with a fresh basin of hot water and dashed my face and chest with cold water; I was in no mood to prolong the conversation. The crone brought more towels for us to dry on. As I rose to leave, Justin Apollo approached me from the side and said in a low voice, "We will have occasion to speak again, Josiah ben Haggadah."

I bowed slightly and left as quickly as I could.

Chapter 2: The Favorite of His Brothers

I

I left my meeting with Justin Apollo baffled and bitterly disappointed. My expectations had foundered in an instant. Had I blundered? Had I deserved ill of my brother? And what expectations had *he* brought to the meeting? I acknowledged I had invested too much hope in embracing a kinsman, only to find that he was, in fact, a stranger, akin to me in name only. Too much hope, I decided, remembering the precepts of St. Supplicee: *The world is a flame fed by human hearts. If you would see a little through the flames, quench your desire.*

In the midst of this conquered city, I found myself missing the comradeship of the camp. I longed for the sound of reveille at dawn, with ice in the bucket and our gear frozen hard as iron. I leaned into a cold wind as I walked back to the barracks, thinking*: a soldier's duty is a life, and not a contemptible one*—and realizing how much I preferred field duty to serving in this wretched city.

That night I tossed and turned unsleeping on my cot. Toward dawn, I found myself sweating and exhausted, and distressed beyond words. Focusing on the light streaming through my window, I tried to empty my mind and recover a sense of harmony. Perversely, my inner self refused to dissolve. It remained alert, rebellious, observing me and my cold quarters, noting how exactly my room in the barracks duplicated my rooms at the Refuge and the Academy. Worse, if I relaxed my guard but a moment, it became an insinuating voice taunting me with single, repeated epithet: *murderer!* Cursing myself for indulging in self-pity, I threw back my blanket, hurriedly washed and dressed. Many people manage to get through life alone, I reminded myself. I remembered my mother and tried to imagine her life, wishing I had more urgent work to do.

The next morning was the day of First Plantings, and I wandered the city half-hoping to encounter brigands or rebels or amusement of any kind. The air was cold and damp, threatening rain. I longed for the country and the sight of the first furrows. The streets of Esdralon swarmed with a multitude of shabbily dressed and sullen people, and the market was loud with women haggling with vendors and watched over by bored sentries. A single Messiahist preacher scolded the indifferent crowd. "The millennium is at hand!" he shouted as I passed. His message was typical Third Comer fare – doom and destruction and impossible promises. His kind made ludicrous claims to knowledge of another world, while their views of this world were little short of absurd. In any case, it was *this* world, and not a realm erected by superstition, that interested me.

Walking further, I marked the points on the south wall where the October assault had breached the defenses, reconstructing the attack in my imagination. The ramp, famous in Israel, still lay against the east wall. A soldier pointed out to me the spot where Captain Apollo had fallen. My brother was, I saw, a legend among the common soldiers. However, I knew more about the attack than my guide. The assault here had been a decoy to draw the defenders away from the real attack. The main assault, which was made with ladders, had come against the south wall. My brother's bravery had been expended in a mere sideshow against the enemy. Had he been aware at the time of the real point of attack? The only answers that occurred to me further depressed my spirits.

After Hebron and New Jerusalem, Esdralon was the largest city in Israel and the capital of Benjamin. It had many buildings three and four stories high, of brick and stucco and dressed stone, with tile roofs. Nearly all the streets were cobbled and equipped with drains. Even the poorer sections of the city were constructed of brick. Those parts of the city that had been spared the devastation of the sack were well laid out and in perfect repair, as if no assault had ever taken place. But, to my surprise, virtually nothing in the damaged areas had been repaired. I walked whole sections of the town through streets of burned-out buildings, where bricks and rubbish still lay in the streets.

Away from the waterfront and the main plaza, the city had a desolate, empty look, as Benjamites still tended to keep indoors and out of harm's way. Until peace was negotiated, the citizens were, in effect, prisoners of war, held in their own homes. Israel's policy of occupation was clearly not conciliatory. The metal workers' quarter was devastated, though it lay far from the area where the breach had been made. Everything of value had been carried away or smashed in the streets. The area seemed empty of inhabitants, but as I passed fire-scarred buildings with broken shutters and gaping doorways, I saw evidence of people still living within. I caught glimpses of women's faces at doorways and heard children's voices. When they saw I was not a provost guard, wretches of all sizes and stages of emaciation showed themselves to me. A woman approached me boldly from a doorway and announced, "We have no bread."

Passing out of the city walls, I explored a mile or so beyond the south gates, and was surprised that the devastation extended into the countryside. Whole orchards and vineyards had been cut down by the besieging army – or so I assumed until I saw with my own eyes a work party of Home Guards chopping down an apple tree that was just coming into bloom. A middle-aged woman was pleading with them, wringing her hands. A flock of crows was settling in the orchard and their clamor drowned her words. Shocked by this impiety and by such flagrant contempt for the Law, I drew my sword, but the three fled at my approach, cursing me. The old woman cursed me too.

Farther out, many farmsteads were burned to the ground and a small village had been completely emptied of inhabitants. I saw fresh graves in fields and many graves along the road. The destruction of the wealth of the region was continuing under the occupation. Was this policy? And if so, policy to what end? Where were the teams of mules and oxen and plowmen? Why was next year's bread not being sown in the fields? I returned to the city mystified and dismayed.

That evening, I made arrangements to explore other parts of Engedi, not so much to study the enemy as to observe the effects of our occupation. I found my way to the barracks well after dark, having been solicited by a half-dozen prostitutes and scanned by several persons I took to be thieves too timid to attack an armed officer. I went to bed without eating and again slept fitfully.

The next morning I arrived late to work and sat for a while in a reverie, remembering the three Home Guards despoiling a living orchard for firewood.

"So, feeling the effects of a carouse last night, ah?" Major Cohn-el was leaning over my desk. "We were beginning to wonder if you had any of a young man's habits. The staff was beginning to talk. This should keep you busy," he said, handing me a sheaf of papers. "By the way, you had a visitor this morning. Major Glanz, a famous figure around here. I assume he is your brother. Or half-brother, rather."

I replied noncommittally, not appreciating his attention to the details of my kinship bonds. I acknowledged that I had met brevet Major Justin Glanz Apollo two days before.

"Just met? I see. Kin, but not kind, as they say." Major Cohn-el seemed inordinately interested in my personal affairs this morning. "Well," he said, "he is a gallant officer; I'll say that much for him. Reckless as the Devil. Never catch Major Apollo on a Commissary staff, I'll wager."

I scarcely smarted at the Major's jibe, so surprised was I at the news of my brother's visit. I sat at my table recording receipts of barrels of salt beef and hundredweights of dried peas, puzzling at Justin Apollo's motives for coming. I maintained a bearing that was correct and formal, but my heart was fluttering like a schoolgirl's.

An hour later I heard his voice, recognizable but pitched to carry and be heard. Major Apollo was exchanging friendly insults with one of the officers in the hall: "It's the truth," he was saying, "I swear it! We'll all be drinking out a ditch before April, just because Mathias here can't count his cards."

Major Apollo strode into the room, handsome, immaculately uniformed, and seemingly an intimate of everyone on the staff. He embraced Major Cohn-el familiarly and casually dropped a small gift-wrapped package on my table. "You left the other day before I could ask you to dinner. You mustn't refuse me." He spoke quickly, moving to the window without meeting my eyes. "I've gone to incredible bother about the meal," he continued over his shoulder, in the voice he had used in the hall. "You must come. I've bribed two-thirds of the Commissary for the wine alone, and I've been to this miserable office twice already. I can scarcely afford to pay them all off! Not on a brevet major's salary!" He slapped his braided quirt on the table where three staff members were at work, and they smiled at his interruption. "But I must have a moment of the Major's time," Justin said, sweeping Major Cohn-el out onto the balcony. "Serious business," he laughed, and was gone, and dust and paper and small objects seemed to settle in his wake. I found the rest of the staff staring at me, perhaps with new appreciation of my exalted connections.

"Aren't you going to open it?" one of them asked.

I remembered the package. Inside was a pair of gloves of finest kidskin, and a note that read:

> *Do me the honor of accepting this small token of my regard. Monumental rudeness seems to run in the family. But let us get to know one another, properly, starting now.*
>
> *Yours,*
> *Justin Glanz Apollo, Brvt Major*

I stared at the page, at the closing of his letter and his signature, and I felt again, as I had on the docks of Hebron, that my life was beginning anew.

As it happened, I was not able to accept his invitation, as I had made arrangements with a captain of the fleet to inspect the Harlech installations at Gath. But after a few moments of private conversation with Justin, I felt we had arrived at a better understanding and that our relationship could indeed begin anew and on a proper footing. We agreed I should come by in the evening two days hence, when I returned from Gath.

II

My arrangements were with a Captain Haddis of the merchant fleet. Rough in manner and uneducated, like many of the fleet captains, Haddis had obviously come up through the ranks, acquiring no small estimation of his own merits in the process. I gathered that he was a son of a craftsman's family and not likely to be keen on young officers who bore Israelite names. Gath lay a few miles west and down river from Esdralon, on the Jordan's shore. The city was famous for its large windmill, a mechanical contraption of great complexity that could alternately turn a huge millstone or hoist water out of wells. Gath had a number of such wind machines, which existed nowhere else in Israel. I wanted to have a look at them, to sketch the mechanism for later reference, and also to get an impression of our occupation outside the capital city.

Nothing I had seen so far in the war prepared me for Gath. The town was leveled; the houses and shops warehouses had been razed; the House of Assembly lay in ashes. Even the famous windmills had been torched, and only a blackened skeleton of one such structure stood silhouetted against the sky. On a whitewashed wall nearby was scrawled: *This is Beli-az's work.* The ambiguity of that message impressed itself upon me as I inspected the great tanneries. The place was uninhabited except by stray dogs and a flock of grackles, which flew up noisily as we entered the ruined plaza.

I walked the site with Captain Haddis, trying to reconstruct the town as it had been by its foundation stones and rubble piles. I asked him what motives could have produced this destruction, but the good captain had no answer and had not been moved to ask the question. Gath had been famous as a leather-producing center. All of the facilities were gone, but their foundations and the pits for dipping hides revealed the extent of the operation, which covered several acres. The peculiar stench of leather making lingered among the ruins, and as we walked the site, the huge scale of the operation became evident. From the size of the production facilities, I tried to estimate how many thousands of hides could be processed in a season: a thousand? Ten thousand? Captain Haddis replied that even my higher figures were off the mark. But how? Hides from where? All of Engedi could not hold so many cattle! I was tantalized by the evidence of an enormous operation whose basis I could not imagine and whose consequences within Israel were quite invisible.

The captain was a bluff, competent man not much interested in idle questions about hides: "They get them from the Kuhlans, so I'm told," he replied. "Raft them down the Snake every fall, in high water. Field dressed hides, packed in brine in barrels." He dismissed it all with a wave; it was ancient history.

From the Kuhlans!

Here it was, then! Here at last was a piece of evidence from which I could uncover the foundations of Benjamite power, which had, by one means or another, provoked the war. I began to fancy that whoever had selected me to serve the Eyes of Israel was an extraordinarily shrewd judge of character. The Captain, however, regarded me dubiously and pressed me to return to his vessel, so he could get on with his patrol.

I recall nothing of the return voyage, rapt as I was in sorting out the meaning of what I had seen. The tannery at Gath was surely the largest enterprise in Israel. As I drew out the implications from this single fact, I found they led in a single direction, like the threads of a loom, and connected to other facts that I did not yet have, could not yet surmise. To the tannery at Gath must have come annually a small forest of bark. I visualized the hundreds of cords of wood – and behind the wood, an army of toiling loggers and sawyers – like a column of ants – stretching in a line from invisible Benjamite enterprises in the west, up the Great Jordan, to this spot. I tried to estimate the quantities of brains and gall and whatever else was used in the tanning process and was forced again to contemplate the annual slaughter of more cattle than I had ever seen in my life. And the salt. A mountain of salt! An absolute fortune in salt. In my boyhood, packets of salt circulated as currency in Asher.

As our ship plowed through the dark waters of the Jordan, it came to me that somewhere down the river, past the great lava flow where Israelites were forbidden to venture, the Harlech had a source of salt – cheap and abundant salt, beyond anything imagined in Israel. At the same time, I realized why Harlech salt made no great showing in Israel's markets. The Harlech neither flooded the market nor enforced a monopoly, even though every household, down to the last slave and poor landless peasant, required salt to survive. *Why not?* Because they had more valuable uses for it. They used it to make leather in Gath. And to salt the beef taken in the same place where they obtained the hides. Far up the five reaches of the Snake, *in the heart of the Kuhlan lands*.

Which meant that both the source of their abundant salt and their uses of it were secret – and secret because their uses were illicit. Harlech salt came from the Nova lands to the west and the products of its use were sold to Israel's hereditary foes. *So, then, the rumors were true!* The bold apostasy of it made me shiver a little. Benjamin's wealth was based on outlawry, on trade conducted with the Kuhlans, a race of predators who had ravaged Israel for generations.

That realization led me to another question: For whom and to whom did the Harlech produce and sell all this raw leather and finished leather goods? I had inspected the ruined foundations of Gath and wandered through the shops and warehouses of Esdralon. I knew what employment those workshops had had: nearly a tenth of the population were leather workers. But Harlech leather, like Harlech salt, was not a remarkable commodity in Israel, though immense quantities of it were manufactured every year. Where did it go? To whom did they sell all these mountains of leather products. I addressed myself to my worthy host, Captain Haddis.

"The same place we'll be selling our goods," he replied.

The Captain's words chimed with my recent discoveries in the archives and allowed me to weave all these separate strands together. Parts of the Benjamite archives were written in code, but in one so simple—merely a substitute alphabet—that even a child could decipher it, let alone someone trained as I had been. Obviously, our enemies had not expected any outsider to have extended access to their records. But merely by knowing a bit about our language, I was able to identify articles and a few unusual words—such as "Kr" and "wool," that occurred with great frequency. And I would have been a fool to miss the significance of these haphazardly protected passages. I spent a few idle hours breaking their codes until I was confident I could read them all.

What I found in the archives completed the picture I had begun to draw of Benjamite wealth. Engedi is continually threatened by the wild nomads who live in the interior, in the region we call Moab. Moab is an arid, inhospitable country, broken up by mountains and ravines and dry riverbeds, with scattered stands of scrub and Ponderosa forest. The remote uplands are inhabited by a people Israel calls Moabites, though in their own language they call themselves "Kr." They raise sheep and goats and keep to themselves, avoiding Israel's settlements unless bent on mischief. Having perused Benjamin's secret archives, I began to acquire a new view of these savages from south of Engedi. What none of the ancient accounts even hinted was that the presence of the Kr and their flocks on the edge of Engedi was the wealth of the country!

Benjamite wool dominates the trade and sets prices all over Israel. Their merchants sell bales of it in the market of Hebron, while caravans deliver sacks of it strapped across the backs of mules as far north as New Jerusalem. The source of this precious wool, the secret archives revealed, was the Kr, the savage shepherd-folk of Moab. The archive's sparse records of weights and values and grades of wool could only mean that an extensive trade was being carried on with these savages. At some point, apparently, the Kr had acquired the custom of bringing their fleeces north to trade for objects made in Benjamin. This trade occurs precisely at the summer solstice, when all human life is at a low ebb and the dreaded mountain fever is at its height. And occurs at no other time.

I could only suppose that at this mutually agreed upon date, the Harlech and Kr observed a truce and engaged in mute barter of goods, since neither—so far as I could ascertain – spoke the other's language. The whole arrangement came together at the spring of Elion, some three days south of Esdralon, and the quantities of wool involved were astonishing. This huge trade was – *had to be* – a recent invention of the Harlech and the source of their sudden wealth. It was another proof of their resourcefulness, the brilliance of these renegade Israelites, who could turn deadly peril into advantage.

As I thought about this illicit commerce, it occurred to me where the greater part of the immense quantities of Harlech leather from Gath went. The invisible sinews of Harlech power had suddenly become visible to me. I felt elated as I scribbled my findings in my journal and wished to boast to someone of my insights. To boast, in fact, to Justin Glanz Apollo, my elder brother.

III

Justin Apollo chose not to live in the officers' barracks but had billeted himself, as he put it, in the fashionable part of Esdralon near the government buildings. His quarters were just off the main plaza, a few blocks from the Hall of Assembly. On a whim I rode a cavalry mount, hoping we might go for a ride if the evening was fair. It was late afternoon when I arrived; the low sun was gilding the tops of buildings and the damaged citadel. Justin was waiting outside the two-story block of buildings where he had an apartment. I reined in the black stallion I rode before him and drew back the hood from my face. He appeared to be staring wide-eyed at me.

"So, it *is* you!" Justin exclaimed. "I thought I had seen an apparition. Welcome, brother!" He was the hearty soldier of his visit to the Commissary. He took hold of the horse's bridle and I swung down. I did not altogether trust his manner, but I preferred it to the haughty staff officer I had first seen.

"Let me show you the stable," he said affably. "There is a courtyard in back." He led me through a lofty archway. "I can't tell you how you gave me a start." He let the horse into a stable and poured a measure of grain into the manger. "I thought you had stepped out of one of the old chronicles. Do you have any idea how much you look like a Dolomite?"

I smiled uneasily. At one time, the kind of robe I wore was the uniform of the novitiate in all the orders of Old Believers. I had worn such a garment since leaving the Refuge of the Brothers for St. Anthony's military academy. It was one of my few links with the past, and I treasured it. The one I now wore was a parting gift of my commanding officer, General Mac Dogol, who apparently forgave me my eccentricities of dress and manner.

At the door of Justin's lodgings a small boy took my robe and sword and led us upstairs. He appeared about eight years of age, small, dark, and well formed. His eyes fastened on the sword as he held it in both hands; then he remembered himself. Withdrawing a step, he bowed deeply and with a poise and dignity surprising in one so young. I followed Justin Apollo into his spacious quarters. "Your boy is well trained," I remarked.

"He's not mine exactly," Justin replied, frowning. "He is the son of the former owner of this house. His widow is my housekeeper now, but she was a great lady among the Harlech." I was reminded simultaneously that the Benjamites kept no slaves and that Major Apollo was rumored to have taken a Harlech mistress. "In fact," he continued, "she *is* a Harlech. It is her clan name as well as married name."

Just as my mind was opening to the implications of his words, a woman appeared before me, obviously the former mistress of the house. She was tall and dressed in black, as befitted her widowhood. She greeted me modestly, even deferentially, as becomes one in her position, but with an innate pride and sense of worth as well. I was struck by her beauty and gracious manner, and I had difficulty taking my eyes off her. She seemed serene, but secret, with a hint of sadness about her eyes and beautifully molded cheekbones.

To my astonishment, my brother Justin Apollo then introduced us, as if she were still the lady of the house. I bowed awkwardly, barely grasping her name: Senyora Michal-Rebekah *Harlech*, which I repeated, lacking presence of mind to say anything else. I was astonished that her husband had also carried the clan name, wondering what this could mean except incest, but at the same time sensing that she must indeed have been a great lady among the Benjamites. Was her son therefore of Apostles' blood? Or a monstrosity? My mind was reeling. But her eyes, rather than cast downward, rose to meet mine and held them – not boldly or impudently, but like a free woman. Justin continued his formal introduction of her as the widow of Colonel Elgin Harlech, late of the Esdralon Guards.

Before I could quite recover myself – *if I have ever quite recovered myself* – Justin introduced me to the boy, her son, whose name was Appian, and who greeted me with the self-possession and good manners of a well-brought up heir. I shrank from the implications of their situation, but said nothing.

"Well, here we are, then," Justin Apollo said, feigning cheerfulness. "Fortunes of war!" His phrase took in the whole impossible situation. My mind does not encompass new things quickly; Justin's remark told me that he sensed all that I was thinking and feeling, and that he was offering, quite unembarrassed, another, though unspecified, perspective for me to consider. But I could only ponder the questions that rose in my mind: does Israel enslave the heirs and widows of Apostles' kin? Abominable! Yet, on the other hand, do heroes of Israel consort with the enemy? I could not decide which prospect was the more appalling.

Michal-Rebekah Harlech and her son retired, leaving us in a spacious living room. Justin's quarters were furnished rather austerely, but there were a few tasteful and precious objects – Blue Drawings from the time of the Governors and glass objects from the Ancients. The rugs and wall hangings were expertly woven and of rich, harmonious colors. I wondered whose taste – his or hers? – was represented in the room.

Justin and I seated ourselves, and he looked at me appraisingly. "I have to tell you that when we met the other night, I was certain I knew everything about you. That, among other things, as a son of Tephlin Glanz, you had been raised up to be my bitter rival and nemesis. But now I see I know nothing at all about you. Nothing! I wonder if I have even prepared a meal that you can eat."

I saw that he was concerned that I was a Devotee with strict dietary restrictions – and that he entertained other assumptions about me that I could not fathom. "I have bound myself by no vows," I replied. "I will eat what you have prepared with pleasure." Wanting both to put him at ease and to change the subject, I explained that I had in fact been educated by a strict order of Old Believers and had come to adopt some of their habits, but I was free, within the general constraints of the Law, just as he was. *Had he, I wondered, been making inquires about me in the mess? And why should we be bitter enemies?*

"Will you have some wine then?" he offered. "I've gotten hold of an excellent vintage especially for this occasion."

"With pleasure."

The woman, Michal-Rebekah Harlech – whatever her status or relationship to my brother – reappeared with a crystal decanter and glasses on a tray. She placed them before us and disappeared into another room. Justin poured, offering a silent libation. The wine glowed like a jewel in the glass. I had never put such a costly object to my lips before, and the wine, a rare Judean red cardofan, seemed doubly precious in such vessels.

"Nice aroma," Justin said. "But a little tart." It tasted delightful to me, though I am a poor judge of such things.

Justin Apollo was animated and friendly and committed small awkwardness that suggested he was eager to please but not entirely certain how. I realized with surprise that I was to be the only dinner guest. I was flattered and soon put at ease by his obvious good will. He wanted to know all about how I had been brought up, how I had lived as a boy. I started to tell him about my grandfather and his far-flung but barren possessions in Asher, but he soon interrupted: "I saw immediately when we spoke the other day that you are the real thing. That insight, at least, has been borne out."

"What do you mean?" I asked.

"One of the warrior caste," he said, as if his meaning had been obvious. "And a perfect expression of the class. I mean the old-time warriors, when it meant something to be one. Your manners, your way of speaking. You seem, if you don't mind my saying so, to have sprung fully armed out of the last century!"

We laughed together, I a little self-consciously. I had not thought much about how I must seem to others. I had supposed myself invisible in the thicket of my everyday roles and assumed that, if noticed at all, I must appear like everyone else.

"Tell me about your education," he said amiably.

"I expect it was an education like no other in Israel, now that I think about it." I told him a little about the Refuge and the discipline that, even I knew, was a relic of another age. "Apparently, from what you've said, I've spent too much time in old books and meditation and not enough in conversation with the living!"

He nodded, seeming to intend no rudeness. "I'm afraid I pressed you the other day," he said, "behaved quite badly, really, because you caste warriors are so. . . well, so predictable. Or so I had thought. But you, at least, are *not*!" He spoke quickly, as if anxious not to offend. "In fact, nothing of the kind!" he finished, apparently trying to reassure me.

I was not following him, but I smiled politely.

"That is an amazing sword you have," he remarked, making an obvious change in the subject. "Can you speak of it?"

"Of course." The boy retrieved the sword, and I explained that it was the parting gift of the Order to me when I had left for the Academy. "I was their prize student, I suppose."

"I imagine you were!" Justin said, admiring its balance and heft. "There are not twenty such swords in Israel."

"There are about a hundred," I replied, not wishing to appear so especially set apart by the Order. "All from the same period, about two centuries ago, when Israel had steel and techniques for working it. There are only a few of these particular swords. Perhaps the best of them are by the same master, Eliphaz of Hazor. I am fortunate to have one of his masterpieces." I showed him the craftsman's identifying mark near the hilt. "Each of his swords is named," I explained, wondering how much he knew about sword craft. "It's an old custom, a superstition really, that is supposed to give extra power to the owner of the sword."

"I am familiar with the custom," Justin said. "And this sword, its name is secret?"

"Yes," I admitted.

He looked at me closely. "Well," he said, slipping it back into its sheath, "it is a beautiful piece of work." He lifted the sheathed sword and saluted me: "May it serve and protect you against all enemies."

Dinner was roast lamb with carrots and potatoes. While I ordinarily avoid eating flesh, the very scent of this dish made my mouth water. To my relief, the woman and her son only served the meal and did not join us. Apparently, even Justin Apollo abided by some limits and conventions.

Justin remarked as we ate that he had an informant, a Captain Mathias in the Commissary, who had given an account of me. "They didn't know what to make of you at first, a Glanz right in their midst. He says you are a modest young man, attentive to business. Aloof perhaps, but more shy than arrogant."

Faint praise, I thought.

"A northerner of the old school, Mathias says. And he can't see a speck of Glanz in you. He says you're every inch an Asherite warrior who perhaps doesn't know he's living in the tenth and last century of the Third Tribulation." Justin laughed at this characterization of me. "He meant that as a compliment, by the way, which is most unusual, coming from an officer in the Commissary. He regards you highly."

I knew Captain Mathias slightly; I chewed over his characterization of me as I sampled the lamb.

"I see I am still apologizing," Justin said, "but I have to tell you by way of explanation that in my time at the Academy, I did not have reason to admire people who claimed descent from the landed classes."

"I understand," I said, wondering if I truly did. "I imagine you must have suffered a great deal."

He made a dismissive gesture. "One should ignore slights. But unfortunately I was a Glanz on top of being the son of a poor merchant's daughter." He laughed ruefully. "My time in the Academy was, I suspect, a foretaste of the Messiahist's Hell. It made me a believer – in their Hell at least!"

I confided that my own time at the Academy had been somewhat less congenial than the present war. He was silent a while, and I had occasion to wonder how much he knew about me and my time at the Academy.

"Do you mind if I ask," he said at last, "what our father said to you? In Hebron, just before you came to Esdralon?"

The question had come suddenly out of no context, as if it had lain at the back of his mind as we talked of other things. At last I knew something about him. I chose my words carefully: "Why should I mind? Our father said nothing to me. Nothing at all. I called at the palace when summoned. I expected an interview, as I had reason to believe Tephlin Glanz might have influenced the granting of my commission. I wished in any event to pay my respects, as custom requires. As it happened, he was too busy to see me. I met with his aid, General Simon ben Gurion. Ben Gurion gave me my commission and my orders assigning me to Headquarters of the Southern Host here in Esdralon, in the dual role, in fact, that you have surmised." *I wondered if I was breaching security by admitting my role in the Eyes.* "Ben Gurion politely wished me good fortune and showed me out." Justin continued to gaze at the table between us, so I added: "I have never seen Tephlin Glanz or spoken with him, though his actions have affected my life often enough."

"So, you've never met him? Our doting father?"

"Curiosity was one of the motives for my visit – more than filial gratitude, I admit."

"Forgive me," he said. "Truly." He looked at me in a way that acknowledged the many masks that he wore, and at the same time said that in this moment he wore none. "I thought that I was the only legitimate son who had never been acknowledged. But I see we are brothers in experience as well as in blood." He rose and embraced me. "I see also," Justin mused aloud, "that we have both been raised as orphans – though with the inconvenience of a living father!" We laughed together, I a little uneasy at his irreverence.

He looked at me fully and frankly; then I noticed his eyes sought out the serving woman's.

After dinner I wanted to broach the subject of Gath and my conjectures about Harlech trade with the Kuhlans and the Kr, but I was reluctant to speak in front of the woman. I asked Justin – we had reached a first-name basis early in the meal – about his experience in the war, but he dismissed the topic. He wanted to know more about my childhood on my grandfather's estate. This was a subject in which Justin seemed particularly interested, but I had little to tell. He, on the other hand, was a child of Hebron, raised on the street and in the busy marketplace, and he had a wealth of colorful and amusing anecdotes. I had nothing to match them.

"My childhood ended when I was about seven," I said at one point. "Since then I have been waiting for my life to. . . ."

"To what?" he asked, seeing me pause.

"To knit together again. To become something else."

We talked long into the night. I was not used to brandy and fell asleep on his couch.

IV

Justin and I saw each other frequently after that, both of us eager for a relationship that should have been ours from childhood. I had a sense of having been deprived of much, and I felt a need to catch up, to use the time to best advantage. Like me, Justin had had a difficult childhood, and that, together with our mutual shame at our origins, was a bond between us. Still, I had moments of uneasiness about our first meeting. What had motivated his hostility? That I was equally a son of Tephlin Glanz? Because I was a Haggadah? Jealousy was not a plausible motive, since he had fame and glory enough for any man. And neither was fear. Justin was a man, not a child; such explanations demeaned him.

I remained uneasy as well about the Harlech woman and her child. What did they mean to Justin? And therefore what should they mean to me as our friendship ripened? Justin explained to me the Harlech custom of honoring distinguished service by adoption, so that the clan name was now spread widely among people who were not blood relatives. I was relieved that the rumors of Harlech incest were false, based on our misunderstanding of their ways. But what social forms could one use for Israelites who had been reduced to virtual bondage by defeat and occupation? Was Michal-Rebekah Harlech a great lady or a prize in a captured city? A slave or an honored matron? I could deal with an enemy or an unfortunate widow with a child to raise, but not with some status in between. Israel's customs were complex, and I had had little experience of society. I could scarcely make out the nuances of this situation, which seemed repugnant in all of its features. But I knew the Law, and the Law was plain. If she was Justin's mistress, he had put himself – and her – in grave danger.

In the meantime, my fascination with the Kr and their trade relations with Benjamin grew, and I searched the records available to me, grateful to have a diversion from thoughts about Justin and his living arrangements. The most reliable chronicler of a century ago reported that the Kr of his times used poison arrows and feasted on human flesh. In his day, the plain of Engedi was densely settled with many towns and strongholds and was one of the most prosperous districts belonging to Israel. Nevertheless, the Kr were a terror to the settlements. It was partly to avoid dealing with these savages that the whole of Engedi was later ceded to Benjamin, a concession thought at the time to be empty of value.

In the year 881, during the Second War of Investiture, the victorious Conclave of the Messiahists declared the Kr anathema and defined them as beings without souls, incapable of salvation. This Conclave was important in our own history as marking the earliest assertion of Messiahist pretensions to rule the nation. Their power had grown steadily over the past century. Pondering their theological dismissal of a whole people, I wrote in my journal: "We Old Believers are less presumptuous about defining the spiritual status of others. We neither yearn after salvation nor deny its possibility to others." Beyond these few facts, I could find very little information about the nomads of Moab. As a people outside the Law, the Kr are, by definition, utterly repugnant to Israel. And what Israel defines as unclean, it is not likely to examine. Still, I was dismayed that the Harlech, who are after all Israelites, could hold intercourse with such a degenerate race. "It is hard to say in this situation," I wrote, "which party is the more repugnant."

Nevertheless, I felt nearly as attracted as repelled by these renegades. I was particularly tantalized by one detail. How, I asked myself, did the Harlech control the actual contacts with the Kr? How did they manage to deal with such savage and, theologically speaking, soulless partners?

To repay his hospitality, I invited Justin Apollo to dine at the Orion, reputedly the best Inn in Esdralon. I was aware that the Headquarters and Commissary staffs often spent their evenings there in company with the richest merchants and highest-ranking Messiahist clergy. Justin was obviously a regular there, for he led me immediately to a back room where a game of chance was in progress. Players and spectators alike greeted him familiarly and regarded me coolly. Justin seemed to be looking for someone. "Do you come here often?" he asked as we returned to the dining room.

"Never," I said.

"I didn't think so. There is a brothel upstairs, very nice," he said. "And the highest stake games in the city as well." He put his hand on my shoulder. "It would please me to eat in a quieter place. Perhaps you have somewhere you usually dine?"

I usually took my meals in the mess hall, but there was a small brandy shop just off the main plaza that served the simple foods I was used to. I suggested it to Justin, and he seemed pleased. Justin paused at the Orion long enough for the proprietor to wrap up a loaf of bread for him, and we then made our way to the Cup and Saucer, a much humbler establishment. We shook the rain from our garments and enjoyed its steamy warmth. Their evening fare was turnip and onion stew served in earthenware bowls with hot cornbread. They brought us a cruet of vinegar and dried hot peppers – a southern dietary custom I had picked up campaigning in Judah. Justin fell to with a good appetite, asked for more chopped onions for the stew and a pitcher of their best beer.

Over dinner I broached the subject of Gath and my discoveries about Benjamin's trade with the Kr. As I had expected, Justin was already well informed on the subject. After making sure our conversation would not be overheard, he filled in all the details I had not yet discovered or inferred. The hide and leather trade was indeed centered here in Esdralon and at Gath. The source of hides was their trade with the Kuhlans. "The Kuhlans are permanently hostile to Israel," Justin explained. "They allow no buildings on their territory, but they have allowed the Harlech to establish temporary base camps up the Snake River at its confluence with the Clearwater. That, apparently, is a remarkable concession on their part."

"But how could the Harlech trade with such filth?"

"They don't trade with them, exactly. The Kuhlans cull their herds in the fall as part of a ritual demanded by their religion. They happen to do that just at the juncture of the Clearwater and the Snake – and have done so, apparently, for centuries. By an arrangement that goes back to old Jonas ben Harlech, seventy years or more, the Benjamites collect the hides, field dress them, pack them in brine, and raft them down the river to Gath, where they are processed. Thousands of hides are taken there each year. The Benjamites also salvage hundreds of barrels of dried beef and salt beef – the same beef, I expect, that your grandfather fed his slaves." The thought of Kuhlan beef on our tables brought an exclamation from me.

"Few would guess," Justin added, seeming pleased to have surprised me, "how large a portion of the diet of Israel comes, courtesy of the Harlech, from our werewolf neighbors to the east. For years, no one even suspected it. The Harlech are incredibly secretive. I don't see how they manage."

"That is exactly what excited Israel's hostility," I remarked.

"One of the causes, certainly," he conceded. "But Benjamin aroused Israel by being so successful." Justin, I saw, enjoyed taking sides against the obvious. However, he was as fascinated with the illicit Harlech trade as I was, and he had studied it longer.

"I cannot imagine how they managed this 'exchange' – as they call the trade," he continued. "For the most part, the Benjamites don't have much contact with the Kuhlans. The Kuhlans won't allow it. As I understand it, their religion forbids nearly all intercourse with outsiders. On the other hand, I've heard that some of the Harlech clan – wild young men, the companions of Zachariah ben Harlech – have adopted Kuhlan ways and their manner of dress. Even their religion."

He enjoyed my shock at this news. Zachariah ben Harlech was famous all over Israel. It was the attempted assassination of Zachariah, the heir-apparent of the Benjamite Apostle, that had started events moving toward the present war. I had always regarded him sympathetically. To hear him described as a partaker in savage rites was disturbing.

"In any case," Justin said, "the Benjamites don't actually trade for the cattle; they leave gift offerings. It's a technicality, really, but important to both sides. It maintains appearances."

"Gift offerings? What manner of gift offerings?"

"Blankets and garments made of wool. And linen cloth – their women like linen for sacred garments. And leather goods. The Benjamites make – I should say, *made* – all kinds of leather goods right here in Esdralon: coats and leggings, leather clothing of all kinds, lariats, harness, fancy bridles, and the high-pommeled saddles preferred by Kuhlan warriors. They also trade metal goods – kettles and knives and other tools. No swords, however! It is a point of honor with the Harlech that they do not trade iron or steel weapons to the Kuhlans."

"Honor among the Harlech?" I interjected. But I was surprised at Justin's knowledge, for I was beginning to connect information with sources.

"The Kuhlans live apart from their women most of the time," Justin continued. "So I suppose it has become convenient for them to have their leather tanned and turned into useful objects by Esdralon's workshops. The Harlech also leave salt and grain offerings. It is all pre-arranged, of course." Justin explained that the Harlech bring the Kuhlan hides back to Engedi and process them and then turn about and trade a good part of the leather goods to the Kr. "The miracle," he said, "is how they set it all up in the first place."

I began to sense how deeply our views of the trade might differ. The waiter brought another pitcher of beer.

"Trade with the Kr," Justin said, "is especially lucrative, as those savages know the value of nothing. The Harlech barter everything they can manufacture and that the Kr can carry off. Woolens, for example – mostly woven into blanket cloth, since weaving is not a high art form among the savages. The Kr, too, seem bereft of women to serve them, although I believe their custom is not to exalt their women as priestesses as the Kuhlans do, but to savage them so thoroughly in childhood that only a handful survive to child-bearing age. In exchange for these excellent Harlech products, as you have inferred, the Kr leave them mountains of unwashed wool."

"I see." For the first time, I saw this triangular exchange in my imagination like a campaign in a war. "So, for three generations, Benjamin has grown fat off of this commerce with savages—with both of Israel's mortal enemies." Justin nodded. "And Israel's Second Army," I continued, "now waits at the junction of the Clearwater, hoping to take over where Benjamin left off."

"That was the intention, certainly, but the Kuhlans never appeared. They have chosen to perform their annual cattle sacrifice elsewhere, or not at all. We simply do not know what happened. Several hundred Benjamites who served this trade are stranded upstream somewhere, perhaps wintering over with the Kuhlans. Or perhaps massacred by them. Again, we do not *know*!" Suddenly he struck the table with his fist. "Israel's intelligence has failed completely! That's why we are stalemated! But I can tell you that Montevideo's expedition up the Snake will fail – just as our occupation of Engedi is likely to." He sat musing a moment and then leaned over and put his hand on my arm. "By the way, do you understand now the timing of the war? Last fall?"

I wondered at the sudden change of subject. Israel had struck the first blows of the war in late autumn when Harlech manpower was absent, engaged in this peculiar exchange at the junction of the Snake and Clearwater, one hundred and fifty miles to the east. Israel's attack, Justin was intimating, had been timed at their moment of weakness.

"But what do you mean," I asked, "by saying that our conquest of Engedi is likely to fail? I see no evidence that the Harlech have the power to contest it."

"These outcasts from Israel," he said emphatically, "have kept the Kr at bay for over a century while simultaneously separating them from their fleeces. But Benjamin has also maintained a steady war against them. Except briefly during the season of actual trading, which occurs at the summer solstice, these two trading partners were constantly at each other's throats. *Constantly*," he repeated, as if I were incapable of understanding.

"I don't understand," I admitted.

"*No one* in Israel understands! I'm telling you that the Harlech knew how to deal with these partners of theirs; they understood that the hostility of the Kr, like the hostility of the Kuhlans, is unrelenting – and that the trade changed nothing. *Nothing!*"

I waited for more explanation.

"Except for the period during the actual exchange of goods, the whole of Engedi is a war zone. *Permanently.* The Harlech never relaxed their guard when dealing with the Kr. In fact, they regularly mounted expeditions against them in the autumn, as soon as the tick season abates. They were *at war* with the Kr!"

"Against their trading partners?"

Justin heaved a great sigh, seeming resigned to my incapacity to understand. "War is war," he said. "Trade is war conducted by other means."

We ate in silence for a while, but I could see he was agitated. "So you see, by seizing Esdralon," Justin continued, "Israel has inherited the Kr as trading partners and as enemies. But meanwhile, the Kuhlan leg of the triangle is missing – sawed off, so our stool cannot stand. That leaves us with the menace of the Kr as raiders but with *nothing* as trading partners!" Justin was well into his fourth pitcher of Engedi beer, and his voice had unconsciously grown louder. In spite of the amount he had had to drink, he remained completely lucid. But I was growing uneasy. "The Kr are not familiar with us, and they are completely unknown *to* us," he declared. The truth is, we know nothing of how to conduct the exchange. That is dangerous, Josiah. Very dangerous!" I was surprised to hear that his thoughts, coming from such different premises, so closely paralleled my own. "And the Harlech aren't *telling*, either," he said, seeming particularly incensed.

I related everything I had learned from the archives of Esdralon, which was not much. "Yes," he said, his eyes gleaming, "together, you and I have acquired an excellent overview, but the Devil is in the details!" He slammed his empty mug on the table.

I flinched at his use of the Messiahist expression. "What a shame," I said, expressing my view of the whole business, "that the Harlech have wandered so far from the Law and from the community of Israel."

"I disagree!" Justin replied emphatically. "The Harlech are able to deal with these two peoples whom the rest of Israel holds in dread. I count that as quite an accomplishment. Remember, this is not trade, exactly, and it all falls within the letter of the Law. The Kuhlans do what Kuhlans do; the Harlech conveniently appear, salvage the remains of a sacrificial rite, and leave polite gift offerings. Nothing so contemptible as commerce is transacted between them."

I saw he mocked my disdain of trade, my Haggadah pretensions. Perhaps justly. Justin had an unsentimental, calculating, merchant's intellect which seemed to serve him surprisingly well as a soldier.

"There are lessons here," he insisted, suddenly sober. "Israel has always looked inward and enforced a fierce conformity on its members. Israel's identity lies in that conformity. But the Harlech clan of Benjamin, who were pushed out to the margins, have been forced to live on other terms. They have had to make their own rules and find their own salvation."

Salvation! I must have winced visibly at the word.

"Granting that fact, you must acknowledge that they have succeeded, and succeeded brilliantly, in turning their disadvantages into wealth and power."

"And into this war!"

"Ah, the war!" he said, wiping his mouth. "The war. I agree in part with what you imply. But it was not Benjamin's wealth alone that brought about this war. It was their independence, their going their own way indifferent to the rest of Israel."

"And to the Law?" I demanded.

"And their indifference to the Law," he said steadily, looking at me. "And I for one admire them for it."

It is not possible, I decided, for brothers to remain always in harmony or to see things in the same way. And I knew that we both had had too much to drink. But I also knew in my heart that *the Law is not mocked*, and I feared for Justin. Remembering the warnings of nighttime violence in Esdralon, I saw Justin home, supporting him on my shoulder. On my way back to the barracks, I thought it possible I was being followed, but no one offered me any harm.

V

The next day at Headquarters I heard that Justin was ill, so I stopped by to visit him as soon as my duties permitted. I had had news that the Council of Apostles was gathering in Hebron, and I was anxious to ask Justin what this meeting might mean. To my surprise, the Harlech woman informed me that Justin was out. Before I could inquire what errand would take him out of a sick bed, she drew me inside in a manner that was both shy and confidential and asked me if I would assist her with a favor.

"What favor?" I asked, perhaps a little abruptly.

"Major Apollo often brings things here from the barracks – food and other items. Your brother is very generous and kind, as you know."

I did not know, so I waited for her to continue.

"We – my son Appian and I – regularly distribute food to less fortunate people here in Esdralon. To those who have no means, because of the war, and to those who are sick or otherwise helpless. There are many such in Esdralon." She had a soft, rich voice and an expressive manner. Since our awkward moment of introduction, I had never spoken to her.

"I was told Justin is ill today," I said warily.

"True, he complained of his stomach and head when he awoke, but the discomfort passed." She looked at me sternly. It was clear that she felt that Justin's illness was related to the condition in which I had returned him the night before. "Major Apollo would not say where you had taken him." Her eyes had more than a little rebuke in them. *Exactly like a protective wife*, I thought. Then she brightened as she recalled the favor she wanted to ask: "Would you be so kind," she said, "as to accompany Appian on an errand? We promised to deliver a basket of food to some elderly people just a few streets away; they depend on us." Her dark eyes were wonderfully eloquent and her voice like a melody. "I am afraid to send Appian alone, particularly carrying a food parcel. Major Apollo sometimes accompanies him if I cannot, and there is no one else I can ask."

"And *you* are unable to go with him?" I was suddenly suspicious and determined not to be taken in by this dangerously appealing woman. My question startled her; she cast her eyes down and twisted her shawl in her hands. She seemed suddenly embarrassed.

"Yes," she said; her large eyes turned on mine an instant and then away. "Since you ask, the time of women is upon me. It is not customary to go abroad."

I was shamed into silence, paralyzed with embarrassment. After a moment, I began to babble apologies, knowing that only one raised as I, entirely apart from women, could have made such a blunder. My entire body clenched in shame while she instructed Appian to fill a basket with bread and cheese and fruit preserves to carry to her dependent countrymen. Eventually, emptied of all the words of apology I knew, I escorted Appian on his errand, still feeling firebrands of remorse in my heart. An elderly woman answered his knock and took the basket, darting a hostile glance at me as she closed the door. She had a large tumor on her throat, and she scowled at me even as she took the basket from my hand.

We returned through the narrow streets in silence, buffeted by wind and sleet. I had intended to flee as soon as I had seen Appian safely home, but Justin was waiting in the street. "I heard a strange story about you today," he began, and my heart fell, revolted at what I had done and dreading to be confronted with it. "Someone told me today," Justin said, "that you had been in Lagash. Can it be?"

I was relieved that he was not rebuking me for my awful discourtesy to the Harlech woman.

"You *have* been to Lagash!" Justin repeated incredulously, taking my silence as assent.

"You *are* that same young Glanz offspring with an Israelite name – surely there cannot be two such persons in the Army of Israel!"

"Yes," I admitted. "I led a patrol into Lagash."

"Into the very lion's mouth! Well, you must tell me about it. No buts. Come up with me and share a meal, and tell us everything." Justin was insistent, taking me by the arm. "We're having something simple enough for even your tastes tonight. Michal-Rebekah thanks you, by the way, for helping Appian on his errand."

He used her first name familiarly, I noted.

"I must say," Justin went on, "I can't begrudge these poor wretches a crust of bread now and then. They've suffered a good deal, there's no denying it." I found myself at the top of the stairs and in his living room. "But it is against regulations, you see, to give Benjamites bread!" He laughed in his humorless way while helping me out of my cloak. "Charity itself is against the regulations of the Army of Israel, " he added, "so I wouldn't mention this to anyone. I want to hear all about your epic journey to Lagash, but first, tell me what you think of infantry. I was at the Field of War all afternoon, suffering intolerable miseries from a hangover, for which I have you to thank, just to see the First Apostles go through their drills. I watched them maneuver through sleet and storm, nearly freezing to death myself. They looked impressive, I thought, even so. Is there anything in it, do you think?"

"Infantry? Not likely," I replied. Israel's wars had always been fought by mounted warriors. Horsemen could be hurled swiftly and with great force at an enemy's weak spot. Infantry seemed to me impossibly slow and clumsy, weighted down with all their armor and equipment. "I don't see how infantry can even arrive at the contested point before the issue has been decided," I said.

"Decided by the real warriors!"

"Yes, exactly!" I laughed. "Maybe the infantry can man our fortified posts and guard the baggage trains."

"Perhaps," Justin said. "They looked quite impressive, I thought, nonetheless – as if wherever they placed themselves would *be* the contested point."

The apartment was warm and inviting and smelled of freshly baked bread. I soon felt at ease again. The woman made no sign that anything had passed between us earlier. She was more the proper retiring servant than at any other time I had visited. Justin and I supped on chicken broth and vegetables, warm bread, and a dry white wine. His stomach, Justin said reproachfully, required great care this evening. Afterwards, Appian brought us a salad of fresh greens in a mild dressing. "I'll wager these are the earliest greens in Engedi," Justin said. "Michal-Rebekah has a few plants on the roof she forces in the spring. I don't see how she manages in such miserable cold weather."

The troubling familiarity again! Of their alleged adultery, I had compelling evidence from their manner together, and I had no evidence at all. I had nothing but nagging, insistent doubt. Because of it, I saw with regret, I could not hold my feelings for Justin or my sense of him as a man steady.

Justin was unimpressed by my news of the Council. "So let them meet," he said contemptuously. "The whole Confederacy is just an empty shell—and has been for some time. This war seems only to the ignorant a decision of our Council of Apostles. They were tools, as the world knows. Or *will* know."

I reminded him gently that war had come when the Apostle from Benjamin refused to attend the Council sessions. "The Council chose to consider that a grave affront, a breach of the covenant. They declared war."

"So it was announced to the world. But the Apostle of Dan, who is opposed to the war, has not been to a Council meeting since the war began. Do we see the Council urging war against Dan? Hardly! And consider Naphtali, which our elder half-brother Hanford holds tight in his embrace. That tribe, if tribe it is, hasn't sent an Apostle to the Council for years. Hanford is himself the sole government of Naphtali. Everyone knows that. But again, no declaration of war against the private fiefdom of our eldest brother. The Council of the Apostles is a ghost and a mirage, I tell you; its time is past."

Justin had grown fond of lecturing me, and I could see he was acquiring energy for a major performance.

"Surely you see," he said, "that the old landed families like your grandfather's are impoverished, and that power now emanates from the cities rather than from the tribes. Do you imagine," he demanded, "that the legion in which you and I serve could have existed a generation ago?"

Justin's point was undeniable. In the past decade, the Council had established two national legions apart from the tribal levies. The action was unprecedented, and the decision had, in fact, been implemented over fierce opposition. To the more conservative elements in Israel, the idea of a military force separate from the tribes and answering directly to the Council was highly subversive. But the Council had, nevertheless, succeeded in imposing its will. *Or someone behind the Council had succeeded.* In spite of myself, I was beginning to think like Justin.

"New men are making decisions in Israel now," Justin declared. "Men who are not of noble blood and whose wealth is based on commerce rather than land. Yes, merchants like my family – like our father, whom I believe you despise even more than I do!" It was my turn to seek the eyes of the Harlech woman, but her gaze was cast demurely on the floor. "What must be understood," Justin continued, "is that Tephlin Glanz's career is not the story of a single individual. A whole group, a class, has been secretly waxing in power and has risen with him. These men have risen inside a society that officially despises them and bars them from office, but they are coming into power nonetheless. We won't accept being shunned forever, you know." Justin looked at me accusingly, and then broke into his most charming smile. "That's why, my brother, we live in such interesting times!"

As usual, there was a great deal to digest in what he said, but before I could reply, Michal-Rebekah had cleared the table, making an obvious point of picking up the wine. I rose to leave. Justin asked if I would tell the story of my journey to Lagash, but I begged off. "Another time, perhaps."

"Tomorrow then," he said, following me to the door.

VI

The next morning the army was called out to witness the execution of eight Benjamites. A wooden platform had been erected in the main plaza in front of the Hall of Assembly, which lay only a short distance from Justin's quarters. Israel's forces were drawn up in formation to witness their deaths and to overawe the crowd. Justin and I were placed among the Headquarters staff very near the scaffold. Six men and two women were garroted one by one, to the flourish of drums. The first two men were very brave, but their struggles unnerved the later victims. The women were last, and I had to stare straight ahead and try to close my ears to their cries. Their bodies were stripped and disemboweled and then thrown on a huge pyre in the center of plaza and burned. Afterwards, as the fire diminished and emitted a black oily smoke, Bishop Bon of Manasseh, reputedly the most strident voice among the churchmen, delivered a Messiahist harangue from the balcony of the Governor's residence. Justin whispered to me that Bishop Bon had come down from New Jerusalem especially for the event. I scarcely paid attention to his words, for I was seething with revulsion.

As soon as we were dismissed, Justin took me fiercely by the arm, and spoke into my ear, "Did you hear that, Josiah? Did you *hear* that?"

"Yes, of course, a thousand times over. The same familiar rubbish – another bloodthirsty churchmen vowing the destruction of all who oppose their god. What of it?"

Then you *didn't* hear!" he exclaimed. "Zaiyah, Zaiyah!" he said, using my childhood nickname. "The Bishop – Bishop Bon – he spoke of a date, an actual date!"

"What are you talking about?" I thought Justin's excitement about dates very unseemly, given the events we had just witnessed. "What date? The date of what?"

He looked at me with an indescribable expression on his face. "Judgment Day!" he exclaimed, "Bon gave the date of Judgment Day!"

I shook free of his arm. "I don't believe in their Judgment Day, and you are a fool if you credit it."

Justin had already started to turn away from me, preoccupied with this new information. "But what does all this mean?" he asked. "What does it reveal, and what does it disguise?"

My thoughts were on the Harlech woman and her son – how I wished they had been spared this revolting barbarism. I followed Justin through the crowd. "Why were the two women put to death?" I asked.

"Heretics, I think," he answered quickly over his shoulder. A crowd of ragged Benjamites, both men and women, began shouting and making a commotion off the square. I heard cries of "Bread!" and "Justice!" and then missiles began to fly overhead.

"This was not on the Bishop's itinerary," Justin remarked. "Interesting. . . ."

I was too furious to wonder where his thoughts were leading this time. "This meddling by the church," I said, 'this savagery—calling out the army to witness the deaths of these heretics! As if we approved it, as if we could *tolerate* these black-robed swine! I don't believe I could live in a nation ruled by these churchmen!"

"You think not?" Justin said, giving me a strange look.

We encountered Colonel Asad Shevren in the midst of the square. His command was drawn up in formation; lines of mounted troopers reared like a wall in front of the crowd. The cavalrymen were tense and ready, but Colonel Shevren had a leg thrown over the pommel of his saddle and his helmet pushed back on his head, to show his contempt for such a rabble. Colonel Shevren was in an ugly mood. "I care nothing for the mob," he said, spitting on the cobblestones. "But the Bishop practically invited the soldiery to sack the city again. Bad for morale, shedding civilian blood."

"There will be hell to pay tonight, that's for certain," Justin said. He was no longer the eager curiosity-seeker of a moment ago. He saw what was about to happen.

I repeated my question about the women who had been executed and flinched at Shevren's answer: "I heard they were spies," he said.

As we spoke, we heard hoarse, shouted commands and the tread of hundreds of feet in unison. It was the First Apostles infantry. Their units maneuvered in step, stamping fiercely while they wheeled their formations toward the crowd. Like Justin, I had seen them perform on the drill ground, but at this moment I began to see them with new eyes. The measured tread kept their ranks tightly together. A thousand men stepping as one has, I discovered, an ominous, unsettling sound, suggestive of power and determination. We watched as the infantry, shield to shield and three ranks deep, swung into the crowd. The angry shouts quickly turned to cries of terror; serious blood was about to be shed. The mob dispersed down the side streets like flocks of sparrows.

"Damn!" Colonel Shevren said, "and it's my watch today!" He seized the reins and set spurs to his horse as he turned to his command. Worse was about to follow. Justin and I took ourselves quickly out of the square.

The rioters fled along the narrow streets of the city, pursued by both infantry and cavalry. Many people lost their lives that day. Fires were set in abandoned dwellings along the western wall, but were quickly contained. A pall of smoke hung over the city.

That evening, Justin asked several officers who were friends of his and myself to stay at his quarters in order to protect the building and the people of the block. A half-dozen of us clustered around the fireplace, warming ourselves over a tiny fire, for the spring had turned cold again. Fuel was scarce, and to use a fire except for cooking was a luxury. I thought with sudden repugnance of the huge fires in the plaza that morning that had consumed the bodies of those executed. Michal-Rebekah, who had said not a word to either of us, set a pot of tea brewing over the hearth. We shared some bread and cheese, and soon we soldiers were cheerful enough. To pass the time, Justin asked me to tell the story of my patrol into Lagash. Glad to let my mind wander from our present gloom, I consented.

"It was last December," I began, "soon after I joined the Second Apostles. It was very cold. Morale in the Second Apostles was still low after Beth-Shan." Outside we heard a commotion, and then a bugle call and drums and the clopping of horses' hooves.

"That's the First Apostles Horse," someone said.

"What idiocy!" another of the officers declared.

"Headquarters," I continued, trying to keep my mind on the story, "was expecting Benjamin to follow up their victory with an offensive into Manasseh. Information about their intentions was needed, so I volunteered to lead a patrol into the Lost Horse Hills." *I had volunteered, and Mac Dogol had accepted my offer, but no others stepped forward to go with me. Whether this reluctance stemmed from knowledge of my disgrace at the Academy or from my name, I could only speculate. How could I know? How would I ever know?* "That evening, four young troopers – young boys from the north, probably driven into service by poverty at home – came forward." *They were not really warriors, but they were from Asher and would not let one of their own, as they saw it, bear a disgrace. It was snowing when they led their horses up to Mac Dogol's tent. Mac Dogol grimaced, but did not forbid us to go.*

"We left the next morning before reveille. Heavy snow had fallen, so we had to lead our horses that first day. We feared that a Harlech patrol would cross our track and follow us, so we circled back and laid ambushes several times. We lay in the snow under scrub pines to watch our back trail, but no one was following us. It was apparent that such caution was getting us nowhere—and we were freezing. After that, we went forward boldly –

perhaps I should say recklessly." I paused a moment, looking at the other officers. "Sometimes one relies on luck."

"That night we made camp in the lee of a cliff. A storm blew up and dropped more snow on us. The next morning, the others wanted to turn back, but I persuaded them to cook a double portion of beans and dried beef and wait it out. They were more than happy to gorge themselves, so we tarried there all day, feasting. The next day the sun came out and we could feel the thaw, so I was able to persuade them to go on. The enemy were encamped on Clamas Creek as we had expected. We made our approach after dark and crept up very close. I thought once we had been discovered, but the whole affair came off without incident. We counted their horses and were mystified: why were there so few of the enemy and with horses in such poor condition? If the Harlech intended to come through the pass, they must be encamped somewhere farther west, laying up food and supplies. But where? We pulled back and spent the night without a fire, miserably cold. The next day one of the troopers scaled a ridge top but saw no smoke rising to the west. Nevertheless, we decided to press on and find the enemy encampment."

The group appeared to be waiting expectantly, but my tale was over. "That's the story, really; three days later we were a hundred miles southwest and inside Lagash. There was no encampment. No invasion was in preparation."

"But you must have suffered great hardships," Justin said, prompting me. Apparently, I had told a very dull story.

"One man got a case of frostbite and suffered a good deal. We grew quite hungry, because we had eaten nearly all our rations the first day."

"So what happened to you in Lagash?"

"Nothing of importance. We penetrated only the northeast edge of Lagash, of course. And even there we found no troop encampments, no trains of wagons, no herds. The first horses we saw were on a ranch – just a small, dilapidated shack with barns and corral, not an army depot. Of course it should have been obvious that the Harlech were not intending to push through the pass to attack Manasseh. If they had been preparing an invasion, we would have seen signs of it."

"You didn't realize that?"

"Not immediately. I must have been stupid with fatigue. All I could think of was our failure to find the enemy. Then it began to dawn on me what the absence of enemy preparations meant – and only then that we had a long way back and no certain means of returning with our information."

Justin prompted me to continue, anxious to find a story somewhere in my account.

"We decided to raid the ranch and replace our horses, which were played out, and to take whatever supplies we could lay hands on. We started toward the ranch the next morning, but we encountered a boy, perhaps fifteen, on his way to care for the animals. We rode right up to him in a dense fog, both of us equally surprised and alarmed. I pretended that we were a Benjamite patrol and that we needed fresh horses. The boy saw through us immediately but played along to save his life. The others privately urged me to kill him, but I said wait, maybe this encounter will make things easier for us. We picked the animals we wanted out of the pasture and changed saddles." *Our hands were so stiff we could hardly cinch the girths.* "I took the boy aside, and by this time he was not able to hide his fear. I pretended not to see, and I said to him, we both know that this is irregular. We have to have fresh horses and we can't wait. But I don't want you to get into difficulty with the Provost. I'll write out a requisition, and you can give it to the District Commander, and you and your family will be reimbursed." *He nodded but he was very afraid.*

My story, I realized, had begun to move in a direction I had not intended. *I had asked the boy, menacingly, who is at the ranch? Your sisters and mother? St. Supplicee! Your father? In the army. Do you have any food? Yes? Give it to me.*

"I scrawled out a letter and said, take this to the District Commander." *But first ride hard back to your house and get your mother and sisters to safety. There are enemy patrols nearby. Do you understand? He understood.*

"What was it that you wrote in the note?" Justin asked.

"Just a note," I said. My audience seemed to think this a good joke. I recalled vividly the misery on the face of the boy, expecting to be killed, and my own misery, expecting to kill him.

> *"This young man is loyal to Benjamin; when we exchanged horses with him, he acted under coercion. Be good enough to reimburse his family for five moderately good horses, pending the settlement of claims for war damages at the termination of hostilities. . . ."*

They were waiting for me to continue. "I scrawled a signature that no one could possibly read, but wrote very plainly under it, 'representing the First Army of Israel'."

"That's all?" someone asked.

"I had some difficulty explaining all this to my comrades, but I assured them that I had gotten some food, which I had." *I told them I had scared the boy out of his wits about the safety of his family. He would get them to safety before he sent anyone after us.*

You should have killed him, they said.

Yes, and gained a few hours start at best.

But if alerted, the Harlech will easily overtake us! Have you thought what they will do if they capture us?

Yes, and it is very possible that they will capture us, and that will bad for us. But they will do less than if we killed the boy.

I realized I was staring off into space, absorbed in the story I was not telling. "So, with the fresh horses and a little food," I said, picking up the thread of the tale, "we started back."

"But you had no grain or fodder for the horses," Justin said, still anxious to squeeze some drama from the tale.

"True. We had to walk part of the way back. We had some close calls, but we made it. That's it. Or rather, that's all."

"Still," one of the officers remarked, "you received the Red Oak Leaf for valor. That is something."

We drank our tea by the fire, six Israelites and two Harlech, thrown together by the war. I had brought candles from my quarters – a gift that would cost me dearly in time and reflection in my journal. Nevertheless, the warmth of the moment was precious because of the memories my story had evoked. I looked at my hands, which were tinged with the color of the circulating blood beneath. Recalling our hardships, I treasured the warmth of the fire burning brightly in the hearth and each tendril of aromatic steam rising from our cups. Justin said something to the Harlech woman, who brought out small glasses and a stone bottle of apple brandy. We warmed the brandy near the coals and held our glasses in the palms of our hands. As I sipped mine, it suffused warmth though my entire body. I sat lost in thought, enjoying the moment and the low murmur of conversation.

Appian was fidgeting behind us, pacing back and forth. Justin motioned him to come and share a seat with him close to the fire. Instead, the boy approached me. Appian looked at me intently, his dark eyes reflecting the fire. "Why did you not kill the boy?" he asked cautiously. I had not realized he had been listening. "He was your enemy. It would have been safer to kill him."

"Appian! be still!" His mother's eyes were wide with surprise and alarm. "You must be still!" she hissed.

I was surprised by his question, but puzzled more by his mother's response. Appian knew a great deal for a boy his age, and his mother must have realized by now that I was no zealot against the Harlech. I replied as if Appian were a man, which is what he seemed at the moment. "Perhaps you are right," I said, "but it is hard to know. That young man seemed to me not an enemy, but someone who was supporting his family while his father was away." I looked around the circle for assistance. "Perhaps," I said, "I should have been born in other times, when there was no civil strife."

"Hah!" Justin sneered. "Landed warriors and civil strife were hatched from the same egg!"

Appian continued to regard me silently, and I knew he was not satisfied with my answer. "Perhaps," I said, "I would have felt otherwise if we had been captured, and I had to watch – if I had seen my men interrogated." He nodded, understanding me and ignoring the others, including Justin, who has still gesturing for him to sit down and be still. "When you are an officer, Appian," I said, "you may confront similar situations. Let us hope by that time Israel will be whole again."

He was not to be mollified so easily. "Mother says that I am to be a slave all my life and not an officer," he replied in his boy's voice but man's manner.

Michal-Rebekah's eyes were downcast and her hands were clenched tightly together. I recalled Justin's remark when I met her: *"Fortunes of war"* – a phrase that covered so much that was otherwise inexplicable. "This war cannot last forever," I said. "And when it ends, we will have, not justice perhaps, but some abatement of this cruelty." Justin and the other officers nodded, looking acutely uncomfortable. Appian's mother raised her eyes to gaze at me in such a way that I felt compelled to add: "Appian, you are the son of an honored father and a gracious lady; you must not" – *I hesitated, seeking desperately for what it was he must not do, for a way to finish my sentence of advice.* "You must not give up hope." I felt the hollowness of what I said. It was the best I could do.

Appian seemed also to feel its inadequacy. "You are an enemy of my people," he said. "How can you tell me to have hope?"

I sat upright, feeling extremely awkward. "We soldiers do what we must," I said. "You will be an officer someday too. That is what you *are* and will be, whatever happens temporarily." I glanced at Justin, who seemed even more uncomfortable than before. "And if we should chance to meet someday as enemies on a battlefield, I would say to myself, there is Appian, the son of Elgin Harlech, both men who are great Names in Benjamin." I paused, for I could not say what I felt easily. "They are men whom I would wish for friends, but who are worthy and honorable enemies, if enemies we must be. In the presence of such men, whatever befalls, there is no disgrace" – *I stopped, feeling embarrassed and exposed* – "but honor," I finished lamely.

Justin snorted, "Spare us, please, your antique warrior philosophy! Your ethics of caste!" I was startled by his vehemence, but Appian regarded me as if he had understood.

"That is the consolation of a soldier's life," I said, speaking to Appian, "that it be honorable. That possibility survives, though all else may not." *I recalled my Master Ebenezer at the Refuge speaking earnestly of these things that are so difficult to put into words: "If the time comes when you must throw your life away as a thing of no value, then all that remains to you is the style with which you do it. The style of your death may be the only way of saying that your life is valuable. That all life is valuable, is infinitely precious, though the world spills it like so much dirty dish water."*

"You mean," Appian continued relentlessly, "that you would give us, my father and me—that you would give us our deaths, too. Honorably. If necessary."

I turned round and round in my heart, looking for some escape from the question he had put me. "If necessary," I replied at last.

Justin continued to rail under his breath against the mores of the old clans, but I scarcely noticed him. Appian had my full attention, and it was as if two men in the midst of a potentially lethal difficulty had come to an understanding. I could tell that what I had said was sinking down in him, and that it had brought him a kind of relief. Or at least a kind of clarity. Then his eyes narrowed and I understood that we would be enemies, not friends. I felt his father's death hovering in his mind, and I suddenly felt a pang for Justin and for whatever hopes he entertained of a future that involved these two. Both of them, mother and son, nobles of the tribe of Benjamin, were members of a tradition alien to him – and, it was equally clear, *not to me*. The degree of difference between them and myself was negligible compared to the distance that separated them from Justin.

The boy's mother filled our cups again in the near darkness; we could still hear the sounds of tumult and drunken revelry in the streets outside. When she filled mine, she put her hand on the cup so that her fingers encompassed mine around its rim; then she knelt a moment before me, never looking up at me. Her breast moved under her gown with an emotion she struggled to suppress. In that moment I understood a great deal about how my brother had come to transgress the Law.

VII

On the next market day, when I had no regular duties and I was making a few notes in my journal, Justin stopped by my quarters – which he did only on rare occasions. "Come," he said. "Arise, make haste! We must continue your education."

I looked at the sun, which was scarcely half an hour high. This early visit was not Justin's usual behavior, and it intruded upon one of the rare occasions when I had time to myself. "Not until I finish my exercise," I protested.

"Well, hurry then; this is the first market day since the new policy of occupation."

Though Justin and I spent as much time together as possible, we were continually discovering new things about each other – usually in the form of contrasts. Justin's habits were as irregular as a magpie's. The times when he would choose to sleep, eat, or work were daily mysteries to those around him. My routine, on the other hand, was still governed by the discipline of the Refuge and was orderly enough for both of us. I hurried through my ritual ablutions of cold water and performed a very abbreviated exercise. Justin's companionship and my practice of meditation had proven almost entirely incompatible. But there was a mental discipline in my exercises as well, and I insisted on practicing them regularly. Justin watched me curiously. Strength, quickness, and flexibility were values in the old disciplines, but the goal was balance – balance in all things. At the same time, I could not help but be aware that my breathing exercises, stretches, and held positions must appear ridiculous to the uninitiated.

"Very interesting," Justin said. "What were you doing just now? What was its purpose?" He often inquired about my education and training in martial arts; I avoided the topic as much as possible and put him off with an innocuous answer.

"I heard something about you recently," he said. "About your time at the Academy." I stiffened – rather too quickly – into the folded bat position. He seemed not to be watching me. "Someone said," he continued, "that you were reluctant – or rather, that you *refused* to practice swordsmanship at the Academy."

"I practiced swordsmanship quite rigorously at the Academy," I replied, somewhat evasively.

"Yes, of course," he said. "I meant, more precisely, that you refused to engage in contests of swordsmanship with the other cadets – which were held, routinely as I remember, to develop skill in this essential warrior's craft. Is that true? Did you ever actually draw swords with one of your fellow cadets?

"Once," I admitted.

Justin appeared to examine the folds in his outer garment. "That would be . . . unusual behavior at the Academy – bound to attract notice, I suppose." He regarded me for a moment. "While some may have misunderstood your motives," he said, "both then and now, I believe I can understand them. You were already expert and wanted neither to show up your fellow cadets nor injure them.

"I would not have been so clumsy as to injure them," I said heatedly. I had finished my exercise and was splashing the last of the clean, cold water over myself. The topic was painful, and I longed to be done with it.

"Tell me something, Josiah," Justin continued in his relentless fashion; "how in the world did you gain permission to be exempted?

"I spoke to the instructor."

"Spoke to the instructor in swordsmanship?" He appeared puzzled. "And gave a private demonstration, I should think."

"Yes," I admitted.

"Ah!" Justin exclaimed, as if everything had become clear. "So your real motive was secrecy! Fear of revealing the ancient secrets of the art in which you had been initiated."

"Perhaps my real motive," I said, "was to avoid being questioned constantly about my previous education. My behavior was unusual, I'll grant you. And capable of supporting many interpretations. Perhaps my education has in fact made me strange, but"—I suddenly paused, not knowing how to finish my sentence. Justin was capable of worrying me like a sore tooth; at times he exasperated me.

"Well, brother," he said; "Enough of this subject. But I should warn you that your reticence only makes it more interesting to me."

The market was crowded and noisy. Sentries and armed patrols were everywhere in evidence, but I was not certain what Justin had meant by a "new policy." I looked around curiously at the crowd, which seemed to contain everyone in the city, from high to low and both Benjamite and Israelite. The mood of the crowd was tense and sullen, but there were many items for sale besides the usual foodstuffs. We wandered slowly among the pavilions.

"What do you see?" Justin asked in a low voice.

"Well," I replied, uncertain what he was trying to elicit from me, "I see a set of goblets of rare blue glass and a carved, inlaid box of great value."

"No!" he said impatiently. "Look around. What do you see?"

I was not always content to be cast in the role of Justin's naive protégé, but I decided to be patient and see where his questions would lead. "There are many precious items for sale – more than usual. Jewelry, cook ware and furniture, cloth and clothing of all kinds."

"Yes!" he exclaimed, and I was pleased to have hit even by accident on his line of thought – though as yet I could not fathom its significance. "Yes, and what for? A few peck of grain or a sack of moldy potatoes. Look around." His gesture took in the food stalls, which, in truth, seemed to offer a meager array of choices. "I would estimate," Justin said, "that every third person here with something valuable to sell is named Harlech."

"You mean," I said, "those who bear the clan name as well as those who hold membership in it?"

"Of course." He pointed out several stalls as we moved through the crowd. "Today the clan leaders left in Esdralon seem to be trading their accumulated wealth for a mess of pottage. If I am not mistaken, they are buying food for their poorer brethren. There is hunger in Esdralon."

I thought of the small amount of acreage that had been plowed and seeded on the outskirts of Esdralon, and I recalled the hungry people I had seen in the damaged sections of the city and believed him. "I don't understand," I said. "It is true that the absence of planting around the city will mean that this region cannot support itself this year. But I see the invoices every day in the Commissary; there are plenty of stores in Esdralon. The warehouses are full."

"Exactly! And that's why Israelite policy is such a disgrace!" Justin's voice was unnaturally loud and I feared we had been overheard. I glanced around, fearful not of the populace but of the sentries. Justin had a jest that everyone, without exception, was a member of the Eyes of Israel, but those who were patriots did not report to anyone. This morning I did not find his jest amusing.

We left the market and headed for Justin's quarters. On the way, he described how the Harlech were trying to get their people out of the city and down to Lagash safely. "But escape has become nearly impossible with Israelite patrols on both land and river, and now the Kr are loose to the south. There will be starvation here by the solstice. In the meantime, as you say, the warehouses are bursting with supplies."

"Someone should bring this problem to the attention of Headquarters," I said. "A tragic oversight, certainly, but this can't be deliberate."

"*Of course* it is deliberate!" Justin exclaimed, again too loudly. "It cannot be other than deliberate." I was certain that Justin's comment had been overheard by Provost's guards, so I steered him down a side street. "There continues to be conflict at the highest level over how to conduct the war. You mentioned that the Apostles were meeting in Hebron. It is true, and the meeting of the Council drags on as they fail to reach a consensus on how the war is to be fought – what objects to pursue and what measures to take."

"Justin," I demanded, keeping my voice as low as possible, "how is it that you *know* these things?"

"Bishop Bon is there," he continued, ignoring my question, "and the policy of hard war is his. He means to depopulate Engedi."

"You can't be serious!"

"Come tonight to my quarters," he said, squeezing my arm; "I'll tell you what I know." He hurried off after an officer of the Home Guards.

That evening, Michal-Rebekah met me at the door, seeming agitated. "Justin left you a note," she said, handing me an unsealed envelope. "He had to leave suddenly. He asked me to convey his regrets and insist that you stay for dinner." She patted her hair into place. "I do insist," she said, managing a smile.

Justin's note was brief and not very informative:

> *Josiah, I had news today that requires my presence in Hebron. If I call at the Palace of Ingots, as I intend, I shall of course convey your regards to all concerned. I expect to return in a few days. Regrettably, I will miss the pleasure of your company this evening. Please look after Appian and his mother while I am away.*

The note was unsigned, but I recognized his handwriting. If Justin had left after midday, he had already missed the packet – which meant that he probably hired a private boat to take him over to Achish, on the north side of the Jordan. He would have to ride hard to make Hebron by nightfall. It was all so hard to imagine – Justin taking such pains, making such an uncharacteristically strenuous effort. Why? What news had he had? Clearly, something was amiss.

I stood rapt in thought, pondering what this sudden urgency of Justin's might mean until my remaining in place was taken by Michal-Rebekah as an acceptance of her invitation to dinner. In fact, I wanted to stay and question her; she seemed to know more than she was saying. On the other hand, I felt uncomfortable to be alone in her presence. I had never settled in my own mind the nuances of our relations: was it proper to eat a meal at table with this woman and her son? As if reading my mind, she remarked, "The weather is mild; why don't we take the meal up on the portico?"

I had to concede that Michal-Rebekah was a wise woman with an intuitive sense of the proprieties. Israel takes very seriously the ritual of putting ones knees under a table for a meal; it prescribes very strictly with whom one may sit down. Merely taking food in an informal way, on the other hand, can be accomplished however is most convenient. It is not the table, I reasoned, but the ceremony that is critical. Our own times were very lax compared to ages past. How strange is change, I thought. A century ago, a Haggadah would not have sat down to bread with a Glanz! Michal-Rebekah and I were of the same class, after all. I tried to picture her former life as the wife of one of the first men of Esdralon, but I could imagine little of it.

We sat discretely apart on the upper portico; Appian moved between us with the serving dishes and teapot. The meal consisted of vimosh, the flat unleavened bread of the south, and a salad of cracked grain and parsley served with vinegar; for desert we nibbled dried fruits and hard cheese, and washed it down with strong, sweetened tea. It was delicious, and something more besides, something with which I had very little familiarity: it was gracious. I wanted to ask Michal-Rebekah about Justin's sudden departure, but I could not think how to begin. Consequently, we ate in silence. Spring weather in Israel is notoriously unpredictable, but this evening was milder than the day had been, and it ended with a spectacular sunset playing upon masses of moving clouds.

Appian was not at all subdued by our awkwardness. "Can you tell us another story?" he asked as we lingered over tea. I had not seen Appian and his mother since the evening after the executions – the night I had told my tale of the patrol into Lagash. "Major Apollo," Appian said, "says that you are very soft-headed for a warrior. He says you show compassion even to your enemies."

"Appian!" his mother said sharply.

I smiled at his mingled impudence and insight. "You and Justin may be right," I admitted. "General Mac Dogol once said that very thing to me – and for that reason, he was not sorry to see me packed off to the Commissary here in Engedi. He said that to me when we parted."

"Remember your manners, Appian," his mother chided.

"As I think about it, it is odd that I have been in the thick of several fights and have never shed any blood." *No Benjamite blood, that is.* "And furthermore," I reflected, "I am not eager to."

"How could you be in a battle and not shed blood?" Appian asked. "Did you run away?"

His mother attempted to hush him, but I was not offended. Appian and I had arrived on familiar terms in our last conversation, and in any case I found it easier to talk to the boy than to his mother. "Not exactly, Appian. But I did a strange thing once. I threw my hands up in the midst of a battle – a small skirmish, really – and stopped the fighting. We were contesting a ford of the Yakima, and I halted the fighting because a Harlech officer had fallen into the river and was about to drown. It *is* very strange, now that I think of it."

"Yes," Appian said.

Michal-Rebekah turned to me, the sunset tinting her features with gold. "I would like very much to hear about this episode," she said, placing her cup on the saucer in her lap.

"Well, I suppose there is no harm in telling it now," I said, "though I might have been court-martialed at the time." I described the course of the winter campaign, which was by now common knowledge, and explained the movement of several legions from Manasseh down to Judah during January to counter the Harlech threat there. "One brigade of the Second Apostles Legion was sent on ahead; the second, to which I was attached, came later, in company with the army's trains. One night I was detached with a patrol to guard a ford across the Yakima. The convoy of wagons was using the Ancients' Road, which runs along the bench about a mile east of the river at that point. A hundred wagons and the army's beef herd were encamped above us on the bench just back of Solomon's ford, it is called. In hindsight, I see that we should have had a stronger force guarding the ford. The crossing is fairly remote and seldom used, but you learn to expect the Harlech to know about things like a little-used ford."

Michal-Rebekah listened politely while Appian fidgeted with the teapot. "But here I am," I said, "describing our skirmish as if it had been a significant event. It was all very simple, really. At dawn, a company of Benjamite cavalry started across the ford toward us with one of their officers in the lead. The Yakima was running high then, and the ford was treacherous, so he and two aides were feeling out the bottom of the river. With the Army's wagon trains strung out behind us, I had no choice but to try to brush them back while we raised the alarm. We attacked, and in the melee, just as it began, this officer, a very fine, bold fellow of middle age, got knocked, horse and all, into the river. We stopped fighting, politely fished him out, and gave him back to his men."

"That is remarkable," Michal-Rebekah said. "To do what you did."

"We had an unofficial truce for about an hour. Mac Dogol came down toward the end of it, furious and ready to sack me, but he saw immediately that the delay had probably saved the trains. The Harlech seemed more interested in getting the officer to safety than pressing their attack, so everything worked out."

"Tell me more, please, about this officer," Michal-Rebekah said.

"I don't recall much," I said. "The encounter took place at first light. My men and I were waiting back from the ford, invisible in the woods, where we could see the river and move quickly to the ford. We were all quite numb with cold. We heard the enemy before we saw them – muffled cavalry sounds, quite unmistakable. A mist was rising from the river, but we could see the three riders scouting the ford. Luckily, their horses were having a hard time in the water, and the main body had halted on the opposite bank to see if it was fordable."

She nodded, so I continued. "As they approached, I could make out a big man on a palomino; in the half-light, its coat looked gray and its mane silver. When they reached the bank, the man turned and whistled to the rest of the command to come forward, the ford was safe. Immediately, I signaled my command to attack, and we charged out of the shadows. However, scarcely anyone followed me. Perhaps my order had surprised them, or I had bolted forward without it being heard. At any rate, only three or four of us met the Harlech riders as they emerged from the river. In the collision, the palomino went down; horse and rider were tangled for a moment and then the horse kicked free. I saw the man's face, helmetless in the water, as he struggled. He was hurt, probably kicked by his horse. He was in great pain."

"Please," Michal-Rebekah said, leaning forward, "go on."

I searched my memory for details, uncertain what she wanted to hear. "He was handsome, bearded, with a little gray in his beard and hair, but not much. I noticed these things afterwards, as he lay on a litter. The event is almost dream-like as I remember it. The enemy stood on the opposite bank, surprised by our sudden onslaught, and meanwhile the rest of my own command had not come up. So there were just a handful of us engaged on both sides. At that moment, I saw the current catch the injured officer and carry him down stream. He cried out for help, and a few yards away his cloak caught on a low-hanging branch and he was dragged under. The water was shallow, but I knew he would drown; he had crushed his thigh."

I was looking at the last rose-colored thread of sunset as I spoke. I heard a crash of crockery to my left.

"What is it?" I asked. "What is the matter?" Michal-Rebekah had dropped her cup and saucer.

Instead of answering, she summoned Appian to help her. They swept up the pieces and she sent Appian downstairs to dispose of them. When he had gone, she turned to me. "Josiah ben Haggadah," she said, "I must tell you something – tell you against my better judgment, though I believe I can rely on your honor. I ask that you do not repeat what I am going to tell you, but you are a man and can do what you like."

I waited for her to continue, wondering.

"You know that news circulates in war-time in spite of the lines. You may not know that there is great concern among us who remain here in Esdralon, because our forces seem idle and directionless and without offensive spirit. The winter campaign, as you know, came to nothing."

Michal-Rebekah amazed me; she seemed to have a soldier's command of events in the war.

"Rumors," she continued, seeming to choose her words carefully, "insist that this inactivity is because Jonas II Harlech, the Apostle of Benjamin, is gravely injured. He lies in his bed in Lagash and there is no one to take command. One son is dead in Achish; the other, Zachariah, is somewhere in the Kuhlan lands."

It was my turn to listen intently.

"It is also said," Michal-Rebekah continued, "that Jonas II Harlech has a wound that will not heal. . . ." She paused, seeming to regret that she had started. "He has a wound in his thigh. A crushed bone that will not mend."

My breath stopped in my throat. "Probably a coincidence," I stammered. My head swam.

"Yes, probably," she said, her eyes brimming. "Except that it is also reported that the Apostle was wounded in January, at the beginning of the fighting in Judah – and was saved through the extraordinary compassion of an Israelite officer!"

Shrouded in mist, we burst from the woods. In the shock of collision, my horse rears, slips, its hooves skidding on the wet stones. Blows and screams and the shrill neighing of horses sound around me. Hoarse animal cries burst from my own lungs. Beneath me, the palomino rolls and kicks in the water, struggles riderless to its feet, and then I see the pale face, catch a glimpse of surprise and agony contorting the features; and then, unseeing, absorbed in his own pain, he turns away from me, moving, then rushing away to his death beneath the water, to suffocation in black, icy nothingness. Then the willow catches the hood of his cloak and the current drags him under.

What was there about his death that I could not bear?

I wave my arms, shouting frantically. But what did I shout? Halt? Cease fighting? Truce? I cannot recall. The enemy on the opposite bank has not moved; I sense my own men around me pause uncertainly. I am off my horse and the shock of the water knocks the breath from me. I have his cloak in one hand and my horse's bridle in the other, calling for help. One of my sergeants is in the water beside me and he takes the reins from me; in a moment we have the officer in shallower water, his head above the surface. "Truce," I shout, and others repeat it.

I drop shivering on the gravel, but others have taken up the burden. "Watch the leg!" the sergeant shouts. "Put him on a bedroll and bring blankets; we'll have to splint the leg." Somehow our feelings have changed; it is as though there has been an accident rather than a skirmish. Someone waves a cloth and motions the enemy across the ford. A half dozen men come forward warily, feeling their way through the swirling water. It is beginning to be light enough to see well. I sit beside the Benjamite officer, who wears a simple officer's field outfit and no insignia. He has vomited on the stones and part of it clings to his beard. Someone puts a blanket around my shoulders, so I am on my feet and able to greet the Benjamite cavalrymen when they emerge, horses dripping and shivering, from the Yakima.

Chapter 3: A Lion at the Gate

I

"Now it's dysentery!" Major Cohn-el exclaimed. The news from the Second Army was not good. Tales of a clash between Montevideo's expedition and the Kuhlans far up the Snake River had come back with the merchant fleet, hard on the heels of earlier rumors of poor rations and frustrated plans. Justin was the first to glean the story of the renewed fighting and brought it to the Commissary, where there was consternation, followed by a great deal of shrewd speculation. "Fighting *and* dysentery – on top of the influenza that the army suffered in mid-winter." The major paused, calculating. "There'll be hell to pay!" he said. "We'll have to audit Montevideo's pay vouchers, for sure."

As soon as we could get away, Justin took me down to the docks to talk to the river men who had come back from the Snake River expedition. A good intelligence officer, Justin wanted to go directly to the source. We failed. There was a subdued murmur of conversation in the shops we visited, but no recently arrived sailors. We walked along the docks, surveying the ships in harbor.

"Too late!" Justin said. "They must have been arrested."

"Arrested?"

"Yes," he replied. "And that tells us that the Eyes of Israel are alarmed, so the stories the sailors were telling must be substantially true. This is all the confirmation we can expect to have for the time being, but it is enough."

I was astonished. We ourselves were members of the Eyes of Israel. What could he mean? Justin was in a familiar but exasperating mood – distant and sardonic and impenetrable. He seemed to be deriding me even as we discussed this new development. We skirted the harbor fortress and walked along the Jordan until we were well outside the city. Of his recent trip to Hebron, Justin had told me nothing except that it was a false alarm and a waste of time; he had accomplished nothing, he said. On many issues Justin seemed reluctant to take me into his confidence.

"I have often speculated," he said, making one of his conversational leaps to a new topic, "that it must have been particularly useful to heap the blame for Israel's decline on our most successful rivals – a people who seem more alien than Israelite anyway."

"What are you talking about? Useful to whom?"

"To our doting father, Tephlin Glanz. Who else? I was thinking how much the Harlech unwittingly helped him by being so secretive. Gradually, they became strange to Israel – and then they acquired so much power, took so large a role in our commerce, that it virtually compelled the rest of the nation into hostility toward them." I inferred that Justin was moving back onto the familiar grounds of our discussions, but suddenly he turned to confront me: "For you it is *still* a merchant's war, isn't it?" He seemed actually to sneer at me. Justin was in one of his perverse and cantankerous moods, but he surprised me both with the question and with his vehemence. "Your warrior caste is unimaginative," he said. "And why not? You have your duels and affairs of honor and amuse yourselves with an occasional massacre of rebellious slaves, and you are content with that. It affirms who you are. You live like pampered children and think like them. You live from one cockfight to the next, and everything is *personal* to you. Everything touches your honor."

I was baffled to find myself the object of this sudden wrath. I did not have to reply to feed his indignation.

"This war," he declared, "is not personal! And it is certainly not honorable. Listen, Josiah, I respect greed. Greed is a force of nature, like hunger or desire. To fight a war for grain in the bin or gold in the treasury is a motive I can respect. What's more, that's what I thought this war was about. I admit that. But you still think our father is behind everything – that he plotted it all!"

"Well, is he not?" I asked. "You have suggested as much to me yourself. What are you saying now? That he is *not*? That he and his merchant allies have not embroiled us in a war over Benjamin's commerce? What have we been talking about these several weeks?"

"Yes, yes," he said impatiently. "There *is* the merchants' war. There is that aspect of it, I mean. And the merchant conspiracy was, in fact, the means by which the war came about and took its initial form. I don't deny that."

"Then what in the world are you talking about?"

"Complexity, Zaiyah. Wars have many causes, and many intentions meet in them. There is the merchants' war, as you suggest. But then there is the church's war. That is the war I am beginning to see more clearly – and one concerning which you never speak. *You* of all people!"

"What do you mean, *me* of all people?"

"Don't you see?" Justin said, exasperated. "Haven't you yet *seen* the war? The very manner in which we fight the Harlech – this ruthlessness which we inflict upon the population here in Engedi. . . ." He paused, as if I were too dense to make the connections he was showing me: *"The church's war!"* he almost shouted. "The church's war makes settlement of the other wars impossible."

Justin's mind was far more nimble than mine, but I followed his latest leap: to secure the advantages seized in the war, Israel's merchants needed a peace settlement that confirmed them in their new possessions. But under present circumstances, it was true, negotiations seemed impossible. I wondered if the cost of the war had already exceeded the profits the merchants expected to reap.

"What I cannot fathom," Justin continued, "is the religious motive itself. What does Bishop Bon or the Primate hope to derive from all of this? Or our cousin Bulavar, who, by the way, is one of the chief henchmen of Bishop Bon."

"Bulavar? Our *cousin*?" My heart knocked in my chest. "I *know* him!"

"Possibly even our half-brother," Justin remarked indifferently. "He is said to be one of a host of our father's unacknowledged bastards – allegedly the eldest – gotten by him on a niece of his, so the story goes. Bulavar is a terror, I assure you, and I take no comfort in our alleged kinship."

I recoiled from the thought of being kin to such a man – and to be descended from such a father.

"I understand perfectly well what Tephlin Glanz hopes to gain from the war," Justin declared. "I can even calculate it. But what the Messiahist clergy fight for is incomprehensible to me. I believed their aim was simply to advance the their faith, as we might expect our trade or increase our profits. But I see that their aims are different; their motives are different– different in kind – from ours. For instance, we would be willing to kill some number of people to increase our wealth; I admit that. That's what we've been doing, in fact. But the churchmen are willing to kill *everyone* to achieve their goals. They are quite seriously intending to exterminate you heretics – all of you! They want you gone, dead, obliterated– or converted. And they mean to do it soon, very soon, so the world can end. Will you explain that to me, please? But as a heretic – even an arch-heretic in their eyes – you probably find their behavior mystifying as well."

We walked along silently for a while, and then Justin abruptly stopped and turned to me: "You are more than just an Old Believer, aren't you?"

I stammered a little answering him; Justin's question had came out of nowhere, startling me. "No – well, no, as a matter of fact. The Edict of Restitution says that we are all of one faith. But that, as you know, is a lie. The Law handed down from St. Supplicee is one thing, and this new Messiahist gibberish is quite another. But I don't know what you mean by *more* than an Old Believer."

"Nor can I understand," Justin replied, again changing the subject, "why you Old Believers do not regard the Benjamites as co-religionists. Did not and do not. Or why the north stood by in the Religious Wars while Benjamin was slaughtered by the Messiahists."

Justin seemed to hold me personally responsible for decisions of a century ago. "Benjamin was the first tribe to break with the Law," I replied, my own temperature beginning to rise. "How can they possibly be considered our co-religionists? Then *or* now?"

"Yes, but the Benjamites hate the Messiahists with the same fervor that you Old Believers do. Doesn't your St. Supplicee say somewhere that the enemy of my enemy is my friend?"

"He says nothing of the kind!" I exclaimed. Asher and the other law-abiding tribes had in truth stayed out of the conflict too long, until the outcome was decided, before they joined their efforts in a lost cause. But the Benjamites were apostates; they had made a common cause impossible.

"Well, perhaps he should have said it," Justin said petulantly. "After all, the power of the Messiahists has grown steadily since then, and now they are using this war to eliminate their southern rivals. This, too, is a religious war. And so far, the Messiahists have used and manipulated the merchant class with great skill. They induced them to commit all their prestige and resources to the war, and to take all the risks, and now the merchants are taking the blame for the failures. The merchants do the church's bidding, spend their blood and treasure – all the while believing that the war was their own idea! Devilishly clever, don't you think?"

"This is preposterous, Justin! Where do you get such notions?" My head was spinning as this new perspective began to sink into me.

Justin turned to me and demanded: "Josiah, you are a Devotee, are you not – perhaps even a Dolomite?"

"Dolorite," I corrected him.

"All right, Dolorite!"

I felt hot blood flow into my cheeks and forehead, and I was grateful for the formula I had memorized. "Everyone knows the Dolorites no longer exist."

Justin was not to be put off so easily. "The Dolorites are a secret military order of the Old Believers, are they not? Fanatics, like the caste warriors who used to chain themselves to a stake and refuse to surrender?"

I felt my skin prickle. "Not at all," I said. "Chains and stakes are nothing, a gesture. Anyone can throw his life away in the heat of battle. The Dolorites are serious, and they take deliberate, irrevocable stands. And when they do, they have no need to chain themselves." *The Dolorites, I thought. What does Justin know about the Dolorites?*

"The military orders of the Old Believers were outlawed a long time ago," Justin said. "But don't tell me they no longer exist! You Old Believers never relinquish anything."

I stopped and faced him, my blood pounding. "You speak of things you don't know!" I exclaimed. "The Dolorites are men who take a vow unto death; they accept the pain of the whole nation as a burden upon themselves, willingly. By doing so, they acquire a power like a force of nature. I cannot explain that power to you; I doubt that anyone can. But they cannot be deterred or defeated by ordinary means. On the other hand, neither can they hope to survive the burden of their vow. The weight is too much for a human being to bear. That is the cost of the vow, and it is accepted willingly. There are no chains or stakes in the ground."

Justin was not impressed and seemed not to be listening.

"The Old Believers," I added, "lost the Wars of Investiture a century ago because there were no true men then who could assume that vow. And there have been none since."

I expected Justin to mock or contradict me, but his reply was serious, even grave: "Zaiyah," he said, "these times do not permit foolish adherence to lost causes. I fear for you."

His changes of direction always threw me off. "Forget about *me* and what I am! If I am in danger, that is a burden I must carry, and I will carry it gladly. But where do your own thoughts lead you? I fear for *your* safety, brother. For your allegiance. I fear where your thoughts are leading you." *There! It was out. What I had worried over silently for so long had found voice.*

Justin did not reply. We walked a while in silence. "I care nothing for allegiances," he said. "Nothing at all. After all is said and done, I wish merely to be on the side of intelligence. Yes, that's it! Justice not having much role in this war, I will settle for intelligence." After a while, he added: "Frankly, I don't see much of that either."

We turned back toward the city, following an ancient path beside the river. After a time, Justin remarked, "Zaiyah, I am sick to death of all this charade and deception. I want to see what *is* with my own eyes. I want to speak what is. Does not your St. Supplicee say somewhere that now we see as through a glass darkly, but then—*eventually* – face to face?"

"He says nothing of the kind. That sounds like more Messiahist nonsense. Through a glass darkly is all we Old Believers expect."

Justin turned and glared at me furiously, and then he stooped and picked up a stone and hurled it into the Jordan. It raised a flock of ducks out of the reeds; a pair of blackbirds with blood-tipped shoulders also fluttered up and scolded us, and then returned to their nest.

"Through a glass *very* darkly," I heard him mutter as he turned away.

II

More and more churchmen made their appearance in Esdralon. Black-robed clerics thrust themselves into every crack and corner until the army was infested with them. Justin warned that a young priest had been installed at Headquarters – ostensibly as an aid of General Boseth, but in fact to keep track of all who came and went in Headquarters. The partly ruined citadel of Esdralon, which housed the archives and the dungeon, was taken over as a barracks and was soon a hive of Messiahist activity. Repairs on the damaged upper floors – the first such project in the city – were soon under way. Clerics swarmed on the scaffolds like beetles on a carcass.

There was much grumbling in the army and a bitterness beyond description in my own heart. But ensnared in events I could not control, I could do little but wait out the season. I sought ways to pass the time. Through Justin, I was invited to banquets hosted by aspiring officers to honor these black-robed "guests" – affairs in which I had no interest other than as a component of my larger study, which was the war. These occasions all seemed to feature the same tedious succession of flutes and guitars, toasts, and speech making, and protestations of mutual admiration. And through them all, no matter how exalted the company, was a pervasive thread of rancor and suppressed resentment. After the last course was served and the Messiahist clergy departed, there was usually gambling and drunkenness, followed by worse drunkenness and brawling over the same women and sometimes duels the next day or within the week.

Justin also had contacts with the richest merchants, and we attended a few of their more sedate affairs. After a short while, I found their habitual caution as repugnant as the brawling and whoring of the officer class. *Intelligence*, says St. Supplicee, *should find a use proper to itself.* While it was not clear to me where those uses lay in the Israel of my day, I was certain that the frugal weighing, parsing, and retailing of gossip in the most minute quantities was not such a use. Their never-ending quest for advantage was oppressive without consideration of the question: to what end? *To what end?*

One afternoon we visited a weaver's establishment not far from Justin's quarters. A Judean family, the Calderons, had recently taken over a Harlech operation. Twenty ragged Benjamites of both sexes were kept busy in a large room weaving cloth, both flax and wool, on fantastic contraptions where the warp and the weft threads were controlled by foot pedals. I had never seen anything like these machines. We had a brief chat with the family, and I became duly apprised of the efficiencies to be gained from specialization of tasks and improved looms.

Afterwards Justin remarked, "I believe people in their station are most likely to find real happiness. No religious excitements or false hopes in their lives, but solid comfort and tangible achievements."

"What do you mean?" I asked. "These people are making bolts of cloth."

"That's it, precisely!" he said impatiently. "They are producing a great deal of cloth, by making use of the clever Harlech inventions and taking advantage of a situation they found here. Simon Calderon came down to Esdralon seeking their runaway son, who had joined the army and gotten himself into trouble. And now the family, which had virtually nothing in Hebron, has quite a nice establishment."

I said nothing, but I wondered that the man would risk his wife and daughter in this hostile land for a few bolts of cloth. Should Israel's army ever depart Esdralon, his investment would be worth last year's dung heap.

"In Hebron," Justin continued, "when I was growing up, Simon's family lived in meager, difficult circumstances. That may be, in fact, the ideal life situation, when you think of it. In such a situation, everyone must contribute, or all suffer. And it is *clear* that they suffer!" he added emphatically, as if to batter down my obtuseness. "In that situation, in precarious circumstances if not in actual want, there are obvious consequences to actions; everything is simple. Everything is real – unlike the lives of the rich or those with Israelite pedigrees. The lives of the Calderon family must seem much more"—he searched for a word—"*interpretable* to them. No spoiled and languid young men wasting away in ennui and melancholy!"

"I thought you said their son had run away."

"Well, yes, he was always a wild stallion. I knew him in Hebron."

"But the Calderons are struggling to become rich – that is, to be *other* than they are now. And it appears they are succeeding. So. . . ."

"Well, yes, I see your point," Justin acknowledged. "But theirs is a life I could have had. Perhaps should have had. My mother's family was similarly situated. Less stable – less decent, I have to admit. My grandfather drank more of the products of his distilling than he ever sold, and my aunts were not as honest as they should have been. But there was a young woman of the neighborhood, a pretty sparrow of a girl with bright, lovely eyes—wonderful eyes! Our families talked of marriage when we were young, though no arrangements were settled on. Then fortune intervened, and I was off to the Academy, and her family found her another match."

"And you feel the attraction of such a life now?" I asked.

"Yes, I suppose so. I am curious about how things might have turned out."

I nodded, but Justin struck me as very poor material for a life in a weaver's loft. "How was it that you married" – *I searched for a tactful phrase* – "otherwise than you expected? You have never told me the story of your courtship."

He grimaced. "There is not much to tell. It's the commonest sort of story among my class. It was a marriage arranged with the daughter of a wealthy family. Simon ben Gurion was the go-between; that is its only unusual feature. I believe it came about as a result of a compact of some kind between my father and her father – a business alliance. It was not, by any means, a love affair. And the young woman, though pretty enough, turned out to have no qualities that would endear her to anyone. I was young and knew nothing of marriage – and still less of how long a life can be in an unhappy union. I suppose the main attraction for me was – not her wealth, although that was a consideration to someone as poor as myself – nor even her beauty, as I had not found beautiful women inaccessible. It was, strangely enough, a desire to please our father, who was the prime mover in the arrangement – Tephlin Glanz, whom I should hate and despise above all men."

We walked along together in the lengthening evening shadows. "I thought father must be breaking his long silence and taking an interest in me," Justin said. "As you know, he has never been a father to me, ever, and I should have long since become accustomed to his indifference. Oddly enough, his silence is deafening; it drowns out other things that I should be attending to. The strangest part is that I feel as though *I* am the guilty one, the one who needs to make amends. I never leave off trying to please him."

"I think I know how you feel," I said.

"Sometimes," Justin said, "I believe I should seek him out and rip his throat for what he did to my mother."

His words stopped me in my tracks. "Do you actually know what happened? Do you have certain knowledge of what he did or how your mother came to die?"

"No, of course not," he said. "And so, how can I lift my hand against him? It's not possible for me!"

"You cannot act," I conceded, "though he may deserve it. But not from your hand. I

see it clearly." In the twilight, my heart was beating like a swallow's throat.
"I expect you may," he said.

The violence in the streets, the arrests and executions continued unabated in Esdralon. A row of hooks was added to the scaffold to accommodate the increased number of victims. The drum call to parade filled us with dread and loathing. We never spoke of the executions at Justin's. His quarters had become a refuge from the war. We four, in our bizarre situation, developed a mutual friendship made stronger, I suspect, because of the barriers to it.

III

I met Justin on the Field of War on an afternoon in late April to watch the First Apostles drill. We were drawn to observe the evolutions of the heavy infantry, which was a new thing in Israel, and because watching them took us out of the cursed city. Justin informed me that he had arranged for us to accompany a patrol into the south of Engedi. He was eager to look for evidence of the Kr intrusion into Harlech territory and, I think, anxious to be distracted. Since his injury, his primary service had been staff work, so the prospect of duty with the cavalry filled him with enthusiasm. For my part, I was sick of the city and longed for active service. Across the Jordan, the hills were green and the leaves were well out on the trees along the river. The spring countryside calls to a man, ticks or no ticks.

"I want to see the Kr for myself if it is the last thing I do," Justin said. And then, as we parted for our respective duties at Headquarters, he added, "Come by tonight. We have planned a special occasion – a small celebration—in honor of our coming expedition."

I flinched at his use of "we," but accepted his invitation.

As I mounted the stairs of Justin's quarters, I was greeted by familiar aromas and a pleasant murmur of voices. My appetite was whetted before I even identified the smells.

"We have salad!" Michal-Rebekah met me at the door smiling and displayed a large bowl of fresh greens and a cruet of oil and vinegar.

"First blessings of the fields," I said. "The land is coming alive." She smiled at me, looking demure and pretty, and she seemed happy at pleasing me. Justin was dressed in a robe of white lamb's wool and wore a matching headband of twisted wool. The contrast with his dark skin and hair was striking, and I thought again that he was the handsomest man I had ever seen. He looked like a king's son.

Justin was in a cheerful mood. "Michal-Rebekah has been using me to spy on you," he said. "She wanted to know all about the ordinary fare of Asher. Not the fancy dishes, mind you, but plain, unpretentious meals, simple enough for a Devotee. Imagine me," he added, "the hero of a thousand hands of cards, seeking out the gruff warriors of the north and asking them about recipes! 'But only the plainest, please and thank you! Nothing that would offend a Dedicated One!' You owe me dearly for this meal, brother!"

"You do a fine imitation of yourself," I replied. But I was touched by the thought behind the meal and the impulse to make me feel entirely welcome and at home. That the impulse must have come from Michal-Rebekah also delighted me.

Served on simple earthenware, the meal was a perfect replica of daily Asherite fare: mixed beans and lentils in onion broth. Michal-Rebekah set the steaming tureen and bowls before me along with a fresh loaf of black rye bread and a square of mild white goat cheese. How many such meals had I had at Tirzah at my grandfather's table? I had not been served so since childhood. I thanked them both, taking Justin's and then Michal-Rebekah's hand in mine, feeling as I did so how soft her hand felt. Her skin was like a sensation from a world other than the one in which I lived. *How long had it been since I had held a woman's hand – any woman's hand – in my own?*

"I hear that Asherite cavalry are arriving in Esdralon," Justin said as we seated ourselves.

"That would be a triumph for the Council," I said, "if true. But I doubt that it is. The heart of Asher is not in this war."

"The heart of Asher?" Justin laughed. "The heart of Asher is on this table! And soon to be in your belly."

The stew was hearty, delicious, steaming in the bowl; it was cooked exactly in the northern style. The bread, still warm in my hands, gave off a rich rye aroma. Beaming, Michal-Rebekah offered me a dish of butter.

"How in the world did you find fresh butter," I asked. The butter melted into the bread and was salty to my tongue. I seemed enveloped in warmth and good will and delicious aromas.

"I believe you are actually converting me," I said between mouthfuls. And indeed, here I was savoring what I ate like a gourmet, rather than merely feeding with my mind busy elsewhere, as was my habit. The greens, served as a second course, were fresh and mildly bitter, the flavors of the several plants set off perfectly by the dressing of mixed herbs and garlic and the first wild onions of the year. The vinegar made me salivate, and as I swallowed, I remembered the name of one of the herbs I was tasting: fennel. *From my grandmother's garden.*

Suddenly I felt a constriction in my throat and a sensation of choking; hot tears sprang to my eyes and I was wrenched by an emotion fierce and painful, but which I could not name. I gasped and choked again, wracked by spasms of pain. It was several moments before I began to regain control of myself. Through a blur of tears I glimpsed Justin, looking alarmed and confounded, standing over me. Michal-Rebekah had risen, her hands pressed to her face in horror as if I had been poisoned.

"No!" I said. "Please!" I could not speak more. I attempted to apologize, but instead choked again; my voice was paralyzed. There were no words in me, but an overpowering grief and pain, fresh as the bread I had just broken in my hands. I left off trying to explain and made my apologies as best I could, feeling foolish and ashamed.

I was truly baffled. When I recovered my composure, I explained, "Something came to me just now, very vividly – from another time. . . ."

Justin wanted to know precisely what had overwhelmed me: "*What* came to you?" he asked. "What other time? Can you recall the incident? Perhaps it was the moment a long time ago when you last ate a meal like this. . . ?"

I could only shake my head. I wept like a child.

Afterwards, Justin and I retired to the roof to watch the sunset. The evening chill comes rapidly in Israel; we wrapped ourselves in soft wool robes and leaned against the rail of the upper balcony. "So, brother," he said, "it would appear that you had a childhood after all."

"So it would appear."

He asked me about my mother, if I knew what had happened to her.

"Not really," I admitted. I tried to conceal my hands, which were still trembling.

"Well," he said, "I think you must find out."

In the twilight, Justin and I talked without restraint, perhaps for the first time in my life, of intimate things I never dreamed I would discuss with another human being – of matters I dared not put down in my journal for my own eyes. With Justin, however, I felt no embarrassment. He had, I knew, lost his own mother without knowing her and had never stopped grieving for that loss. Much of what I found objectionable or irritating in Justin, I had come to realize, was scar tissue from that wound – or from our father's indifference.

The conversation turned eventually to my time at the Academy, and I told Justin the story of my disgrace. Michal-Rebekah brought us up tea and stayed within hearing, and I was relieved to have her as well as Justin know the truth. "If you know these things, you may as well know more," I said. "And know why my commission was delayed."

Justin nodded, encouraging me to continue. This tale had long lain like a weight on my heart; I was eager to be free of it. "At the Academy," I began, "a young man chose to make himself my enemy. His name was Senesh Velco, and he was the son of one of the great families of Manasseh, and he had influence and a following. To my knowledge I did nothing to offend him, but he took offense. He sought every occasion to engage me in a quarrel, but I was determined not to respond. I attempted by all honorable means to pacify him and to turn him from his hostility – and failing that, to ignore him. Nevertheless, he persisted. I held back. Twice I refused his challenge, intending to refuse all of his challenges, ignore his insults, and be quit of him when we received our commissions. Not because I feared him, but because it was a point of honor, as well as an . . . obligation. To others."

"I see," Justin said.

"But then, just before commissioning time, he gave me an offense I could not endure. He actually struck me in the face, before witnesses, but it was his taunt that stung me." I paused, searching for the right words, but there were no such words. "Then and there I cut him down. This in spite of my resolutions. In spite of my deepest commitments."

"A duel?"

"No, I cannot fairly say in a duel, though we were both armed. There were no seconds, no ceremony. I killed him where he stood. With a consecrated sword." I shook my head. "Even yet I cannot believe it."

Justin lowered his head; Michal-Rebekah regarded me with her large dark eyes.

"And what followed?" Justin asked.

"I was arrested and held for a time and then released. I was not commissioned with the rest of my class of cadets, as you know. At the time of the commissioning ceremony, I was lying in custody deep within the citadel of New Jerusalem. Shortly after, I was released without explanation and assigned to the Second Apostles Legion. That was in November, not long after the Legion's disgrace at Beth-Shan." *Released and assigned but not commissioned. Not consecrated as a warrior and a Name in Israel.* I knew that my story was often retold as a simple duel – a relatively minor infraction of the military code – and knew that as many would approve it on those grounds as would condemn me. I longed to assure Justin and Michal-Rebekah that I was not just an arrogant caste warrior leaving victims to his honor strewn in his path.

"Curious," Justin remarked. "Can you say why you were released without a hearing or court-martial?"

"I have assumed that it was the crisis after Beth-Shan that earned me the reprieve. Men were needed to defend Manasseh." He nodded, but seemed unconvinced. "For months," I continued, "I had been expecting the incident to overtake me and to find myself summoned to a court-martial. Instead, I heard nothing. Then, six weeks ago in Hebron, I received my commission as if it had never happened. I was commissioned without reference to the incident, and without explanation."

"And the Velcos – you, or someone, has made restitution to the family?" Justin's question was one a kinsman would ask; I was pleased.

"Not to my knowledge."

"Senesh Velco," Justin mused. "I'm surprised you have not been murdered for it. How did you survive in the northern legion?" He rose and walked about the balcony. "By whose authority were you released from prison? Do you know?"

I shook my head.

"Can Tephlin Glanz reach even into the dungeons of New Jerusalem?" Justin said, partly to himself. "But if he could – begging your pardon, brother – why would he *want* to intervene in your case? Your commission I can understand. Your service in Judah is explanation enough for that."

"Nevertheless, I feel the disgrace of my offense very keenly."

But it was not the disgrace that was the worst. It was not knowing the meaning of the event. It was as though it had all happened in someone else's life.

Justin looked at me enquiringly, and then, his question, whatever it was, repressed, remarked, "I have heard several accounts of the incident. Israel's army is small, and its mouth and ears are large, and it gossips endlessly about its members. You have no doubt heard many outrageous stories about me as well. Believe half of them, at best. But the one thread in all the stories that rings true to me, true to what I sense about you, is that the offense given to you was a killing one, and the cadet who provoked you was armed and capable of defending himself. That you acted honorably in this affair is as certain to me as your standing here before me."

Honorably? The scene rose up in my mind with startling vividness: Senesh Velco glowered before me, hand on his sword hilt, smiling a cruel, sardonic smile. . . .

"No!" I exclaimed, feeling the salt of unappeasable anger well up in my eyes. "No, Senesh Velco had no chance at all!"

That was the truth. But another truth lay coiled around my disgrace, and that was my inability to remember it; I had no memory of the act itself. That I cut Senesh Velco down, severing the life from him, I do not for a moment doubt. But, mysteriously, I recall nothing of the event itself – nothing of the blow I struck. What I retained of the event was an accusing voice in my head. "Murderer!" the voice declared insistently, "you have betrayed everything entrusted to you!"

When I left that night, Justin and Michal-Rebekah and Appian saw me to the door downstairs. Justin embraced me. I turned as I walked away and saw them framed in the doorway – saw also what Justin and Michal-Rebekah were to one another. More than that, as Justin stood holding a lantern in one hand and tousling the hair of the boy with the other, I saw that they were a family. In this sudden clarity of mind about them, I felt a rush of pain because of the danger they were in. But as I looked deeper into myself, I knew that much of the ache in my heart was envy. I walked the silent streets back to the barracks, searching the dark alleys of my mind. I found many things there, some good and some not, but nothing of the condemnation of their situation that the Law requires.

IV

The next day, I embarked with Justin on our long-awaited foray into the hinterland of Engedi. Attached to a troop of the First Apostles cavalry, we set out to scout for signs of Harlech activity. I had yearned for a taste of the active life, and I was proud of my skill as a cavalryman and anxious to display it before my brother. But somehow, in the event, Justin and I had very little to say to one another. Justin was not interested in Harlech activity, but was intent instead on finding the Kr and assessing their numbers and intentions. Thus, each of us conducted the patrol wrapped in his own thoughts.

The first day of our patrol, the sun was bright and unobstructed by clouds. There was a softness in the air, a mildness like a warm breath. The earth was warming, moving in its cycle from darkness to light. The hidden life in the soil was quickening and reaching upward, sending up pale shoots that darkened and toughened as they reached the light, turning the land the fresh green of fertility, the color of brides and promises kept.

I felt a deep ambivalence, almost a sadness, with the returning spring. Israelites speak of the "spring mourning" because the season carries with it the knowledge that the first hatching of ticks would soon be upon us. Even the tumors, so common in our polluted land and descended to us like a curse from the Ancients, were less terrifying than the threat of this diminutive enemy. The ticks themselves are no larger than a speck, a mote in our eye, but the plague they carried looms gigantic in our vision. It is partly the speed of the illness and partly its fearsomeness. The swelling of the brain makes the victim tear at his own scalp and skull, and the fever breaks the mind itself upon the rack of madness. In comparison, the tumors seem a natural death concerning which it is bad form to complain.

More than we wish to acknowledge, this plague has made us what we are: strangers in a strange land. Israelites crave the desert and barren ground and frost deep in the soil; we dread the warmth of summer and shun the forest and quiet shade. Our peculiar customs – our summer nudity and frequent body inspections, our obsessive cleanliness – all reveal our dread of this relentless enemy.

Ebenezer, my Master at the Refuge, taught us that Israel glories in its own weaknesses, mistaking them for strengths. Israelites pride themselves, he said, on the smallness of our circles of acquaintance. We walk with eyes on the ground and averted from strangers, stiff with our sense of self and hostile to everything that does not confirm it. Israel prefers austerity in all things, he explained, *because it is afraid.* Above all else, afraid of the plague. And because of it, all else – politics, love, war – were merely diversions for us. Ever mindful of this threat, we struggle not to understand or rejoice or even to *live*, but merely to survive. Thus, though our Teacher calls us to fulfill our higher natures, we descend to a craven and brutish existence. *Only the Dolorites*, Ebenezer said, *are truly free.*

But Israel's spring sadness involves more than the hatching of deadly ticks. The turning of the season reminds us of our essential difference from other life. The May fly lives a single afternoon, and, together with all other unconscious blood in the world, lifts its gossamer wings as an anthem of praise to the renewed sun. Gray geese and the multitudes of ducks rejoice in their migration, each after their kind, scorning the distance and hardships. But what if the hatchling flies could, as we do, see the shadow of the trout hanging in the current? Or watch the sun poised just moments above the horizon? We grieve in the midst of play because we foresee and because we remember. Burdened with far-seeing consciousness, we are reminded by spring of all those things that constrain and eventually extinguish us.

Fools! St. *Supplicee said. Can you see only the door by which you came in and the door by which you will leave? Leave these thoughts of birth and death and be free!*

Freedom, the precious gift of truly understanding the Way. But how is it that only we are burdened with the necessity to *find* the Way. Can it be that only we are lost?

The third day of our patrol, the fickle Israelite spring turned against us, and we encountered a cold, wet wind blowing out of the west. We followed one of the Ancients' roads past heaps of stone and stands of wild plum, descendants of once cultivated orchards. Justin pointed out the signs of still more ancient ruins and the faint traces of roadways etched across the plain, which sage and rabbit brush had reclaimed ages ago.

Topping a low rise, we encountered row after row of earthen mounds that stretched along a south-facing slope. The mounds were of uniform size and symmetry, about thirty feet in length and perhaps eight feet high. The south ends of the mounds were tapered slightly, while the ends that faced north were cornered square and abrupt, like the end of a loaf that has been sliced. Judging that their regularity implied human builders, I inquired about their origin and purpose.

"The place is called, U-mah-ti-yah, or the Hill of the Tumuli, on the oldest maps," Justin said, "but I have never seen a plausible explanation of them."

So, they were grave mounds – but so many! There were a multitude, a great host arrayed in ranks and stretching from horizon to horizon. It was as if many dynasties of kings or a race of giants lay interred here. We paused, resting our horses and watching the scouts move warily ahead of us and at the compass points.

"There is no word of this place in the early histories," Justin said, squinting against the rain. "Clement is silent on the subject, but he scarcely mentions the South Bank. Jacob of Achish, who surely saw them, speaks of them in connection with the Plague of Seizures in 563. He places their origin in the time of the Ancients, but not very confidently."

I was surprised by his knowledge of the chronicles; Justin had never struck me as a man who had drunk deeply of the scholarship of Israel. But getting to know my brother had been a continual surprise.

Surrounding this precinct was an irregular barrier of stones, crudely built, with rock cairns and huge monoliths positioned at intervals. We examined the largest of these upright stones and found carvings of the figures called "Transmitters," which in the ancient tongue means the "Messengers" of the Ancients. They were rendered in stiff line drawings such as a child might make, with square, box-like bodies and dangling arms. Some appeared armed with weapons, some had clearly discernible heads, and in others the head appeared subsumed into the chest.

"They say the Kr revere these figures as deities," Justin said. "And even in Israel, the superstitious imagine they can cast spells with them and believe that the Transmitters have the power to ward off evil."

I recoiled at the thought. "We Old Believers do not acknowledge these or any other images; neither do we invoke their assistance or presume to curse." I spoke these formulas with more confidence than I felt. Some think that the Transmitters are vaguely human in appearance, but they seemed to me overwhelmingly alien. These were forms that could never wear flesh.

"Some claim," Justin continued, "that men who tread on these mounds have sometimes perished suddenly, in mid-stride – and animals as well. Even birds flying overhead drop from the sky."

I looked at him skeptically. Nevertheless, the gusting wind raised the hairs on my neck. My horse, suddenly skittish, tossed his head and tugged at the bit. Inwardly, I too shied at the thought that these silent mounds remained lethal to intruders.

"Legends, no doubt," Justin said. "But the nomads shun this place and will not go near it." We rode on a while in silence, skirting the barrier of stones. "Our Messiahists, on the other hand," he continued, "claim that these Transmitters were angels – divine Messengers to the Ancients – and that they rebelled against God. It was their seduction of the Ancients that summoned the Savior to the world the second time. The Dissolution was a judgment upon them, so the Messiahists claim."

I made a face. I despised all the claims of the Messiahists. "I suppose, then, that they believe the host of rebel angels lies buried here. What nonsense! St. Supplicee says, let the things of the Ancients remain buried with the Ancients."

"Yes," he replied, "and would they could stay buried!"

Contemplating the mounds as we rode on, I wondered what fury against life lay interred here. We Old Believers reject the idea that the soul is immortal and disbelieve in ghosts and spirits. But I noticed that some of the mounds were deformed and cratered from within, as if the non-existent souls of the departed had taken violent leave of their resting places. Though I rejected all forms of superstition, I had the uneasy feeling that if evil could take a tangible form, the Transmitters might be that form.

"I hate these claims that the Messiahist make," I said, "that have no basis in evidence and always work to justify their faith."

"Indeed, I've noticed!" Justin said. "Nevertheless, the mounds cry out for explanation. And not just the mounds. We, too, have a history concerning which the chronicles do not speak."

"What do you mean?" I demanded. I was annoyed, as always, at Justin's claim to superior knowledge, and I sensed that in this instance he was taunting me. But in spite of my protests, he would have nothing more to say, and I had to be content with my ignorance about what we had observed. As for the Messiahists and their explanations, I would not believe a claim by them that the sun rises every day.

As we continued our patrol, the mounds and the crude Kr images of the Transmitters lingered in my mind. If a particle of what Justin had reported was true, then these mounds remained lethal even after millennia. I asked myself what that could mean for our world, and whether these mounds were truly connected to the Dissolution of the Ancients? If so, then whatever had destroyed them remained alive here to plague us. Our own lives for many generations had been played out over a vast graveyard of the Ancients; the mounds were a vivid reminder of that. Could this evil, I asked myself, awake and devour us? I marveled that the Kr could actually wish to evoke the malevolence buried there. Far better, I thought to myself, to learn how to live so as to let it sleep!

Until this moment, I had not given much credence to any account of the fall of the Ancients. *Let the things of the Ancients remain buried with the Ancients,* our Teacher says. But seeing the mounds left me unsettled. Justin was right; whatever lay buried here was neither explained by the Messiahists nor accounted for in our histories. I resolved to pursue the question until I had some better understanding. I could not tolerate the idea of a menace that neither tired nor faltered as a man does, and for which there was no remedy.

We reached our appointed rendezvous in late afternoon, just as the weather was brewing into a storm. Dark masses of clouds rolled overhead, and only a streak of gold showed on the horizon. The camp was a welcome sight. There was a circle of tents and wagons, a rope corral, and pickets in place by a small stream. About fifty head of horses grazed under mounted guard on a bench above the camp. As we descended into the valley, the wind rose at our backs. "Just in time," I said to Justin. "Tents and dry beds. We'll find them welcome tonight!"

Justin, who was haranguing the captain of our troop about the direction of our patrol, ignored me. "What can Headquarters be thinking of! Do they imagine that the Kr will bolt at the sight of a few cavalrymen? I cannot believe that the First Apostles do not venture toward Elion. *There*," he said gesturing southward, "is where the danger lies."

At that moment, I saw the golden ensign of Asher flapping above one of the campaign tents – a bound sheaf of wheat on a pure white field. So, it was true: there were cavalrymen from my homeland serving in Engedi. Justin galloped after me to the great tent where the Asherite standard snapped in the wind, and we dismounted and introduced ourselves. My fellow tribesmen gathered around us – ragged, hardy fellows, most of them scarcely more than boys, though there were a few grizzled veterans among them. Their dress was colorful and eccentric, and their speech – to my ears, at least – was without accent.

Captain Elias Neccho, adjutant to the commander of the Asherites, shook our hands and greeted us formally. In my enthusiasm, I had forgotten military protocol. "Sir," I said, "Brevet Major and Under-lieutenant Glanz, at your service."

"Ah, the famous Glanz brothers!" he said, looking us over. "Except one is a Haggadah, and the other"—he said, returning Justin's salute – "is an enigma."

Justin smiled at this dubious compliment and bowed slightly.

"Then you are the one with the Hazorite sword," one of the young men said, equally unconcerned with protocol. "Will you show it to us?" I was pleased that we enjoyed such notoriety, and I was glad to oblige them. They clustered around and examined it, making appraising clucks and ahs.

I could not express my delight at finding a contingent of troops from Asher in Engedi. I asked them about soldiers I had served with in the Second Apostles. Yes, yes, they knew them. Of those present, many had family names that were familiar to me from boyhood. Asher was a very small place.

As we lingered, another returning patrol came cantering down the slope. I caught my breath: the personal ensign of the commander was a heron in full flight on a green field. I recalled the omen I had received on my first descent of the Yakima and marveled. The group came to attention as the horsemen approached. The commander was obviously a man of respect. He was tall, well formed, broad of chest, and in the prime of life. Captain Neccho took the reins of his horse as he dismounted and introduced me to Major Elkiah Vashon. Under-Lieutenant Erech Vashon, who seemed almost a younger twin, was his son.

A wave of excitement passed over me. The Vashon clan were near neighbors of ours in Asher. Their stronghold lay just east of Tirzah, my grandfather's estate, and part of their lands were adjacent to ours. Here were people whose lives were interwoven with the life of my family, who knew me, who would remember me! Even so, it seemed a miracle when Major Vashon's countenance lit up on hearing my name, and he greeted me warmly. "Josiah ben Haggadah!" he said in a deep, resonant voice that seemed somehow familiar. "Can this be the child I saw tagging along after old Samuel?"

Erech Vashon, a young man about my own size and build, swung round and seized me by the shoulders, embracing me. "Do you remember me?" he asked. "I stood by your side at your confirmation."

He was very insistent, but I could not recall him. "Forgive me," I said, "my memory is faulty."

"Josiah was in mourning then," the Major said. "His grandfather had just passed away, and his grandmother too, not long before. His mind must have been in great turmoil."

The young man continued to hold me by the shoulders, looking crestfallen. "I remember when they draped the shawl of consecration around you," Erech said. "You looked as though you were being prepared for sacrifice." He smiled, and I recognized the face of my old playmate behind the man's mask.

"Erech!" I exclaimed. We embraced. No wonder I had failed to recognize the quiet boy in this full-grown warrior standing eye to eye with me! My childhood had been in another life, and I did not visit those memories often. Justin, standing beside me, regarded Erech and me strangely, but said nothing.

"Enough, Erech," his father said. "Let the past lie. I see we have another guest." He greeted Justin cordially, obviously pleased at our unexpected presence. "What a stroke of fortune this is," he exclaimed. "Come along, and let us hear about yourself, Josiah, and how you two came to meet. It is always good for parted friends and family to find one another."

Major Vashon invited us to mess with them. Justin and I accepted gladly, and no sooner had we put up our horses than a gust of wind carried the first drops of rain into our midst. Moments later, rain began to fall in torrents, driving us inside the Major's great tent. We sat in a circle around the fire and shared a meal, drinking sparingly from a stone bottle of apple brandy, while the smoke and an occasional spark ascended through the roof hole. The food was plain, but Major Vashon broke the flat bread with his own hands and passed it to each of us. We cut portions from a round of cheese to eat with the bread, and a steaming pot of beans and lentils was placed in the center of the tent, which we shared in common. Justin seemed aloof at first, then curious. On my part, I reveled in the presence of these fellow tribesmen, who knew me – knew my family and my history for generations. *Had they perhaps known my mother? I felt suddenly close to her, as if she were present.* And I had a new feeling, impossible to describe.

Our hosts and the company were, on their part, fascinated to have a Glanz among them – Justin, that is, for they instantly counted me as a Haggadah. They respected Justin as the conqueror of Esdralon, but were puzzled that he could be a Glanz at the same time. Justin seemed uncomfortable with their questions at first, but gradually warmed to them. He leaned toward me during a lull in the conversation and whispered, "The warriors may be abolished in name, Josiah, but here they are."

Justin and I were obliged to describe the rows of mounds we had seen earlier and to say something about the savage inhabitants of this place. They knew nothing of the Kr and cared less, as they preferred telling and retelling tales about the Ancients, full of great deeds and fantastic miracles. My fellow tribesmen were a talkative lot. When they were pleased or excited they drummed their quirts on the ground as a kind of applause. They were candid about their displeasure at serving here in Engedi so far from home.

"This is a hard land," Elias Neccho said, "but service here is bread."

"In the old days, this land must have been like Eden itself," Major Vashon said. He quoted from memory a few lines of poetry celebrating Engedi at sunset, with a storm coming on. I was impressed by his learning and taste.

"I don't believe Eden ever existed," Justin said, rather abruptly. "But this place, before the war, was good enough for men."

"The pastures here are fat," one of the older men remarked, "with grass enough to feed thousands of cattle, and yet it is as empty as the Desolation."

Justin seemed suddenly pensive. "This is indeed a strange land," he replied. "So close to us in Judah – and yet lying at the very edge of what we know. Of what Israel knows. Like the war itself," he said, "this place is unknown territory."

I was moved both by what he said and by his manner, which was candid and troubled at the same time. I was anxious to hear more, but he fell silent. We resumed our talk of the Ancients and the great days of the Governors, of ancient battles, and of Israel's never-ending war with the Kuhlans. We speculated why the Khulans crossed the Jordan when they did and not at other times, why there were intervals between their depredations, and what controlled their timing. The last full-scale invasion of Israelite territory had been over seventy years ago. One young fellow, his beard scarcely grown but with shoulders like an ox's yoke, asserted that the Kuhlans worship the Moon and drink blood. "And when the Moon is full, they turn themselves into wolves."

The rest of the group laughed at this old superstition; I had heard it myself as a child.

Elias Neccho claimed that the timing of the raids was due to the peculiar customs of the Khulans: "They have no women," he said. "They live solitary and brutish lives because they allow no female infants to survive, and so they are driven by desire and the need to replenish their numbers to ravage other lands and take their women."

"Only once in seventy years?" an older warrior snorted. "No wonder they're savage!"

Another voice disagreed, saying that the Kuhlans were ruled by their women, "And when the women say to, they cross the Jordan and lay waste our country."

Neccho dismissed these speculations in his sharp, caustic way, speaking the opinion of most of Israel: "The Kuhlans are all murdering catamites, and Israelites have a duty to slay them wherever found."

The conversation turned to the present war. Major Vashon remarked that Asher had no quarrel with Benjamin, but had obeyed the summons out of respect for the Council. "There is no proper employment for young men in the north," he explained. "No means to set up families. There is so little trade in the north that I have taken my friends and kinsmen to war out of necessity. Asher will perish if things go on as they are." *So, I reflected, my people are reduced to acting as mercenaries in a war in which they have no stake.*

This subject seemed to arouse Justin. "Israel's wealth," he remarked, "has been declining for generations. You northerners have seen hard times for years, and now there is poverty on the middle Yakima, where the land is salting up and will no longer yield. Want is visible in Judah also, although it often lies down beside great wealth. The Population Law has been flouted there for years, especially in the breeding of slaves. And now we see hunger in the countryside, beggars in the streets, children with thin limbs and big bellies."

"We live in the midst of painful changes, to be sure," Major Vashon agreed.

I began to anticipate some of our recent conversation, but Justin paused, as if his mood had suddenly turned. "Some complain," he said, "of wealthy merchants commanding from palaces and dictating to the Council of Apostles." The casual side conversations died away with Justin's words; he had the full, if not friendly, attention of the group. "It may be, of course," Justin added, "that Israel is as wealthy as ever, but Tephlin Glanz has garnered so much of Israel's riches that all others are poor. Some say he has the nation in his purse."

I was not certain how my fellow-tribesmen would take Justin's humor, if humor it was, but one of them, an elder with streaks of gray in his hair, replied amiably, "Come peace or war, good times or bad, the big merchants make out well enough."

"A merchant's war is it?" Justin seemed fully roused from his earlier torpor and was strangely aggressive, as he had been at our first meeting. I began to feel uneasy. "I used to believe that myself," he said. "In fact, that is exactly how the war was *intended* – a surprise blow to break the Harlech's monopoly and to seize their wealth for Israel."

Justin and I, of course, had had this discussion before, but I was curious why he would speak of it now. "The main blow fell right here in Engedi," he continued. "The first phase of the war was brilliantly planned and executed. It will be celebrated in the chronicles just for the timing of it! When the summons to war was declared, a disguised force of Israelites already lay inside Achish, ready to seize the city."

All this was news to me; I wondered what our hosts would make of it.

"Achish fell to a sudden, almost bloodless coup," Justin continued. "And Ziklag met a similar fate, surprised and overwhelmed while it was virtually undefended." Judah's fleet had gathered as if for the fall festival at Hebron and then swooped down on Ziklag on its way south to Engedi. Esdralon had fallen before Benjamin could recover from the surprise.

"How could this be?" Major Vashon asked, frowning. Justin's account was clearly at odds with everything Major Vashon believed about the war—and about Israel.

"When these blows fell, nearly all of Benjamin's defenders were at the junction of the Clearwater and Snake, conducting the annual trade in hides with the Kuhlans." These circumstances were of course familiar to me, though the rest of the group seemed ignorant of them. "Benjamin's strongholds were practically undefended," Justin explained. "The planners at Headquarters – or those who do the planning *for* Headquarters – knew all of these things, to the last detail. They knew that most of Benjamin's soldiers were hundreds of miles away on the Clearwater."

"You make it sound as if a deliberate surprise attack was launched against Benjamin," Major Vashon said. "But the Council – "

"The Council vote was merely a sham, a cover," Justin declared. *I saw Major Vashon's face change slightly.* Justin was obviously excited, but so sure of himself he gave no thought to his reception. "The decision to attack Benjamin had already been taken, and for other reasons. I repeat: Judean troops were already in the city of Achish before the Council's vote."

"So," Major Vashon said, picking his words carefully, "you insist that the war was not a just rebuke to a rebellious Benjamin, but. . . "

"A sharp cuff, I like to think, such as you'd give a servant – or a barking dog – to silence it. Or to take something out of its mouth. At any rate, a sudden blow that changes your enemy's perspective. And then peace negotiations and business resumes again as usual – only on our terms. Or rather, *our father's* terms." His eyes flicked in my direction, startling me again.

Justin had the style of a city man, flippant and jesting about serious things. I was not sure how his words were being received. I suspected that Asherites did not regard our father as a joking matter, but I was more unsettled by his correcting our host than by the story he told. Justin seemed to enjoy this verbal fencing, but I was uneasy at his breach of courtesy. As for the rest, they listened quietly, without expressing either enthusiasm or anger. They were not sure what to make of his criticism of the army he served, or of the Council, or of his own father. We had wandered onto dangerous ground, and I was not misled by our host's mild manner.

Justin, however, continued his train of thought oblivious of all else. The topic held him with a strange power. "Israel's attack was a thing of beauty – if it were not for the treachery of the whole thing. But one cannot ignore the stupidity of it, either. Wars," Justin added, preoccupied with his own inner conversation, "are defined in part by how they begin. The nature of the strike against Benjamin – the devastating effectiveness of it – along with, as I say, the treachery of it, must surely determine how it is fought and how it is concluded. What I ask myself now is: where is the basis for ending a war begun in such a manner? How can the Harlech negotiate with us? They cannot! They know they cannot. *We* know they will not. What can the Harlech do other than fight us to the death? How would any people respond to our high handedness here in Engedi? How can we ever bring them to the bargaining table? *Must we go on until we exterminate them?"*

Justin's obsessive topic was released among us in the great tent; it lay among us like an unbidden guest. For the first time, I saw where his thoughts were leading him.

"Sometime, when we are at leisure," Major Vashon replied after a long silence, "I would like to hear more on this subject. But there is a story to tell of a great deed, and the doer is here among us. My son Erech will tell the story as it passes in the campfires of the legions and throughout Asher. And you, Josiah, can emend his words and add whatever has been omitted."

To my surprise, Erech Vashon recited the story of the scouting party I had led into Lagash as if were a warrior's tale from ancient times. I had had no idea that this affair of mine was known in the army. But my four companions had been Asherites, so, of course I should have known. Our patrol had become a tale among my tribesmen. I was pleased to be praised among them in the old way, particularly by family friends—and peers. I was also immensely relieved by the change of topic, which had become dangerous.

There was a distance between Erech and myself, however, that I could not name. Looking at him was like gazing at a twin. And yet our lives had diverged so far and there was so much that could not be spoken of in mine, that I could not even visit our shared memories without pain. Nevertheless, I felt drawn into the warm circle of their attention.

Turning to Justin, I realized with a kind of wonder that, for the first time since my boyhood, I was again in my own element. In all of our prior acquaintance, Justin and I had met on his familiar ground and on his terms. But in this moment, I sensed we regarded one another in new circumstances, unacknowledged but mutually understood. Justin, I was pleased to see, had relaxed and was enjoying the story, helping himself to extra bread and dipping from the pot of beans and lentils. His eyes met mine across the fire, and – as certain as one can be of anything in this realm of shadows – I knew that we both liked what we saw.

Listening to Erech Vashon recount our hardships, I could feel again the sting of snow on my face, and I remembered the fear, always in my thoughts at the time, that another storm, coming by chance when we were exposed on high ground, would leave our frozen carcasses parching for years on some wind-swept slope.

At the end, there was much rapping of quirts on the ground. Then Colonel Vashon raised his hand, saying, "My friends, I will add something else, which is not about the courage of these five sons of Asher, but speaks of the consequences of what they did. The information you and your companions brought back told us that Israel's preparations for an invasion had been misplaced. No blow was being readied against Manasseh. That knowledge saved Judah. The Council of Apostles concluded that the invasion was coming there. Three legions were moved south, accordingly, to ward off the attack. When the blow fell, Israel was ready to parry it."

There was a good deal more of quirts pounded on the ground and many guttural "Bwen! Bwen!" – a term of approval in the old tongue. I thanked the teller of the tale, as was customary, and said, "May it truly be that the hardships we endured saved one life in Israel."

I turned into my bedroll after the evening's entertainment as happy as I ever remember being. The rain drumming on the roof of the tent only made me more conscious of the comfort I had found inside it.

That night a great crashing of thunder and lightning descended upon us. After a particularly violent clap, I found myself sitting bolt upright, fully awake and alarmed in the pitch darkness. My mind was slower than my body: *Why was I awake? What was it that had alarmed me?* Then I remembered. The lightning flash had illuminated the tent; the bedroll beside me was empty. Justin was gone. I rolled out of my blanket and sat shivering a moment in the blackness until another flash confirmed what I had half-perceived in my light drowse. Yet another flash and thunderclap showed me the way to the entrance flap, and I peered out. The wind was still gusting and big drops of rain were falling, but the worst of the downpour seemed to be over. The storm was passing over us and was rolling and cracking to the east. I slipped on my robe and oilcloth and stepped out into the rain. I could see no one among the tents – not even the sentries along the picket line. Tracks in the mud led toward the picket rope where the horses were tied, and I found him there, under a flapping tarpaulin.

"It's best to leave these duties to the sentries," I said. "You are not dressed for it." He did not reply for a long time, so I stood nearby and helped him quiet the horses. We rubbed down the most agitated ones with dry blankets and gave them each a handful of oats. The storm was receding, flashing, into the distance.

"I was thinking of the tale that Erech Vashon told," Justin said. "Your story has passed into legend. Or rather you have. I see how it works, how the tales preserve the value of an event, if not its details. Or its ironies. I liked your version better, but I was impressed by his. Truly impressed."

I was not sure how to reply. "You also told a story tonight that held everyone's attention – of how the war commenced and. . . ." As I spoke I felt a sudden inward chill; I drew my cloak more tightly about me and my sentence died unfinished. I said instead: "You have told me before how the war began, but I found your account tonight even more. . . compelling." Although my mind works slowly, I found myself not entirely surprised by his reply.

"You boast yourself one of the Eyes of Israel," Justin retorted. "Has it not occurred to you yet how I came to know that story so well?"

I felt a great sinking sensation inside me. "Yes," I admitted. "Just now."

"So," he said, "it is better that you know some of my secrets, at least."

I knew this secret before he spoke it: As he explained how it had come about, how he had been part of a small group in Hebron, its junior member, though one of its leading minds; how the authorization from Simon ben Gurion had convinced him that his father, Tephlin Glanz, had finally anointed him for some special purpose – I saw it all, saw the story unfold in my mind's eye slightly in advance of his telling: his pride in his intellect, his ambition to shine in a service and among comrades who only partly accepted him, his desire for some belated recognition from our father, and the prospect of high office and command to come. . . . *Justin had planned the war.*

"It was a trap for you, cunningly laid," I commented lamely when he had finished.

"It was indeed," he agreed bitterly. "A noose! And it was a perfect fit, made just for me. And made in part *by* me. Made of what I am. And I walked into it with my eyes open, willingly, even eagerly. That is my shame. My everlasting shame. It will be the story they tell of me."

Again, I knew of what he spoke. He had come to see the war through Michal-Rebekah's widow's eyes as a great evil; he saw its consequences in the orphans and the helpless destitute and in the desolation of the land. He had come to despise his own ambition and his desire for recognition. I could imagine his delight at the early successes of the war, his pleasure in his secret knowledge, an insider at last. But later, the pleasure died. *Base triumphs become unhealing wounds*, St. Supplicee says.

When had he felt his secret joy turn into a stitch in his side?

As we returned wordlessly to the tent, I thought of Justin's reckless exposure of himself on the ramp during the assault on the east wall of Engedi. I felt his desolation as if it were my own. I felt, in fact, closer to him at that moment than I had ever been. Even so, there was no calling out across the abyss to him.

VI

By morning the weather had cleared and the sun shone brightly. Major Vashon announced it would be a good day for tracking as soon as the ground firmed up. Justin seemed a little subdued; otherwise, he showed no sign of what had passed between us the night before. We traveled southeast, the intervals and points of the patrol loose and customary and efficient. These Asherites made the rigid discipline of the First Apostles seem clumsy and amateurish. Asherite horsemen are famous in Israel, and we were treated to a show of their skill. They could shoot arrows at a full gallop from under their horse's neck with only a leg exposed to the enemy, and they could swing down into a moving dismount and vault back into the saddle at a reckless speed. Whatever they did, they expressed a gaiety, a sheer delight in soldiering as if they had been born to it – as indeed most of them had. I wondered how much Justin felt as I did.

Erech Vashon rode at my side, laughing at the pranks of his companions and describing the particular virtues and eccentricities of each. A young trooper named Kimieh, who rode like a fury and whose smile showed toothless gaps was, he explained, a former indentured servant. "Almost a slave to a man who had not much to live on himself. But he has spirit," Erech explained, "and peculiar abilities. He can find water with a peeled willow wand and buried iron with a forked ash twig."

"If he can find buried iron with an ash twig," Justin, who had overheard the conversation, said, "his former master must be a very rich man by now." Iron sometimes passed for currency in Israel; it was far too precious for any use but money and weapons.

We searched the gullies and watercourses for sign until the trackers became persuaded that anyone wishing to hide their presence would seek drier ground well up the slopes. The Asherites, for all their high spirits, were as intense as wolfhounds. After noon our patrol crossed a trail. It was more than a day old, and nearly obliterated by the heavy rain. I was gradually regaining my war senses, the special acuity of sight and hearing that comes from prolonged exposure to danger. In an hour they had followed the invisible spoor to a cold camp, where even I could read the signs. A small party of horsemen had spent the night here without a fire, weathering the storm as best they could in only their blankets. The grass had been trampled down and cropped by their horses where they had been hobbled for the night.

Kimieh knelt on bowlegs and measured the hoof prints precisely with his hands. "Ponies," he said. "Six riders."

"Then they can't be Benjamites," Major Vashon said. "Not if they are riding ponies."

"Then they must be Kr!" Justin said.

Kimieh stooped again to examine some horse dung, which he kneaded in his hand, broke apart, and sniffed. "They are hiding their trail," he said. "They know we are close by"

"I don't wonder they know we are here," Justin said impatiently, "with all the hallooing and racket you've been making!"

Kimieh wiped his hand on wet grass. "Five or six hours, maybe," he said to Major Vashon.

"Let's have a look over yonder," the Major said. He was searching the sky to the south. I saw a black speck high in the sky and then another and another. "Mount up," Major Vashon ordered, his manner suddenly stern. The points fanned out and our column moved forward, following the contours of the ground to avoid revealing ourselves. We moved swiftly, confidently, but differently than we had, aware that we were not alone in this empty-seeming expanse.

The ancient willow, just leafing out, was full of magpies. The ravens on the ground let out a raucous clamor, and the vultures flapped clumsily away and upward. Beneath the willow lay three bodies, clustered together near a stream. Beside them was a dead horse with a distended belly and outstretched legs.

"Benjamites, do you think?" Major Vashon asked Justin, whose jaw was clenched tightly.

"Difficult to say, sir."

The Kr we were trailing had led us to this site. It appeared that our enemies had a sense of humor. The bodies were stripped and mutilated in the familiar Kr fashion. Headless, with hands and feet and other appendages lopped off as trophies, the bodies lay in tall grass, surrounded by swarms of insects. The corpses had been partly flayed, and opened from chest to groin in order to get at the organs – heart and liver – which the Kr relish. The entrails of one victim were festooned on the branches of a willow. Three people and a single horse lay pincushioned with arrows, and the carrion birds had begun their work as well.

"I think this one was a woman," Kimieh said. "A family killed here yesterday, maybe." The smallest victim looked to be about Appian's height, but there was no telling what sex it had been.

Major Vashon looked around the scene, taking in the small valley, the height of the sun, the disfigured dead, the ravens strutting at a distance. "Where are they now, Kimieh?" he asked grimly.

"South, maybe," Kimieh said, squinting up at the sun.

"Southeast," Justin corrected. "The Kr have a base camp at Elion."

"Benjamites or not," Major Vashon said, his face darkening, "these were Israelites."

We performed over the bodies a brief but ancient ritual. Sky burial is permitted on appropriate occasions, and this seemed one of them. I dismounted and took a handful of earth and sprinkled it over the corpses and said the words of the liturgy, which I had by heart. *"All flesh is grass, and its goodness is as the flowers of the fields. . . ."* Their flesh would indeed be grass in a short time. The energies comprising their lives would be diffused here in this draw and would ultimately circulate through the whole universe. Most Old Believers favored cremation to release those energies as quickly as possible. But this was not, I reflected, the worst place for the transformation. Not that it mattered.

The horror of physical dissolution, I kept reminding myself, is an illusion – simply a phase in a process of transformation in which we are always immersed. *"Death is necessary so that the life of things and the eternal flow of energy may continue; therefore death is the servant of life and not its master."*

I had the words by heart, but the whine and buzz of insects in my ear and the stench of the dead distracted me. Our teacher reminds us that life is precious, that all lives are infinitely valuable, not just our own. That is our fundamental intuition of the nature of things. That this intuition is nowhere confirmed in our experience except in our hearts is the paradox in which we move and have our being. *"The eternal flow of energy," St.* Supplicee acknowledges, *"has no discernable purpose."*

Gagged by the stench, I longed fervently for higher powers of discernment.

Kimieh had no difficulty picking up the trail again, and we rode hard. But even though we had correctly inferred their direction of flight and their trail grew gradually easier to follow, we failed to catch the elusive Kr. They were traveling light and fast, and they knew of our presence on their back trail. Two hours before dusk, Major Vashon gave the order to break off pursuit. Justin stood up in his stirrups and cursed.

All the way back to camp Justin harangued Major Vashon. He was still at it when we had our supper. "The Kr wintered over at Elion, south of here." Justin said, pointing to a map. "They hung on our flanks while we conducted the siege of Esdralon. Human vultures, looking for carrion. The Harlech would never, *ever*, have allowed them to do that."

"Do what?" Elias Neccho had wandered into the conversation at the wrong moment.

"Winter over in Engedi!" Justin was impatient with the obtuseness of all Israelites on this subject. I was afraid he would give offense, but Major Vashon was a patient man as well as a quick study. "The Harlech traded with the Kr in the month of the summer solstice," Justin explained as calmly as he could. "But they were never at peace with them. And the Harlech never let them winter over north of the Blue Mountains."

Later, when we gathered around the fire in Major Vashon's quarters, the Major seemed to be reciting his lessons from Justin: "So the Kr are gathering here," he said pointing at the map, "presumably in anticipation of the exchange of goods. Perhaps for other reasons as well. They come north for the trade as soon as the grass is up and they have shorn their flocks. But how they manage to make that migration, I cannot make out. There are solid mountain barriers to the south, and this map shows a belt of forest they have to cross, which would be fatal in May."

"Then even the best maps must be wrong," Justin said, "because they have been coming for three generations."

"You make them sound very dangerous," Major Vashon said.

"They are, believe me!"

"I should think Israel could handle a horde of lawless shepherds," Elias Neccho declared. "After all, the Harlech managed them."

"The Harlech," Justin declared, "never let them winter north of the Blue Mountains!"

"Our merchants can deny them trade goods if there is any difficulty," Necco replied loftily. "They'll know how to deal with a pack of filthy savages."

"Our merchants!" Justin erupted. "This is quite a handful of filthy savages you are talking about!"

"I still don't understand," Major Vashon said, "what you mean when you say we have made these brutes our allies." He turned to me; "What does the Major mean," he asked.

"All I know," I said, hearing myself repeat what Justin had convinced me was true, "is that the Kr wintered north of the Blue Mountains this year, and now they are coming toward Israel in greater numbers than ever before." *Recalling our conversation from the previous evening, I wondered how Justin knew that the Kr were at Elion in such numbers.*

VII

Major Vashon invited me to stay awhile after the group dispersed to their tents. As the evening was fair, we sat outside his tent by a small fire. Erech remained with us, and we chatted pleasantly for a time. Soon, however, Major Vashon leaned forward to stir the fire and said in a low voice, "I know your family. Our families are quite close, in fact, and their histories are intertwined in many ways."

"I remember," I said. "Not well, of course, but I remember. Kadesh-Barnea sits atop a hill and your orchards spread below it practically up to its walls." My grandmother had been scandalized by the risks the Vashons thus took with ticks, planting trees so close to the great house, but I kept that information to myself.

"Your grandfather was a colorful figure, Josiah, and a good friend of my father."

"In what way colorful?" I asked. I had always seen Grandfather through a child's eyes, as a great and awesome figure. This was new light.

He smiled and rubbed his knee. He was being careful to avoid giving offense. "Do you remember a slave of your grandfather's? A great red-haired brute?"

"Lukash?" I thought of a gross, freckled body that turned crimson in the summer. For fear of ticks, Lukash always worked in the orchards stark naked, wearing only a broad-brimmed straw hat.

"Yes, the very one. Complexion like a beet in the summer, or if he'd been drinking. He and your grandfather had some times, I'll tell you."

I began to fear that my view of my grandfather might be fragile and perishable.

"How old were you, Josiah," the Major said, "when . . . you last saw your mother?"

I saw the polite circumlocution. "Seven, I believe."

"That means," he said, seeming to calculate in his head, "you are now twenty – and nearly twenty-one."

"I'll be twenty-one in December."

"Yes, you and Erech are only a few months apart." *So he was aware of my age; he was only bringing it to my attention.* "And what will you do, if I may ask, when you reach your majority? About the Haggadah property, I mean?"

"On my grandfather's death, Tirzah came into the possession of my uncle, Brandon ben Elath, whom you know.

"Yes."

"Under a trust agreement, or so I have always assumed. I was a boy when Grandfather died; I never saw a will. But under the Law, I am the heir." I was becoming uneasy at his questions.

"And upon reaching your majority," he continued, "you intend to return and take possession?"

"I had always assumed so. As soon as my duties with the army permit." I began to suspect that I was about to be told my assumptions were seriously flawed, if not entirely wrong.

"Has your uncle – do you correspond with your uncle?"

"I write him once a year, but I have not had a reply in several years," I said, sensing his drift.

"Josiah, it saddens me to say this, but it may be more difficult for you to regain your inheritance than you imagine."

"Why?"

"Your grandfather was, well – he was not a prudent man. He had strong appetites and a taste for brandy. And he was, even by his own account, addicted to gambling. In short, your grandfather ran up debts, large debts, which he entailed on his property. And, in a sense, on his descendants. Therefore, I am not certain on what terms your uncle Ben Elath holds the property, or presumes to hold it, although you may, as you suggest, have title under any arrangement he may claim." He cleared his throat, looking uncomfortable. "But I begin to feel like a meddlesome neighbor here, Josiah."

"Please continue," I said. "For someone as ignorant as I, a friend must sometimes perform a painful office."

"Exactly so," he said. He seemed relieved but uncertain how to proceed.

"I know nothing of these matters," I said to encourage him. "But the family stronghold is not, as I understand the Law, relinquishable. As the heir of Samuel ben Haggadah's only daughter, I inherit Tirzah and the homestead, even if Grandfather threw everything else away." Major Vashon nodded. I reflected a moment and asked, "Who were his creditors?"

Erech and his father exchanged glances. "It would be easier for me if you did not have to hear it from my lips," he said. I was beginning to fear that Major Vashon had more than, or *other* than, a friendly interest in my family property. "Tephlin Glanz," the Major said at last, clearing his throat and starting my heart hammering in my chest. "Everyone was your grandfather's creditor in small ways, Josiah, but Tephlin Glanz had him in a vice-grip."

I put my fist to my forehead, and breathed deeply, trying to compose myself. *He had just explained to me the circumstances of my mother's marriage.*

"I regret touching upon these matters," Major Vashon said, "that must be painful to you – and some of this, I see, is news to you. But I did so for a good purpose. It was to offer my assistance, whatever it may be worth. You are indeed the heir to Tirzah. Allow me to play the role of elder if you wish, when the time comes. Or a second if you have need."

His words had thrown me into a tumult. There was much – too much – to reflect on in what he said, and much of my life to understand in new light. *My mother! I saw her now as a hostage to my grandfather's weakness – a sacrifice to his folly! He had sold his daughter to ransom his estates!* But I could not accommodate this new view of him without pain. It was as if a portion of my life had been wrenched away and replaced, poorly – like a young man's leg traded for a crooked stick. And there was much unsaid in what had been revealed. It was clear enough that he meant to say that my uncle was my enemy – perhaps mortal enemy – and that the Vashons would stand with me in the quarrel. But the quarrel was over Tirzah, the Haggadah family property. What interest did the Vashons have in that? How is it, I asked myself, remembering Major Cohn-el's smug voice, that my uncle, my kin, was not kind, and these strangers, the Vashons, were offering to act as kin to me?

Before I could settle any of these questions in my mind, Major Vashon added: "There is one other matter, Josiah, that is even more urgent. Again, I am at a loss. In some sense we are strangers, in that we have not seen one another for years. And in another sense, we are quite the opposite. Your family were like kin to us. And you—well, I was present at your circumcision as well as your confirmation." He paused, and then moved abruptly to the new subject. "You had a quarrel, an affair of honor, at the Academy." It was not a question; *he knew, and Erech Vashon knew, and their knowledge made my face burn.* I opened my mouth to explain, but he held up a hand. "You need not speak of it now," he said. "I know enough. Israel knows enough – although I am sure there is much more to know."

I waited for him to continue.

"The question I must ask," he said, "is this: did Brandon ben Elath offer to make restitution for the death of Senesh Velco? No? I thought not."

My uncle's silence through my crisis, the absence of some offer of assistance from him in my hour of need, confirmed, as I reflected on it, the general tenor of what Elkiah

Vashon was telling me about my uncle. *My uncle was my enemy.*

"Again, in the matter of restitution to the Velco clan, let me offer you my services as – well, as your uncle, since your maternal great uncle, Brandon ben Elath, has neglected his duty." Major Vashon seemed embarrassed to have to broach these matters, but was at the same time entirely earnest and forthright. "I am acquainted with some sensible men of Manasseh," he continued. "With your permission, I will approach them and see if they are willing to make discrete inquiries. This matter cannot be allowed to fester unattended."

I wanted to ask why he would put himself at risk in my vendetta with the Velco clan, but I was overwhelmed, thinking of my mother's fate.

"I have reason to believe you are in grave danger from the Velcos," he continued. "For that reason, my son Erech will be constantly at your side until this matter has been resolved. And then we will deal with Tirzah and your uncle." I startled at his use of *we* in regard to Tirzah, but he misread my surprise as selfless regard for his family. "No matter," he said. "Erech understands and accepts the hazard along with the responsibility."

"With pleasure," Erech said. He had not spoken for a long time, but I saw that he was informed of everything regarding my affairs—*far more than I was myself.*

Major Vashon rose, signaling an end to the conversation. "I must tell you also," he said, "that relations between your uncle and myself are not good. Not good at all. He is leader of the war party in Asher. And I – even though I lead my people to war – am for peace. Your uncle also seems ambitious for the Apostleship, which may fall vacant soon. With his connections, he will be a formidable candidate – and a disaster for our people if he succeeds. I mean no disrespect to Major Apollo when I say that your uncle Brandon appears to be entirely the agent of Tephlin Glanz. That I am no friend of Tephlin Glanz you have surely gathered by now."

I awoke early next morning after a troubled, fitful sleep. In a half-doze I heard Major Vashon's voice and then my brother Justin's reply. "Yes, of course," Justin was saying. "He is brave and incorruptible. If only he had a sense of humor – and were capable of lying – he would, I believe, be the most dangerous man in Israel."

"The most dangerous man in Israel!" Major Vashon said. "Exactly the words I have heard used to describe you."

"Well," Justin replied, "I suppose brothers must compete in all things."

VIII

When we returned to Esdralon, there was a great stir and excitement in the city which we could sense as we approached. From the rise above town, skiffs and cargo boats of every kind in the fleet were visible lining the quay in tremendous numbers. For a moment I could not imagine what it all meant.

"It is Admiral Montevideo!" Justin declared. "See, that's his ensign flying over the harbor, the red sturgeon on a blue field." Seeing the ensign, I recalled the comments I had heard in the officers' mess disparaging the Admiral as a fishmonger. Indeed it was Admiral Baldwin Montevideo and his entire expedition returned from the confluence of the Snake and the Clearwater. Regimental flags and ensigns of fleet units fluttered along the landing. Ragged rows of tents were being set up outside the walls along the Jordan. As we passed into the south gate of the walled city, the bells of St. Eli's began to toll. Our horses' hooves clattered on the cobble stone streets, but scarcely anyone attended to our return.

"But why put in here, at Esdralon, rather than at Hebron?" Major Vashon remarked. "It strikes me as odd that the fleet and army have come here."

"Of course!" Justin exclaimed.

If the army and fleet had been victorious, they would naturally have decamped at Hebron for a triumphal procession and celebration. There was no celebration in progress in the streets, no sounds of jubilation, but something dejected and hangdog about the army's return, visible even from a great distance. We parted company with our new Asherite friends at the main plaza. Justin and Major Vashon reported to Headquarters; I returned to the Commissary.

Major Cohn-el mopped his face with a cloth as he examined a stack of documents and waved me away; he had no time to talk to me. I sensed an undercurrent of anxiety among the staff, but it was apparently bad form to show it. News was sketchy, but I gleaned bits of information from the others. The fleet had labored over the portages of the Snake and reached the junction of the Clearwater, but there had been nothing to capture there. No base, no Harlech expedition. There had been little fighting of any kind. Instead, the army had struggled with dysentery and pneumonia and returned with them. Part of the warehouse district was being converted to house the sick, and the area would be quarantined.

"There is no need, however, to fear an outbreak here in Esdralon," Major Cohn-el announced in his most official manner.

The next morning the drum roll summoned us not to executions of heretics and spies but to a ceremony of thanksgiving. Montevideo's army passed in dispirited procession from the Field of War to the main plaza. From the balcony of St. Eli's, Bishop Bon, the famous Messiahist cleric from New Jerusalem, conducted a solemn thanksgiving. The great bells pealed over the assembled throng, and we sang the anthem, "Brave Dead of Israel." Afterwards I recorded the gist of Admiral Montevideo's speech in my journal:

"The expeditionary force has served with great courage and distinction in overcoming many difficulties. Regrettably the enemy fled rather than give battle, which prevented a decisive engagement. The expedition has accomplished all it could have, all that is necessary for the next stage of the conflict. Circumstances require flexibility in plans. . . concentration against the weakest points of the enemy. . . seizing the opportunities which God gives us. . . exercising patience when opportunities are not present. We are redeploying our forces for a new offensive, for the final struggle. It is time to strike boldly in a new direction."

The dejection of Montevideo's officers and men was apparent at the ceremony, and I learned that that something else, something worse, had happened as well. Word went round that a troop of Issachar Light Horse sent to scout up on the plateau had not returned; eighty-six officers and men had been lost without a trace. Worst of all, Montevideo had not had the courage to send a relief force to learn their fate or recover the bodies. Captain Mathias remarked to me that if the rumors were true, Montevideo was a ruined man. "The old Names in Israel will never tolerate this," he said. "Moreover, the churchmen are incensed at his failure. They seem on fire with indignation."

I felt saddened, not by the lack of progress in our war effort, for I had been shaken in my convictions about the war, but by the loss of so many good men. Justin, who joined us in the officers' mess, was almost cheerful, seeming to take his own private view of the matter. I had learned to defer to his judgment on many things, for he typically considered carefully before forming his opinions. Still, it seemed to me that he was taking a strange view of this disaster.

Afterwards, we gathered with our Asherite friends at the Brown Pitcher, which was crowded and noisy with Montevideo's soldiers. Justin insisted, perversely, on defending the return of the army. "It's obvious that Montevideo could have accomplished nothing more on the Snake," he asserted. "Winter is the only time you can deal the Kuhlans a blow on their own ground. That's how Israel fought them in the old days. Once their pastures green up again, and they can scatter, there is no way to catch them. And it's a foolish general who tries."

Justin seemed remarkably knowledgeable about how to wage war against the Kuhlans; he had informed himself, apparently, on all topics. But my own mind was in turmoil. Israel had suffered a grievous defeat. Admiral Montevideo's expedition up the Snake River had represented the greatest extension of Israel's military might in over a century, and I could not regard its failure coolly. As the details of the mission's failure emerged in overheard bits of gossip, the hollow space in my stomach grew. The Admiral had taken the cream of the army – many of whom were now quarreling and drinking themselves into a stupor within our hearing. The expedition had had some initial successes in forcing the portages, but the hope of a decisive battle on the Snake had been frustrated as the Benjamites moved upstream ahead of the fleet. By mid-December, the expedition had reached the Clearwater. Their intention had been to seize the heart of the Harlech trading empire, but there was nothing to seize. No one came to trade hides or beef – nor to dispossess them of their provocative outpost. The Kuhlans never appeared to conduct their cattle-sacrifice. Israelite patrols observed a few scouts along the edges of the bluffs and a few columns of smoke. Otherwise: nothing. Where were the Kuhlan herds? Where were their winter campsites? Toward the last, there was much sickness among the troops. Finally, in March, the single armed reconnaissance party that was sent out to find the Kuhlans disappeared into the cold mists of the plateau.

We listened while a Judean officer at a nearby table raged at the cowardice of the Admiral and his staff and heard loud murmurs of approval from the crowd. Justin whispered to me, "This begins to look like trouble." He seemed intensely interested yet detached, as if at a play. "Think of it!" Justin exclaimed in my ear as we walked homeward. "The whole expedition was stampeded by one small ambush! The reputation of the Kuhlans is beyond anything!"

IX

In the morning, the Commissary was a hive of activity. There were thousands of soldiers to feed and re-equip, and a mad confusion of inventories to sort out. I had just returned from the docks with a ship's lading when Justin, feverish with excitement and exalted with brandy, burst into the office. He strode by Major Cohn-el and Captain Mathias and others of his acquaintance as if they were invisible. "So, my brother," he shouted, throwing a letter on my desk, "it seems that a Glanz is to be lifted up before Israel like a piece of vermin on a pitchfork!"

Justin had never seemed more a stranger to me than in this mood. He stood before me, chest heaving, as I read the letter. It was an official document, sealed by the Council. It announced that Justin had been selected to receive the Order of the Sacred Heart of the Constellation, Israel's second highest decoration. I read the document aloud. A circle had formed around us, and there were murmurs of congratulations.

Justin sprang back as if stung. "Say nothing if you value my regard. Headquarters has culled out a dozen other officers from Montevideo's host – probably at random – who will be similarly treated, along with one dead colonel of Issachar Light Horse." His features were twisted and angry, and I understood the mockery of his hopes in the timing of this decoration. "This is a skewer in Montevideo's heart," he said, crumpling the paper. "It is no honor to me!" I rose quickly, fearing he had said too much and would say more, but Justin turned on his heel and was gone.

The ceremony, which I attended that afternoon in the cavernous gloom of St. Eli's, was everything that a show of honor to a brave man should not be. Bishop Bon in the garments of his Order officiated at the Messiahist rigmarole at the front of the hall, while the audience stood fidgeting in the back. It was not even a military ceremony, but a strange affair of gongs and cymbals. I felt unclean afterwards and wanted to be purified.

"None of this can detract from what you did," I assured Justin. He said nothing and strode furiously along the street until we turned into the Brown Pitcher. Our conversation that afternoon is burned into my heart.

"It's true," Justin said, "I bear honorable wounds on my front – as if that means anything. And now I have this little heart with stars on a string at my neck – Messiahist nonsense, as you would say – placed there by the will of the Council. I myself designed the siege engines at Esdralon and built the ramp – and I left half my life's blood upon it! So the Army of Israel toast me and sometimes even cheer me. And of course they obey me, as they must. But I am not of them, little brother. I drink and brawl and whore with them, and bet on their cockfights and races, but they know I am not one of them. Never! Among the great landed families of Israel, the name Glanz does not appear. Neither does Apollo, my mother's people. My family is, to speak the truth, conspicuous for their absence from among Israel's great Names. The Apollos, makers and purveyors of a plum brandy so vile that only by a device of great cunning by my father, have we foisted this awful stuff upon Israel as ritual drink. The Apollos now make a special vintage, suitable for great occasions like today, which pain and distaste make memorable."

He was soon drunk. I said nothing, felt nothing – except a numbness and something like despair on his behalf. Justin seemed to be performing at a great distance from me, like someone observed through the wrong end of a telescope.

"When you spoke to me about your disgrace at the Academy, " Justin continued morosely, "I understood your shame. But when I think of my great deeds, as they call them,

I feel a worse disgrace. Far worse! You acted out of natural and honorable feelings, while I am made a hero because of my own foolish and degraded hopes. Because of my ambition to be known in Israel, to enjoy a small fame, to advance my *career!*" He spoke the word as if it were an obscenity. "A marriage gone sour, a wife distant and – no, I'll speak the truth – a wife unadmirable in any way, a wife whom I dislike intensely and who dislikes me equally. So, a motive for leaving home, yes. For cynicism, perhaps. And divorce – difficult as they are to come by. Even motives for drunkenness and debauchery, out of frustration of being denied a divorce." His speech had become rambling, difficult to follow.

"But is there reason in any of this," he demanded, "to sack a flourishing city? Basest of all, my merchant's heart, ashamed of my origins and anxious to win the admiration of the nobly born of Israel. To be approved by men I know to be mindless brutes – my God, how repulsive! And for the sake of their approval, to bring down the towers of Esdralon and to bring widowhood and misery to Michal-Rebekah and an orphan's life to Appian! Josiah," he said with a sadness I could not bear to witness, "I am the most despicable of men. When I wear my Order of the Sacred Heart of the Constellation, I will wear it to remind myself of that. I wish I had died on that ramp."

That night I called on the Vashons at the cavalry encampment outside the city, for we had an invitation to Justin's. I accompanied Major Vashon and Erech to his quarters, all the while fearing Justin's state of mind. I informed the Vashons about the circumstances behind Justin's decoration and his bitter disappointment. Major Vashon suggested we delay our visit, but I explained that I would rather be with him than leave him alone in this mood.

"It is better for soldiers to keep out of politics," Major Vashon said as we dismounted at Justin's. "Too many distractions when the heart and mind must have a single purpose."

Recalling Justin's greeting on my first visit, I grieved that this time the street was empty. Michal-Rebekah met us at the top of the stairs, her manner grave but hospitable. I was reminded that this was her home into which she invited us. Major Vashon greeted her with perfect courtesy and introduced his son Erech. When we were seated, Michal-Rebekah informed us that Justin was indisposed at the moment but would join us later. Major Vashon arose protesting that we should not trouble the household, but she gently restrained him. Appian quickly brought a tray with tea and unleavened bread. Conversation proved difficult, so we turned to the war, which had at least the quality of being impersonal.

Major Vashon had been to a briefing at the Field of War, and he recounted what had transpired, speaking as confidently as if Michal-Rebekah and Appian were good Asherites. "The plan now," he said, "is to send an even larger expeditionary force down the Jordan, to strike the Harlech in Lagash. They will wait until June, until the fever season is well under way and the ticks block the land routes from Lagash into Israel. Headquarters doesn't want Jonas II Harlech flying across the barrens at Judah when our strength is concentrated on the river. General Boseth will use Montevideo's troops as the core of the next expedition. The question remains if they can persuade the northern tribes to come in."

Major Vashon had traced these plans on a map of Israel on the wall; we followed the logic of what he said with our eyes. "It's a good plan," Major Vashon said. "It allows us to make use of the fever season for waging war. The Jordan is the only approach to the enemy that is free of ticks. The plan also seeks a decisive victory and an end to this stalemate. Since everyone is eager for an end to the war, that hope alone will carry many along. Finally, on the Jordan route, we can use the fleet to supply the army."

"A brilliant plan!" Justin interrupted; he had joined us unnoticed. We looked at him in astonishment, and I was shocked at his puffy face and disheveled hair. "There are only three things wrong with it," he said disdainfully. "The Harlech, the Kr, and now the Kuhlans!"

The Vashons glanced at me uneasily while I studied Justin.

"Consider the Dall Fortress which guards the portage to Lagash," Justin continued, clearly drunk. My heart felt like a cinder. I knew his childhood dreams of glory and realized that, while disparaging them, he retained them still.

"I mean no disrespect to my northern warrior-guests," Justin said, gesturing at the map, "but it cannot be taken. It's built on solid rock and surrounded by swift water on three sides. Water that is unclean and which our attacking soldiers, in their superstition, will fear more than the Harlech. The fourth side is a cliff 800 feet high. We can't undermine the fort, and we certainly can't go over it, and I can't imagine a way around it." Justin slumped beside me on the couch. "I have seen this place myself, scouted it thoroughly. The Harlech made no attempt to keep us from seeing it, I can assure you. They practically invited us up to measure the walls. The walls are high and of smooth masonry. The Harlech spared nothing in its construction. And, I repeat, it is the single gate into Lagash from the south, from the Jordan."

Erech attempted a polite entrance into this monologue by reminding Justin that Esdralon had also seemed impregnable until Justin himself had helped capture it. Justin glared at him with bloodshot eyes.

At that moment, Michal-Rebekah appeared, either to call us to dine or to interrupt an embarrassing scene in the making. Justin rose awkwardly and waved her away. "Israel is beaten." he said hoarsely. "It's as simple as my standing here. We are beaten before we start, and not just at the Dall Fortress. Come, look here!" Justin gestured toward the map on the wall. "First, consider the Kr lying at our doorstep in Engedi. All of Engedi lies open to them. They mean to knock the door in at any moment, although I am apparently the only man in Israel who has eyes to see it."

"Second," he resumed, unsteady on his feet, "consider the Kuhlans. As if the Kr were not enough, now the Kuhlans are aroused. Montevideo has just pulled back from above the fifth cataract, abandoning a 150-mile stretch of the Snake River. The entire Kuhlan horde can now concentrate against us and invade our homeland. That, my friends, is the single wretched accomplishment of Montevideo's expedition. We have kicked a wolf in the ribs, and we are about to repent it."

I marveled how Justin, so overcome by brandy that his speech was slurred and his hands shook, kept a tenacious hold on lucidity. As always, what he said made sense. I thought his anger would subside, but he continued. "When the Kuhlans came against Israel in the past, they struck across the clean reaches of the Jordan." Justin pointed at the river north of Chinnereth, in Danite territory.

"That's where the fleet needs to be," I interjected, trying to mollify him.

"And if the Kuhlans *but use their senses!*" – Justin turned his glare on me – they will know what I know and realize they can cross anywhere. *Anywhere!* The river will not stop them."

Belatedly, I understood the import of the conversation Justin and I had had as we walked along the banks of the Jordan. Whatever had poisoned the river during the Dissolution of the Ancients' civilization had lost its lethality.

Justin grinned wolfishly and collapsed on the divan. "Can you imagine what General Zillah confided in me at Headquarters today? 'This in strictest confidence, of course!'" He mimicked Zillah's voice and pompous manners. "Zillah said he had no idea that Kuhlan warriors were so impious as to cross the Forbidden Zone. No idea! My friends, the Plain of Sharon has already been penetrated – a small raid, only a reconnaissance. But no doubt more to come!"

The Vashons flinched visibly at this report.

Justin then turned his intense, almost furious attention back to me: "Why should the Kuhlans confine themselves to the clean reaches of the Jordan, when they know what we know, or *should* know. The Jordan no longer kills those who touch it! The Kuhlan are ruled by experience, by what is, not by what was proclaimed to be centuries ago. They will come straight into the heart of Israel, forbidden reaches or no!" He turned to the others, but whether furious or despairing, I could not tell. "Israel," he declared, "lies open as it has never been in history!"

Major Vashon, who had been sitting passively to one side; now gripped his chair to control himself. "I feared this," he exclaimed; "I have dreaded it! And now it has come to pass. For three generations," he said, "no Kr, no Kuhlan, no foreign enemy has set foot on Israelite soil except in chains."

Justin turned to listen, his head balanced unsteadily on his neck.

"It was always Israel's goal," the Major continued fiercely, "to keep the barbarians out. Generations of Israelites suffered the depredations of the nomads until the Twelve made the Jordan into a moat and Israel's fleet into a fortress. Behind these wooden walls, Israel has slept secure. This, for my lifetime and my father's father's lifetimes." He paused, gathering his breath, and then rose. "Until now. Until *now*! Until that son of Beli-az, that spawn of shame and outcast darkness – may his name live in infamy and his seed perish before his eyes – *Tephlin Glanz!* The dog who brings the nomads across the Jordan. I know of a certainty it is he!"

Elkiah Vashon's was an ancient and conventional curse. Feeling among friends, he had forgotten who we were, Justin and I. The Major was afterwards distressed almost to choking by his words, his face so twisted with pain that I felt compassion for him. No eyes could meet in the aftermath of his words. Justin's face was red with emotion but not with anger. Michal-Rebekah had shrunk into the shadows, sunken within her own sorrow and habitual reticence. There was nothing to say; we saw exactly what Major Vashon saw; felt what he felt. In any case, words cannot be recalled. *"May his seed perish before his eyes!"*

And of course there was merit in Major Vashon's view. Could either Justin or I deny it? Already cursed in our patrimony, we felt this additional burden no more than a feather. There was nothing to say, no apology or restitution to be demanded. Elkiah Vashon marched down the stairs straight as a spear, but Erech touched his forehead to my hand in parting, and I felt his tears on the back of my hand.

After a long while in which we neither moved nor spoke, Michal-Rebekah stirred herself to leave us in privacy. "Stay a while," Justin said softly, reaching out and taking her hand. So much had transpired, I was not even shocked by this open display. "Sit with us a moment." Justin seemed completely himself again; the effects of the brandy had evaporated. "You see how things are," he said gently, holding her hand. "How they are about to turn out. You see them as well as we. Perhaps better. Truly, my beloved Michal-Rebekah, I have longed to see justice for you and your people. I still long for it."

"Justin! Be still!" she cried, trying to pull free of his hand, but he held her.

He lifted his eyes from the floor and gazed at her. "Justice. Truly, I long for it. Do you believe me?"

She shook her head fiercely, eyes shut tight, tears flying. In this agonizing moment in which I was an intruder into their innermost private life, it was as if I could reach into the minds of each and hear the unspoken words pass between them.

I have longed to see justice for you and your son and your people. But what is coming will not be justice.

It was as if an irreparable breach had opened between them – or a gulf always present had suddenly yawned visibly at their feet. As she glared at him, it was as if she touched the raw heart of the matter. Did she speak, or did the words form only in my mind?

You served Israel, aiming at the destruction of my people. Now you will suffer what I have suffered, and you will understand how I have longed, longed to see the slaughter of your people Israel!

Alone, hours later, in the sleepless hours just before dawn, I realized how hard are the truths of the Way – how events may be seen to grow out of one another until the fundamental order of the world can actually be glimpsed in them. But the world's order is not a moral order; it is not made for us. And there is no comfort in it.

Chapter 4: The Kr

I

The next morning Major Vashon was waiting outside my quarters with an apology. "Josiah," he said, "forgive me. I spoke unwittingly of your brother; I regret my words from the bottom of my heart."

I took some consolation that his apology was directed at Justin. Major Vashon apparently took for granted, on the strength of our friendship and tribal ties, that I had forgiven him, which of course I had. "Justin understands, just as I do," I replied. "If we could choose another father, we would do so."

"And if I could choose another son, it would be you," he said, his voice full of emotion. I was so astonished that I watched him disappear around a corner before I could speak.

General Boseth turned from his pacing and scowled at us. "You call yourselves members of the Eyes of Israel?" he demanded.

Justin had persuaded me that we must approach Headquarters and lay the dangers we saw before them. It was our duty, he assured me, as officers and members of the Eyes of Israel. General Boseth, however, was not pleased. The General had invited General Zillah, his second in command, to be present at the interview. To my dismay, the young churchman who had denied me use of the archives was also present as a scribe. The meeting felt immediately hostile – more like my long-expected court-martial than a report by earnest junior officers.

"The Harlech," General Boseth said, pointing his finger at us as if we were the authors of the policy, "refused to let Israelites share in the trade at Elion or the harvest of bulls at the Clearwater. They went so far as to deny entrance into Esdralon to all foreigners during their trading seasons with the uncircumcised."

"Exactly!" snorted General Zillah. "One of the many provocations that brought about the war."

"The Harlech kept their business to themselves, kept their trade secret," Justin acknowledged, "and that was offensive to the rest of Israel. But the Harlech also knew how to conduct it—and knew how to conduct themselves with these savage peoples. I submit to you that we, who must deal with them now, do not know how to conduct ourselves. And that is a danger. This ignorance could well prove fatal to us." Justin seemed supremely confident, his manner an open rebuke to his superiors. "Or, more likely," he continued boldly, "now that the trade is in our grasp, our ignorance may cause it to evaporate like mist. It is quite possible that we've won nothing for our pains. Nothing but trouble!" To my astonishment, Justin actually leaned forward and spat on the floor.

"Granted, we may encounter problems," General Zillah replied, ignoring this incredible breech of etiquette. "But surely these are problems that can be overcome. Trade makes its own way."

Justin waved his argument aside. His manner of speaking with the highest officers was no different from his manner with me; he did not know the meaning of deference. "By seizing Esdralon," he argued, "we intended to make ourselves partners of the Kr. In order to do that, we were willing to make ourselves enemies of Benjamin—who, by the way, are enemies enough for anyone. But we underestimated both the Kr and Benjamin. And if this were not folly enough, the expedition to the Clearwater has almost certainly roused the Kuhlans against us. That, I believe, is Montevideo's sole achievement."

Again, General Boseth interrupted, not to address Justin's point, but to recite Israel's grievances against Benjamin. I thought him foolish or mad – until I noticed the pains that both he and Zillah were taking to get their views of Harlech transgressions into the record that the Messiahist clerk was unobtrusively scrawling in the corner of the room. This desultory business might have gone on forever, but, grown suddenly impatient, Zillah snapped at Justin, "Well, then, what is your point?"

Justin replied instantly: "Sir, we have in a practical sense allied ourselves with the Kr – or *appear* to have done so."

"Appear to whom?" General Boseth demanded. "I do not see it so."

"To the *Kuhlans*!" Justin exclaimed.

"Israel may use," General Boseth replied solemnly, "but it never forms alliances with unconvenanted peoples. Besides, the Kuhlans have always been Israel's enemy."

"True, the Kuhlans are always Israel's enemies, sir, but they are not always *active* enemies. We are always mortal, but we are not always having our throats slit, if you see the difference. There is a difference, sir! There is a difference."

General Zillah leaped indignantly to his feet, but Justin, also rising from his seat, continued undeterred: "And that is why this army must immediately – *immediately*, I say – turn its strength against the Kr encamped south of Esdralon! That must be our first task. Second, the fleet must stand watch on the central reaches of the Jordan, to intercept any Kuhlans who attempt to cross over to Israel. Which means," he added almost casually, "abandoning this foolish effort toward Lagash." His words shocked me; our auditors were transfixed.

"This is outrageous!" General Zillah stormed. "This is insubordination!"

'This is treason!" General Bosheth added ominously, glancing at the cleric.

"And third," Justin added, tenacious to the point of insolence, "the Council must open negotiations with Benjamin with a view of putting an end to this war."

The General of the Host sputtered a moment before he had the presence of mind to shout: "Major Apollo, you are dismissed!"

To my everlasting surprise, we left the meeting and the building without being placed under arrest. On the balcony of his own quarters, Justin removed his headgear and robe and washed his hands in a basin of water. He ran his wet fingers through his hair and then dried them on a towel. He stretched himself comfortably on a couch and turned to look at me.

"No one," I said, "but the son of Tephlin Glanz would have dared to do what you just did. And no one else could have gotten away with it!"

"Fools, the pair of them," he said. "Blustering fools! And they are both frightened half out of their wits." He stretched, yawned, and rubbed the bridge of his nose. "But what troubles me is that they were not afraid of *us*."

"Why in the world should they be afraid of us?"

"Zaiyah, Zaiyah," he said in his most condescending manner. "They know who we are, even if you do not."

Justin not only got away with his insolence at Headquarters, he received permission next day to take a patrol down to Elion. General Zillah instructed him to take a troop from Colonel Shevren's First Apostles Horse, but, as Shevren and Justin were having a tiff at the time, Justin coolly rejected the offer, saying that he preferred the mixed battalion commanded by Major Vashon. "More reliable," he said.

Justin chose to deal with the breach between himself and the Vashons by ignoring it. City-bred men have their own manners, which they seem to make up as they go along. In this case, as in so many, what Justin decided to do succeeded well enough.

As our patrol rode southward toward Elion, Justin regaled us with his version of the meeting the previous day. His imitation of General Boseth was masterful. "'The Primate and the Council of Apostles'," Justin said, gesturing pompously, "'have declared the Kr to be utterly without souls, incapable of salvation or of human intercourse of any kind. Therefore, the Kr are to be treated as the rest of inanimate nature, as objects for our use. Israel's use, do you see?' Boseth was watching that scribbling churchman out of the corner of his eye the whole time! The Primate, he announced to us, 'has recently confirmed the Sixteenth Utterance of Polamur IV, given a century ago in the 882nd year of our Tribulation'."

"Well, then," Major Vashon laughed, glad to be on good terms again with Justin, "I suppose we need feel no concern about the Kr, and you've brought us on a fool's errand."

"Ha! No concern about the Kr!" Justin laughed with a cruel twist in his face that I associated with officers in a losing game of chance. "As a rational man," Justin went on, suddenly sober, "I fear death. Any man who says otherwise is a liar or a fool. But I would rather die any death than be taken by the Kr. So let us keep our eyes open today."

Later, his mood lifted and he amused himself by disparaging me and my assignment in the Commissary. I endured him patiently, relieved to be in the field again and away from the intrigues at Headquarters. We rode in bright sunshine; tufts of cloud drifted overhead, driven by a steady breeze from the west. I would have been content to abandon myself to the impressions flowing over me and the steady, hypnotic gait of my horse, but Justin's mind was, for reasons I well understood, continually upon the rack.

"Victory," Justin resumed, "has not given us Engedi, but rather the shadow of Engedi. What Israel actually controls, as you will see today, my friends, is that portion which lies within the moving shadows of our horses' bellies. You may observe it beneath your horse, there, Erech: secure Israelite territory. Mark it now and treasure it in your memory. We have seized the fabulous wealth of Engedi, but somehow the trade and these fertile lands do not yield any profit to us. Is this not a paradox, my warrior friends? Rather than a prize, Engedi is a wound in our side, a hole that bleeds away our blood and treasure."

As we rode, Justin continued relentlessly on his theme: "When the Council of Apostles granted monopolies in Engedi to Jonas ben Harlech at the time of the Religious Settlement, no one wanted them. They were thought to be worthless. These lands were worthless then, and are worthless again. That is the secret of Engedi," he declared. "The wealth of this place is smoke. Smoke!"

Suddenly Justin spurred his horse and wheeled to face us, his mount dancing and champing at the bit. "Zaiyah," he exclaimed, "I see, I see it all now! *The fools!* I see now why Boseth and Zillah were not afraid – not afraid of us and not afraid of Tephlin Glanz."

"What are you talking about?"

"Yesterday, the tone of the meeting. That whole strange business with the Messiahist scribe taking down everything we said. It is Bishop Bon! They fear Bishop Bon, who proclaimed the Judgment Day will come with the new millennium! The millennium! Boseth and Zillah *believe* him! Can you imagine?

The Vashons and I reined in our horses; the Major turned to me for explanation, but I had none.

"Or," Justin mused, "they are afraid of the power that Bishop Bon has acquired by announcing the date of Judgment Day. That's it! Yes, that must be it! Bold, very bold, you must admit! I should have realized what it meant that day in the square after the executions, when Bon gave his speech to the army. Yes, that's it! That must be it! 'When I remember that God is just,'" he intoned in imitation of the Bishop, "'and that Day of the Lord is nigh, I tremble for the Doubters! But for Dissenters and heretics I have only derision! Derision and God's curse!'"

"Please, go slowly and explain yourself," Major Vashon demanded.

"If Bishop Bon announces that the date of Judgment Day is two and a half years away – no, if he *says* that Judgment Day is coming at that moment, he is claiming that God speaks to him. To *him*. And if revelation comes to him, and thus through him, he is by right head of the church. Of course! Bishop Bon is claiming that the power of God sanctions his authority; his voice is God's own. Therefore, the church must be his as well. Bon was implicitly making that claim that day in the square."

Major Vashon frowned. "I think I begin to see."

"Something is afoot," Justin said. "Generals Boseth and Zillah know about it – and I must find out what it is. I wouldn't be surprised if the Primate is about to be deposed. Bishop Bon is not one to wait patiently for God to stir up a bit of slaughter and tribulation. Bon stands for hard war, war without stint or pity or possibility of compromise, and in his view no one but himself quite comes up to the mark. Josiah, I need to get back to Esdralon!"

"And the Kr?"

"Damn the Kr! The Kr can wait!" Justin shouted.

I respected my brother's intelligence above that of all men, but I was beginning to doubt his stability. Apparently, Justin had just acquired a new obsession, and he was immediately consumed by it. Nevertheless – as I was forced to make plain to him – we served under orders and had our patrol to complete. Reluctantly, he agreed to proceed a few more miles as ordered, so as to be able to report what we saw.

Topping the crest of a low rise some hours later, we saw below us the grassy plain of Elion. We rested our horses while we scanned the valley. It was an impressive sight, spacious and green. The surface of a small lake glittered in the center of the depression, miles away, and there was timber to the south. Haze obscured part of the valley, and a mirage seemed to dance and shimmer just above the horizon. This was Elion, the spot where the Kr would exchange their wool and hides for Israel's goods.

"Here is grazing for more cattle than all of Israel possesses," Major Vashon observed.

"Yes," Justin replied, "and here is the reason why the whole of Engedi is no longer ours. Look yonder; that is not haze in the valley, but smoke. If the wind were not at our backs, you could smell it. Smell the Kr. *There*," he said, rising in his stirrups, "is Moab come to us. Damn the fools at Headquarters for their blindness! They refuse to see, stubbornly refuse to acknowledge what is! Why can't they see the danger?"

We strained our eyes to confirm what Justin was telling us, but the distance was too great and the haze impenetrable. For all I could tell, the valley was empty. Major Vashon motioned us forward. We followed a small spring-fed watercourse down hill. Clumps of sage filled the valley where it opened out, and hawthorn and aspen grew along the stream. *Good cover*, I noted, wondering if we might flush a mule deer. Instead, a hundred paces ahead of us a horseman suddenly erupted out of the ground. Then another, and then a dozen, all with the same astonishing speed and a clumsy twist of the body as they jerked themselves and their mounts erect.

"What on earth!" I heard Justin exclaim.

Compact, ragged figures on small horses, they confronted us like specters, like a previously unknown form of life. *At last,* my mind reported, *the Kr!*

Their effect was almost supernatural. "There is not cover enough for a rabbit!" Major

Vashon exclaimed. I felt my hair stiffen like a cat's. Then another group of horsemen broke from behind a line of brush on our right, and both groups moved forward to attack. There was no signal, no command – just a common will for our destruction. The horsemen were swathed head to foot in ragged, pollen-colored cloths, and as they broke into a gallop, they emitted high-pitched hooting war cries that perfectly chilled my blood.

Are these creatures human? I asked myself, feeling unreasoning terror grip my heart as they closed with us. A moment before collision, I was enveloped in a sickening, miasmic stench – a mingled smell of Eucalyptus, wood smoke, and a rank odor of human filth. More than that I cannot remember.

II

When I returned to my senses, I was swaying in the saddle, my mount unsteady beneath me. I shook myself to clear my vision, and wiped a trickle of blood from my eyes. A wave of violence had passed over me, leaving me stranded and bewildered. I patted my horse's neck to steady him, wondering dimly how badly I had been wounded. I was struggling for breath, and I felt a pain swelling in my forehead and an ache in my left side and arm. A riderless horse lay nearby and several straw-colored heaps were sprawled on the ground. *Kr*, I reasoned.

There were more figures in the distance that I could not make out clearly. The horizon danced and surged in my head; blue, white-tufted sky and sage-colored earth shaking together and parting, unfamiliar and ominous. A strange repulsive odor lingered in my nostrils, and I longed to vomit forth the acid taste in my stomach. I could not see straight.

My horse tossed his head fretfully, sawing at the bridle. Through my lifting fog I perceived gradually that my horse's right ear was a bleeding stump. I felt a thrill of horror. *St. Supplicee!* Had I slashed off my own horse's ear? Bewildered, I stared at the twitching stump and then realized his mane, too, was flecked all over with blood. My own left hand, entangled in the mane was likewise sticky with gore. And then, unbelieving, I gazed down at my arms and legs and equipment, and at my sword clenched in my right hand: all of my body that I could see was drenched with blood as if I had splashed at a gallop through a brook of it.

My horse took a few steps and stumbled. Feeling his giddiness between my knees, I swung down. Blood was spurting from a large gash in his chest and splattering on the ground between his forelegs. I glanced frantically about, while the great heart of the beast continued to pump its life onto the ground. Knots of horsemen moved in several directions and a commotion sounded below me, but I could not guess its significance. Trembling on spread legs, his large eyes imploring me, my horse groaned in terror. I knelt and scooped up a handful of the bloody mud beneath his feet and packed it into the wound. He stood under my hand unresisting, eyes rolling, while I packed a second handful of mud into his wound. I tried to hold him still, pressing my hand onto the wound to stanch the bleeding. Instead, I felt the mud poultice dissolve in my fingers, the pent-up blood spurted outward, splash, splash, on the ground. There was nothing to be done. I stripped off the bridle and released the saddle girth, freeing him from those burdens. I stepped away, avoiding his gaze.

Gradually, I became aware of what had transpired in the past few moments. I remembered the attack, the sudden ambush. Kr swarming toward us, having leapt up out of the very earth, and our troop – or part of it – fleeing as I turned to rally them to our aid. I recalled rising in my stirrups, my sword unsheathed, the overpowering stench of the Kr in my nostrils, as both revulsion and battle fury mounted in me like delirium. "Arribe!" I had shouted. My battle cry. Nothing else of the scene came back to me, so I began to search for clues.

A Kr pony lay sprawled a few yards away. Astonishingly, the horse's neck was severed halfway to its chest. Its head and upper neck lay apart, intact as a roast in a butcher shop. The horse appeared to have been decapitated cleanly in one stroke. Its rider – or a Kr, at any rate—was sprawled just beyond it. Two more Kr bodies, or pieces of bodies, lay nearby, partly hidden by sagebrush.

It came to me then that I was isolated on a battlefield and in great danger. Stumbling about, I picked up a discarded lance and tried to sort out the clumps of milling figures. Following my training, I looked on the ground and in the brush for other weapons I might use, searching slowly but purposefully for a bow and arrows. My legs moved clumsily, as if I were wading in knee-deep water. *Where is Justin*? I asked myself. *And Major Vashon?*

Below me and about two hundred yards away the ground was strewn with bodies, Kr and Israelite, dead and dying horses. I began to make out riderless horses and figures here and there on the ground. Wounded or dead, safe to ignore. To my right, up the slope, mounted Kr and Israelites sparred and maneuvered. As I watched, a group of Kr detached themselves from the mass and began to approach me at a gallop. At that moment, as blind chance would have it, I found what I sought – my intact and unstrung bow on the ground alongside my dying horse, which was stretched now helplessly on its side. Rising with the bow in my hand, I felt something approaching clarity of mind.

The bow was short and deeply curved and of a powerful composite construction. Striking the butt of the lance into the ground, I pulled a handful of arrows from the quiver. I crouched as low as possible behind the body of my horse, stringing and testing the bow. The Kr were loosing arrows at me, coming at a gallop. Two arrows whizzed harmlessly past and a third buried itself in the ground. The sound of the hooves rose in my ears like thunder, and from somewhere, faintly, beyond them, came the sound of a command whistle. The four of them came onward, and I prayed like a Messiahist that they would remain bunched together for another heartbeat. The pull of the bow was like the flex of a good sword in my hands; I released quickly and notched another arrow.

My horse, whose body partly shielded mine, suddenly neighed shrilly and reared upright, struggling to gain its forelegs. Its sudden movement knocked me sprawling on the ground. I heard arrows pass overhead and the impact of another that struck the horse. The beast reared up, screamed like a man, and collapsed. By rising on its forelegs, the horse had taken arrows meant for me; its single convulsive effort had saved my life. I sprang up and released another arrow and then lunged to the right, slipping into cover behind a clump of sagebrush.

I heard rather than saw my arrow strike home. I released another quickly, and frantic neighing told me I had hit something. One horse was down and its rider sprawled on the ground. I rose from the brush and released another arrow, this one carefully aimed at the tangle of horsemen and wildly plunging horses. I targeted the rider of the other wounded horse, off-balance and preoccupied with his mount, and my arrow took him squarely in the chest. I had hit the two center riders; the other pair had split apart to pass me on either side. Choosing instantly, I pivoted to the right, notching another arrow just as one of the circling Kr released his own. I dodged – or rather flinched – away, and felt a hot stab of pain in my neck as I released my arrow. The blow had spoiled my aim. Immediately, I felt another shock, another stabbing pain, this one in my back. The impact threw me forward on my knees. In the haze that threatened to envelop me again, I tried to fathom what had knocked the breath out of me. Still on my knees and hands, it came to me what had happened: the fourth horseman. I had turned my back to him and taken his arrow. I knew I was finished.

There was a din of shouting and the sounds of approaching horsemen—and then the shrill war whistles of Asher. Staggering to my feet, I confronted the fourth horseman, who had wheeled back for the easy kill. He had come broadside of me and but thirty paces off, on a small, leather-mouthed bay. He was sure of me; I could see it in his eyes. He turned for an instant to measure the distance between himself and my approaching comrades, and I loosed my last arrow at him. The shaft penetrated his thigh. His horse reared and kicked, and he jerked his bridle savagely and turned away from me.

I flung away the bow and turned, reeling, to face my last assailant, bearing down on me from the other side. He was almost on top of me, poised for an easy kill. A half-dozen helmeted Israelites were galloping hard toward me; I heard their cries, my comrades coming to rescue me, and realized that they were too late. Raising my sword Singer in both hands over my head in the crane position I croaked my battle cry – *Ai Ai arrib Isra-el!* – and, miraculously, this last Kr veered away and fled from my companions.

In a flash I recollected how the Kr horse had come to be decapitated. Then the sky darkened and the sandy soil hit me square in the mouth.

". . . Erech is down, and Asahel is dead. And here are the brothers."

I heard these words as I struggled to regain my senses. Kimieh was on the ground beside me, slapping me and poking roughly at my wounds. My head was throbbing. They raised me to a sitting position.

"You must get up, Josiah! Your brother Justin is gravely hurt. Can you stand? We're not out of danger yet; we must hurry."

Remembering the Kr, I lunged to my feet, and Major Vashon caught me in his arms. I saw only Israelites, sweating and bloody, surrounding me.

"My son has a head wound," Major Vashon was saying. "I think he may recover, if. . . ."

Justin lay nearby, unconscious. His tunic and armor had been cut away from his chest. Seeing the effects of the war club on my brother's body, I recovered another sharp fragment of memory of the first onslaught: the Kr coming up out of the ground, so it seemed, slashing at us with clubs with smooth cobblestone heads. *Dangerous enough, but not as lethal as an axe with a blade.* In addition to the wound on his chest, Justin was bleeding from the mouth and nose, but no other injuries were visible. He had taken a hard fall.

"We thought his neck was broken, but he moved his leg a moment ago. We have to move him, but if the sternum is fractured I am afraid it will kill him."

Erech Vashon was unconscious from a better-aimed blow of a Kr war club. The blow had landed squarely on the crest of his helmet and split it asunder. I wondered if Erech's skull had fractured like his helmet.

The event was coming back to me in disjointed segments. Justin and I, trained in the tactics of the Apostles cavalry, had stood our ground at the head of the column, Erech standing with us. We had taken the shock of the Kr attack while the others, using the age-old tactics of light cavalry, fell back from the assault like a bending bow, regrouping as they gave ground, appearing to flee but gathering themselves for a rebound. Justin and Erech had been struck down in the first onslaught. I had survived a glancing blow to my head and my horse had been killed under me. The Asherite cavalry had then counterattacked, cut through the Kr, and rescued me. The whole action had transpired in a few moments.

"Sir, the Kr are gathering."

"Josiah, *come!* We must make haste."

"He'll need a travois," I said. "They'll both need travois." Several other men also had wounds, but they were mounted double with comrades.

"All right, all right! We'll make the travois. Get blankets and picket ropes. But hurry!"

I knelt by Justin and spoke some encouraging but not very coherent words. He seemed unconscious, though his face was clenched with pain. I touched Erech's forehead gently as they lashed him to a travois. I was dizzy from the blow to my own head, and the horizon was vibrating like a drum.

"Are we ready then?" Major Vashon's voice was strained. I discovered my saddle and bridle clutched tightly in my left hand. I handed them up to Kimieh and walked along beside Justin, who was strapped awkwardly in the makeshift travois. Every jolt and bounce of the poles was agony to him; I could only hope for a clean break that would not tear his flesh to pieces as we moved. Clumps of Kr horsemen shadowed us on the ridge tops, but they did not choose to molest us.

III

"So, you remember nothing?" Elkiah Vashon asked me more than once. "I have heard of the battle fury, but I have not seen it. Yet many have it, they say."

"I remember a little," I said. I visited the Asherite encampment frequently as my wounds healed to see how Erech fared, and each time Major Vashon questioned me about the skirmish with the Kr. He was always complimentary, but he seemed troubled as well. On several occasions, he gathered the other members of the patrol to describe the encounter for me, to see if their accounts could stimulate my memory.

"Surely you remember, Josiah, how you scattered the first onslaught of Kr and then fought like a fury over Erech and Major Apollo's unconscious bodies. Elias says you pursued a group of Kr alone, striking down three of them and decapitating one of their horses with a single blow." He shook his head at my answers. When I confided in him that I had no clear recollection of this event or the one that caused my disgrace at the Academy – the death of Senesh Velco – he frowned and bit his lip, saying, "Battle fury," as though it were a question rather than an answer.

The Asherites and the other troops of his battalion, however, lionized me for the feats attributed to me and demanded to see my Hazorite sword. I felt like an impostor, as though these imputed deeds had really been performed by someone else. In the meantime, I spent as much time as possible with Justin and rested and tried to regain my sense of balance.

It was little short of miraculous that Justin survived both the rigors of the journey back to Esdralon and the shock of the operation. The hospital was still quarantined, and neither I nor anyone else was allowed to visit him there. So when Justin emerged on a stretcher, pale and wasted but alive, I had to call him a fortunate man. He had, however, re-injured the same bones crushed in the assault on Esdralon, and his collarbone had required surgery to be set properly. When I saw his body encased in bandages, I feared that, even if no infection appeared, he would be crippled by his wounds.

Michal-Rebekah ministered to Justin's needs faithfully, with a firm touch that warmed my heart and increased my esteem for her immeasurably. She also insisted on caring for me, which she accomplished in a determined but gently competent manner, which I suppose is the peculiar gift of women. Compared to Justin's, my own wounds were unimportant: a concussion from the blow of a Kr war club; a deep cut on my forehead below the line of my helmet; a sprained left elbow from another blow taken on my shield; and superficial arrow wounds in my back and neck. My armor had saved my life. Fortunately, the arrows had not been poisoned.

The news of our fight with the Kr occasioned much indignation in the army. But it was a cause of consternation at Headquarters and in the merchant shops. In both, it was claimed we had jeopardized the exchange of goods scheduled for the summer solstice. Called to Headquarters to report on the incident, Major Vashon was severely reprimanded. To my surprise, however, Major Vashon was indifferent to the reprimand. Incensed at the blindness of the high command, he had adopted Justin's views of the dangers of the Kr presence in Engedi, and he was not reticent about stating his opinion. Though a cautious man, the Major was tenacious when aroused. I was sorry that we had entangled him in these difficulties, but I feared Justin's punishment might be very serious.

Ten days after our encounter with the Kr, I was well enough to attend a feast Major Vashon held in my honor. I expected a small affair involving his immediate circle of Asherites and perhaps a few other northerners. The Major had hinted to me that he would use the occasion to announce that in my quarrel with the Velco clan, the Vashons were now a concerned party. This was a precaution he felt necessary to deter assassins. Knowing a little of vendettas, I was grateful to have his assistance. As I readied myself to leave my quarters for the encampment on the appointed day, a dozen cavalrymen appeared at my door with a litter, in which they insisted I be carried to the Field of War. This honor guard of veterans, be-decked with all their ribbons and medals, accompanied me on horseback.

At the Field of War I was greeted like a hero and paraded around the drill ground where a crowd of several hundred had gathered. Still astonished, I was then taken to a sweat lodge for a brief purification. Afterwards, my face was painted red for the ceremony, which I knew by this point was an initiation into the Order of Mighty Men – the warrior lodge of those who had slain seven or more enemies in battle. Finally, I was arrayed in robes of white linen and led to a pavilion over which flew the white and gold standard of Asher.

I had never seen such a ceremony, which was a colorful relic of the old days – an affair of tents and of the fields and not of the city. There was much speech-making in my honor. Sheep and cattle were roasting in great pits, and bread and hominy and bulgur wheat were set out in abundance, with casks of good wine and beer. The great war drums throbbed like the pulse of the earth itself, and I became dizzy with all the activity, although nothing was required of me but to recline under my pavilion and receive the homage of well-wishers. My deeds were recounted and embellished, and singers made ballads praising my prowess. Major Vashon himself placed the crimson sash of the Mighty Men across my shoulder and took that occasion to announce the entry of the Vashons into my affair with the Velcos. Honorable restitution would be forthcoming, he declared, and he invited those present to witness that I was under his protection and under the protection of the Order of Mighty Men as well. As the assembled warriors voiced their deep-throated assent to this arrangement, I was elated beyond any saying.

In the afternoon, young warriors performed a horseback pantomime of the engagement, which was highly stylized and resembled a kind of equestrian dance more than the fight itself. But it was a thing of beauty, and the crowd roared its approval of the splendid horsemanship and the grace of the riders. At the end of the performance, there was wild applause and the clashing of swords on shields as the young man who played my part uncinched his saddle and strode with it from the field. Finally, the landed cavalry passed in jangling review, arrayed in all the splendor of their clan colors and accouterments.

All of the members of the Mighty Men present then took their turn and recounted their famous deeds. It was both an impressive and exhausting performance, as several were quite long-winded. But I was especially moved that three elderly Harlech wearing the crimson sash had come out from Esdralon to honor me. They boasted of their feats of arms and then seated themselves and partook of the feast, knitting up by their presence, if only for an hour, the frayed fabric of the nation. Many among the Israelites wept at their presence and loaded them with gifts when they departed.

Major Cohn-el appeared briefly – the only member of the Commissary to attend, as this was one of the ceremonies still belonging to the caste warriors. "Well, well," he said. "It's not every day that one of our office is inducted into a barbaric lodge. I came out to see if this gathering was just a cover of the old warriors for a rising against civilization itself. I'm still not convinced that all this is innocent."

I welcomed him and accepted his ironic congratulations. He shook my hand, stepped back, and saluted. "This ceremony is everything that half-cooked meat and sour beer could make it," he said in parting. "Enjoy the praise today, Under-lieutenant Glanz – or should I say Haggadah? Headquarters takes quite another view of your affair with the Kr."

IV

"Impossible! Quite impossible!" General Boseth was indignant, his voice soaring. "Do you imagine I can find two hundred cavalry mounts overnight, let alone *two thousand*? Montevideo's cavalry need rest and refitting, as well as remounts. Do you take me for a magician? There are not two thousand cavalry mounts in all of Engedi." The members of his staff all nodded somberly and General Camero Zillah glared at us. "No!" the General exclaimed. "You'll make do with the troops here in Esdralon. I've given you the cream of those forces for this little adventure. I'm assigning General Zillah and the First Apostles infantry, with Colonel Shevren and the garrison cavalry. Enough, and more than enough. But that's *all*, mind you!" He paced the room, hands clasped behind his back. "The High Command has other matters to consider. The entire Southern Host must be brought up to the mark for more important things, as you well know."

He stopped abruptly and waved my report at me, as if to single me out as the cause of all this difficulty. "I must say, Under-Lieutenant, the Council does not look favorably on this expedition at all. Not at all! It represents at best – at *best*, I say – a serious diversion of our strength at a most inopportune time. The High Command does not *like* it."

Major Vashon contained his wrath until we were outside. "Does the Council imagine we provoked the Kr attack? That Major Apollo somehow contrived to get himself wounded, perhaps mortally, just to interfere with Headquarters' plans? This is outrageous!"

I was too angry to speak, still absorbing the instructions given by the General of the Host: *"Never mind your report. You have permission for a punitive raid, and you have the means to accomplish it. Those are your orders; carry them out!"* The three of us, Major Elkiah Vashon, Elias Neccho, and myself, were survivors of the brush with the Kr; all of us bore wounds, and together we had the best conception in Israel of what a punitive raid against the Kr would encounter. We should have been involved in planning the expedition, but we had been deliberately excluded. As a result, General Zillah's plan appeared to send us on a fool's errand.

"We're to conduct a reprisal against the Kr *with infantry*, "Neccho exclaimed. "But unless the Kr consent to be caught, we'll never see them." All of us had bitter things to say about the army's high command and the new priestly influences on it. "The Messiahists foist this gullible fool on us and call him a general!" someone added, and we were suddenly on dangerous ground.

Major Vashon regained his composure first. "We have our orders," he said quietly. "Let us see what can be done."

I returned with them to the cavalry encampment, where the Major set about assessing our strength. The General of the Host had assigned the First Apostles infantry, amounting to better than a thousand infantrymen who knew the value of their formations. Of cavalry, there were three hundred men of the First Apostles Horse – Colonel Shevren's command – and two hundred more of the mixed battalion from the north, including fifty Asherites, all under Major Vashon. Good men, well trained and mounted. Fifteen hundred effectives all told, plus two cohorts of Home Guards. I sighed aloud, and the Major read my thoughts: "That's right," he said, "not half enough strength for the task. The First Apostles are a formidable weapon. Nevertheless. . ." he began, but did not finish. He was thinking of General Zillah, who had been recently appointed to command the legion and whose merits were unknown. "I wish we knew more about our commander, whether. . . ."

"General Zillah is a Messiahist lackey!" Neccho interrupted. "That's all we need to know about him."

It was difficult to estimate the enemy's strength. All of us had the impression that the Kr were present at Elion in overwhelming numbers. Perhaps only I was conscious that this impression was Justin's doing more than anything we had observed.

But what if, I asked myself, Justin had intended to provoke an incident with the Kr?

"Do they intend us to fail, do you think?" Neccho said.

I shrugged, still thinking about Justin. "It's more likely that Headquarters believes that we exaggerate the threat posed by the Kr. They fear that the exchange of goods has been endangered by this encounter of ours. They intend that the exchange take place, no matter what.

"Even over our dead bodies!"

"The exchange is only a month away, I said. "The Council would prefer to forget our skirmish with the Kr, but concede that the honor of the army must be placated. So, we will have our reprisal."

"But with infantry?"

"They see the expedition as a gesture, as a concession to our blood. They expect us to march out and back untouched, but with the army's honor satisfied."

"Ah, they take us for fools, these merchants!" Neccho snorted. *I agreed, but it seemed to me that it was the churchmen who were influencing events.*

I knew that Justin was convinced that both the Council and Headquarters misunderstood the Kr; I spoke what I had heard many times from him: "They believe that a desire for trade is the Kr's governing motive and that, given their need for our goods, they will allow themselves to become tools of our policy."

Major Vashon grimaced and then looked at me sharply. "What do you believe about the Kr?"

"I have nothing on which to make an estimate," I admitted. Justin's views of Kr strength and intentions – however obtained – were the most plausible we had. But my question about Justin's intentions had opened a box I could not close.

Late that afternoon we returned to Headquarters for a council of war with our new commander. General Zillah was a stout man of middle years with square shoulders and only a trace of a neck. "We have the orders of the General of the Host before us," he announced, glowering at the assembled officers. "Any questions?"

Colonel Shevren was lounging across two chairs, his sword propped on the bench next to him. "I don't mind running over a few savages," he declared. "Damned nuisances, if you ask me. Prowling around the city, interfering with patrols, pillaging the countryside." The Kr had taken to raiding close to the city in recent days; the Harlech population had fled inside the walls, leaving the countryside deserted.

General Zillah looked sternly over his assembled officers. "We will march straight down to Elion and deal with whatever is there. Put your commands in order; we start at dawn the day after tomorrow." He then bid us kneel and beseech the blessings of Almighty God upon our endeavor. Those of us of noble blood stood stiffly at attention, as though we had been slapped.

Afterwards, one the infantry officers stayed to question me. He towered over me like a tree. I recognized him as Colonel Hezekiah, one of the two brigade commanders and one of the tallest men in the army. "So what can we expect from these goat-buggers?" he demanded.

"That depends," I said. "If the Kr are few in number, they will run and we'll see nothing but their dust. In that case, we destroy all signs of their presence and march back to Esdralon. In a month, the truce will prevail, and they can return to Elion with their wool. The trade will proceed as usual, with Israel picking up where the Harlech left off."

"And what if these murdering trough scum are gathered at Elion in strength?"

"Then they will choose what happens. In that case, I expect the Kr will come out and fight us."

"And then?"

"I don't know." I described everything I had learned about the Kr – their weapons and tactics, the range of their bows, even their war cries, which I had found so unnerving. "The Kr are fierce fighters," I said, "but they have no discipline in our sense. They will flow around and through a formation like water, but they can't break through it by main force. They fight in small groups and as individuals, but will be reluctant to press a charge home. They are dangerous to patrols like ours, but will be baffled by larger formations. However, everything I've learned of how the Harlech fought the Kr leads me to encourage you to keep the tightest formations at all times, en route to as well as on the battlefield."

As we filed out of the meeting, Colonel Ahaz, the other brigade commander of the First Apostles, took Colonel Hezekiah by the sleeve. "One legion and a handful of auxiliaries are not much to work with," he said. "Not enough strength to push a determined enemy around, and yet it is too many lives to throw away. I don't like it."

Later, I paid a brief visit to my Asherite friends. Erech Vashon, his head swathed in bandages, embraced me and his father did likewise. "Josiah," Major Vashon said, holding me at arm's length, "see to your brother. I will brief the First Apostles. The two brigade commanders seem to have better judgment than most. I'll drop round and talk to both tonight." He smiled. "I may be suspect, however, as the friend of you and Justin."

"A friendship that is much appreciated."

"Josiah, you are truly my friend," he said seriously. "But you are also my kinsman."

Major Vashon's comment was the highest compliment I could imagine. We were fellow tribesmen, but kin only in the most rarefied sense. I knew that in extending to me the privileges of blood kinship, he had given an unqualified pledge of support. I longed for a way to acknowledge and reciprocate the bond he had affirmed, but sometimes there are no words.

V

Justin was in pain but cheerful. The old woman with the tumor, to whom I had delivered bread, was a healer of some reputation, and she had come the previous day and placed leeches on his flesh where it was swollen near to bursting. The swelling had subsided; nevertheless, I feared an infection so near his heart. Justin and I spoke for a few moments while Michal-Rebekah sponged his forehead with a damp cloth. I mentioned that plans for an expedition against the Kr were underway, but told him no details, for fear of rousing him. He was weak and easily tired, and soon he fell asleep.

Michal-Rebekah took me firmly in hand and insisted on examining my wounds and changing my dressings. She had me remove my tunic to examine where the arrow had penetrated my back – actually only piercing the skin a little. The wound had filled with pus a few days after I returned, and the woman had lanced and drained it. A poultice of healing herbs and aloe had drawn out the infection. "It looks as though your wounds are healing now," she said. She reminded me sternly to keep clean bandages on them and to stay out of the baths.

"But I need to be purified."

"Nonsense; not with an unhealed wound. You'll take your death at the baths." She had water boiling on the veranda, where the smoke and heat would not trouble Justin.

"What about your headaches?" she asked when she returned. She took my head in her hands and bent me backwards into the light. "Has your vision entirely cleared?" She looked into my eyes searchingly.

"It's fine," I said. I could not return her gaze. Almost two weeks after the encounter with the Kr, I could move about and my head was clear, though I still suffered headaches.

"This looks as if it might scar," she said, rubbing aloe sap on my forehead. "It's a pity," she said, stepping backward to look at me again, seeing me this time. "You are not a bad looking young man."

It was the first compliment I had ever had from a woman. I must have blushed. She blushed also, just for a moment, and then busied herself preparing hot cloths for my sprained arm. I watched her as she worked, oblivious of me, although I was nearly naked. She had a common-sense manner that spared me any further embarrassment. I thought how strange it was that I had originally disapproved of her – and still disapproved of her in an abstract way – as a snare for Justin and an enemy of Israel. And yet I was no less grateful for the kind attention she gave to Justin – and to me. I was conscious also of her woman's body near me, of her graceful arms and neck, and the strands of lustrous black hair that had come loose from her coiffure. Michal-Rebekah Harlech, wife and daughter of our enemies, had cared for both of us competently and, I think, tenderly. What did she really feel about Justin, I asked myself – suppressing the other question that lay behind it: *what did she really feel about me?*

When Justin awoke he was feverish. I helped him swallow some lukewarm tea, but he made a face and pushed it away. The effort made him grimace. Then he grasped my hand and pulled me close. "Josiah," he said, "you must listen to me and do as I say." He was emphatic to the point of fierceness, and I thought at first it was the fever speaking, though his words were distinct. "Listen, Zaiyah, *always*," he said, speaking as if we were alone on a vast plain, "keep the Kr away from the Jordan! Do not let yourself be lulled asleep for any reason; do not let the Kr see any kind of boat on the south shore." He tried to raise himself from his pillow, winced and lay back, perspiring heavily. "You still don't understand! Zaiyah, the Kr are *dangerous*! The Primate hasn't the ghost of an idea, back in his palace. Nor do Glanz and Ben Gurion." He paused for breath. Justin was clearly overwrought, and I was moved at his distress, though far from understanding it.

"No idea of what?" I asked.

"Above all," he continued as if I had not spoken, "do not carry any living Kr, prisoner or not, in any form of vessel. If you see Kr in the water, *kill them*! Kill all of them! That was the first rule of the Harlech, and we must adhere to it. The Kr must never cross over to Israel. They must never *conceive* it is possible!"

My brother spoke with such urgency I could only nod in assent.

"Because," he said, turning his fever-wracked eyes on me, "they can cross."

VI

I used my office in the Commissary to commandeer extra wagons and water barrels for the expedition. The land south of Engedi is not well watered, and a host such as ours could easily deplete the wells along the way. Since we would be less mobile than the nomads, we might easily be cut off from water. I also located several of the smaller ballistas and catapults used in the siege of Esdralon and had them mounted on wagon beds, and I filled yet another wagon with arrows, pikes, and javelins from the arsenal.

I returned to Justin's late that night to say good-by. Justin was sleeping and was obviously not to be disturbed. Nearing exhaustion myself, I turned to go.

"Do you really intend, then, to accompany the expedition?" Michal-Rebekah asked. "With your wounds not yet healed?"

Her question did not seem to require an answer. I inquired about Justin's fever and appetite and nodded at her replies. There was an awkwardness between us. It occurred to me that if Justin was correct about Kr strength at Elion, this could be the last time I ever saw her. I longed to say something, but could find no pretext for such an utterance and did not, in any case, know what I wished to say. I dismissed the thought.

"Tell Justin," I said, buckling on my sword, "that Colonel Shevren quarreled with General Zillah today. The General is in a foul mood, and Shevren is furious. Headquarters finally sees Justin's point that the Kr will threaten our flank if we move" – I stopped abruptly, realizing I was giving secret information to a Harlech. "I'll say good-night, then," I concluded awkwardly. I was already moving toward the stairs.

"Wait!" she said. "*Wait.* Please!" Her voice was soft but urgent. She looked at me with her large eyes, her hands clasped loosely together at her waist. "Tonight," she said, "of all nights, you forgot who and what I am. For this one moment of forgetting, I thank you, Josiah ben Haggadah." I stared at her, seeing her eyes brim with tears. In that moment and in that long gaze that held us, many things passed through my mind: my brother's hope (vain, I believed) of obtaining a divorce from the Elders and his plans for a future with Michal-Rebekah and Appian. Would Michal-Rebekah consent to marry and bear another child, I wondered. *Justin's child? Could she, the widow of Elgin Harlech, truly love an Israelite?* I thought of Justin's wife and child in Judah and the prospect of endless war before us. Woven among these thoughts was a sense of the meagerness of my own life prospects. I felt the weight of responsibility that had been hoisted onto my shoulders by other men's hopes – a burden I had worn like a garment since – *since when*? My mind flew back to the day my uncle and I came upon the death fetish of the forest people in Grandfather's pasture. How many strands of my present life led back to that moment?

Michal-Rebekah spoke at last, and it was as if a spell was broken. "Will you accept a gift from me, Josiah?" she said quietly. Her voice was normal again, except that she spoke my familiar name as if it had always been hers to use. "Wait here, please; I will only take a moment."

She returned with a bulky object wrapped in fine cloth. I could tell it was a book, and when I removed the cloth I saw it was a journal – the chronicle, in fact, of Jonas ben Harlech, the founder of the clan's fortunes. I was unaware such a journal existed. When I opened it, I found a layman's scrawl on yellowed parchment. Was this, then, the original manuscript I held?

"I want you to understand my people," she said to me in parting. "You, of all the people in the world."

Back at my quarters, I knew that, exhausted though I was, I would not find sleep that night. I lit a candle and took up the chronicle Michal-Rebekah had given me, pleased to hold in my hands something that belonged to her – and yet hopeful that the book would offer some measure of distraction. The chronicle was written in a fine bold hand, slightly marred by the tremors of age. It was an old man's reminiscence. I had before me *The Chronicle of Jonas ben Harlech*, the founder of Benjamite fortunes. It was an account of the establishment of Benjamin's trading empire.

In the midst of the siege of Beth-Walula, the garrison town that the Harlech had boldly planted in Kuhlan territory, Jonas ben Harlech had an insight born of desperation. Despairing of a successful outcome of the siege and unwilling to see the consequences of his having led his friends and kinsmen so disastrously into danger, the first Jonas Ben Harlech rode forth through a sally port and turned his horse in the traditional tight circle which is a call for parley. The Kuhlans stared for a moment, and in that instant of hesitation, Jonas Harlech cried out, in a language they could understand: *"I see that we are one people. Let me speak to the women."*

Curious, I thought. The Kuhlans speak a dialect of the old language of the Governors.

Jonas repeated the formula he had spoken: *I see that we are one people. Let me speak to the women.* The Kuhlans remained stock still, until one of their leaders rode forward and turned his big bay horse in a small circle. The two approached each other and spoke briefly, and then the Kuhlans retired a respectful distance and waited.

We are one people, spoken in the language of the Governors. What did the words mean to the Kuhlans? A magic formula? A charm? Or were they merely surprised to hear an Israelite speaking, however imperfectly, in their own tongue? And the request to speak to the women: what was the nature of Jonah Ben Harlech's insight? What did he understand about Kuhlan customs? And how had he acquired that understanding? Dizzy with fatigue, I read on, skipping whole sections, understanding half of what I read.

Tonacarloche. Jonas Harlech remarks repeatedly upon the man's manners, his mildness and courtesy. Not until they entered the sweat lodge and disrobed for the purification, he says, did he recognize the man, the ogre, with whom he was dealing. He describes his host as a small man, well formed and muscular. *"The skin of his face, arms and upper body, darkened by years of exposure, was very like my own; his hair and beard, though graying, were dark as my own. Only his lower abdomen and legs, white as a fish belly, as he stood naked in the light penetrating the boughs of the sweat lodge, betrayed his identity as a Kuhlan. But then, by the whiter streaks of scars on his body, the long thin scars on chest and upper arms, I recognized him: Tonacarloche, the terror of Israel. The realization lifted the hair on my head and arms, and I could not speak a word."*

The ceremonies of purification, the long-drawn out preparation for negotiation, were unfamiliar to Jonas Harlech, but quite recognizable in their intentions: "*surprisingly like the customs of Israel,*" "*surprisingly refined,*" his narrative proclaims. When the moment for speaking arrived, his host, the relentless Tonacarloche, the foremost despoiler of Israel in previous decades, was somehow transformed into a mild-mannered diplomat of mature years. He came directly to the point: *"What do the intruders wish to say to the Grandmothers?"*

Jonas ben Harlech describes himself as a gambler with only one throw, and the stakes were a thousand lives, his own included. He had memorized his speech beforehand, which he uttered in broken Kuhlan: *"Let the women speak. Jonas ben Harlech, the author of this expedition into Kuhlan lands, sees now with clearer eyes. And let it be done to him as they see fit, but spare the others who came with him. We are one people."*

That was it. But they understood him.

What had *he* understood? What was the meaning of what he said?

On the basis of that single meeting, the relationship of the Harlech clan and the Kuhlan nation began. Why the words of Jonas ben Harlech, great-grandfather of the present clan-baron, struck precisely the right chord at this time, when it was in the power of the Kuhlans to destroy them, and what the motives of the Kuhlans were in reaching a peaceful accord with these Benjamite interlopers on their lands, when their usual policy was ruthless massacre, his account does not explain. Who the women were that he wished to speak to, I could not imagine. I fell asleep with none of the answers I sought.

In my sleep I had a vision of savage horsemen clothed in pollen-colored rags desecrating Israel, putting all to flame and sparing neither mother nor infant. Under their pitiless hooves, all things of value to the children of St. Supplicee were trampled and defiled, and in my dream I grieved at the sight. Then a purifying fire, like a wind, swept across the land, and it shriveled the nomads like spiders on a burning log, but left the land unharmed. Miraculously, rather than scorching the earth, the fire healed it, dissolving into a spring rain and then into a morning dew, sparkling with light.

Afterwards, the earth seemed radiant but empty, and then I heard a voice, a woman's voice, saying, "This is the holy day of First Plantings." I looked, and there was a team and a plow; and I took up the plow and followed behind the team, and the earth was soft and yielding and the furrows opened beneath me. At the end of my labor, I saw a woman, dark-haired and comely, the most beautiful of all the daughters of Israel, arrayed in white linen, and she said, "Come, you must be purified and exalted." And she took me to a couch and reclined there, and she opened her garments and drew me to her, and her body was like a rich field after rain, or a spring of clear water to the parched traveler, and her mouth was like the best wine.

I awoke with a start, breathing heavily and shivering, aware of the identity of my partner in the dream, and sick at my new knowledge of myself. *So,* I said to myself, *where is the righteous man who rebuked his brother?*

Brother, what have you done? I lamented.

And what far worse thing would I do to you?

If there is darkness in your heart, St. Supplicee says, *it is far better for you and for the world to acknowledge it than to keep it hidden.* So I acknowledged the truth about myself, acknowledged who the woman of my dream had been, but I vowed that no one else, not even Michal-Rebekah, would ever have occasion to know this of me.

VII

So it was a relief when the day appointed for the expedition dawned. It was the mid-May, and Esdralon was adorned with lilacs and honey-suckle and many kinds of flowers, and the air was fragrant as a festival. The day was a balm to my exhausted senses, but my heart, secluded in the deepest dungeon of my being, was in mourning.

The expedition was late in starting. The Guards units were ill prepared and in disarray. The delay allowed me to commandeer two more wagons which I filled with iron-tipped arrows and lances from the arsenal. I had spent the intervening time imagining as many contingencies as possible. Two of Justin's ballistas from the siege were mounted on wagons and could be used without dismounting them. I managed to fill three more wagons with barrels of water, but there were still too few casks and wagons for a host our size.

Just before noon, with all last-minute arrangements completed, I joined General Zillah's staff, arrayed as gorgeous as peacocks, under the city wall. The General, visibly impatient, was dressing down Colonel Pasco for the delay. I had discarded my sling and fastened an extra strap on my light cavalry shield, which I passed over my left shoulder. That way I could rest my arm on the handle of the shield, and its weight would not pull on my strained tendons. I found it served nearly as well as a sling. I reported to Colonel Pasco and took an inconspicuous place at the rear of the staff.

Someone had gathered the rudiments of a military band from among the Home Guards, so the expedition assembled on the Field of War with horns and fife and drums playing and banners flying. But by the time we were assembled, only a few men of Montevideo's command remained to jeer at us and to insinuate that our success would be no larger than their own. Our mustering for battle, in fact, occasioned no more public interest than an ordinary drill. I was already hot and thirsty long before the bugle summoned us to march.

Because of the late start, we made only a few miles before dusk. The army encamped in a broad meadow at Beersheba Wells, a stronghold recently abandoned by its Benjamite inhabitants. The wells had been fouled, so we were waterless. I heard General Zillah loudly cursing his staff until Colonel Ahaz took it upon himself to deal with the problem and sent a party slogging off in darkness after more water wagons and barrels. Waiting on the water would delay us again in the morning. As it grew dark, we could see the glow of the city Esdralon on the northern horizon. Beersheba Wells was, I fretted, not a third of the journey to Elion.

As soon as the main camp was secure, I visited Major Vashon and my Asherite friends. The mixed battalion of cavalry was bivouacked in orderly fashion, their tents pitched in the van of the army, and their small fires shining brightly. I found Major Vashon tending to his command, alert to every detail. Kimieh was doctoring a lame horse, and Neccho was making a last check of equipment. Instructed almost from birth on how to soldier, the Asherites were the elite of the detached cavalry. I was proud of my association with them and pleased at the contrast between them and the pervasive incompetence of the expedition. I helped myself to the soldiers' mess, waiting to converse with the Major. When he joined our circle by the fire, the Major looked grave. He had bad news, he announced. "Colonel Shevren has informed me by courier that he intends to camp about five miles forward of this position."

Neccho swore and exclaimed that Shevren was a stubborn fool. "This is no time to quarrel with Zillah," he declared. "We need the cavalry together *here*! Tonight!"

"Unfortunately, he is heedless of the danger," Major Vashon said. "I've tried everything I know. I've sent a courier to Shevren with a personal message, and I've talked to General

Zillah, but he will not interfere. The General is an obstinate man. He does not see the danger."

I was trying to estimate the consequences of this recklessness when I was startled by a deep voice behind me: "So what the name of Beli-az does Shevron think he is doing!" Colonels Ahaz and Hezekiah and several captains of cohorts appeared out of the darkness. Apparently, there were others who shared our views of this ill-conceived expedition.

The next morning I felt stiff and my head ached. I was far from recovered, and I knew that this exertion would take its toll. Fortunately, I had no special duties to perform; the Commissary functioned smoothly without me, so I was able to move about slowly, dwelling in my own thoughts until the camp was struck and we commenced the march. The sun warmed quickly, first increasing my discomfort and then bringing on drowsiness. The slow rocking motion of my horse lulled me until I must have fallen asleep in the saddle, for I had a vision of hordes of savage horsemen streaming towards us, darkening the earth and making a sound like thunder. They carried bloody heads aloft on their lances, and they were hooting in triumph. I awoke with a start, oriented myself, and blew the dust of the column out of my nostrils.

At the mid-day pause, we lay down to rest in fields gorgeous with white and yellow blossoms. I felt detached and without appetite and still oppressed by my dream. Then, under a bright, crystalline blue sky and amid all the flowers of the field, my nightmare descended and enveloped me again. There was a shout and some confusion forward, and I saw three horsemen beating their blown and lathered mounts down a slope towards us. More shouts; then a young staff officer from Judah came running back: "Colonel Shevren is engaged," he announced breathlessly; "he is surrounded and attempting to fall back. His couriers report overwhelming numbers." *It was my dream again; only this time I was awake.*

The command formed quickly, and we moved forward more than a mile. Then the column came to a halt, and I chafed at the delay. Riding forward, I observed General Zillah on his white war horse. The huge stallion was pawing the ground – a proud, obstinate animal as oblivious to the General's bulk as the General was to the situation. I was too distant to hear his brief conversation with Colonel Pasco, but I saw General Zillah order the remaining cavalry forward to relieve Colonel Shevren. *I was aghast!* The disaster was taking shape, just as I had envisioned it. Major Vashon saluted without a word, his face drawn and grimly set. Summoning his bugler, he formed his command and led them forward at a trot, his lines dressed and banners flying.

Rousing myself, I drew the General's chief of staff aside. "Colonel Pasco," I said urgently, "surely you recognize the danger. General Zillah has just thrown the cavalry away; we are now totally without support. I beg you, form the infantry brigades into a square and get the wagons inside; the Kr will be on us any moment. Get the Home Guards inside too."

He glared at me as if he resented my impertinence and turned away. Without waiting to see if he would speak to the General, I galloped back to warn the wagons to close up as quickly as possible. On my way, I found the commander of the Home Guards and fell in beside him, explaining what he should do. "Close up as quick as you can. Get your men inside the square. They can be of use there as archers when the Kr attack. No point in having all of you run down and killed in the first few moments."

"What?" he demanded. "What are you talking about?"

"You'll see soon enough," I said. "When the Kr attack, they will smell like death itself." *Their strong medicinal smell, mingled with a musk-like odor, returned vividly to my mind.* "Their smell alone will make you want to vomit and run. Warn your men about it."

"Who the name of Beli-az are you?" he demanded, his indignation mingled with apprehension.

"Get your men inside the square," I repeated. "Use the men as archers. But close up the wagons first."

As we spoke, a lieutenant of General Zillah's staff sawed his horse to a halt beside us; he was plumed like a cock pheasant and highly indignant. "General Zillah demands to know why you have interfered with the order of march," he shouted, his voice carrying the ire of the commander.

I took hold of his horse's bridle and pulled him along side me so that I could speak plainly but for his ears only. "Tell General Zillah to imagine what happens when thousands of cavalry strike an infantry column that is spread out over a mile. Never mind," I said, releasing his bridle. "I'll tell him myself!" He seemed considerably taken down by the prospect I had offered him, but he accompanied me to the head of the column. I saluted Colonel Hezekiah as we passed his command and called out that he should look about him.

When I tendered my report, General Zillah exploded in wrath. He raised his entire bulk in his stirrups and shook his quirt at me, threatening to end my career for this insolence. Strangely, I felt wholly detached, and as his rage increased, I only grew calmer. But my manner seemed to enrage him further. When he paused, finally, florid and out of breath, I leaned forward and spoke quietly in his face: "Sir, you have thrown away the First Apostles Cavalry. You must now look to what is left of your command, which you have just left naked."

"I'll have you court-martialed!" he began, but the sound of distant tumult – no more than a low vibration in the air – interrupted our conversation. I dismounted and felt the earth thrilling like a drum-hide underfoot. Colonel Pasco, who had listened to our exchange impassively, came up to request that staff officers be sent forward. His eyes did not meet mine, but I felt that the precariousness of our situation had at last dawned on him. General Zillah seemed confused by the interruption. He looked this way and that and turned his horse in a circle, leaning heavily to one side. "I'll deal with you later," the General said at last, focusing his eyes on me. The air was now filled with a low, indistinct murmur of sound. "Traitors to Israel!" he muttered, scowling at me. Colonel Pasco quickly dispatched two riders forward.

From the crest of the next low hill, we saw the cavalry fail. My heart caught in my throat at the sight. The valley was dark with horsemen; the whole unimaginable host of the Kr lay before us. *Justin had been right!* A tumult of shrill cries and galloping hooves rose up and engulfed us. Then, what I saw froze my blood; I stared in horror and utter disbelief. The masses of horsemen were forming the distinct crescent with two horns that every Israelite child recognizes as the dreaded Kuhlan attack. *Kuhlans! This could not be! I could not believe my eyes!* As we watched, the dark masses converged around the small compact formation of horsemen that was Major Vashon's command, the horns sweeping beyond and then closing behind them. I fumbled with my glass, my lame arm hindering me. "Ah!" I exclaimed to no one in particular. "They *are* Kr!" The yellow-brown garments and small shaggy ponies were unmistakable. *But they were fighting like Kuhlans!*

There was consternation among the staff. Colonel Pasco was shouting, "We must extricate the cavalry! We must *ex-tri-cate* them!"

No one moved; the entire staff seemed paralyzed. I nudged my horse forward and saluted. "General Zillah, sir, if it please you, we must move forward and relieve the cavalry. Shall I notify the brigade commanders?" The General glared at me and looked to Pasco, who nodded imperceptibly. Saluting, I wheeled my horse as hard and fast as one desperate arm could do.

Ahaz and Hezekiah closed up with their brigades very quickly and seemed fully aware of the situation. The musicians, when I found them and brought them forward, looked dismayed and fumbled with their instruments. "Make as much noise as possible," I instructed them. "Never mind the key." I hoped that the Kr, being unfamiliar with infantry maneuvers and with the sound of martial music, might grow wary and draw back, giving Major Vashon and the cavalry precious time to disengage. Ahaz and Hezekiah formed their cohorts on either side and the wagons came thundering up, mules braying. "Forward!" Colonel Pasco shouted. "Forward, by brigade square, march!"

We moved down the slope in a solid mass, drums pounding, fifes shrilling, and bugles blaring. Our formation moved like an angry porcupine, deliberately, and with all its quills bristling. The maneuver appeared to make an impression—more than a thousand men moving as one, pikes erect and glistening, shields swaying together. Martial music skirled around us and solemn drumbeats marked our every step. The Kr flowed around us, swooped in close to loose arrows at us, and then quickly withdrew out of bowshot. In this manner, the masses of Kr dissolved away from our front and gave the cavalry an opportunity to withdraw. We covered the ground quickly, and the leading edge of the formation opened to admit our horsemen. Our troopers came pouring back, their formation broken, the men panting and dejected. I was relieved to see that Major Vashon was unhurt. He reported to General Zillah only a few yards from me; in the din I could see his lips move but could not hear a sound.

Amid the confusion, I instructed the Home Guards to position themselves inside the moving square and to shoot as targets presented themselves. I wondered if there had been a day in Israel with so many targets in bowshot. Immersed again in the Kr smell and the sounds of their cries rising above the dust and tumult, I realized that we were surrounded. The thought was a constricting sensation in my throat; I coughed and choked, knowing it was fear and not the dust raised by thousands of Kr ponies that threatened to close my throat. I glanced quickly around, expecting to see the command dissolving in a similar panic, dropping their weapons and preparing to flee. Instead, the infantry brigades looked rock-solid, their sergeants berating the rank and file over some flaw in their drill, exactly as on the parade ground. Instantly I was relieved and heartened. The first two ranks of the legion stood facing outward, with a double row of pikes level and steady. The third rank, inside the square, had planted their pikes and were shooting arrows into the swirling masses flowing past us. The officers were shouting; we were pelted with arrows. The mules began to bray and rear and looked to get out of control, but a group the Home Guards threw themselves on the teams to hold them, while others lined up behind Ahaz's brigade, stringing bows. With the infantry between them and the Kr, the Guards were steady, and their captain, the one who had cursed me, seemed alert and watchful. I was suddenly deeply ashamed of my fear, but over it. I went to see that the cavalry were accommodated into our formation.

We extended our lines to make room for Major Vashon's troops. His men dismounted, with every third man holding the others' horses, as they formed an extension of Hezekiah's line in the rear – if a surrounded unit has a rear. No one seemed to be in command, but the brigade leaders and Major Vashon were resolute, and their commands were not panicked. As I had no assigned duties, I tried to stay in the center of the square, in visible contact with all units, in order to relay messages. On Colonel Pasco's command, we surged forward again – slowly, but with admirable cohesion – to occupy the ground where the cavalry had been engaged. We were hoping to rescue the wounded, but found none. The bodies of our fallen troopers had been carried off. Dead and dying horses littered the field, and there were many Kr dead.

Clouds of horsemen were moving on all sides of us. The Kr had drawn back a little, but whether uncertain of us or gathering for a strike I could not tell. Like us, the Kr seemed to be trying to decide what to do. I took advantage of the lull to ask a teamster to fetch me water out of a barrel. Colonel Pasco found me as I was emptying a canteen down my parched throat. He relieved himself of a great volley of curses and informed me that General

Zillah was dazed and useless.

I had no urge to challenge his estimate. I felt strangely calm again, as if I were still re-living these events in dream and had only to play out my pre-determined role. Nothing was demanded of me, it seemed, except that I finish my dream. The feeling of walking through already completed actions made everything simple and easy. Best of all, I found that I had forgotten myself in the excitement. I was neither afraid nor overcome by my peculiar mind-extinguishing malady; my mind was, in fact, quite clear. I had feared that the battle fury would overwhelm me as before, and I would do something ludicrous or harmful. My relief was so great I felt almost elated.

"Let's give the men a rest," I said. Pasco looked at me as if I were mad. Undeterred, I suggested that he have the staff summon Major Vashon and Colonels Ahaz and Hezekiah. "Have the teamsters take water to the infantry," I shouted in the din. In fighting any but professional troops, the impression one makes on the enemy early in the fray can be decisive. I hoped the sight of our legion taking a rest and having a drink of water would impress the Kr with our coolness. In any case, I knew that our composite bows gave us the advantage of a longer bowshot, and I was confident that undisciplined savages would have little stomach for trying to break into our formation.

Major Vashon reported briefly what he had seen, which was little enough. He had been engulfed and nearly swallowed by vastly superior numbers before he had gotten a glimpse of Colonel Shevren's command. He feared the worst, he said. He had not even come within signs of the fighting when the Kr burst upon them – in relatively few numbers at first. Then there were thousands. We had seen the rest.

Ahaz was grimly confident. "We have an edge in discipline," he said, "and their arrow-heads won't penetrate our shields and armor."

"Thank goodness someone had the sense to equip the infantry!" Colonel Pasco exclaimed.

"The Kr know nothing of fighting infantry," Ahaz declared. "If they try to come to grips with us, we'll cut them to pieces."

"What worries me," Hezekiah said, "is that they won't try. They are more likely to pick us to pieces – wear us down like coyotes on a lame heifer."

When asked for my opinion, I said, "It's obvious that they can't break us with an assault. They aren't disciplined for it, and Colonel Ahaz is right, they have no experience, no concept, I believe, of throwing masses of men and horses directly at a formation. We have the catapults and ballistas if they attempt it. They can't break us; I doubt that they will seriously try."

Just as I spoke these words, the turbulent sea of horsemen suddenly gathered itself and threatened to fling up a gigantic wave against us. They came from all directions, loosing a hail of arrows and raising a wild din, punctuated by the blare of rams' horns. The mass seemed thickest directly ahead and opposite Ahaz's brigade. I moved the Home Guards right behind them and instructed the musicians to play like madmen. Our great bass drums beat a steady, tenacious rhythm, more felt than heard in the melee. The mass of horsemen seemed to coil and thicken as it launched itself toward us, a furious unstoppable horde. When they came in bowshot, our disciplined volleys took a terrible toll on the densely packed horsemen. At 30 paces, Ahaz's front ranks hurled their iron-tipped javelins into the wall of horsemen. The screams of men and beasts, tumbling riders, impaled and outraged flesh, assaulted my senses. And then, unbelievably the mad crush of bodies, men and brute, the massed Kr horsemen, pushed from behind by an irresistible will, flung themselves against the pikes of Ahaz's infantry.

The collision I thought impossible, unimaginable, unfolded before my eyes. At the shock of the impact, Ahaz's line seemed to stagger backwards as if under a great weight, stabbing and thrusting. The furious crescendo of sound, the cries of men and horses, the frantic lunging against iron pikes, was like a physical force, irresistible and overpowering. And then, just as it seemed to overwhelm us, the wave receded – or rather ebbed and sank into the sandy soil at our feet. I could not believe my senses.

After the charge had spent itself along our front, the survivors recoiled, sullenly and in almost total silence. The Kr who were out of bowshot also drew back; a multitude lay in tangled heaps in front of us. A lone and riderless horse cantered past me inside the square and collapsed, its entrails out. The ranks of Ahaz's brigade seemed to draw breath again and look about them, unbelieving. The coiling mass of Kr had formed again, but lay far out of bowshot. Our archers methodically picked off anything, man or beast, that rose to its feet.

All had happened in a moment, but the carnage was terrible. The Kr had attempted what I had believed impossible for savages, a concerted mass assault. I was dumb-founded. My mind could not register what I had seen. For the first time, I had witnessed the horror of modern warfare on a large scale. It was as if a saw-blade had been drawn across the advancing, seemingly unstoppable mass, drawn back, and drawn again across unresisting flesh and blood. I was appalled and revolted and relieved and grateful. *Infantry!* I thought. *What a blessing!*

"Their timing was off, that's all." Colonel Hezekiah was drenched with sweat and gloomy. "Had they waited until we were exhausted and the formation thinned a little. . . ." Pasco and Hezekiah and the other officers gathered toward the center of the square to assess our losses.

Suddenly I heard Ahaz's furious voice behind me: "I *want* the son of a bitch who said the Kr could not break an infantry formation!" He slammed his fist onto his thigh; he was covered with blood from head to toe. "I want him!" he shouted. It was clear who had aroused his wrath. Just then a Home Guard astride a terrified mule, bucking and kicking, intruded between us. There were shouts and curses, and then the man went sprawling in the dust. "What the hell is this," Ahaz snarled, "officer training? Somebody think this is the Academy?" The suppressed laughter from those nearby who had heard his words spread rapidly through the ranks as the comment was repeated. Ahaz, still in a rage and unamused by the laughter, shouted, "By God! I want the son of a bitch's ears on our standards who said that the filthy Goddamned Kr could not charge!" This comment provoked gales of laughter that drowned out the other uncomplimentary things he was saying about me.

Battles are won or lost on trivial accidents, and it occurred to me that this might be one of them. As infantry, we were a novelty to the Kr, and I believe our laughter after their charge may have made an impression on them. I watched a small group of horsemen detach itself from the swirling mass as if they were observing us. Meanwhile the standard bearer of the First Brigade was waving the standard like a madman, the soldiers hooting and shouting "Ears! Let's have the ears!" *Let them believe we are laughing at them, I said to myself.*

Nevertheless, I took myself out of Ahaz's section of the field as quickly as I could. I went to the rear where Major Vashon had placed what was left of the cavalry. Major Vashon was glum; his command had suffered a great deal from the rain of arrows from the Kr. "I don't think I can mount an effective force," he reported. "Nearly half my men have wounds." He had a cut on his left hand that needed attention.

"You must have that looked at," I said. "I'll fetch a surgeon." He waved me away and turned to see to his men.

Among the infantry, casualties had been remarkably light. Their armor and heavy shields had protected their lives. Of the seriously injured, however, many had been struck in the face, where they were most vulnerable. The Home Guards had lost almost as many casualties as Ahaz's brigade, and many maimed horses and mules were being destroyed.

I found General Zillah near the head of the column, dazed and leaning against a wagon.

I reported what I had learned, but he seemed not to hear. "Sir, I think Colonel Shevren's detachment is lost," I said. "If we can move forward a mile or two, we may be able to verify it – and perhaps recover some of his wounded, if any have survived." I spoke as much to Colonel Pasco and the staff as to the General. I felt little sympathy for General Zillah. The responsibility of command is an awesome one, but he had not exercised it. I privately vowed never to go into battle without all the contingencies available to my imagination thought through and accounted for. My own coolness surprised me. To be sure, I had knowledge that the General lacked and would not accept, and I had had the leisure to consider these eventualities, which were working themselves out not far different than my expectations. It is possible, I thought – perhaps a little smugly – to avoid, even in great adversity, being dismayed to the point of paralysis. I felt simultaneously detached and full of energy.

The brigade officers and staff gathered around us, and we considered our next move. "I see no more danger in going forward than in going back," I said to Colonel Pasco. "If we have to share Colonel Shevren's fate, we may as well share the same field with him."

Pasco objected that my plan was folly, given that we were outnumbered and less mobile than the Kr. I countered that it was important to seize the initiative and to maintain any advantage it gave us. "It might well be more dangerous to seem uncertain than to advance. We have six hours till dark, when the Kr are likely to break off the attack. If the Kr have slaughtered Shevren's cavalry, then they must surely expect to do the same to us – more easily, since we are on foot on the prairie. But we have repelled their first charge and we laughed at them. Now if we move forward briskly. . . " Such was my argument. There were not many other factors to ponder, and no one offered an alternative.

Colonel Pasco rubbed his chin with a grimy hand. Although he had assumed the role of commander, he seemed willing to defer to the group. After a brief discussion, we agreed that going forward was the best we could do. Knowing the contempt that Admiral Montevideo had earned by not retrieving the bodies of his dead or even learning their fate, we knew we could not retreat with Colonel Shevren's fate unknown. Two such craven acts by Israelite armies would not be tolerated.

Not to be outdone in boldness by anyone, Ahaz moved his command forward fifty paces, dragging the rest of the formation with him, his men clambering over the mounds of dead, giving a quick finish to the wounded and retrieving their bloody javelins and arrows. I heard him cajoling his men and at the same time railing at me: each of them, he shouted, must slay a half-dozen Kr or be forever shamed, "bettered by a skinny whelp of a Commissary under-lieutenant! Mighty Man of Israel!" he stormed, "By St. Supplicee, this is intolerable!" His men seemed to draw confidence and fighting spirit from his outbursts. They roared and pounded their bloody weapons on their shields.

I requested one of the staff to inform Colonel Ahaz that there were more weapons in the wagons. "Be sure to tell him," I said, "that they are courtesy of the Commissary."

Once the weapons I had taken from the arsenal were distributed all around, the wounded could be placed in the wagons. We had almost a hundred injured men, but only four ambulances and a dozen wagons. We packed the most seriously hurt four to a wagon, which was a cause of great agony to them. The rest were forced either to walk or straddle horses. I was not used to seeing wretchedness on such a scale, but we could not remain where we were, and the wounded could not be left on the field.

We had advanced no more than a mile when Colonel Hezekiah shouted, "Look out! They're working themselves up to come at us again!" The deep bellow of rams' horns was calling them to our destruction. This time the Kr circled and probed at us, a vast swarm of pollen-colored riders loosing arrows at us as they galloped and emitting their queer malevolent war cries. A choking dust cloud enveloped us. Men dropped in the ranks and were dragged backward into the square by their comrades. Horses and mules were particularly vulnerable to the storm of missiles, and our formation ground slowly to a halt. Seeing our confusion, the Kr pressed us, showering us with arrows. Still, the enemy seemed shy of closing with us, and, in the narrow glimpses I had between helmet and shield, we appeared to be giving better than we got in the exchange of deadly missiles. I pushed the catapults forward toward the closest and densest point of their swarm. The crews loaded heavy cobblestones into the carriages, cocked them, and let fly. The range of the missiles was a surprise to the Kr. The stones whizzed through the air and into the mass of horsemen, creating an incredible havoc of plunging horses and spilled riders.

Suddenly, a team of mules, crazed with terror, burst through Hezekiah's ranks, dragging a wagon on three wheels. I leaped after it, putting all my strength into a single blow of my sword between the ears of the near lead mule. The results were horrific in blood and mule brains, but it stopped the plunging team in its tracks before it could trample a larger swath through the legion. The catapults reloaded and released their missiles a dozen times, and the Kr withdrew out of range.

Colonel Pasco limped toward me out the dust, his eyes bulging, his forehead bandaged with a dirty cloth. "Thank Heaven for those machines," he said hoarsely.

We moved forward into a shallow draw which opened out into a larger valley; ahead a small stream meandered through the valley and there was timber on the north slope. It was, we saw instantly, Colonel Shevren's battlefield. A single glance sufficed to take in their fate. His command had been cut to pieces. Dark clumps that had been men were strewn across the valley amid the larger and darker shapes of their dead horses. Our men broke into lamentation at the sight. Over two hundred Israelites and perhaps an equal number of Kr, lay scattered across the valley. We searched for survivors but found that the Israelites had already been stripped and mutilated – more evidence of the peculiar Kr passion for desecration. "This is a dark day for Judah! " Colonel Pasco lamented. "A dark, dark day!"

As we marched onto the battlefield, two of Shevren's troopers emerged from the timber. Slightly wounded in the melee, they had fled and hidden themselves in the brush—running from one danger into another. We immediately stripped them and searched for ticks; one of the surgeons poured doubly-distilled medicinal brandy over their hair as they wept and hugged our knees. They would have stories to tell, if they lived.

"How in God's name," Colonel Pasco exclaimed, "are we to find Colonel Shevren's body among all these? His whole command, dead!" General Zillah turned his horse away, apparently no longer in control of his feelings. He pulled up at the edge of the field, and the reins of his bridle fell loose to the ground. He held his hand pressed to his chest, while one of his staff helped him dismount.

We surveyed the field. Debris of all kinds littered the ground. I picked up a Kr shield with a Messenger painted on it, recalling the images Justin and I had seen near the Tumuli. "Sir," a sergeant of the Home Guards spoke up near by, "this looks like the Colonel right here." He was pointing at a naked, headless corpse that lay in a tight clump of dead men and horses, all the bodies mutilated and pin-cushioned with arrows. We saw the wisdom of his remark and exchanged glances. The sergeant was a Judean; his judgment would count for something at home. Colonel Pasco limped over and ordered a group of soldiers to lift the body.

"It certainly could be Shevren," he said. He had the body placed in one of the blood-soaked wagons with the wounded. When the wretched men protested, the sergeant taunted them, saying "Make room for him, muchachos; you're not half as bad off as he is!"

With Colonel Pasco's permission, I prepared a brief ceremony for the dead. Major Vashon assisted me, explaining to uninitiated soldiers that sky burial was an ancient and honorable rite. His Asherites, who knew of the practice or had seen me do it previously, helped arrange the dead. The Messiahist clergyman attached to the legion also seemed eager to help, and not inclined to dispute fine theological points. He filled a censor with sacred cedar resin and accompanied me, swinging the sweet-smelling smoke over the corpses as I sprinkled them with dust. Apparently relieved to have something to do, he soon ceased his dazed cringing. The musicians played "Retreat" and the men in ranks beat their spears on their shields in time to the drum. The corpses were arranged as neatly as possible, and each was given its handful of dust. It was the second time in three weeks that I had recited the liturgy for sky burial.

Afterwards Colonel Pasco drew the men together and spoke to us: "This is what we came for," he said. "What was required of us. Now let's get back to Esdralon alive."

VIII

We now had more wounded than we had wagons to carry them, and fewer mule teams than we had wagons. We fashioned rude litters for the rest of the wounded. The Kr had withdrawn a space, watching us, but now the sounds of their presence, like the howling of beasts of prey, increased in volume. We looked about, exchanging glances, mindful of the ordeal to come. Nevertheless, the legion re-formed and swung out stolidly, singing "Brave Dead of Israel" to the accompaniment of martial music and drums. The music stiffened every man's back and lifted our spirits. After a quarter of a mile, our formation was moving smartly. We marched in this fashion, resolute and undaunted, backwards on our track. Miraculously, the Kr horde drew back and let us pass. Individuals approached close enough to shoot arrows and curse, or to shake the severed heads of our comrades at us, but the mass of horsemen kept back, hovering on our flanks but not interfering with us.

By dusk, we had covered six miles and returned to our previous night's campsite at Beersheba Wells. Having made it thus far, it was not clear what to do. The ruined stronghold afforded some defensive protection, but an all-out assault by the Kr was still possible. We were all nearing exhaustion, and the craving for water was like a madness in many of the troops. We broke into the last barrels, but it was not enough. The officers warned the men sternly about drinking brandy, which would set their thirst on fire, if not kill them outright. One old-timer fell down at my feet, his breath stinking of alcohol. Colonel Ahaz, who had seen him collapse, announced in his drill master's voice: "The next man that falls down drunken, unable to perform his duties, will be staked out where he falls and left for the Kr." Ahaz glared about and many nodded approvingly. It was easy to understand why even the bravest would wish to escape into a drunken stupor. But this was no time for weakness. I rejoiced that Israel's discipline was strict.

The sun was going down. The legion formed into ranks, into a hollow square again, and the men in the first rank fell out inside the square, stripped and examined each other in the usual fashion. The other two ranks did the same in order. Three men were found with ticks; they were bled at the site of the bites and hot alcohol applied. Pasco ordered fires built to lift our spirits, even though we would eat cold rations. The troops carried the pounded dried beef, suet, and dried fruit that were the army's emergency rations, and they were ordered to make do with them. Army pemmican was barely palatable, and the men complained bitterly. Still, such food has value, and when the loudest objectors scooped it from their pouches and licked their fingers, I saw their dull eyes brighten.

The wounded were carried inside the ruins of the stronghold where there was shelter from missiles. The surgeons set up their tables on the west side, where the light was best. A shallow trench was dug for those who had died in the wagons during the march and for those who would die during the night. We quickly interred Colonel Shevren. A fire was built over his grave to disguise its presence from the Kr.

Failing to find Major Vashon, I searched for him in the ruins where the wounded lay. An exhausted orderly was giving brandy to a man who had been run over by a team of mules. I inquired about the Major, but he only looked at me with vacant eyes. The soldier he treated was in a bad way; his legs were mangled and his back broken. Two of his comrades were tending to him and trying to make him swallow brandy, but the liquor only spilled out the side of his mouth. The surgeon seemed unaware of my presence. He drew back a pace and searched in his kit. One of the assisting friends turned away. At a signal from the other, the surgeon reached forward with a scalpel and deftly nicked the artery just under the man's ear. The poor wretch flinched slightly as his blood escaped, and his groans subsided in time with his jetting blood. It was over quickly, and at the end he expelled a sigh which sounded like relief.

"Everyone who can live we will take back with us," I said, feeling obliged to comment but having nothing useful to say. The surgeon nodded, his eyes glazed with fatigue.

I propped myself against a ruined wall facing the sunset, intending to think through what to do next, but I must have fallen asleep instantly. I dreamed again of Kr hordes in uncounted thousands swirling around us, now like the waves of the Great Jordan, sucking us down in a whirlpool, and again like the coils of a giant serpent, crushing and suffocating us. All the horror of the battle, the tumult and the shouting, passed before my eyes again.

I woke with a start. It was dark, and a small fire reflected on the faces of Colonels Pasco and Hezekiah and Ahaz, who were gathered around me. I made out Major Vashon and Neccho and all the members of the General's staff.

"So, he's awake," Colonel Pasco said.

"Make no mistake," Ahaz said. "He feared the Kr just as we did."

"Kr?" I said, rubbing life back into my left arm. "I dreamed that my ears had been nailed to the standard." There was a low chuckle from the group. Ahaz lowered his eyes and looked at the ground; when he raised his eyes I knew that the incident was closed.

Colonel Pasco had called a council of war, and the officers had gathered, not merely including me, but waiting patiently for me to awake. I was moved and embarrassed at the same time. How long had they waited? But there was no time for such vanity. Colonel Pasco brusquely summarized our predicament. "We need to reach a decision about how to deal with the Kr," he said wearily, pausing for breath. "I wish to hear everyone's views of what we should do. For myself, I believe the safest course is to turn these ruins into a fortress and hold out and wait for help. The problem is we have very little water. The sheep carcass the Kr dropped into the well has been removed, but the water is not wholesome. Nevertheless, it can be boiled and mixed with brandy."

"There is not enough, even so," Ahaz said. "The men will sicken and die in a short time. I say we should cut our way through the Kr, just as we did today."

"But we can't move rapidly and carry our wounded with us," Pasco objected. "Burdened as we are, we cannot possibly maneuver. General Zillah is dead," he added as an afterthought. "His heart failed him."

When asked for my views, I drew attention to how little we knew about the Kr. "We fought an unknown enemy today. Everything the Harlech knew about the Kr has been useless to us. On this field, there was a directing will, an intelligence. We saw the Kr attack in the formation the Kuhlans use, the double horns – a tactic they have never, to my knowledge, used against Benjamin. Then they closed with us. That, too, was unprecedented. The enemy we fought today were not the people the Harlech have fought. Our enemy has found a leader—and a dangerous one at that."

Hearing murmurs of assent, I continued. "I was wrong," I admitted in an aside to Ahaz, "about the Kr's willingness to attack in mass. But I was right that the Kr could not break our infantry. The only thing able to do that, I believe, is another formation of Israelite infantry."

"God forbid," he said.

The implications of our predicament emerged more clearly as I spoke. Justin, prescient as always, had observed the First Apostles drill on the Field of War in the blustery March winds, and he had seen immediately the significance of highly trained infantry. Here was a new Queen of Battles, a new way to win victories, that would replace the noble cavalry of the past. Infantry composed of ordinary men, but highly trained and disciplined, heavily armored, and armed with pike and javelin and stabbing sword, had just proven its worth. The future lay with such solid formations of commoners, trained to move as one, backed by archers – and *supported* by cavalrymen. Yes, from now on, the noble cavalry would be reduced to a supporting role. I searched Elkiah Vashon's face to see if he discerned any of this – if he knew we were in the presence of yet another sign of the death of the way of life that he embodied with his whole being. Expressing his congratulations to Ahaz and Hezekiah, he seemed serenely unaware. I roused myself from these thoughts. "Where are the Kr now? What are they doing?"

The answer was in the thousand campfires ringing us and in the solid glow of fires beyond a hill north of us, on the route we must take to reach Esdralon. From a distance came the sound of drums and harsh discordant voices; we could hear individual howls and cries above their savage chants.

"Will the Kr attack at night?" Hezekiah asked.

"It is not their custom," I said. "But with a leader, anything is possible. Where is their pony herd?" We examined a map by firelight. The nearest water was in the low ground to the northwest. That was where the Kr ponies would be grazing. The moon had not yet risen; when it did, it would be three-quarters full.

We begin to hear shrill screams, the agony unmuted by the distance, and we knew the torture of the survivors of Shevren's command had begun. As we listened an idea began to form in my mind; it was less a plan than a vision, like my dream. I saw what we had to do. I urged that we attack at once, at moonrise. "Better to die attempting to rescue our comrades," I said, "or to avenge them, if we can do no more. I fear this leader of the Kr. Every Israelite life he takes tonight increases his prestige and therefore his power to harm us."

To my surprise, the group agreed. Perhaps it was easy for all of us to imagine ourselves in the hands of the Kr, enduring the torments that assaulted our ears. We quickly formed a plan. We determined to hold Beersheba Wells with four of Hezekiah's cohorts and the Home Guards. Our wounded secure, we would then attack with Ahaz's troops and the other cohort of Hezekiah's brigade, while the cavalry, now scarcely a hundred men, slipped around to the left. They would stampede the Kr ponies and then break through to Esdralon. Ahaz's command would march straight north, engage the main body of Kr in their camps. If repulsed, the infantry could fall back on Beersheba Wells. If successful, the whole attack force would push on north to Esdralon through the night.

"It might just work," Colonel Pasco said, his ragged bandage drooping over his eye.

"Troops from Esdralon can come out to meet us in the morning," I continued. "We will have seven hours till daylight; if we are lucky we can march nearly to Esdralon before the Kr can organize to do us serious harm. Admiral Montevideo's men can rescue the remainder of the legion by late tomorrow."

"But do our men have stamina enough?" Pasco objected. "We're asking them to fight again and then march all night." It was true. Exhausted ourselves, we had to wonder what the men were capable of.

"I don't intend to give them any choice in the matter," Ahaz swore, struggling to his feet.

As the moon rose, the commotion in the Kr camp reached a feverish crescendo. Their camp on the summit was lit by an orange glow. At the foot of the slope, six hundred Israelite infantrymen formed ranks in close formation and a hundred cavalrymen stood by their mounts.

"Lead off," Colonel Pasco said to Ahaz, and the iron ranks of infantry surged forward silently.

"Give us a little start," Pasco said to Major Vashon, "make a quick swoop on their pony herd and then ride for Esdralon. Don't stop for anything. Hezekiah is depending on you." Major Vashon saluted and turned to his command.

I placed myself with Ahaz's infantry, with the troops guarding his flanks and rear.

We moved forward several hundred yards before the Kr discovered us, so intent were they on their fiendish revels. We burst in among their camps like furies and scattered them. Undaunted, the Kr gathered themselves in the darkness and came back at us, howling and leaping up and down.

"They have a leader all right!" Ahaz shouted to me.

The Kr fought like demons, curling around our flanks. They might have stood; they might even have overwhelmed us, had not Major Vashon disobeyed his orders to ride directly on to Esdralon. Instead, he brought his command, one hundred weary but vengeful horsemen into the rear of the Kr at precisely the right moment – just as they threatened to envelop us. They had not sensed his presence, and the surprise in the darkness demoralized them. We smashed them then, broke their spirit of resistance and scattered them to the four winds, and the slaughter afterwards was perfect exhilaration. We paused only to search for surviving comrades of Shevren's command and to gather up our wounded. Then we pressed on in the moonlight toward Esdralon.

Chapter 5: The Citadel

I

News of the army's plight caused panic in the city. There was, these events announced, a new and terrible danger on Esdralon's doorstep. Commandeering a fresh horse, I accompanied the column sent to extricate Hezekiah and his men at Beersheba Wells. I can say nothing of the march because I rode asleep for most of it. When we arrived at the Wells, our stranded garrison rushed out to embrace us and to empty our water pouches down their throats. We saw to the wounded as best we could and brought all who still lived back to the sanctuary of Esdralon. On our return homeward, we marched unmolested, just as we had in coming. A great host of vultures could be seen circling above the hill of Beersheba, where our night battle had been fought. The soldiers in the relief column marveled at the numbers of the slain.

I have no recollection either of how I returned to my quarters that night; I was too thoroughly spent. Early next day, however, I was summoned to Headquarters. As I waited in the anteroom, a friend on the First Apostles staff slipped me a note: *"Josiah, you saved the legion; surely you have earned a medal and a promotion!"*

My interview with General Boseth, however, proved far from laudatory. I believed I had been invited to report to the General of the Host, evidently to supplement the accounts of Colonel Pasco and the other senior officers. Even after a night's rest, I was dizzy with fatigue; my wounds ached, and my head felt like an over-ripe melon. After a long wait, I was ushered into General's Boseth's private office. Ominously, I was not invited to stand at ease. As I stood stiffly at attention, the General and his staff began to question me closely about the conduct of the battle and the death of General Zillah. After what seemed an interminable period and a host of repetitive questions, the General paused to confer with his Messiahist clerk. Then he turned back to me and asked what I imagined would be the long-range consequences of our provoking the Kr.

"Provoking the Kr? Sir," I replied, more emphatically than was prudent, "the Kr were our enemies *before* the battle; their attack was an expression of that enmity, not its cause." I perceived that my reply did not please the General and his staff. "It may be," I added, "that the trade with the Kr will be re-established at some point – provided that we are not pushed into the Jordan in the meantime. But unless we respond and drive the Kr back south of the mountains, there will be no future for us here – no trade, no viable settlements. The Kr will make a desert of Engedi."

I perceived that this reply did not please him either, but I was exhausted and did not much care. "With the force Israel now has in Engedi, we have barely strength enough to hold Esdralon and patrol the Jordan. But I doubt that we have men enough to contest the countryside, let alone drive the Kr back into their own country."

"You actually imagine the Kr intend to cross the Jordan?" the interrogating officer asked. "That is absurd!"

"I would have thought so too, a few days ago," I said. "But yes, I think they may cross the Jordan. We will require the fleet here to prevent them."

"Are you aware, sir, of the forces already in Esdralon?"

"Of course I am, but even with Montevideo's troops, we have nothing like the strength we need."

"This is nonsense!" the interrogating officer exclaimed, seeming to think me deranged. "Mere defeatist fantasy! The First Apostles just inflicted a smashing repulse on these savages. We demonstrated our complete superiority over the Kr, and you blather about our lack of strength? This is cowardice!"

"Cowardice? The First Apostles just barely escaped annihilation. A portion of the cavalry did not. Call it victory if you like, but I was there, and I say we escaped – and were very fortunate to escape."

"If you are intimidated by these savages," the officer sneered at me, "General Boseth can have you relieved."

My anger brought me back from a near swoon from exhaustion. "You say 'we' demonstrated this or that," I said, "but I was on the field. While the Kr could not break our infantry, it's true, we lost two-thirds of the cavalry engaged at Elion. Besides those survivors, we have in Engedi only a few hundred of Montevideo's cavalry without proper mounts. Hence, as I said, we have a military problem."

"This is intolerable!" General Bosheth exclaimed. "A timid Commissary estimate!"

"What about the prospects of resuming trade with the Kr?" the clerical scribe suddenly interjected – apparently forgetting his ostensible role. I was appalled that he was allowed to question me directly. *Had army protocol slipped entirely into an abyss? Had Messiahist domination extended so far?* I refused to answer.

"Are you deaf?" the General demanded. "Can we expect to trade with the Kr or not?"

"Trade? You ask about *trade*? Sir, if the army does not take prompt action, we will trade Engedi for a desert!"

General Boseth snorted and turned his back on me. Clasping his hands behind him, he bent to confer with the Messiahist cleric. Then he turned to me and told me to remain outside. I was to hold myself ready to discuss the situation at greater length with other members of Headquarters staff. He was not pleased with my report, he said, "Not pleased at all!" and dismissed me. I waited outside on a bench. Shortly an officer and four men approached me. The officer told me curtly that I was to accompany him to the citadel. We descended the stairs and stepped outside into dazzling sunlight. Down the street the citadel of Esdralon loomed like a mountain of black basalt. I did not like the look of it. The soldiers walked on either side and behind me as though I were already in custody.

My interrogation, however, had nothing to do with the Kr.

"I find him . . ." *I ransacked my mind, growing embarrassed as the precise word failed to rise and present itself. Fatigue and apprehension had left me tongue-tied.* "I find him unorthodox, perhaps, in his methods. However, I know very little of mind war," I finished lamely.

Previously as noncommittal as stone, Brother Bulavar appeared to agree with this last statement. The quill pen of his secretary, the same Brother Rodrig I had encountered in the archives, scrawled furiously across the page, rose, and hung poised in the air like a hunting hawk. We were in the tower of the citadel of Esdralon. Down the stairs on another floor were the archives I had used; three floors below us were the dungeons.

"Justin is unorthodox – about gathering information," I continued, withering under his baleful gaze. "Major Apollo is concerned about the success of our strategy. He considers the war as a problem to be solved, abstractly as well as practically" – *wondering, as I spoke, what I meant.* "And so he requires the freedom of movement, mentally speaking, to . . . to examine the case – any case – from all sides."

The recording scribe looked appraisingly at me and then at Brother Bulavar.

"Major Apollo," I continued, gathering a little confidence, "asks questions – of everyone, of everything – including himself, of course. He is mercilessly – rigorously – logical. He has a fine intellect, his insights honed by his recent experiences, I should think. In the war. Some could, perhaps, interpret his . . . his questioning, as criticism in the wrong sense. But I assure you he is a patriot, an officer of unquestionable . . . unquestionable gallantry and devotion. I have often heard the story of his –"

"Yes, yes," the Brother interrupted, "a few wounds, the heat of battle. An Order of the Constellation." He waved his huge hand dismissively. "Your brother's gallantry, as you phrase it, is not at issue. As for his devotion . . . . "

"Justin sees everything; he drives himself." I felt compelled to interrupt, to put the best face on affairs that I could. "He allows himself almost no rest or sleep, he. . ."

"No sleep?" Brother Bulavar inquired, eyes wide. "Pity!" *Try as I might, even my praise of Justin indicted him.* "Doesn't *sleep*, you say? So intensely does he engage his duties? Well!" The scribe was enjoying this repartee.

The import of Bulavar's irony was painfully clear; it pressed like the weight of a wrestler against my chest. I decided to broach the dangerous subject first, but to make no admissions. "The Benjamite woman" – *in spite of myself I hesitated* – "and her child are – are among his best sources of information. They know the customs of the Harlech." *I found myself repeating and nearly choking on Justin's own deceptions, the very language of his flimsy self-justifications, which earlier had wrung only contempt from me.* "Knowing her – knowing *them*, Justin can discover their. . . capabilities."

Brother Bulavar did not bother to raise his voice to express his contempt for my rationalizations; he merely raised his eyebrows and glared at me. But when he spoke, revulsion was in every syllable and inflection: "Your brother, as if you hadn't noticed, lives openly and flagrantly with a Harlech whore!"

His voice pushed me back a pace.

"That woman," Bulavar waved his thick palm in an angry gesture, "that daughter of destruction, is an enemy and a heretic, a blood enemy of Israel. And *wife* to a Harlech! Perhaps your brother was too busy to notice! Too devoted, you said. And your brother's wife and child, *his* own child, not three days sail away! Oh, this is vile, vile!" Brother Bulavar suddenly shrank back from his desk as if Justin's acts of concupiscence were being performed before his eyes.

"I condone nothing in my brother's behavior – or of any man's – which the Law does not condone. But the fact remains . . ." *What fact remains? I felt my own career, public and secret, my standing in the Order diminishing, and my own worldly disguise, my own safety, melting like a glob of wax over a flame.* "The fact remains that to perform his mission, Justin has to search out every – he has to explore – and the woman is – he uses her to test . . ."

"*Uses* her? I should say, *uses* her! And she *him*, no doubt! And all in the line of duty. Convenient, convenient! A channel of communication, you suggest? Of course! A channel! The imagination runs riot! But channels, don't you see, run both ways. And just how much information has she passed the other way to the enemy? Ah? Can you answer me?"

I said nothing, suddenly aware of an intolerable tickling in my scalp as beads of sweat trickled down my temples. "Your brother is a fool, don't you see? He has but to question this woman along a line of thought, and the Philistine harlot immediately infers his drift, and hence our intentions. As clearly as if our gallant Samson had blurted them out to her, she has our plans and prospects! What a perfect canker and corruption in our midst!" He leaned on his desk, breathing heavily. "And do you wonder, then, at Israel's lack of success?"

"No!" I protested. I felt compelled to resist, but felt the very ground under me slip away. "Not so, my brother Justin is. . . no fool."

"No fool? Hah? You trifle with me. No *fool*, you say? Can you prove my allegation wrong? Do you imagine this woman loyal because she lies at night with your brother in her dead husband's bed? Do you imagine she loves our cause, drops tears of joy praying for Zion's victory? Blesses the day her husband's life spilled out on the ramp in Esdralon and left her son an orphan? Hah?"

Bulavar rose up, his neck and eyes bulging, and he grasped the large oak table at each end as if to lift and hurl it at me. Then, relaxing suddenly, he dismissed the secretary and approached, his manner familiar and confidential. He too was perspiring, as if from strenuous effort, and I breathed in his sour, musty odor. "Your masters report that you have sense—and some signs of manhood, some glimmerings of faith. Mark me, a man of the church – or of the Law, as you prefer it – does not see only what his heart desires. He looks, he penetrates, he *discerns* what is true. Do you understand me? And a man of faith, worthy of this poor cloth and the vows that the church holds out like the cross itself to those who are willing to mount it – I say a man of faith puts no loyalty, no earthly tie, no family interest, above loyalty to the church and its just cause!"

I stood silent, sweating profusely.

"Josiah, you disappoint me. Do you think I cannot see through this pathetic tissue of deceptions that you weave – not for me, my son, but for yourself? You believe yourself honest – yes, I see that. Your teachers, old Josephus of the Refuge and the rest, testify to that." *I flinched, thinking: Impossible! He cannot have spoken to Josephus!* "Yes," he continued, "they believe you honest. They believe you show promise. Promise, yes. But you must learn to *be* honest! You must learn to be wise."

I attempted to think nothing, to acknowledge nothing.

"You must understand that your brother Justin is lost to us," Bulavar continued. "Lost! Mark me, as long as he wallows in Elgin Harlech's filthy sty, he is not of Zion's cause. He is not right with God. His heart is stone, he is unfit. Do you not *know* this yourself? *He* may not know it, but it is necessary that you should know it. Mark me, child, you know the truth of what I say, though your boy's heart denies it."

My entire body clenched to resist him, but my heart was sinking like a stone.

"Your brother Justin is lost to us. Lost! But of you, great things are expected. To whom much has been given, much is demanded. So, you must gird yourself and put away these childish notions."

Bulavar suddenly shook himself as if waking; his huge shoulders bulged against the cloth of his surplice. "Let me be candid. There are plans afoot," he said, in a manner that severed the present conversation from the one that preceded it. "Let me tell you about the operations underway, and then you can judge for yourself." He led the way to a map on the wall of his inner office.

As I followed his finger on the map, Bulavar outlined the grand strategy of Israel's war with the Harlech as if every detail were his personal possession. The Strike South against Engedi had, he emphasized with a tap of a huge finger, ended in victory. The Strike North, however, had been turned back at Beth-Shan before it got well under way. "The work of traitors," he muttered angrily; "heads may still roll!" The Strike East, he acknowledged, had ended on less than satisfactory terms. "More has been accomplished than meets the eye," he hinted, his voice suddenly low and confidential. "Conditions for the final struggle have been established. Now the Strike West, into the heart of Lagash! Down the Jordan and completing the circuit of the four cardinal points of the compass. The circle, as you know, means completion as well as perfection. Thus, how can Israel fail of complete and perfect victory?" He looked at me expectantly, perspiring heavily.

I had always feared the Messiahists, acknowledging the power of their doctrine even as I rejected it. For the first time, coming from his lips, it sounded like a lunatic's gibberish. I pointed out the fortresses Beth-Lagash and the Dall, which guard the approaches to Lagash. "Difficult objectives," I said, "even if not impregnable. What would happen if Israel's army were still outside the walls of Beth-Lagash when frost comes, and the Harlech slip through the Lost Horse Hills and strike Judah?"

Bulavar ignored my objections, seeming rapt by his own vision of the war. "It is true we did not accomplish all we had hoped in our Strike East," he conceded. "Admiral Montevideo failed the test of wills. He took counsel of his fears – excessively, I'm convinced. That he faced difficulties, I doubt not. That he would have triumphed, had he put himself to the test, I am virtually certain. But Montevideo shrank from the final jar and collision." His eyes found me again. "Thus, if we are to succeed, Israel must rid itself of such timorous souls. We must expose them as the heretics they are. For from what does timidity spring but lack of faith?"

Finding my voice, I asked if he thought it was wise to provoke the Kuhlans before we had defeated Benjamin. I asked him if he was aware of the Harlech policy of simultaneously conducting trade with and war against the Kr, but he scarcely glanced at me. I then repeated one of Justin's remarks, that the Kr were rabid dogs lying across our doorstep. "And to think," I dared add, "may our descendants forgive us, we opened the door to them!"

My comment failed to rouse him; he continued to stare at the map. "Do you seriously doubt that the High Command knows what it is doing? We have a threat to our flank, to be sure, in the Kuhlans, which we will eliminate, once and for all. The Kr, wretched scum that they are, are a flail delivered into our hands, and with God's help, we will use it to scourge our enemies. The Kr will serve God's purposes in serving ours – and then be fit like straw for the fire. Don't give a thought to the Kr; you are wasting your time."

He turned to me suddenly, as if the conversation about the map and the war had never happened. "Your brother Justin," he said, "was an intelligent man, even a brilliant one." *I froze at his use of the past tense.* "And a promising officer, once. His courage has never been in doubt, any more than his mind. It was his faith, the ground of action, the source of vision and purpose, that was lacking. Tragically lacking! Especially to us, for we who are his blood kin know what he could have been."

Blood kin! So, it is true! But what have you done with Justin?

"We know also what he is, what he has become. Sad, sad! Without faith, without the fiber of lasting commitment, eventually the will falters. The eye sees only obstacles; the brain conjures up terrifying and repulsive scenes; darkness penetrates everywhere, chilling and enervating the will. Yes," Bulavar continued slowly. "Yes. Your brother Justin lacked a vision of what must be; he lacked faith in that vision of the future. Without it, he became dangerous to Israel. Like the foolish milkmaid, to whom all things seem impossible, his dark imaginings overwhelmed him."

I hung on his words, every fiber of me denying the import of what he had just said.

He inspected me carefully. "But those who serve God, those who submit their wills to His will, cannot fail. Your brother, Justin Apollo," Bulavar continued evenly, "was arrested last night." He spoke as if it were only a transition to a new topic on which he could turn inexhaustible reserves of energy. "I brought you here to tell you that. Things may go hard with him, I'm afraid. I am not optimistic. But I am instructed to tell you that you are permitted to petition his Excellency Bishop Bon, in whose jurisdiction the case lies, on Justin's behalf. If that is your wish. . . ."

"And the charge?" I managed to ask, my voice slipping from my control.

Bulavar raised his eyebrows: "The charge? Let me think. Sedition, perhaps? Consorting with the enemy? Adultery! Spying for the enemy! Treason! Heresy! Inciting

Israelites to rebellion!" He stopped to glare at me. "The list goes on. Are you quite sure you wish to trouble his Excellency on his behalf? Yes, of course. I was expecting you would. I have taken the trouble to have Brother Rodrig prepare a petition for you."

A hand appeared with a piece of parchment.

"The legal language," Bulavar continued, "the precise charges, all the niceties, are already inserted – to spare you the trouble, of course. In anticipation of this desire on your part, I asked Brother Rodrig to take careful note of what you said on Justin's behalf. You'll find your own arguments – your own words, in fact – inserted into the document, if you now care to sign such a petition. A useless gesture, in my opinion. The evidence against Justin is quite compelling, quite complete. I'm not certain I would want my name on such a document, if I were you. Your association with Justin has already brought, let us say, some interest to bear upon you. Such interest can rapidly become scrutiny, as you know."

I stared at the document in my hands, a petition in my own words and, incredibly, in my own handwriting. "But—" I stammered, not knowing how to frame a response. I stood speechless.

"Ah," he interrupted, as if he felt a need to spell out my own chaotic thoughts for me, "you wish to plead the chain of command and the officer's sacred right to trial by his peers? I see. Indeed, things have changed of late, Josiah, and changed for the better. You'll find this to be true in due time. In the meantime, I would not advance a claim based on rank or the so-called rights of officers—still less on privileges of birth, if I were you! All that has quite gone out of fashion—and suddenly. But who among us," he said, smiling grimly, "can properly boast of his birth?"

I stood rooted in place, dumbly holding the document.

"The army answers to the church now, Josiah, as you shall see. Of course, if you do not wish to trouble his Excellency in this matter, I can have Brother Rodrig burn this letter and all the notes of our conversation. And all this can remain confidential between us."

II

I found myself in the hallway, still staring at the parchment the scribe Rodrig had thrust into my hand. The handwriting was perfect; *it was my own.* Yet not my own. I could not discern myself that it was forged. I recognized my own thinking, saw my own words, even the eccentricities of my speech. Then I realized: *my journal!* So, they had my journal and had studied it minutely. If so, then they had had access to every thought I had formulated since coming to Esdralon. And now the churchmen had seized power. They had not destroyed the existing government, but had taken control of it nonetheless. I felt myself staggering, not from a blow, but from a cold paralysis that invaded my mind. My enemies had crawled inside my ear. No wonder I had not been asked to report through channels to the Eyes! The Eyes of Israel was now merely the tool of the Messiahist hierarchy. They knew everything I knew – *everything I thought* – as soon as I did. I wondered if I had unwittingly betrayed Justin in my journal. I was certain I had betrayed myself.

My reverie was interrupted by two armed guards, who escorted me unresisting down the stairs of the citadel. We took an unfamiliar turn on the stairs and down another flight and I was suddenly aware of the nearness of the dungeon, for I could hear the muffled cries of prisoners. Fearing I was about to join them, I drew violently back, but one of the guards led me, almost gently, to a small door, and I found myself outside blinking in the bright sunlight. Scaffolding reared above me, where workmen busied themselves repairing the damaged fortress. The sound of hammers and chisels and ordinary voices sounded from the empty dazzling sky.

I stood trembling in the street, hearing the hammer blows of the workmen above me and thinking: *nothing in my life will ever be the same again.* Justin? *He was doomed!* And Michal-Rebekah? And Appian? Hope and fear swept over me in waves. I could not think clearly enough to comprehend what had happened; still less could I face what these events meant. *Hope is a fire that consumes all.* I have to put it aside. *Understand that they are dead: Justin and Michal-Rebekah and even Appian, dead.* Or if not dead, beyond your power to help. Make your mind accustomed to it.

And you? What about you? Are you less doomed than they?

I tried to think as Justin would have thought – not about the event itself, but its meaning within a larger pattern. Step back and see what it reveals, what it hides. What patterns emerge? I pounded my temples with my fists. Nothing came to me. *Nothing!*

Eventually, I found myself outside the walls of Esdralon, wandering through a devastated vineyard, my mind in a tumult. I had come halfway to the Field of War, unconsciously seeking the company of friends. Major Vashon and Erech and Elias Neccho, however, were nowhere to be found. A sentry informed me they were attending a meeting. News had come that Admiral Montevideo had been put to death in Hebron, and the officers had gathered to discuss it. I scarcely attended to his words. I borrowed a scrap of paper, intending to leave a message for Major Vashon.

With the paper in my hands I hesitated: *Your life is over,* I thought. *You are already dead. It only remains to warn your friends.* Gathering my wits, I wrote: *"Beware. Justin has been arrested; prospects uncertain,"* and handed it to the sentry. Then as a darker impulse took hold of me, I demanded it back and added: *"I cannot express my gratitude for your assistance with the Velcos and for your other acts of kindness. But you must now separate yourself from my fate. Farewell. Josiah."*

"Will you see that the Major gets this?"

The bells of St. Eli's tolled the hour. I looked about me, uncertain what to do. The sun was setting. It occurred to me, crazily, that I would not have to return to the Commissary till tomorrow, giving me time to compose myself. Then I realized: *Fool; you will never return to the Commissary!* If Justin is guilty of heresy, so are you, a thousand-fold, and they have all the evidence they need, plus whatever they have concocted. They have your journal; *they have always had your journal!* In their eyes, your thoughts have condemned you from the very moment of their birth.

Then why arrest Justin? I asked myself, trying to find some solid purchase for my thoughts. *And what had they done with Appian and Michal-Rebekah?*

Justin was a hero of the army, idolized by the soldiery. He was also the son of Tephlin Glanz—and therefore. presumably, under his protection. Glanz was allied with the Messiahists; the merchants and the church were allies. The war was built on that alliance, and Israel's merchants had virtually carried the Messiahist banner into the war. *So why would Justin be arrested? Would his detention not be a challenge to Tephlin Glanz? To the very alliance on which the war was based?* Nothing made any sense.

I recalled my conversation with Justin as we walked along the banks of the Jordan. He had hinted of a divergence of merchant from Messiahist interests in the war. The merchants had had enough of the war, which was proving unprofitable, and had begun to wish for peace. *Is that it? But why Justin?*

I had wandered to the end of the docks. The Jordan lay like a crimson tide beneath a crimson sky. Because he is a heretic, I said to myself. *But it is not Justin who is the heretic; it is you!* Death lapped at my feet as I struggled to find the connecting thread in these events. Both parties, merchants and churchmen, regarded the Law of St. Supplicee as repugnant, as part of the old world of landed aristocrats and hereditary warriors that must be swept away. *It is you who most offends them! Moreover, the charges against Justin will not be heresy, but. . . .*

I could not, for the present, countenance this line of thought—even with Bulavar's voice ringing in my ears. Justin's arrest, I concluded desperately, must be an effort to discredit him before the nation – and with him the Army that revered him. Justin was arrested to discredit his faction. *But discredit how?*

Discredit by treason! Discredit by the charge of spying. It was a conclusion I could not escape. And that meant, I realized with more pain than I thought could be contained in a living heart, Michal-Rebekah is truly lost, doomed, dead already perhaps. *Dead!*

But with what justice? Was she in fact a spy? Had she turned Justin to the Harlech cause?

Has she turned you as well? The thought blew like shattered glass through my brain.

I found myself opposite the southwest gate; it was dusk but still light enough to see if anyone was following me. I skirted the city wall through small gardens and fields, wandering aimlessly and occasionally stopping to listen. Then suddenly I knew where I was going, where my feet were carrying me. I needed time to think this through, but I knew where I needed to go, where I had to go. *I knew what I was going to do.*

But of course they would know too. They would be waiting there expectantly. That's why they had not bothered to have me followed.

When I reached the gate, I was cold with apprehension. It was the site of executions of adulterers by stoning. I dreaded to find Michal-Rebekah's body there, lying in a crumpled heap. I saw it all in my mind's eye. But there was no one, no crushed and battered body. The place was empty. I shivered with relief.

The gates were locked for the night; I had to beg admission to re-enter the city my brother had conquered. The southwest gate was not far from the dwelling of the old woman where Appian and I had delivered foodstuffs. I decided to visit her quarters, longing for contact with someone who had known Michal-Rebekah and Justin—but wondering at the same time what else had been delivered there besides food.

A crowd had gathered before the old woman's tiny lodging. The door was slightly ajar. I shouldered past the crowd and pushed it open and saw her on the floor in the shadows. *She is dead*, I noted dully. The contents of her head had spilled onto the floor. *She could tell me nothing*, I said to myself, though I knew in my heart exactly what her death meant. I pushed back through the crowd, feeling their hostility on my face like hot breath.

Justin's quarters were only a few blocks away. I covered the distance in a trance, not caring if I was followed. At the top of the stairs, the door was open and the setting sun cast its golden light into the room and onto a wall, where, head-high, small dark drops were visible. I reached out to touch them but stopped; my hand shrank from the wall: *it was blood!* I imagined the blow of a soldier's hand on a woman's face and the fine resulting spray. I shuddered.

Meditate, I ordered myself. Grief could come later. I heard Josephus saying, *desire is a raging fire*. I sat facing west, the setting sun in my eyes, my legs folded beneath me, my hands open, resting on my knees, chanting the ancient words.

When I came back to myself it was dark. I lit a candle and felt the ashes in the hearth. They were cold. Bulavar said Justin's arrest had occurred the night before. I calculated the hours that had passed and what I had been doing when my brother met his fate. I had been asleep in my quarters, exhausted from the battle with the Kr and the rescue of Hezekiah's men. I roused myself and resumed my attempt to comprehend this event. What did the timing mean? Justin's arrest coincided with the battle with the Kr—and thus with the First Apostles' absence from Esdralon. A coincidence? The First Apostles Legion was Justin's old unit, the comrades with whom he had won his glory. Were the Messiahists not certain of the Legion's loyalty? Had they timed Justin's arrest when the Legion was absent and engaged?

Conflict with the Kr marked the defeat of important hopes in Israel – chiefly the hope of wresting easy wealth from the war. But that was a merchant issue, not the church's. What other hopes had been dashed by the outbreak of war with the Kr? I had no idea. By his own admission, Justin had been a central figure in planning the war. In addition, he was the son of Tephlin Glanz. I tried to weigh what that meant. Perhaps it meant nothing to Glanz; most likely it meant nothing. Only Justin knew for certain. Others might expect that Justin acted with his father's consent and direction – and might well regard Justin as an extension of Glanz's will. *Was it possible that Justin's actions were in accord with Glanz's will? Was his manner with me contrived to appear otherwise? Was he serving Glanz? Or pursuing some object of his own in secret?*

My brother was a man with many facets, like a jewel with multiple reflecting surfaces. It diminished him to read his actions as I was doing. Still. . . . *The world is a trap baited by desire.* Justin had taken the bait once. Had he taken it again?

I concluded that Justin's arrest must signal a fatal breach between the merchant faction and the Messiahists. Always cautious, the merchants wanted to cut their losses and negotiate a peace. But the churchmen, with their very different motives for waging war, wanted it to go on, to the death, as Justin had foreseen. They intended to exterminate the Harlech heretics, so that they could fasten their fanatical religion upon all Israel. A dreadful prospect, but not an impossible one.

But only if the army does their bidding. I surmised from the timing of Justin's arrest that the Messiahists were not sure of the army. Indeed, at this point neither side could be sure of the army.

Justin's significance began to dawn on me. For very different reasons than those of our father's faction, Justin longed for peace and reconciliation. Thus, whether or not his views projected Tephlin Glanz's, he represented an emerging peace party within army circles. To the churchmen, however, the peace movement had to quashed, destroyed. The very idea of peace-making had to be killed – and one can kill an idea only by discrediting it. And so to discredit Justin was to discredit the peace party, so that the war could continue. But first, they must discredit Justin with the army. Thus, they would charge him with treason, with spying.

Had Justin opened his own channels to the Harlech? From what I had observed myself, I had to admit the possibility. Was Michal-Rebekah that channel? The old woman whose body I had just seen – was she a link in that chain of communications? Were preliminary contacts—even negotiations – in progress? And if so, were they authorized or not? And if not authorized, where had Justin wandered? Or been *led*?

My entire experience of the war suddenly seemed a shadowy thing, acted out by shadowy figures behind a screen. As Justin had foreseen, there had been a coup by the churchmen – quite possibly triggered by the need to ward off his peace initiative. He would have appreciated that irony; I could not. In recent days, the first group of figures, whoever they were—had been swept away and replaced by other shadowy figures belonging to the church hierarchy: Bishop Bon and Bulavar and others whom I did not know. Had Justin been the tool of the first group, or had he led them? I knew as much of these things as a miner in a cave knows of the weather outside.

My questions dredged up another, more personal one: was Justin really as estranged from our father as he pretended? Or had he feigned hostility to Tephlin Glanz to mislead me? And draw out *my* attitudes? These were dismal thoughts, but I had to sort through all the possibilities. But why would Justin deceive me? *My brother!* And why, when we first met, had Justin assumed that a brother and a son of Tephlin Glanz must be his enemy? As I sorted among these questions and their possible answers, I felt as though I had been loosed from earth. Truly it is written, *we move among shadows and are ourselves only shadows.*

I felt suddenly restless; my legs were stiff and bloodless. I had to move about. With the light of another candle, I wandered through Justin's quarters, which had been ransacked. His clothing and personal belongings were strewn about his bedroom. The same violence had spent itself in the room where Appian and Michal-Rebekah slept. I stopped at the door, inhaling her aroma for a moment. A terrible grief welled up in me again. I retreated back into Justin's room, which was safer for me.

In his scattered belongings, I had a glimpse of Justin's private side that I had never seen before. In spite of my questions, I looked over his possessions reverently, savoring the man he had been. His wardrobe was elegant and costly and even more extensive than I had imagined – a forgivable vanity in one so graced by nature. A trunk had been split open and its contents thrown in a corner. I found memorabilia of his childhood and his time in the army. To commemorate his moment of glory at Esdralon, there was a small model of a siege weapon and his drawings for its construction. A complimentary note from a superior was scrawled on a corner of the drawing. I decided to keep these objects as mementos. Still in the trunk was a grappling hook with a rope attached—presumably another souvenir of the siege of Esdralon. I found nothing among his effects of his wife and son.

I sat on the floor amid the detritus of Justin's life and thought of the contradictions in the man. Justin seemed, in retrospect, layered and divided and constructed of separate boxes hidden within other boxes. But take him all in all, there was much, very much, to admire. His death meant that there was an infinite amount that I could never know about him. But as I recalled our brief acquaintance, everything I knew about him began to take on new and different meanings—contrary to my will and affections. I remembered his opposition to the Strike West plan and his insistence that the Kr were the chief threat to Israel. In spite of myself, I speculated on his motives. In the midst of grief, I felt an additional measure of pain at the distance that had opened between us. I recalled again the occasion of our first meeting, for which I now, for the first time, had a context for understanding.

I continued to rummage through his belongings, as if searching for an answer to all my questions. Instead of answers, I found his military dagger, which he had worn constantly, lying by his bed, covered by the unmade bedclothes. I drew it from its sheath, intoxicated by the sudden thought of oblivion, but the blade come out of the sheath queerly, distracting me. Examining it, I found a piece of paper wrapped around the blade. Suddenly, I was anxious, almost frantic, to see what it might contain. As I unfolded it, my own name caught my eye. It was a message from Justin to me, undated. Frantically, I tried to read it, but the candle was guttering. I found an oil lamp and lit it with the butt-end of the candle. The handwriting of the letter appeared labored and unsteady; Justin had written it after his injury.

> *Josiah,*
>
> *So young, and already a legend! Two stories are circulating about you; soon there will be a third. The third will claim that you befriended an evil and treacherous brother, who was the spawn of Tephlin Glanz and Glanz's agent. The evil brother is both a Glanz – and therefore a monster of greed – and a motiveless wrecker. The story glosses over incompatible elements, but never mind. The character of legends, as we know, is to give expression to perceptions of events, not their truth.*
>
> *Still, they are not without truth. Truths are braided in the rope, among many strands of falsehoods. And it is we ourselves who braid the rope, though the rope hangs us in the end.*
>
> *Truly, my brother, I think you are singled out by fate for some remarkable thing. The truth of your tale is that you survive the uses others would put you to.*

The letter was unsigned but in Justin's handwriting. I had a sense that the ink was scarcely dry. Had Justin known what was coming to him and managed this last communication with me? *Or could this be more of Rodrig's work?*

I read the letter again. Hearing his voice in the words of the letter, I missed my brother immeasurably. He had left me a message that could only be construed as a confession and apology to me, but which at the same time was as opaque and ambiguous as only Justin could make it. I sat immersed in these thoughts until the oil lamp began to flicker. I recalled my own unacknowledged secrets, and I had had similar moments of absolute loneliness and despair at the Refuge – when, as a boy, I lay grieving in my cell, with a sense of total abandonment and absence of any desire to live. It was my teachers who had drawn me back and given me a purpose and a set of tasks and renewed my will to live. Brother Josephus with his quiet voice and gruff old Master Ebenezer had set me on this road. Perhaps they had foreseen a moment such as this.

I stirred and shook myself. My earlier determination returned to me fully-grown and sharp as a blade. I found a black linen cloak among Justin's clothes and took an iron hatchet from the wall. I picked up a coiled rope with a grappling hook, Justin's souvenir of the siege, and made my way back to the central room by the hearth. I refilled the oil lamp and blackened my face with charcoal. I covered my entire face and neck carefully, observing my reflection in a shard of broken mirror. I would need to encase and protect myself from the acts I was going to perform. The flickering light of the lamp was hypnotic. I saw the image of the flame in the mirror, multiplied endlessly in reflection, until the fire seemed to gleam from my own eyes. Then an image of the ruined citadel rose up like a vision in the mirror; it was the site where the archives were housed, where the churchmen lurked in their vipers' nest, and where Bulavar had informed me of Justin's arrest. It was Bulavar, I inferred, who now directed the Eyes of Israel. If so, it was time that this Eye was put out! I recalled the scaffolding alongside the citadel where repairs were in progress, and I heard my own voice say, *this is what you were trained for.*

I had been distracted by ambition, by hopes of a career and by friendship with Justin and Michal-Rebekah. But I had been prepared well, and my lessons now came back to guide me. The Kr, the Kuhlans, the war with Benjamin were of no account. I dismissed them. My heart was of no account. Nothing was of any significance but the Messiahist enemy!

I had let my Master's words fall asleep, but they had awakened: "The Messiahists are your enemy and our arch foe," Ebenezer had warned. "They know nothing of divine things; they hate the world, and, in expectation of another to come, they destroy the one we have. Only we have the courage to oppose them and expose their falsehoods. Therefore, they lie in wait for you. They will pursue you and hound you to death. They will deceive and pretend and then ambush you without warning. Therefore, my son, be wary! Understand the times, and steel yourself to strike first if you must. Strike like a bolt of lightning! Make yourself the hammer of our people. Strike hard and never cease from striking! It is you who must become the vengeance of our people!"

I left the lamp burning and went to the roof, searching the streets for any sign of movement. *This is what you were trained for. Think nothing, acknowledge nothing. Act!*

Heeding my training, I left over the rooftops, heading south and away from my target. I had the hatchet and the coiled rope over my shoulder, Justin's dagger, and my own sword in my belt. I felt invisible in the night, inseparable from it. As I approached the Citadel, I focused my mind on Brother Rodrig's hand, the hand that had cunningly contrived a petition in my own handwriting – a petition that said that Justin was doomed, and that I would follow him into oblivion if I protested.

I saw his hand clench and open, as if trying to ward off a blow, and thus my anguish transformed itself into action.

I came to myself only gradually. The fire burning in the citadel so mirrored the blaze behind my eyes and in my heart that I could not at first distinguish between them. From somewhere, perhaps from the heart of the fire itself, I heard a howling, drawn-out cry, pitched as much in sorrow as in anger. I did not know what I felt – unappeasable rage or inconsolable grief. My mouth was parched, my tongue swollen; I had a taste like cotton in my mouth. I did not know where I might search for understanding.

But it was a familiar voice that had summoned me from my battle trance, the sound of my name being spoken. *My name! But spoken by whom?* I turned, searching the crowd—discovering, for the first time, the presence of a crowd.

"Josiah Glanz ben Haggadah, come; I have orders for you."

I found myself face to face with a small, withered figure perspiring in the heat of the flames. I recognized him: *Simon ben Gurion.*

Coming to myself, I discovered I had been somehow stripped of my clothing—I was naked in the midst of a host of people, strangers, who peered at me with bloated and distorted faces. Was I awake or dreaming? And should I hide my nakedness or pretend nothing was amiss? A riot or battle seemed to be in progress; much wreckage was strewn about. I saw soldiers – infantry, First Apostles infantry, and an array of other uniforms—milling about in the fire's glow. The citadel was in flames, and there were fires in progress elsewhere in the city, southward, toward the great plaza. A great crowd surged in the streets. I found my sword in one sticky hand and my scabbard in the other. I was covered with soot and blood and filth, and a noise like a cataract roared in my ears.

"Can I hold these for you? Yes. Yes. That's it. Thank you." Simon ben Gurion led me gently by the arm through the mob, which drew back from us, and also through the encircling infantry. Dazed as I was, I thought it strange that the soldiers made no attempt to interfere in the chaos that roiled around us.

"Come, you must leave this behind you now," Ben Gurion was saying. "You have a great task before you. A task only you can perform. *Come with me!"*

Book Two:
The Desolation

Chapter 6: Meribah

I

When I was a child, I was visited by terrors in my sleep, but my mother was there to comfort me. "You've been dreaming," she would say, placing her cool hand on my forehead and smoothing the bedding. But in the dream I was having, I myself am the horror, and there is no one to comfort me.

I awoke in a small room gray with early morning light. I was drenched with sweat and I had a terrible thirst and a weakness such as I had never felt before. My legs seemed nailed to the cot; below the ankles I had no feeling. The same heaviness enveloped my wrists, and when I tried to raise them, I realized that I was confined in iron shackles. I tried my bonds as far as my strength would allow, which was very little. By moving and clenching my muscles, I gradually restored a little circulation, and with it sensation. But as sensation returned, so did pain; the slightest movement caused exquisite agony. Ignoring the discomfort, I flexed my toes, fearing that lying motionless would cause renewed numbness. Quickly exhausted, I slept again.

When next I awoke, the pain in my feet and ankles was intense, but I managed to struggle into a sitting position so I could massage them. My wrist manacles had been removed. My cell was gray with light again, and I could make out objects indistinctly as my eyes adjusted. My room was plain, whitewashed, with one window and a door, and with no furniture except a bed and an old ceramic pot for necessities. Outside, I could hear women's voices and what seemed to be the miscellaneous sounds of a large household. Gradually, the room grew lighter, until, by the light streaming through cracks in the shutters of the single window, I judged it to be mid-day. It was strange beyond belief to be held in isolation, in iron bonds, with all the familiar sounds of life going on around me. Where was I? How had I come to be here, and why? I searched my mind, which was a dark closet, and found nothing. *I had no memory!* More than for life or liberty, I feared for my sanity.

I called out, my voice croaking. There were footsteps and then the door rattled open, and a soldier appeared in the doorway. "He's awake," he called over his shoulder. Three other soldiers and an officer appeared and crowded around my bed staring at me. "Call the Senyora," the officer said.

The soldiers trussed me up in a sack-like garment with sleeves into which my arms were thrust and then tied across my chest – a clever constraining device superior to my strength and yet less cruel to the flesh than iron manacles. Then they removed my leg irons, and I was carried outside and placed on a divan. I lay blinking painfully in the bright sunlight trying to orient myself in these new surroundings.

"You fools," a voice behind me said, "put him in the shade. Over here, on the portico."

It was a woman's voice, commanding and confidant though raspy with age.

It appeared that I was being held in a stronghold much like my own family compound at Tirzah. I lay in a sunlit, open square with a large well in the center. Around the square was a walled enclosure with barns and outbuildings and great house. I had been carried from a room in what I judged were the servants' quarters. There was a cloth canopy in front of the quarters, in the shade of which several women, both slave and Israelite, were washing clothes. A dozen children of all ages played nearby.

An elderly woman – apparently the woman who had spoken – approached me. She was small in stature, dark, with wrinkled skin and black intelligent eyes. Her hair was pulled back in a bun, from which strands of gray emerged. Though simply dressed, she had the air of a person of consequence. She scrutinized me intently for a moment and then said, "You are welcome here."

I found this greeting fantastic in the circumstances. I would have laughed, but anger stifled my humor. I tried to raise my arms to protest my restraints, producing what must have looked like a maniacal shrug.

"You have been ill," she said. "When you are recovered enough, your restraints will be removed." Her voice was low and uningratiating. It reminded me of someone whom I could not quite place.

I shook my head as vigorously as I could, clenching my teeth to avoid outcry.

"In good time," she replied. "All in good time. What you need right now is rest. Therefore you must be calm."

These words, spoken without any particular warmth, yet conveying something like kindness of intention, moved me powerfully. Something in me steeled to resist relaxed infinitesimally. My eyes filmed over, and I heaved several great sighs. I was at the point of losing control. "Water," I whispered, to cover my real agitation.

"I'll send someone to see to your needs, and then we'll talk. In the meantime, rest and compose yourself."

I turned my face away. Clearly, this formidable woman, whoever she was, saw through me like glass. As resolutely as I could, I tried to regain command of my breathing. To distract myself, I lay for some time observing the sunlight and shadows and listening to the ring of a hammer from a forge play a rhythmic counterpoint to the sound of children's voices. The familiarity of the scene was comforting, and these images of life's normal routine gradually formed a barrier to the things in my mind that were clamoring to get out. I was soon asleep and slept without dreams.

The next day this routine was repeated. I lay in the same place on a divan in the shade of a portico in front of the great hall. My guards said nothing to me and treated me with rough indifference. Soon, however, half a dozen children were bold enough to form a ring and stare at me. "He stinks," one of them said. Later, two slave women appeared with basins of water and, under the supervision of my guards, began to wash me as thoroughly as they could, given my confining garment. I felt humiliated to be thus exposed. The guards eyed me warily, but I was no way inclined to resist. Indeed, my spirit was quite broken. I was unsure of my tongue and reluctant to use it, so I remained silent through the entire procedure. The cloths that the women used to bathe my face came away black, and I remembered suddenly how I had darkened my face with charcoal from Justin's fireplace. Then I remembered why, and my heart nearly burst.

As soon as I recovered myself, the elderly woman appeared and seated herself beside me. I sensed the guards hovering at a discrete distance. *This is a powerful person,* I thought.

"In the absence of my brother," she said without prologue, "I am lord of this stronghold. Therefore, you will not be offended if I read the liturgy of purification." She took the *Sayings of St. Supplicee* from a handbag and announced, "Since the ceremony of purification is a means to compose one's mind and to accept what is, it will do no harm for you to hear the words prior to an occasion for the ritual." She read the words in a quiet, dignified voice.

That afternoon I remained awake, reclining on a couch in the shade of a portico, watching without seeing the activities of the household as the sun passed overhead. In my mind Justin and Michal-Rebekah were vividly present before me. For several hours I took my fill of grief and then, for sanity's sake, laid it aside for a time.

There was a racket of dogs and chickens out of my line of sight, which prevented any attempt at meditation, so I allowed myself to lie watching the life of the courtyard – the feeding of livestock and other chores, the waddling hostility of geese toward the children. Again, the mere movement of shadows across the enclosure and the sounds of daily life seemed to work as an antidote to what troubled my sleep. Fearing a descent into those depths, I struggled to keep my eyes open. I oriented myself on the sun and could see bare brown hills to the west and specks upon them that must be grazing cattle. Were these the hills of Judah? It seemed likely.

As the shadows lengthened, I watched as sunburned slaves hoisted water out of the well and carried sloshing buckets to a large trough near the barn. Soon the gates of the enclosure opened, and a dozen huge draft horses were let in, their hooves clopping on the cobblestones. The late afternoon sun shone on their backs and rumps; their tails whisked ceaselessly at flies. When they had drunk, they were led to their stalls in the stable on the north side of the compound. Immediately afterward, a herd of spotted cows came in through the gate, ambling in single file, lowing to be milked, and took their place at the trough. This routine pleased me greatly, and when my guards came, they allowed me to walk a few steps before they carried me to my room. The pain was terrific, but the scene had touched some wellspring in me.

The following day, I was allowed to take my meals outside, and my guards exercised my legs by half-carrying, half-dragging me around the shaded portico. One of the slave women who had washed me the day before massaged my legs and rubbed an unguent on my ankles.

"So," the Senyora said to me as I awoke from a drowse, "the light begins to show again in your eyes. Tell me your name, and I will answer such of your questions as I am able to. My brother will return shortly, and then you and he may speak freely of all things."

This contact was abrupt and unexpected, like much else in my immediate past, and I felt an impulse to shrink away from it. But I was desperate to know where I was and why. "I believe," I said, moistening my cracked lips, "that I am. . . ." The voice was still not my own; I hesitated, unconvinced of what lay on my tongue. "Josiah Glanz ben Haggadah."

She nodded. "Good. Josiah Glanz ben Haggadah. You have had quite a difficult time, and, quite frankly, Josiah Glanz ben Haggadah, you have been difficult for others as well. But you are mending now, and you have a young man's health and spirits." She gave me a penetrating look. "There will be no more nonsense. . . ."

I stirred in my confining garment, and gestured my wish to be free of it.

"Not just yet, young man," she said. "I have strict orders from my brother, who is lord here, to keep you in restraints – for your own good, mind you – until he returns and says otherwise. Be patient; he will be here soon and you may make your peace with him then. In any event, we will await his decision. I will send him word that you are ready to speak. My brother is not a man to trifle with, as you know."

"Your brother . . . ?"

"Ah, I have neglected to introduce myself. I am Senyora Eliza Hadash-Gurion. This is Beth-Gurion, the stronghold of the Gurions, and my brother, as you know, is Simon ben Gurion."

Simon ben Gurion! I remembered the burning citadel and a voice calling me, summoning me back from the abyss. Flames soared and crackled in my mind's eye.

"I see you are remembering," she said. "Do not attempt to take in too much too quickly."

When I awoke from a nap, I found General Simon ben Gurion seated opposite my divan, waiting with seemingly infinite patience for me to come to my senses. "My sister tells me you are recovering," he said calmly, as if he conversed with bound prisoners daily. "You will want to know of your brother, Major Justin Glanz Apollo. Sadly, I cannot confirm whether he is dead or alive. You know of his arrest. And you know also that he was not among the prisoners of Esdralon's citadel. . . ." That this was a question he indicated with his eyes.

"No," I confirmed.

"Well, this is a bit of a mystery. Given his condition, it does not seem likely that Major Apollo could have been removed secretly from the city – nor is it possible that he could have remained in custody but hidden since that time. Esdralon is, by the way, now in the hands of forces loyal to us. Happily, the Messiahist clergy and their faction have been put to flight." He paused to let me absorb his words. "Brother Bulavar. . ." he said, watching me, "was not among the Messiahists found in the citadel. So," he continued, clearing his throat, "we must assume that in some fashion he made his escape. I anticipate, in fact, that my contacts will soon report Brother Bulavar safely arrived in New Jerusalem. Most regrettable, I must say. But unfortunately I have no news for you of Major Apollo. No news, I'm afraid, is not good news in this instance. In all likelihood, Major Apollo was executed immediately after his arrest or died quickly under interrogation." He paused again, hummed to himself a moment, and went on. "Given his connections and his popularity with the army, I imagine that his body was disposed of secretly. Does this seem plausible to you?"

It was some time before I could speak. "Yes," I said finally, "that is the way I have imagined it." *Michal-Rebekah and Appian,* I wanted to ask.

"I have no news," he said, as if anticipating my question, "of the Benjamite woman and her son. I assume a fate no better than his has overtaken them." I turned aside to conceal my emotion. At some point the thought occurred to me that *he knows too much about you and Justin and Michal-Rebekah*, and I was put on my guard. His voice and manner were unperturbed; he might have been a farmer describing a moderately good crop rather than the deaths of those close to me. Thus, I scarcely heeded him when he remarked in the same tone: "As things turned out, they would have done better to arrest you."

He left me to my grief. When I was aware of him again, General Ben Gurion was speaking quietly to the guards. Several departed, taking the weapons of the others. "You see, Josiah – may I call you Josiah?" Ben Gurion said, turning to me again. "You are aware of very little that has transpired, or your own role in events." He seated himself beside me. "It will be difficult for you to trust me, Josiah, but I have, in fact, saved your life – albeit against your will. But I have saved it nonetheless."

He paused as if he expected I might challenge him.

"I saved your life for a reason, not out of sentimentality. You have a great task before you, perhaps many such tasks, but we can speak of that later. First I must bring you up to date. Israel is now involved in a great civil war. I do not refer, of course, to the war between Israel and Benjamin, but to the new conflict between Judah and its allies and the Messiahist faction in New Jerusalem." I was taken aback at the news.

"You must allow yourself," he said, "to consider the amount of time that has elapsed."

"Since when?" I asked.

"If you recall, it was early morning of Saturday, May 20th, that I found you before the burning citadel of Esdralon. What day might it be today?"

His question filled me with anxiety: "I'm afraid I have lost track of time. Is it Tuesday or Wednesday? Is it the 24th of May?"

"It is now June 10th," he replied. "You have been delirious for over two weeks. I ordered drugs administered, which may have prolonged your disorientation. Yes, you may remember a little as we speak."

Dread took hold of me; the loss of so many days was beyond comprehension.

"You have been through a difficult experience. Exhaustion from battle, the loss of your kinsman, and your own violence against the Messiahists – each of these has, I expect, exacted a toll from your life-energies. Nevertheless, one must go on. Death comes as no surprise in Israel. Neither does injustice – though I see you feel it keenly." When I was silent he added: "Justice is a young man's fancy; you outgrow the need for it. Some say that justice can be wrested from the teeth of the world, but only by accident. It has no part in the scheme of things, I assure you! But enough of this; I should leave such ramblings to the scholars and churchmen."

I listened silently as the Lion of Judah assured me he was only a simple soldier.

"You need to know," he continued, "that I have placed you in restraint to keep you from harming yourself. But you seem to have recovered your senses. Come," he called to the guards, "unbind him."

The abrupt and seemingly random nature of this transaction took me by surprise. I felt unable to respond, even to thank him. The guards removed my restraints, peeling the garment over my head like a skin, while Ben Gurion described the civil war that had broken out during my period of oblivion. The leading circles of Israel, as he put it – by which he meant the merchants – had had a falling out with the clerics. "We had thought we could work together because we wished to see Israel change. But as the war progressed and we encountered difficulties, we discovered their interests and ours diverged. Fatally, as it turned out." By his account, the Messiahist faction had overreached themselves, first in executing Admiral Montevideo after a secret trial in Hebron, and then in arresting Major Apollo. The Admiral's execution was an unmistakable signal that failure in the field could mean death. That, he pointed out, had alienated the army: "The generals, you see, are well acquainted with failure." He smiled benignly. "Then, by arresting Major Apollo, the Messiahists struck at one of the popular icons of the army, incensing many of the ranks. That, too, was a mistake. Both of these actions were destructive of morale. They undermined the war effort itself. In this sense, their actions could be considered treason. In fact, it has been convenient for us to consider them so." He rubbed his knees with satisfaction. *His cynicism reminded me vaguely of Justin.*

"This all has to do, at bottom, with the date of Judgment Day," Ben Gurion continued. "With the date of Judgment Day, can you believe it!" He might have been describing a large fish someone claimed to have caught. "Do you believe it?" he asked me suddenly.

"Do I believe that Bishop Bon has claimed the world will end with the millennium? Yes, I believe he has made such a statement. I heard him make it in Esdralon, in the great square of the city. Do I believe his claim that the world will end? Of course not! That is insane presumption and superstition. Justin thought that this claim of a special revelation was part of a struggle for power that Bon was intending to replace the Primate."

"And so he has. Bishop Bon is now Polymer XII."

I drew a breath; Justin had seldom been wrong about anything.

"So, then, as you know and no doubt approve, the legions in Esdralon rose and put down the Messiahist faction, whose fanaticism – 'insane presumption,' as you put it – had infected the army."

"Why do you say 'as you know'? I know nothing of this."

"You should know, young man. You led the rising."

"I *what?*"

"At least, the chronicles will say you did." He ignored my astonishment and went on: "Hebron and all the rest of Judah are with us. The First Apostles, now under the command of General Pasco, routed the churchmen out of Esdralon and then out of Hebron. The south is ours, firmly in control. The Messiahists are, however, still very much entrenched in New Jerusalem, and now we have a three-way war. Which means, I suppose, that the three sides have a powerful motive to negotiate." This prospect seemed to him mildly amusing.

Which means, I thought to myself, that two of the sides have a motive to unite and fall on the third. But which two? And which will be the odd side out? "Justin Apollo would be very useful to you in this situation," I remarked.

"Ah, you believe so?" he said, folding his hands. "Indeed, I have thought so myself."

Ben Gurion and I talked on several other occasions as my body slowly mended. As soon as I was able to exercise, I noticed him observing me. "Tell me about your education in the martial arts," he said.

This was not a subject on which I was willing to dwell. "Tell me about my father," I countered.

"Tephlin Glanz? Strange you should ask," he said. "I was just thinking about him. Thirty years I have stood at his side. And now the rumors – you may have heard them yourself. How ironic it is!"

"What rumors are you talking about?"

"People say that I have done away with him," he said. "Murdered him."

"Murdered him!"

"Yes. A strange man! Now more the legend of himself than the man I knew. As a young man, Tephlin Glanz was everywhere, seeing and doing and taking control of things. Now he seldom goes out of the palace – except in disguise, some say. Do you find that strange? The truth is, he's become a recluse and a bit of an eccentric, in my opinion. Some people – malicious persons, I imagine – not having seen him for some time, assume that Glanz has been murdered and insinuate that I carry on in his name. Do you find that amusing – the thought of me secretly pursuing evil schemes of my own?"

"I find that remarkable," I managed to say.

"Not at all. In fact, such tales always have a degree of plausibility about them, and this one makes a wonderful story. I suppose the tale satisfies a need as well. But here is something I'll wager you do not know about him." He described Glanz as a young man, a commoner with no fortune or prospects, but cunning and bold and above all impatient of the constraints of birth that kept him outside the circles of power. "The young Tephlin Glanz was a genius," Ben Gurion declared. "He saw opportunities where others saw only danger, and he founded his fortune not on the dowry of his first wife, as is the common report, but on metal recovery from the ruins of Old Pasco, on the Kuhlan side of the Jordan. The metal had always been there, waiting, but others were too afraid of the Kuhlans to venture over."

"But Pasco has been excavated off and on for centuries," I said. "There cannot have been much metal to recover."

"True, there was not," he admitted. "But there was some, and if one used prison labor, as he did, and fed them on close rations and held them to their tasks, there was profit to be made. One had to take risks, of course, both from the Kuhlans and from the prisoners. But he did. He had some losses, and he had some luck – but most of all, he had the sense to see that the real profit lay in mining the ruins for brick and cut stone, which he ferried across the river. And he made himself useful to an impoverished state by relieving it of the troublesome burden of all those prisoners."

"Ah," I said, "I had not known of his role as benefactor!"

He smiled. "In this way, Tephlin Glanz became one of the greatest builders in Hebron. He built the Palace of Ingots, you know. And grown wealthy, he began to enter into the councils of the great in Judah. He even loaned the money to the lord who built the Palace – and then took possession of it when the same lord went bankrupt. Critics claim the nobleman went bankrupt with some subtle assistance from Tephlin Glanz, but that is old and quite unreliable gossip. I always hold that a man is responsible for his own actions."

"A fool and his gold are soon parted," I replied, quoting the proverb.

"Exactly so," he said. "Tephlin Glanz excavated every yard of Old Pasco, salvaging every scrap of usable material, and at the same time building roads and fences with broken stone. He built no buildings, mind you! He never tempted the Kuhlans so far! But he planted gardens and fields and orchards and laid a network of roads to get the produce to market. It was Tephlin Glanz who brought about the tilling of the Kuhlan side of the river. And now Pasco feeds most of Hebron, and every apple and grain of barley belongs to Glanz."

"An interesting tale," I said, "but I want to know something else about him."

"Yes?" he said.

"I need to know what Tephlin Glanz *wants*."

"I imagine," he replied evenly, "that Tephlin Glanz would like to know that himself." I waited to hear more, but he said nothing else. At that moment, the captain of the guard appeared with a long bundle wrapped in wool. I recognized the hilt of my sword. I watched with surprise and anticipation as he lay the sword on the table between us, hilt toward me. Ben Gurion looked at me placidly as the sword was placed on the table. It was wrapped in a cloth; all but the hilt was covered and bound. My heart leapt! I had an impulse to reach out and take it from its scabbard to examine it, but another interior voice told me to ignore the sword and to watch the old man.

I fixed my eyes on Ben Gurion, wondering what was afoot. "I thank you for your consideration in this matter," I said. "The weapon is precious to me."

"I must ask you a question, Josiah," he said mildly, "and it is important that you speak the truth."

"As you can see, I am at your disposal," I replied. *And I too have some questions that I would like to have answered, I thought to myself.*

"Had you, prior to undertaking your – your mission against the Messiahist clerics, received instructions to do so?" I frowned, not certain that I understood his question. "Come, come," he prompted me. "After your interview with Bulavar, you went to the Asherite encampment?"

I nodded.

"And there you requested to speak to Major Vashon, a close connection, I believe, of your Asherite kin?"

"Yes."

"But the Major and his son were not present at the camp. They were in fact attending a meeting of the officers of the Third Army, discussing what to do in light of Montevideo's execution. A meeting you did not, according to reports, attend. . . ."

"I was not aware of such a meeting."

"I see. Interesting. But I believe you left a message for Major Vashon. What did it say, please?"

"I don't recall exactly. I wrote telling him what Bulavar had just told me – that Justin had been arrested. The implications of his arrest were only just dawning on me."

"I see. And what else?"

"I thanked Major Vashon for the role he had taken upon himself to mediate between myself and the Velcos. I. . . "

"Yes, yes, I know all about that."

"I said that restitution to the Velco clan would not be necessary. Would no longer be necessary."

General Ben Gurion's eyes narrowed as he heard my reply. "And what would the good Major have understood by that?"

"That I was very grateful for his generosity. I have expected that the Velcos would demand a huge sum for the blood debt. I did not see – I still do not see – how I can ever repay Major Vashon."

Ben Gurion seemed highly displeased with my answer. "Josiah, people who do us favors have in mind very definite ideas about how we may clear our debts to them in the future. Very clear ideas! You may consider that at your leisure. But you have not answered my question: what would your Major Vashon have understood by your comment that this recently assumed obligation on your behalf was no longer required?"

I resented both his condescension and his imputation of improper motives to Major Vashon. I could not imagine what he wanted to extract from me or why he was so intent on it. "First of all," I replied heatedly, "he is not *my* Major Vashon, and he sought no advantage of me. He accepted me quite generously as a kinsman. On my part, I simply hoped he would understand my intentions – that's all."

"Ah, are we coming at last near an answer? What precisely were your intentions, which you conveyed so succinctly in the note? Come, you must stop trifling with me. What did you intend to convey to the Major? He is a deep one, this Major Vashon of yours."

It occurred to me that I did not like this minion, or possibly murderer, of Tephlin Glanz any more than a black-robed Messiahist. Enemies or allies we might be, as chance determined. But friends, never!

"I had just heard the news about Justin's arrest and had barely time to digest what it meant—to realize that his case was hopeless. And mine as well. I could have been implicated in anything Justin was charged with. More, in fact. Bulavar had this creature named Rodrig who can perfectly imitate people's handwriting. He handed me a letter during our interview written in my own handwriting. Only it was a clever forgery, you see. And they had my journal – they had seen all my thoughts about the war and other matters, which were not, in their view, orthodox. So I was conveying to Major Vashon that Justin was doomed, and – it was just beginning to dawn on me – so was I. I had realized by then that they could do anything to us, prove anything, however false, against us. The Messiahists were playing with us – with me – like a cat with a bird."

"And you intended to convey all this in your note? In so few words?"

"No, I'm just recounting how I felt, as a way of explaining my state of mind."

"At last, some progress!"

"Even a rabbit may turn and leap at the dog's throat. I had just decided – no, I had just realized what I would do. It was not really a decision."

"I see," Ben Gurion said, leaning forward and piercing me with his gaze. "So this was a signal to Vashon? And he was to respond – how?"

"Signal? No. It was not that kind of message. I wanted him to know, as a friend, so when he heard what had happened, he would understand."

"Come, come, Josiah! You are speaking nonsense, babbling. Is it because you are not telling me the truth?"

I felt my blood rise at his chiding, and we both found ourselves looking at the hilt of my sword, which lay between us. "I wanted Major Vashon to understand that I had chosen to defy my enemies, to resist what had been prepared for me. That way, he would not grieve, nor see what I had done as dishonorable. He would understand that I had chosen my way."

"You are speaking of a determination on suicide?" The old man looked at me shrewdly, dubiously. Then his eyes told me that there were people behind me of whom I had not been aware. "Your Major Vashon, you know, counseled patience in the meeting of the Third Army officers – the meeting which you say you knew nothing about. He expressed himself as a sensible man, not anxious to take rash actions. Very clever. Of course at that moment, he may not have known of Major Apollo's arrest – or of your own so-called determination."

I was suddenly tired of his questions and insinuations. Mild mannered though he was, Ben Gurion was the most arrogant man I had ever met. "It's very simple," I said, controlling my temper. "It was a farewell message to my friend. Is that so difficult to understand?"

"In my experience, Josiah, very little is simple. Did you know, at that moment, the mood of the army? Or the army's reaction to the news of Montevideo's execution?

I shook my head, recalling that Major Vashon's sentry had told me about Montevideo's death and the Major being at a meeting. But no, Montevideo's fate had scarcely registered on my mind. I had had much closer, dearer losses to assimilate.

"So, you contemplated your little mission in the citadel – why? For revenge? Did you intend to free Justin from the citadel? Or had you another motive. . .?"

I shrugged. "I would have risked anything to free Justin if he were still alive. I knew the citadel was used as a dungeon. But whether Justin were there or not, I knew that that was where my enemies lay. When I left Bulavar, I saw the scaffolding by the wall and realized I could reach the top floors without interference. What I intended, however, was born of the realization that I was doomed. It was a leap, as I said, of a cornered animal." I paused, remembering my mood. "What I cannot understand is why I am here, still alive, and not dead in Esdralon."

"There may be many things that you do not understand," he said sharply. "But I ask again, Josiah, were you given instructions by anyone to do what you did?"

I shook my head, meeting his gaze directly, and he appeared to be satisfied, even slightly relieved, if such impassive features could register any emotion.

Then I spoke what had been lying in the back of my own mind: "Now I have a question to ask of you." "Yes?" His gaze flickered past me to whomever was standing silently behind me.

"What was it that I performed that night in Esdralon?"

Ten days later, Ben Gurion's private bodyguard escorted me to Hebron. I rode one of the General's finest horses, and we passed with great pomp and formality along ruined streets lined with cheering soldiers and a dazed and anxious citizenry. With his taste for irony, Ben Gurion had arranged that I receive a hero's welcome. In honor of my role in the battles with the Kr at Elion and Beersheba Wells, I was proclaimed the savior of the First Apostles Legion. In the ceremonies that followed in the great plaza under the fortress, I was promoted two ranks to captain and received both a battle citation with shield and the Order of St. Gideon, Israel's highest decoration – the latter from Ben Gurion's own hand. Then, among the still-smoking ruins of the city, I was acclaimed as the scourge of the Messiahists and the firebrand of the rising against them. For two days thereafter, the army celebrated my honors and its victory over the unarmed churchmen in Hebron with drunken revelry.

But in midst of this adulation from my comrades, I knew that these honors of mine, so called, were contrived for my father and Ben Gurion's purposes. That was only a trifle; much closer to my heart was the knowledge that all those closest to me were no longer among the living. And I knew in my heart that I could never become clean again.

But I had formed another realization as well: Simon ben Gurion had not been pleased at my question: *what had I performed at Esdralon?* The general had grunted in exasperation and ended our interview with a wave of his hand. That was the first moment I realized that an officer of the guards had been standing behind me with his sword out of his scabbard. So our conversation had been a test with my life hanging in the balance. I had much to take in and digest. But, judging from his manner, so did he. And part of what he did not know involved myself.

But I had accepted the mission.

II

They say that stories are journeys – movements through time and change that return at last, triumphant or exhausted, to the point of departure. The tale I tell of my own life, altered now almost beyond recognition, commences with a journey – my second, in fact, by sail and oar on the Great Jordan. And it began, as had the first, on the docks at Hebron, under the shadow of Techsaymun, the great citadel of Judah. But how different it was from my first journey to Engedi, my first embarking on a man's life, and how strangely altered was the world in which I journeyed. But it was I, rather, who had changed. This time I went on another man's errand, not my own, and there was nothing in my mission that could rekindle my vanished hopes.

The Yakima in July was barely a trickle; the dry season heat oppressed like an oven. We embarked at dawn, dipping our oars into the dregs of the river. I scarcely noticed the great fortress or the ripening fields slip by in the early morning haze. My gaze was inward and backward, reaching toward another segment of my past that had been wrenched from me violently. I kept to myself, bitter, laden with grief, contemptuous of life and ready for it to end.

Israel was changing, sloughing its old skin as it outgrew it. That these changes, having the force of a natural process, must be and could not be averted, I accepted. That the process was grotesque and dangerous to passers-by, especially to those who would observe too closely, I had come to know also. I sought consolation in the thought that the new Israel would have its own awful beauty. I strained to discover signs of renewal in the events I had witnessed, the diamond design of new scales. But the Israel I knew seemed to be dying, its transformation a death, a dissolution, not a renewal. The body might writhe till sunset, but the brain was gone. Meanwhile, those I loved had already perished in the coils, and their lives lay behind me. With every oar-stroke they moved irretrievably away, receding like froth and detritus borne away by the current. One can turn and watch wistfully as objects diminish with distance, but no more.

At the confluence of the Mother and Father, we were to turn north. My destination was Hammoth-Wenatchee, the chief city of Naphtali, where I had a rendezvous with my elder brother, Hanford Glanz. It was a gossamer thread of curiosity about him that kept my mind engaged with my surroundings and focused on my mission. I held myself erect, rigid, disconsolate on the thin deck of a carrack, listening to the rhythm of the boson's chant and the beat of the oars on the river, my feet on the fragile planks between myself and Father Death flowing below and against us.

The oars lifted; the captain ordered the sails furled; we drifted in the current. We were at the junction.

"Young sir, young captain, sir!" I was startled from my reverie by one of the passengers, who was tugging at my sleeve. He had a round perspiring face the color of wet clay. "The rites," he said. He held a rooster, bedraggled and heat-dazed, aloft in one hand and an empty sack in the other. "Here, young sir, perform the sacrifice for us." The ship captain gazed impartially at me from the tiller; the oars were raised and dripping.

"You mistake me!" I replied as soon as I found my tongue. "I am no Messiahist magician. Fetch another for your childish rites!"

He stared at me slack-jawed and some other passengers seconded his plea, urging me to spill the cock's blood for Beli-az. "For safety's sake," one of the passengers added.

I drew back involuntarily as the man persisted in dangling the rooster in my face. The bird opened in its beak soundlessly, its eyes glazed. "Fools!" I shouted, "How much blood do you think you must spill to make the Jordan run backwards?"

There was an intake of breath from the passengers and crew. "It's a fee he wants, then," an oarsman sneered. "Give him half a kanz."

Before the act formed in my mind, my sword leapt out and flashed across the space between us. The white body of the rooster flopped to the deck and then raced madly about, spurting its meager life-blood in all directions. The man stood with his mouth agape, holding the rooster's head in his hand and gazing at the body of the cock, thrashing in its the death throes. Then his eyes lighted on me and widened in terror. The bird, fallen on its side, was still twitching. Revolted, I kicked it over the side. "Let Beli-az come up and take this morsel, if he likes!" I shouted. "If he exists! You fools, you imbeciles! You play at children's games. No amount of blood will make the Jordan flow backward or lift you from its depths. You cannot buy good fortune or escape the past; you cannot bribe away the consequences of your actions. Not even with human blood—for that is where the Messiahists are leading you! The future comes on as it will, undeterred, and the past lies upon our heads forever."

My outburst had shocked many among the passengers and crew, and they gave me dark looks and glanced at each other as if to find the courage to rebuke me. Inwardly regretful but still angry, I challenged them, "If any here believe in the efficacy of blood, let him come forward and volunteer his own, and I will gladly spill it over the side."

". . . And your arrogant carcass over with it!" I heard someone mutter. The captain, still at the tiller, intervened quickly. "Put up your weapon," he said. "There will be no bloodshed on my ship. If there are rites inoffensive to the powers that be, let them be performed."

I was relieved that another Old Believer stepped forward and said the brief requiem of the juncture. We then scattered the ashes of the dead we carried on board. There were many urns, and then many more. Apparently a multitude had died in the recent fighting in Hebron. No wonder my fellow-passengers were sullen and quick to take offense – but no more than I. After the events in Hebron, I was surprised that Third Comers were still so bold about revealing themselves. In these times, it should not be so easy to know a man's thoughts.

My traveling companions chose not to trouble me again. I spent the rest of the day in perfect isolation, meditating alone on my corner of the deck. The beat of my heart against the planks of my ribs answered stroke by stroke the rhythm of the oars. But instead of transcending my pain, I relived with perfect clarity all the most anguish-inspiring moments of my past.

Truly our Teacher wrote: *consequences lie upon our heads forever.*

III

The Great Jordan is hot in July; the sun glares off its surface like a reflection off a blade. For two days we had a stiff wind at our backs in the morning, and then a dead calm all afternoon, during which we made little headway. Our military escort of water striders, however, moved smartly even with their sails limp or furled, and I began to understand the boast of Judean sailors that they had built a wooden fortress wall around Israel. The clumsier cargo vessels and the passenger carrack in which I traveled could only wallow along behind.

The Jordan is navigable at all seasons, but in winter and spring the current is too strong to travel easily upstream. Only when the flow has diminished after mid-summer can trading vessels make progress against the current, which accounts for the ebb and flow of Israel's trade. Much cargo of all kinds comes down river. Naphtali and further Lebanon are rich in timber, hides, and furs, brandies and dried fruits, and cedar resin for sacred incense. Most of the products that the Glanz interests provide Israel came, in fact, from their holdings in the north. The far-flung Glanz enterprises also had access to gold and silver and metal for weapons, which came down to Israel from those distant regions.

Thus, I was able to observe the busiest season of Israel's commerce. We passed barges pulled by mules along the shore, small flimsy sailing craft, and, sad to see, barks filled with the ill and dying, making pilgrimage to Meribah, the miraculous healing well in the midst of the Desolation. The part of me tenacious of life and consciousness fastened on these details. In spite of myself, I watched and learned. As a landsman, I was baffled by the river traffic and the skills necessary to maintain it. But even the most difficult voyage by water was obviously easier and cheaper than transporting the same weight by land. As a soldier, I saw what can be done in a military craft with a skilled captain who used the oars sparingly and kept in the wind, saving the strength of the crew for the dead calms that set in as quickly as the gales.

The Great Jordan was a tireless adversary, but our crewmen were unawed either by its power or its uncleanliness. The crew stripped to the waist in the heat and pulled hard at the oars, levering our clumsy vessel northward at the pace of a slow walk. Sweat glistened on their backs, and the sun darkened them like bricks in a furnace.

In a few days, I grew accustomed to the features of the summer voyage, which have their own special annoyances. Using my scabbard as a tent-pole, I made a shade out of my outer garment and endured the heat as best I could. Though I longed a thousand times daily for the company of my brother, I never missed him more than in the silence that had followed the requiem at the junction. No one had spoken to me since our first day out, when I had lashed out at the man who asked me to make a blood sacrifice.

On the third day, I admitted to myself that I was lonely.

"Take him along," Ben Gurion had admonished me.

When I received my orders in the Palace of Ingots, General Ben Gurion had instructed me to take a certain Rehab Gill, a Judean and captain in the Commissary, with me on my mission. By Ben Gurion's account, the man was bright enough, but unmilitary. His name betrayed his humble origins, and Ben Gurion had intimated that the man had not prospered in the Army. "Take him along," he urged me, as if my mission were only an outing. "You'll find him useful when it comes to accounts and ledgers. Hanford Glanz could fool you with his books – in fact a child could fool you with accounts. But Rehab Gill is a wizard when it comes to figures. Use him! Use him! This mission will be his chance to redeem himself." I had resented the intrusion, as I resented everything about my mission, and I suspected Ben Gurion – and Tephlin Glanz behind him – of having ulterior motives in sending another officer to accompany me. But whether they intended to set a spy on me or merely to hang a dead crow around my neck for sport, I could not decide. *What did it matter?* I thought at the time. But now, after nearly a week of isolation, I thought differently. It seemed to me that a companion, even a poor one, would be a comfort. But the fool had missed the departure of the fleet. Unmilitary indeed!

I used the time in the days that followed to ponder the civil war that had broken out. The coup by the Messiahists had been met with a violent counter-coup by my father's faction. I had unwittingly participated in the latter—had led it, according to Ben Gurion's ironic account. This new conflict would affect the tribes of Israel differently. Justin would have been able to predict exactly how the opposing forces would align themselves; I could only guess. The Third Comers were strongest in New Jerusalem. The Messiahist faith had started there, and New Jerusalem was its bastion. In the north, Ephraim, Gad, and Issachar always leaned as Manasseh did. My people Asher would stay aloof and hope that fortune favored Judah. Dan and Naphtali were too remote to be easily coerced into taking sides in any of Israel's quarrels; they too would bide their time and stay aloof. In the south, Reuben and Shimeon would stand with Judah. Benjamin was the tribe least disposed toward the Messiahist faith, and the recent war could only have deepened that aversion. I wondered whether Judah could seek common cause with Benjamin against the Messiahists. Such a course would be expedient, if either side could put aside their enmity.

The new war would not only split the tribes, but divide individuals against themselves. It was a cruel situation in which it would be difficult for many to know their own hearts, let alone their neighbor's. After the slaughter of the churchmen in Esdralon, reconciliation with the Messiahists would be impossible. And a peace agreement would require a radically new ordinance governing the practices of faith and holding the Messiahist hierarchy in check. Such an accord would be difficult to achieve and even more difficult to believe. Since genuine peace was not possible, any agreement now would only postpone hostilities – and if that were so, who would derive advantage from that postponement? In my estimation, the Third Comers stood to gain more from delay. The Messiahists were naturally secretive, superb organizers, and they tended to take the long view. The merchants were temperamentally disposed to do the opposite. Judah's merchants would therefore do well to strike swiftly, while they controlled the bulk of the army and before the churchmen could organize.

Victory would require a ruthless extirpation of the church hierarchy. Could tradesmen, used to shifting ground with every fluctuation in the market, find the will for such an effort? For such bloodshed? I believed my father capable of anything, but doubted that his faction as a whole would be capable of such decision. Judah's merchants had, after all, managed to hold the exchange with the Kr at the solstice. Their warehouses were full of wool; the weavers were busy; and a new basis for wealth had been laid in the south – albeit none too securely. Hostilities with the Kr had resumed immediately after the exchange. Judah was being hard pressed to hold on to Engedi. As Justin had foreseen, they had a wolf by the ears. So, I concluded, there would be no offensive out of Judah, but rather a cautious waiting policy that would unwittingly favor the Messiahists.

Lastly, I asked myself, where would the landed nobles stand? A purge of army officers was no doubt taking place on both sides, even now. The survivors would carry memories, hold grudges, and await a propitious moment. Eventually they would choose. Justin would have had informed opinions on how they would choose. But without Justin beside me, what did I care about any of it?

We camped along the river at night. The sight of food nauseated me, so I decided to fast and drink only bitter tea. I kept apart, and found that the mosquitoes bothered me less than those who took food. I lay on my back and looked at the stars. That the old ways were ending and some new way of life was coming into being seemed beyond dispute. I meditated on the saying of St. Supplicee: *Except the Way, all things change. Even the Law.*

The next day was unbearably hot. The water from the barrel tasted of mold, and some of the passengers and crewmen began to sicken toward afternoon. My stomach rumbled and growled, but remained intact. The sky turned bright yellow and I thought I would faint from the heat. I determined to drink no water that had not been boiled. As I dozed off under the small canopy of shade I had made in my corner of the deck, I had one more fugitive thought of Justin and Michal-Rebekah: if Justin were alive, he would see what had to be done.

The morning of the fifth day we had the White Bluffs on our starboard. As the day wore on, we alternately tacked and rowed, making ragged headway against the current. The river was low with many sandbars, and the water stank. The Jordan in this reach was dead, inhospitable to all life. When we stopped for midday rest, I climbed the west bank to stretch my legs and observe the terrain. Hereabouts, the Jordan flows through a plain nearly as low and level as the banks of the river, and the land is arid. A few miles above us, on the west or Israelite bank, lay the Desolation, a region hostile to all life and forbidden both to us and to the Kuhlans.

Preoccupied with my own thoughts, I startled when one of the crew, who had climbed the bank after me, exclaimed and pointed across the river. I strained my eyes to the utmost, regretting that I had left my glass in my baggage. Eastward the plain shimmered in the heat, monotonous and empty. Then I saw a small cloud of dust like a smudge on the sage-covered plain. The captain and others of the passengers and crew climbed up beside us to have a look. We shaded our eyes and peered intently into the glare. One of the passengers, a man tall and lanky and very dark, stood nearby examining the dust trail with a telescope. He glanced at me once, but did not offer to loan me his glass.

"Antelope," the captain said after a time. "Only antelope." His voice was quiet but decisive, and at his words the group relaxed visibly. But I wondered if his eyesight was truly that keen and he could tell what creatures raised the trail of dust, or if he spoke to reassure us. I looked to the tall man with the glass beside me, but his impassive gaze neither confirmed nor denied what the captain said.

Kuhlans on the move near the border; that was something to think about.

I sat apart from the rest, taking some hard crackers with my tea, and I exercised afterwards. The crew and passengers finished their midday rest and meal and returned to the carrack. I sensed that the men put new energy into the oars, as though to distance themselves from that menacing thread of dust on the Kuhlan plain. I too began to see the Great Jordan with new eyes: the river seemed suddenly smaller. Its narrowness oppressed me, and I resented the fickleness of the winds that took us tacking toward the eastern shore.

Ordinarily, the Kuhlans do not bother travelers on the river or interfere in our trade. The nomads usually stay as aloof from us as if they inhabited another world. But sometimes, capriciously, they do attack vessels going up and down the river, and every few years, or decades – but always unpredictably – they cross the Jordan and lay waste our land. The river thus marked the narrow boundary between two hostile worlds. I realized that my calculation of the contending forces in Israel had omitted the most dangerous factor of all: our hereditary enemies, the Kuhlans. Thereafter, all the length of shallow bank that we sailed along seemed like a treacherous screen that concealed what I most desired to know. And I began to search the Kuhlan bank as if the future lay in ambush there.

Determined to turn my isolation to good use, I set myself to examining the Kuhlan threat. The nomads could fall upon us at any season, but they tended to cross in the late summer, timing their attacks with the lowest ebb of the river and with a full moon – a

"Kuhlan moon" in the folklore of Israel. They always struck suddenly, by stealth, and then slipped away. Israel was so in awe of these phantom raiders that the ignorant attributed supernatural powers to them. The truth must surely be that they were men like ourselves, but operating without humane constraints or inhibitions. It was our very fear of them that gave the Kuhlans their greatest advantage. Try as I might, I could think of no way to counter or prevent their raids. All the chronicles described, and no doubt magnified, their uncanny mobility and speed. Once on our territory, the Kuhlans appeared to be everywhere at once, and Israel never knew where to concentrate to stop them. But unless we concentrated, our forces were helpless, perishing in their twos and threes and dozens until all Israel was a funeral pyre.

In the old days, Israel had manned watchtowers and prepared signal fires in Ephraim and Dan. But now that the confederacy was torn by civil strife, such a degree of organization appeared to be out of the question. Israel's fleet was its best defense, but it was needed to patrol this reach of the Jordan continually, for if the Kuhlans alighted on our soil, they could travel like the wind and strike wherever they pleased. But the fleet was also needed now in the south, to block the Kr from crossing the Jordan – a barrier that, my brother had persuaded me, was no longer fatal to cross in that reach. Justin had been right: Israel was ripe for invasion and probably helpless to repel it. *My brother had been clear-sighted about everything but his own life.*

We camped that night on the west bank. I sat apart and reflected on my mission and the larger events developing invisibly around me, like heat lightning brewing over the horizon. We would be passing the favorite crossing sites of the Kuhlans in the next few days. It saddened me to think of Israel's plight, but not even the prospect of danger could lift me from my torpor.

On the seventh day, in mid afternoon, the wind died, and we were becalmed in the midst of the region Israel calls the Desolation. The captain ordered the anchor dropped and offered purifying incense and a litany. Afterwards, the oars were plied with vigor, for the men had to struggle to make headway against the current. To the west we could see the giant structures that mark the center of the Desolation. Great rectangular blocks, bare of decoration and blue with distance, loomed in the shimmering heat. It was hard to believe that human beings had built such gigantic structures. I wondered what purposes lay concealed behind their immense geometry—or reared them here in a lifeless desert. Unable to conceive any other use for them, Israel has always assumed that these were sacred monuments and marveled at the spiritual power of the Ancients, manifest in the very scale and symmetry of their projects.

By tradition, however, these structures are also linked with the Dissolution of the Ancients and are therefore known as the "Temples of Destruction." It occurred to me that if these huge structures were indeed connected with whatever destroyed the Ancients, then they had obviously failed in their purpose to deter or propitiate. In truth, however, I doubted that Israel had any concept of what happened to the Ancients. Nonetheless, I gazed upon their ruined monuments with awe. They are like the world, it seemed to me – vast and menacing and impervious to our understanding.

The river at this point braided into many shallow channels through sand and mud bars. The captain stood in the bow to make the best way through, barking orders as he felt for the riverbed with a pole. In spite of my general indifference, I appreciated his skill. At a brief rest stop one of the crew exclaimed, "Look," pointing upward. We could see dark specks circling overhead in the afternoon sky. "It won't be long now," another of the crew remarked. The river in this reach stank of death, and the men covered their faces with cloths and muttered protective charms. One crewman claimed that we would see bones in the sandbars from now on, but I observed none. A column of smoke on the horizon marked our destination, and the crew exerted their best efforts to attain it.

After more weary hours, while the sun appeared to hang motionless above the mountains, we made the bend where the Great Jordan turns from east to south flowing. Here, for centuries, has been the pilgrim site where Israel comes to confront its mortality: Meribah, the sanctuary of healing waters.

IV

The sanctuary of Meribah lies on a narrow strip of land in the Jordan; it is neither Israelite nor Kuhlan land, but suspended between. The island is three miles in length and low-lying – hardly more impressive at first sight than a sand bar that survives long enough to sprout sagebrush and cottonwoods. But the base of the island is solid basalt, and thus it belongs to the land rather than to the river. Meribah lies in the heart of the Desolation, where both banks are forbidden to Kuhlan and Israelite alike, and thus the shrine serves as a way station in the river commerce as well as a site of pilgrimage. The route upstream would be impracticable without this layover, the only hallowed, unpolluted ground and the only fresh water in the Desolation.

On the lee side of the island was a harbor built of stone and capable of sheltering a considerable fleet. We secured the carrack and made a brief ceremony of thanksgiving for our safe journey. Then I set off alone, leaving the captain and crew to pitch camp near the landing. As one of the most sacred places in Israel, Meribah was a curiosity to me, and, had Justin been my companion, I would have been eager to explore it. Here the old and infirm, and especially those suffering from the tumors, come seeking a miraculous cure – or, failing that, a peaceful death on holy ground. I noted many children, wan and disfigured by disease, who had come to face their untimely fate – or to seek miraculous rescue from it. It is said that St. Supplicee himself visited here, not to preach but to see, and seeing, to weep. Legend has it that the famous healing waters of Meribah are his tears. Much cause for tears was visible from where I stood, but such stories of the origins of shrines are for children and the credulous.

A more likely account of the origin of the shrine dates it from the age of the Governors—from Governor Posedas, in fact, and his infamous quarantine law. All those suffering from the mysterious wasting disease, ayudas, were exiled here with their families, even their children. The disease was particularly insidious, in that parents often passed it to their children at birth, and one might carry the disease for years and spread it without exhibiting any symptoms oneself. Spread by intercourse and blood, it was invariably fatal and therefore threatened the existence of the nation. Governor Posedas was reviled for his harsh policy, but the disease had eventually disappeared. The first priesthood of Meribah consisted of the uninfected children of the diseased who were forced to live out their lives here. Gradually the site become hallowed by their suffering and by the many deaths here, and eventually it became safe to visit. Over time, the emasculation forced upon the male victims of the disease became a sign of holiness and a mark of its priesthood.

As I approached the central shrine, I passed camps of invalids and sufferers from every kind of malady, but especially age. There appeared to be a host of the sick, all dwelling in tents according to their infirmities. Further up the path lay a stone corral as large as that by my grandfather's stronghold, with many head of sheep, cattle, and goats. Surely, the business of blood sacrifice and burnt offerings was thriving here. *A Glanz enterprise, no doubt!*

Near the center of the island stood a jumble of buildings, low and crudely made. The buildings were of rough basalt and housed a permanent priesthood as well as wayfarers and pilgrims, of whom a considerable number were present. A small tent city had been erected outside the compound, as the number of pilgrims had outgrown the permanent facilities. The sanctuary itself was unimpressive, even ugly, though its very starkness seemed to compel reverence and to hush the voices of pilgrims and rough sailors alike. The low stone buildings opened onto a plaza, roughly rectangular in shape. In the center was the well, the source of the mysterious healing powers of the place. It was in appearance a well such as any town in Israel might possess, or many a wealthy stronghold. It was unroofed, and marked by only a low stone enclosure. The well was surrounded by stone benches, erected for pilgrims waiting to be healed. Behind it lay the altar, a long low slab of unhewn basalt where sacrifices were conducted. I judged that the altar was a Messiahist innovation, probably not more than a century old.

The sanctuary, still baking in the late afternoon heat, was swept clean and empty. The low voices of two priests conducting a blessing ceremony about the altar were barely audible beneath the drone of flies – the inevitable presence at, and, in my view, the chief beneficiaries of blood rites. There was a heavy stench about the place, like that of a shambles. I was greeted by three members of the Meribah priesthood, who were covered with gore and dressed in the filthy rags that are a famous feature of the site. They invited me by gestures to exchange my own outer garment for a moth-eaten surplice, of the kind which pilgrims don and wear until they leave the Desolation, but I refused. As weapons were not permitted inside the plaza, I bowed curtly and retired, happy to place a distance between their vocation and myself. I determined to sleep in the open that night. The thought of entering one of the wayfarers' disease and fly-infested inns was over-poweringly repulsive.

The northwestern end of the island was relatively empty. I found a trail and followed it through the sagebrush. Twice I had to assist rattlesnakes off the trail with the tip of my scabbard. Clearly, this would be no place to walk after dark. I found a small clearing suitable for my exercises and performed them. As I returned, somewhat refreshed and wanting a swallow of water, the sun was just sinking behind the western mountains. I saw some apparently healthy travelers perched on an outcropping of rock and joined them. They were examining the landscape of the Desolation, which lay to the southwest. The Temples of Destruction were still visible in the twilight, along with one very large crater nearby.

One man, whom I recognized as a passenger from the carrack, was scanning the area through a telescope. A slender, plain-looking man, he had attracted my notice before, when we observed the ominous dust trail on the Kuhlan plains. He was unusually tall and thin for an Israelite and was of a type commonly seen in Judah but seldom elsewhere. His skin was the color of basalt, and his hair was curly rather than straight, dull rather than glossy. I seated myself near him on the rock, and he silently handed me the glass. I nodded my thanks and had a closer look at this mysterious landscape. I saw no sign of life anywhere. The large crater on the western bank had filled with water, perhaps eons ago, but dark-colored trails of debris were still visible radiating out from it. I searched carefully and saw that there were no swallows above the Jordan. No swallows meant no insects. The land and river were dead.

"No sign of life anywhere," I said, handing back the glass. It was my first comment in several days. I coughed, finding my voice strange in my ears.

"Perhaps I should introduce myself," he said.

"Yes," I replied. "I recognize you from the carrack. My name is. . . ."

"I know very well who you are," he interrupted. "I am Rehab Gill."

I stiffened. Here was the companion Ben Gurion had ordered me to take with me to Naphtali. I examined him carefully, suppressing a host of questions. He was dressed in shabby civilian clothing; truly, there was nothing military about him. He seemed loosely connected at the joints and a little stooped, although I noticed that his neck and arms, though slender, were muscular. His face and eyes were perfectly impassive.

"I had intended to introduce myself earlier," he said, "but I was afraid that you might mistake me for a sacrificial beast."

His words were an ironic reference to the incident at the junction. Their hostility was muted just enough for a jest. I chose to take it as such. "Yes," I said, making as if to draw my sword. "You do remind me of something aching to be slaughtered."

He raised his hands, palm outwards in mock dismay – his palms were light pink and contrasted sharply with the backs of his hands and arms.

"So," I said, sheathing my sword, but speaking more sternly. "You deceived me. Why?"

"I merely postponed introducing myself. If you drew unwarranted conclusions from that, that is your affair."

This time there was no mistaking his tone; it was as arrogant as his words. I recalled myself pacing impatiently on the docks at Hebron, arguing with the captain to delay sailing until Captain Gill arrived, and my anger welled up again. "You deceived me," I repeated. *"Why?"*

"General Ben Gurion thought it wise that I try to estimate your character before we began our collaboration."

"Ben Gurion? Ben Gurion told me that you were an accountant." It struck me that this man had very little of the shop or counting house about him. If he truly were of merchant origins, those features had been worn off by recent experience of a different kind. I decided it would be unwise to underestimate him. "So," I said, "what is it that you do for the Eyes of Israel?"

"Ah," he replied, "you are not as obtuse as the General implied."

We regarded one another in the deepening twilight. "Whatever your mission may be," I said at last, "it surely cannot be to assist in mine."

"Perhaps I shall assist you," he replied. "It will depend. . . ."

I had already learned to detest him; I was imagining with grim pleasure the act of throwing his decapitated body into the river, when a procession of pilgrims and priests passed us. The priests carried many litters of unfortunate people who appeared wasted with disease, and all lying motionless on their pallets. Each had been marked with a seal on his forehead. Then I saw with horror that each person had a cord tied around his neck; they had been strangled. The priests set the litters down and held a brief ceremony on the riverbank, which they conducted impassively. Then the bodies of the slain pilgrims were thrown into the Jordan like so many pieces of driftwood.

"Your health!" I said to Captain Gill, and turned my back on him.

V

Wishing to be as far from such rites as possible, I walked back toward the landing and joined a group of woodcutters around a small fire. To my relief, they all appeared to be hale men engaged in the river trade, not pilgrims with fatal illnesses. Visitors who are not themselves seeking a cure are expected to split wood for the burnt offerings and the many cremations that take place here. A dozen or so such men were roasting stick bread, and they invited me to join them.

Before we could introduce ourselves, we were joined by a small, agile old man. He was bald, with a few coarse hairs on his chin, like a goat, and was naked to the waist, wearing only an ephod in the night breeze. He was obviously a Third Comer priest, but of what particular persuasion I could not tell from his garb. He introduced himself as a second-class servitor of the sanctuary, mentioning no tribe or homeland or patrimony. He chatted with us a while, asking shrewd questions of each of us, and I soon realized what he was about.

Shortly he arose and stood with both arms outstretched toward the fire, as if warming his skinny limbs. Then he began speaking in a high-pitched, monotonous voice, as if what he said he had by memory. "Some come to Meribah to be healed," he announced; "some come to die. You are all welcome. May the merciful Lord grant you peace, whichever you seek." It was none of his affair, his manner said, if the merciful Lord chose to be patient with fools. "Those who come here," he said, "draw near to God. Whether you seek Him or not, He is here. This is the place of His judgment and His fiercest wrath, on the day He made the Earth his footstool. Who can look on this place and not believe?"

I recognized in this last reference the Third Comer doctrine of Judgment Day. "In ancient times," the priest continued, "the Son of Man returned in glory and gathered the faithful up into His Kingdom. Thus," he declared with some asperity, as if he were aware of doubters in the audience, "the evildoers were dealt with on the Day of Wrath. The Lamb gathered them all in this place – you can see it across the Jordan yonder, in daylight. The wicked were utterly destroyed in a single great cataclysm, the effects of which are still plain to behold around us."

The crowd murmured their uneasy assent to these premises. The sunset had faded. In the west, just above the horizon, a dark line of clouds announced an approaching storm. As it grew dark, distant flashes of light played above the mountain crests.

"Judgment Day," the priest repeated softly, and several in the group stirred and nodded, glancing toward the core of the Desolation. A cool breeze raised the hair on my arms. "On Judgment Day, the Son of Man and His Angels had combat with the Prince of Evil. 'And I saw an angel, ascending from the east, having the seal of the living God; and he cried with a loud voice to the four angels, to whom it was given to hurt the earth and the sea, saying, Hurt not the earth, neither the sea, nor the trees, till we have sealed the servants of our God in their foreheads.' And He split the earth and imprisoned the great dragon, Beli-az, in the Bottomless Pit beneath – beneath us here, where we sit. The great dragon, Beli-az," the priest repeated solemnly, as if anticipating our skepticism, "stirs in the depths, and his struggle to free himself makes the earth tremble; his rage is the fire that splits the mountains. He is impatient to come up again."

I found the naiveté of his tale laughable, but most in the group listened avidly. I noticed that Gill had joined the group and was sitting quietly to my left. I had to admit, the setting lent a certain grim credibility to the story. The unimaginable violence visited upon this spot at some moment in the past cried out for explanation. The priest then described the turning away of the Messiah's face from the earth: "The land and rivers and oceans, all originally created clean and wholesome for man's use, He cursed eternally, because of the evil that men had done to the earth. He cursed the earth and the sea and the trees and the rivers, forever more."

While it was a performance the priest must have given countless times, and he made no special effort to work upon the emotions of his audience, his words nevertheless moved many of our small group to lamentation. I longed to have Justin's impressions of what I saw. I must attest to the power of the tale, which resonated with so much of ordinary experience. The despoiling of creation is a story enacted in each of us, in large and small ways, in the misuse of what is good. An eventual Judgment Day lends our stories a principle of symmetry and a kind of account-balancing at the end. I wondered if Captain Gill, with his accountant's heart, would be drawn to that aspect of the tale. The doctrine of Judgment Day is an explanation of considerable power: it tells us why our world is spoiled and promises its recovery. It imposes meaning on a life experience that is otherwise baffling and unsatisfying. I recalled Ben Gurion's words to me as I lay trussed like a fowl at his hacienda: "Justice is a young man's fancy. But you outgrow the need for it." I believe Ben Gurion wrong; many never put aside their desire for that perfect alignment of rewards and desserts. For them, that hunger is a deep, unsleeping need. At the same time, however, I acknowledged with Ben Gurion that justice has no part in the nature of things. There is no single point in time when everything will be made right and even. There is no Judgment Day.

Captain Gill nudged me, and I turned my attention to the priest. The old man, suddenly seized with passion, stooped and took up a handful of earth. "What remains for us," he demanded, "for those who live on after Judgment Day? What but this," he said opening his hand: "a handful of dust."

Afterwards he told his tale in a whisper: "With the faithful gathered into Paradise with the Lamb and the evil-doers destroyed, there was left on Earth only a pitiful remnant of the Unsealed – those who were neither good nor evil. Those who, because they did not choose, were not chosen. Their destiny was to survive and replenish themselves endlessly – to endure miserably and without hope among the ruins of creation. *Here,* in the Desolation!" The priest paused for dramatic effect, his eyes searching his listeners. "Abandoned by the Creator and Savior, living in a world accursed, *we* thus play out our pathetic lives generation after generation, after the end of time." As the crowd contemplated its desolate plight, the old man shouted in a great voice, "Salvation to our God, who sits upon the throne, and to the Lamb! Come, Lord Jesus! Come quickly, again!"

"Amen, amen!" responded a number in his audience.

In spite of my disbelief, I admired the priest's eloquence, his dramatic shifts in tone, and the pathos of his delivery. He was a skilled performer who invited his auditors to underestimate him and then swept them up in his artful rhetoric. I had to acknowledge that his tale, even apart from his flair in telling it, had a certain resonance with experience. My own life had aspects from which I could wish to be rescued. The Messiahists have a special word for it – *redemption* – which they do not define very clearly. Its original meaning, I am told, is to "buy back," a phrase not very helpful in grasping the concept.

But the tale the priest told has its objectionable side as well: "It is only in these latter days," he said, "that men have begun to hear again the voices of Angels and Spirits and to prophesy a great mercy. For centuries, the message was only a whisper, uncertain and unconfirmed. But further revelation of God's will remained the last and only hope of a degenerate race, poised, perhaps forever, in this wasteland between good and evil. Whether the earth would be destroyed or simply abandoned to serve as the eternal prison of Beli-az was not clear. Some said that the sign of the Last Days would be the release of the Dragon and that the very sun itself would diminish and wink out. Others said a great flood of healing waters would well upward from Meribah, cleansing the faithful from all stain. All was uncertainty and dread and anxious waiting. But then came the discovery of the lost *Book of Bezor* and the *Meditations* of Polymer I, blessed be his name, the holy Messenger of all Messengers, who foretold the Lord's coming yet again a third time, seeking His lost sheep."

There were mingled sighs and groans from the audience. "And the sign," he continued, "now known to all, shall be the recovery of the faithfully departed from the depths of the Jordan. Released from the Waters of Death itself, they shall live again in the light of His countenance!" The priest ended his tale with a request for alms – or, failing that, for assistance in the cremations, which, he explained, took place at night to avoid troubling the devout. There were many poor, and no one could be cremated without a fee.

The priest had articulated perfectly all I detested in Messiahist doctrines. Aside from dividing the world into simple dichotomies of good and evil, which seemed folly to me, the Third Comer beliefs rested on scriptures of doubtful provenance and therefore carried with them the troubling issue of authority. Believe in those who hear the voices, they demanded, or be branded a heretic. Their claim to knowledge of the world's fate, if not accepted at face value, defined any who rejected their claims as rebels. The Messiahist creed was intrinsically an act of aggression and a threat. To accept their claims was to yield to the power of the claimant; to reject their messenger was to define oneself as an enemy of their god.

The priest and his small audience had left Gill and myself by the embers of the fire. "You lack the enraptured look of the convert," Gill said to me. "What is it that has kept you straying from the fold?"

My anger at him had somehow evaporated, and I found myself almost eager for conversation—anxious, perhaps, for an opportunity to explain what I so opposed in the Messiahist creed. "I am no Third Comer," I said, "and I reject all claims to revelation and all authority derived from them. There is no perfect knowledge and no revealed Word. What we Old Believers possess, though imperfect, is adequate to human needs. We live by the teachings of St. Supplicee, which have come down to us through the commentaries of his disciples. Not actually disciples in the sense of men who were his contemporaries and sat at his feet, as many of the ignorant believe, but men who lived close after him in time, and who received his teachings devoutly and reflected upon them deeply." I explained that we neither needed nor desired absolute truth, and we rejected all Third Comer claims as fraudulent.

"I see," Gill replied. "And you say that only Third Comers live by mindless slogans?"

"Ours are not slogans," I said, "but principles of action. Clement condemns these very excesses in Messiahist doctrine – the excesses in all revealed religion. They demand implicitly that you trust the revealer, the individual who claims the revelation. If that is not dangerous, I cannot imagine what is. Clement warned that

> *"There are no obstacles to understanding greater than those*
> *that the mind itself engenders:*
> *first, the harlot Superstition, which is the daughter of Fear;*
> *then Prophecy, which is the daughter of Hope;*
> *third, Piety, which is the daughter of Grief.*
> *If you would overcome them all, you must avoid their embrace.*
> *You must avoid the embrace of Fear, of false Hope, and of Grief.*
> *Know that they are begotten by Ignorance upon Desire."*

"Thus, we Old Believers do not live by false promises; it is understanding we seek—

the wisdom to live in the world as it is."

Captain Gill affected to scoff at Clement's words—and mine. "Avoid fear and hope and grief? Give up living, in other words! I've studied your doctrines, and you Old Believers can justify anything you choose from your texts," he said scornfully.

"Our rules which have come down to us from the Masters are all contextual and demand application. We do not live by lists of simple-minded commands."

"But surely you see that if a saying such as Clemont's is not clear as a rule, it is ineffective as a guide to life."

"Not at all," I rejoined, confident that Clemont needed no defense of mine. "Clemont says: *'Call an action good if it sustains the beauty, integrity, and harmony of the world; evil those actions that tend to do the opposite.'* A simple, terse command, such as the Third Comers love, may seem clearer and appear to be universally true, but you must in any actual case decide whether the rule applies. Our precepts are a guide to responsible thinking, not an escape from it. Our tradition invites us into acts of interpretation and application; it does not pretend to do otherwise."

"Perhaps," he conceded. "But what about the gibberish of Master Israel Zhen-Gwo? *'Cleave the wood, break the stone; enter the fire. There am I.'* What can that possibly mean? Who and what in your creed could call itself *I*? And if this adage means anything, what use is it?"

Gill seemed to betray his accountant's heart, demanding the unambiguous and practical application in all things. "We ourselves are an expression of the Way," I explained. "It is natural for us to seek understanding and harmony. In doing so, we clear away the clutter and illusion in our minds and lead a life natural to ourselves, purged of falsehood and vanity and fear. That is the essence of pursuing the Way."

"Hah!" Gill retorted. "You call contradictions instruction? Negations insight?"

It occurred to me that anger would be my natural response to such provocation, but, for some reason, I was not at all stirred to passion. "Each of us enters upon the Way in our own time and of our own accord," I said.

Gill looked at me a moment as if my answer had surprised him; then his eyes narrowed. "What about the teachings of Master Ebenezer," he demanded, "a sage who advocates extinguishing the self in action – even in violence – as the best means of discovering the Way? Do you not find Ebenezerism as dangerous as the claims of Polymer?"

I sat bolt upright as a log snapped and flared. *Ebenezer had been my teacher, my Master at the Refuge.* The reason for our conversation—and perhaps the reason for Gill's mission to accompany me – was suddenly clear. "Master Ebenezer. . . ," I replied cautiously, searching for words. "I am surprised that you have heard about such an obscure rural teacher. Master Ebenezer has been much maligned and even worse understood. The world has nothing to fear from him."

He would have replied, but we were interrupted by another procession passing by our fire. The old priest, assisted by a subordinate class of clerics, was leading a group of pilgrims to the river. Those pilgrims who seemed whole or nearly so, would, I assumed, be washed in the Jordan; those who were past all hope would be taken to the river later, after another kind of ceremony. The sight filled me with unutterable sadness. I thought again of the changes coming over Israel. In the old days, it had been the duty of the landed families to provide for the afflicted and to care for their dependents. In those days the sick had found solace among loved ones and friends and had died among familiar surroundings. In these days, of course, such amenities were impossible; the number afflicted with the tumors was staggering. And those with means – increasingly the rich merchants – lacked that sense of engrained responsibility that the landed lords had possessed.

Then I remembered my grandfather.

"Interesting sentiments," Gill interrupted. "I had expected to find you an ignorant devotee of the old cults, for such is your reputation. Instead, I find a religious antiquarian – well informed, but a relic of a bye-gone century. But like all the Unsealed, you hunger and are not filled; you thirst and are not satisfied."

I shrugged, thinking of the sick and dying.

"You might be interested to know," Gill continued, "that our fellow passenger, Won Datzen, miller and grain factor – the man whose humble sacrificial offering you violated – suspects you of being a Dolorite. There is similar talk back at the camp. The First Mate accuses you of being an agent of one of the suppressed secret societies. The evidence, I admit, would seem to point that way."

A sudden fury blazed up in me, and I found myself standing over Gill with my sword half-drawn. "Tell him – tell your Won Datzen and the First Mate – tell them that they'll find out soon enough what I am. And tell them that Dolorites who have not declared themselves are not forgiving of those who provoke them. If this Won Datzen feels my blade on his throat tonight, he'll *know* that I am a Dolorite. But that is the *last* thing he will ever know. Tell him *that*!"

VI

I stalked away in the darkness. My feet found the trail to the sanctuary and, after a time, mindful of snakes, I approached the first encampment I came to, hoping for a place by a fire. I bitterly regretted my outburst, which was foolish in the extreme, but words cannot be recalled. My night of surprises, however, was not over. My greeting was answered by the clank of metal chains and curses. I heard a woman's voice and saw the form of a man struggle into a sitting position, his motion betraying the presence of an iron collar and chains. I had stumbled onto a slave coffle bedded down for the night. I groaned, feeling as though I had wandered into a nightmare from which I could not awake.

"Get out of here, scum!" a voice behind me said, and I felt myself pushed violently in the back. I nearly collided with a large man with a pointed beard and a rank, sweaty odor who had risen before me. As I struggled to regain my balance, he tapped me menacingly on the chest with a large bullwhip, and I felt the rough grip of the man who had pushed me from behind. "You have no business here, get out!" the man with the whip growled in my ear.

A moment later I was standing over both of them, my chest heaving, the whip in my hand. The man who had held the whip was sprawled on the ground, holding his bloody mouth and nose; the other man lay face down and appeared to be unconscious. "I am an officer and a Name in Israel," I said to the conscious one. "I have a right to expect courtesy, *and I demand it*." When he lay silent, seeming to ignore me, I gave him a kick in the ribs, and he said, "Yes! *Yes!*" very quickly.

"Don't be alarmed," I said to the chained figures lying near me. These wretches lay about me clad only in rags, without cover. Some of them failed even to stir in all the commotion. It was beginning to be cool, so I put wood on the fire. I knelt by a robust middle-aged man, intending to ask why they were all in chains when, in the light of the flames I saw the answer: "You are Israelites!" I exclaimed.

"Benjamites," he said. My heart jumped to my throat.

"From?"

"Esdralon."

Israel's own flesh sold into slavery! My heart recoiled from the cruelty of it, to subject those not bred to servitude to such humiliation. I had a sudden, horrified thought of Michal-Rebekah and Appian. Could it be possible? I seized a burning brand and searched the group, but only succeeded in terrorizing the women and children. There were more than twenty of them, all twelve years of age and upwards; no elderly and no young children. It was not a good sign. *The world does not weep*, St. Supplicee says. But to act more cruelly to one's fellow beings than nature does, that is beyond understanding.

I hushed their whimpers as best I could and begged them for news of Michal-Rebekah and Appian. The two were in fact known to them, though their fate was not. I spoke with each separately. They were dazed and depressed and could not give a good account of themselves, let alone speak of the fortunes of others. They reported that arrests and enslavements had been going on for two weeks in Esdralon; a multitude were being shipped northwards. I was staggered. "So this is Messiahist policy," I said. "To depopulate Engedi by enslaving and selling off the population who were spared by their cruel occupation!"

"Messiahists? No, this is Ben Gurion's doing. Tephlin Glanz's doing!"

I sat down heavily on the ground, wishing it would open and swallow me. So, then, was there nothing to choose between the two sides? After a moment, I collected myself, bowed to the Benjamite elder, and then hurried back to the camp where my baggage lay. I returned with provisions of bread and dried fruit. I made each of the Benjamites rouse themselves and eat; they had been poorly treated and were not over the shock of their enslavement. If they did not take in nourishment, they would begin to die. I made them all drink abundantly as well. Above all, I tried to leave each with a message of hope. The war would be over soon, I told them. The Harlech would ransom them.

"They'll never find us," a man said bitterly. "We are being sold beyond Lebanon into the metal recovery mines. The Glanz mines."

"Even in Lebanon or beyond," I assured them, "the Harlech will find their own." I made a list of their names and the names of others they knew who had been taken. They asked to know who I was, but I was ashamed to speak. "I am a soldier who served in your country," I said, "but I am no enemy of Benjamin."

Before departing, I knelt before the Benjamite man and held his hand to my forehead, to witness the vow I whispered: never to raise a hand or weapon against Benjamin again. I left these unfortunates reluctantly, feeling that the differences that divided me from the crew of the carrack were of no consequence whatever compared to those that divided me from my father.

When I awoke in the morning, Rehab Gill was waiting nearby, leaning against a stone fence, his head tipped back. He was drinking water from a leather bottle in long, deep swallows. When he noticed me, he stopped the bottle and set it on the wall. "I have spoken to the First Mate," he said, without preamble. "And to Won Datzen. I have some good news and some bad news. Datzen and the First Mate no longer think you are a Dolorite."

"No?" I replied groggily.

"They think you are a fool."

I started to make a harsh reply, but I stopped myself, reflecting that my argument with this tactless, provocative Gill was the first time I had spoken in several days. Our debate and his sarcasm reminded me vaguely of Justin – a Justin without grace or charm, but with the same sharp tongue. "Very often," I replied, "I am of the same mind as they."

I roused myself, feeling a sudden determination to end this foolish enmity with Datzen and the other passengers. I washed myself and then sought out the tents where the passengers and crew had camped. I found Datzen standing beside the captain's tent and called out his name. My determination, but not the nature of my intentions, must have been clear, for he shrank back and looked frantically about for assistance. Gill had doubtlessly spread my foolish words about vengeful Dolorites through the camp. Datzen would have fled, but I caught his garment and held him. The first mate and others began to raise a cry, thinking I meant to do him harm. "Don't be such fools," I shouted, exasperated to the point of forgetting my intent.

Datzen struggled weakly in my grasp. As I held him at arm's length, I noted suddenly his unsymmetrical, slightly misshapen face. There was a bulge under his right eye, a puffy, slightly discolored area in his cheek. I stared at his face, recognizing what I should have seen immediately. Under the skin a tumor was gnawing at his face. Had it penetrated his skull? Was a malignant tendril reaching even now toward his brain? Had the man come here in desperation for a cure, or had he made provision for his family and come to Meribah to die? I recalled the saying that *the parent's tumor marks the child's face*. What dowry would buy his child a marriage when the father's face announced so publicly his grandchildren's probable fate? In all likelihood, it would be better for his children if he did not return from this pilgrimage. I knew that these things must be clear to him as well. So much was certain, and yet still unresolved was the question of his own courage: whether he could find enough of it to face the cord and the garrote.

Datzen continued to struggle weakly, his eyes bulging. He was trying to apologize, to turn away my wrath, as he imagined it. I held him fast with both hands, seeing him cringe in terror, and said, almost furiously, "It is *I* who owe you an apology. My discourtesy was unforgivable, but I ask you to forgive me." Seeing his eyes still wide with fear, I released him and bowed before him, touching my hand to the ground. "Truly," I said, trying to reassure him, but seeing his mouth still gape as wide as his eyes. "It is I who owe you an apology. I ask you to forgive me."

Knowing even as I spoke of forgiveness that consequences follow us forever.

Chapter 7: Crossing Over Jordan

I

What weighed on my heart like a stone was not the fate of this foolish man. It was his flabby hand raised to ward off, as he thought, a blow from me, that took me back to the citadel of Esdralon and the bloody work I had done there. Though I had acted in a trance, goaded beyond my powers of reason, I had raged through the citadel without mercy, like a butcher in the shambles. I was not born to shed the blood of my fellow beings in a pitiless fury, but I had been trained for it. I saw the truth of that reflected in Won Datzen's eyes.

Rehab Gill and I began our mutually unwelcome collaboration that same unhappy day. "We are effectively stranded on Meribah," Gill announced with evident distaste. "Hanford Glanz has declared an embargo on all trade with the south of Israel. No ships are going north to Chinnereth. I just had the news."

"This is impossible! We have already engaged our passage." Appalled as I was at my own fatal temper, I was nonetheless roused near to violence by this news.

"It's true," he said. "The embargo must be a counter-move in Hanford's struggle of wills with your father. It seems that things have come very close to war. For the moment, no traffic is going north, and none will be coming south. "We'll see about that!" I retorted. But when I insisted that our ship captain continue the voyage to Chinnereth as agreed, he refused. "Israel keeps its contracts," I said angrily. "Or it did before we played with prophecy and sacrifice!" Gill pulled me aside before I could say more.

Not desiring to add to my reputation for rashness, I let him have his way. Abandoned by the captain and crew of the carrack, we were unable to find any further passage. No ships were going forward, and there was no land route through the Desolation, so we were at a loss as to how proceed. I suggested that we show my orders from General Ben Gurion to the captain of a military vessel, preferably a water strider, and commandeer their services. "I have my authority from the Council itself," I reminded him. "I suppose these Judean ship captains still take orders and respect the chain of command."

Gill demurred, saying that Judah's fleet had strict orders not to proceed beyond Meribah. "Besides," he added, "given the nature of your instructions, it would be best not to make them known. You never know who is in the pay of Hanford Glanz."

"Is he so dangerous?"

"Dangerous enough that I have taken the trouble to identify you to everyone who would listen as a discharged and deranged veteran. That's what the Captain and Datzen and the others believed of you at the end. It was, by the way, an easy story to establish."

"Why trouble yourself?" I retorted. "Who cares who or what I am? And why am I different from any other pilgrim to this charnel house?"

He shook his head in disbelief. "You are unlike other men. Surely you see that. But it is better that you be thought somewhat dangerous and unpredictable rather than to be recognized for what you are."

"And what's that?" I demanded, suddenly fearful.

"Someone who is extremely dangerous and unpredictable." Gill had clearly found a vocation in taunting me. Nevertheless, I felt relieved that his comment was only a taunt. "The scars on your forehead help establish the story," he continued soberly. "Your head-wound is a convincing detail, but your whole manner is what carries it through." He had spread about that I was a fanatical Old Believer conducting a pilgrimage in the footsteps of St. Supplicee. Ill fortune had thrown us together, and he intended to complain widely and bitterly about me as he arranged transportation for us northward.

"Complain away!" I replied. With great effort, I bore his arrogance and consented to his arrangements. That my instructions represented both a rebuke and a threat to Hanford Glanz was obviously true, and if he were only half as ruthless as reported, he would surely resist the order of the Council.

To my surprise, Gill showed himself energetic and capable in renting a small skiff and purchasing provisions that same day. At his suggestion, we spent the afternoon and evening as widely separated as possible. I spent the day on the rocky outcrop contemplating the landscape of the Desolation, thinking on many things and, truth to say, brooding on many more. I thought of Esdralon and its suffering, hoping against hope that Michal-Rebekah had somehow escaped both the malice of the churchmen and my father's cruelty. I grieved for my dead brother, and I thought of Major Vashon, my new friend and ally. I had not seen the Vashons since our expedition against the Kr, or communicated with them since my note after Justin's arrest. The attention Ben Gurion had given my innocent message to the Major alerted me to the dangers of corresponding with them. After my elevation by Ben Gurion as the "Scourge of the Messiahists" in Hebron, I felt as if I had a target painted on my back. It would obviously be best to separate the Vashons from my fate, if possible. I missed them, but it was better to go forward into this wilderness alone. Fortunately, there were few Messiahists where I was going.

Meanwhile, the Vashons evoked memories of Tirzah, where I had spent my earliest days, and I wondered if I would ever return to claim my inheritance – my Haggadah inheritance. My Glanz inheritance, I reflected bitterly, lay all around me, imaged in the Desolation itself.

Putting these thoughts aside, I turned my attention to my mission to Naphtali. I had received my commission from the hands of the fragile old man who served as Shepherd of Israel and Elder of the Council of Apostles. My task, to "restore harmony and justice in Naphtali," had been given to me in the very language of the investiture rite of an Apostle. I had been honored and entrusted with responsibilities far beyond my years and experience. And yet, at the same time, I could not but recall, this entire charade had been arranged by Simon ben Gurion, one of the most cynical schemers in Israel. And it was not hard to imagine my father's shadowy presence behind him. Was my charge authentic, or was the Council merely a tool of my father's? Was my mission a jest or a death sentence? And upon what foundation could I hope to restore justice in such a world? Justin would have liked the irony, but the sacrilege of it made my head swim and stars flash and dazzle before my eyes.

Remembering my discipline, I visualized my anger as sand in an hour glass. I watched the grains flow through several times, and then at last, empty of both rage and grief, I was able to focus on the problem to be solved: my mission. I could understand the importance of Naphtali in the events that were unfolding. Because of the plague of ticks, Naphtali was accessible to the rest of Israel only via the Jordan, which Judah controlled. Thus, Naphtali, the northern-most territory of Israel, lay for all practical purposes adjacent to Judah, to which it was closely tied by blood as well as by commerce. Naphtali was a gateway to other lands and other peoples to the north – the only other peoples, besides the Kuhlans and the Kr, that Israel knew. The regions to the north had abundant resources. In addition to its wealth, Naphtali possessed a fleet that could patrol the Jordan's dangerous middle reaches where the Kuhlans liked to cross. That fleet could figure mightily in Israel's defense if the Kuhlans came over against us. Or, if the Messiahists lay siege to Hebron, Judah could be supplied indefinitely by Naphtali, or their fleet could disembark an army to relieve the city. Thus, control of Naphtali and the upper reaches of the Jordan could be decisive in defense from Kuhlan *or* Messiahist attack. No wonder Tephlin Glanz and his faction desired to re-establish control of the north. *But why had they dispatched me to accomplish it?*

I could see the strategic possibilities quite clearly, but I had no answers to my questions. Neither I nor anyone else could foresee the outcome of this new war, other than the immense suffering it would bring. Who would prove stronger, the churchmen or my father's faction? The nobles still led the army, and they had yet to speak in their own behalf. How would they choose, when the moment came? And how long, I wondered, would Israel continue to savage itself, to unravel the fragile ties that held it together as a community?

In the midst of these uncertainties, a tantalizing thought occurred to me: *Whoever held Naphtali might be able to answer these questions.*

II

We cast off that night, hoping to avoid detection. It was a day and a half sail to Chinnereth. Our course was due west from the great bend of Meribah, and we made fair progress in the moonlight. At dawn, a steady breeze blew up so that we made good time. Gill minded the sail and I the tiller, each of us swallowing a handful of pemmican and a few gulps of water as we went. In this reach, the river flowed through a barren wilderness uninhabited by human beings. With the ban on northbound travel, the Jordan was deserted. Gill and I had little to say to one another and spoke even less than we had reason to. My companion did, however, prove a competent sailor – a skill unknown to me.

Once, during a calm, Gill asked me why I pulled so hard at the oars. I replied that I expected to overtake slavers such as I had seen at Meribah, and I intended to free all Benjamites that had been sold into bondage. "I intend to free all slaves taken into Naphtali. I have the Council's authority, and I intend to use it."

He shook his head in his arrogant way. "Good," he said. "Excellent! But I should point out to you that Ben Gurion and Tephlin Glanz would not approve. Not while the Council is trying to force the Harlech to negotiate."

"By enslaving fellow Israelites? The fools! The Harlech will never negotiate under such conditions. Can the Council not see that?"

"Glanz and Ben Gurion want the Harlech flank secured so they can deal with the Messiahists; they are in haste to do so. Thus, they are ruthless."

"They are *always* ruthless! They know nothing but force. These new men, these would-be rulers, do not know enough to break a colt to a bridle. They demand power, connive to have it, and squirm their way into office, only to use their power without responsibility. Their arrogance breeds terrible consequences for the nation."

"Perhaps," Gill said. "But don't forget whose commission you carry. Like it or not, these are men to whom you must answer." When I declared that I did not fear them, he said he was glad of it. "And I hope," he added, "that you may live to use your power – whatever it is, from whatever source it may derive, though I doubt that you will." He adjusted the sail expertly, swinging around to the other side of the skiff so that he faced me. "You seem anxious to use what is yours by gift and training only to destroy yourself." He would have pressed me on this subject, but I would not hear him.

Long before we hauled in sight of the stronghold, we heard the roar of the Jordan raging through the cataract of Chinnereth, site of the fifth dam of the Ancients. For a mile below it, the breeze above the river was cool with spray. At Chinnereth, the Jordan emerges from its deep canyon and turns sharply from southward to eastward. Chinnereth itself commanded the portage from the Desolate Reach of the Jordan northward. Steeply sloping canyon walls towered above it, barren and brown. It was a forbidding and isolated spot.

As we approached the landing, the thunder of the cataract rose like a storm in my ears. "What's this?" I asked Gill as we hove within good sight of the fortress above the broken dam. "Is this how Israel's borders are kept nowadays?" Fully garrisoned, the fortress could hold several hundred men; at the moment it looked deserted.

Gill said nothing, shading his eyes with one hand and holding the tiller with the other. Clustered about the south wall of the fortress were a group of ramshackle huts. Empty stone corrals stood below the village, and trash and wagon parts and other debris lay scattered about. The portage itself was paved with cobblestones and ran from the landing past the fortress and northward around the ruins of the Ancient's dam. The road alone seemed in decent repair. We tied up at the dock and transferred our luggage and provisions to the shore. There was no one to greet us or inspect our goods; the village seemed empty of inhabitants.

"Well, a more desolate, fly-infested heap of dung I never hope to see," I said. "Behold, Israel's first defense, alert and ready to repel the Kuhlans – if our good citizens chanced to notice their crossing!"

"I expect that the Kuhlans would by-pass this place," Gill said, eyeing the cliffs above the fort. "No sense stepping in shit just to massacre these people. Strange," he continued, "I don't see any military presence here. Where is the Guards Legion? Where is the assessor?"

It appeared that Naphtali had pulled its military forces back from the border, just as Judah had done to the south. At the moment, not a soul was in sight; not even a dog barked. A few speckled hens pecked at dung in the road. A tremendous feeling of depression settled over me. As we approached the main gate of Chinnereth, however, we heard a sudden commotion inside the walls and a babble of voices; then a cry of alarm rang out. "The place is inhabited after all," Gill said, touching the hilt of his sword. Then we heard shouts and wailing and a high-pitched woman's scream. We froze in place as a woman burst out of the gate, weeping and tearing her hair. I called to her and she stopped, her eyes flaring wide, like a horse in a burning barn. Tears had washed muddy streaks through the dust on her cheeks. When I tried to extract an explanation, she tore loose from me, stronger than many a man I have grappled with, and continued frantically on her way. Like the place itself, she was dirty and disheveled to a degree not often seen in Israel.

We hurried forward and entered the open gate of the stronghold. A ragged crowd had gathered in the center of the small plaza. There was much weeping and lamentation. In answer to our questions, a woman tearfully explained: "A child, a little girl, has fallen into the well!" Then she, too, ran through the gate, apparently in pursuit of the other. "Her child! Her baby!" she cried over her shoulder.

We pushed our way through the throng. The well of the stronghold lay near the center of the courtyard. Not even a retaining wall separated it from the plaza; any number of children or unwary beasts could easily disappear into its depths. "How long has the child been down there?" I asked, but no one paid any heed to me. Gill cleared a path for us and commanded silence. The crowd looked us over and then resumed its gabble. We exerted ourselves to clear a space around the well, attempting to quiet the wailing. I knelt over the well and listened for faint cries coming from below, but I could hear nothing.

"She's alive, but she's hurt," a man said to us. "She may be twenty feet down or more."

Just then a large drunken man lurched forward and pushed Gill aside. "Damn the luck! Damn the day!" he moaned. "I can't bear it! Oh, my little girl! It's my daughter trapped down there, fallen and entombed alive, and suffers! Oh!" His breath was hot with alcohol. Suddenly, he left off beating his breast and lurched through the crowd to the well. "Her voice!" he cried, his hands to his ears. "I cannot hear her cries and live! This is torture!" He seized a large stone and seemed about to hurl it down the well, apparently to crush the life out of the child. The women howled in horror, and several men lunged at him. Before I could move, Gill had sent him sprawling with a kick. The man let out a roar and rolled on the ground, clutching his hip. I motioned to two stout fellows to hold him down with their staves while I doused him with a bucket of water. Shocked and spluttering, he subsided and began weeping noisily. Several women began beating him with sticks, but he appeared too dazed to notice.

I looked around, searching for something effective to do. The crowd of villagers was in a panic. "You, there," I shouted at a pair of ragged but brawny men. "Fetch some large timbers! Quickly! There can't be much air down there." As I shouted instructions, I felt my own blood rising; their panic was infectious.

"But where, sir, begging your pardon, sir? There is no lumber here," one replied. "There is nothing," the others repeated. "There is nothing we can do!"

"Nonsense," I shouted, and drew my sword, taking one of them by the collar and motioning to half a dozen capable-looking men. "Captain!" I shouted. Gill responded briskly, and we managed to herd them like so many sheep out through the gate. I ordered them to demolish the first hut we came to, a sorry, falling-down affair that leaned against the fortress wall. It was the work of a moment. A man, apparently the occupant of the hut, jumped up and down shouting at me and frantically objecting to our labors. "Stop!" he shouted. "This is unjust! This is unlawful!"

"Your house is illegally placed," I replied. "The walls of a fortress must be kept cleared for defence. Stand aside." When he tried to interfere, Gill threw the man into the road. The hut came down in a cloud of dust. The roof timbers were about the right length. We carried the usable lumber to the courtyard, and I ordered two sets of three timbers lashed together at one end and set up as tripods on opposite sides of the well. The longest and sturdiest timber I placed horizontally across the tops of the tripods. It held my weight when I tried it, but it did not inspire confidence.

"Cottonwood!" Gill spat. "And rotten besides."

"It will have to do," I said. "Now we need a pulley. And rope. You there! Be quick about it!" I sent the villagers packing with curses and blows. Every portage on the Jordan has block and tackle and cranes to lift logs and other cargo out of the water. I knew that even this worthless rabble could find a pulley and ropes. In a short time, they returned and we rigged a pulley over the well.

"Well done, Captain," Gill said.

"Now for a harness," I said. I took the rope and looped it over Gill's torso, crossing from shoulder to groin and back again.

"What! Wait," he protested. "What are you doing?" He saw clearly enough that I was rigging a harness. I tied a knot securely at his waist in back, and then looped a torn blanket around the ropes where it would pull against his shoulders as he dangled upside down.

"It has to be you," I said, ignoring his protests. "You see the size of the hole, and you are the leanest man here, with the narrowest shoulders. Your shoulders will fit down the well, and mine won't."

"All right," he said, the white part of his eyes showing unnaturally large. "All right, then!" He shook himself. "Shit!" he said, staring at the well.

The makeshift harness was finished in a moment. In spite of his fear, Gill crawled headfirst down into the hole without a murmur. We lowered him slowly and waited tensely until he cried, in a voice muffled and strange, "I have her; pull me up! Pull!"

It was more difficult pulling them up than I anticipated. Gill was caught twice in the narrow passage, his body wedged against outcroppings of rock. We tugged gently to free him, shouting for him to hold onto the child at all costs. I feared he would lose consciousness from lack of air or from the pressure of blood in his brain and thus perish there himself. Somehow he held onto the girl until we could drag them both to the surface. As we raised them from the hole, a woman even more ragged and dirty than the rest swooped in and seized the little girl. We helped her lay the child gently on a soiled blanket. Gill drove back the crowd so she could have air. The child was breathing, but unconscious. She was delicate, almost bird-like, and looked to be about three years old. She had, under a layer of dirt, fair skin and light, almost blonde hair, betraying the slave blood in her ancestry. Her hands twitched and she turned her head back and forth, whimpering softly. She was badly scraped and bruised in several places. I ran my hands along her chest and then her limbs. She flinched in pain when I touched her hip and cried out for her mother. I noticed then that the woman, obviously the mother, whom we had seen run frantically through the gate, was standing to one side, hair awry and fingernails pressed into her cheeks. I motioned, and she came forward timidly. When she saw the little girl was alive, she sprang forward and would have caught her up in her arms, but Gill restrained her.

"She is alive," Gill said. "Be content she is alive. We need to examine her. Her hip may be dislocated."

I was surprised at his knowledge. "What do you make of her injury?" I asked, moving aside for him. "Is the joint intact?" Gill knelt beside me and slowly raised her knee; the child cried out, but her hip seemed in place. Then he pressed gently against her abdomen and lifted her eyelids to peer into her eyes. The child was gradually coming to herself and began to cry. Gill whispered reassuringly as he completed his examination. Then, satisfied that her injuries were superficial, he allowed her to be wrapped in a blanket and placed in her mother's arms. "Hold her carefully, carefully!" he said. Many hands helped to soothe the child and to wash her face and arms and hands with fresh water. At that moment, it occurred to me to wonder, for the first time, if Gill had a past – a family and children. And as I observed him cradle the young girl in his arms and pass her gently to the women, I knew that he had.

Once the child had been reunited with her mother, the excitement dissipated rapidly and the courtyard emptied. The distraught father of the girl still sat in the dust, weeping drunkenly and bleeding from small wounds on his face and head.

"Do you suppose we can get a meal in this place?" Gill asked, dusting himself off and looking around the small plaza.

Suddenly I was not feeling well. I bent over in pain, holding my stomach. The bad diet of the trip north was taking its toll; I needed rest and lawful food.

"So," Gill said, standing over me, "the consecrated warrior has a variety of emotions after all."

"I'm sick, that's all. I think I have a fever." I settled myself on a stone bench while Gill fetched up our luggage from the quay. My stomach purged itself violently, and I broke into a sweat and then was seized by a chill. As the sun slipped behind the canyon rim and enveloped the plaza in shadows, I felt intolerably cold and shook all over like a wet dog. One of the women covered me with a dusty blanket. I was miserable, but after a while I slept.

When I awoke, it was dark, and I could smell an unfamiliar odor from an outdoor brazier. A group of women were at work preparing the evening meal in the courtyard. The smell was not wholly repulsive, even though my stomach was churning as if it was being ravaged by wolves.

"You need food." Gill was leaning over me appraisingly.

"I need tea – herbal tea and tannin bark. Whatever is cooking, I don't want any."

With an efficiency that I was beginning to appreciate, Gill had brought up our luggage and negotiated a meal for us. When Gill brought me a plate, I saw what it was: fish. *Fish!* I recoiled and pushed the plate away.

"Remember yourself!" Gill hissed in my ear. "This is Naphtali."

I had forgotten that this stretch of the Jordan north of Chinnereth was clean. Nevertheless, I could not overcome my revulsion. Gill ate with apparent relish. There was dry bread on the plate, which I soaked in wine and swallowed, and a kind of paste made of warmed-over lentils. I managed to get a few mouthfuls down. Swallowing made me hungry, but I needed lawful food. I paid a woman to gather some lamb's quarter and chard out of a garden plot, which she boiled for me. The fresh greens tasted good, and I drank the broth as well. In a few moments, however, it acted more like an emetic than a tonic, and I knew I was truly ill.

For the next several days I lay feverish and weak. Gill prepared my food for me, partly for health's sake, as the standard of cleanliness in this outpost was little better than a stable. Cautious and alert to appearances, Gill wanted to disguise what he called my fastidious attention to the dietary laws. "No point in advertising who you are," he said. "You have a strange kind of fame, and it has undoubtedly preceded us. Keep in mind that where we are is the dragon's country." I consented to his precautions, but when he pressed me to eat fish, my gorge rose and I refused. "It is clean, after all," he said frowning. "This squeamishness does not become you."

"Later perhaps," I replied, knowing he was right.

In the meantime, we had become celebrated in Chinnereth. Gill was very popular with the women – who seemed, however, a woeful, bedraggled lot. He chatted with them in the mornings as they ground the day's masa on large flat stones in the plaza or sorted out onions and potatoes and the few other foodstuffs available at Chinnereth. While I recovered, Gill busied himself with bringing the stronghold into better order. His first act was to supervise the building of a stone enclosure around the well, so the accident suffered by the child would not be repeated. He also set the inhabitants of Chinnereth to salvaging timber from the sand bars and logs lodged among debris of the great ruined dam of the Ancients. This was dangerous business so near the cataract, but he set about the work with determination and saved much valuable wood. The women he instructed to clean up the stronghold. All obeyed him unquestioningly, even, as he reported to me, with a kind of eagerness. "Vicious brutes," he remarked. "But they respond to direction."

After a few days I was able to take a short stroll outside the stronghold, accompanied by the child we had rescued from the well. Her name was Susannah. She hobbled along beside me assisted by a crude crutch, and once, when she stubbed a toe, she swore like a sergeant. She was four years old, but poor diet had left her small and thin-boned. Together we observed a new and tidier hut being built to replace the one I had ordered demolished. Returning the child to her parents, I reflected that flowers bloom even in the desert, even from the face of the rock.

I soon felt well enough to continue our journey, and announced my intentions to Gill. "Have the women bake unleavened bread. We'll need it for the next stage of our journey."

Gill seemed hesitant to comply. The townspeople, he explained, had planned to hold a feast in our honor the next day; they were particularly insistent. I consented to the delay reluctantly, and he reminded me: "Don't let them see you refuse to eat fish."

"Damn the fish!" I said. I disliked the delay, but acknowledged another day's rest would do me no harm.

I felt well enough the next morning to resume my routine, and Gill insisted on exercising with me. His awkwardness in the movements of the discipline almost made me laugh. "When they speak of us," he panted, "they will say the two of us did exercises. That in itself may help disguise you. If they describe only one, it will identify you immediately and warn Hanford of your presence."

That afternoon Chinnereth offered up its grateful hospitality. It was not much of a feast; I had fared better on half-rations under General Mac Dogol. But the townspeople were eager to make a show for us to demonstrate their gratitude. They had musicians and a huge drum of ox-hide. The racket they produced inspired them to lurch about in a crude dance. We watched politely, and I managed to eat a portion of fish – which I trust had come from the clean reaches of the Jordan. The flesh was white and somewhat oily, but not nearly as bad as I had anticipated. One could probably learn to tolerate it.

After the fish course, the parents of Susannah knelt before us and touched our hands to their foreheads, loudly praising our kindness and generosity. The wife, who may have been attractive at one time, was marked at this moment by a freshly blackened eye and bruises on her forehead. We accepted their homage and distributed several handfuls of kanz from my luggage – worth, I estimated, at least three times the cost of their hospitality.

Then I led their little girl to the well, where I carved on the largest stone of the new enclosing wall the saying of St. Supplicee to women: "Be thou a well of ever-flowing water." I inscribed the name of the child, Susannah, after it. The crowd applauded lustily and found in the occasion a reason for breaking into the stronghold's last reserves of cheap brandy. I watched the ensuing revelry with sadness as the afternoon progressed. When Gill seated himself beside me, sweating after a vigorous round of dances, I remarked to him that while all this was distasteful, these people had no livelihood without the usual flow of trade.

"They were the dregs of the earth to begin with," he said. "Half of them must have been sentenced here for their crimes, and the rest must have followed because they could hope for no better bedmates."

"Well," I said, "perhaps they are as degenerate as you say. That would account for the remarkable impression you've made upon these forlorn creatures! Half the women of Chinnereth must have offered to be your comfort woman in the past few days."

"More than half," he replied. "And you forget the men."

I was a little taken aback at his words, but Gill abruptly changed the subject, leaning forward so we would not be overheard. "This revelry is not what it seems, Captain. I heard by chance that a river patrol is due here tomorrow from Hammoth-Wenatchee. Hanford's soldiers will be here before noon. That's why they have delayed our departure."

I stared at him.

"I suggest we slip out of here tonight, when the fire and the howling die down and everyone is asleep. In the meantime, act like you are enjoying this."

I nodded, observing the spectacle unfolding around me in the plaza with new eyes.

Not long after midnight, we slipped out of the stronghold. We had a full moon with small patches of cloud. Gill had purchased a pair of burros for our use, so I unhitched my pack and set it in the road by the livestock corral and slipped into the pen. Any two burros would do, I reflected. We had paid good money.

Gill called out my name in a hoarse whisper, his voice registering surprise.

"What is it?" I whispered.

"The boat," he said; "we're taking the boat."

"What?" I demanded. "We can't take the boat. We're going north."

"North?" he repeated in a voice loud enough to wake the town. "Hell and Beli-az! We're going back south, and as fast as we can!"

"North!" I repeated. "You take the boat if you want. My mission is in Naphtali."

"Your *mission*! For the love of God! You and I have got to talk."

"Later," I said. "Help me with the burros."

III

A steep trail led northward along the bank of the Jordan, and we would have made good time in the moonlight, but I was still weak and had to stop frequently to rest. Toward morning the trail climbed the ridge above the river, and I found myself at the end of my tether. "Let's stop here a while and let the animals graze," I said. "They look like they have had poor forage." I was panting and out of breath.

"As you say, Captain."

By mid-morning I could go no further. We had climbed high above the bed of the river and had a view of the canyon. Gill had seemed restless all morning, eager to be making better time and yet reluctant to push me beyond my strength. We tied the burros where they could browse and shared a skin of vile-tasting water. As I recovered my breath, Gill scanned the river below. "Look," he said. "Two water striders!" We watched through his glass as the oars of the two craft made delicate traces on the water. "They are military, all right. Northern Lights Guards, just as my Chinnereth sweetheart confided to me!"

"Why don't you go down and hail them?" I said. "I don't know how much farther my legs will carry me."

"Are you mad?" he cried. "Those are Hanford's men. They are searching for *us*!

We need to talk about this mission of yours," he added impudently. "In my opinion, Captain, what you are doing is madness. In fact, you seem more intent on throwing your life away than carrying out orders."

"So you have said. Believe what you like, but I have a mission to perform. If I die in the performance of it, well, a man can do worse."

"What exactly are your orders?" Gill insisted, refusing to be put off. "What precisely are you expecting to do? I must know. It is necessary that I know."

"You pretend to me that you do *not* know?" I retorted. "Did Ben Gurion not brief you himself? My orders are sealed, but I suspect that before I had a copy in my hands, he had placed them in yours." Gill had spoken with some conviction of the folly of conducting my mission; he clearly did not want to pursue this errand. Yet knowing whatever he knew about the obstacles we would face and the circumstances surrounding my orders, he had accepted a mission to accompany me. Nothing our joint effort to accomplish my mission made sense. "So, what are *your* orders from Glanz and Ben Gurion?" I demanded.

"My orders are sealed as well," he said. "I am not to open them until I reach Jezreel."

"So, then, check and countercheck, and we get nowhere. Nevertheless," I said, "I must know at least your verbal instructions from Ben Gurion."

"They make as little sense as yours," he said. "I admit, however, that I accepted this task from Ben Gurion on false assumptions. I was instructed to serve as your companion, protecting you from your own follies, and to serve as investigator into company affairs in Naphtali. . . ."

"But you believe," I interrupted, sensing that he had glided over things unsaid, "that I have no chance of surviving if I appear in Naphtali. Then you are not telling me something."

"I needed to get out of Hebron. Accompanying you on this absurd mission was a means of doing that."

"Indeed, you must have had desperate need!"

"I assumed that you were being got rid of – sent north on a hair brained scheme of the Council to depose Hanford Glanz. And that meanwhile, your father and Ben Gurion had other ends in mind for your journey." He paused, seeming wary and evasive. "Ben Gurion did not *say* that one troublesome brother was being dispatched to cancel out another – that whoever dies, it is no loss to Glanz, no loss to Israel. But I inferred as much."

"You flatter me; you have the habit of flattery."

"Forgive me," he said, suddenly vehement, "but your butchering the clergy in Esdralon has not endeared you to us!"

"To *us*? To whom? What are you talking about?" I was surprised at his sudden show of anger.

"I am a Messiahist," he said. "Have you not guessed that? Why else would I need to leave Hebron?"

"A Messiahist! St. Supplicee! Does Ben Gurion know that?"

"Of course he knows! How else would he know I'd come with you!"

I turned away and scanned the steep gorge of the Jordan, and eastward, the barren plateau of Moses, in the Kuhlan lands. The wind was sweeping fiercely through the gorge, its howl voicing many of my thoughts about Gill. "So," I said, drawing the obvious conclusions but wishing to hear him speak the words: "You accompany me as an assistant, an expert to help me in my – as you term it – absurd investigation?"

"Yes."

"Which you admit was doomed from the start?"

"Yes."

"And to act as my bodyguard?" He nodded. "Not a very congenial role for a Messiahist!" I said angrily. "But rather – in case my brother Hanford should fail to live up to his reputation – to act as my assassin!"

He regarded me coolly. "My orders are, as I said, sealed. But I admit, you have about covered the possibilities – all that was implied but unspoken. Except for one."

"What was that?"

"I did not anticipate playing your nursemaid."

The road south was blocked by Hanford's men, so we had no choice but to go forward. We made our way cautiously along the high trails along the canyon rim. On the occasions we had a sight of it, the Jordan was a mere ribbon below. We made a few miles, but by late afternoon, I could go no further. I made no pretense or apology, and Gill, to his credit, made no complaint. We pitched camp, tethered the burros nearby, and I made a small shelter from the sun out of my outer garment. I had no appetite but dutifully chewed unleavened bread and dried apples. I dozed fitfully until dusk and then roused myself. Gill had built a small fire and was brewing tea. I drank a cup of it and felt somewhat calmed and ready for sleep. Rest, however, eluded me. I had only just fallen into a drowse when my familiar nightmare tore me from sleep. I believe I awoke before crying out, which was a point of pride to me. Nevertheless, I felt shaken.

Darkness fell, and with it came a refreshing cool. Eventually, I found myself able to relax a bit. I took comfort that I was now able to acknowledge what had happened in Esdralon and recall some of what I had done. The events had become part of my life, rather than a horror that visited me from elsewhere. I turned on my side, assuring myself that this misery too would pass eventually.

After a time, I heard one of our burros bray and pull at its tether. In a moment, I was alert, my senses awake and combing the darkness. The burro snorted again and struck the ground with its hoof. What had disturbed it? And why were both of the beasts not *more* disturbed? One had resumed cropping the dry grass. Suddenly the ears and heads of both turned toward the way we had come. Then I heard a crackle on our back trail such as a heavy animal or a man might make, stepping in brush. My blood burst like fire in my veins. "Gill," I whispered, "Alarm! We have intruders."

Sensing that they were almost on us, I rolled out of my bedroll, not waiting to see if Gill had followed, and crawled on my hands and knees towards the picket rope. Beside the animals, the sound of movement would not betray our presence. A cloud passed over the moon and it was very dark. Gill was right behind me and bumped into me as I paused and turned. From his reaction, I knew that he had not panicked.

"Are you armed?"

"Yes," Gill whispered. He held his drawn sword at the ready. I had my Hazorite sword and my bow and quiver. I strung the bow and notched an arrow as we peered into the blackness. Our campfire had died down to embers, and I avoided looking at it, trying to accustom my eyes to the surrounding dark. We waited, listening, knowing the intruders waited as well. Our bedrolls were barely visible; I wondered if it was possible to mistake the rumpled bedclothes for sleeping men.

The shape of a man materialized suddenly out of the darkness and strode forward into the dim glow of the fire. Another followed and another, and the first thrust a spear into the bedroll where Gill had lain a moment before. The man grunted with surprise, and I heard the *thunk!* of my arrow in his body. Gill let out a shrill howl and hurled himself forward, startling me and spoiling my aim; my second arrow strayed off into the darkness. Shrieking like a madman, Gill slashed at the intruders. Drawing my sword, I leaped into the fray, wondering how many assailants we faced. It was over in an instant. I parried one clumsy spear thrust and slashed the throat of its owner. His hot blood sprayed my face and clothing. Gill struggled lustily on top of another, and I heard a cry and footsteps diminishing, running away down the trail.

"Four of them! Were there only four of them?"

"Yes," Gill panted. "Here is one accounted for!"

I took off in pursuit of the fourth. After a few yards our intruder had, in his haste, left the trail and was struggling blindly through brush and over stony ground. His panic told me that there were no other companions waiting nearby in the darkness. I could have followed his thrashing flight blindfolded, by sound alone; I had only to bide my time. Suddenly, there was a loud crash and a howl. The intruder had apparently fallen down a precipice. I approached cautiously, but there was no trick. My quarry had blundered off a small outcrop of rock. His moans located him below me, though I could not see him.

In a moment Gill came up. "Four of them," he said. "Lucky you were awake." He was still breathing heavily. I indicated that the fourth lay below us. We listened to the sounds of moaning below us for a moment, wondering what to do, and then Gill took up and hurled a large stone in the direction of the cries. It produced a scream: "Merciful God, have pity!"

"No!" I said, seizing his arm. "Not that way!"

"Don't be a fool," he said. "Think a moment."

I could not answer him. The man had come to murder us in our sleep. We could not approach him safely in the darkness. We owed him no mercy. And yet this manner of death, like that of a wild beast, filled me with revulsion.

"Go back to the camp and get a torch," Gill said. "See who these men are." I did as he said, but as soon as I was back on the trail, he resumed his grisly task. I heard the muffled impacts of stones and a few screams and then only the impacts of stones.

I returned with a stick of firewood I had coaxed into flame. I blew on it until the flame blazed up brightly, and Gill scrambled with it down the rocky face. I heard him whistle in amazement. When he climbed back up, he had a water bottle and a purse. "He's dead all right; look at this." He counted out twenty-five kanz, the large coins making a soft rasping noise. "This is a down payment on your head," he said, "courtesy of Hanford Glanz. I'd bet my life on it!"

We returned to the camp. It did not seem prudent to awaken the fire, but Gill was curious about the attackers. "Look!" he exclaimed as the fire blazed up. "This man is from Chinnereth!" Indeed he was; I recognized his features. He also had a purse full of coins.

The first intruder, who had speared Gill's bedroll and taken my arrow, lay on his side. He was a huge brute; together we turned him over, and Gill held a glowing brand close to his face. I drew back in revulsion. "So," Gill said, clucking his tongue in disapproval. "One of many in Israel who needed killing!"

It was the father of the child we had rescued in Chinnereth.

IV

By the embers of our fire we took careful stock of the situation. One of our intruders was a Northern Lights Guardsman – one of Hanford's soldiers. In all likelihood, then, a patrol was only a short distance behind us. The four men who had stumbled onto our camp were no doubt scouts; a dozen pursuers might be only a few hours on our back trail. We needed to flee immediately, but in what direction? We had so little water we could not even cleanse ourselves of the blood we had shed. I wiped my sword on the garments of one of the slain, swallowing my revulsion and cultivating patience until such time as I could perform the rituals.

"We need water," Gill said, "but we can't descend to the Jordan. No doubt the other water strider is down there waiting for us. We can't go ahead, where Hanford is waiting, and we can't go back. But without water, we can't risk climbing out of the canyon either. The wilderness of Dan is a desert this time of year, and we have no map."

"We'll have to risk the canyon rim, " I said. "Reaching Dan is our best hope, but we'll have to march cross-country." Gill began to raise objections, but we were without other options. I was desert-bred, however, and was confident that if there was water along our route, I could find it. I convinced him of the necessity to leave at once. The moon was fully up, and we could see well enough to follow game trails, which would be our only paths. Gill assented, grumbling. We gathered the weapons of our enemies and their full purses and packed them on the burros along with our scanty equipment. I judged that the water they had carried would supplement our own and might last two days. The main road from Jezreel to Hazor was, by our best estimate, three days away across very rugged country. "We must be wary of ticks," I added as an afterthought.

"Ticks!" he growled. "On top of everything else, ticks!" Gill complied but he was furious. He followed along after me, struggling with his beast in silence until we had put a safe distance between ourselves and our campsite. Then he began complaining bitterly about the treachery of the man to whom we had done a kindness at Chinnereth.

"Necessity is a hard thing," I said. "No doubt it was a powerful man who placed a spear in his hand and set him on our trail."

"And that man was your brother, Hanford Glanz!" Gill retorted.

"Perhaps," I said. "But Ben Gurion warned me that many people desired my death. I did not realize at the time that he might be referring to himself."

"What do you mean by that? Are we speaking in riddles now?" We were both panting from exertion, and conversation was difficult. Nevertheless, there were things I wanted said.

"Do you believe my father is alive?"

"Tephlin Glanz? Of course! Why not?"

"Do you believe it possible that Ben Gurion has murdered him, as people say?

"*What* people say that?"

"Malcontents, gossips, seditious people, I imagine. I heard the story from Ben Gurion himself. He laughed at the tale but did not deny it."

"What are you driving at?"

"I'm only trying to divine the purpose of my mission – as Ben Gurion would conceive of it."

"So?"

"Consider this: if Tephlin Glanz *is* dead . . . and Justin is dead. And if Hanford is soon to be disgraced or put to death . . . ." I stopped on the trail to catch my breath. Gill turned to face me. "Then I am the heir of Tephlin Glanz."

"I see," Gill said, his eyes narrowing.

"But if *both* Hanford and I die, then Glanz is heirless, and it seems to me possible that somehow the wealth and power of Tephlin Glanz would pass to his long-time companion, Simon ben Gurion."

"I see," Gill said. "I do see."

We paused for breath in the bright moonlight. "I see also what necessity is, and if I were a Messiahist who had a family in Hebron, and they were hostage to the good will of Ben Gurion, I might do many ugly things, if put to it by a powerful and ruthless man." Gill regarded me closely but said nothing. "All these considerations," I said, "make me very curious about your orders from Ben Gurion."

He did not reply, but I felt we were no longer entirely at odds as before.

In spite of balky, stubborn beasts and difficult terrain, we managed to climb out of the canyon by daybreak. We rested periodically and examined each other for ticks. We were below timberline, but there was much low brush and a gusting wind that could carry the tiny messengers of death for miles. When the sun was high, we halted and made sun-shelters for ourselves, and let the burros graze. I was very tired, but felt my health returning.

I gazed out over the baked and barren land to the east, at the plain of Moses, the land of the Kuhlans. The soil itself looked sterile. Above us, on Israel's shore, there was timber at higher elevations, but the sun-drenched foothills where we lay were eroded and yellow with dry grass. I felt completely alone, cut off from all human ties, with enemies in front and enemies pursuing, and my only companion a potential assassin. Only a few weeks before, sheer loneliness would have driven me to befriend whatever companion chance had thrown my way. Now I had no need or desire for any human contact whatsoever. I lay down under my sunscreen and slept like one of the dead.

When I awoke, the sun was far to the west, but its heat was unabated. Gill was seeing to the burros, who seemed little affected by the journey or by the heat. We nibbled our rations of bread and dried fruit and sipped tepid water out of our foul-smelling water skins. I showed Gill how to cover his head and neck with a loose head cloth. In the desert, the main thing was to keep one's body from the direct rays of the sun, thus preserving moisture and energy.

"We will not be difficult to track," Gill said gloomily, "if they are determined to catch us."

"True" I said. "But we have a head start, and they have no horses. This is the border of Danite country. Only a fool would relish an encounter with the shepherd clans who live here." We studied the terrain before us. It was only a few miles on a map, but the country was rugged. There would be water holes even in July, but we would have to find them.

We trudged along, angling slightly to the west of north and keeping a watch on our back trail. Gill lectured me as we climbed the narrow trails about the folly of pursuing my mission in the face of Hanford's power to do us ill. "You suspect Ben Gurion of evil intentions," he said. "Did it ever occur to you that you may be more useful to your *father* dead than alive?" Gill seemed drawn, as much as I, to finish our earlier conversation. "I do not claim to know what your father intends," he said, "but allow me to speculate. You grew up apart from him, and from your own family, your mother's people, in that isolated, preposterously antiquated Old Believers' Refuge in Zoar – the Wayfarers – is that what you call it? And with no contact with Glanz and no prospects. But then suddenly – and coincidentally with his other sons straying over the fence – you are summoned by your father to attend St. Anthony's Military Academy."

"You are incorrect." I said. "I was a fellowship cadet at St. Anthony's, but it was the Refuge that opened the way for me. As far as I know, Glanz played no role whatever in my admission to the Academy."

"You do remarkably well at the Academy," he continued confidently, "but on the eve of receiving your commission, there is a quarrel, an encounter, between you and another officer candidate – which, forgive me, we may not label a duel, because dueling is strictly forbidden at St. Anthony's, and because the other cadet was killed with his sword still in its scabbard."

Gill had scuffed with very heavy boots across these old sores of mine, but so much had transpired since then that I hardly winced. "True," I replied. "Senesh Velco spoke words to me that he should not have uttered without a sword in his hand."

"I see. But your commission is delayed; there is an inquest, rumors of charges being brought, perhaps for murder, but no trial occurs. Instead, you are allowed to serve in the winter campaign, and you served with distinction, so it is said – but without your commission."

He took my silence as affirmation.

"You were then assigned to the First Apostles Legion, after your service in the Second. Which is curious, very curious. The First Apostles Legion, like the Second, exists apart from the tribes and therefore violates centuries of precedent. To a cynical observer, such a force could serve as an instrument for someone – let us say Tephlin Glanz – in an illegal usurpation of power. You could, as a Haggadah – even as a half-Haggadah – have served in the Asherite Legion. Correct? But you accept the assignment, and at this point you receive a summons from Glanz – and this time you actually meet him?"

"Yes – and no. I was summoned, but I met with his aid, General Simon ben Gurion, known to us both."

"So, then, you have never seen Glanz? Even you."

I shrugged.

"Ever the obedient son!"

I did not like Gill's levity and I liked the subject even less. But he seemed either fascinated by my situation and or a very determined inquisitor.

"And next," he continued, "you are assigned to Esdralon. Let us consider for a moment the case of your brother, Justin Apollo." Gill paused, "Excuse me, your late brother, who had in the meantime made a name for himself in the army. Popular beyond expectation, brave, and enterprising, he is an engineer of genius, and he is credited by many with the capture of Esdralon. Major Apollo not only builds the ramp and the engines, but leads the assault, in which he is wounded. Some say heroically. At any rate, he becomes the idol of the First Apostles Legion; his fame spreads throughout Israel."

"And rightly so," I avowed.

"Eventually, Major is recognized for his merits and receives, though somewhat belatedly, Israel's second highest decoration. . . ."

"Which he richly deserved," I interrupted, "though the circumstances of receiving it were repugnant to him."

"At the same time," Gill continued, "I must point out that your brother was not notably tractable to your father's wishes. His difficulties with his wife are well known, as are the causes. And the scandal threatens to upset one of Glanz's critical alliances."

"Again, I would challenge your assumptions. Tephlin Glanz has no need for marriage alliances. He can take whatever is not given willingly. Besides, I am not certain myself on what terms Justin and our father maintained their relationship. Justin may, in fact, have done his bidding." *It pained me to acknowledge that, even to myself.* "It is just as plausible, however, that Justin's best qualities would have aroused our father's ire. Justin's fame and reputation would make him offensive to a man like Glanz, even if not dangerous."

"You anticipate me, but have my point precisely!"

"Then none of your speculation is exactly news to me, Captain Gill."

"But you," Gill continued, wagging a forefinger at me, "in the meantime, have arrived in Esdralon. And while you wear the insignia of the Commissary, you are in fact attached to the Eyes of Israel. True? And your mission, as the world knows, is to gather information not concerning the enemy, but concerning your brother, the wayward hero of the siege of Esdralon."

"That is a lie!" I exclaimed, pulling up short and confronting him. "I reported to no one! And I certainly never spied on Justin! Nor did I ever betray him. Never! And what do you mean, 'as the world knows'?"

"Of course not," Gill said, almost soothingly. "Of course not. Although the fact remains that there are reports in the archives at Hebron about Justin's unfortunate liaison with the Harlech woman, and they are in your hand-writing."

"Forgeries!" I exclaimed. "It was Bulavar!" The landscape spun around me. *My handwriting! Brother Rodrig! It was Brother Rodrig!* "They forged my name!" My head seemed to float from my body.

"Doubtlessly so," he conceded, his eyes like dark pits. "A precaution, merely, should either of you rise so high as to become dangerous."

My interrogation by Bulavar and Rodrig returned vividly to mind, and for the first time I felt something other than shame about what I had done in the Citadel of Esdralon. I had performed nothing worse than had been intended against me – or *performed* against Justin. It seemed, in fact, that I still had wrongs to avenge.

"None of your brother's actions, certainly not his – *devotion* to the Benjamite woman, was unknown to Glanz. Surely you have realized that. Glanz has a thousand eyes; what need had he of yours? Nevertheless, he sends you to Esdralon to observe your brother and to report to him what he already knows. I find this puzzling and unsatisfactory as an explanation."

"That is because it is not an explanation. It is foolishness. I was not sent to observe Justin. In fact, no one gave me any instructions, and I reported to no one."

"And regarding that, *no one* will believe you."

"Nevertheless, your whole construction collapses; you have missed the thread." I was pleased to be able to puncture Gill's explanation, even though I had asked myself many of the same questions.

"Um, yes, I suppose so," Gill conceded, frowning. "Unless," he continued, "we suppose, through all of this, all the while, that Glanz is really observing *you*."

"Not likely! Why would he want to observe me? Believe me, it is unlike him to show any interest in me. I am the least of his concerns, as I am the least of his sons."

"Yes? Then how do we explain this commission that you carry in your wallet?"

"I cannot explain it, I admit. It is a wise son, the saying goes, who knows his own father."

"From Glanz's point of view, "Gill continued relentlessly, "what is most disturbing about your brother are not his flaws of character, but his virtues – his potential to become a power in his own right. To become other than Tephlin Glanz's instrument."

"True," I said. "I once heard Justin described as the most dangerous man in Israel. For myself, if he were alive today, I would regard him as the most valuable man in Israel."

"Consider this," Gill continued relentlessly. "At the same time you arrive in Esdralon, the troubles with the Kr erupt, and *you* – quite unexpectedly, from Tephlin Glanz's point of view – distinguish yourself in battle. Suddenly, the two younger Glanz brothers are both heroes to the army, winners of the most coveted honors that Israel can bestow, and worst of all, inseparable friends, like David and Jonathan. That this could be seen as a problem by your doting father – well, does this seem plausible to you?"

I admitted that his speculations made sense.

"Of course they make sense! Can you imagine anything more threatening to him than two sons such as you are, with minds of your own, with fame and a following in the army –

and *allied* to each other by unbreakable bonds of trust and affection? Think about his eldest son, Hanford, the one you are to investigate, if not replace. Sons go astray; they prove unworthy of trust; they betray their father. It is an old story."

"But Justin and I have never been connected with him, as sons with a father. Why should I believe my life matters to him? He has made it clear over my entire lifetime that it does not."

"He may indeed wish it so. But you have, you see, made yourself a Name in Israel. Your actions have had an effect; you have set certain things in motion – all of them, unless I mistake you entirely, without reference to his interests or desires. So now you are a fact, something to contend with, like a troublesome entry in a ledger."

I smiled in spite of myself. "At last, Captain Gill, it may be that you speak the truth."

"Truly, sons are both a blessing and a plague," he replied. "The adage is true. But what Tephlin Glanz cannot control he often destroys."

I pondered Gill's words, measuring them against the little I knew of Tephlin Glanz and his role in my life. I of course had no certain knowledge of his attitude toward me. I found it difficult, in fact, to attribute normal human feelings to him. "It is easier to believe that Glanz is indifferent rather than actively hostile toward me. I have always believed he may have had a hand in the granting of my commission. If he did, then – whatever his intentions, good or ill – he created an opportunity for me."

"And this mission of yours to Naphtali – is this another opportunity?"

"I think that neither of us knows what is intended. Before, I believed I alone was in the dark, but I see I may have company."

Gill indeed seemed as genuinely puzzled as I: "Your brother Hanford's doings, no less than Justin Apollo's, are already known to Glanz. That Hanford is a vile and greedy man, that he tips the scales with his greasy thumb and keeps two account books, is, I dare say, universal knowledge. That he rules the North through terror and extortion and stubbornly defies his father's requests for assistance in this war with Benjamin is known to every child in Israel. Glanz does not need an inquiry into the matter, he needs an assassin!"

I stopped in my tracks.

"And now," he continued, his voice rising, "are you not sent again to uncover what is already known? To discover the sins of an elder brother? The pattern quite teases my imagination."

I had to admit that Gill was astute. With Israel wracked by religious dissention and by a war that split north and south, Hanford's power in Naphtali had suddenly become of great and perhaps even decisive importance. *But why, I asked myself, had Glanz not sent an assassin?*

"What you can observe of Hanford's doings in Naphtali, or what an encounter between you will produce, is a mystery to me," Gill said. "But you must know, and I will say no more about it, that this mission cannot be intended for your good. Instead, Ben Gurion, or your father – or perhaps both – have sent you to your death. That, in my opinion, is what your orders mean."

Then what do your *orders mean? I asked myself.*

As if he had heard my unvoiced question, he stopped and reached into his robe for his dispatch case. "My orders were to give you this at Jezreel; take it now. I do not trust what lies ahead there, and I have no wish to see the place. I strongly recommend we abandon this mission immediately. We can seek refuge in Dan. They say Hazor is a considerable place; we may even find service there." He thrust his orders into my hand. The seal was unbroken. When I asked why he would disobey orders, he grimaced. "I accepted these orders on false assumptions, as I told you. Though I have served your father often enough, I thoroughly despise him. I expected you to be like him, but I find you are not."

He would not speak further of his motives, so I took my own dispatch pouch from inside my robe, unlocked it, and removed a parchment document. "You are curious about the details of my mission? Then see for yourself. I had this from the Shepherd of the People, from his own hand."

Gill scanned the document and whistled with surprise. "From Moshe ben Hadith himself? Ben Gurion said nothing of this to me."

"My commission from the Council of Apostles is written in his hand." I recalled the Shepherd of the People as a frail little man with a gray beard and a quavering voice. Gill read the document aloud:

> *"Josiah Glanz ben Haggadah, captain in the Army of Israel, attached to the First Apostles Legion; In the name of the Council of Apostles, you are empowered by this, the Writ of the Council, to go up in Our Name and acting on behalf of the Council, to re-establish justice and harmony in Naphtali. Using all appropriate means and authorized to call upon the assistance of all loyal sons of Israel, wherever they may be, go forward and faithfully execute Our will; amen. Sealed this day, etc., etc., by the Shepherd of the People,*
>
> *Moshe ben Hadith."*

"St. Supplicee!" Gill exclaimed. "What kind of a commission is this? Re-establish justice and harmony? You are commanded to do all but empowered to do nothing!" He seemed genuinely surprised. "I have never seen the like! And your orders from Glanz and Ben Gurion – what do they say?"

I took another document from my pouch and read it to him:

> *Sir: It having come to our attention that the affairs of the Northern Lights Enterprises are in jeopardy, and that the agent of record, Hanford Glanz, has willfully disobeyed commands to give an account of his actions and has remained unresponsive to all inquiries; you, Captain Josiah Glanz ben Haggadah, the bearer of this note, are empowered to establish the true nature of affairs in the company; in pursuit of which to investigate and peruse all accounts, records, and documents of the company; and, if your findings warrant it, to relieve said Hanford Glanz from his duties as agent, thereafter serving yourself in that capacity in his stead; and to take other such actions in defense of the property and interests of the company as you see fit.*

The document had Simon ben Gurion's signature at the bottom and his seal, affixed on red wax. "Accountant's language," I said. "Perhaps another accountant can explain it to me."

Gill rubbed his forehead. "Two completely open-ended authorizations! Not even an Apostle"—he stopped abruptly and looked hard at me. "Not even an Apostle," he exclaimed, "is granted such discretion! I don't like – I don't *trust* either of these documents. Where are the constraints? Where is your accountability? Where are the means by which you are to accomplish these things?

Again, Gill but spoke my own reservations about the mission; I had asked those questions myself.

"What if Hanford resists?" he asked. "Suppose your brother wishes to retain his power – which he surely must. Hanford has killed dozens of people whom he thought merely inconvenient to himself, but you are actually dangerous."

I retrieved the document and returned it to my dispatch case.

"Consider this," he continued: "if your father has a spy system in Naphtali – which he does – be assured that Hanford also has one in Judah. There are few secrets in Israel, and I doubt that you are one of them. I see these orders as more dangerous to you than to him."

"Perhaps," I said. "Let's see if your instructions shed any light on these questions."

I broke the seal of his dispatch and read it aloud. We were both amazed by its contents: his "orders" were in fact a letter of authorization for me to withdraw, on the credit of the Northern Lights Enterprises, a sum up to the amount of 200,000 kanz, as needed. That was a figure beyond my power to imagine. Gill tore the letter out of my hands and read it himself.

"This is no jest!" he exclaimed. "It is truly a draft bill for 200,000 kanz! So much for my theory of a conspiracy against you! And my sinister interpretation of your mission! Here are the means, the tools, to accomplish miracles. You have not been dumped like a naked foundling on Hanford's doorstep after all – however much you may deserve to be!" He laughed, and I joined him, but I was both elated and mystified. Here was power to act, power mysteriously condensed and concentrated in a few scrawls on a piece of parchment. Still, as I turned the draft over in my hands, it occurred to me that there were no accompanying directions – no explanation of the draft or its purposes. Gill had received no instructions whatever concerning it – or myself.

"Wait!" he suddenly cried. Gill seized the letter again and seemed to devour it with his eyes. "To be valid, the draft must be counter-signed – by you, yes – and then *sealed* with the stamp of Tephlin Glanz. The seal. Surely you have the *seal*?"

His words deflated me instantly. "I have no such thing," I stammered. "I was given nothing of the kind. Two hundred thousand kanz! And you tell me that all I have to do is get Tephlin Glanz's seal into my hands and affix it to a draft, and the money magically appears. A miracle! *But I have no such seal!*"

"Wait," he cried. "Wait. You said you also had sealed orders, not to be opened till you arrived in Naphtali." I started to protest but he seized me by the shoulders, "Surely," he exclaimed, "*surely* a bit of clarity on the nature of your mission and your means to accomplish it could do no harm!"

I dug quickly into my dispatch case, tore the seal off the parchment, and scanned the message. "St. Supplicee!" I cried, disgusted. "I can make nothing of it. It is all written in code, and as I have no seal, neither do I have the key to this message!"

"Let me see it." Gill scrutinized it for several minutes. "It is not a coded message," he announced at last. "These are account numbers. These are accounts in banking houses, I think, related somehow to your mission. But nothing is explained." He turned the paper over and upside down. "Not a word of explanation."

"So Glanz and Ben Gurion have given me a sword without a blade – only an empty scabbard!" The afternoon sun bore down on me like a weight, but at the same time I felt a chill, a shudder, pass through my flesh that lifted the hair on my head. "The means given to me are only a mirage."

Gill seemed as baffled as myself. He raised his arms as if to say, what shall we do then?

"I shall have to do everything myself," I said.

V

The Jezreel-Hazor road follows the Ancient's double highway. Our path intersected its arrogant ramp of earth late in the afternoon of the second day, and we followed it westward. In the first vale we came to, we found a well surrounded by stone sheep pens arranged for the spring shearing. There were no dwellings nearby, as the Danite shepherds live mostly in tents, and their flocks were widely scattered in this season. Though the road was empty, we scanned the horizon for any sign of life. Nothing stirred in our field of vision but two hawks circling in a sky of brass.

Gill dropped a bag into the depths of the well and pulled up fresh cold water, brimming over. We drank our fill and poured water into a trough for the animals. Then I removed my bloody garments and washed them. The stains were well set and stubborn. Gill stripped and doused his lean body with water. We had traveled well together of late; I was beginning to feel reluctant to part from him, but I knew we had come to a fork in the road.

"The shepherds will not like us using their well," Gill said, drying himself. "I say we press on to Hazor while we have light. It could be dangerous to tarry here. Jezreel is only a day east of here, so Hanford could have cavalry out this far. And if that were not trouble enough, I have heard that Danite shepherds can be surly to strangers."

"I have no business in Hazor, Captain. My business is in Hammoth-Wenatchee."

"Fool!" he exclaimed, pitching his garments at me. "Madman! What do you take upon yourself? You are the purest arrogance that God ever let strut about."

"That may be," I said, ignoring his anger. I thought of my state of mind after Esdralon, as I lay recovering at Ben Gurion's estate. I believed then that if I were to endure and carry this mission forward to some kind of success, it would benefit Naphtali—and perhaps all Israel. I tried to explain as much to Gill.

"So you must press on," he said, "to rid Israel of a great evil. So that is the temptation in your orders?" Gill paced before me like a huge cat.

"Perhaps it is only something to do."

"I see. Only something to do!" He swiped at the air angrily with his arm. "I would wish nonetheless," he added in a different tone, "to strip away the veil that separates one mind from another and read your true intentions in this matter."

"So would I wish with you."

He continued to regard me soberly. "I really cannot tell," he said, "whether you are a fool or a madman."

"Nevertheless," I said, "I'm going forward. And it is best that you do not."

I tended to the burros, trying to ignore the awkwardness between us. Still hoping to dissuade me from my purpose, Gill continued to upbraid me for my pride and blindness. Suddenly, he glared at me accusingly: "Some say you are the disciple of Ebenezer of Zoar, and that the secret orders of the Old Believers are alive again in you. Is it true?" I pretended to scoff in reply, but he was not put off. "Ben Gurion himself expressed an opinion to me on this subject. He wondered, he said to me, if you were Ebenezer's shepherd dog, trained to savage enemies of the old faith at a whistle from the Master."

"Ah," I said, remembering with a pang a similar conversation with Justin as we walked along the bank of the Jordan. *Even my brother Justin had harbored such suspicions; they had always lurked beneath the surface of our relationship.* "What was it," I asked, "that could make Ben Gurion entertain such foolish notions?"

"What indeed!" Gill said. "Could it be," he said, peering at me intently, "that *you do not know* what you are?"

"Are *you* mad?" I exclaimed. "What do you mean, do I not know what I am? What is this mystery about me? I eat and drink and suffer diarrhea like other men. What is mysterious about me?"

Gill stood before me, his body stooped a little as he peered at me. He seemed to be panting with excitement. "The other night when we fought our assailants," he said, "had you learned that sword play at the Refuge?"

"Of course. Why not?"

"Your man was a Northern Lights Guardsman, heavily armed."

"Surprise was on our side."

"He wore armor. His throat above his neck guard presented a very small target. Yet. . . ." I made a dismissive gesture, but he pressed on: "Is it true that in Engedi you killed eight men in one engagement?"

"If Kr are counted as men. It was" – I searched for words of explanation – "no great feat of arms. The Kr were poorly armed and wore no armor."

"It is said that you have no recollection of these acts. Is that true?"

I had not expected his question. I felt the hair rise on my neck.

"Is it possible, then, that you truly have no memory of what you were trained to do at the Wayfarers? No memory, at least, of *some* of the things you were taught?"

I shook my head and said nothing. *Gill's words had sent a chill through my body.*

"I am told," Gill added, his eyes glinting, "that your friends fear you as much as your enemies."

"You lie!" I cried, suddenly furious.

He stepped back quickly. "I only repeat what I hear," he said, warily. "Except –" He paused and would not finish. Gill regarded me for a long time and then raised his hands and dropped them, as if in resignation. "You are a stubborn mule," he said. "Still – for someone who is so damnably foolish—you seem a good enough officer."

Gill had suddenly become the hearty, plain-spoken soldier. I knew it was time to part. We shook hands and divided the provisions and the money we had taken from our attackers. I was not certain whether I was happy or sad to part with him – nor was I altogether clear in my own mind why I persisted on this errand of Tephlin Glanz.

VI

Gill's words lingered in my mind long after we had parted. I had only a vague plan of how to proceed – and as many doubts as he about my mission. Perhaps my orders were straightforward, and I was meant to put an end to Hanford's rule in Naphtali and restore the area to peace. Perhaps instead I was merely a tool to be used for purposes that I could not fathom and then be discarded. There was no trusting Tephlin Glanz or Simon ben Gurion; I knew that much. Yet on the other hand, I had been entrusted with serious means. Money is a powerful persuader and a weapon as well. Men like Tephlin Glanz and Ben Gurion do not part with it lightly. Yet I had only the appearance of that weapon in hand – and therefore perhaps only the appearance of trust. Had someone been instructed to contact me in Naphtali, bearing the necessary seals, so that, having passed some test of will or ability, I would find the missing puzzle-piece in my hand, and with the seal, the power latent in a few scrawls on paper might spring to life? That was a tantalizing prospect.

Or was I, after all, only a slave on a fool's errand, unwittingly bearing the message: *slay the bearer of these tidings*? It seemed more than possible that I had been sent to my death, out of sight and hearing of the rest of Israel. *But why?*

In the final analysis, I reflected, the outcome of my mission mattered very little. I had accepted the mission at a point in my life where I had neither pleasure nor, apart from this ambiguous directive, purpose in life. I determined that in performing this mission, I would either find some reason for being or I would cease to be. As Gill's figure diminished and then disappeared in the distance, so too did my reservations. I resolved to go forward and do this thing – whatever it was – or die trying. The simplicity of purpose was a balm to my thoughts, like sunlight on water. And it began to dawn on me for the first time in my life what else it meant, or might mean, to be the son of Tephlin Glanz. I was familiar with the disgrace and humiliation of my status, but I began to see it might also mean power. *Power to effect my will and not submit to his.*

I had no sooner pitched camp and performed a ceremony of purification when I noticed a cloud of dust, no larger than a man's hand, on the western horizon. By the look of it, it was raised by a large party. I thought of fleeing or concealing myself, but decided against it. Hanford's cavalry would come from the east, not the west. As the procession drew near, I was relieved to see livestock and wagons, which made the group seem less threatening in aspect. To announce my own presence, I added wood to my fire and fanned it into crackling flame. Chance meetings in the wilderness are always perilous, so it seemed best to make my presence visible from a distance. It occurred to me that the large purse of coins taken from our assailants might be difficult to explain, so I quickly buried it under a stone by the campfire. I wrapped a cloth around my Hazorite sword and bundled it securely with my luggage. Then I seated myself in plain sight by the well. I had a quiver and bow at my side, and I leaned one of the spears we had taken from our would-be assassins against my shoulder.

As the procession came into clear view, the sun was barely an hour high, a crimson disk behind them. The careless noise of the group was reassuring; the creak and rumble of the carts, the whistles of the herdsmen, and the voices of folk mingled with the lowing of the animals, all proclaimed the peaceful nature of their journey. The presence of oxen meant they were not of the sheep-raising Sevfolk clan, which postponed any difficulty about my use of the well. I rose to greet the procession and was enveloped in its dust.

I recognized their headman by his clothes. He rode a tall, spirited buckskin, and his manner told me that he was a man of substance. All of his companions wore versions of the same checkered head cloth, apparently their clan colors. Stripped as I was for the cleansing ceremony, I had only a plain linen cloth bound around my middle. Without my robe and tunic, none of my affiliations was visible.

"You are dear to the Sevfolk," the headman said to me, swinging down from his horse, "that you use their well so boldly?"

"That is my wish rather than a fact." I replied, bowing low. "I am a fugitive and a sojourner. I have relatives in Naphtali, which is my destination, and a blood debt for manslaughter in the place where I was. I seek asylum and assistance from my kin, once I get there." That I omitted the rest of the formula of introduction must, I thought, seem natural owing to my pretended status as a fugitive. I was gambling that Danites would have little interest in the quarrels of their southern brethren.

He looked me over. He was a man of middle age, still powerful and active, with a face that was deeply lined. Accompanying him were half a dozen mounted men and another dozen on foot; there were four women and half a dozen children in the wagons. "I am Joash, son of Jabeth, of the Dekali clan of Dan," he said, observing the customs. "We are cattlemen. Nevertheless, we are kin to the Sevfolk and have permission here." I bowed low to him again, thankful that the traditions were kept in Dan. The courtesies would place us on a cautious footing with one another. After the preliminaries were concluded, each of us would know better what to expect from the other.

"Call me. . . Won Datzen," I said. The name had leaped into my head, and I was grateful for it, though bemused by the ironies it carried. My hesitation and my omission of my father's name and tribe would tell him I had adopted a fictitious name, owing to my fugitive status. I was in fact a fugitive, though not for the reasons I pretended. "I served in Israel's army," I added.

He nodded but regarded me suspiciously. "It is said that a young man in trouble can find employment in Naphtali. They say that Hanford Glanz always welcomes new men for his Guards."

"Employment would be welcome," I said, seeing his eyes narrow at my words, "but I must lodge far from Hanford's gaze. It would mean my life to be known to him." Again, I gambled with candid-seeming half-truths; I guessed what his own sentiments toward Hanford must be.

"Very little in Naphtali is far from Hanford's sight," Joash ben Jabeth said. "But may you have your wish." He motioned his people to pitch camp. The difficult part, I felt, was behind me.

Joash explained that his party was traveling to the harvest games at Jezreel, held annually to celebrate the feast of First Fruits. Like the rest of old Israel, Danites celebrated the year's bounty in the leisure time after the grain was up and the earliest fruits were ripening. The new masters of Jezreel discouraged the custom, but it was a way, he asserted candidly, of maintaining the Danite claim to the territory.

"They keep the tradition of the games even in Jezreel?" I asked. I was considering the prospect of entering Jezreel undetected in the company of these strangers. "What events do they preserve?"

"The full events," he said, as if he wondered at my ignorance. "Dan does not stint. We honor excellence in the old way. And we do not forget to whom Jezreel belongs."

The Danites watered their animals and pitched their camp alongside mine. The men examined my burro and all my equipment minutely. I noticed Joash eyeing my clothing drying on a rock – the rust-colored stains had not been entirely effaced by my scrubbing. All my insignia of rank and the gold shoulder cloth of Asher were, however, packed in my luggage. At n opportune moment I took the headman aside and pressed a few coins into his hand. "I have no claim on the hospitality of the Sevfolk," I explained, "and no one to speak for me. Yet only with their good will can I pass through their country to Naphtali. If you could speak on my behalf. . . ."

He regarded me and then the gift and, to my great relief, nodded. This small gesture established me on a somewhat better footing. Not that Joash was a venal or grasping man, but rather that he recognized me as a law-abider – someone who knew the customs and terms of respect and followed them. I had shown myself willing to pay my way, thereby acknowledging established rights in Dan. He would be much more inclined, therefore, to accept my account of my difficulties – my plight as a fugitive with a blood debt – as a misfortune merely, and none of his business. Suspicion of me relaxed somewhat thereafter, and soon a number of the party came forward and engaged me in conversation. The women seemed particularly curious about me. The wife of Joash asked me shrewd, roundabout questions to determine where I had served in the Army.

"I served with the First Apostles," I answered truthfully, knowing my answer would not identify me or my tribe. "But army life did not agree with me."

She frowned, as if by anticipating her questions, I was denying her a rightful pleasure.

"The First Apostles I know of. But you are no Judean. Your speech is –"

"Very like your own," I admitted. "I am a near countryman of yours, but I have lived elsewhere for several years. But I beg you, do not ask me more concerning my origins or seek to know my identity. It is not wise to involve others in private misfortunes, especially since" – I recited the adage – "blood stains everything it touches."

She was alert to the pointed nature of my comment, which, I was sure, only made her more curious. I had donned my white tunic in the cool of twilight, and its stains were visible. "I need to purchase new clothing," I said, and her eyes widened slightly, and she nodded. "If you wish for any reason to end my life," I added, seizing the moment, "you need only speak of me and my troubles to any of the garrison in Jezreel." I spoke candidly to her, judging that she was a woman of sense – and no friend of the Glanz enterprises. Whether she was also a woman of good will remained to be seen.

She called to the other women, and they soon had spread a modest array of trade goods before me: fine and coarse linen of many colors, woolen cloth, knives and cooking utensils. I selectd a Danite head cloth, useful to cover the scars on my forehead that could otherwise identify me. I added a light tunic of undyed brown wool. Then it occurred to me to wonder how I would pay for these goods. I had money enough and more, but I was concerned about the large purse I had from Ben Gurion for travel expenses. To have so much money would not look well. A man in my pretended situation could plausibly have so much only by theft, and such a view of me would be dangerous in the extreme. On the other hand, I had a burro from Chinnereth – a burro that might identify me to Hanford's men. "I have a burro," I said hesitantly.

"Ah, you have a burro, do you? But you are about to tell me, young man, that you have no true bill for this animal you want to trade?" She looked at me shrewdly.

I did in fact have a bill of sale for the beast from Chinnereth, but the bill had Gill's name on it, and that would require an explanation. I did not wish to reveal my own identity under any circumstances – not to folk who had good reason to resent the Glanz family and would be unlikely to distinguish among its members. "Perhaps," I offered, "I could assign you the lifetime use of the beast, but not sell it to you outright." She shook her head. I took another chance of being candid even while I dissembled: "I have a bill of ownership for the burro, but I would not like my name revealed – nor might it be safe to you to hold such a bill in Jezreel." She frowned, eyeing me suspiciously. In spite of the advantage she had of me, she would not trade on those terms. Following a sudden flash of insight, I rummaged through my goods and produced the bill. "I speak the truth," I said. She squinted at it a moment and then looked at me. As I had guessed, she could not read.

"It looks like a true bill," she said. "But it might be anything."

"True, it could be. But it is a bill of sale, and it is valid. I swear on my honor as a soldier."

The woman gave me a long look and then inspected the animal with equal care, examining it both for its health and previous marks of ownership.

"You'll carry my luggage to Jezreel in one of the wagons," I said. "And speak to no one of what I've just told you. After that, we are clear."

"Done," she replied, deftly notching out the animal's earmarks with her knife. The burro brayed and kicked, but she had stepped back out of harm's way.

The Danites and I shared a meal of hot porridge as the sun was setting. "Is it possible for a stranger to enter the games?" I asked. "I can throw the javelin and shoot with a bow. If there are decent prizes, I might win my fare to Naphtali."

He grunted in affirmation to my question, but obviously did not approve of my plan. It was a good sign. I had established myself as a young man open about his difficulties – even foolishly so – and I wanted to maintain that appearance. Talkative people are not dangerous. At least, that is what the proverbs assert. These were good people who had invited me to sit by their fire, and I did not like deceiving them. Though my need was great, I felt a pang nonetheless.

"Truly it is said," Joash remarked after a while, "men are prone to evil as the sparks fly upward." So apt was his remark that I startled a little.

As we settled down for the night, I thought of Rehab Gill and why no one had mentioned meeting another lone traveler with a burro on the road.

VII

Jezreel lay a thousand feet below the interior of Dan. The ruins of the Ancients' double road descended down an arid canyon to the Jordan. There a massive ramp of earth thrust out into the river, and great pilings, the remains of a bridge of unbelievable size that the Ancients had built, still stood in the river. Jezreel was sited at a natural crossing, with low banks on the Israelite shore of the river. Elsewhere in the Danite reach, the Jordan flowed between sheer canyon walls and basalt ramparts. The town had once been a considerable place. Dan had sent its grain and hides and cattle to market in Hebron from Jezreel; thus, its loss was a festering wound to them.

Far more than a port, Jezreel was a fortress. Some of its former greatness was visible in the stonework of the stronghold. Its citadel, the Vantage, was a massive work with huge exterior walls of rough stone. It rose like a natural outcrop from a basalt cliff above the Jordan. The Vantage guarded the most obvious crossing place for the Kuhlans when they came over against Israel. In addition to the citadel itself, a long defensive work ran from the citadel south along the river's bank, ending where the walls of canyon rose to form a natural barrier. Recent settlement had spread down the hill from the citadel and the old enclosed city.

The vale of Jezreel was a garden set in the midst of arid land, and I was reminded vividly of the heart of Israel. Fields of maize lay alongside the river, and the foot of the valley was terraced with crops of many kinds. Vineyards skirted the lower hills and orchards were planted above, as if in defiance of ticks. Small channels for irrigation ran this way and that in the valley and on the lower hillsides. Above the cultivated zone, the tents and livestock of the shepherd folk who had come for the games covered the hillsides. Our party had joined those already camped on a ridge overlooking the town and pitched our tents in the late afternoon sun.

Shortly after our arrival, a great commotion arose as a group of horsemen galloped into our half-made camp, raising dust and scattering livestock in every direction. The intrusion provoked alarmed trills from the women. "Sevfolk!" I heard someone shout. I made myself as inconspicuous as possible, but it was soon apparent that these were allies of the Dekali, and that the indignation of these shepherd warriors had a source other than ourselves. The leader of the group swung down violently from his horse and embraced our chieftain, Joash. The man, roughly of the age and rank of Joash, ceased his violent imprecations of Northern Guardsmen and Hanford Glanz long enough to exchange compliments with Joash and his kinsmen.

"They leave us nothing, the swine!" he exclaimed, returning to his rage. "Not our horses! Not our honor! And now our women!" I strained to hear what the present indignity involved. I gathered from the talk that the headman's name was Jerub, and that he was the sheriff – which is their term for patriarch – of the Sevfolk clan of the Danites. Apparently fearing trouble at the games, Hanford's lieutenant in Jezreel had doubled the garrison and brought in a troop of horse as well. "And this morning they took hostages!" Jerub protested. "Hostages! My daughters Ester and Tamar among them! My daughters' lives as surety for our 'good behavior'! God damn them!" Jerub roared, his robes flying. "We'll show them good behavior!"

Joash and his clansmen whistled with indignation, and the women keened in sympathy for the hostages. Joash eventually invited them all to partake of his hospitality, and the men settled down under an awning while the women prepared a meal. I slipped away, not wanting to be brought to the attention of the angry Sevfolk.

It was evening, so I walked abroad to spy out the land and enjoy the sights. It was pleasant to be among cultivated fields again. From Hebron to Jezreel, I had seen nothing but arid land and then the Desolation in the midst of it. I relished the smell of fertile soil and sweet water. The scent of curing hay on the evening breeze positively sent a pang through me. There were gardens of beans and tomatoes, peppers and greens of various kinds, squash and melons in abundance, and aromatic herbs planted near cottage doors. In the larger fields green corn stood well tasseled out, rustling in the breeze. I descended the road into the village, savoring the smell of cooking and the murmur of conversation from the huts.

At the harbor, the fishermen were preparing their nets for the nightly runs, and the nearby market place was hung with bright awnings and humming with voices. I heard singing, accompanied by drums and guitars. A crowd had gathered in the market and, in the center, young men and women whirled to the music. I paused, making mental notes for the journal I now carried only in my head. The prosperity of the place and the number of its inhabitants surprised me. For an outpost, Jezreel was a considerable place. I was also taken by the handsome appearance of its people – so different from the loutish folk of Chinnereth, a place that seemed a mere dunghill in comparison. I was drawn to the music and the gracefully moving figures. Jezreel was famous for a gemstone found nearby that had a grain like wood but, when polished, shone in brilliant, unexpected hues. On close inspection, I saw many examples of this jewelry on display among the dancers, but none, I thought, shone as brightly as the dark eyes of the young women who wore them.

Long after dark, I returned to our camp with the rhythms of the songs still throbbing behind me in the valley. I was saddened by the festivity, feeling somehow barred from the circle of gaiety. The life of my people seemed more like a memory than a present reality in which I could partake. Why was I unable to step into the line and move my feet to the music and return the flirtatious smiles of the young women? What was the invisible screen that separated me from ordinary life? It was too painful to think of. I resolved to sleep as quickly as possible and put this mood behind me.

VIII

The morning was spent in preparation for the games, and I was surprised at the absence of Messiahist taint in all the proceedings. Here in Jezreel was the Israel I cherished. I rejoiced that in the remote corners of Israel, at least, the ancient customs were still respected. I wore only a clean ephod, the linen undergarment, and the Dekali headband I had bought to cover the scars on my forehead. The distance events were held in the cool of the morning, and although the number of athletes was small, they did credit to themselves. I competed in archery, but lack of practice and a lingering weakness in my left arm from the blow of the Kr war club diminished my performance. In the javelin throw, however, I performed creditably in spite of my lack of conditioning. I felt elated by the cheers of the crowd and exerted myself until my chest and limbs were bathed with sweat. I managed second place.

Events were suspended for the mid-day meal. Cattle and sheep were roasting in pits for this evening's feast, when the prizes were to be awarded, and the aroma was stimulating. For this lighter mid-day meal, beer and vegetables and freshly baked bread were set out on long tables. An elderly Devotee, frail but possessed of a great booming voice, held forth during the meal about the meaning of the games and the importance of striving for excellence as a path leading toward the Way. When he finished, the guitars and drums took up a traditional harvest song, and the crowd began to move in rhythm with the song.

I felt myself being pulled away from the table into the throng; I turned and saw, to my astonishment, a pretty Danite girl had seized me by the hand. "Come" she said smiling at me, but in the din I saw rather than heard her invitation. The steps of the dance were new to me, but the crowd was so thick and we were both so hedged in and bumped about by other dancers that it scarcely mattered. Through all the confusion and flurry of movement, she held my hand and fixed her eyes on me, her gaze merry and mischievous and her lovely face upturned in a smile. She had shining black hair and eyes like garnet. I was too absorbed in her presence to feel awkward or embarrassed – too pleased at being singled out and chosen to be shy. We moved to the music as best we could in the dense throng, her small hand firmly clasping mine. Occasionally, the steps of the dance brought her close to me, and she held her skirt in one hand with a winning and graceful flair and brushed me lightly with it as she passed. At the end of one song, I drew her close again and asked her name, but the music started up again and drowned her reply. I found my heart beating as though I had run the mile race.

Just as I was again about to speak, a huge lumbering fellow, apparently overcome with drink, lurched violently into me and sprawled at my feet. The Danite girl's fingers slipped out of my grasp. I had a glimpse of her laughing face as I bent to assist the man. I raised him to his feet, straining to lift his bulk, and felt my head cloth snatched suddenly from my head. I looked up and saw the girl, no longer smiling, but gazing at me with curious intensity and holding my Danite head cloth in her hand.

The drunken man pushed against me, belligerent and confused about what had happened. For a moment he seemed bent on attacking me, but I succeeded in calming him. Turning from him, I hastily scanned the small crowd that had gathered around us, feeling something akin to panic when I failed to find my lovely partner. I pushed through the ring of curious observers, but she was nowhere to be seen. I roamed the area around the dance, looking for her, with dread and anxiety mounting in me. Where had she disappeared? Had I found this beauty, this enchantment, only to lose it by a moment's inattention?

For the next several hours, I felt an indescribable distress amounting, as time passed, almost to desperation. I continued to search for her, alternately despairing of ever seeing her again, and expecting her to appear at any moment laughing before me, my head cloth tied around her shoulders or knotted like a belt at her waist, in the manner of Asherite girls who have taken a sweetheart. Nothing in my life had engaged my attention like this smiling Danite beauty; she had taken me out of myself and away from my brooding preoccupations in a moment. Her smile and the promise in her flashing eyes had pulled me into the festival, into the spirit of thanksgiving for the bounty of life in a way that I had never imagined possible.

At sunset, a long roll of drums and a trumpet blast interrupted my search. The sprint, the last event of the day, had just ended and the crowd was cheering the victor, an athlete of unusual talent. A herald mounted the judges' platform and, in honor of the feat just performed, announced that the garrison commander of Jezreel had issued an invitation to the winner and to all those who had won a prize today to drink a health with him in the citadel. Those who had excelled in the events would receive from his hands additional prizes of value.

The crowd cheered. The festival atmosphere had, for the moment at least, prevailed over the tensions between Dan and Naphtali. But I was bereft of my companion. Though I was curious to see the interior of the citadel, nothing meant as much to me at that moment as finding the girl and learning her name. The citadel was one place I had not searched for her. When the crowd hoisted the winner of the sprint onto their shoulders and began a torch-lit procession up the slope toward the citadel, I fell in with them, still hoping to find my mysterious dancing partner. Near the gate, as if by magic, I caught a glimpse of a young woman carrying a basket on her hip and dressed exactly as my dancing partner had been. As I gazed at her, she turned and I saw her face: *it was my partner!* I was certain of it!

I crowded forward, hurrying to get into the gate, which was clogged with people. I was just inside when suddenly another body lurched violently against me from behind. Thinking it another drunken reveler, I whirled angrily about in the press, catching a glimpse of a Guardsman's helmet and feeling a strong grip on my arm and separate fingers clamp like a vice on my flesh. "Captain!" a voice hissed in my ear. I turned my head and gasped, recognizing the voice. *It was Rehab Gill!* "Get out any way you can," he whispered. "They know who you are!"

He thrust a bundle into my arms and deftly pushed me to the right, toward a corridor leading off from the main entrance; then I saw him rudely shove a man in front of him. "You oaf! You fool," he shouted, pushing the man again. "Watch where you are stepping!" The man turned angrily and the two moved forward and away from me with the crowd, jostling each other and shouting. All eyes were on them as I ducked into the corridor, grateful for Gill's cleverness. Out of sight of the crowd, I examined the package he had thrust upon me: it was a uniform cape of the Northern Lights Guards and, bundled within it, a helmet.

In the recess of a doorway, I put on the helmet and slipped the cape over my shoulders – I was naked except for the ephod in which I had competed. My mind, like my heart, was racing. What was Rehab Gill doing in Jezreel? And what was he doing dressed as a Northern Lights Guardsman? Had he doubled back on the road in Dan and seen me join Joash and his band? Had he followed me here? If so, *why?* Moving cautiously down the corridor in my disguise, I felt for the first time an appreciation for what Rehab Gill was – of what he *must* be: a trained agent of the Eyes of Israel. And knowing that, and realizing at the same time that I had been trapped by my enemies as easily as a yearling cub is led with a honeycomb, I was furious at myself.

My first task was to get out of the citadel. I was weaponless, and I had no inkling of the layout of the fortress in which I was trapped. Around a corner, the corridor led to a stairway ascending to the next floor. There were no windows. I paused, wondering if I could turn back and bluff my way out the front door, and then I heard footsteps from the floor above, approaching the stairs. Thinking it better to seem resolute on some errand rather than be seen hesitating, I moved toward the sound, climbing the foot of the stairs. An officer and two soldiers passed me on the stairs, talking, paying me no attention. The upper hallway was empty; doorways were sited at intervals along the hall, which appeared to be officers' quarters. Hearing loud voices and footsteps behind me, I hurried down the hall. One door had been left ajar. With no better option available, I slipped into the room and closed the door quietly behind me.

I examined the room, which was bare of hiding places. It was the quarters of a junior officer. The bed was unmade and the room had the bare, impersonal look of a barracks. There was only one door – the one by which I had entered. I was on the second floor. The single window opened out over the basalt cliffs above the Jordan. It was a sheer drop to the river. I leaned out as far as I could, trying to estimate my height above the river, and searched for window ledges or climbable surfaces. Of the latter there were none, but below a floor and to the left, there was a window ledge. The window might be open or openable, if I could reach it. From there I might negotiate a way down to the cliff-base – and either climb down to the river or, if the narrow ledge at the base of the fortress permitted, edge my way to the end of the wall and make my escape. An ancient woodbine covered the stone up to the second story. It was just possible that, with luck, the vine could support my weight. I recalled the saying, *Only a fool trusts to luck.* But he who is trapped in the citadel of his enemies has few options.

I was panting and sweating like a blown horse; my hands were slippery. I willed my body to relax and relinquish this panic, to breathe deeply and easily, so I could think. My best chance was to wait until dark and then try to make my way out. I pressed my back against the wall by the door and listened, breathing quietly and thinking nothing.

An hour passed, and then footsteps sounded in the hall and loud voices; the sounds swelled and subsided, swelled again, and then a fist banged on my door. Several voices shouted demands to open up. Gill had spoken the truth: *They know who I am. The invitation to the athletes to enter the citadel had been a trap.* I thought with a sudden pang of my lovely dancing partner. The banging increased, rattling the bolt in the jam. I looked about frantically. The door appeared fairly strong. To increase its power of resisting force from without, I smashed a chair on the floor and wedged the broken legs under the door. I heard curses outside. From their voices, I judged there were at least half a dozen men – too many to overcome without my sword, which was bundled in my luggage in Joash ben Jabeth's camp. *"Never forsake your Hazorite sword,"* I recalled my Master Ebenezer saying earnestly, *"and it will never forsake you!"*

Regrets, the saying goes, are worthless currency. I searched the room for some tool I could use and some idea to save myself. There was a dagger on the table. For a rope I had only the bedding, a wool blanket, which I cut in half and twisted. I knotted the two pieces together and tried them, but I could not trust the knot, which wanted to slip. I tore down the drapery along the wall, but found the cords were rotten. The door in the meantime was shaking with blows. I heard the men curse and call my name. In a few moments, they would attack the door with axes or a battering ram.

There was nothing to do but use the window, and I had only the blanket for a rope. I retied the blanket ends, tightening the knot with all my might. Then I tied this makeshift rope to one of the window bars. I cut the soundest part of the drapery cord and tied the dagger to my belt. Last, I fastened my sandals to my belt. The assault on the door appeared about to succeed, so I flung the end of the blanket rope out the window and squeezed through the bars. The hilt of the dagger caught on one of the bars and it nearly cost me my life to untangle it. For a moment, I perched on the ledge, holding tight to the bars, feeling as vulnerable as it is possible to be. The moon was already up and three-quarters full in a cloudless sky; a night breeze was blowing up the Jordan. The confused tumult outside my door had been replaced by the steady blows of an axe; I had only moments to escape, perhaps only moments to live. The first stars of evening were tranquil and bright.

I took a deep breath and released my hold on the bars, slipping over the window ledge and down the blanket-rope. My feet felt the knot between the blankets, and then my hands gripped tight just above it. I had to force myself to go on and will myself to put my weight on the lower half of my improvised rope. The knot tightened and slipped simultaneously; but it held. *It held!* Sweat trickled down my forehead and into my eyes. I lowered myself further until I judged myself even with the window below mine. It was about six feet to my left. If I held to the very bottom of my makeshift rope, I judged I might be able to swing gently to the left and get a foothold on the ledge. I began to lever myself to the left with my bare feet, putting as little strain on the rope and its treacherous knots as possible. The rock was rough and warmer than I expected, its surface covered with lichens. Gradually I inched my way toward the ledge. I had estimated the distance accurately and my blanket-lengths seemed long enough, but my grip was already tiring and my hands were aching from the strain. I took several deep breaths and shifted my grip, relaxing my muscles for an instant, one hand at a time.

By careful effort, edging to the left, I reached a point where I could touch the window ledge of the floor below with my left foot. I reached out with it, willing my aching hands to hold tight to their grip, and stretched out my entire body. I could hear the sound of axe-blows against the doorway of the room, and I knew I had only seconds to escape. I touched the ledge lightly, then pressed the ball of my left foot firmly upon it, feeling for an instant an enormous relief. Just as I did so, I felt the purchase of my right foot on the wall suddenly slip, and my body swung back to the right like a heavy sack. The abrasive surface of the stone scraped my elbows and knees. Then the rope gave way entirely and I soared backward into thin air, sheer terror sucking the breath from me.

Chapter 8: In the Presence of My Enemies

I

For an endless moment the rough basalt wall seemed to drop away from me. Then I had a sensation of tumbling backward, my heart and lungs lifting and floating inside my ribs as I came loose from the earth in a dizzy, terrifying descent. The shock of collision slammed the air from my chest; pain stabbed my back and shoulders. I plunged into mind extinguishing cold. Stunned, I hung suspended for a long moment, enveloped in a halo of bubbles. Slowly, the pounding in my eardrums grew into a roar, and I came to myself, and then I kicked and thrashed, clawing for the surface, starved for air. Mad with terror, my lungs bursting, I shot up out of the water as if launched from a bow. I sucked in great lungfulls of air and choked as the Jordan closed over me again. I sank down helplessly. The dark waters rolled over me, and my desperate thrashing gave me no leverage, no purchase against this resistless medium. It sucked me downward and squeezed the breath from me. I was trapped, powerless. Then I was gasping for air again, slapping the surface with my arms, glimpsing the great cliff and lights moving on the water.

In a moment I slipped under again, descending this time into a strange lassitude. My limbs continued to struggle, to flex as if an unappeasable desire to live survived somewhere still, though not in me. A heavy, limb-numbing coldness penetrated my body; my legs and arms grew leaden, and I felt my will ebbing with my strength. A profound resignation, a stillness, invaded my senses. Only a faint throb of energy beat in my ears. *This is death, some part of me reported.*

My trance was interrupted by a sharp blow to my head and then the violent sensation of being lifted by the hair. I was seized in a powerful grip and yanked upward. My face collided violently with a solid surface; I was stunned. But I could breathe. I inhaled a great lungful of air, coughed, and took in more water, sputtering, my lungs burning. Then my hair seemed to be pulled from its roots.

"You fool, why didn't you take hold of the rope?"

My back was slapped and clawed. Hands pulled at my shoulders and arms; I glimpsed a man with a torch above me; again my face was crushed against the side of a boat. Slowly, and with great effort, I was hauled wailing and slippery out of the water. The wood bumped and rasped against my body and I flopped like a catch onto the deck. I lay face down and was slapped and pounded. I vomited sour-smelling water and lay in it, sobbing painfully. Aching in every part of my body, I wondered into what world I had emerged.

I was poked and shaken until I began to discern that questions were being asked of me. "Escaped," I gasped. "Don't take me to shore."

"Damn! Damn the luck!" a voice complained.

I was wrapped in a rough blanket and my limbs and body were chafed hard. There seemed to be two of them; their accents were harsh and unfamiliar. I was enveloped in fish-smells.

"This is trouble!"

"I believe it! Lucky he was not tangled in our net.

"We may have been seen, do you think?"

"Es possible."

We were suddenly in darkness, and I heard the remnants of their fire hiss in the water. As my eyes adjusted, I could see other fishing craft at their night's work and lights on the water. Above us, the stars were out and the moon had freed itself from the clouds. Gradually, in response to their questions, I recovered my senses and explained my situation as best I could, haltingly, like a child discovering the words for things. I had fallen from the wall of the Vantage, I said, escaping from Hanford's men. I begged them for help. I was past all shame, broken in spirit. It was difficult to speak sensibly.

They listened, saying little. They were Danite fishermen. While not eager to come to the attention of the authorities on my account, they were even less anxious to assist them. Their problem was what to do with me.

Getting my bearings again, I told them that I thought I might have a chance of skirting the town on the south and make my escape that way. I reckoned I could make my way up the valley, if they could only drop me on the shore below Jezreel's landing. By that route, I might reach the camp of Joash undetected by Hanford's men. Surely the Danites would extend hospitality to me, feed and clothe and hide me if necessary.

My two rescuers grunted their assent, glad for a way out of the danger in which rescuing me had involved them. We floated silently with the current, watching the lights of the town pass on shore. They offered me food, and I took a piece of hard cornbread, declining a kind of fish paste they kept in a jar. I began to shiver uncontrollably. They debated a while about the fire and then relit it, drying my clothes as we drifted. They resumed their fishing, casting and drawing their net in the darkness. I began to think a little more clearly, and I focused on how I would go about making my way past the garrison and finding the Dekali. I needed to recover my sword and gear, my orders from the Apostle and Ben Gurion – but above all my sword. Then I could continue westward toward Hazor. But for the moment I had to put myself out of the grasp of Hanford Glanz.

I wrapped myself in a tattered blanket at the bottom of their boat, realizing that I had nothing to give them to pay my fare. I had nothing at all in my gift at this moment – except a lesson that I could not share. I began to shudder violently and clenched my teeth against the cold.

I made my way up the slope, stumbling through the irrigated fields and across ditches, avoiding inhabited places. I tripped over a hoe carelessly left out, and, mindful of dogs, decided to borrow it, as I had no weapon larger than a dagger. I climbed steadily, pausing frequently to catch my breath and to listen for signs of pursuit, but I heard only the pounding of my own heart. The scent of the fields lay heavy about me; the dew had fallen.

A dog barked by a hut, and I froze in place. I waited for the racket to subside, but it persisted. Music drifted up from the town; some vestige of the games and the harvest celebration lingered there. I caught my breath, reflecting that, if I were fortunate, Hanford's men might assume that I had died of the fall or drowned in the Jordan. But that would be too much to hope. Patrols would be looking for me. Perhaps they would be lazy and confine their search to the near shore under the Vantage. But if they were diligent or imaginative, they would seek me right where I was. So far, there was no sign of pursuit, and the dog finally left off baying at me.

I skirted an orchard with houses nearby. The local inhabitants would not betray me intentionally, but any loud commotion could bring Hanford's garrison down upon me. I stopped frequently, scanning the dim landscape. The valley was luminous in the bright moonlight. I tried to estimate where the garrison might have posted sentinels, but they might be anywhere. In this shadow land, there were few obvious landmarks to guide me. Fortunately, my course was straight up the valley. All I had to do was keep moving and avoid attracting attention. If the Northern Guards were on horseback, the sound of their hooves would warn me in time to slip aside and hide. But if they used hounds to track me, I was a dead man.

It was difficult labor climbing the bench to where the Danites had camped. I made my way through the cultivated land and into the sagebrush, feeling the temperature change. Atop the bench, I stopped, panting, and rested on the ground. The campsite was empty, and signs of a hasty departure littered the area. The Dekali must have learned of my detention in the citadel and realized that their association with me meant danger for them also. I drew a great gulp of air, longing for my gear, for my Hazorite sword, and a good wool robe to ward off the chill. A night wind had begun to whistle down the vale of Jezreel. I chafed at my weakness. My strength was nearly spent and I was cold. I regretted too that I had exposed my innocent hosts to danger. Remembering my recent habitual mood, my flirting with death, I reflected: It is easy to despair. Despair is a weakness. Worse, it is self-indulgence.

Amidst these thoughts, the memory of Rehab Gill crossed my mind. What was *he* doing here? And what was he doing in the uniform of a Northern Lights Guard? I had to know. I pulled myself to my feet, realizing that I was finished with death longing. Under the sheer cliff of the Vantage, in the depths of the Jordan, I had gotten hold of a simple truth—or it had gotten hold of me. In the water, helpless and half way down death's gullet, I had nourished no griefs. I had wanted only to live and draw in lungfuls of air. To live! *Respect the infinite preciousness of life*, the Master says. I vowed that I would. Too bad about my Dekali hosts, I reflected. But I must live.

I looked around, casting about for some idea of escape. By all appearances, the other Danite groups camped along the ridges had also taken hasty leave of the place. I could make out a few abandoned tent poles and other rubbish in the moonlight. Then I heard voices and the sound of horses' hooves coming up the Ancients' road. I slipped behind some sagebrush and lay quietly. It was a fair-sized party, a dozen or so, moving quickly, but unwarily. Cavalry, I thought. *Looking for me*.

I crouched in the shadows and considered my options. Hazor, my only possible refuge, was two or three days to the west. But I had to climb the hills above Jezreel, and they were both steep and arid. The wells of the Sevfolk lay a day inland. I had no water bottle and no food. Hanford's cavalry would be scouring the brush for me. *Not this group, however; they passed me chattering noisily among themselves and looking neither to the right nor the left.* So, my case was not hopeless. A party the size I had just seen would not risk an encounter with Danite warriors on their own ground. My best chance would be to continue up the ridge above Jezreel, staying south of the Ancients' road but parallel with it, until I either found a friendly party of Danites or reached the wells. I stumbled along the bench, looking for an easier ascent up the ridge, and feeling myself close to exhaustion.

After a brief effort, I was totally spent. I had to lie down. The wind was rising and I shivered hard in my damp clothes. My head was still clear, but I knew that if exposed, wet and unprotected as I was, I could die over night. It was already becoming difficult to concentrate. I looked about for cover. Seeing none, I knelt behind a clump of sagebrush and scratched a shallow trench in the sandy soil with the hoe and lay down in it. I covered my legs with a few inches of sand, and scooped it over as much of my body as I could manage. Drawing my borrowed scrap of blanket over my head and shoulders, I nestled down into the earth, trying to preserve the warmth of my body like a log in the ashes, wondering if I would ever rise from this cold bed again.

The sun awakened me out of a tumult of dreams such as I never hope to experience again. Then I remembered where I was and realized my dreams had been the events of the night before. I stretched cautiously, flexing my muscles, and then began to disinter myself by degrees from my bed of sand. I was painfully stiff, and I ached to my very bones. Carefully, I brushed the grit from my eyes and looked about. The sun was well up and mercifully warm. My clothing and skin were crusted all over with sand. I brushed myself off as best I could with hands as clumsy as roots. My fingers were shriveled as if I had stayed too long in a bath. My head ached behind my eyes, and I was feverish. But I was able to stand erect, if unsteadily; my legs worked and I had my bearings. I meditated silently a moment and started west up the slope.

The terrain rose steeply toward the summit of a ridge, but its eroded slopes also gave me many declivities in which to hide. The hoe was a good walking staff, and I crossed the summit by mid-day. By afternoon the staff had become a crutch to lean on, and the hot sun a burden on my shoulders. I grew gradually desperate for water, and panted until my tongue swelled. In a small depression I found stagnant water and cattails. Falling to my knees, I pulled several and chewed the fleshy inner stems and the roots, wallowing in the muck. The taste was putrid, and I knew I would pay later on with dysentery.

An hour later, descending the ridge along a ravine, I found a small spring – a lonely spot of green in the arid landscape. I was elated, recognizing that my mind was beginning to wander dangerously. I needed food as well as drink. As I approached, I tossed a few stones and set the resident rattlesnakes buzzing. I killed one with my hoe before it could make off into cover, intending to make a meal of it after I had drunk. The water tasted sweet, and I drank until my stomach was distended uncomfortably, and then I rested a while and drank again. I must have dozed in the shade of the gully. When I came to myself, I was still hungry, but when I saw my headless prey stretched out beside me, I realized I had no means of making a fire. I gazed at the plump, muscular body, feeling frustrated. Hungry as I was, I was not quite ready for raw rattlesnake. Still, my stomach was making its needs felt. Objects in my sight began to move and swim together; I was beginning to hallucinate. I was so hungry that I could smell smoke and food cooking.

Then I realized that it was in fact smoke I had detected. I rose quickly, looked about, and then tossed a handful of dust into the air. The wind was from the southwest. It was the scent of cooking all right. I had only to follow my nose.

II

Ignoring my churning stomach, I settled down to wait until dusk, until the sun had slipped behind the high ridges and would not be in my eyes. I could see fires glowing among the tents and occasional movement. The air was filled with the tantalizing aroma of cooking meat. I tried to summon up the hunter's patience I had learned as a child at the Refuge and bent all my self-discipline toward solving the problem before me. Surely there must be sentries, visible or not. I searched the terrain. The camp lay in a canyon along side a small creek. The tents were pitched on a bench, well back from a clump of cottonwood and willow trees. The ground was broken and afforded a good deal of cover. I traced potential paths to the camp in my mind's eye, eventually satisfying myself that there were no guards posted between the camp and me. These had to be Danites, I assured myself – probably Sevfolk shepherds, who claimed this territory. No one else would be so confident of their safety here. The sun dropped slowly behind the western mountains. Then I began to move.

I crept through the sagebrush on hands and knees. I stopped for long intervals to watch and listen. Insects whirred and clicked and jumped so ostentatiously out of my path I was certain that they would give my position away. Everything in the camp, however, remained peaceful and oblivious to my presence. I saw horses hobbled near the tents, but no sign of flocks nearby. I thought it just possible that these were the tents that had been pitched at Jezreel – perhaps even the camp of Jerub. I approached nearer the camp, exercising all the care in stalking that I could command. The wind was still favorable and, I hoped, would not betray my scent to the camp dogs. In spite of my best efforts, however, a dog stirred near the edge of the creek and commenced a high-pitched barking. Several others took it up and I knew the moment I dreaded was at hand – and I was not yet close enough to seize a tent rope. The camp began to stir; angry voices sounded within the tents.

Crouching low and using the cover, I moved quickly forward. Then, out the corner of my eye, I caught sight of a shape, a blurred form, coming at me. Reacting instantly, I swept the hoe upward and to the right, solidly whacking the body of the attacking dog in mid-air as he sprang at me. The shock of the blow knocked me off balance, but the dog missed with his teeth and went sprawling beyond me. He made no sound, and had uttered no bark or growl of warning. Gaining his feet, he sprang at me again, and I spun backwards to strike another blow with my full weight transmitted to the hoe. This time, the dog retreated yelping. In a moment, however, a pack of dog was baying me furiously, circling close, but there were human forms behind them now; I would not be torn entirely to pieces. I lunged forward a few paces and seized the nearest tent rope, throwing myself on the ground. It felt as if my last energy departed from me, and the hoe dropped from my hands. "Hear me, Danites!" I shouted with all my remaining force. "I claim protection as a suppliant. I claim the protection of Jerub, Sheriff of the Sevfolk."

The melee of dogs and angry humans closed on me; I covered my eyes. I was prodded with sword and spear points. Someone thrust a torch in my face. "Who are you? What do you want here? Who calls on Jerub the Sheriff?"

"I am a son of Asher," I exclaimed, still clinging to the rope. "I have fled from the river, from Jezreel and from Hanford Glanz and his soldiers. Do what you will with me, if you have no honor and despise the Law!"

"Speak your business, stranger. You tempt fate to intrude upon us this way!"

"I am a son of the Haggadah, of the tribe of Asher; I am descended from eminent men; the brother of my great-grandfather was an Apostle. Ask me no more"

I may have lost consciousness for a few moments. When I came to myself I was lying propped by a blazing fire, surrounded by a circle of faces. A woman offered me a water skin to drink from; as I drank it came to me what I must say, how I must dissemble to save myself. "The sheriff's daughters, Tamar and. . ." *I searched for the other name.*

"Ester? You speak of Ester?"

"Yes, Ester! Have the hostages been released? Are Ester and Tamar here safe with you?" The woman who spoke to me seemed beside herself with astonishment at my knowledge of these names, but she nodded.

I heard a deep but familiar voice behind me: "You speak of my daughters? How do you know of my daughters?" I recognized the square, robust figure of Jerub, sheriff of the Sevfolk.

What under the wide and empty sky could I tell them that would dispose them to help me? I could not truly say that Hanford wanted war with the Danites, but I had to imply it. "There is still time," I said, feigning relief. "I was a guest yesterday of Joash ben Jabeth. I was at the Dekali camp when you called." I hesitated, not knowing what to say next. "After I competed in the games, I was trapped in the citadel. I escaped with my life, but the Northern Guards are bent on murder. You must not linger here," I warned. "You must get your people to safety. Hanford looks for a provocation, for blood to spill."

My listeners made mingled expressions of outrage and disbelief. "We are on our own ground," someone said. "Hanford Glanz dares not intrude here."

"There is safety in numbers," I cried, exaggerating my gestures. "If you rouse the other camps and leave here together you may be unmolested. Otherwise, the cavalry –"

"The fool is talking gibberish," someone interrupted. "He is delirious. We are safe here. We brought the hostages out with us last night. The games were completed without incident; the garrison commander told us to go in peace."

"Who is this fool?" another male voice demanded.

Watching myself lie, seeing myself willing to deceive these people in order to save myself, I felt my previous despair and death longing – and all the forms of grief for Justin – swell up again like a bubble in my heart and felt the bubble burst. *Harmlessly. Thus, I cast them off, all my scruples, all the pain of my past.* I felt them slip from me like bedclothes in the morning. *I wanted to live!* Having discovered life on the far side of melancholy and despair, I would not deceive myself further nor pretend to stand on scruple. In the depths of the Jordan, I had encountered a part of myself that valued existence above all else—a self that would spare no effort, endure any pain or humiliation, to continue to live. To *live.* I had decided to respect that impulse, stronger than any other, and obey it.

I gazed at my host-captors, and they gazed back.

"Fetch Joash," the Sheriff said. "His camp is not far."

III

I spoke warily, knowing that my life hung upon my words, but now I was more ashamed of having dissembled than afraid. I had no stratagem by which to manipulate or deceive them, and I wanted none. I decided to plunge ahead, relying upon simplicity, upon the truth. *Thus, I reflected, even expediency leads back to the Way.*

Piled upon rugs in the Sheriff's big tent were all the worldly goods that I possessed – all that I had left in Joash's care when I took part in the games. The firelight played on my Hazorite sword, on my uniform tunic and wool surplice and other clothing; all my military insignia and decorations were laid out for display. My leather pouch with the documents I carried was turned inside out; the charge from Tephlin Glanz and from the Council of Apostles lay open to view. Even more difficult to explain to frugal shepherds was the large wallet containing my travel money from Ben Gurion, which was spilled over the rug. The coins shone in the firelight. To my hosts – or captors, as the case might prove – the money must represent a huge fortune. Everything I owned or had accomplished or aspired to was contained in my scattered effects. What I was lay exposed to view. It remained to be seen what the Danites would do about it.

The tent was full of Jerub's angry kin crowding close about me, and the sides of the tent were pulled up and tied so that the entire camp could press close around and hear what transpired with me. The women were trilling in excitement; their shrill voices rent the air. Joash's features were set in an impassive mask as he alternately searched my face and prodded at my belongings with his quirt. "Who are you?" he demanded. The crowd grew silent.

I drew a breath. "Earlier, it seemed necessary for me to deceive you. I did so, reluctantly. But my intent, I admit, was to deceive."

I heard the sharp intake of breaths around me; Jerub's eyes were narrow slits. Several people clamored for explanation, threatening me, but Jerub silenced them.

"I am in fact a fugitive, as I said. And bound for Hammoth-Wenatchee. Only I was fleeing *toward* danger, as well as away from it." Joash frowned, not understanding. "Hanford Glanz," I explained. "I left four of Hanford's men dead on the canyon rim two days before I met you."

There was a stir in the audience. Joash nodded, indicating for me to continue.

"Deception seemed necessary to my mission. I was – I *am* – under orders." Reluctantly, I made the sign, touching the tips of my forefinger and thumb together in the shape of an eye, the universally recognized symbol of the Eyes of Israel. There was a collective gasp and then muttering in the group. I could only guess at their view of the Council of Apostles and its instrument, the Eyes. My charge from both the government of Israel and the Northern Lights Enterprises lay before them; I scarcely knew what else to say. I gestured toward the papers: "As you see."

Joash looked to the Sheriff and they exchanged glances, then turned to me expectantly.

"It is true, as I told you," I continued, somewhat puzzled, "that I have a blood debt – though not for the worthless lives of Hanford's men, who came in the night to murder me, but rather for the accumulated wrongs of my kinsmen. Men have carried heavier burdens, though it seems that many lifetimes will not suffice to clear myself from their deeds." I thought it best to distance myself from the Glanz family policy, though I spoke only what I felt to be true. Instead of reacting to this information, however, the two clan leaders exchanged puzzled glances.

Is it possible that they do not understand? I plunged ahead, blurting out what I most hated to say: "My father is Tephlin Glanz and Hanford Glanz is my brother." The universal gasp that greeted my words confirmed their ignorance, which I could scarcely credit. I continued doggedly; there was no turning back: "I am Josiah Glanz ben Haggadah. Captain, Third Army of Israel, on detached duty. On a mission from the Council of Apostles."

Joash's impassive face had crumbled and Jerub was staring open-mouthed at me, pulling his beard.

"Keep my goods, my provisions, all," I said over a rising clamor of voices, "but give me my Hazorite sword. The sword is dedicated; its name is my possession and my power, and any who use it unlawfully will feel its edge turn against him." I could not have created more astonishment and consternation if I had turned into fire and vanished up the smoke-hole. The son of Tephlin Glanz stood in their midst – and at their mercy.

The Sheriff signaled for quiet, but had to shout repeatedly to silence the group; everyone was speaking at once. Gradually they grew quiet and stared at me. Jerub conferred a moment with Joash, and then said to me, "If you are indeed his kindred," he said, rubbing the stubble on his face, "then why would Hanford Glanz seek your life?"

"Because of my orders," I replied, still mystified at their ignorance. I could not understand why we were talking at cross-purposes. "I have a commission from the Council of Apostles and another from Tephlin Glanz. Even Tephlin Glanz knows that his son's evil is an offense to Israel. My orders are to relieve Hanford from power and to hold him accountable." As I spoke the answer came to me: no one among these shepherd folk could read. I paused, looking about the group as they digested what I had just told them. The Sevfolk were poor and isolated and clung to the old ways. It must be so. They were illiterate, all of them! But the import of what I had just said to them had sunk in clearly enough; the tent was suddenly filled with their clamor.

"Read us the orders you carry," the Sheriff said. "I would hear the words of the Apostle."

I read my orders to them, and they marveled.

"So Hanford's evil is at an end?" the Sheriff said.

"If I am successful."

Joash played his quirt over my possessions, frowning. He leaned forward and tapped the tip of his quirt on the papers I held. "Read them again," he said. "Read the papers to us." I saw he had set me a test, to see if I could repeat what I had just read – or if I would stumble over the words, forgetting – and thus reveal myself a fraud.

I read both commissions again, slowly and distinctly. The crowd was still; they listened intently, and looked to Jerub and Joash for guidance. I proceeded with a little more confidence, understanding their previous incomprehension. "Knowing how the Glanz name is hated among you, I was reluctant to reveal my identity. My mission itself obliged me to travel in disguise. But Hanford somehow learned of my presence as well as my intent. He is determined to kill me if he can. And for my part, I will tear him from his seat if I can."

The hostility I expressed toward Hanford elicited some sympathetic murmurs, but Jerub eyed me warily. "What help do you seek from us?"

"A good horse and free passage to Hazor and your blessing upon a guest-friend." I knelt before him and touched his hand to my forehead, and then I did the same before Joash ben Jabeth. The crowd voiced its approval: here was a Glanz abiding by the customs, humbling himself before Danite clan chiefs!

Jerub and Joash were not so easily swayed. They saw clearly that, as kin of the hated Glanz family, I was dangerous business. And I might well be dangerous in my own right. Nevertheless, as they pondered what I had said, I was besieged with questions from the crowd, and their inquisition gradually turned friendly. I explained – exaggerating, perhaps – that the Council of Apostles had finally acted to redress their grievances; Hanford would pay for his crimes. The Danites were elated. Jerub, however, demanded to know if Jezreel would be returned to Dan. I explained that my commission did not extend so far. He understood and did not press the matter, but I laid up his question in my memory.

The women had pressed forward among the crowd, and their questions superseded the concerns of the two clan chieftains. My belongings were being passed around the tent, and most of my audience seemed more interested in my oak leaf of beaten gold, won in the winter campaign, than in my kin or my purposes. They handled my St. Gideon's medal, which I wore on a string like a signet, and they unfolded the scarlet sash of the Mighty Men. But, surprisingly, the item that most fascinated them was the memento of the battle with the Kr that I had received as a campaign decoration – a miniature shield with an image of a Messenger etched on it. "Tell us of the Kr and how they fight," a young man demanded. "Tell us how you came to be one of the Mighty Men," said another. It occurred to me that word of the wars to the south, and perhaps some account of Justin and me, had traveled even unto Dan.

They were eager to examine my sword, so I drew it carefully from its scabbard. The sword's beauty and craftsmanship had their usual effects. The fine polished steel and the ornately worked handle and guard glittered in the firelight, causing awed intakes of breath. I believe I could actually hypnotize many in the crowd simply by drawing the sword slowly from its scabbard. I noticed some, however, who were not absorbed in my sword but were observing my scars. One handsome young woman came forward and put her hand on my forehead, where the wound I had received from the Kr was still swollen and purple. Her boldness excited me, but I was suddenly conscious again of my ragged, filthy appearance – and also of my exhaustion. I turned to Jerub and bowed and said, "If it please my host, let me rest and purify myself. Then, after a little food, I will answer all your questions."

A group of young women accompanied me to the stream where I was bathed and inspected for ticks in a manner not at all customary to me but apparently amusing to them. On the whole I felt their behavior wanton and somewhat unbecoming, though I was greatly stimulated by it. I gave them my few clothes to be washed, and half a dozen young women jostled each other to dry me with rough towels. Afterwards, they wrapped me in a light woolen robe. In the meantime, a sweat lodge had been prepared for my purification. I lingered only a few moments, hardly long enough to break a sweat, for the Sevfolk were impatient to hear my story. In any event, sounds of revelry had broken out, and the noise would effectively prevent any meditation I might attempt. I sat in the darkness, inhaling the steam and thinking: sooner or later, they will reflect on whether they really prefer me – or any Glanz – to rule Naphtali and the Northern Lights.

IV

"I will not boast before men who are warriors themselves and sensible men." I used the stilted language of the old storytellers and all the ancient formulas I could remember in telling my tale: "Who here does not know how it is? How in the thick of the fight, a man feels a sudden strength, like a giant, and has a courage not his own, and it comes about that he does surprising things. It is a gift, a mystery. The next day the man is himself again. On the third day, the terror may come while he is in his tent with his blanket warm upon him. Or the dread of death may steal up by his fireside, and the shaking takes hold of him, and his knees are like water. This too comes to any man."

Though my storytelling sounded absurd in my own ears, the curiosity of my hosts seemed inexhaustible. Jerub had proclaimed a feast, and while the food was being prepared, there was a good deal to drink. In response to their questions, I told them of the battle against the Kr at Elion, of Shevren's men strewn in pieces across the valley floor, and of our night attack at Beersheba Wells. Tears welled in their eyes when I told them how we set out in darkness to break through to safety or die to the last man, and they recoiled as we had to the hideous sights and sounds of torture that met us as we overran the campfires of the Kr.

Speaking these things brought them back afresh to my mind's eye. Thereafter, I spoke artlessly, describing what came to mind with no more consciousness than a bubbling spring. Justin had had a gift for articulating a perspective capable of capturing his listeners; his words connected things – made sense in new ways. Sometimes his own private view of events was as elusive as a swallow's flight, but he could make you see an event as he intended you to see it. The typical warrior's gift was simple narrative, to tell a tale of things connected by a string of "ands," much as I was doing at the moment. But Justin Glanz Apollo went at the causes of things and interpreted events as passionately as a Messiahist glosses one of their texts.

As I wondered about the style of my own story telling, I lost the thread of my tale. I had been speaking of my winter patrol into Lagash, only this time instead of being snow-blind and drunk with fatigue, I was a master of strategy, staving off the Harlech offensive into Judah by my discoveries. When I paused, bewildered, my hosts offered me a drink of a bitter rye beer much favored by the shepherds, to clear my throat. It was strong, head-spinning stuff. Whatever the style of my telling, I seemed to have my audience spellbound, particularly a young woman of fine, open features and ample figure, who sat close to me and listened intently to my tale, flashing me smiles of encouragement and praise. It was she who had touched my forehead earlier. She had also accompanied the young women who had bathed me so wantonly, but had hung back, watching.

As I paused for breath and to collect my thoughts, a young man rose and offered a toast to our host, Jerub. I enthusiastically agreed and downed another bowl of a concoction the Danites made of fermented mare's milk and brandy, and which suited my tastes far better than their beer. The warmth of these simple folk, exemplars of a kind of hospitality from Israel's past, touched my heart. I felt cheered by their kindness and by my great good fortune to be here alive and feasting among them rather than fish-bait drifting on the bottom of the Jordan. The contrast appeared so palpable to my imagination that as I looked at the friendly crowd, my eyes misted with tears. "To our hosts," I shouted, downing another bowl of fermented milk. My goods were nearby, and on impulse, I emptied all the money I had in my pouch and divided it into two equal piles. "For my hosts and protectors," I declared, "Jerub, sheriff of the Sevfolk, and Joash ben Jabeth of the Dekali. Generous men both, and pillars of the old Israel! I owe my life to them; therefore I share my substance with them without stint."

The revelers cheered my generosity, and several rounds of toasts were raised and enthusiastically downed. Other storytellers took over and entertained us as we feasted on lamb and cracked wheat in oil and vinegar and rolled up in hot flatbread. The tales grew increasingly ribald and I found them outrageously funny. The various articles of my personal property were still circulating through the group. After I had eaten, I regathered as many items as possible. I was particularly anxious about my dispatch pouch and the letters, my original orders and the authority from Tephlin Glanz to draw 200,000 kanz in his name. Eventually everything seemed to find its way back to its proper place. My hosts were honest Israelites, salt of the earth. One man, somewhat befuddled, handed me my battle decorations, saying, "This one is broken."

It was my miniature statue of St. Gideon, which I wore around my neck on formal occasions. The base had become separated. It was made of green gemstone and it had come apart into two pieces. I tried to fit them together, noticing that my own movements had become uncoordinated as well. The base had come away, but it did not seem to be broken – but rather made that way. The edges were smooth to the touch and seemed to fit together. Curious, I brought the base up close to my eyes in the poor light and squinted at it, and then noted how the image of St. Gideon, turned upside down and aligned with the base, fitted perfectly. The bottom of the image was deeply grooved. I felt it with a clumsy finger and squinted at it again.

I dropped my hands immediately to my side and glanced about. No one seemed to be paying me any attention. I was suddenly dizzy with elation, breathing hard and feeling perspiration run down my face. As the storyteller finished his tale of the adventures of a goat, a pig, and a cock, I laughed with the group and then slipped outside as if to relieve myself. Indeed, the need was on me. The cool air was a relief in itself, and, unable to contain myself, I urinated a torrent into a clump of sagebrush. *That drunken fool, I thought, has handed me my destiny!*

I could see nothing clearly in the darkness. The stars overhead and the moon seemed to shift in and out of focus, and I could barely make out the shape of my St. Gideon medal. But I knew what I would find. My mind reeled. Every object in view seemed in motion, as if I were gazing at reflections in moving water. *How can I be sure? How can I know it is so? Am I as drunk as the fool who handed me the medal!* Befuddled though I was, my hands in the darkness easily fitted the base to the statue and twisted it tight. It was made to do so! It was no illusion. Inside the detached part of the image was the carved seal of Tephlin Glanz, and it screwed cleverly into the base. The juncture when closed was almost invisible. General Ben Gurion had presented the medal to me in Hebron with his own hands. The seal screwed into the base, which perfectly concealed it. I had had the seal all along!

So my father had given me something useful after all – a sword more powerful and with a great deal more reach than even my Hazorite blade. I returned to the feast elated as I had never been in my life. I seated myself in the circle, watching the smiling faces and shadows, hearing nothing but my own racing pulse, knowing what I knew and savoring it. Someone brushed against me and I turned, and it was the young woman, her eyes shining at me. I was enveloped in her presence, in her scent. "Tell me your name," I said.

"Tamar," she replied, smiling at me.

"Surely, Tamar," I said, not certain I could still speak clearly, "you must be the most beautiful of all the daughters of Israel."

Someone handed me another bowl of brandy and mare's milk, and I drank it, gazing deeply into Tamar's eyes. The clan had started a rousing song of ancient deeds and triumph; it was unfamiliar to me, so I clapped my hands in time with it, smiling at my companion. But even in the midst of this excitement, exhaustion soon took possession of me. My attention wandered, and I must have drifted off at some point.

It was the sensation of cold wetness that roused me, and my first thought was that I had spilled the bowl of milk and brandy in my lap. I sat up, confused, trying to get my bearings. To my surprise, I found myself outside and some distance from the tents. The stars, as well as I could make them out by rubbing a fist in my eye, were getting on towards dawn. Beside me, on a wool robe, a figure stirred. It was, to my further astonishment, a young woman – perhaps the Tamar who had spoken to me and sat beside me at the feast. Whoever she was, she tugged at my sleeve and then put her hand into my robe familiarly. "Shhhh," she said, and pulled me toward her, brushing her lips against my face. The warm scent of her was overwhelming. I was rigid with surprise, trying to remember what had happened while I was in a stupor. "Tamar?" I said. My heart was knocking in my chest.

"Shhhh!" she whispered again, kissing me very lightly on the lips. In the darkness, I could not even be sure that this was the woman who had spoken to me and not another. "Here," she said softly, "come here." She snuggled her hips against me and placed my hand on her breast, which was uncovered. I marveled at the softness of it, at the texture of her nipple, which hardened under my touch. "Here," she whispered again, moving my hand to her hips and then down her belly. She moved again, drawing my body over on hers.

Without any conscious intent on my part, my body settled gently on top of hers; I felt her hand lifting my robe so that my bare legs and belly pressed against her. I experienced a paralysis of will, such as I had felt in the Jordan. I could no more withdraw from her than I could rise unassisted from its depths. She placed her hand on the small of my back, pressing ever so lightly, and then her hand slid down my buttock and squeezed, pressing me more tightly against her. She awakened in me the most delicious sensations I had ever felt. Abandoning my resolution to leave her, I moved instead infinitesimally against her, with her, contracting my muscles and feeling with disbelief the exquisite friction of myself, suddenly tumescent again and eager, moving resistlessly within her. I heard her sharp intake of breath, and then her mouth was on mine, devouring me. Her hand moved down my buttock again and touched my scrotum, and I cried out in the fierce pleasure of the moment, unmindful of where we lay. She cupped her hand over my mouth to silence me, still clasping me tightly with her legs, rocking me, and then she turned my head aside and thrust her tongue into my ear.

V

The next morning I departed from the Sevfolk as soon and with as little ceremony as I could manage. I collected my belongings, pulled my damp clothing off of a tent rope, and accepted the loan of a horse from one of the sheriff's kinsmen. I hoped my hosts would attribute my gloomy silence to the effects of drink, but I was wretched beyond words This was *shahat*, filth, that I had done. I stole a brief look at my nocturnal companion in the dim morning light. Snoring softly, with her mouth ajar and a trickle of saliva on her cheek, she seemed infinitely less alluring than the night before. Good features, but not beautiful. And certainly not elegant. Still, I gazed at her longingly. One soft breast lay exposed and rose and fell gently as she breathed. I thought with a pang of the softness of her skin, the yielding female textures of her body. I rebuked myself for these thoughts and hurried away.

Once out of sight of the camp, I turned my horse off the road and climbed into the high country. Within a few miles I found what I sought. The summer sheep pastures of Dan exactly resembled those of my native Asher. Danite flocks were scattered over the highlands. On ridges round about, I saw armed shepherds rise up from their vantage points. I guided my horse toward the lowest-lying dell where water must lie and where, inevitably, I would find the main camp. I approached openly and unhurriedly, thus announcing my peaceful intentions. I soon came upon the encampment and saluted the elder who stood by the well: "Brother, I have need of purification. Great need."

He was an old man, and, I earnestly hoped, someone wise in the ways of the world. He nodded slowly and introduced himself as Micah, and I was relieved to hear the Israelite name. The young boy at his side was his grandson.

The rites lasted until sundown. Emerging out of the sweat lodge into the sights and sounds of the world, I felt my skin tingle as the air enveloped me. My hair lifted in the electric contact of re-entry. The boy placed a robe over my shoulders and motioned me to a place by the fire. The wool of the robe felt rough and familiar against my skin. As I gazed at a streak of red sky fading above the ridgeline, my mind gradually returned to me. Birds called, insects buzzed and chirped nearby, and a breeze stirred the cottonwoods. The air was cooling with the end of day. I drew deep breaths into my lungs, drawing in the world, inhaling again my familiar thoughts and feelings.

When I came fully to myself, Micah and the boy had disappeared, the flock apparently needing their attention. Down in the draw the soft shapes of the grazing sheep resembled outcroppings of stone. Dogs were working the flock expertly, moving the outliers back into the safety of the fold. I knew they would be gathered and counted before bedding down for the night in the stone pens, and the familiarity of it all was a great comfort. As I waited vacantly, night began to descend out of the twilight. The sounds of the pasture were changing as subtly as the light.

I felt myself drifting away again. I went out into the dusk and hovered light as a strand of spider web; I floated away from my body, riding the wind, the form and color of my thoughts flowing away from me. I hung there remote from all life, including my own. From a distance came the evening call of the cock quail drawing the covey together, and I returned.

Micah stepped into the firelight. "Perhaps I failed to do the rites properly," he said, glancing about anxiously. "The sayings – I may have forgotten. . . ."

"Truly," I said, "nothing was lacking." I groped for more to say, unable to explain my feelings, which he had seen so easily.

The old man bent to stir the fire, throwing some sweet-smelling sage and dried hemp leaves into the flames. For an instant, the pungent smoke burned my eyes and nostrils.

"You have done the part of a brother, without fault," I said, repeating the formula of completion. I began to feel better then, and wished for some word to reassure him. "I believe in the ritual," I said. "It has power, but it is not magic." For us, no ceremony, no depth of repentance, no sacrificial blood comes between the doer and his act. There is no wiping the slate clean. As surely as a broken tile fallen from a roof will hit the ground, so do consequences follow from our acts. Through our rituals, we seek to put our minds in order, to see more clearly and to recover harmony – the better to deal with what is, including the consequences set in motion by our actions. Our rites also teach us to avoid harmful acts in the future. Nevertheless, as our Teacher reminds us, *surely the past lies upon our heads.*

I felt purified and whole again, but the possible consequences of what I had done weighed on me. At the same time, I could not keep my mind from dwelling upon the indescribable pleasures of contact with the woman, and I was not certain whether I would be immune from them in the future. As I recalled what I had done, desire stirred in me, and I knew I would not be. For a moment, I felt despair to be so powerless to enforce my will. No wonder the ignorant are drawn to salvation, to promises of rescue, I thought, and I felt again the power that the Third Comers drew from their faith, false though their assurances are. I knew that in the face of desire such as I had felt the night before, I could not set one foot before the other away from it. How, then, was I to find the Way and follow it? How keenly and with what painful new knowledge I understood the Master's words, *"the world is a trap baited with desire!"*

But I seemed to see other things as well. I had accepted the mission from the Council and Ben Gurion without real hope of accomplishing it, and in truth, as a form of self-destruction. Grieving for Justin and Michal-Rebekah, I had accepted that my life was over. I had longed for death and had moved toward it with unshakable certainty – or so I had assured myself. But two days ago, in the depths of the Jordan, I had discovered that my life possessed a will of its own, apart from that wish. *Apart from what I thought of as my own will.* Apparently, I had deceived myself – *or something in me had deceived what I think of as myself* – with this false and foolish death longing. I could not easily pull these thoughts together, but I had grasped one certainty: desire for life moved in me stronger than any will of mine. I – whatever *I* was – served *it*; it did not serve me. Suspended in the depths of the Jordan, something in me had awakened, and this something had taken note, without fear, without alarm, of the elemental flux of things outside pressing in, and inside me pressing out. This something had brushed against me in that pitch-darkness. I felt its wake roil in my heart. *This is death,* I had said to myself, but it was a reality deeper than death or life itself that touched me. Then I had been hauled back into the air, and into new life. I felt humble and blessed and possessed of something beyond any value, beyond any words.

But then, to my consternation, within the span of a day I had deceived the Sevfolk, innocent women and children among them, putting them at risk to save my own life. I committed acts which, even hours earlier, I would not have believed myself capable. So craven, and yet so easy after all! And then, after a bout of drunken bragging, I had taken my host and protector's daughter – whether Tamar or Ester I could not be certain. I had had full, uninterrupted intercourse with her, with the possibility of starting a new life in her belly, in flagrant violation of the very heart of the Law. *Twice!* If she was pregnant, the consequences of this act of mine – this act, at any rate, in which I had participated – would go forward, time out of mind. I could not even compass the implications in my mind.

I had always seen myself as a Law-abider. As a child at the Refuge, I had sought to please my elders with a willing obedience. As a youth and as a man, I had lived and breathed the Law. It defined all things and gave me their meaning and value. It was a shock, therefore, to observe myself behaving like a wild animal.

But when I considered the means by which life is begotten, I could not but marvel at its lawlessness. How strange and all consuming is desire! It is a purpose that uses us, like the life-thirst that I felt in the Jordan's depths. No wonder the great teachers of mankind have railed against it and sought to suppress it. They fear it. St. Supplicee warns that the world is a flame fed by human hearts and bids us quench our desire in order to see. And yet is it not our fate to burn continually with desire, and to be seared and scorched and eventually consumed by it?

None of our teachers denies it. But if desire is a stratagem of life to triumph over death, then it is not quenched, cannot be quenched. And if we see at all, we must see *through* it, not in spite of it. Perhaps this eternal tumbling together of desire and death opens to the Way itself. Or do we merely wear out our human hearts and call our exhaustion wisdom?

I could not make these ends match up. Pondering these things, I began to feel the weight of conventional wisdom as merely a feather, as mere timidity, and I thought of the teachings of my Master Ebenezer and of his Master before him, Israel Zhen-Gwo: "We live," Master Ebenezer says, "an existence that lies beyond any concept of existence. Our lives have, or *may* have, a beginning and an end – or may extend beyond any concept of beginning or end. Therefore, Master Israel Zhen-Gwo has truly said 'we must understand at last that understanding is not necessary'."

I savored the words. *We must understand at last that understanding is not necessary.*

Micah and the boy shared the tasks of preparing our evening meal. With old-fashioned courtesy, he shared out the flat bread and lentils and greens, served in the ancient way with salt and vinegar, the bread tasting a little from the ashes.

VI

In the morning my spirits had returned, though I was no clearer in my mind than before. I parted from my hosts and set my horse's head toward Hazor. The day was bright and clear and promised to be hot, like the summer days of my childhood. The trail was easy, and rest had restored my energies. My blood began to sing along with the gait of my mount, and I let him break into an easy canter when we intersected the Ancients' road. I remembered my shame vividly enough, but it co-existed with pride in my new knowledge—vague though it was. And, to say the truth, I felt a smug pleasure in my memory of the Sevfolk woman, a memory that the motion of the ride excited in me. Is this the way it is, then? We move from the few simple truths of childhood into the vast confusion of manhood? I put these thoughts aside. Though incomprehensible, the world seemed good to me this morning.

The trail took me to the Sevfolk wells where I had parted from Rehab Gill, and I remembered the kanz I had buried under our campfire. I needed the money, as I had foolishly given away all of my travel allowance from Ben Gurion. Shepherds were watering their flock at the wells, but I rode forward boldly, my horse pressing through the throng. My borrowed head cloth identified me as Sevfolk, and when I waved familiarly and seemed intent upon my own business, no one paid me any attention. In the dust and din of bleating animals, I may even have gone unobserved as I found the hearthstones and quickly unearthed the pouch of coins. *Blood money*, I recalled grimly. But I had earned it. I waved farewell to the two shepherds, who were intent on their labor of drawing water from the well, and went on my way.

As I resumed my journey, the thought of starting a pregnancy in the woman gave me a moment of sick fear. I thought too of the anger of her relatives, and the public infamy and disappointment among my teachers and kin. But ignorant as I was of women, I knew I had not taken a virgin. My partner had evidently broken the Law before lying down with me. *Perhaps many times*, I thought, feeling relieved. She had been at least as knowledgeable as I was ignorant. The more I thought of it, the less culpable I seemed – or, in case of a pregnancy, the less identifiable. There must, I thought, be others closer to home for her kin to suspect. And in retrospect, the revelry of the Danites seemed provocative and licentious. These Sevfolk were more lax than I would have believed – or would have expected to find anywhere in Israel. I thought of the garrison life in Esdralon, which I had observed but not partaken of. I had much to learn, obviously, but I felt a little contemptuous of my hosts. It seemed possible, on the other hand, that I over-estimated the extent to which the Law was kept in Israel.

I thought of Michal-Rebekah and of married life as an estate. It gave me a sharp twinge of sadness to think of her in this intimate way, through my experience of the Sevfolk woman – though I had thought of her in intimate ways many times before. I was simultaneously proud and a little ashamed of my new knowledge of womankind. Still, I felt beyond doubt that it would be a good thing, with the Law's consent and public approval, to start a life in a woman's belly – given a wife like Michal-Rebekah. I wondered if I would ever have the opportunity. Then the memory of what I had done came back to me vividly, and I shivered in the hot sunlight.

I knew something of Dan, having traveled there as a boy with my Masters, Josephus and Ebenezer. I knew its southern boundary, at least, and its capital and chief town, Hazor. I was approaching Hazor through its arid eastern region, the Sevfolk hills, which were fit for pasture but not for crops. Dan occupies the upper Yakima valley, and it is separated from Israel proper by forty miles of wilderness – the Wilderness of Zoar. The Wilderness is an arid stretch of bare hills cut by the canyon of the Yakima, and it forms a no-man's land between Dan and Israel. I had been schooled in the heart of that barren waste. The Wayfarers Refuge, where I received my education, lies in the very center of Zoar, deep in the canyon of the Yakima. The Refuge was, in fact, the chief stop over and resting site on the road between Dan and Manasseh.

Behind their wilderness barrier, the Danite clans keep to themselves and cherish their distance from the rest of Israel. Old Believers had deep roots there. My sword was the product of the last great master of the craft, Eliphaz, whose forge had been at Hazor. A small college still flourished there, dedicated to the old lore and the discipline. Unless it had changed greatly in recent years, Dan lived closer to the old ways than any other part of Israel. Here, I thought, were people like my own, like-minded and suspicious of the Messiahists. I felt that coming to Hazor would almost be like coming home.

Late in the afternoon, I topped a rise that afforded a view of the country, and I reined in abruptly, in awe of the sight. Dan lies in a hollow between two ridges that descend like enfolding limbs from the Cascade Range to the west. I was unprepared for its beauty. Even in this season, the plain was green and inviting. The curving bed of the Yakima glowed like a jeweled necklace in the summer haze. From the heights where I sat, the notch of the Yakima canyon was visible in the west, and Dan lay below like a table spread with great bounty, or a palm-full of precious gold. All the chief inhabited places of Dan were visible from my vantage point. Hazor lay in the northern-most arable portion of the Yakima valley, mother of Israel. Smaller strongholds and villages dotted the plain. Dan, they say, is one of the blessed places of the earth, where the land yields faithfully and in good measure. Seeing the valley lie before me like an open horn of plenty, I thought involuntarily of my Danite sweetheart of two nights before. As my horse descended the ridge I felt a wild elation and something like lust to possess and hold this bountiful place.

As I approached the city, ruined towers of the Ancients rose up like sentinels outside the walls. Hazor was a fortress town with a sprawling settlement growing up outside its walls. Its low outer wall of rough stone seemed no formidable obstacle compared to the walls of Esdralon. A higher wall of dressed stone twenty feet in height encompassed the Old Town, and within it, the citadel of Dan rose like an eagle's eerie. It looked to be five stories tall. There was a market in progress at the south gate. Not knowing whether Caleb Boz, the Apostle of Dan, would be disposed to greet me as a guest-friend or to hang me up in one of his towers, I paused at the market, leading my horse past stalls and peddlers shouting for custom. No one paid any attention to me. Nevertheless, I felt a shadow pass over me as I entered the gate of the outer wall. Caleb Boz was no man to trifle with. His temper was dreaded throughout Israel, and he was indeed known to hang people in his tower. I chewed on a corn fritter and considered my options.

I was an enemy of Boz's enemy, Hanford Glanz. That was one thing in my favor. *Sometimes the enemies of one's enemies are friends.* Second, I had resources at my disposal. I fingered the image of St. Gideon at my throat. Third, I carried the writ of the Council of Apostles. I searched for other factors in my favor, recalling my charge from Tephlin Glanz. But Glanz was doubtless an enemy of Caleb Boz. *No help there.* My assets seemed meager. Nevertheless, one must begin somewhere. I approached the guard at the gate and announced boldly: "I have business with the Apostle of Dan. I am the guest friend of Jerub, sheriff of the Sevfolk. I have a mission from the Council of Apostles that your master is honor-bound to assist. And tell him that I am empowered to discuss with him certain grievances he has with the Glanz family and with the Northern Lights."

The guard stared at me vacantly for a moment and then ran to fetch his officer. I might have guided my horse through the open gate, but I chose to wait, growing less and less confident of my reception. As I waited, I continued to mull over my prospects. Suddenly, a surge of energy swelled within me. Previously, I had intended only to seek refuge in Hazor and inquire quietly about things in Naphtali until I had formed a plan. But I saw now that I had weapons and could act. I had, in fact, the germ of a plan already. My policy was born in that instant.

My brother Hanford was a tyrant who had betrayed those who had given him authority. The wealth he had amassed maintained a fighting force, but Hanford had failed to legitimize his rule. Having misused what was given him, he could build nothing of his own. He was hated by those whom he ruled as well as by those who had lent him power. It was he who was vulnerable, not me. No one would lift a finger to save or sustain him who was not paid or coerced to do so. Formidable as he seemed, his power was brittle. I determined to break it, to wrest Naphtali from him. Glanz had placed the power to act in my hands, if I had the wisdom to convert his script into action. It was thus settled in my mind, a decision taken as I entered the dark inner city of Hazor and inhaled the dust of its streets and the smoke of its cooking fires: *I would take possession of Naphtali – but for my own purposes, not Tephlin Glanz's.*

I followed the Danite officer to the House of Assembly with possibilities blossoming in my mind. Naphtali was the key to defending Judah against either Kuhlans or Messiahists. With that power in hand, I could bargain for things that mattered to *me*. Perhaps I could bring about an end to the war with the Harlech. I pictured myself as broker of a peace among the contending parties – and I imagined myself finding and rescuing Michal-Rebekah and Appian from slavery, should they still be alive. Alive or not, the very prospect of my friends' enslavement filled me with revulsion. When I acquired power in Israel, I vowed I would seek freedom for all Benjamites reduced to slavery – and the end of slavery itself in Naphtali, where my father and brother had introduced it. As for the Messiahists and their claims, we had a score to settle.

A handsome young officer with the insignia of a captain approached and saluted me and then led me to a small apartment across a narrow street from the House of Assembly. I tied my horse to a post and followed him inside. The building was such a modest place I was unprepared for what followed. The captain knocked on the door and opened it without waiting for a reply. I stepped inside and found a group of men, well dressed, sitting at a low table. A single oil lamp burned above them; a candle sputtered on the table.

"What insolence is this?" a voice demanded. It was a harsh voice, and it belonged to an angry hawk-faced man with a deep scar down one side of his face. "You permit a trained assassin to come armed before your father?" I recognized Caleb Boz, the Apostle of Dan, by his blind eye which scowled sightlessly at me. And I saw that he recognized me also.

"I beg you," I said quickly, "do not let me be a cause of rebuke to your son." I unbuckled my sword belt and handed it to the captain who had escorted me – evidently the son of the Apostle. "Do me the courtesy of standing nearby," I said in the young man's ear. The four companions of the Apostle had risen; one, a stout elderly man in the uniform of the Danite Guards, had his hand on the hilt of his sword. "Forgive me," I said. "I have lived in peril of my life for some time, and I have lost the custom of being apart from my weapons. But I mean no harm to any of this company; your safety is assured alike by my honor and by the absence of any motive for hostility. So do not rebuke your son for my sake."

I searched for some way to get on a proper footing with these men, obviously the elders of Dan. I had come upon them too suddenly; neither of us was prepared for the encounter. A foolish mistake. And worse, Boz somehow knew who I was. I put the best face on things that I could: "It is true, I repaid an insult to my mother's name, and I avenged my brother's death. But if there is blood on my hands, none dare claim that it is innocent blood." I ended on a more challenging note than I intended, but I would not wear the name of assassin.

"Is this the tedious fool Jerub warned us of?" Caleb Boz glanced at me and then turned his attention back to documents on the table. "Be brief, young man. If we want horse shit, we have wheel-barrows in the stable."

The others looked me up and down. I was conscious of my youth and inexperience as if both were branded on my forehead. "I am Josiah Glanz ben Haggadah of the tribe of Asher, and captain in the Army of Israel, on special assignment. It is my fate also to be the son of Tephlin Glanz. You know who I am, and that I stand before you as a suppliant."

"The Law decides which is innocent and which is guilty blood," the stout old soldier retorted vehemently, "not some bastard whelp of a Glanz!"

I drew in my breath with a rush, glancing at my sword in the hands of Boz's son. I had killed a man for a similar taunt. I was not amused by this man with his paunch and his bluster, but I suppressed my anger. I noted for future reference that this must be General Malachi, commander of the Danite Legion. "I am here on an errand of the Council," I announced as confidently as I could. "The Shepherd of Israel has set me before you, and I carry the writ of the Apostles. Though it is true that I stand before you in need, I do not come empty-handed."

"Ethan, make this windbag come to the point or have the guards let the air out of him with their spears."

"I come on two missions," I explained quickly, feeling the group harden their hearts against me. I handed them my commissions to read. "I have a mission from the Council of Apostles to investigate excesses in Naphtali and to restore justice to that region. I have another from Tephlin Glanz to depose a rebellious son and to repossess the Northern Lights Enterprises." I waited impatiently while they perused my orders, thinking to myself: *but I intend to seize Naphtali for myself!*

"Your brother Hanford will not relinquish anything to you willingly," said one of the elders, a man dressed like a prosperous merchant. "It would be unwise to underestimate him, particularly since you have no means of wresting anything from him."

"Perhaps I have."

"Perhaps you are a fool and meddler!" the Guards commander said. He had obviously taken a dislike to me.

"One Glanz seems very like another," Boz said. "What have we to do with any mission of Tephlin Glanz?"

"The wrongs that Tephlin Glanz has done in the past," I replied as confidently as I could, "I have the power to undo."

"Or to extend his evil sway even further!" General Malachi retorted. The Guards commander and Boz had arrayed themselves firmly against me. I had blundered badly in coming here unprepared.

"Even so," I replied, "you would do well to be concerned with any mission pertaining to Hanford Glanz and the Northern Lights." I could not tell if my pretended confidence had whetted their curiosity or merely tried their patience.

"I wonder what you will do with the Northern Lights" – it was the merchant who spoke, breaking an awkward silence – "if you manage to take it from your brother?"

I hesitated, not having had a chance to think through this or any other eventuality. "That is a matter I am willing to discuss," I said.

Caleb Boz raised an eyebrow but said nothing.

One of the two elders who had not spoken took his cue: "I wonder why this business of yours concerns the Elders of Dan?" he asked. "And I wonder why an officer with a charge from the Council of Apostles stands before us as a suppliant?" The other followed his lead: "How is it that you intend to restore justice to Naphtali if you cannot reach there? We understand an attempt was made to murder you at Jezreel."

"Like Dan," I said, "I have need of an ally."

Caleb Boz laughed harshly. "You arrive on a borrowed horse, in borrowed clothing.

Yet you claim you do not come empty-handed?" He leaned forward and added with casual menace: "Speak your business plainly, or I promise you, you *will* swing in my tower."

"Accept me as your guest-friend until I repay the sheriff of the Sevfolk for his kindness to me," I said quickly. A flicker of amusement crossed the Apostle's face; perhaps Jerub's account of me had been less kind than I imagined. "Meanwhile, I have business with the Brothers of the College here in Hazor, a few days of business, and then we will speak again of what I have in my hand to offer you."

"Speak now if you have business."

"I have spoken my business; I have shown you the orders I carry from the Shepherd of the People and from the Northern Lights Enterprises. If Dan no longer respects the writ of the Council, it may well fear the power of the latter."

"Why should we fear the Glanzes?" General Malachi sneered. "Let alone help one! One Glanz litter-mate is very like another, it seems to me, and the Northern Lights wage unrelenting war against our merchants."

I was ready to flee in despair, but the man I had identified as a merchant remarked thoughtfully: "I wonder whom we offend by helping you. It is said that the Velcos seek your life. We are near neighbors to them, and their reach is long and their memories longer. Thus, young man, you have the look of unnecessary trouble."

I recoiled from his words. I had not included my enmity with the Velcos or my own war with the Messiahists in my calculations – but they had, and correctly so. "It is good to speak with people who are not ignorant," I replied. But in fact I was unprepared to discuss any of these issues. I was not sufficiently informed, and I had formed only the most rudimentary plan. I needed time to decide how to proceed. The Devil, as Justin liked to say, always lurks in the details. I vowed never again to walk into negotiations without thinking through all possible issues.

"For now," I said, "I ask only that you allow me to remain safely in your city. I have co-religionists here in the College of Hazor. With your permission, I will lodge with them a few days. And when you are ready to hear me, I will lay before you certain matters of importance, and you can then decide what is good and prudent to do."

Suddenly business-like, Caleb Boz granted my request and set a time when I could come again. "We must know more of you and your doings," he said in dismissing me. I took his remark with relief, as if it had been a blessing, and got myself out.

I was not pleased at my maiden effort at diplomacy. I had thought myself shrewd when I was only revealing myself as an ignorant whelp – a "bastard whelp of a Glanz" at that, the General had said. I had believed *Boz is a vain man, whet his curiosity.* But it was my vanity that had been on display in the room. I was ashamed. Things could have gone very badly. Perhaps they had gone badly! I recalled General Zillah's confusion at Elion and saw myself in him, with pain.

But I had come away with a valuable lesson: I had learned that the common report of Dan was wrong: it was not the old Israel, law-abiding and righteous. It was an outlaw state, estranged from Israel and its troubles. Boz was its brigand chief, and the Apostleship was as dead here as elsewhere in Israel.

It was also clear that these Danite outlaws wanted none of me. As an emissary from the Council and a son of Tephlin Glanz, however, I was too important to kill with impunity. I was lucky for that. I had, I felt sure, not even aroused their curiosity.

VII

So it was with mingled foreboding and relief that I found my way to the College of Hazor, the surviving fount and center of Old Belief. I had blundered badly, but I had colleagues and co-religionists who could help me recover my balance. I knocked at an ancient door set within a decaying brick and stucco wall. An old man, bent and seemingly as weathered as the door itself, opened to admit me.

"Peace be upon this house," I said.

The College of Hazor consisted of several buildings built solidly of brick, but badly kept, in the center of the Old Town. The inner compound was merely an overgrown garden surrounded by a crumbling wall. A rambling structure at one end housed the commons. I let my horse drink from a trough near the fountain, and then the old man took me to the Master of the College.

"I seek bread and shelter and an opportunity to meditate upon the Way," I announced, repeating the formula of initiates as I was shown into the library. The college library was hardly larger than my quarters in Esdralon and seemed to have fewer books. The Master of the college remained seated behind a bare table – as if, with nothing to do, he was still annoyed at being interrupted. He introduced himself as Brother Peter. When I gave my name, however, he and a half-dozen ragged devotees suddenly rose with an excited clamor and knelt before me. To my amazement, they reached out and touched their foreheads to my hands, paying me zealous homage, as if I were one of the great masters of the past.

"Stop!" I exclaimed. "What is the meaning of this?"

"Can it be true then?" Brother Peter exclaimed. "It is said that Master Ebenezer has raised up a sword out of the Old Believers. Do we have reason to hope?"

I startled at his words, for they called to mind every probing question of Justin and every accusation of Rehab Gill about my special status among Old Believers. My discipleship to Master Ebenezer was suddenly cast in new light – and with it, Ben Gurion's interest in me also. They all had had intelligence to the same effect: that the last sages among the Old Believers had raised up a special servant to be a weapon against their enemies. And it was no very shrewd deduction that that weapon was myself. *But why had I not realized it? "You of all people!" Justin had said to me. And I had understood nothing!*

I broke free from my reverie and bade them all rise. I rebuked their homage as gently as I could, saying I knew nothing of what they meant, but that I desired their hospitality and was in need of their assistance. All the time my mind was whirling.

I spent the evening in a daze. I turned my face toward the world – walked through introductions, discouraging homage of all kinds, and arranged for the repayment of Jerub's hospitality. I then sat down to dinner in the Commons with as much composure as I could manage, but all the while my attention was furiously concentrated on the possibility at hand: *Was I in fact trained up to be the Sword of the Old Believers?* I ransacked every aspect of my education at the Refuge: *Could I be the Sword and not know it?* My lapses of memory maddened me; they were a door I could not open.

I ate what was put before me, tasting nothing, responding to but not hearing the conversation. I absorbed only an impression of the shabbiness and disrepair of the College. It had few students and a ragged, hangdog look; it seemed more ruin than establishment. The devotees who shared the table with me seemed as much a reproach to our discipline as practitioners of it. It was a bitter disappointment that even in Dan few heeded the teachings of St. Supplicee, and fewer still presented themselves to learn the discipline and the lore. Old Believers had truly fallen upon evil times.

During the meal, I leaned over and said quietly in Brother Peter's ear: "I desire to speak confidentially with a person knowledgeable about Dan and about the affairs of the Apostle Boz. I need someone with a head for figures and for dealings in the marketplace – and someone who also knows the affairs of the Northern Lights and Naphtali, as far as any outsider may."

Brother Peter stared into space for a moment, then replied: "There is a benefactor of our order, a merchant who is licensed in Naphtali. He would be knowledgeable."

"And is he trustworthy?"

"Wholly."

"Can you bring him to me? Tonight, if possible?"

Nathan Lander was a handsome man of middle age, small of stature but expensively dressed. He was ushered into my presence in the tiny library of the College. As clearly as an officer's insignia, the metal chain around his neck signaled both his calling and his wealth. His hair was cut short, after the fashion of the merchant class, and he was dressed entirely in black, except for an undershirt of fine white linen – almost like a dandy, I thought, who wished to pass for a Messiahist. He nodded familiarly to Brother Peter and then, being introduced to me, knelt dramatically before me, just as the Brothers of the College had, making the candles flicker. "Are you then indeed the Sword, or should we look for another?" he asked, addressing me as Master.

"Peace," I said, bidding him stand and feeling both embarrassed and annoyed. "Let us not misunderstand one another. I am a captain of the Army of Israel, and I am here on an errand of the Council of Apostles. I claim no title except that rank which you see on my tunic."

The two of them exchanged glances and regarded me quizzically, so I felt compelled to say more, to put an end to these ludicrous expectations about me. The small possibility that their expectations might be founded upon the truth, however, made a great hollow in my stomach. "How good it is," I said, "that not everyone is offended that Masters Ebenezer and Josephus have been my teachers. I am grateful to be among men like yourselves, who revere the old ways and respect the teachings. But understand, Master Ebenezer *gave* me a sword when I left the Refuge; he did not forge one." They continued to wait expectantly, so I added: "I learned at my Masters' feet that we Old Believers wait for no redeemer. In our tradition, we struggle to understand the world as it is. Salvation, escape – these are the stuff of children's tales. We enter into the Way and awaken to its truth each in his own time and each in his own manner."

They nodded intently, as if hearing pearls of wisdom, so I reminded them: "I am here on the business of the Council of Apostles and on a related mission for the Northern Lights Enterprises, and for those tasks I need your help. Other than that," I said, speaking with more confidence than I felt, "I bear no commission." I left the group puzzled and apparently determined to plumb the hidden meaning of my words while I turned my attention to the merchant. When left alone with me, Nathan Lander was more than happy to tell me about Dan. He was a veritable fountain of useless information. Dan, he explained, was blessed by its fertility, as well as by its isolation from the rest of Israel. Outside of Hazor and the rich farmland of the Yakima valley, the Danites lived mostly in tents, as shepherds. In times of emergency, the clans resorted to their stone forts and strongholds in the central valley around Hazor. Dan had often been ravaged by invading hosts or torn by internal strife, but had never been conquered. He went on in this vein for some time; I waited for him to pause for breath, searching for some thread of order in his words.

"Dan," he continued earnestly, "is not wealthy in goods, and the merchants here are a more modest lot than elsewhere in Israel. Wealth is still measured in land and its products, and the owners of the land are the men of influence and rightful leaders."

Is he a fool that he expects me to believe that?

"Dan's strongholds are capable of withstanding the most determined sieges. Hazor itself has wonderfully thick and well-made walls, the legacy of Caleb Boz's Apostleship. The present Apostle brought the fortifications to a high state of perfection soon after his elevation." He looked at me expectantly, and then launched into another topic: "The ground water lies near the surface, so Dan has the best wells in Israel. The soil. . . ."

I grew impatient, drumming my fingers on the table between us. "I am not planning to invade Dan, and I have no time to hear an encomium. I want something I can use."

Lander hesitated, as if I were a problem he did not know how to solve, and then broached the subject of Caleb Boz's women. "The Apostle, as everyone knows, has the coarsest appetites. . . ."

"No! Enough of this! I want to know what makes Caleb Boz afraid. I want to know what wakes him up in the middle of the night, so that he sweats and tosses and cannot sleep."

"I was just getting to that," Lander replied. "Boz is in debt. His government is insolvent. It was the cost of the fortifications. He. . ."

"Insolvent?" I interrupted, suddenly interested.

"Yes, it was the fortifications. To pay for them, he borrowed at an exorbitant rate years ago, knowing nothing of usury. The rates have eaten up the bounty of Dan for years. The Apostle has taxed the landholders and, uh, we who are merchants and bankers, most cruelly. It has occasioned much ill feeling. The Apostle Boz means well, but now he cannot help but squeeze the well-to-do citizenry of Dan, of which there are fewer and fewer, in order to pay his creditors. And the debt still grows. And the clan chieftains say they will bear no more, not a straw's weight of additional taxes."

"Who are his creditors?

"Chiefly the Velcos and their associates in Manasseh." He paused, blinking at me.

For the next few days I had leisure to ponder my good fortune. Nathan Lander was indeed well informed, and he had given me information I desperately needed. With his assistance, I could estimate Caleb Boz's difficulties with some precision and use the knowledge to advantage. Lander also visited Naphtali frequently on business; he was acquainted with my brother Hanford and was able to give me valuable insights into the man and the far-flung Northern Lights Enterprises. With this knowledge, I was no longer helpless.

With the assistance of the College, I also purchased a good horse and arms and tack as a return gift to Jerub. I made a brief tour of the market and added a lyre and several lengths of fine cloth for his women. I made certain that the Apostle Boz learned of these transactions, so that he would know that I honored the customs and kept my end of a bargain. In all of my doings, however, I told my co-religionists nothing I did not want Caleb Boz to hear.

To my surprise, news of my presence in Hazor had spread, and men from Asher and Manasseh and Ephraim who sought refuge from the religious strife engulfing Israel, began to appear at the College. They begged to see and converse with me, and occasionally they would stretch forth a hand to touch me. I was moved by their accounts of hardships and dangers endured, and I comforted them as best I could. But I told them nothing of my alleged identity as the Sword of the Old Believers, saying only that our discipline called us to exert ourselves, not to look for either an escape or a protector.

On one occasion, Brother Peter took me aside and warned me that Hazor was full of Messiahist spies, and that any one of these visitors might be an assassin. "No doubt you are right," I said. "But those who are true men could be enlisted to protect the College in the troubles ahead." I asked him to examine the refugees and to select such men as he could vouch for. Those who were willing and able-bodied could defend the College and could also act, if need be, as my bodyguard. He agreed and set about it with what I suspect was unaccustomed energy.

VIII

I walked the short distance to Lander's establishment accompanied by a half-dozen newly armed men – the core, I hoped, of a self-defense force for the College. Lander had a counting house on the best street in Hazor and spacious apartments above it. He had seemed a bit pompous and full of himself when I first met him, but I had quickly put aside my first impression. On his own ground, describing what he knew, he was very sound. And he had, I felt certain, delivered Caleb Boz into my hands.

Lander greeted me affably in the street, posted my new guards at all the entrances, and led me inside. We spent several hours working out the details of the offer I would make Caleb Boz and establishing safeguards to retain control of the remaining funds entrusted to me for my mission. Banking, I discovered, is its own mysterious world, aloof from the struggles and suffering of Israel. Money continued to cross hostile boundaries in the form of notes on slips of paper and seals and coded messages as if the war did not exist. With armed men raging about on all sides, business went on as usual.

Nathan Lander was clever and full of ideas, and he made many helpful suggestions as to how my funds should be disposed. While we had in an important sense become partners and allies, I chose not to show him the list of accounts (as Gill had reckoned them) among my orders, nor did I ever use my seal in front of him. The seal was a potent source of power, and I had had ample experience of treachery in the past.

His wife brought us tea and bread as we worked in his down-stairs office. He introduced us in a casual way, after the manner of his class. His wife was named Miriam, and though she greeted me informally, she had the dignity of a noblewoman. I was impressed by her speech and manner, which were gracious and refined. Some years older than Michal-Rebekah, she nevertheless had the same confident presence. She chatted a few moments with us and then left us to our business.

I questioned Lander closely about Naphtali, concerning which he seemed an inexhaustible fount of knowledge. His wife's knock on the door an hour later reminded me that I had overstayed. I apologized and rose to leave, but she invited me to dinner in a cordial but insistent manner. Lander seconded her invitation, assuring me that we could continue our discussion after the meal. He seemed so eager to be of assistance that I accepted their invitation. They showed me to a bath and sauna in the rear of their courtyard, and I refreshed myself and dressed in one of Lander's robes.

"I have dismissed the servants so we might speak freely," Lander announced when I came from the bath. "Miriam will serve us, so we may protect the confidentiality of our conversation." I must have betrayed doubt in my expression, for he said, "Rest assured she is with us – with your enterprise – heart and soul."

During the meal, I grew gradually less wary of speaking in front of Lander and his wife. Lander seemed genuinely eager to be of service – though even more eager to have me speak of my plans. Even had my plans been formed, however, I would not think of revealing them. I deflected the conversation toward the future of Israel in general, concerning which I could speak freely and yet reveal nothing.

"I share your fears," I said, "that if the war continues, it may engulf Dan." At the moment, Rueben and Gad were being ravaged by opposing cavalry forces, and both sides were conducting themselves like savages.

"Why would you expect the war to spread?" Miriam Lander asked. "Surely the destruction gives all sides a motive for ending it—and for Dan to remain aloof."

"None of the contending parties is powerful enough to win outright. Nothing in the existing situation – neither the array of forces, the character of the leaders, nor the nature of their ideas – seems likely to prove decisive. Meanwhile, each side wants victory more than it wants peace. Thus," I explained, "I expect a protracted war."

"That would be disastrous for Israel," Miriam said. "Both sides seem willing to go to any length to injure each other."

"To *win*!" Lander said.

I had acquired most of my views of the war from Justin, but from what I had observed myself, I could see little grounds for optimism in the present situation. I thought of my own father's extra-legal dominance of Judah and the virtual dictatorship of Caleb Boz in Dan. It was clear that the war was not just a crisis of the institutions of Israel, but proof they had been swept away. I shared part of what I was thinking with the Landers, including my view that while the name and outward form of the Apostleship lived on, the living heart had died.

To my surprise, Lander agreed with me. He described with evident distaste the arbitrary authority that the Apostle Boz exercised: "He acts the tyrant – when he can be moved to act at all. But mostly, he does not act. He does not *see*! Meanwhile, Messiahist influence is rising here in Dan."

"The Messiahists are powerful here?"

"Yes," Lander replied bitterly. "While Boz does nothing. Unless, of course, he wishes to squeeze the merchants."

"Boz will regret it if he lets the Messiahists get established here," I said.

"No doubt! No doubt he will. But he who would set up as a petty tyrant," Lander declared, "should not become a prisoner of his creditors!"

Ah, I thought, *here is the man speaking*: Lander is contemptuous of Boz for failing at things any merchant would understand. I thought to myself that when I ruled Naphtali, it would be well to keep the merchants' perspective in mind.

The meal was excellent – an affair of several courses that reminded me of many pleasant, but more frugal meals with Justin and Michal-Rebekah. Miriam Lander managed to serve with skill and flair and to converse with us at the same time. Watching the dishes come and go, I marveled at the wealth of the merchant class.

"So, supposing we have a protracted war, as you suggest," Lander said, "who stands to gain, and who to lose?"

"The Messiahists are most likely to succeed," I said. "They possess the most powerful ideas. Benjamin has leadership and organization, but lacks resources. My father controls the bulk of the army, but has no idea what to do with it." *Three groups were contending for supremacy in Israel. In addition – though I suspected the Landers were unaware of it— Israel's foreign enemies, two rival wolf packs, waited in the shadows. The Kuhlans and the Kr might well intervene in the conflict, and either could prove more dangerous than any of the Israelite factions.*

"The outcome," I said, keeping my thoughts of the Kr and Kuhlans to myself, "will depend on whether the Messiahists can turn their fanaticism into military discipline. For my part, I expect that they can."

"I'm surprised to hear you say that," Lander replied, his face full of emotion. He described himself as content with the Law, but acknowledged that the younger of his two grown sons had embraced the Messiahist faith and was living in New Jerusalem, a stranger to his father and mother. I looked to Miriam Lander for confirmation and saw sudden tears in her eyes. "How has this Messiahist faith grown so attractive" Lander asked, "that it can seduce half of Israel?"

"I would give a great deal to know that," I admitted. "I find their beliefs repugnant, but I have also seen the lengths to which men go to serve them." I told them of the speech of Bishop Bon in Esdralon, announcing that the Judgment Day and the Third Coming would occur at the end of the present millennium. "The prospect of Judgment Day terrifies the gullible. I imagine a great many people doubt the truth of these claims, but the signs, as the superstitious think of them, are grim enough to portend anything."

"The times are harrowing," Lander agreed. "But what if the Messiahists are right?"

"Nonsense!" I exclaimed.

"Nonsense perhaps. But nonsense that gives strong men pause," Lander said. I could not dispute his point. I thought of the priest I had heard at Meribah and the effect his harangue had on his audience.

"What has happened to us?" Miriam mused. "What has happened to the nation? How do the Messiahists dare claim that the world will end with the century and demand that we bow to them!"

"They dare and they do, "Lander said. "And credulous fools accept their claims."

"Superstition rules more of Israel than the Council ever has," I said. "Perhaps more than the Law as well. I suppose many go along with the Messiahists, fearing they may be right and the Day of Judgment is at hand – but waiting, too, until the millennium comes, to see if things go on as usual. As they surely will. At some point, there may be an accounting with the Third Comers over their claims. But in the meantime, the idea is very powerful."

"So you see the power of the Messiahists as growing out of that fear? From their claim about the end of the world?"

"In part. The Messiahists excite fear and then offer relief from it. But that does not wholly explain their power. I cannot explain it. I wish I knew, for example, whether Bishop Bon—or Polymer XII, as he calls himself now – believes what he says. I could understand a fraud, if he were one. But I think he is not – even though his alleged revelation about the Third Coming was the basis for his seizing power."

"But the previous Primate had died," Miriam Lander said.

"Yes, and quite conveniently."

"I see," Miriam said, as her eyebrows arched gracefully on her forehead. I could not tell if she was genuinely surprised at this news or merely wished me to think her surprised. "Still, the Messiahists would not have grown so dangerous," she ventured to add, "if the Law had retained its stature."

I had to agree with her. Even here in Hazor, the College of St. Supplicee was more a mud hole than a fountain of the Law. The decay of our teachings was only too obvious. "It appears that the Law no longer suffices," I conceded. "People look elsewhere for answers and nourish other hopes. I do not understand it."

"And who is to blame that Israel wanders from the Law?" Miriam said, her eyes smoldering, "And who allows the Messiahists to exploit our fears like hucksters in the market?" She darted what seemed a hostile glance at her husband.

I gazed at her thinking, *this is a woman of sense,* and at the same time I was reminded vividly of Michal-Rebekah. Miriam Lander was smaller and perhaps less regal in manner. And there were fine lines etched around her eyes. *She is after all a woman with grown sons, I reflected, rebuking myself.* But she was a beautiful woman, with fine sculpted features and lustrous black hair. I had held her gaze too long, and she looked away modestly. I returned to the conversation as gracefully as I could. "I expect many are to blame," I said. "Not least of whom are we Old Believers. Where there is no vision, the people perish."

Miriam stared at the table. Lander, however, could not refrain from interrogating me further in his clumsy way. He wanted to know about the forces in Judah and particularly about the leading figures in the army. He seemed well informed, and he aroused my curiosity just enough to distract me from the grief that these memories had engendered, for the conversation reminded me continually of Justin. Colonel Pasco, Lander noted, had recently been promoted general and commander of the First Apostles.

"A good man," I said. The First Apostles was the core of my father's power. Pasco, however, was not the man who could size up the moment and turn the legion into his own weapon. It had struck me that the officer class in Hebron had seemed uncertain, as if, unwittingly, they too were deciding something. I thought of Ahaz's surly presence. When the time came, Ahaz would not need to decide. *The force that fuses the clay in the furnace is the same that smashes the pot into pieces.* Ahaz would do nothing until the moment arrived, and then he would act. "General Ahaz is the man to watch in Judah," I remarked, realizing my reverie had created an awkward silence. "He is a force to contend with. Or will be, when events thrust him forward."

What would Justin say? The dialogue in my own mind had been conducted almost in his voice. My grief for him was again fresh and painful, for I could not think at all without remembering him. Yet to think in his characteristic way seemed to bring me closer to him and to pay him homage.

Our conversation turned again to the idea of Judgment Day and the coming of the Messiah—an idea so preposterous and, at the same time, I was forced to admit, so compelling.

"Our tradition has nothing in it of a *first* Judgment Day," Lander complained. "The chronicles speak only of a terrible time, the Dissolution, coming between the Ancients and ourselves. There is nothing in the records about a gathering up of the righteous into Heaven *or* the destruction of the wicked. Frankly, I'm at a loss to explain how the idea ever gained currency in Israel, and why we commonly call our times the 'Third Tribulation.' The whole concept is alien to our traditions, and yet I use the term all the time."

We agreed that this was strange and that there was no certain dating of when this usage began to pervade Israel. I knew from my studies that Governor Posedas, who founded New Jerusalem, had also established the new calendar. But of a Second Coming or Judgment Day in the past there was nothing in our records.

"There is talk," Lander added, "that in the early days of Israel, the Old Believers suppressed the remnants of the Ancients' religion. What do you know of that?"

"Nothing," I admitted. "The beliefs of the Ancients were not part of my education at the Refuge. I doubt that real knowledge of their religion has survived."

"I suppose not," Lander said. "Nevertheless, the Messiahists claim that it has survived, and that the Ancients' faith is now recovered in their own creed – this in spite of the Old Believers' persecution of their ancestors and the destruction of their texts."

"It may be true, but I doubt it. There is nothing in the chronicles that supports their view. Whatever the Ancients believed, the fact that they were destroyed proves that their religion failed them—and spectacularly at that." *We Old Believers hold that the wounds to the Ancients' civilization had been self-inflicted, either through some excess on their part or some stupendous folly. Hence, we strove for wisdom and self-restraint.* "The churchmen," I said, "make many absurd claims about the past, and if the chronicles say nothing about the events that they allege, then they claim that the chronicles lie. As the Messiahists describe it, the past is full of impossible things. We hold that the world the Ancients inhabited was essentially like our own—a world of natural law."

"Yes, exactly," Lander replied. "But that view also runs counter to a great deal of evidence."

It was true. There was no way we could envision our world except in terms of a baffling declension from Ancient times. Our cities and towns sprouted among ruins on a far grander scale—like toadstools out of the roots of a dead tree. The Ancients had been far more numerous and infinitely more powerful than we. That much was beyond dispute, though we could not explain it. But a Judgment Day in the past? The very idea begged more questions than it answered. But what did we know of the past except what the chronicles told us? *Uneasily, I recalled Justin's doubts as we pondered the images of the Messengers in Engedi.*

The Landers and I pursued these questions for a time but gradually fell silent before the mystery of our declension. Suddenly I found I was growing weary and had had too much wine. I made my apologies and rose to go.

"What will you do now?" Lander asked, pressing me again. "What are your plans?" His manner was so obvious that I sensed that Miriam Lander recoiled, though she tried to conceal her embarrassment.

I was annoyed by his brazen interrogation, but I chose to ignore it, realizing that I was suddenly very tired. "I plan to sleep," I replied.

In spite of his eagerness to know my plans, Lander had discussed all matters I had raised so frankly and with such an obvious desire to assist me that I felt grateful to him – and only a trifle annoyed. I thanked them for their hospitality and took my leave. Miriam, as she said good-by, held my hand for a moment while Nathan told a not-very amusing story about a servant. Her perfume lingered in my senses as I walked to the College.

IX

General Malachi rose as I entered the Council Hall and immediately accused me of fomenting disorder in the streets of Hazor. "Since you arrived," he stormed, "there have been brawls between the factions and two murders. Two lives lost to fanaticism since you arrived in Hazor! Our very streets run with blood!"

"And you wish to attribute these disturbances to me?"

"Do you pretend that they are coincidence?" General Malachi seemed genuinely indignant, but the rest of the Council regarded me neutrally. I looked around the group, trying to fathom what I was up against. The Danite Council had survived long contact with Caleb Boz, I reflected, so there must be few fools among them. Nevertheless, I suspected there was one. I looked again from Malachi to the group; I wanted to find the right tone with them. This charge hurled by General Malachi seemed to be a test of some sort.

"These disorders," I replied, "have been going on for some time, as is common knowledge. Do you mean to say that Old Believers now defend themselves against Messiahist provocations? If you wish to credit me for that, I am pleased to accept your praise."

"So," the General retorted with unconcealed triumph, "you admit that Old Believers are emboldened by your presence!" Malachi believed he had trapped me into revealing my identity – and I inferred that the issue of the moment was my alleged identity as the Old Believers' promised leader.

"Emboldened? I hope so. But to admit that a stranger could effect such a change would be a rebuke to you all. It would imply that the Elders of Dan have done nothing to protect your own countrymen from outrages in your city."

Malachi scowled at me, but several of those present seemed mildly amused by our exchange. Given an opening, I announced boldly: "I can tell you things about the war in the south which will be useful to you. At Elion, I saw five thousand savage cavalrymen turned back by catapults – the same engines that broke the siege of Esdralon. My brother Justin Apollo built them. With his death, I am the one who best understands their use."

They were indeed interested, and they questioned me at length about the war in Engedi and the fighting with the Kr. I described the power of Justin's long range weapons to protect formations and to break masses of horsemen. I repeated that Justin had, with weapons of the same design, taken a city larger than Hazor. "It is not the weapons alone nor the tactics alone," I emphasized, "but the two conjoined." A couple of the younger clan leaders and young Captain Boz came forward to see the drawings I had made. Boz the elder remained impassive as a stump.

"I have no knowledge of what the future may bring," I continued, "and if I were Danite, I would wish my people to stay clear of this slaughter – but to prepare themselves for the worst." I pressed my point as boldly as I dared. Caleb Boz was peering intently at a crude copy I had made of Justin's drawing of the weapons he had designed and used at Esdralon. "I could help you build such weapons and show you how to use them."

"Dan is a poor country," General Malachi interjected quickly. "We cannot lavish money on new-fangled weapons. And who, after all, would be likely to come up against us, unless we foolishly allow ourselves to be drawn into others' quarrels?"

"Wise counsel," I said. "Obviously it is best to stay detached from Israel's wars if one can. Dan has done well to remain aloof. But even long-tested principles of conduct eventually fail. You, for instance," I continued, gazing at General Malachi, "would not wish to ask the garrison at Jezreel, dead these thirteen years because Dan was unprepared, who would come up against us?"

Malachi flushed and glared at me; he had been commander of the Danite host when Hanford seized Jezreel.

I turned to Boz. "The truth is, I could provide you with weapons that would make Hazor impregnable almost without cost."

Boz stared impassively at his cup. "I heard you say *almost* without cost," he remarked.

"Nothing is without cost," I said. "But I came seeking help and prepared to give it in return. Value for value."

Boz appeared bored, preoccupied with the wine cup that he revolved in his massive hand. "Speak," he said finally.

"I seek protection and friendship," I said, trying to seem self-assured. *Protection and friendship because I had no inkling of how to proceed with my mission and I had no other place of refuge. How I might take Naphtali and unseat my brother Hanford was, at the moment, wholly beyond my powers of imagination. Thus, I had no choice but to remain quietly in Dan and bide my time, waiting for something to turn up. I had, in the abstract, ample resources, but I had to discover a way to transform them into tools I could use.*

"I want Dan to continue to be a sanctuary for Old Believers, and for Dan to take no role in the religious struggle now taking place. As for the war with Benjamin, I wish to end it, not draw Dan into it. I have in addition specific and private needs." I paused, giving them time to absorb the fact that I had no intention of involving them in the Harlech war. That left, of course, the Messiahist war, the religious war, which was a far more dangerous matter. They were deeply suspicious of me on that score. *And rightly so.*

"Too many eyes and ears are fatal to secrecy, and hence, to success. I will need the advice and experience of the Mayor of Hazor, Nisan Lot, as well as the Apostle Boz, for this is in a sense a financial matter that I wish to lay before you." It was easy to estimate the likely sources of resistance to what I would propose; General Malachi was still red-faced and glowering. I needed to disarm him somehow. "Since these weapons would be central to the defense of Dan," I added, "I have need of another ear – that of the most seasoned warrior on the Council."

Boz did not raise his shaggy eyes from his cup. "He wants our help against his brother," he remarked to the Elders. "To which I say, yes, conditionally. And he wants our help against the Messiahists and the Velcos, to which I say *no*!" He glared at me balefully. But he had taken the bait. So, I thought, it is settled. The Apostle, the Mayor, and the aged but noble General will make whatever deal is to be struck.

Boz nodded slightly at each item in my list except the last. "Impossible! Extending protection to the Refuge would be a provocation to Manasseh. The Refuge lies in the Wilderness of Zoar. Danite territory does not extend so far!"

"Then I request sanctuary for the Brothers, in the event of Messiahist aggression."

"Understood. What else?"

"Assistance against my brother."

"You waste our time. What *else*?"

"Beyond these items," I hesitated, genuinely unsure, "I don't know—except that I desire your advice and counsel." The three Elders of Dan looked at each other in disbelief as I pressed on. "I have been given a task that is too big for me. I cannot see a way to perform it. It may be that I can learn from you how it can be done. In the meantime, what I have in hand will surely be useful to you." I showed them Justin's original drawings. "I can supervise the construction of these machines. Larger versions can be mounted on the city walls. With the superior elevation afforded by the walls, you can out-range any opponent. A besieging army cannot even bring its machines or its troops within range of your walls without being destroyed."

"Dan has no money for such foolishness," Boz said scowling, but he was also licking his lips. I knew he would like to have these engines of destruction mounted on his fortress walls. And I knew how sore a point was his government's debt.

"Dan is not a poor country," I said, "but its government is poor, because it is in debt. Deeply in dept. Dan needs breathing room from its creditors and capital to maintain its independence. Therefore, I will ask no money for the engines, provided that you build an equal number for my use."

My offer had given me the full attention of the three Elders.

"I admire your policy of independence," I began.

"No alliance against the Messiahists!" Boz roared, slamming the table. "You heard my decision!"

"Hear me out," I interrupted. He paused, eyeing me suspiciously. "You Danites are famous for your independence, but Israel is now torn between the churchmen and the faction that my father controls. You play one side against the other, as far as you are able. And you have done admirably so far, the world knows."

"But you are about to express a reservation about the wisdom of our policy," the Mayor of Hazor said mildly.

"Only that," I admitted. "For years you Danites have pretended that a choice between two masters is liberty. The game you play is a clever, but I believe a losing one. In the long run, it is a desperate game. Only the preoccupation of your enemies with each other keeps you in the circle with them. Years ago, you accepted the loss of Jezreel to Hanford Glanz because you hoped some day the Velcos and Glanz would have a falling out, so that you could avenge yourselves and take back what is yours. Behold, they have had a falling out. But you cannot act because in the meantime, the Velcos have become your creditors; they have you at their mercy. And just so far are you free to act as the Velcos permit."

Boz and Malachi scowled at me. I watched the banker, Nisan Lot: if there was an agent of the Velcos in Dan, it would likely be this man. *Or, I reflected, if there was an agent of Tephlin Glanz in Dan. . . .* Lot stroked his beard but said nothing.

"The costs," I continued, "of retaining even this much independence have been dear. The Apostle of Dan has made Hazor into a nearly impregnable fortress, but the price of its construction has driven many among his people to hate him. Meanwhile, the debt to the Velcos has constrained Dan's freedom to act." I glanced at Boz to see the effects of my words. *Is it any wonder that you must hang an occasional kinsman in your tower?* "Is it any wonder," I continued, "that clan leaders who value your wisdom are uneasy – or that others curse you as a tyrant behind your back?" *You are not a tyrant really; you are merely constrained by your debts.*

I lay the draft for 200,000 kanz before them.

So we entered into an agreement, the Elders of Dan and I. With the Mayor's assistance, I wrote a draft for half of the money in my trust, to be deposited in Hazor's chief bank (his own). He in turn arranged that, on a specific day at a designated moment, agents of his would present drafts of withdrawal on the accounts of Tephlin Glanz for 100,000 kanz all over Israel. Once the transactions were completed, I would loan that money to Caleb Boz at a ridiculously low interest for the period of one year. This would grant him his breathing spell from his Messiahist creditors. The remainder of the money I put in a separate account in Nathan Lander's counting house, with the promise that I would withdraw no more than a quarter of it within six months. This gave the counting house capital it could safely loan or invest, and thus afforded the Danite government needed operating funds. No new taxes need be levied. The Apostle Boz could rebuild his tattered relationships with the clans of Dan and at the same time prepare for whatever lay ahead.

General Malachi would designate craftsmen to work with me on the siege weapons and lighter ballistas. It was agreed that I would take possession of half of the machines constructed. Meanwhile, I was free to lodge at the College, as a refugee and guest-friend of the Apostle.

It was, as the merchants like to say, a sweet deal. Oil and butter and honey all around.

X

Once I had reached an agreement with the Elders of Dan, however, I felt as if I were treading water in the Jordan again. I could not proceed with my mission until I had perfected a plan – and I could not perfect a plan until I had cemented my relationship with Caleb Boz and the Elders of Dan. With the money I loaned him, Boz was renegotiating his debts, trying to free himself to act, and until he accomplished that end, I was, I soon realized, virtually his prisoner in Hazor.

In the meantime, word of my presence in Hazor continued to spread, and men young and old came to seek me out. The Messiahists had made themselves feared and loathed all over Israel with their campaign to cleanse Manasseh and Ephraim of unbelief, and refugees flocked to the only city of refuge available. Hazor was crowded with strangers, and the sense that something unprecedented was afoot seemed to pervade the city. Repeatedly, I encountered the same troubling question from those who stopped me in the market or sought me at the College: "Are you the one we wait for? Are you the Sword of the Old Believers?"

I fashioned a brief reply to such questions: "It is the Messiahists who wait for a redeemer. We Old Believers search for understanding, not for escape. *This* is our world. In times of danger, we exert ourselves" – and so on, ending with an exhortation to shun the idea of a supernatural deliverance and to search within themselves for the grounds to act. Many seemed disappointed with my words, but others went away contented enough. It puzzled me that the rumors about me – or about the alleged Sword of Israel – could gain any currency whatever. A savior figure was alien to our whole tradition. Perhaps in times like these, very different traditions mingle together like images in a cloudy mirror. No doubt the need for hope was great. I longed to sit at the feet of my Masters and take direction from them again, but that too was forbidden me. In the meantime, my own lack of direction weighed on me like a stone.

I was not concerned about the ultimate outcome of the war, nor with the alleged end of things at the millennium. It was the immediate future that baffled me. I could not for the life of me see what my next step might be. Subsequent steps were clear enough. Somehow I must wrest Naphtali from Hanford Glanz. With the resources of Naphtali at my disposal, I could accomplish a great deal. I would create a legion of infantry trained on the lines of the First Apostles and build a fleet to transport it. If I could form an alliance that would give me the cavalry of Dan, I would indeed be a power to contend with. But how I might seize Naphtali or maneuver Caleb Boz into such an alliance was beyond me.

Nevertheless, I was certain that if I could only bring those forces under my hand, I could speak as an equal with any who intended to remake Israel. Against those who intended to change her utterly, I meant to champion an Israel renewed and purified, but still recognizably Israel. Moreover, as ruler of Naphtali I might speak with the Velcos and arrange honorable restitution for the death of their son, Senesh Velco. Or not, as they chose to play out the quarrel. I could even stand against Simon ben Gurion and Tephlin Glanz and say yea or nay as I pleased. Finally, I could inquire of my uncle Brandon about my mother's fate and his part in it.

But I could not envision the first step.

So I was relieved when Nathan Lander came to me with a proposal that I accompany a trading party into Naphtali after the earliest frost. He described a mountain road from Hazor into the interior of the Wenatchee valley that was little used, and, because of the ticks, impassable in summer. The road led into Naphtali near its second city, Cashmere, deep in the interior of the Wenatchee valley. "The back door of Naphtali," Lander called it. In the brief opportunities for travel in fall and spring, Dan traded for horses, furs, and recovered metal by that route. "The danger, of course," Lander explained, "is being caught by snowfall in the mountain passes, so we must time our journey carefully. We must prepare ourselves," he said, "but wait for the frost in late September."

Lander's plan gave a period to my enforced inactivity; I was grateful for that. Boz would surely negotiate the relief he needed from his debts by then, and I could seek his assistance. He had promised as much. But to remain inactive so long! September was two months off! What on earth was I to do? I could not imagine. My patience would be severely strained, I knew that much. In the meantime, Lander remarked, business trips would take him frequently out of the city.

I accepted an invitation to dine at his house that night very gladly. I had come to enjoy his company and took special pleasure in the conversation of Miriam Lander. Social life exerted a great attraction for me, and there were many times when I would have preferred an ordinary life on a country estate to playing the role of champion of the old Israel. I looked forward to the evening, intending to bathe and put on fresh clothing for the event.

That afternoon, however, yet another disturbance in the marketplace left a refugee dead and two others injured. The injured men were carried to the College, where their wounds were attended to under my direction. A crowd of exiles and Danite Old Believers gathered, vowing revenge. I quieted their mutterings as best I could, but I arrived at the Lander's late and angry. I gave them a brief account of the incident.

"You will get no satisfaction from Caleb Boz," Lander said. "He will keep Dan out of the war, no matter what."

"Dan is already in the war!" I exclaimed. "Messiahist priests harangue crowds on every street in Hazor, and now they shed blood even here. Dan has the power to act decisively, but keeps its eyes shut, as if these troubles will go away. Mark my words: Dan will soon be just another victim of the war."

"Ah!" Lander said, his eyes gleaming. He believed that my anger had flushed out my secret intentions.

I dashed his enthusiasm as quickly as I could: "I have considered the advantages of Dan's involvement in the war, but I do not seek it. As likely as Dan's involvement seems, I would prevent it if I could."

"Why prevent it?" Miriam Lander asked. "You owe nothing to Dan."

"If Israel is to survive," I said, "some parts of the nation must remain unscathed. Dan may have to be the seedbed of the new Israel."

"Do you believe it will come to that?" she asked.

"Yes, I do."

"This war consumes everything it touches!" Lander declared dramatically, leading us into his spacious living quarters. "Meanwhile, Boz has no policy, no ideas!" It seemed to me that Lander made a great show of criticizing the Apostle on every occasion.

"If it continues as it has," I said, "the war will devastate Israel more thoroughly than the last Kuhlan invasion. And if Dan clings to its foolish isolation, it will ensure its own destruction. And Dan will go to its fate unmourned, believe me!"

"And so you. . . ," Lander began, obviously trying to interrogate me.

"I fear for our whole way of life," I retorted, weary of his questions. "This war is being fought to define Israel anew – or perhaps to break the old mold into pieces. Such a war is fed by many motives and will be fought without pity."

"I fear you may be right," Miriam said at last. "So much is passing away here in Dan, even without war. So much that is good in Israel has rested on our ancient traditions – the honored office of the Apostles, the landed families. The Confederation of Tribes has embodied our highest values and given dignity to life. What will replace the life we have known?"

I was skeptical of her professed attachment to the old ways; she was a merchant's wife, after all. "In all likelihood," I said, "our way of life will vanish."

"To be replaced by what?" Lander demanded.

I shrugged. "The Messiahists believe in a theocracy ruled by themselves for their own purposes."

"I despise their purposes!" Miriam exclaimed.

"Magic and superstition!" Lander said. "We'll have the Primate defining reality anew with every fresh revelation. What a prospect!"

"The churchmen are infatuated with blood sacrifice," I remarked, speaking my own fears. "Before long, human blood will be spilled to appease their god." *There were, in fact, rumors that the elder son of Jonas II Harlech had met such a fate at Achish at the beginning of the war, though I had never credited the story.* "To think that blood poured out on the ground could change the course of events," I said. "It is a perverse conception of the world. For myself, the most intolerable burden of Messiahist rule would be to have to submit to their beliefs. Their whole faith is repugnant to me. Under them, the Law would be extinguished, and our freedom with it. No man could hold opinions contrary to the Primate and live. And every sensible person *will* hold opinions contrary to the Primate!"

"So," Lander mused, staring at me again, "you have a great task before you."

I ignored his clumsy probing. "Unfortunately," I said, "the countervailing power in Israel at the moment is the merchant faction, and they desire an oligarchy based on wealth to replace the Council of the Apostles. The merchant class lacks vision. They desire an Israel without protected property in land and with the landed warriors transformed into buyers and sellers like themselves." I kept forgetting that Lander belonged to the same class as my father. "And they will tolerate no constraints of the Law that interfere with trade. I, for one, cannot embrace their schemes either."

"Ah, you see us too clearly!" Lander said, smiling. "We want an Israel ruled by ourselves, for *our* purposes."

"Precisely. Your class longs for an Israel unfettered by privileges of birth, but bound instead by privileges of wealth. Are you all blind to this fact?"

Lander laughed, but did not dispute my point. "And it is your belief," he said smiling, "that there must be another alternative?"

"Exactly so!" I said. Turning to Miriam, I added: "Your husband has spoken my deepest wish." I wondered at her change of expression, but could not read it.

"In that case," Lander exclaimed, almost exulting, "we must now look for a new side to emerge in this civil war – the party of the Sword of Israel." He paused to assess my reaction, and then said, "Let me raise a toast to that!"

I shook my head, but felt my skin prickle. Lander had hit upon on my own thought just as it was taking form. I resolved to be more careful of him; he was not as foolish as he seemed. Lander followed up relentlessly, inquiring how I intended to realize my own vision of the future. I replied evasively, injecting the army into the conversation: "All sides of the war see the army merely as a tool to use against the others. But as I read the chronicles, armies have a way of asserting themselves in events like these. The fourth party in the war will likely be the army."

"That sounds like an opportunity as well," Lander said, "for a man like yourself – a military man of great spiritual power."

Lander's role, apparently, was to flatter me at every turn in order to pry out my heart's secrets. But in truth I dreaded the army's intervention, just as I dreaded Dan's entry into the war. The army had intervened almost accidentally in Esdralon, turning an incident in the Harlech war into a religious conflict. "The army is divided," I said. "Even those who turned against the church last May were not certain what they had done or what they should do next. The army can add to the bloodshed, but cannot end it."

"Then why did you lead the rising against the churchmen?" Miriam asked sharply.

"Be wary of such rumors," I cautioned, not wanting to discuss my role in those events. I quickly turned the conversation away from myself. "What little I saw convinces me that the army has power but no direction. At least not yet. For it to assert itself now would only postpone what is coming." *My own words surprised me; I had not formulated this thought before.*

"And what is that?" Nathan Lander's eyebrows rose on his forehead. "What is coming?"

"There is something underneath events that is trying to reveal itself, trying to be born." *Instantly, I regretted having said this; again I had spoken my private convictions.*

"But what?" They looked at me expectantly.

I felt chagrined, as when the priest at Meribah set out deliberately to play upon my emotions and had succeeded in doing so. These two, interrogating me blatantly without even pretending to do otherwise, had similarly plumbed me to the bottom. I clenched my teeth together angrily.

"What do you feel is coming?" Miriam asked, seeming as determined to interrogate me as her husband.

"What I meant," I said evasively, "is more like a change of seasons. Like summer into autumn."

"I don't understand," Lander said. "Summer into autumn?" He looked at his wife, who kept her gaze fixed on me.

"It must be the wine speaking," I said, anxious to end the conversation. "I am no seer who claims to know the future. In any case," I added, intending to be facetious, "it's likely that the Kuhlans will cross the river again and put us out of our misery long before these things come to pass!" But as I spoke, the latter prospect seemed suddenly very real. At the same time, my strong sense of Justin's presence in our conversation connected inwardly with my thoughts of blood sacrifice, forming a vision that took sudden and fierce possession of me. Involuntarily, I flinched and dropped my cup of wine. As the dark liquid spread outward, I gasped, seeing with perfect clarity my brother and Michal-Rebekah under a sacrificial knife, trussed like sheep on the altar, their throats arched to receive the knife.

After I made my apologies and the table was cleared, Lander led us into the garden. "Why not enjoy the evening cool?" he said, doing his best to put a good face on things. I was excruciatingly embarrassed, and their spirits seemed equally dashed to the ground. Not having acquired the useful diplomatic habit of dissembling easily, I had spoken too frankly—and alarmed my hosts. Miriam would have excused herself, but I asked her to stay. Even though I had dismayed them both and disgraced myself, I felt she might lighten the situation with her presence—if anything could.

I knew that my glimpse into the fate of my brother and Michal-Rebekah was not a true revelation – only a possibility that I had not fully contemplated before. My imagination was over-wrought. Surely I was poor material for a champion of Israel when I could neither control my emotions nor hide my innermost thoughts. In the meantime, I could never know what had really happened to my brother and Michal-Rebekah, and thinking on them could not bring them back.

Shortly, I bid the Landers goodnight and walked to the College, yearning for some distraction.

XI

I had several weeks to wait until frost made travel to Naphtali possible. In the meantime, the grain harvest was beginning, and I found employment on Lander's estate. I marveled that a merchant could hold an estate in land. Dan was not the old Israel at all. Lander's possession of an estate in land was just another piece of evidence about the larger changes taking place in Israel. Yet it was good to work in the hot sun, cutting and binding the golden sheaves of next year's bread. I emptied my mind and focused on the tasks of my hands, moistening the sacred soil of Dan with my sweat.

Refugees continued to arrive in Hazor and seek out the College. Our defense force grew as hostility between the Messiahists and Old Believers sharpened. At my insistence, however, we took a very passive role in events, in acknowledgment of our dependence upon Dan's Apostle and Council of Elders. But incidents of violence in the city increased, and when blood was again shed outside the city gate, I determined to complain to Caleb Boz and demand that the Law be kept.

As I was admitted into his presence in the Hall of Assembly, I saw with surprise that the Apostle Boz and Nisan Lot sat engaged in close conversation with Nathan Lander. When I entered, Lander rose in embarrassment, excused himself, and was quickly gone. My blood burned in my skin; I was angry rather than shocked. I should have expected what the scene so clearly revealed. Lander was a traveling merchant and banker; he was well connected throughout northern Israel. Such men are useful eyes and ears for the powerful. Every word I had spoken to Lander – to *either* Lander, I presumed – had been poured into the ear of Caleb Boz.

I set my disappointment aside and addressed the task at hand. I had learned the value of brevity in dealing with Dan's Apostle: I described the recent incident at the gate, which had involved a violent beating of an Old Believer by a crowd of Messiahists, and then waited.

Boz had not bothered to look up from his papers. "So?" he grumbled. "The man was a foreigner; the matter is of no concern to the Council."

Lot explained that the Council of Elders had to exercise caution until emissaries from Manasseh arrived and the details of Dan's schedule of payments were worked out.

"Understood," I said. "But understand also that the Law provides remedies for injustice when the authorities sleep – or are incompetent."

I went immediately to Lander's. I had no wish to rebuke him. If I had spoken indiscreetly in his presence, no one was to blame but myself. But I wanted to see his face, I wanted to read his emotions, now that he knew he had been exposed as an agent of Boz. I thought of how easily the loan of the money entrusted to me had been arranged with his help. *No wonder!* I thought ruefully. He had been Boz's agent as well as my own. Still, I was forced to admit, the arrangement had value to all parties.

I found Lander in his counting house. He met my eyes boldly, and I saw in them a hardness and pride that I had not seen before. He motioned his assistants away so that we could speak privately. Without waiting for a word from me, he spoke imperiously, almost insolently, as if I had at last learned my place and was expected to observe it: "You have never once communicated with your Masters Ebenezer and Josephus, who are only a day's ride south of here in Zoar. Why not?"

His question startled me. It was not surprising that he knew these things, considering his role, but I pondered his reasons for asking. "I am forbidden to," I said at last.

"Forbidden by whom? And why?" He persisted in his new manner with me, taking a graver risk than he knew. My senses were raw and my muscles tensed, anticipating anything. Hearing a sound behind me, I whirled, with my sword flashing out of its scabbard. Miriam Lander emitted a shriek and dropped the tray she was carrying.

We stared at each other, absorbing our new knowledge of each other. I sheathed my sword.

"I am ordered to ask," Lander said, breaking the silence, his breath irregular. "Who forbids you to communicate with your Masters? It is better that you speak."

I watched Miriam Lander on her knees, retrieving the broken pottery. She did not raise her eyes.

"I intended to contact my Masters immediately after I arrived in Dan. But when I spoke of it, Brother Peter said I was not to visit, nor to send a message, nor even communicate by word of mouth. He was quite emphatic about it, so I have assumed he spoke with authority from my Masters. I did not think to verify the truth of it or ask whence the order came. In any case, I have abided by his instructions."

"I see," Lander said. "And why not communicate with the Refuge?"

"I am told," I said, "that there are spies everywhere."

"Good advice," Lander said gruffly. He sat at a table and began writing furiously, meanwhile repeating to me what I had heard from Nisan Lot that morning: negotiations with Manasseh were at a delicate stage; it was imperative that Dan give no offense. I was to keep my followers, as he termed them, well in hand. Miriam kept her eyes on the floor. "Here," he said, rising and thrusting a paper at me. "This will give you authority on my estate. It is best that you take yourself and your followers out of the city for a time. Safer. You understand. You can manage my estate if you wish. This gives you authority to dismiss my servants there, and you can replace them with your own men and enjoy complete privacy and security there."

I started to refuse him, seething with pent-up anger, but he held up his hand.

"I am not your enemy," he said, and I felt, strangely but very forcefully, the truth of what he said. He took his leave, explaining that he had business elsewhere.

I was left alone with Miriam, who seemed, in her husband's absence, less embarrassed than relieved by these revelations. "My husband," she said, as if in explanation, "is ambitious. He loves to be near great men and great events, hovering in the shadows, influencing and assisting. Spying. But what he said to you is true; he is not your enemy."

"And you? Are you my enemy?"

"I despise Caleb Boz," she said forcefully. "And I despise my husband for serving him. I am with your enterprise heart and soul."

I was more than a little doubtful of her words. I recalled her husband's comments about her the day we met, and it occurred to me that her words were more likely rehearsed than sincere. But she *seemed* in earnest.

"My husband is a fool," she said quietly. "I was afraid you would say something that could harm you, if you did not learn what he is. It is better this way, now that you know. I dislike dissembling."

My thoughts were in a tumult, and I was as surprised by this revelation as I had been at my first sight of Lander at Boz's ear. Nevertheless, I regarded these seeming confidences of Miriam Lander warily. She had set herself decisively apart from her husband and had declared herself my friend and ally. But how could I believe her? Somehow, without my being aware of the steps we took, I found myself in the Lander's private quarters with Miriam brewing tea and conversing with me as if nothing unusual had happened.

"I suppose you take my Masters' order as proof of my identity as the Sword of Israel, as some like to call me."

"Whose order? What proof?" Miriam Lander was busy with small cakes and the fire and the service.

"The order that I not contact my Masters. I assume you take it as proof that I am the Sword of Israel." She remained busy at her tasks, her back to me. "I take it as proof of the contrary," I asserted.

She turned and looked at me as if I were a troublesome child. "Proof of the contrary? How so?"

"I admit I have pondered the meaning of my Masters' intentions toward me long and hard. I believe I may have been singled out by them and prepared for some great task. But, to speak to you candidly – perhaps more candidly than you deserve – I believe I failed them. I believe I failed their last and crucial test."

"I will ignore your remark about what I deserve," she said. "And you will, I hope, learn to distinguish my views from those of my husband. What test did you fail?" she asked without evident curiosity.

I wondered whether I should tell my story. I was at a loss to know what might harm and what might save me. "Ebenezer," I began, "was my Master in the ancient martial arts at the Refuge. The art was one of his methods of teaching the Way." I hesitated, despairing of a way to explain these matters to an outsider. "He was nearly fifty years old, but possessed an amazing strength and quickness. He was, strange to say, gentler than any of my other teachers. I was his best student, his favorite. I progressed rapidly through the secrets of his art until I achieved an unusual mastery of both the discipline and philosophy of the Mano. But I failed his last test for me."

She served me tea as I spoke and seemed to follow my story with at least a semblance of friendly sympathy.

It was my last day at the Refuge. I had prepared rigorously for the ordeal; I had fasted and meditated a day and a night on the eve of the contest. I was prepared – but not, as it turned out, for the test in store for me. *Today, they announced, you must overcome your Master. Here are the rules, and observe them well: there are no rules. You fight to win, to defeat your Master. It is you or him. Live or die. Prove yourself!*

"How cruel," she said quietly as I paused in my account. "How impossible!"

"Impossible for me," I admitted. "I refused to participate in the match. No, to speak truly, I could not participate. I could not raise a hand with such an intent against my Master. I sat on the floor, and Ebenezer ordered me to stand and fight, but I sat silently, and the Brothers came and reviled me and beat me with sticks. I said nothing, did nothing. Ebenezer eventually turned his back on me and left. It was the last time I ever saw him. The next day I left the Refuge for the Academy."

We sat a long time together without speaking. "I'm glad you told me that," Miriam said at last. She added, almost as an afterthought: "And I'm glad you know what my husband is."

She led me to the door. "You must come by tomorrow," she said, suddenly businesslike. "My husband is right, you know. You will be safer at the estate, and so will your followers. I can arrange all the details, if you need my assistance. And you will."

Chapter 9: Out of Strength, Sweetness

I

The Lander estate lay northwest of Hazor under a bare ridge of the Cascades. It was a sprawling expanse of fertile land, well watered and surrounded by pasture and woodland. Reluctantly, I took both Nathan Lander and Miriam's advice and withdrew there, accompanied by two dozen of the men I had recruited. It stung my pride to be beholden to a man who, if he had not actively betrayed me, had proven unworthy of trust. But I had no better idea and no other prospects. I dismissed Lander's servants and set my men to work the land, so as to pay our way and leave none of the bounty of nature unappropriated by our labor.

I inspected the estate carefully, enlisting the knowledge of one my earliest recruits, a man named Burgos, who had been steward on an estate in Ephraim. He showed me the merits of the ripening grape harvest with an expert eye, and he identified which fields should lie fallow next year and which required manure. The maize was yellow on the stalk, but it would stand until November. It had been a good year; the ears were over a foot long. Pumpkins and squash were ripening in every field. At Burgos' suggestion, we turned over a barley field and sowed turnips for a winter crop. "A precaution in war time," he said. Burgos was a man of sense and discretion, though coarse in appearance. I congratulated myself that I had sense enough to value him despite his peasant origins.

We whitewashed the buildings, repaired roofs and fences, raked and burned the refuse of the fields. It was good to sweat and see the results of our labor. We let the black, sturdy cattle of Dan glean the fields after us. The Landers had a small dairy herd as well, so we fetched hay for them by the wagonload and built stacks by their pen. The men chided me for setting up as an old time patriarch, and I saw the justice of their criticism. "For the moment," I explained, "I must wait." They waited with me. In the meantime, there was the harvest to get in. The last wheat and barley had already been cut and the grain winnowed and stored. We gleaned the fields and raked straw into stacks and wove Harvest Men for the approaching Feast of the In-Gathering.

Our second week on the estate, the apple harvest began. To aid with the heavy work and the sorting, the College and all its adherents, men and women and children of all ages, came out of the city and worked with us. Burgos assigned them to a hundred tasks with the skill of a general. The Lander orchards grew several varieties of fruit, and it was a trick of timing to bring them in at the moment of optimum ripeness. There was danger, too, from the ticks. The work took on a reckless and festive air, such as I remembered from my childhood at Tirzah. It was the knowledge that life was good and might end suddenly that gave the Feast of the In-gathering its special flavor. Burgos and I sampled mugs of fresh cider as baskets of culls and windfalls tumbled into the press. I wiped the sweat from my forehead, surveying the results of our labor and mentally contrasting this bountiful land with my family's estate in Asher. "This is good land," I said. "One could have a good life here."

"None better, my lord."

I had many invitations from Miriam Lander over the course of these weeks, and she proved helpful in many ways in what she termed "my enterprise." She was knowledgeable about the Lander estate and, without being intrusive, made many useful arrangements to get the crops safely to market or into storage bins. Occasionally, she would visit the estate on horseback, and she and I would take a meal together under a canopy in the garden. She was as informed as her husband about the affairs of Dan and probably his superior in intellect. Thus, I learned many valuable things from her.

Occasionally, she entertained me in Hazor, with her husband absent. She was indifferent to such circumstances, so I followed her lead. Miriam Lander was a woman of substance who, in some areas of her life, seemed to make her own rules. Perhaps it was a characteristic of her class, newly come to power. In spite of my lingering suspicions, I soon realized that I had not had conversations of such candidness and friendly intimacy since I dined in Esdralon with Justin and Michal-Rebekah. My discussions with Rehab Gill and Nathan Lander had been contests, mental wrestling matches in comparison. With Miriam, I experienced the delight of conversation even as she worked to educate me for my new circumstances. Rather than struggling with each other, as men might, we fused our energy to move toward greater insight. It was a relationship like none other I had ever had, and I valued it.

In every situation, whether in private or on the occasions in which she introduced me to Hazor society, I found that my merchant hostess was as polished and courteous as a daughter of the most ancient landed family. In all other ways as well, she seemed my peer and fellow. As we walked from her well-kept grounds to her spacious apartments, I almost expected to come upon a family shrine with portraits of warrior ancestors and weapons buckled to the wall. I had to keep reminding myself that Miriam Lander was daughter of a merchant family and not a Name in Israel. *It might be a good thing, I reflected, to live in a land where such distinctions were meaningless.*

But it was another aspect of my education that most concerned her. It became gradually clear to me from her attentions and the drift of her conversations that she desired a greater degree of intimacy with me. She was inviting me by stages into a special relationship, carefully prescribed and condoned in Israel, of the mature wife's friend. *His wife has taken a young friend*, the saying goes.

Israel is strict about the marriage bond and stricter still about the legitimacy of heirs. Adulterous wives are sometimes put to death if it can be proven that they have had intercourse with a man other than their husband. But it is the Reproduction Law, not an abstract virtue, that is at stake. A license to produce an heir is everything to a family; authorization to bear a child means its survival or extinction. The value of that authorization being nearly infinite, the privilege is rarely squandered or abused. Thus, it is the pride of Israel's wives to keep their agreements, to bear a child or two – three at most – as legitimate heirs, within the house and in the bloodline. Under the Reproduction Law, an unauthorized pregnancy *within* a marriage is only slightly less serious an offense, as the family must petition the Elders for an unused license and pay an exorbitant fee. Careless wives and husbands can thus use up their inheritance and turn their children into paupers merely by exceeding the allotted limit on births. Not everyone can reproduce, of course. The legacy of defects and cancers from Ancient times requires that blood lines and family histories be scrutinized carefully and that marriages be arranged to optimize the chances for healthy offspring. That is the meaning of legitimacy in Israel. For these reasons, the Reproduction Law is very strict.

But not all of life is reproduction, as the saying goes, and therefore every wife in Israel knows a hundred ways to please her husband – and herself – without risking pregnancy. Once the heirs are born and safely raised, the Law relaxes somewhat. Custom permits much freedom of association to both sexes later in life, and intimate friendships outside marriages are common. It is even a matter of pride in the great families that the wife be admired and sought after in her days as a matriarch. Family alliances are often cemented by such relationships, when honorably and discreetly conducted. Usually the friendships are between peers in age and status, but, though frowned upon in some quarters, they frequently involve mature women and young men. Such relationships are seen as having social utility, as an outlet for women and as a school for young men—and perhaps a necessary preoccupation for them as well, since Israelite girls of good family are closely supervised or even sequestered until marriage. It is an open secret that many relationships are also formed between members of the same sex, but it is the spring-autumn relationship between a young man and a married woman that concerns me here. Miriam Lander, as I was to learn, was a woman with much to teach.

Miriam was describing the benefits of such a relationship for a young man such as myself as I bathed prior to the evening meal. I had just come from the fields and was hot and covered with dust. Hearing an urgent summons from her, I had ridden as fast as I could to Hazor, without stopping to change my clothes or wash the dust from my body. Instead of imparting some news about Caleb Boz's negotiations or events in Naphtali as I expected, however, she greeted me playfully with a kiss. "Time enough to talk," she said, "when you have bathed and refreshed yourself. You work like a peasant out there!"

I work like a landed noble, I thought to myself. But I was content to humor her. She poured the water for my bath herself, explaining that she had dismissed the servants. This familiarity in itself was not unconventional. Because of the danger of ticks, frequent nudity is a necessity in summer, and Israelites are compulsive about cleanliness. I suppose we have learned to be casual about nudity, as long as certain proprieties are observed. I often bathed at the Lander's, and Miriam had come into the bath once on a prior occasion, casually, to ask me a question. I had the distinct sensation on this occasion, however, that proprieties were not being observed.

"Three wounds," she said pensively, making a point of passing her eyes over my body. "And barely healed. Yet, nothing repulsive so far, thank goodness! You still have everything essential to a warrior." She affected a humor in all this that seemed incongruous with her usual manner.

I mumbled something incoherent in reply, very conscious of my nakedness.

"My dear, Josiah!" she said laughing, handing me a towel and pressing, I thought, the limits of modesty, even for the summer season. "Beautiful young man that you are, you are obviously in need of a tutor. You know the truth of what I say. Yes," she said, "you need instruction from someone versed in the law within the Law that actually governs Israel. You have learned nothing of these things tucked away at the Refuge. I'm surprised an interest in women survived such an education. Yes, you do like women; I see that much."

Miriam had broached the subject with a boldness that I associated with the landed nobles. She had nothing about her of the circumspection and timidity of the merchant class. I was as much flattered as disconcerted by her attention, but I did not know how to respond to her.

"Don't be alarmed," she assured me. "I ask nothing in return. I know that a young man of your fame and personal charm could never feel anything for a woman my age."

I stood silent as she searched my body for the dreaded ticks. I had, in fact, considered her attractive at our first meeting and told her so. But she would hear nothing of what I had to say.

"You possess great charm," she said, stepping back to gaze at me as I reached for a fresh robe. "And great physical beauty. Your scars," she said, tracing the marks on my forehead and neck, and then turning me, holding my arm, to touch the scar on my back. "Oddly enough, your scars only enhance your beauty—ah, you are impatient at hearing such things." As if to dismiss her own words, she seized a towel and briskly rubbed my chest and back. Then she had me bend forward so she could reach my hair, which she dried vigorously.

When she finished, I felt that her mood had changed again. "Such a man as you," she said, "must have many sweethearts and no time for friendship with a woman almost your mother's age. I know, I know, you are willing to flatter me, but time is our enemy; it is a woman's foe. It destroys our beauty. No one knows that better than myself." Her face as she spoke seemed as serene and unconcerned as a bird singing on a branch, but I sensed an undercurrent of sadness in what she said. I wondered, at that moment, if she were really aware of me or expected a reply.

I said something to the effect that she was very beautiful still. She ignored me and stepped away and turned her back. For a moment I thought I had offended her.

"Do you know," she said turning to me, "what gives us away? What first reveals the triumph of time?" I confessed I had no idea what she was talking about. "It is not the wrinkles about our eyes and mouth." She touched her face with both hands. Her skin was smooth, and she had fine, even features and large dark eyes. "Men can tolerate a few wrinkles – even young men. It is the backs of our arms!" she exclaimed, raising them both for my inspection, gathering up the short sleeves of her wilpa to reveal them to me. She grasped her upper arm and said, with what seemed unfeigned distress: "See, the difference between a firm young girl and a matron like myself! A *matron*! How I hate that word!"

Her flesh was as firm as that of any young woman I had ever seen, although, to be sure, I had never been invited to contemplate the arms of any young girl, or any woman, for that matter, so freely. As she turned, I saw that the large sleeve lay open at an angle that revealed part of her breast, a full voluptuous swell. I gazed at her boldly and she met my eyes, and then she lowered hers deliberately down my body. I found I had difficulty swallowing, my thoughts bounding like deer in all directions.

"You have much to learn," she said. "It's time a woman of sense took you in hand."

The first occasion of our taking pleasure together was a clumsy and self-conscious affair; I had little delight in it and no doubt gave even less. In truth, I knew nothing of women and their desires. Miriam was gracious and patient and practical, chatting about a young man's needs and health, and afterwards we talked of her upbringing and her life as a young bride. *She is angry with her husband, I thought, but she is too proud to complain.* Miriam told me many things outright about women and married relations and let me infer many more from the stories she told of her own life.

"I know you fret about your honor and the burden of responsibility you carry," she remarked one day. "You and I break no rules here; we violate no principles. My husband's honor, such as it is, and the honor of his house are intact."

I acknowledged that I knew nothing of the rules that really governed relations between the sexes in Israel.

"Which is why we have such friendships," she said gaily. "My husband, if it makes a difference, has many such relationships. He often travels for weeks at a time; it is practical for him. Almost a necessity."

"And you don't object?"

"I would object," she replied vehemently, "to his getting a bastard somewhere and paying half of his estate to make amends! His children's estate!" She paused, seeming to forget my presence, and only with difficulty restraining her feelings. "I have done my duty by him as a wife," she said. "I have raised two sons and kept his house. I have a right to friends of my own choosing."

II

In spite of this change in our relationship, Miriam and I went on in other ways as before. She often shared her disparaging views of Dan's chief figures with me, and I delighted in her satiric gifts. I acquired much of Dan's recent history, in fact, listening to her stories. I found her an agreeable companion, clever and entertaining and possessed of a rich sense of humor. And she apparently found attractive qualities in me. While I felt no passion for her, I felt gratitude and respect—and to speak the truth, affection. I enjoyed her very much. We did not speak of love, but of my education. Or rather we talked about love in the abstract, with Miriam taking the role of a general, coaching me for the encounter with potential brides, as well as for the ordeal of Israelite marriage. I began to feel how strange my education had been, and how poorly it had prepared me for ordinary life. Obviously I had much to learn.

Often she talked of her own life, of painful, though intensely private losses and disappointments. I learned that she grieved continually for the son who had embraced the Messiahist faith. And for reasons that she did not reveal, she nourished a resentment of her husband for that loss. I came gradually to understand that her usual gaiety of manner masked a hard, stoic strength that any man could admire.

One evening I found myself speaking of my own childhood at Tirzah and the loss of my mother and of other painful memories. She was as understanding and sympathetic as I could have wished, and I felt no shame imparting these things to her.

"My dear Zaiyah," she said to me afterwards, embracing me and using my childhood nickname, "I see that your life has not been easy."

"Not until now!"

"Your story explains a great deal of what I sensed about you. Yes." She traced my features gently with her fingers. "I see now what your life has been, the obstacles others have placed in your path. Worst of all, the uses to which you have been put by others."

I reminded her that the plans others had laid for me had not worked out as intended.

She was silent as she considered the implications of what I said. Then she leaned toward me, her lips almost in my ear: "It may be that you were called to some special task after all," she said, taking my face in her hands. " Yes, I believe it."

"Believe what?"

She detached herself from me and picked up a brush and began grooming her hair, which was thick and lustrous. "Never mind," she said. "It's probably only a woman's intuition. But one must hope that so much pain was a preparation – and not merely ill fortune."

"I believe more in blind chance than in fate," I said, wondering what she was driving at. "Master Josephus taught me that. Things fall out by chance, he said, just as the dice turn over at random."

"Perhaps," she said, turning to me and laying down her brush, "but he raised you up to be the champion of the Old Believers, Josiah. Is this not an attempt to guide events and not rely blindly on chance? He prepared you, and Ebenezer gave you all the wisdom of his heart and head, and the skill of his hands and feet, and he set you forth armed. I feel the idea of intention in this – and not of dice turning over which ever way they will."

This was a point I had never considered. "But I failed them," I said. "I told you the story."

"Josiah," she said, kneeling on the divan beside me. "Josiah, my dear one, has it never occurred to you that you may have passed their test?" She gazed at me a moment and then kissed me passionately. The import of what she said, though delayed a moment, struck me like a blow.

"That's impossible!" I exclaimed, rearing up from the divan. "Ebenezer turned his back on me!"

"Could he have turned away because he had no more to teach you? Can it be that you had met his expectations and surpassed them? Think of the test, Zaiyah: what you did shows that you had acquired his power, but could not be induced to misuse it. Does it not? Josiah, I beg you, open your mind and consider what I say."

When I could converse sensibly again, she asked if I would tell her what had passed with me on the occasion of our last meal with Nathan, when I had blanched and spilled my cup of wine. "You were seeing Israel's future, weren't you?" she asked. "What did you see that caused such revulsion?"

"It was not that," I said. "Nothing of the kind." She pressed me to explain. "It was my brother," I began. "We had been speaking of the Messiahists, and I was remembering him vividly, as I often do. Suddenly I had a vision of Justin and" – *I started to say "and his family"* – "I had a vision of my brother and some others lying under the knife on a Messiahist altar."

"Sacrificed! So he died a sacrifice?" She pressed her palms against her temples, seeming aghast at the thought but not surprised.

"I don't know. I know nothing for certain. Perhaps – perhaps the others are alive. I doubt that Justin is. It is a torment not to know."

"I understand," Miriam said. "But you do see the future sometimes, don't you?"

"Nothing of the kind," I assured her, though she persisted relentlessly in her belief. It occurred to me that women are like Messiahist priests in their fondness for occult explanations. "I think about the future often enough – mostly conjectures about what is coming. Sometimes I think I see a pattern in events – in the changes. It is as if this process is directed—but I have no idea by what or whom, really. I am not even certain that I am making sense. But I feel – I have felt for some time – that things are moving. That Israel is coming to a turning point."

"I knew it!" she exclaimed, clasping her hands together. "Summer into autumn! You must tell me what that means."

"Miriam," I said, shaking my head, "I cannot well say. I lack the words to express it."

"Try," she urged.

I felt embarrassed. I was speaking of an intuition based on long study and observation, and she was treating me as if I had supernatural insight. "A thousand small changes are going forward, all foreshadowing *something*," I said hesitantly. "We are coming to a season of turning, like summer into autumn. I feel certain of that. And if this is so, as I believe it is, then"—*I paused, at a loss for words*—"then it cannot be otherwise." I felt, but did not say, that events were moving like a game in which the dice were rigged to come up sevens over and over again. All the combinations gave the same sum.

"You mean to say," she said, "that fundamental changes do not come about casually, and so they are not forestalled or hurried along by anyone."

Her words almost startled me—as did her tone. I had an uncanny glimpse in my mind's eye of Miriam sitting among the highest councils of Israel and speaking and being heeded.

"Something is coming to birth," she said, her eyes wide with the thought. She placed her hand unconsciously on her womb. "I pray it will not be a monstrous birth."

III

As we grew more intimately acquainted, Miriam seemed willing to share her feelings on any subject, large or small, and this spontaneity, this freedom of discourse, was entirely new to me. I had never imagined it possible with a woman. She was particularly candid about what gave her pleasure, and she was free with directions and praise in our private moments together. As clumsy as I had been initially, under her tutelage I apparently grew more adept. On her part, her initial patience warmed into passion, and I found her increasingly eager for my embraces. What we had together, while short of full intercourse, made me burn for more. I sometimes felt as though I had wandered into an exotic pleasure garden designed expressly for my use. Nothing seemed to be required of me; my life-long habits of discipline dropped from me like a garment. On her part, Miriam seemed to embody desires that could not be quenched. She was expert at exciting my desire and satisfying it, yet always stimulating my imagination for more. These pleasures, her manner always implied, were merely the threshold to much greater ones. Thus, the gratifications she offered whetted rather than sated my appetites. No matter how many times she brought me to release, I was eager for more. Day after day, an aching hunger brought me back to her.

And strange to say, while we never talked of our relationship as love, I nevertheless became attached to her by feelings I could not label. Occasionally, as I labored under the hot sun on the Lander estate, or toiled, stripped and sweating, in her orchards, I rebuked myself for a fool who had become addicted to pleasure. But it was not just pleasure she offered, but delight—a joy to which I was hitherto a complete stranger. So try as I might, I could not raise my gaze beyond my next meeting with her, or our next embrace. It occurred to me often enough that I had acquired this dumb, puppy-like dependence upon a woman who was another man's wife.

It occurred to me also that I did not care.

Nathan Lander's face was dark and lined from his recent exertions and exposure to the sun. He looked as though he had lost weight as well. "When the trees have turned gold halfway down the mountain, it will be safe to travel, and we can visit Naphtali," he announced. "I will make all the arrangements. It will be a trading expedition like many I have led in the past. You will accompany me disguised as a Danite Guardsman. The mountain road has many brigands and other dangers, so a military escort will not arouse suspicion."

Some part of me was still mindful of my mission and my duty to investigate Naphtali. But to speak the truth, I was no longer eager to journey there. I could scarcely attend to Lander's words.

"Negotiations with Mannasseh are not going well," he said, "and the churchmen are making demands on Dan. The Apostle Boz is hard pressed."

I stared at my hands, unable to summon up any sympathetic feelings for Caleb Boz. Instead, I questioned Lander closely on his purposes for the journey and his contacts in Naphtali. "Who are the leaders of the opposition to Hanford? To whom would I speak, and for what purpose?"

"I cannot reveal those things in advance," he replied.

"Why not?" I insisted. "My mission is to depose Hanford. Any enemies of his will be potential allies of mine. If I am to learn nothing, why bother to go at all? Why should I run unnecessary risks?" Though Lander found many arguments to persuade me to go and even chided me for a lack of manhood, none of his reasons seemed very compelling. On my part, I did not have to feign reluctance to undertake the mission. "What is it that I am to learn by all this?" I complained. "The dangers seem overwhelming." It was not the risks of the journey, but the charms of his wife Miriam that filled my mind. I sat across from him, recalling vividly the warm sensations of her embrace.

He eyed me narrowly, and I wondered how much he knew about Miriam and me. Condoned or not, such relationships must necessarily excite jealousy.

"I have assumed," Lander said impatiently, "that you must have a contact in Naphtali whom you have not revealed to me. Otherwise, your entire mission against your brother makes no sense. I have assumed that you would initiate contact with this agent of Tephlin Glanz once we are in Naphtali. Is this not the case?" He expressed his annoyance with me freely, and his manner did not endear him to me.

"No, it is not," I replied, adopting his tone. "I have also assumed that a contact has been arranged for me – an agent who can give me further instructions about my mission. But the identity of the contact has never been revealed to me. This is yet another piece of the puzzle I have been handed. And so I have not been able to imagine how I should make myself known to this person. Do I stand in the square in Hammoth-Wenatchee and read aloud my charge from the Council? How many moments would I survive there after that?"

Lander looked at me and shook his head.

I pressed him for more information, for clues about the probable identity of Tephlin Glanz's agents in Naphtali. I pressed him hard, sensing that I had an advantage over him and enjoying the reversal of our usual roles of interrogator and interrogated. I saw that he wanted to convince me of the necessity of going to Naphtali, and that put me on my guard. He seemed also to be caught up in the intellectual game of my mission, which, after all, put him at no personal risk. And most of all, he wanted to learn the identity of my contact. Eventually, pursuant to that goal, I learned the names and characteristics of the chief men of Naphtali and the officers of the Northern Lights Guards and something of their politics and predilections. We talked into the night, almost on our original footing. He had a vast store of information and a good memory, and I was fairly sure he did not suspect that I had a better one.

"I have learned through an important and reliable source," Lander remarked at one point, "that a companion of yours, a certain Rehab Gill, a Judean of the rank of captain, is held prisoner in Hammoth-Wenatchee. What do you know of him?"

I sat upright at this news. "Gill, alive and a prisoner? And in Naphtali? Rehab Gill is an agent of Tephlin Glanz rather than an associate of mine. Still, this is important news. We must free him. Who is your source of this information? Does he have power? Can he be bribed?" My mind was racing. Lander, as I expected, made many objections to revealing his source. Finally, I threw up my hands, telling him to forget about the reconnaissance into Wenatchee.

"Solomon Glass," he acknowledged reluctantly. "Glass is the Controller of the Northern Lights Enterprises. He is a powerful man, and I cannot have you jeopardize his standing—or expose him. You must swear to keep this in confidence."

I feigned reluctance. *He had just revealed to me the identity of my contact in Hammoth-Wenatchee.* I could not tell if he understood what he had revealed or not—and I wondered simultaneously why Ben Gurion and Tephlin Glanz could not have given me clearer instructions in the first place. What kind of game were *they* playing with me? "Gill has answers that I need in order to complete my mission," I said, diverting his attention from Glass. "You make the contact with Glass, but get Gill for me. Have him waiting at Cashmere or nearby. But get him for me. I won't go to Wenatchee without him."

Lander hemmed and hawed, but at last consented. It was all I could do to conceal my elation. "For the sake of Gill," I said, "and the answers he has about my mission, I'll conduct this stupid reconnaissance into Wenatchee, as you wish."

"The frost comes late this year," Lander said, bringing our interview to a close. "We'll plan on the second week of October—three weeks hence."

IV

The Feast of the In-gathering fell on the last day of September. It was an ancient celebration, deeply entwined with the traditions of Old Believers. We had arranged the straw Harvest Men and the wicker Giant to be burned, and we had assembled tables heaped with the bounty of the year's harvest. In late afternoon, however, as we prepared for the festivities, a carriage driven with reckless haste appeared at the estate. It was Miriam. "Josiah!" she cried, alighting from the carriage, "my dear Josiah! Make haste, protect yourself!" she exclaimed, heedless of our audience. "Your life is in danger!" A cloud of dust raised by the carriage enveloped both of us.

I was astonished that Miriam could so entirely shed her usual composure. She seemed more distressed than I had ever seen her. In front of my bodyguard and a crowd of workers gathered by the commotion, she embraced me and explained breathlessly that a plot to assassinate me was afoot. I was to be struck down that very evening by Messiahist agents just arrived from Manasseh. "At the height of the festival, here on the estate," she exclaimed. "You must take measures to protect yourself!" She was excited, almost frantic, so I took her inside the house and tried to calm her. She would not reveal how she knew of the plot but urged me desperately to believe it. "Let me rule you in this," she said. "I have a group of soldiers on the way here from Hazor. They can reinforce your bodyguard. The festivities can be moved to the College. There is still time."

Reluctantly, I accepted her view of the seriousness of the threat and began to make the arrangements she wished. There was a vagueness about her knowledge of this alleged plot, however, that ill accorded with her excitement. I sensed that she was withholding something. If the Messiahists had a spy among us on the estate, I noted, she had just thrown away important advantages. Miriam continued to insist, however, that the festival be moved to town, to the College, and she begged me to stay at the estate, surrounded by a picket of armed guards. It seemed foolish to me—and disappointing to my men, who were looking forward to the feast and the dancing.

Eventually we compromised. The festival would go on as planned, with the adherents of the College coming to the estate to enjoy the feast we had prepared, but I would not show myself. I would stay barricaded in the house, with guards posted all around. After many protests, she consented, and we picked up our tasks of preparation where we had left them.

I posted the sentinels and saw to last-minute details of the festival while Miriam made up a divan on the low roof of the hacienda from which, out of harm's way, we could survey the surrounding countryside. I paced the house, bolting doors and windows, wondering if her story were true and what it meant if it were. What other dangers might this threat portend?

I climbed the stairs to the roof. Dusk had fallen; soon it would be dark and moonless. The air felt almost cool enough for frost. Miriam seemed calm at last and had recovered her usual self-assurance. She invited me to sit by her, somehow making herself alluring in the midst of danger. In the candlelight, her eyes shone with unfathomable depths of both feeling and reserve. We bundled ourselves in soft blankets to ward off the evening chill. From our vantage point, the lights of bonfires of the harvest celebration glowed in every direction. Soon music and voices sounded from below. I could easily have forgotten her warnings, but I had never felt in a more incongruous position. Miriam attempted to engage me in small talk while I tried to form a view of possible approaches to the house. I arose again and paced the portico. "You've said nothing about numbers," I repeated to her. "How many assailants can we expect? Or do you think our preparations will deter them?"

"Sit down," she urged. "The tea will get cold." I seated myself beside her, and she embraced me. "You must believe me and do everything I say tonight. You take no care for your own safety."

"I need information to defend myself, but—"

Miriam moved my hands to her breasts, opening her garments, and I felt her warm, tantalizing softness. She reached her own hands to my belt, which she unfastened. Feeling her touch, I responded to her like a trained pony.

"I'll be in strange shape to defend myself from assassins," I said, beginning to doubt the seriousness of the threat.

"You are truly the hope of Israel," she said, kissing my neck. "Incomparable, irreplaceable man. Sword of Israel." She often said such things to me in jest in our intimate moments, but I could not begin to read her mood in this moment. I embraced her and kissed her on the lips. She responded passionately, though in a moment I felt her hot tears on my face.

"What's this?"

"Your life is in terrible danger, darling. Why can't you see it? Why can't you understand?"

"I understand well enough."

"No, you don't, you can't!" She spoke with great urgency of the danger threatening me, all the while removing her own clothing and tugging at mine. I felt uneasy at this lack of her usual discretion. While we had sometimes taken our pleasure together within the house, in carefully contrived privacy, we had never done so on the upper portico—especially with a festival in progress below on the grounds of the estate. Fortunately, the night was pitch black. My men, augmented by her guards, were standing sentinel in pairs around the house to protect me. Fires burned at intervals, illuminating the scene below; the house was dark and empty. I wondered again if the danger were real, or if this was some strange whim of Miriam's. Anxiously, I tried to estimate the time by the stars. The star road glowed in the heavens overhead.

"You do not understand the mortal danger you are in, you don't!" she repeated, all the while covering me with kisses. She guided my hands expertly to touch her, and I soon lost all sense of disparity between her manner and her words. "If only you hadn't told me that story," she whispered. "If I hadn't known. . . ." Her voice was full of emotion.

"What story?"

"If I hadn't known that you refused. . . ."

"Refused *what*?" Her kisses had turned to bites and her tongue thrust itself into my mouth.

". . . to harm your Master Ebenezer."

Suddenly, her mouth moved over my chest and down my belly. She tugged at my last garments boldly, almost frantically. *I suppose I can fight as well naked as clothed, I thought to myself.* In a moment, she was moaning and moving rhythmically against me; I was sure she was coming close to her own release. I had lost almost all curiosity about how her sentence would end when she suddenly rose up, slipped her bare legs around me, straddling me, and left off, for a moment, devouring me with kisses:

"Then I would never have loved you as I do. Oh, Zaiyah!"

As she spoke she put me inside herself decisively, completely. For a moment I was rigid with astonishment and disbelief that she could cross this line, this barrier, from condoned forms of intimacy to actual intercourse.

"Miriam!" I said, but she smothered my protests with her breasts and then arched her back and neck in ecstasy.

There are many actions, I reflected later, as we lay warm in our blanket, which, once in progress, are difficult or impossible to stop. War was one of them. Surely this was another.

"What about pregnancy?" I asked cautiously when she had come to herself again. "Are you not afraid of pregnancy?"

"No!" she replied emphatically. And then, less stridently: "We women have ways. Don't give it a thought."

I pondered what she said, hoping she was speaking the truth. Miriam had not ceased having her monthly cycle, so I knew she was capable of bearing children. Perhaps women have secret knowledge of these things, I thought. I hoped she knew what she was talking about. With the urgency of the moment past, I was anxious and more than a little appalled at what we had done. I recalled my drunken encounter with Jerub's daughter the night I discovered the seal of Tephlin Glanz in the base of my statue of St. Gideon. Again, the potential consequences of our coupling seemed overwhelmingly vast.

"What about your husband's honor?" I asked.

"Go to sleep now, love," she said, kissing me and snuggling down into the blankets.

Sounds of music and laughter faded gradually as I fell asleep.

Three days later I was telling myself that I had become tired of the teasing and roundabout ways Miriam had previously coaxed me to release. *For my health's sake, she always said. For my education's sake.* Now nothing short of the total intermingling of our flesh could satisfy me. Embracing to the hilt, in the vulgar saying. I embarked on a new course of instruction with my beloved tutor. I had not imagined a man and a woman's body could touch and conjoin and entwine in so many exquisite ways. All forms of sexual embrace intrigued and fascinated and compelled me. We abandoned ourselves to the most reckless acts, discovering sensual heights and depths of feeling that I had not imagined possible. I believe it was the same for her, though she retained the power to laugh at me. At times, she was fierce as a lioness, and at others, her wantonness would fade into a look of infinite softness. She flattered and aroused and pleased me in every way I could imagine a man could be pleased.

I was captivated by her. Thus, when she teasingly called me her stallion, I could conceive of no purpose in life beyond my serving her in that fashion. If she had called me her cock or gander or lion or young bull, I would have leaped to the fray in whatever manner she desired. I would have joyfully embraced her as eagles mate, hurling myself from a great height in free fall with her. I was possessed by a kind of madness and a wild energy that she easily matched and exceeded, until we both lay spent and wrung out and exhausted.

"I love you, Zaiyah," she would say in our quiet moments. "Love *me*!"

And so I would. I was lost in this rite without beginning or end.

V

When it occurred to me that my men might want some direction on the estate and that Miriam and I might need some solid food, I dressed and went outside, searching for Burgos. It had been three days since I had set foot out of doors. I was thirsty and tired. The sunlight dazzled me and my head ached. Nevertheless I felt marvelously empty and sated. I left Miriam asleep on our bed, but I carried her scent, and the scent of our lovemaking, with me.

I found Burgos supervising the turning of a field that had grown wheat. He had a fistful of stubble in his hand and a straw hat on his head. His lined face and the slight stoop to his body betrayed his age, but belied his undiminished strength and endurance. His expression did not change as I approached.

"My lord," he said, touching his forehead.

"Burgos, I have asked you to call me captain."

"Captain," he said. He was not his usual respectful self, in spite of the ancient usage he affected, as though it were a century before and the landed families were still entitled to respect.

"Say what's on your mind, Burgos," I commanded, a little gruffly. The sun was glaring in my eyes and beat down on a world entirely separate and infinitely less appealing than the one I had just left.

"I don't like to say, Captain," Burgos said, "but the men are complaining. The work here on the estate is not bad; it's good in fact. But how is this of any use?"

"How is *what* of any use?" I was impatient with this ugly, tiresome man, this emissary from the workaday world.

"This plowing with another man's heifer."

"Watch your tongue," I said sharply. I began to feel a pain in my skull like a toothache.

"What is the Sword of Israel for? What is it that we do here?"

His words sank into me like a spearhead. His question demolished the walls of my private quarters and let light flood in. My mission, Miriam's marriage, the whole larger horizon of my life rushed back in to me. I felt the weight of my responsibilities to the refugees from Messiahist persecution—good men who had gathered around me in Hazor. They had put their trust in me, and I had betrayed them. But my words and part of my mind continued in another vein, in pretence and denial. "Burgos," I said, "have I ever told you or anyone else that I am the Sword of Israel?"

He looked at me, raising a woolly eyebrow.

"I acknowledge that there are rumors and that I am the focus of them. I don't know what to make of these tales myself. But I don't believe in superstitions – in miraculous escapes or deliverers. I make no claims."

Burgos released the soil and stubble from his grip and brushed his hands, as if absorbed by the grime on his palms.

"Burgos, I would gladly lead you against the Messiahists if I had the power, if I had some means of doing it without getting you all slaughtered in the attempt. But I am a suppliant, a guest-friend of that scoundrel Boz, and if I act precipitously, this last refuge for Old Believers will be destroyed. And all of you with it."

He mumbled something to himself, looking resolutely at the ground.

"Some times are unpropitious." I ransacked my mind for something that could justify my behavior. "There are different times for different things," I said, fumbling vainly for an appropriate adage.

Burgos appeared to be listening but did not meet my eyes.

"There are times for going to war," I said lamely, "and there are times for preparing for war."

"My lord," he said, looking me full in the face, "you want me to believe that what you do all day and night with the Senyora is preparing for war?"

"I don't know if I want you to think anything about it—and she is not a Senyora!" I was angry rather than contrite. Or rather the contrition I felt was smothered by my anger. "*Some* times," I insisted stubbornly, "are just for waiting.

"The assassins, my lord," Burgos said soberly, "they never came. What are we waiting for?"

"I don't *know*. That's the riddle I have to solve."

He took a while to absorb what I had said, as if I have imparted something of great profundity. I had just tried to be honest with him. Or rather I had been honest in one small thing, pretending to be honest in all.

"Burgos, to speak plainly, I don't know what to do next. I'm hoping something will turn up, or I'll have an idea. I plan to scout out Naphtali as soon as the frost comes. Nathan Lander and I."

He made a sound between a sigh and a groan.

"In the meantime, perhaps it is not completely foolish to seem absorbed in other matters, to seem preoccupied and harmless. As I am in fact virtually powerless to act, seeming so may disarm my enemies."

"It might as easily embolden them, my lord, it seems to me."

"Yes, I have to admit that. As I say, I'm just waiting."

Miriam was awake and had bathed and was brushing her hair when I returned. She had gathered the bedclothes around her, but they had fallen around her hips. I admired the grace of her naked back as she moved, but it was not desire that I felt. I had no name for what I felt.

The strokes of the hairbrush were decisive enough that I was not surprised by her words: "I heard what your man was saying," she said, intent upon her mirror. "I'll be leaving for Hazor within the hour."

When it came time for her to leave, we held each other tightly, clinging desperately and searching each other with our hands and mouths and eyes, and binding each other with whispered endearments. But we could not find our way back to our feelings of the previous days and nights.

VI

I endured for two days on the estate, and then I went to Hazor and to Miriam's arms. Her body was a field I could never finish plowing, a never-failing well of sweet water. We rediscovered the abandon we had experienced at the estate, but not the tenderness. We took our fill of each other like starving travelers. Eventually I was exhausted. Our parting was painful and awkward.

Burgos was waiting for me outside. Though he could barely tolerate my connection with the Senyora Lander, as he called her, he dogged my footsteps everywhere. It was as if he alone had taken seriously Miriam's tale of a plot to assassinate me. This time he tugged at my sleeve, glancing about to see if anyone could over hear us. He frowned, his face as long and as ugly as an old horse, and I expected him to upbraid me again with the folly of what I was doing. Instead, he reported that yet another outrage had occurred in Hazor, this time the murder of an Old Believer. A Third Comer priest had arrived with the delegation from Manasseh who were treating with Caleb Boz, and for the past week he had been haranguing crowds in the market, inciting them to violence and provocations of all kinds. The inevitable had finally happened. "This time," Burgos whispered excitedly, "the victim was a Danite. One of the Garza clan, a resident here in Hazor." When I failed to respond to this news, he added, "The Garzas, they say, are famous hot heads. If you mean to quarrel with them, bring a load of wood for a pyre."

I scarcely attended to what he was saying, feeling as I did the need to justify myself to him. "Miriam Lander is well informed about events; she is my contact with the world," I said as we walked to the College. "Without her I would be completely isolated and blind and deaf, as my enemies no doubt wish."

He looked at me as if I were completely blind and deaf. "And you trust what she says?"

"Not entirely."

Burgos seemed alert and wary as we passed silent shops along the way. His question had disconcerted me.

"It's not always what she says," I continued. "For instance, she told me something today"—*a fuller realization was dawning on me even as I spoke*—"not with words, but with her tears. She wept today and said she wished there were some safe refuge to which we could flee. Together."

I was putting together clues and fragments and seeming coincidences as we walked: the incident in the market, the arrival of a Messiahist priest of high rank, the continued haggling, as it was described to me, of the Velcos over the terms of the debt Boz had incurred. That agreement should have been worked out weeks ago. Something was not right. Miriam's tears alone told me that. The continued absence of her husband Nathan, ostensibly renegotiating the debt in New Jerusalem, confirmed that. Something was not right. Caleb Boz, the Apostle of Dan, was using my money to gain breathing room from his creditors—true. But he was using the occasion to negotiate a broader settlement with the Messiahists as well. This revelation came to me in a flash and I blurted it to Burgos: "Boz is not just renegotiating his debt; he is entering into a larger compact with the Messiahists!"

Burgos grimaced, showing his long yellow teeth. "Do you know that for certain, my lord?"

"Not for certain. It occurred to me just now that this is what was going on, unspoken, behind Miriam's words and actions." I stopped, confronting him and wracking my brain for the full meaning of what a larger compact would entail: "Tell me, supposing I am correct, and Boz is indeed negotiating a broad settlement with the Messiahists, what would the Messiahists ask for? An alliance? Yes, but Boz won't grant them that. He would balk at involvement in the war. A guarantee of neutrality? Yes. That's it! That's just what he wants. That would buy time for Boz, and it would give the Messiahists a free hand to deal with Judah. So, we can imagine an agreement of mutual interests there. What else? What would—"

"The Messiahists would want protection for their faith here in Dan," Burgos said, interrupting me. "They would want the power to suppress us and put an end to Dan's role as a refuge for Old Believers.

"Yes," I said, surprised at his astuteness.

"And they would want you turned over to them, as a token of Boz's good will."

"Precisely," I exclaimed. "And how convenient for Boz! If the matter is handled properly between them, he could avoid repaying the loan I gave him!"

Burgos stopped dead still and looked at me.

"He would need only Lander's help to do it," I finished haltingly.

I was suddenly appalled at the danger I was in. *Imminent danger.* I took it all in at once, and a chill gust blew through my mind, scattering my thoughts like chaff.

"Burgos," I said, "I need to take you into my confidence—even more than I already have. I need one other person to act for me in these circumstances. You must think of the risk it entails before you consent to do this thing I will ask."

"I am with you, my lord. Ask."

"I need someone to contact the Garza's, someone to set up a meeting." At the same time, I recalled: I have a rendezvous with Miriam; I must send her word. But a second thought took hold of me, again shaking me like a fever, and I thought better of contacting her.

The plan was simple enough. It was not unlike the war games I had played at the Refuge. I sorted through all the information we could gather about the recent incident and laid out the possibilities like a hand of cards. All that was needed was a group of men who would risk anything. The Garzas were Danites, after all. The priest Ignacio had blundered badly in provoking the murder of a Danite clan member and a well-known citizen of Hazor. Caleb Boz would do nothing about the incident, fearful of offending New Jerusalem. And his doing nothing would incense the Garzas—and half of Dan—to an irrepressible fury.

Brother Ignacio preached on Sundays in the market. One of the families of the men who had participated in young Garza's death had a house next to the market. It was a simple matter to start a disturbance at the far end of the market, creating a diversion during which a picked group of determined men could break into the house and bind and gag its inhabitants. When the disturbance was quelled and Brother Ignacio returned to his preaching, two men dressed in women's clothing and carrying a basket would go up on the roof. The basket would contain a third man and bows and arrows. At a prearranged signal, the three would throw off their disguises and shoot at the priest simultaneously. Three marksmen at that range should ensure a fatal hit. Horses would be waiting outside. *I had made a hundred such plans at the Refuge.*

The point was not merely to exact revenge; I had another, larger consideration in mind. Under the Law Against Tyrants, an aggrieved party could act in his own behalf, as a rebuke to the ruler who had let the Law fall asleep. The Law Against Tyrants was seldom invoked; its mere existence was a spur to careful administration of justice. But Boz was a renegade who made of the Law what he pleased. This act would announce to the world that he was not a legitimate Apostle. According to the Law, it was necessary for seven citizens, disinterested in the matter at hand, to act on behalf of the injured party and to lay the case before the negligent authority. In the cases of which I was aware, this action consisted of a demand for a trial, however, not assassination. I was on shaky ground, to be sure. But the stakes were high. I felt confident that everyone knew what Boz was.

The danger, of course, was that it would look like revenge, merely, and not an act of justice. But if I could organize the blow precisely enough, the Garza family would have their revenge – an act most of Dan would support. And Caleb Boz would have to face the aroused hostility of the Danite population toward the Messiahists and his compact with them. If the uproar were as great as I expected, Boz would realize he could not enter into his planned agreement with the Messiahists and remain Apostle of Dan. Or remain alive, for that matter. Perhaps in response to these events, the Messiahists would be provoked to break off negotiations unilaterally. It might even mean war.

I had been waiting for something to turn up. *Something had.*

I went to my meeting with Miriam but I said nothing of my plans. She was both passionate and distant; I felt this strange dissonance intensely. For my part, I made love to her with the fervor of a man who expected to be hanged on the morrow. She asked me when she would see me again, and I was evasive. She turned her face away from me when we parted.

Burgos waited with the horses and accompanied me back to the estate; he followed me like a shadow. I told him of Lander's plan of a reconnaissance into Naphtali, on which I would go alone, disguised as a Guardsmen, without my escort of bodyguards. A squad of Danite cavalrymen would accompany me instead.

"My lord," Burgos exclaimed, "can you not see this thing? It is a trap! You will never live past the first bend in the road. Lander is your enemy!"

"I doubt that that is the case," I said. "But in any event, I must go to Naphtali if I am to accomplish my mission. I am under orders." *Even so, I reflected, I have no desire to put myself into anyone's hands to be murdered, if I can help it.*

"What can you do, then?"

"I think I see a way. I must go immediately – and not wait for Lander."

"But how? Who would go with you?"

"Desperate men – or foolish ones. I was thinking of the Garzas – and yourself." I expected him to protest but he was silent, making a wry, ugly face at me. "Sound them out tonight and see if they are serious about taking revenge. If they are determined to shed blood, then they will need to find a refuge thereafter. Their need to escape Boz's wrath will make a perfect cover for our entry into Naphtali." Boz, I suspected, would not be slow to act where his own authority was challenged. I imagined that the Garzas and their confederates would need to hide themselves until all the circumstances became clear and a public outcry on their behalf had emerged.

"This seems both desperate *and* foolish, my lord," Burgos objected.

"We have the Law Against Tyrants on our side," I said.

He snorted, seeming less than entirely reassured by my words. "How soon would we do this?"

"Tomorrow if the Garzas are serious."

VII

By this single, foolish, and wicked stratagem, I plunged my life into chaos and brought death and destruction to innocent people and infamy to my own name. *Revenge is a wanton,* St. Supplicee warns, *a whore that is never satisfied.* I should have heeded his wisdom. I should have been cognizant of the responsibilities I bore, and of my debt to my teachers and the reputation of their Order. I should have had an ounce of sense! In carrying out my plan, the Garzas were not content to bind the family of the house they occupied and to avenge themselves against the Messiahist hireling who had caused the death of their son. Instead, they chose to slaughter the entire family in a fury of self-righteousness. The wife, a young son, and a daughter hardly out of infancy were slain to pay for the loss of the Garza's own wretched son. The husband and father of the family, who had in fact been part of the mob that killed the young Garza boy, chanced not to be at home and so escaped. The Messiahist priest, Ignacio, was assassinated thereafter as planned, but one of the arrows went astray and hit a woman who was standing nearby. Five deaths, four of them innocents, to pay for one. Truly, vendettas are the curse of Israel.

But it was I who was to blame; the blood of these innocents was on my head.

I learned of these things only after the Garzas made their escape and Burgos found me where I waited with extra horses on the road to Cashmere. "This is bad, my lord," Burgos exclaimed, sweating with exertion. "This is evil. These imbeciles, these hot-headed swine, the Garzas were not content with Ignacio; they had to kill the whole family of Valdez, even his children."

In my dismay I actually seized Burgos by the throat.

"They tied them up, yes, and then the middle son, this Rafino—he is a piece of work, my lord!—he had to slit their throats. Ugh!" Burgos spat. "It is unbelievable. Rafino even boasts of it. If the other son was like him, it was no loss to Israel that he died."

For a moment, a long moment, I had a nearly overpowering urge to descend to where these cowards waited and to kill all three of them where they stood. I drew my sword and stood a long moment with my thumb on the edge of the blade. Then I shook myself and sheathed my weapon. It would do no good. *Blood begets blood.* Nothing could restore the Valdez family to life. And no matter what I did now, I would never wear a shining name in Israel again. I realized in a flash of insight how deeply, hopelessly, and completely a fool I was. A reckless, murderous fool! It was clear that however long or short my life stretched out, I would lack time enough to comprehend the full extent of this folly.

"Take them the money," I said to Burgos. "Tell them how to contact Nahum of Cashmere and send them on their way. Let me not see their faces. Tell them to make haste to Cashmere, for if they linger across my path they will surely die."

When Burgos returned, he and I stood contemplating what I had unleashed. "I should have waited and let events unfold," I explained lamely. "Instead, I tried to force them into the direction I wanted them to go. By silencing that miserable priest, I intended to put an end to his provocations and to disrupt Boz's negotiations with the Messiahists. I had hoped to arouse the population of Dan and awaken them to the danger. Striking the priest was to express their anger that one of their own, a citizen of Dan, could be slain and Boz's justice remain asleep. I wanted his people's indignation to shake him and to instruct him that his alliance with the Messiahists was impossible. And I wanted also to defy the Messiahists, to frustrate them in hopes that they would commit some rash act that would drive Dan further into hostility." *I had wanted all these things; I had seen them all so clearly in my mind.* "Brother Ignacio deserved to die," I said aloud to myself as an afterthought; "I shed no tears for him."

"What use are tears in any case, my lord?"

"I had expected we might return in a few weeks," I lamented, "when passions had subsided a little, and then make a claim based on the Law of Tyrants—perhaps even indict Boz for his failure to keep the Law even to protect his own people. I thought we might well raise Dan against him."

"I have heard of the Law Against Tyrants, my lord, but I have never heard it invoked to cover murder."

"Assassination, Burgos!" I exclaimed. "Not murder. Do not say murder! The assassination of a foreign agent and law-breaker was what we sought. True, the Law has never stretched so far. I thought we might make a precedent, while revealing to the world how corrupt and negligent is this one-eyed scoundrel, Boz. That's why I wanted three disinterested men involved in the act itself, and three involved in the escape. With myself the seventh, we would have had the requisite number for a jury of complaint."

"But you didn't get them," Burgos said. "The Garzas are hardly disinterested parties, and you and I add up to two. And now you and I have five murders to account for, not one."

True. The horror of that scene rose up before me again, and I would have wept bitter tears of anger and remorse, had I been able to find my way back to myself. "Burgos," I said, "I should never have involved you in this imbecilic plot!"

"Ya lo creo!" he said.

Burgos was calmer than I could have imagined and not the least sympathetic. "It seems you saw nothing very clearly, young master," he remarked. "Even if you succeeded in provoking the Messiahists against Dan by killing their emissary priest, how do you think Boz would have placated them? He would have given them the college and yourself and every Old Believer in Dan to stave off an invasion. It would have been the very disaster you fear. Perhaps these things are taking place now, even as we speak."

He was right, of course. I had seen nothing clearly.

"But I doubt, my lord," he continued relentlessly, "that the Messiahists want an outright break with Dan at this point. They already have their hands full with your father. Before they risk a war with Dan, they will want to dispose of Judah."

I was again surprised by his astuteness. I was almost ready to feel relief and hope when he added: "In any case, I doubt that Dan will react with a single mind to the murder of the Valdez family. Some will be outraged, to be sure, but many will applaud it. Everyone knows Valdez's role in Garza's death. It may be that this thing will strike fear into the hearts of the Messiahists in Dan, and because of it, Old Believers will sleep easier."

"Fear? These Garza swine are halfway to Cashmere by now. What is there for the Messiahists to fear?"

He looked at me with his peasant's face and shrewd pig eyes. "You," he said. "They will fear *you*. Everyone will see your hand in this. They will see it as a message. Not everyone will approve the message, but they will understand what it means. Harm an Old Believer, and you bring destruction on your house. Many Old Believers will be grateful to you."

VIII

If Burgos had spoken these words to console me, he failed. Still, he remained cool and calculating. It seemed to me miraculous that he could keep his head in the face of all the horror I had set in motion. I was so appalled by what I had done, I could not see which way to turn. Burgos recommended tactfully that we leave the road and travel cross-country, across the mountains. The Garzas, he pointed out, now had a motive for lying in wait for us along the way. If Lander was my enemy—and we had every reason to believe he was—he had likely warned his contacts in Naphtali to expect my approach. No doubt anyone would be rewarded handsomely who could place me within Hanford's reach.

I saw the sense of what he proposed, but I was untrained for mountain terrain; I could not possibly find my way through trackless forests and jumbled ridges. Burgos assured me that as a young man, he had trapped for furs in the foothills of Ranier. He was familiar with mountain country and could find the way. He was stubborn, and being at a loss for what to do, I consented.

The road to Cashmere led through the most formidable mountains I had ever seen. Men did not venture here except in fall and spring, and then only for short times. When we left the road, we left behind everything familiar to me. We plunged into a wild solitude where my senses could not contain the multitude of objects and motions in my vision. We crossed the same raging stream a dozen times and climbed and descended and climbed and descended. The land had a strange beauty, but it seemed more a dreamscape than a journey. In a moment the brightest sunlight was eclipsed by a sudden overcast and flurries of rain and sleet. At other times, we moved in perfect silence amid tall cedars and groves of fir, enveloped in gloom. Then the forest would open up, and we were dazzled, moving through the gold light of aspen thickets. We saw elk and deer in the endless forest and glimpsed bare rugged peaks towering above. Once we happened upon a black bear shuffling through a high meadow, looking to lard his belly for his winter sleep.

We changed horses at each rest stop, and Burgos inspected them carefully for lameness and other injuries. We spoke little and avoided each other's eyes.

By the second night I was exhausted. I sat by the fire hugging my knees and longing for the austerity of desert landscapes. I was haunted by the image of bare crags thrust up into the realm of eternal snow and precipices yawning beneath us.

"The harvest comes late in Naphtali," Burgos remarked, poking the fire. "That means Hanford will not have many timber gangs in the woods yet. That is a piece of luck."

I pulled my blanket tighter and stared at the flames. I could still feel the branches clawing at my face and gear.

"What is it, my lord, that you hope to achieve now by going to Naphtali?"

"Gill," I replied. "Rehab Gill. I paid Lander to ransom him out of prison. He will be waiting for us at Cashmere. We'll find him and take him back with us. Perhaps he knows things that can help me."

"Back with us?" Burgos coughed behind his hand. "What about your mission, my lord; your orders from the Shepherd of the People?"

"I will scout out the country. Make contacts with potential allies. Lander says—"

"Lander says!"

"Yes, Lander says that Nahum of Cashmere is a figure around whom opposition to Hanford seems to be forming. And Solomon Glass—I think he is the man I must see and talk to. But how I am to do this, without danger to him or to me, I cannot imagine."

Burgos doled out the hot beans and lentils. "How will you contact him?"

"I made several copies of my orders, both from Tephlin Glanz and from the Apostle Moses ben Hadith, and brought them with me. I even stamped the seal on the copies of Glanz's orders. I thought I might be able to have them delivered privately to Glass, and"—I looked around for the saddlebag in which I had packed the documents.

"What is it, my lord?"

"The saddlebag! I had copies of my orders—"

I stopped in mid-sentence, my heart in my throat. There was no point in finishing. The saddlebag in which I had placed these documents had also contained the money for the Garzas, the gift that I had planned for them to give to Nahum as they pleaded for sanctuary. I recalled with perfect clarity handing the saddlebag to Burgos and ordering him to give it to the Garzas. My fury at their actions had emptied my mind; along with the kanz, I had given them the copies of my orders!

"Burgos, I am a complete and utter fool!"

"So you keep showing me, my lord."

There were more woodcutting parties in the forest than Burgos had predicted. But fortunately, woodcutters are noisy. The sound of axe-blows announced their presence from some distance, so we avoided them easily. We had several close calls from traveling groups, but in each case we escaped detection. Woodcutters seldom venture far from the Ancients' roads, for they have to load the timber onto carts and haul it back to their homes. Burgos understood this as well as I; he thought like an old soldier and used the terrain like a veteran.

On the fourth day we camped behind a wooded ridge from the top of which we could see the valley of the Wenatchee. We lay on the crest and examined the valley through glasses. Cashmere lay below, a straggling settlement close by the Wenatchee River. The valley itself was narrow, less than a mile in width at this point, with high benches above the river and steep canyons where the river had cut. The fields and orchards looked fertile and well tilled.

Burgos persuaded me that he should descend and scout the town by himself. "They have your description, my lord, but they will pay no attention to an old peasant." What he said seemed sensible, and I had come to rely on him entirely. I described Gill, and we discussed contingencies of all kinds. Eventually, he grew impatient with my instructions and left, grumbling to himself.

While I waited, I assumed the posture of meditation merely out of habit, for I was not capable of meditating nor even of emptying my mind of thought. Instead, I was contemplating the full scope of the disaster I had brought upon myself, feeling for its edges in my mind. It was as if a sudden blaze had consumed every one of my hopes. I could find no prospect in my life unseared by it, no wisp unshriveled by the flames I had unwittingly ignited. I had no real hope of accomplishing anything by this journey. Without copies of my orders, I could not contact anyone who might assist me. I could not even post my orders under Hanford's nose and thus put him on notice that his days were numbered. True, I might find and release Gill from his bondage; I might speak with Nahum of Cashmere—but he was more likely dismiss me as a fool and murderer than embrace me as an ally. But even if I could do these things, where could I go afterwards? Where could I take Gill to safety? The night before, Burgos had caught himself in the midst of rebuking me for my stupidity; he had coughed behind his hand when I mentioned taking Gill *back* with us. There was no *back* for me. I had become an outlaw in Dan, a pariah. What the Garzas had done—what I had conspired with them to do—meant that I could not return to Dan. I would be a hunted man there, an object of fear and loathing.

I realized suddenly that I must separate Burgos from my fate. He might escape harm if he could disassociate himself from me. Then, recalling his insistence on going alone into Cashmere, it occurred to me that he had perhaps arrived at the same view of things earlier than I, and had already acted to separate himself from me. *Perhaps he had gone down to Cashmere to sell me to Hanford.*

I looked around our small mountain clearing; the horses were cropping the sparse grass, pulling at their tethers. The forest was silent. The whole scene brightened intensely and then darkened again as clouds obscured the sun. Just as the sun broke free again of the clouds, I lay my sword across my lap, unsheathing a length of bright silver blade. For a long moment I thought of the options open to me.

Eventually, my mind turned, as if by the pull of gravity, to Miriam. She was never far from my thoughts, and every unoccupied moment and interval between mundane tasks brought her back to me. Since we had left Dan, every detail of our intimacy lived fresh in my recollection; her every touch and endearment tormented my thoughts. When I slept, I dreamed of her, and when I awoke disconsolate her scent lingered in my mind. I ached for her, even as I cursed myself for a fool. In my imagination, I held her again, entwined with her, face to face, her legs around me. Just before we parted, we had gazed into each other's eyes wordlessly, as if we no longer possessed or needed words for anything anymore. Now there truly were no words.

"Wake up! You fool! Wake up!""Master! What in God's—wake up now!"

Burgos was shaking me very roughly and shouting at me. "Thank goodness!" he exclaimed. "When I couldn't rouse you, I thought you'd done some foolishness. Master, wake up." He reached forward, I thought to strike me, but instead he gently lifted the sword from my lap.

"What is it, Burgos? Calm yourself." I spoke gruffly, but I was still groggy and disoriented. *I must have fallen into a trance.* I could tell immediately that hours had passed and the sun was over my left shoulder, low in the west.

"What is it?"

"I have news, master! I have Gill!"

He had Gill. Or rather he had seen Gill, and he had helped drag and carry him from the marketplace where he lay on a beggar's pallet, to the nearest woods. Burgos had concealed him in a pile of brush and returned to me. "He's been tortured—a bastinado, I think," Burgos said. "A mild one—only on the soles of his feet. The flesh is raw. They may have broken some bones. He can't walk, that's for certain. But he'll live, if we can get him out."

"Hanford, that swine! Why torture—"

"And Hanford's dead. I heard the news in the market. Oh, I have other news, my lord. Much news! Everything has happened at once. Thank goodness you stayed here. They knew you were coming; if you had showed yourself in Cashmere, you'd be a dead man."

"Stop!" I seized him by the shoulders and shook him. "Tell me one thing at a time—and in order." He embraced me, chuckling with excitement and speaking incoherently.

Eventually I had the full story. More even than the tale he told, his own excitement was strange to behold. I marveled that anything could so alter his usual demeanor. But the first thing Burgos had seen when entering the gates of the city were the bodies of the three Garzas hanging from a gibbet, in the midst of a scene of destruction.

"It was not good, my lord, the things that had been done to them. Rafino was practically in pieces, and his neck was as long as your arm."

"Why?" I asked. "They had committed no crimes in Naphtali."

"They thought he was *you.* The Garzas had the money you gave them, and Rafino had taken a fancy sword from Valdez—"

"And he had copies of my orders!"

"Yes, and Rafino is your age and about your size. I was told he eventually admitted to being you, after they tortured him. I expect that before Hanford's men were through with them, *all* the Garzas claimed to be the Sword of Israel!" He laughed in a most bizarre and alarming fashion.

"There's an irony," I said.

"Yes, my lord," he chuckled. "It seems that the Garzas found justice even in Naphtali."

We tried to reconstruct how these events had fallen out. Nahum must have turned the Garzas in to the garrison commander, thinking that Rafino was the Sword of Israel in disguise. Lander had no doubt warned him about my impending visit. This inference was not entirely fair to Lander. We considered a number of alternative explanations, but I concluded finally that Burgos had been correct: Lander was my enemy, and he had sought to lure me to my death in Naphtali.

I badgered Burgos for a description of events in Cashmere, and he gave me a vivid account of Rafino's body hanging inside the gate, with a sign reading, "the Sword of Israel" around his distended neck. "They hanged the Garzas the day before yesterday," Burgos continued. "There was quite a stir, apparently. They made a spectacle of it, mocking young Rafino, whom they took to be you, and making a great joke of the orders from the Council of Apostles. They sent your papers on to Hanford at Hammoth-Wenatchee. The whole market was buzzing with these things. 'Justice and harmony in Naphtali.' I heard that phrase a dozen times."

"And then?"

"And then this morning, word came back that Hanford Glanz is dead. Killed in his bed by his own bodyguard. The assassins murdered his wife and two children as well. Everyone assumes that General Huerta, commander of the Northern Lights Guards, ordered the slaying. That news set the ants dancing on the log, my lord! The garrison commander left immediately for Hammoth-Wenatchee and took most of the garrison with him. A riot broke out by mid-morning, and the jail was emptied of prisoners. I believe the jailors were not popular men, and it is their bodies that now hang along side the Garzas. The market is a shambles."

"So Hanford is dead. This happened yesterday?"

"Yes, and something like a rebellion is in progress in Cashmere. There are no soldiers there."

"Well, we must not waste a moment. I must go down and see what is going on, and what can be done."

Burgos seized my arm in an iron grip. "Patience, master. We'll wait until dark. Gill expects us then – and not before. We don't know who is a danger to us down there, or who would aid us. What can be done is that the three of us can get out of this madhouse alive."

IX

Rehab Gill winced as he arranged himself by our fire. Burgos and I examined his feet, which were swollen and bloody. The light was too poor to see much. As we talked, Burgos bathed his feet in spring water. The strangeness of our circumstances was a barrier to speech. There was a distance between us, an abyss of lingering suspicion. And yet there was a bond of familiarity as well. Eventually, without any prompting from me, Gill began to fill in the time and distance since we had parted. "What I didn't tell you when we were traveling together was that I had orders to contact the garrison commander at Jezreel, a Major Gutierrez, when we arrived there. I was told he would have further instructions for us – for me at least – at that point."

"And you chose *not* to tell me this? You chose not to tell me a lot of things, Captain Gill!"

"As I said, I had no idea what my next instructions might be. I tried to warn you about the dangers of proceeding onward. You mentioned yourself that Ben Gurion and Tephlin Glanz might have arranged for your death on this mission. I might have been instructed to—well, my family remained in Hebron, remember?"

"And *were* you instructed to assassinate me?" I asked. Burgos, who was busy with the fire and a pot of beans, looked up and gazed intently at Rehab Gill.

"No, I was not." Gill replied. He stretched his legs, trying to lift his feet into a new position without causing himself pain. "But," he continued, "assassinations were in the wind. Hanford was the target, or I should say the main one. That, at least, is the construction I put on it all now."

"I don't understand."

"I'm fairly certain that you were not meant to understand. You were an instrument merely. But it is still not clear to me for what purpose you were to be used."

An instrument merely? So, my father and my Masters had this much in common! I was suddenly furious. "Gill," I exclaimed, "I'm tired of these intrigues. I want straight talk or I'll have Burgos roll you down the hill into the lap of the Northern Lights Guards." I questioned him minutely about our journey up the Jordan, about what he knew and what he suspected. I wanted answers.

"I knew very little," he insisted. "But of course that is how it was intended. Intelligence missions are segmented like beads on a string. Each segment is only a small part of a larger whole, and the agent or agents in each know only their own role. If the beads are successfully linked together, you have a necklace – or an assassination. But if a segment is taken by the enemy, they cannot, by having it, easily take the other segments or foil the mission. Everyone's knowledge of the roles of others is quite limited for that reason. Typically, there may be several redundant units for each link in the chain, so if one fails, another may try and succeed. There are always alternative means of proceeding built into the chain." Sensing my impatience, he got at last to the point: "I never got to hear what Major Gutierrez's instructions for me might have been, since he welcomed me cordially enough, but put off a private interview for what seemed at the time plausible reasons. But then he ordered your arrest when you were identified – and had me arrested when you escaped."

I asked him what he knew of the man, and he shrugged. "Ben Gurion gave me this part of my instructions orally, not wanting anything in writing that could compromise the Major. But I think this Gutierrez had been turned by Hanford – or was too frightened of Hanford to act as ordered."

"Did you identify me to the garrison?"

"No. But your description was well known to them. I confirmed it, I admit. I had no choice. But I did what I could to prevent your capture. You know the rest. They suspected I had assisted you, so I was arrested and sent northward."

"I do *not* know the rest," I exclaimed. "What else do you know about the mission we were to perform, and about Hanford's countermeasures?"

"I suspect—but do not know—that there must have been a group of officers around Hanford ready to assassinate him once you appeared on the scene. I believe that must have been the plan – to kill him as soon as you arrived, in a way that would have implicated you in his death."

"To blacken your name!" Burgos interjected. "To destroy your power to play the role of Israel's champion." I winced, thinking of the ways I had blackened my own name.

Gill gave Burgos a careful appraising glance before continuing. "Perhaps," he said. "These possibilities are the only ones that make sense to me. I have had little else to think about these past three months in prison, but this is as much as I can explain. I admit that my construction of events seems very paltry and incomplete. It is the best I can do."

We were silent a while. Burgos shared out the hot beans. Gill was ravenous and burned his mouth.

"Hanford would never have relinquished power willingly," I remarked. "I'm certain of that much." I thought of death coming upon him suddenly in his own bedroom and encompassing his wife and children. How strangely the deaths of his innocent family chimed with the deaths of the Valdez family. *It was difficult to discern which patterns held significance and which were meaningless. Perhaps nothing was meaningless.*

Perhaps everything was.

"True, Hanford relished his power, and he would not have surrendered it," Gill said. "He would have killed you in an instant if he had laid hands on you. Strange that he was assassinated immediately upon your arrival in Naphtali – or rather when it was *believed* you had appeared. But perhaps he died as a result of another and different plot, and not by your father's orders at all. This is another one of those strange puzzles that fascinate me about your life. Do you remember the similarity I saw in your being sent to Esdralon to watch over your brother Justin and this mission to bring Hanford to justice?

"Yes," I replied, "and I recall that you were entirely wrong in your construction of those events."

"So you insisted. But I infer in this case that some members of this conspiracy must have been double agents, either loyal to Hanford, or afraid of him. They acted to wreck the original plan, but afterwards, in the confusion that followed, some among them must have had second thoughts. Hanford was not loved, and it must have become known outside the group that orders had been given for his death. Still, it is very interesting that the moment they chose to act was your—or rather an imposter's – appearance in Naphtali."

"Do you believe that Hanford's death was ordered by Glanz?"

"What does it matter? Either way, Hanford is dead. The fact that the assassins killed his wife and children suggests to me that they overreached their orders, assuming they had them from Glanz. Not even Glanz would have ordered the murder of his own grandchildren." He paused a moment to consider what he had said. "No," he concluded. "Not even Glanz. It must have been a group in Naphtali who decided independently to depose Hanford and to seize power. His success in setting up for himself in defiance of Judean interests and ruling the Northern Lights as his private fiefdom must have been a tantalizing precedent."

"I would think his fate might be a deterrent."

"Not at all," he replied. "Nothing compels like the prospect of power."

I pressed Gill for what he knew of the men behind the conspiracy.

"General Huerta is Hanford's successor, so I assume he led the conspiracy. Major Gutierrez holds Jezreel for the General, and a man named Sepulvida commands the garrison in the Okanogan valley and the northern reaches of the Jordan. Those are the leaders. It will be interesting to see who survives the next few days and who does not. That will tell us – by a process of elimination – who was *not* in the conspiracy. Colonel Sepulvida," he added, "has stirred up trouble with the Canadians, and there has been fighting there. So most of the real troops of the Northern Lights Guards are in the Okanogan valley. Given his strength, it's possible that Sepulvida may sooner or later contend with Huerta for control of Naphtali. At least he has the means to do so. Oh, and one other thing – it has occurred to me that the list of bank accounts which was included with your written orders points to another revelation."

"What's that?" I asked.

"Someone knowledgeable about the financial workings of the company would have been your contact in Naphtali. You remember that you were not intended to open that portion of your orders until we arrived in Hammoth-Wenatchee?"

"Yes."

"So it seems probable that this was the case: Major Gutierrez was probably ordered to alert his fellow conspirators against Hanford and to set whatever had been planned in motion as soon as we appeared. I suspect he was also to tell us the name of a man inside the company who could freeze or recover all the accounts in which Hanford had put aside riches for himself. This would also be the man with knowledge enough to conduct the inquiry into company affairs that is part of your orders."

"And who would that man be?"

"I believe it has to be the financial officer, Solomon Glass, Controller of the Northern Lights Enterprises. An interesting character, I'm told. He has a reputation as a mind without a heart – a man totally devoid of feeling. While not greedy himself, he is the willing tool of others' greed. I like to imagine him as an ill-begotten son of Simon ben Gurion."

"Fascinating," I said. "It was through Glass that I arranged your release from prison. I persuaded Nathan Lander, the chief of Dan's intelligence service, to bribe him." I did not mention that I had already deduced Glass' role in my mission.

"Fascinating indeed!" Gill exclaimed. He explained that it was Glass who had arranged for him to be taken to Cashmere and released. Glass had, in fact, interrupted the last interrogation of Gill, one that could easily have proven fatal. Hanford's men had wanted all the information concerning me that they could extract from him—and everything he knew about the Sword of Israel. "I gave them a very minute account of you," Gill admitted, "and I warned them that this young man, Garza, whoever he was, could not possibly be you. Because, while far from brilliant, you would never do anything so stupid as to show up on their doorstep with Glanz's orders in your hand."

I stole a glanced at Burgos, who was watching Gill intently. "And when I saw the sword they had taken from him, I assured them that they had the wrong man. Apparently, they did not believe me. And then Glass intervened, and I was released. Two soldiers took me in a cart to Cashmere, and in the morning, when we heard the news of Hanford's death, they dumped me by the roadside and fled. Some local people brought me to Cashmere. I was proving modestly successful in my new career as a beggar when your man Burgos happened along."

"By the way," he said, addressing Burgos, "I could tell what you are from the questions you were asking in the market. If Hanford's garrison had not fled yesterday morning, you would have joined the Garzas on the gibbet by nightfall."

Burgos spat into the fire.

"You are a shrewd man," Gill said, "but an amateur spy."

"What do you know about Solomon Glass?" I asked.

Gill shrugged. "As far as I know, Glass survives and serves the new masters in

Naphtali. But of course he may be Glanz's man also, in secret. Or his own man against all, in even deeper secret."

So are we all, I thought.

"So where does this leave us?" Burgos asked.

"It leaves me crippled and with no prospects," Gill said, "and it leaves the captain here without a commission and with even worse prospects. Hanford is dead, and others rule in Naphtali. And all you have," he said, gesturing at me, "is a worthless draft for 200,000 kanz that you cannot redeem."

"Not entirely worthless," I said. "It turns out that I have the seal after all. I had it all along."

"What!" Gill exclaimed. "You had it all along? That certainly sheds new light. The seal! So, you had it all the time!" I briefly described my discovery of the seal. He mulled over this news and said: "Nevertheless, seal or no seal, the new rulers of Naphtali want you dead. Tephlin Glanz would probably prefer to be rid of you as well, and your old friends the Velcos in Manasseh and all the hosts of Messiahists surely wish you dead."

"True. And now I have enemies in Dan." We had told Gill about the Garzas but not about my part in causing the deaths of the Valdez family. "I am no doubt the biggest target in Israel. Yet when you had the chance last July," I reminded him, "you saved my life. *Why?*"

"They say that perverse willfulness is my worst quality," Gill said. "And now you have saved mine – if we wish to speak further of willful, inexplicable actions! Are we quits, then? Or are we friends?"

"Even more than Burgos, you have been my severest critic. I suppose that is a role a friend may play. But one of the things you charged me with has piqued my curiosity for a long time. Indeed, I may have saved your life merely to continue that conversation."

"Yes? I sense you on the brink of a revelation." Gill had recovered some of his spirit; I was pleased to hear him banter with me.

"You may recall when we parted, you accused me of being a monstrous creature let loose by the Old Believers, trained to embody their hatred of the Messiahists. You suggested that my Masters Ebenezer and Josephus were somehow hypnotically planted inside my head, to act for me. To control me. Words to that effect. . . ."

"Yes," he replied. *"Yes!"*

Gill had not, I noted, lost his interest in that topic either.

"Since then I have considered your words very seriously – more seriously than you can imagine."

"So? What are you saying?" Gill was leaning forward intently.

"I think it is possible you were right."

The next morning, I had to explain to Gill how disastrously I had erred in conspiring with the Garzas in the matter of the Messiahist priest in Hazor. He listened silently, absorbing it all.

"So you were trying to undermine Boz's efforts to arrive at a settlement with Manasseh," he remarked, unimpressed with the personal tragedy of the Valdez family. "Bold, very bold. You have learned some things since we parted."

"Hardly! I turned a killer loose in a peaceful household. And I turned myself into a pariah. As a consequence, Gill, I have no place of refuge to take you. I have rescued you from the pan only to introduce you into the fire."

"That you have, my lord," Burgos said.

We discussed our prospects for a while, until I was grateful to change the subject by examining Gill's foot: "This swelling will have to be lanced. There is pus under the ball of your foot." In the darkness the night before, we could not tell much about his injuries.

Broken bones may cause swelling, but his foot was clearly infected as well. If we could open and drain it, and soak it frequently in salt water, I thought we could save it. The sole of his left foot was split and bruised, but the right foot was badly mutilated. I doubted that it could heal properly without surgery. "I think you have a bone or two broken here," I said. Gill winced at my touch. Burgos quietly laid his knife by the fire with the blade in the flame.

"What did they use to beat you?" Burgos asked.

"Various things," Gill said. "Mostly unpeeled ash wands, highly regarded for their spring and play." Gill's manner was the same, but he had started to breathe rapidly and perspire. "Trouble is, they break easily. Inconvenient for the interrogators."

"On second thought," I said, "I believe you and Burgos may be able to enter Dan safely. Burgos is known and highly regarded there, and members of the College will surely give you refuge. Hide you if necessary. I'm sure of that. I am the one they will seek for the murder of the Valdezes." *The scar tissue on Gill's right foot will leave him a cripple,* I thought.

"They will seek us both, my lord. Or neither. We need to learn which it will be."

"What about you, then?" Gill asked me. "What are you intending to do? And do I have to call you 'my lord'?"

Burgos laughed, apparently enjoying Gill's humor. He had picked up the knife and was letting it cool. He had his back to Gill.

"Please," I replied, "do me the favor of *not* calling me that!" Responding to Gill's other question, I added, "I have no wish to go back to Dan. The confusion here in Naphtali may be an opportunity. I might be able to accomplish something. It may be that the assassination of Hanford opens the way for me."

"Not likely!" Gill scoffed. "Remember, Hanford's wife and children died also. This was not part of any plan hatched by your father or Ben Gurion. If you set foot in Hammoth-Wenatchee, you will swing higher than your friends the Garzas!"

"That is my thinking, too, my lord," Burgos said. He indicated with his eyes that he was ready. "It is best that you come back with us."

When I had considered all the circumstances, I was forced to agree with Burgos. "I have an obligation to deliver Gill safely to Dan," I said. "I will honor it." To Gill, I said: "Take this stick in your teeth. It helps." I moved behind him so I could hold his arms and shoulders. Gill was trembling; his face twitched nervously.

"I'm going to sit on your knees," Burgos said, "because it is an officer's nature to kick."

"So you believe this young prodigy here is the Sword of—" Gill screamed suddenly, and then shrieked again; I was barely able to hold him, though his shoulders were as thin as a boy's. Burgos was quick and determined; afterwards Gill wept audibly.

Burgos knelt and examined the foot and thrust it into a pan of warm salt water. "Here," he said, "it will draw out the poison. The bleeding is good. And yes," he added, "I do believe it."

Gill's eyes were still rolling and sweat streamed from his face. "I have no – no control," he stammered. "Too many beatings, too many nights and days in the dark will do that, they say. They made a coward of me."

"There are no cowards here," Burgos said, glancing at our provisions. "I wish we had more salt. I'll make a salve so you can travel. You can ride one of the horses; the captain and I will take turns walking."

Gill recovered himself quickly; his breathing slowed, though he trembled still. "So you believe," he said to Burgos. "And that's why you call him lord." *It was as if I were not present.*

"Yes, that's why I call him lord. He objects sometimes, but I ignore him."

"Ignore me!" I exclaimed.

"I see the necessity," Gill said. He was nearly himself again.

"He is young to be a Dedicated One," Burgos said. "He thinks of the burden like a knapsack."

"Ah, you mean like a burden he can carry forever—or put off whenever he wants."

Burgos nodded, busy at camp chores. "He hasn't told you about his lady-love." While I blushed crimson, Burgos gave a brief but surprisingly accurate account of my relationship with Miriam Lander. Apparently, I had concealed nothing from him. "Sometimes," Burgos remarked, "I wonder how the Dedicated Ones are chosen."

"I thought the point was that they are *not* chosen," Gill said. "They themselves choose—what did you say?" he exclaimed. "Miriam Lander? *The* Miriam Lander who is an agent in Dan's intelligence! Perhaps its head! Do you mean to tell me that she actually—that our young friend here was *her* young friend—and *more*? That's hard to believe. What could have possessed her? What was she thinking?" He paused and looked at me appraisingly. "Well, she is a deep one, so I understand."

Miriam—a member of Danite intelligence!

Burgos laughed and shook his head. Then he remarked – again as though I were not present: "He is young. He still trusts. So they think they can capture him, capture his power. Or destroy it."

"Can they?"

"I don't think so. He is acquiring the pain. He does not carry it well, but he will."

Burgos fashioned chaps for Gill out of scraps of cloth, so his wounds would be protected but still be open to the air. The journey back to Dan was strenuous, particularly for Gill, but at every resting point the two continued their conversation avidly. Occasionally, they included me. "I told Hanford's men you were eight feet tall and fell into trances which gave you superhuman strength," Gill remarked on one occasion. "I told them that in this mood, unable to feel either pain or compassion, you chop men and horses in half and then remember nothing." Burgos snorted. "I told them that you took command at the battle of Elion, in your first experience of battle, and coolly saved a legion from destruction. I told them you could never be defeated by ordinary means, and that no one knew the secrets by which you might be harmed."

"Hah!" Burgos swore. "The Senyora Lander knows, if anyone does!"

Their comments goaded me into speech for the first time since breaking camp. "Since that day you accused my Masters of hypnotizing and controlling me," I said to Gill, "I have wracked my memory for some way to refute you. I cannot. I remember nothing of the kind—but of course I *would* remember nothing, I suppose. Still, I doubt your theory. I had a high fever as a child—I survived the mountain fever—and that may have damaged my memory."

"Remarkable," Gill said. "Not one in a hundred survives the fever. How was it that you did?"

I shrugged. "I was only seven at the time. I'm told I was delirious for nearly a week. If the fever did not leave my memory impaired, other events may have done so." *I thought of my mother.*

"Yet it was your famous deeds of war that seem to have triggered your recent losses of memory. How do you explain that?"

"Battle fury, some call it. Or I may simply have a mental quirk that conceals painful things from me. I was, in a practical sense, orphaned at an early age. My mind may have found ways of concealing pain until I can bear it. Perhaps I still react as I did as a child and blot things out."

Gill looked at me thoughtfully and then glanced at Burgos.

"When we fought with the Kr," I said, "they cracked my head with a club; I suppose it should be no mystery if my memory is blurred in that instance. I can recall things now that were dark to me less than a year ago. Parts of my actions in the citadel at Esdralon – even the death of Senesh Velco – have come back to me." I rubbed the scar on my forehead, recalling vividly how I had acquired it. I was reluctant to broach the next subject, but felt compelled to. "Whatever my losses of memory mean, I have to acknowledge that I was trained as an assassin. That was the real import of my education at the Refuge. I realize that now."

Gill and Burgos stared at the fire.

"My Masters prepared me well—and aimed me at the Messiahists. I see that also. What I did at Esdralon when I heard they had arrested Justin—well, I had no need to think about a response. I required no plan, no prevision. I did as I was trained to do. And this latest folly with the priest Ignacio and the Valdez family, I did what I was trained to do there as well. Whether there was more that they trained me to do or expected of me, I cannot say. But this is enough!"

My two companions had listened respectfully and they did not leap to condemn me. I was grateful for that. "Have you ever considered speaking with your teachers at the Refuge?" Gill asked.

"Of course! I intended to contact my Masters as soon as I arrived in Hazor and resolve these questions once and for all. Unfortunately, they would not see me. I cannot write or send by word of mouth. All contact has been denied me."

"Interesting," Gill said. "But it could mean anything."

"Anything but my peace of mind."

He laughed in his humorless way. "Their silence can neither confirm nor refute what you want to know. The Wayfarer's Refuge lies in easy range of Messiahist cavalry, so they did well to be cautious."

"Does the Senyora Lander think you are the Sword of Israel?" It was Burgos who asked the question; it startled me and started me thinking along a very painful line of thought.

"That story is extraordinary," Gill remarked, "and if Miriam Lander does believe that he is the Sword, it would account for her – let us say – unusual interest in our young friend. Imagine it," he marveled. "Miriam Lander!"

"I can imagine the Senyora very well," Burgos said seriously. "A beautiful proud woman. Carriage like a noble lady. Thighs like a cider press."

At the thought of her, my spirits immediately diminished almost to nothingness. I grieved to think of her in this way—to think about our friendship, our attachment, as contrived to serve other purposes. I could hardly bear it. Eventually, I realized that their barracks humor about us was well intended, meant to evoke my laughter and affirm our brotherhood as men. Still, I found nothing amusing in it.

I overheard Burgos say quietly, as he helped Gill to remount: "He will not have much time to sow wild oats. We do not begrudge it. We must leave him be now."

What could I say to them? *What could I say in answer to my own questions?* Miriam Lander, too, it appeared, was one of the Eyes of Israel – one of those who thrive on mind war. They see all and never allow themselves to be seen. Not as they really are. It was excruciating to think that she had entered into our friendship only to manipulate me and to extract information. To control me, or—as Burgos suggested—to destroy my power.

But what power? I had no special powers. I of all people had the least idea of who or what the Sword of Israel might be. I had a sword; I was trained as a warrior and educated to loathe the claims of the Messiahists. I had been turned loose in the world by the most revered sages of the Old Believers—teachers who, in all probability as affairs now stood, would prove the last of their kind. But I had proved a fool, molded and manipulated by all

I met. I had been used continually for others' purposes, not my own. I could claim no sacred calling. Instead, I was deeply attached to a woman whose influence—if she was my enemy – had spread like a brush fire through my heart. Miriam was able to enflame my senses and lay waste my reason like the mountain fever itself. If she was a test, I had failed it miserably.

It seemed that I had bungled and misapprehended and soiled or thrown away everything entrusted to me. As for Miriam Lander, I consoled myself with the thought that she had not acted with the single, calculated purpose of her intelligence mission, but from many motives, some of them, I hoped, unapprehended by her. Whatever Miriam had meant to do originally, I told myself, her purpose had altered along the way. She may well have begun in mere curiosity. She was angry with her husband and had sought an opportunity for revenge. I recalled the steady and unwavering revulsion in her voice when she spoke of him.

Miriam and I had common enemies—and common values as well. Miriam hated the Messiahists, who had turned her son against her. And she resented her husband for whatever role he had played in that loss. She had a feeling for the nation, the old Israel, which was not feigned. I was sure of that. It was visible in her dress and manner and speech, and in the home she kept. Her tastes were a mirror of the noble class. She longed for an Israel that retained the best of the old ways. Miriam differed from her husband in these many ways, and she was never venal or crass. And even though she served Caleb Boz, she despised him. I was certain of that. *I had the evidence of my senses, which could not be wrong in all things.*

Miriam had also wanted to have a child by me. I saw that clearly now, though I had dismissed the idea at the time. How many motives, twisted and straight, had met in *that* desire? I had come back to bed once and saw her under the blanket with her knees drawn up to her breast – the classic posture of the good wife preserving her husband's seed to conceive a child. *What are you doing? I had asked in alarm. Never mind, she said. I'm just resting my back. You rode me like a Kuhlan, darling; I must have strained it.*

No doubt she wanted to recover the child who was lost to the Messiahists. Perhaps she longed to have her youth back as well. Revenge, disappointment, and denial must have mingled in her hopes. Still, Miriam was deeply attached to what she liked to call my "enterprise," and she aspired to a life that touched – or seemed to touch – my own hopes at many points. She had wanted to help bring to birth the Israel of our imaginings. I felt certain of that.

And there was love. She had spoken of love. More than risking pregnancy, this talk of love broke and trampled upon the conventions of the relationship permitted to us. She had said she loved me. I believed she had.

Oh, Zaiyah, she said. I love you. Love me!

Admittedly, she had given me a lesson in the meanings of that word, a sample of the myriad feelings, depths and shallows both, truth as well as deception, compressed into that simple sound. But I could acknowledge that and feel no cynicism about it. My own heart had never been single or pure; I had never quite lost sight of the fact that she was married or forgot the discrepancy in our ages. Yet, I loved her and knew that her feelings for me were similarly real, if alloyed. She could not have feigned it all.

Could she?

How could I know? *Are there no moments when we see clearly? Have we no choice except to see the world through the heart of the fire or through scales of ice?*

Thinking about it, thinking about her, was like looking through the wrong end of a glass; I felt the distance. I felt the change in me. *Already.*

X

We had been in Dan barely a day when troops appeared at Lander's estate. "If the soldiers have come with a warrant, I will go with them. That is the end of it." My bodyguard protested, as did Gill and Burgos, but I was not to be moved on this subject. I would not risk their lives to protect my own. Not in these circumstances. Besides, I needed to account for what I had done. "I am willing to put myself in the hands of the Law," I said. "Even eager to."

"Master," Burgos exclaimed, "this is *Dan*! This is Caleb Boz's law, not St. Supplicee's!"

During our absence, there had been conflict in Hazor and other places in Dan. The College had been attacked by a mob on one occasion, and there had been assaults on Messiahists as well, and lonely murders on the roads, for who knows what cause? No one was safe. Caleb Boz himself had suffered a wound from a missile while riding through the streets of Hazor. It was not yet clear what the Messiahists would do, or which faction would triumph in Dan. Soldiers of the Danite Guard had visited the Lander estate twice inquiring after me, but had not molested my followers there. They were searching for me.

When we returned, Burgos and Gill and I had bathed and purified ourselves and attended to Gill's wounds. We were sitting down to the evening meal when we heard horses outside. It was not unexpected. Nevertheless, my bodyguard sprang up and seized their weapons in a panic. My own heart was in turmoil, but I sat at the table, determined to finish the meal and then face what had to be faced. If I remained calm, I might be able to keep my men from useless violence on my behalf.

"From the sounds, I would estimate a troop of cavalry," Gill said tersely.

"Yes, and we are a dozen," I said. "Resistance is not an option. Come back and finish your meal," I called to the men. We waited and the sounds subsided.

"They are surrounding the house," Burgos said.

I rose and was preparing myself to meet them when we heard a herald's cry outside. Investigating, we found a captain of the Danite Guard waiting to speak. The troop, as Burgos had anticipated, was deployed around the house at a respectful distance.

"Nisan Lot, Mayor of Hazor, desires to speak with Captain Josiah Glanz ben Haggadah," the captain announced. "And to speak confidentially and securely. He will approach the house alone and unarmed, if you consent to it and guarantee his safety."

We agreed to meet outside under the canopy in the garden. It was growing dark, so my men lit fires to make us visible, and then set out a table and chairs.

"I'll stand at your side, my lord. Don't even try to persuade me not to."

"Burgos, believe me," I assured him, "I can deal with any weapon that man may carry."

"It is not a weapon that I fear."

Mayor Lot was grim-faced and dusty; he was not used to exertions on horseback. He glanced at Burgos and me and then sat down heavily in a chair. Like the merchant he was, he came immediately to the point: "I have a warrant," he announced, "for the arrest of Captain Josiah Glanz ben Haggadah and a certain Manuel Burgos of Ephraim, for the murder of four citizens of Dan." *I noted immediately that there was no mention of the priest Ignacio.* "The warrant also names three members of the Garza family. But I wish to speak with you privately first, before dealing with this matter in my official capacity."

I stood ready to listen but said nothing.

"I am tasked with this matter because Dan is in chaos. The Apostle Boz was injured several days ago and his condition is still precarious. You are no doubt aware of the extent to which Dan is now divided and in conflict with itself, and you know also of the reasons for that division."

"Because Boz was making an alliance with the Messiahists," I said. "Because of his own stubborn blindness!"

"That is a possible construction of events," he replied. "Though one that seems to me partial at best. I am proceeding informally in the matter of these four murders because of those very divisions—and because one of the persons named in my warrant is, if not precisely a leader of one of the factions, a person of consequence within it. I refer of course to yourself. In this, as in all things, I seek what is best for Dan." He looked at me. "Do you have the Garzas inside?" he asked.

"The Garzas are dead." I explained briefly what had happened to them in Cashmere.

The Mayor listened attentively; my news had surprised him. "And you will swear to this?" he asked. He rubbed his beard. "This begins to put matters in a different light. But tell me, in strict confidence and in the absence of witnesses, the truth of your participation in the death of the Valdez family. This is irregular, I understand, but, as I said, this is a political matter as much as a legal one. I would not have Dan torn apart over some scruple of the Law."

Burgos nudged me in warning, but I was grateful for the chance to speak. I told Lot very frankly what I had planned to do and what had in fact occurred. The Mayor questioned me closely, establishing my complicity in the murder of the priest Ignacio, and confirming details from several lines of inquiry. He was a skilled interrogator. I admitted that I had assisted the Garzas in making their escape, although I had not known of the fate of the Valdez family until on the road to Cashmere. Other than to omit any reference to Burgos' role in events, I told him the exact truth, without exculpating myself in any way.

"And this Burgos," the Mayor said, glancing at my companion, "he is not responsible for the deaths of the Valdez family either?"

"Burgos had no responsibility for planning the attack on Ignacio nor for any of the unforeseen events that surrounded it. His revulsion at the deaths of the Valdez family is as great as my own." *I had not spoken of Burgos' complicity in the assassination of the priest; I was guilty of conspiracy under the Law, and Burgos was unfortunately an accessory. But Burgos would have to implicate himself in that crime; I would not.*

Nisan Lot rubbed his temples with both hands, his eyes shut. "I believe you," he said. He looked at us both, drumming his fingers on the table. "With your permission, I will summon my secretary, and in his presence, I will ask you a few questions under oath. We will take a formal deposition regarding this crime against the Valdez family."

Burgos put his hand on my shoulder to warn me, but I assented gladly. Lot had not once mentioned the assassination of the priest; he had evidently separated that issue—the death of a foreigner in Dan – from the warrant. He was treating Ignacio's death as a separate crime, perhaps as an act of war.

Lot's secretary was a deferential young man, with slender uncallused hands. He seemed nervous about taking my deposition. Lot quickly led me through a series of carefully structured questions about the deaths of the Valdez family that I could answer with a simple yes or no; the questions did not touch upon the issue of my larger complicity—only on my actions and foreknowledge of the Valdez murders. His secretary scribbled down the questions and answers frantically. Then Lot led Burgos through a similar exercise.

Afterwards, he dismissed his secretary with the document, which we both had signed. "Thank you, gentlemen," he said. "This simplifies my task—as well as relieves my mind. I see I must tear up this warrant"—*which he did before us*. "The case against the Garzas is abated by the deaths of the defendants, while the two of you have established a basis for pleading your innocence in the matter, if you should ever be summoned before the court."

"I have a basis for pleading, perhaps," I said. "But as you know, I am not innocent."

"Nevertheless," he replied, unimpressed by my confession, "I will make the contents of this deposition known to both factions in Hazor. I have hopes that it will have a calming effect. Absurd charges and rumors have been flying about. As for the assassination of the priest Ignacio, I may have occasion at some point in the future to draw up another warrant that would involve the pair of you. Or I may not, depending on circumstances. With the incapacity of the Apostle Boz, I find my own duties much expanded."

"Understand me," he warned. "I have a duty to discharge relative to this matter, and I feel that I have done so, albeit with certain irregularities. My real concerns, as you suspect, lie elsewhere. I have a crisis in my own government to deal with. My people are on the verge of civil war over these recent excitements – which I must say are partly your doing, Captain. Besides the prospect of civil war in Dan, we now face the danger of retaliation from Manasseh. I estimate that that danger is also quite real. They have sent us an ultimatum, which we must answer quickly."

I felt a combination of elation at this news of the collapse of negotiations with the Messiahists and alarm at the consequences I had set in motion.

"You, sir," he said sternly, "are involved in all of these developments. Intimately and deliberately involved. And fortunately for you, in these matters I am not in the least interested in your guilt or innocence."

"I think you can estimate my role in these events pretty accurately," I replied. "I have not concealed anything from you. And you can judge as well that I am not the single cause of putting these events in motion."

"True, I can. The Apostle Boz, however, blames you for everything. Foolishly, in my opinion. Sadly for the nation, he finds it easier to blame you than criticize his own actions. He cannot see that, with or without you, his policy of reconciliation with the Messiahists is dead. And speaking of death, Boz gave me explicit orders to return with your head. He will not be pleased when I return with a deposition."

Burgos stirred at my side; I put my hand lightly on his arm. "Why do you take such risks on my behalf?" I asked Lot.

"They are not taken on your behalf. Your death, or even arrest, would only inflame the situation. The Apostle Boz fails to realize that if I hang you, you become a martyr to half of Dan. More than half. Your death could be the kindling of a very large fire. In my opinion, a violent rising against the Apostle is not out of the question in any case."

"So you do not believe in the accord with the Messiahists either."

"That policy was incorrect from the start," he acknowledged. "You and I are in agreement on that point. The Council is still divided, but it is clear that we will have a rebellion on our hands if we force this alliance upon Dan. I intend to see that that does not happen. Hence, the value of your innocence in the Valdez matter. I need oil to pour on these troubled waters, and this deposition may be that oil."

"You seek to reconcile the Old Believers?"

"Yes. But unfortunately, the Messiahists must also be appeased somehow. They, too, are asking for your head. You are a troublesome young man, Captain."

"If you try to sell the Master to the Messiahists," Burgos interjected, "your neck will experience a violent revolution before you can rise out of your chair!"

Lot did not even turn his eyes. "I note," he said, "that, besides being troublesome, you evoke intense loyalty in your followers." To Burgos he said, "I have no intention of giving the captain to the Messiahists. That would create an even more poignant martyrdom and thus defeat my purpose here at home." He paused and blew on his hands. There was a chill in the air. "It is a difficult case, I must admit," he said, "but I seek a solution we all can live with. But the crux of the matter is that I must get rid of your master, Burgos, remove him from Dan, and that immediately." He raised a hand to silence Burgos: "But in a manner satisfactory to himself and to his faction, if you follow me. I am speaking of exile."

The carriage arrived within the hour. I saw by torchlight the small, familiar figure descend and approach me. At every step she took, my heart rose higher in my throat. Miriam was disheveled, her eyes red and her hair awry, and she seemed actually smaller than I remembered, as if she had shrunk in the two weeks since I had last seen her. An officer of the Guard led her to our table and she sat down, without a greeting and without meeting my eyes, facing me.

"My son Jason, of whom we have spoken. . ." Her voice was low, hardly more than a whisper.

"The one who became a Messiahist?"

"Yes."

"I remember. In New Jerusalem."

"The Messiahists have taken him hostage; he is their surety for our compliance. I must ask you—I *beg* you – to act in accordance with their wishes."

I held up my hand; I could not bear the sight of her pain. "I have the substance of her message," I said to Lot; "it is not necessary to subject her to anything further. I will consent to the arrangements you have in mind."

Miriam was led away without a word. I thought I saw her falter on the path.

Lot explained that the Messiahists wished me turned over to them in exchange for Miriam's son. "They are eager for your blood," he said, "but in my opinion, that is not the best solution. My hope, my basis for coming to speak to you so frankly tonight, is that your enemies may be persuaded to reconcile themselves to some lesser evil regarding you. Given their constraints and ours, I believe they will settle for your exile. Or escape, as I shall present it to them."

"Exile? Where? There is no *where* for me to turn. Asher is –"

"We are speaking of exile in the Kuhlan lands," he said.

My heart almost stopped in my chest. Exile to the Kuhlan lands was tantamount to a death sentence—and death in the most terrifying guise imaginable. I looked for Miriam, for some confirmation of what I was being asked to do, but the carriage was closed and moving away. She was gone.

"I know I speak of extreme measures, but such are all that are left to us." Lot explained in his reasonable-sounding way that Dan, in the days before Jezreel was captured, had conducted a lively trade with the Kuhlans.

"Trade with the Kuhlans? That is forbidden." I spoke almost automatically. Then I thought of Justin sneering at my initial shock—*it seemed years ago* – at discovering the Harlech engaged in unlawful commerce with Israel's enemies.

"It is all conducted through intermediaries—quite legal. Or at least, quite lucrative. Your father and brother have since taken the trade under their control."

"My father and brother?"

"Yes, Hanford and your father – the Northern Lights Enterprises," he replied patiently, as if I might have forgotten their names. "Surely you know that the greater part of Israel's recovered metal comes down the Jordan from Old Spokane. The Northern Lights have a concession there—it is the single most profitable aspect of their business—"

"Enough! So you contemplate sending me to the metal recovery mines in the Kuhlan lands."

"No. Not there. To Moses Town. A village and trading post, just east of Jezreel. A two-day journey on foot, a day by horseback."

"An eternity if the Kuhlans discover me."

"There is that danger, to be sure. Moses Town is an enclave, a settlement which the

Kuhlans allow in their lands, but the inhabitants are not Kuhlans."

"How long must I stay?"

"That depends. Six months or a year. Until things settle down here. Or the larger situation changes. Perhaps you can contact Zachariah ben Harlech and his forces stranded out there. He could, I suspect, prove a valuable connection in your larger enterprise."

I heard the echo of Miriam's phrase describing my vague prospects and was not surprised. It was, in fact, confirming evidence. Strangely, I felt peace rather than agitation. Knowledge so painfully won must surely be valuable.

I had the night to prepare. I spent the time in conversation with Gill and Burgos and the members of my bodyguard, trying to console them and to steel myself for what lay ahead. Burgos would command the bodyguard in my absence and protect those who took refuge at the College. Gill would establish our own intelligence-gathering network while his wounds healed. He was free to return to Hebron whenever he chose.

Nisan Lot had been frank. "You do not want to put yourself in the power of the Apostle Boz any more than in the hands of the Messiahists. But you have friends in the eastern clans, the Sevfolk and their kin. They are at least somewhat well disposed toward you, and deeply estranged from Boz."

Lot had arranged that Sevfolk clansmen would escort me through Dan to the Jordan. The journey would be conducted in secret and as rapidly as possible. We were not to stop. Meanwhile, his own men would pretend to search for me, even to pursue me—to provide a story to tell the Messiahists. *And Boz as well, I suspected.* It was all just barely plausible. I recognized that the Mayor of Hazor was playing a dangerous game. I was grateful I had him to deal with and not Boz or General Malachi.

"Can you trust the Sevfolk?" Gill asked. "What stake do they have in all this?"

"I don't know," I said. "Does it seem as if I have a choice?"

"We could fight," Burgos said stoutly. I shook my head.

"At least the Sevfolk know you," Gill said, "and know that you have defied Boz. For the time being, and for these purposes, that is probably enough. They are Old Believers and will resist a Messiahist alliance with all the power they can muster."

Lot had said as much in explanation: "I quite respect the power of the Sevfolk to do mischief, so I have hopes of regaining their good will by including them in our arrangements."

"What I do, Captain, I do for Dan," Lot had asserted. "Right now, you need to be taken off the board of this game in Dan, or we will have Messiahist cavalry at the gates of Hazor in a fortnight. But I do not desire your death. In fact, in six months or a year, you may become a useful ally."

He had patted me lightly on the shoulder before departing.

I could have predicted the first question the Sheriff of the Sevfolk would ask me: "If you rule Naphtali, will you return Jezreel to Dan? And if so, on what terms?"

Jerub himself had come to escort me, and he brought his kinsmen. He had fifty men on good horses, and they were highly wrought by the recent excitements. It was apparent that they had no use for the Messiahists. They would have preferred to drag Caleb Boz's body to the Jordan rather than escort me, but they had agreed to the task at hand.

I recalled that Jerub had asked me months before, when I first revealed my identity in his tent, if I could treat with him concerning Jezreel. I had deferred the question at the time. I had learned a good deal since that moment, and I considered his question very carefully before I answered. "I cannot give what is not mine," I said. The Sevfolk tensed and bristled, so I hurried on: "Jezreel has belonged to Dan all along. I pledge to you that I will help Dan repossess what is Dan's. I have no terms to offer, just this promise."

It took them a moment to digest what I had said. When they understood, they voiced their approval enthusiastically and pounded me on the back. Jerub went so far as to embrace me. He had the odor of a sheep but the strength of a bear. In their care, I felt reasonably assured I would live to see the Kuhlan border.

We rode hard all night and part of the next day to the Jordan River. Lander and a dozen soldiers were waiting by the shore. Waiting grimly, I thought. There was a boat to take me to the other side.

Book Three:
Stranger in a Strange Land

Chapter 10: A Kuhlan Moon

I

I awoke to find my insides growling and cramping and my mind a fog. As I struggled into a sitting position, my stomach suddenly emptied itself, and I spewed on the ground like a sick brat. I fumbled with my gear, searching for my water bottle. *I could not recall where I was.* I took a long swig, hoping to clear my stomach of whatever assailed it. I vomited again, a sour, wretched-smelling liquid that burned my throat and nose. I rinsed my mouth and spat, leaning on one arm and shaking. Any movement left me dizzy and nauseated.

After a time my mind cleared a bit, and I realized that I was alone. *I must have been poisoned!* The fire had burned down to the embers. Nevertheless, even in the darkness, I could tell that there were no figures stretched out around the fire where they should be. Something stirred beyond the feeble circle of light. I listened intently: it was a horse cropping grass. *My horse.* I remembered crossing the Jordan and eating by the fire with Lander and my cavalry escort to Moses Town, but I could recall nothing further. As usual, my memory was a sieve through which I lost all important information.

I crawled to the fire and blew on it, adding wood until it blazed up. I looked about – and a glance confirmed my fears: I had been abandoned on the Kuhlan side of the Jordan. Lander and the rest of them were gone. I had not been poisoned by them but drugged. Probably by the poppy that healers use for pain. It had, I recalled, an emetic effect in large doses. I lay for a long time with my stomach cramped and my senses reeling. Confusion failed, however, to take the edge off the rage I felt. My supposed exile to the Kuhlan lands was a hoax, a deadfall. The Danites had had no intention of seeing me safely to Moses Town. *Lander had brought me here to die.*

Gradually, fragments of the evening began to come back to me. We had crossed the Jordan and camped at the mouth of a dry canyon leading into the plateau. As we shared a meal, Nathan Lander had described solemnly how my Master Ebenezer had promised that a sword would arise in the north among the Old Believers and chastise Israel. That sword, Lander had avowed – had assured me over and over – was myself. He had told me that to lull me to sleep, no doubt while another was preparing the potion. Justin had been right: examine what speeches signify; do not be seduced by the words.

At the thought of my sword I felt a sudden panic; I searched frantically at my belt and in my bedroll and gear. I put more wood on the fire and scoured the campsite. It was gone! My Hazorite sword! Apparently, the ways in which I could be seduced were without number.

I found my way to the bank of the Jordan, where we had landed. A few lights shone on the far shore. I racked my mind for a way to respond to my situation, to deal rationally with my plight. In crises, St. Supplicee teaches us to retreat to the core of energy within us and rebound from there. But where I sought the teachings there was only silence. I searched my heart, but found emptiness. Where was the core of my being? Where was my energy? I was possessed by a frantic restlessness, but I could not channel it. The energies in me opposed and contradicted and cancelled each other without opening a way for me. Finally, I left off searching and gazed into the dark, watching the lights across the Jordan gradually disappear.

Burgos had said that some manage to find justice even in Naphtali; I would find it in the Kuhlan lands! With that thought my heart slipped again from the wall of the Vantage and plunged into the Jordan. I plumbed its cold and suffocating depths; my heart was a cave of ice, and I wandered there for many hours.

Dawn broke almost imperceptibly behind me. Gradually the hills of Israel turned from gray to rose to gold, until the sky was awash with light. Dark lines of waterfowl moved across the horizon, their cries faint in the dawn. In the light of day it was clear that I would have to find my own way or die here on the Jordan's bank.

I thought of my grandfather and of Tirzah and my mother and the day she disappeared. With these things came a flood of other, unsummoned memories surging into my head. I thought of Justin and Michal-Rebekah and the revenge I had taken for them. I thought of Miriam Lander and the ways we had violated the Law—and of the innocent blood I had caused to be shed in Hazor. Pain and nausea gripped me again till I thought I would faint.

But in the midst of these thoughts, I could not help imagining the scene at the camp after the drugs had worked on me. Had Nathan Lander stood over me in triumph with my sword in his hand? Had he lingered, panting, aching to bring the blade slashing down upon me? Had he hesitated only because he understood that I would suffer more when I awoke to find both my sword and my calling stripped from me?

If Nathan Lander had calculated his revenge with the skill and insight of a sadist, doubling or even tripling the pain he inflicted beyond the pain he had received, I could not fault him. I deserved it all. I, who had been reared to be a champion of the Law, had earned a pariah's portion. I shivered, feeling the justice of my situation. I was outcast from Israel, abandoned in the Kuhlan lands. And if I were suddenly to see a bridge magically spanning the Jordan and leading back to Israel, I would not set foot upon it.

But the emotion that swept over me finally, after hours of meditation, was not self-condemnation, but rage. It rose in me like a well in winter, fed by who knows what subterranean sources. I marveled at the fury that coursed through my veins, recognizing it for what it was, but feeling surprised nonetheless.

Israel Zhen-Gwo wrote: *The leaf moves with the current.* Did he mean abandon your will? Surrender to the forces that move you? I had been moved around like a pawn on a board by the wills of others. *I was through with that.* I vowed that I would never again surrender to the will of another. Henceforth, whether my enemies were evil or foolish or demented, I would defy them all. Even if I was an empty cipher, a man without a center or a core, I would draw my energies from the forces opposing me. I would fill myself with their hostility, move by their malice.

I brushed myself off, gathered my gear together, and saddled the horse. For the moment, it was motive enough merely to defy Lander and Boz. In the long term. . . *I would have to wait and see about the long term.*

As I took a last look around the campsite, I felt an itch under my belt. Urgent and persistent, it forced itself upon my awareness. I saw the cause as soon as I unhitched my belt: a tick, swollen near to bursting protruded from my skin like a black seed. Alarmed, I thought immediately of Nathan Lander. But no, there was no way to tell. There was a breeze off the Jordan and cottonwoods nearby; no autumn frost had yet settled here along the river's edge. Fitting, perhaps, that Lander should assassinate me in this clever way. If he had. But there was no need for human agency in this event. Ticks happen. Bad luck, a moment's carelessness is all that is needed.

I drew my knife. Men, I knew, had been moved to desperation upon discovering the tiny bloodsuckers feasting on their hides. Some took their own lives in fear of the brain fever—and some out of nervous dread, being unable to await the event. But I was, I assured myself, made of sterner stuff.

I coaxed the embers of the fire back to life and placed the blade in the midst of them. No point in excising the tick only to plant an infection in my belly. When the knife was ready I cut the tick out, carefully, taking no more flesh than was necessary. The greatest danger, it was said, was causing them to spew their engorged blood back into your body. Better to lose a bit of one's hide than disturb the tick. But perhaps that was only an old wives' tale. No one knew what the ticks carried that made their bites fatal. Many were bitten, and almost all developed the fever. Of those who did, nearly all died.

I had had it once and lived. That piece of luck—and my own folly – had brought me to this moment.

II

As I moved across the wind-swept plateau, my thoughts swirled like blackbirds trailing a plow. But I was alert, too, and, amid my regrets and self-loathing, I was afraid. This was Kuhlan land, and no Israelite could set foot on it without dread. The Plain of Moses seemed featureless and empty. I searched for signs, for small anomalies in the vast sameness, some detail out of place that could mean the difference between life and death. Death at the hands of the Kuhlans would, I knew well, not be a swift plunge into oblivion. It would mean a universe of pain, prolonged expertly to the last ember of consciousness. I spurred my horse and pressed doggedly ahead.

Here and there among the vast expanse of grass and sage, I encountered deer and elk. Once I surprised a family of wolves resting by a kill. They were smaller than the wolves of the forests and more tawny than gray. I aroused no fear in them whatsoever and very little curiosity; they barely rose and stretched at my approach—though my horse shied and nearly threw me. From all appearances, they might have been shepherd dogs in Israel.

Further inland, the plain was dotted with herds of tall, long-legged cattle—the famous wild cattle of the Kuhlan lands. They were large, formidable-looking creatures, dark along the back and light on the belly, but mottled in various ways. They were of many hues—white and black and roan and buff and sorrel and all mixtures in between. Both sexes are lean and agile and carry long lyre-shaped horns. These beasts are said to be savage by nature, like their masters, and will attack a man on foot without provocation. The groups I saw, however, moved warily out of my way. The bulls sniffed the air and glared at me with red eyes, tossing their horns as they moved away. Of their human herdsmen I saw no sign. Here in the heart of the Kuhlan lands there seemed to be no Kuhlans.

I considered different strategies of approach and concealment, knowing I was in danger of chancing upon the most ferocious race of savages known to Israel – men who were pitiless to outsiders. I had no knowledge of from whence danger might come – or where I could flee if attacked. There was nothing for me to do, I decided, but head northeast to intersect the Ancients' double road and then follow it to Moses Town. Estimating that speed would be my best ally, I determined to proceed boldly. Lander's men had left me my gear – a lance, a dagger, and a good bow. I wore a thick wool surplice, proof against autumn cold, at least, and some protection from rain. I had everything but my Hazorite sword. It was enough; it must suffice. I spurred my reluctant mount onward, ready to contest my path with any who crossed it.

At dusk, I made camp on the prairie, eating dry bread and swallowing down my thoughts. Except for the wind ceaselessly combing the grass, the darkness around me was silent. Without a fire, I was too cold to think much and was grateful for it. I spent the night in a gray doze, conscious only of being alone.

In the morning, I was awakened by the honking of geese overhead. Their formations were headed eastward. I resumed my journey, using their flights as my guide. My limbs were stiff and my belly as empty as a gourd. It took all my will to mount up and turn my horse's head east, and move deeper into the Kuhlan lands.

After many hours, I topped a line of dunes rising out of the sage and came in sight of my destination: the Lake of Moses. The lake stretched before me, glittering in the sunlight. It was one of the largest bodies of water I had ever seen. Reeds grew far out into the lake, and flocks of ducks and geese rose and settled upon it continually; the sky was full of their clamor. The far shore was faded and dull with autumn colors, but, surprisingly, it appeared to be cultivated land. As I skirted the lake, I saw boats on the water and fishermen, but so distant that I had no anxiety about being recognized as a stranger – and no plan of escape if I was.

I guided myself by a column of smoke on the horizon; it rose from what seemed an inhabited place. After a while, I passed through a gate and a tumble-down wall; on the other side the land was a garden, like the finest cultivated land in Israel. I saw the stubble of wheat and barley in fields, and stands of yellow corn and the gleaned remnants of bean and lentil fields, and then beets remaining to be harvested. This was unexpected. In the midst of the Kuhlan lands, I had stumbled onto civilization.

The first people that I saw in the fields fled at my approach. I rode slowly and occasionally circled my horse, indicating peaceful intentions and a desire to talk, but the inhabitants of this place fled upon sighting me, a single figure on horseback.

Moses Town itself was situated on a neck of land jutting into the lake. The town consisted of a cluster of huts with thatched roofs crowded inside a rude palisade. A section of the palisade was thrown down, and some of the huts had been burned. I approached deliberately, settled in my mind to endure whatever there was to endure. A small crowd gathered at the gate. The people were large and light skinned, and they wore clothes made of the rudest woven stuff and skins of animals, They seemed more agitated than dangerous. "Who are you?" they asked in the Kuhlan tongue. "Who are you? Benjamite?" They repeated a term I did not recognize: "men-ish-mah," that sounded like a question.

When I walked my horse boldly through their gate, the inhabitants either fled or shouted at me, brandishing weapons that they seemed afraid to use. "I come in peace, as a suppliant," I said. "I am Israelite, from Asher. I seek Zachariah ben Harlech." I repeated this message as best I could in their own language, which I knew from books. They seemed to recognize the name, though what value they associated with it was unclear. Beneath their fear, I sensed they wished to tear me to pieces, but they could not even meet my gaze. They seemed relieved that I was not a Kuhlan, but they were not made easy or confident. I suppose it was not clear to them *what* I was. I dismounted and stood before a group of them. No one was bold enough to approach me, either to offer harm or to take my horse. I wondered what had left them so entirely subdued.

"Are you Harlech?" the boldest of them finally asked. I recognized the form of the question, as their speech derived from the language of the Governors, which I could read but which was strange to my ear. In my own language, I told them my name and origins, but they had obviously never heard of Asher. They jabbered at me, repeating the word, *men-ish-mah*? with great apprehension, until I said in their tongue, "I do not understand." They appeared greatly relieved that I did not.

They led me, or rather retreated and allowed me to follow them, into their village. The forepart of the village had been torched, and there were burned fields just outside the enclosure. Their houses were crude affairs, made of wood posts with wattle-and-daub walls and thatched roofs. The streets were dusty, rutted paths. There were no large communal buildings and no order in the arrangements of their dwellings.

I could not understand what I was seeing. This was Kuhlan territory, and yet these were not Kuhlans. Nisan Lot had said little about the people of Moses Town. But if these people were not Kuhlans, who were they? Renegades, perhaps? Some of them seemed light skinned, though others were burned as dark as I was. I noticed blue eyes and gray eyes, eyes that were shades of green and brown. The sun tended to bleach their hair out, just as it did the hair of our slaves. There was something slavish in their manner, too. I speculated that they must be descended from Israel's runaways. I could best imagine them as fugitives from a place like Chinnereth who had degenerated even further over the course of many generations. I decided that they were the most wretched group of people I had ever seen. They reminded me of whipped dogs.

I speculated that the Kuhlans might have offered refuge to escaped slaves from Israel, allowing them to remain on their soil to raise food needed to supplement their diet. Perhaps they also used them to act as middlemen with detested outsiders, but without ever truly admitting them into their society. It accorded with the little I knew of Kuhlans that they might prefer to deal with foreigners through intermediaries. Like Israelites, Kuhlans are said to hate contamination.

But what of the destruction I saw all around me? And the fear, visible in every countenance? What possible explanation but the Kuhlans themselves? Even here, then, in their own territory, with people of their own blood, they could not curb their lust to destroy! If the Kuhlans could not refrain from despoiling a people actually useful to them—as well as, from all I could discern, entirely submissive—I wondered what an intruder might expect from them. I recoiled at the ferocity of this detestable race. No wonder Israel shunned all intercourse with them!

As we moved through their primitive settlement, I estimated that at least a third of the town had been destroyed, and that the destruction had been wrought no more than a week earlier. When we arrived in the center of the village, the individual I took to be the chief man of the town offered me water and a little bread to eat. I accepted his meager hospitality, and we sat on log benches and looked at one another. The townspeople crowded cautiously around but withdrew after a few angry words from my host. A half dozen men—apparently men of consequence in the village—squatted in the dust around us. I felt the presence of the rest of the inhabitants in the dark interiors of huts and in the shadows, but most were too timid to show themselves.

I tried out my limited knowledge of their language with simple words such as bread, water, and so on. Their pronunciation was different than I expected, different from Israel's schools, but we understood each other. I found I could make out a few of their sentences. It was truly the old language of the Governors, but worn smooth like stones in a brook. We sat in the warm sunlight, trying to communicate in these awkward ways. What I took to be the headman introduced himself as Meechum, or something near that. They appeared cautiously friendly. But I felt a strong sense of expectancy or dread in the village. The people of Moses Town were waiting for something.

They had not long to wait. A sentry's horn sounded and a gasp of alarm went up from the entire village. Amid cries of distress, the plaza emptied magically and the village scurried instantly into hiding. My host, Meechum, had risen and was looking apprehensively at the way we had come. A couple of armed men ran through the plaza shouting, but I could not catch their words. Meechum stood where he was, his limbs trembling. Suddenly remembering me, he waved, saying—to my astonishment—"Hide yourself" in fair Israelite. *So, he speaks my language!* I thought to myself. One of the chief men led me to a nearby hut.

In a moment we could hear the sound of galloping horses—less than a troop in size, I estimated. They entered the plaza, stirring up a cloud of dust. I pressed against the wall of the hut, peering through a crack to see what would happen. I heard Meechum betray me immediately, saying, in broken phrases in my own tongue, "I have a stranger here, Isra-el, Isra-el!" The intruders crowded their horses into the forecourt I had a glimpse of them through the window slit. There were about a dozen of them – fierce-looking savages. I saw some of them dismount in the dusty plaza and look toward the hut in which I hid.

"Come out!" I heard Meechum cry in a loud voice.

I saw with perfect clarity that I had arrived at the moment of my death. I glanced around the hut, searching rapidly in my mind the layout of the village and the surrounding territory. For an instant my mind and heart churned madly, and then my training asserted itself. I regained control over my breathing, slowed it to deliberate deep breaths. I felt I could, if I wished, achieve the slow rate of the meditative state. Heartened, I looked at my hands, held them steady in the dim light. They would not betray me. There was no way out.

"Come out!" I heard Meechum cry again.

It sometimes comes down to this, Master Ebenezer had warned us. To the manner of one's dying. I determined to end it as best I could, in a way befitting my ancestors. I owed my teachers an honorable death as well. *At least I was armed, which gave me a few choices.* I seized a rope off a peg and looped it around my waist, then tied the other end to my knife. I strung my bow and notched an arrow and held bow and shaft in my left hand. I paused a moment in the shadow of the hut, breathing deeply as dust motes danced in a shaft of light. *So this is how it ends. This is all there will be!*

I burst out of the door and flung the knife into the ground, visibly tethering myself before them. "I see," I shouted, "that your mothers coupled with beasts and suckled wild pigs and wolves! I challenge you Kuhlan monstrous-births one at a time, and I will kill you all!" I continued shouting such insults as came to mind; army life abounds with such filth, and while it was not my ordinary mode of speech, I was surprised how readily the phrases came to mind. I was simultaneously trying to take the measure of the men in front of me, gauge from which direction the first attack would come, and regretting that my life had to end on a note of foolish bravado. I had not expected a long life, but I had hoped for something more purposeful than this. I hated futile gestures. Justin would be chagrined for me, as he doubtlessly had been at his own death. But as Master Ebenezer warned us, one seldom gets to choose. These thoughts passed through my mind with great speed. Meanwhile, I picked what looked to me the most dangerous of my adversaries, raising the bow and grasping the notched end of the shaft with my right hand.

"Hold!" my target said, in perfect Israelite, raising his hand. Surprise froze my fingers just as I was about to release the bowstring. "Hold!" he said again, his body tensed to dodge my arrow. "Meechum," he said, "you told us this was our countryman. He curses well, but he is no Benjamite."

Benjamite!

Meechum gestured at me frantically. "Harlech! Harlech!" he cried, pointing at the others. He was very agitated; perhaps he understood some of the words I had shouted. Their import must have been clear enough in any case. Evidently he did not want to see blood shed on his doorstep. I peered at the ragged, skin-clad warriors before me. They were dark-skinned, certainly, though whether by sun or birth I could not tell, and their hair, where it was not covered with savage headgear, looked as dark as my own.

"You are . . . Benjamites?"

"Indeed, we are!" the man before me said, and, as if to prove his claim, he drew himself up and saluted me in a military gesture that could not have come from the limber, jointless savage he had been a moment before.

"Benjamites?" I repeated.

"Yes, and you are a northerner, are you not? But I can't make out what. What in the name of St. Supplicee are you doing here?"

He pushed his headgear, which was fashioned from a dried wolf scalp and muzzle, back from his forehead and slipped off his horse. Standing before me, I saw him as he was – behind the unkempt beard and weathered face. He had been months without a barber and was ragged as a savage in a nightmare. But he was Israelite, without a doubt. He saluted again, smartly, and said: "Captain Jonathan Amasa of the Esdralon Guards Cavalry. Who in the world are you?"

His introduction put us on an entirely different plane. I was uncertain what to do. Suddenly embarrassed to be tied in a tether of death, I loosed the knot and stepped out of it. I stooped to pick up my knife and sheathed it slowly, to buy time to compose myself.

"You looked like Kuhlans," I said, searching for words. "I thought you *were* Kuhlans. I thought. . . ." I searched the faces of his companions crowding around me. They might all be Benjamites, for all I could tell. Or all Kuhlans. I gestured at the rope apologetically. "Benjamites. . . ," I said, feeling suddenly dizzy. "I cannot fight Benjamites. I took a vow—I made a vow at Meribah, never to lift a hand against Benjamin." Suddenly I sat down in the dust beside the rope.

The officer approached and helped me to my feet. "Lucky for you we aren't Kuhlans! Who are you," he demanded, "and what are you doing here? Are you mad? Who told you you could come here?"

His companions gathered around me, and many voices bombarded me with questions. The man was as stern as his office demanded, but he seemed curious too, and not altogether unfriendly.

"Zachariah ben Harlech," I repeated doggedly. "I must speak with Zachariah ben Harlech."

Meechum pushed his way through the crowd to stand by us. "Countrymen," he repeated over and over, pointing at the Benjamites and then at me.

III

"So, this is the famous son of Tephlin Glanz," the Colonel said, introducing me to his officers. "The son who is a landed warrior and, I'm told, a man of some reputation in the army." Colonel Zachariah ben Harlech was about Justin's age, but taller and more muscular. His skin was dark and his hair straight, but the color of his hair was light brown with lighter streaks bleached by the sun. His beard was fuller than is usual for an Israelite, and it glinted like copper. His eyes were some shade between green and brown. I saw at a glance that the rumors about him must be true. *He was half-Kuhlan. His mother must have belonged to that dreaded race.*

I hid my loathing and saluted him. He returned my salute and greeted me affably. Recognizing my name, he had instantly made the connection between his father and myself. I was astonished that he knew of the incident at Solomon's ford on the Yakima, which I had told only to Michal-Rebekah and Appian. But he did know of it, and I saw that he was also aware of reputations among his enemies. To my further amazement, he generously acknowledged my action toward his father as a blood debt between us. He stepped forward and embraced me formally as a guest-friend.

While I was moved by his gracious behavior, I realized that his knowledge of the event in which I had saved his father could only mean that Michal-Rebekah had communicated the story to her people—and that word had gotten to Zachariah ben Harlech even in the Kuhlan lands. And that could only mean that she had in fact been connected closely with the Harlech intelligence network. *It could only mean that.* This information stirred up my mind, and I wanted to remove myself and re-consider every conversation I ever had with her and every detail of our relationship. I recalled Justin's jest that everyone was a member of the Eyes of Israel. Given Miriam Lander's role in Dan's intelligence and now Michal-Rebekah's in Benjamin's, it seemed not an exaggeration, but rather another of his remarkable insights.

Meanwhile, Zachariah ben Harlech pressed me in a friendly way for details of the incident in which I had fished his father from the Yakima. I hesitated, having just been stung by the revelation about Michal-Rebekkah. Nor did I need a reminder of my recent lesson from Miriam Lander, though it was not clear to me what that lesson was. Nevertheless, I gave a brief account of our encounter at the ford of the Yakima, which seemed to satisfy him. Emboldened by his easy good nature, I cautioned him that I remained a loyal Israelite; that circumstances too strange to relate easily had driven me into his camp. But I was, I insisted, no renegade.

"Be at ease about that," the Colonel replied. "Civil war often separates us from our usual allegiances. One remains a patriot, I believe, only at the cost of great effort and imagination. I confess that I have little of either to spare on the matter. You are welcome here," he said. "I have a debt to pay you on my father's behalf, and I pay it willingly. Hear me, Benjamites," he declared in a loud voice, "this man, Josiah Glanz ben Haggadah, is my guest-friend."

Under the protection of Colonel Harlech himself, my acceptance into the Benjamite community in the Kuhlan lands proceeded smoothly. Captain Jonathan Amasa took me under his care, and I was attached to his company of Esdralon Guards. I could almost believe that his friendly interest in me was genuine, but I reminded myself that this was more intelligence work, surely. Amasa had simply been assigned the task. But what had I to hide? For that matter, what had I left to lose?

Captain Amasa was curious why I had found my way to the Kuhlan lands as an exile, but I had little to say to him about my reasons. He asked me why I had wanted to see Colonel Harlech, but I replied only that I wanted to make peace between Benjamin and the rest of Israel.

"And why would you presume to take such a task upon yourself, a mere captain of the army?" he demanded.

"I took a vow."

Amasa frowned at my words. I suppose he thought I was a little mad. "It's best you keep out of sight and blend with the rest of us," he warned, offering me a buckskin vest and leggings and a fur cap. "Israelites are on uncertain terms with the People right now." He explained that a council was about to take place at Moses Lake, and that the Benjamites were much concerned about its outcome. The fate of all of foreigners in this strange land would be decided over the next few days.

"I thought the Harlech had arrived at an understanding with the Kuhlans long ago," I said, puzzled.

"So did we," he replied.

North of Moses Town lay a plain leveled by the Ancients and paved in an undecipherable pattern. The faint traces of a giant cross or X remained visible in the ground, with additional surfaces connecting to it, like massive roads that started abruptly and went nowhere. There were similar sites of various sizes in Israel; I had seen several myself. While their purpose is unknown, they are presumed to have had a sacred function. Many of the naïve believe that the Ancients used these fields to communicate with heaven; hence, they are called sky roads.

We topped a low rise and got a glimpse of the Kuhlan encampment. Hundreds of white conical tents stretched for miles along the sky road. The prairie around was black with their horse herds. My heart recoiled to see the enemy host arrayed on the plain, but then my blood rose and pounded in my head. While the Kuhlan menace had loomed very large in my imagination since childhood, this was my first actual glimpse of our hereditary enemy. Even at this distance, I recoiled in fear and revulsion. It seemed incredible that I stood on their land and within sight of them.

"How much of the Kuhlan war power is arrayed here?" I asked Captain Amasa, trying to appear calm.

"Most of it," he replied. "I doubt that the People have five thousand warriors altogether, so this is quite a large gathering. All of the four bands will be represented here: Sage Grouse, Camas, Antelope, and Black Willow bands. You're in luck," Captain Amasa added. "You'll get to see the Grandmothers."

"Why should I care about the old women of these savages?" I retorted, savoring the valuable information he had just given me about Kuhlan strength. I was marveling at the smallness of their numbers. At the same time, I asked myself, *how could so few terrorize a quarter of a million of my people?* Out of the corner of my eye, I saw that Amasa was looking at me sternly.

His disdain for my answer gave me pause. Luckily, I recalled the journal of old Jonas ben Harlech that Michal-Rebekah had given me. In his moment of desperation, Jonas had asked to "speak to the women." And he had also used the phrase, "We are one people" – both statements that seemed to me absurd and incomprehensible. Nothing was clearer to me in life than that we were not one people. Still, I could infer from his account that decisions among the Kuhlans lay in the hands of the women.

"You mean to say by Grandmothers," I remarked, hoping to regain the esteem I had lost, "that these women are the government of the Kuhlans?"

"Something like that," Amasa grumbled in reply, "though I'm told that the People have outgrown the need for government. However, this is a gathering of all the bands, which they hold occasionally in order to consult with one another, so the Grandmothers are sure to be present. They'll settle outstanding disputes first and then get down to deciding our fate." He explained that the women do not often mingle with the men; it was always a special occasion when they did. "Thus," Amasa said, "I'll think you'll find the women of the People of some interest, even the old ones."

We camped apart from the Kuhlans on a low rise near the lake. Our group was joined by other troops of the Esdralon cavalry, so there were about a company of us. Colonel Harlech set up camp according to Israelite custom, tents in lines, with a perimeter and sentinels. We seemed to be on a war footing. Benjamites, I gathered, were tolerated in the Kuhlan lands, probably for Zachariah's sake, but they were not welcome here.

I spent hours gazing at our blood enemies through my glass, counting their numbers and marveling that this people could excite such dread in us. Captain Amasa and Colonel Harlech were both absent the next day, so I had no one to instruct me as to the meaning of what I saw. That evening we listened to the drums and singing of the savages in their nearby camp. It was like listening to the fiends of Hell that the Messiahists describe with such relish. The excitement of the savages communicated itself to our camp; the men fidgeted and went about their tasks in a daze, hypnotized by the throb of the drums. In the yellow glare of our fires, my new comrades of the Esdralon Guards and I shared a meal of fresh bloody beef, half-cooked in the savage manner. I had eaten such strange fare since leaving the Refuge that I made no protest. Flesh or fowl, raw or cooked, what was the difference? Nonetheless, to watch blood dripping from the beards of Israelite officers who were dressed in colorful mixtures of rags and savage attire was an experience to remember. In turn, I excited considerable curiosity among my hosts. It was not lost on them that I was the son of Tephlin Glanz and the brother of Justin Glanz Apollo. Tephlin Glanz they hated, of course, but Justin's conduct at the siege of Esdralon had won a grudging respect. They were pleased that their enemies, Judah and Manasseh, had fallen out. But they were more interested in their own fates, which seemed to be unfolding at the great encampment below us.

The next day, in response to my questions, Captain Amasa explained that Colonel Harlech was involved in a blood feud with one of the clans of the Sage Grouse People, and that part of the purpose of the present gathering was to settle that conflict. This cleansing of the blood, as they called it, occurred periodically. "The People tolerate quarrels among themselves only so long," he said. "Then the women get involved. Tomorrow will be a day of reckoning." Amasa made no attempt to disguise his concern.

"So, it's not a good idea to have the women get involved?" I asked.

He raised his eyebrows. "Like surprising a grizzly sow with new cubs," he said. "One does well to avoid it if possible, believe me!"

"How was it that the Colonel got entangled in a blood feud?" I asked. "He seems as even-tempered as any man I know. A blood feud does not accord with what I sense about his nature."

"The feud started about ten years ago," he explained. "It was a quarrel between his father and a prominent figure of the northern-most band, the Sage Grouse People – who, by the way, are the group least disposed to tolerate us on their territory for any purpose whatever. The quarrel turned violent; our people defended themselves, and one of the Sage Grouse warriors was killed—by Colonel Harlech, in fact, although he was only a youth at the time. That's what the present quarrel is about. The Sage Grouse People won't give it up."

"So, the real meaning of this conflict," I ventured, "is that this opponent represents the extreme anti-Harlech faction of the Kuhlans. And the fact that this matter has been allowed to surface again means that the Kuhlans are reconsidering their relationship with the Harlech. Am I right?"

"Something like that," Amasa acknowledged.

I thought Captain Amasa's attitude toward me softened a little after this exchange. I had seen his disapproval of my obtuseness when I failed to recognize the importance of the Grandmothers. I was anxious that he form a good opinion of me.

"Another thing," he said. "We don't use the word Kuhlan here. They find the term offensive. They call themselves the People, and you will call them that too."

The drums ceased in late afternoon. The silence that followed was more tension-filled than the previous din and commotion. It was as if lightning had flashed, and we were waiting for the thunder. After a time, a great cry went up, a deep bass roar of elation and energy, giving voice to emotions I could not name. None of us was immune to it; even I was stirred, who had no understanding of what it signified.

"The women show themselves," Captain Amasa explained.

A great crowd surged out of the camp onto the sky road below us; the drums began again, but this time they beat a more urgent cadence. The crowd resolved itself into several parts, moving rhythmically, and we could catch the strains of a chant.

"This is the round dance," Amasa said. "This is what they have been waiting for."

"The men dance in the middle," I noted, watching through a glass and wondering what I was seeing. The male figures, gaudily dressed, occupied the center of a moving circle. The men moved eccentrically, almost violently, all bright colors and rapid motion, as if to show off their physiques and stamina to the women. Dressed in white, the women moved serenely to the same drum-beat, moving also in unison, in a kind of sideways shuffle that moved them gradually around the rim of the circle.

"This is a religious ceremony," Amasa explained. "The round dance affirms the whole community and symbolizes its unity."

"I don't understand," I said.

"Neither do I," he admitted.

IV

Colonel Harlech returned from the council in the great camp looking very grim. He spoke briefly with his officers, Captain Amasa and Captain Hosea and a dark, somber-faced man named Moriah, who was second-in-command of the Esdralon Guards. Shortly thereafter, the group approached me where I sat by the fire. Colonel Harlech was direct: "Look," he said, "there is no avoiding it. There is a harvest ceremony for me this evening, and then we fight tomorrow. That will be the end of it."

He spoke these things to me as if I had a frame of reference for understanding him.

"This is not good, of course," he continued. "Particularly if I lose. But I have an idea. You and I are about the same size and would look alike from a distance. Listen, Josiah, I want you to stand in my place at the ceremony tonight."

Suddenly apprehensive, I wondered what he was asking of me.

"The ceremony is called harvesting the seed of heroes," he explained. "It's a custom intended to make me immortal through progeny, should I unfortunately fall in battle tomorrow."

"I see. A sacred rite." I recoiled at anything having to do with Kuhlan rites.

"All ceremonies of the People are sacred, Captain. Not much consolation for me in this, however." He looked at me intently. "Honored though I am by these attentions, I'd rather win tomorrow and live. Which is what I intend to do."

"What do you want me to do?"

"We'll dress you in my clothes, and we'll escort you to the lodge prepared for the ceremony. You will go inside and wait. When the quarter moon rises and the dancing is over, they will send the most beautiful young women among the People to you, for your pleasure."

"You must be joking!"

"I've never been more serious in my life. The People," he explained, "do not approve of these quarrels among factions. They heartily disapprove of them, and they don't like factions either. One engages in such a conflict, therefore, only at great peril. But if there is no remedy, if the sides cannot reconcile, then the women hold this ceremony. If a member of the Circle is to be lost, the idea is to save what they can for the future. For the People's sake. That's what the ceremony means. They expect me to die tomorrow, of my own foolish and stubborn will, of course, so they will send the young women to harvest my seed beforehand."

I began to feel very uneasy. "How many young women?"

"As many as you want. As many as you—" he looked at me and laughed. "Don't worry, they come one at a time, and when you're tired—you've been with women before, haven't you? – you just say so. Look, you clasp your hands together like this, and you say [he used the Kuhlan phrase] "My thanks to the Mothers," and open your hands. Until that time, you say to each one, "My thanks to the Mothers" and "Please yourself." That's all you have to say. In fact, it's best that you say nothing else. They may whisper to you all they want, but it would be best if you keep silent. You know neither the language nor the customs, but if you just keep quiet you won't betray your identity. That, by the way, would be unfortunate for both of us."

"You have to undergo this – honor? There is no way to decline?"

He shook his head. "Only if you stand in for me."

"But to subvert the ceremony would—"

"True. It's a sacrilege—if discovered. This ceremony touches the heart of the People's way of life and their sense of what is sacred. It is a sacred moment for me, too. Or would be. But understand that they are doing me no favor. As in all things, the People honor the Circle. The Circle is paramount. The individual fate is unimportant except as it serves the community, knits up the Circle." I must have appeared baffled at this explanation because he added emphatically: "I am being written off, Captain. Sacrificed. That's what it means."

"I see," I said slowly. *I did not see.*

He was impatient but answered mildly: "Need I explain that I cannot perform this harvest ceremony tonight and fight with my full strength tomorrow? The women," he continued, "have ways of influencing the outcome of events. This is one of them." He laughed ruefully: "You may even be able to estimate the extent to which I have aroused the ire of the Grandmothers by the zeal with which these young women attempt to use me up."

These customs seemed bizarre to me and wholly barbaric, as I expected Kuhlan customs to be, but the Colonel appeared very much in earnest. "It could save my life," he said, putting his hand on my shoulder.

"I'll do what I can," I said.

"Good!" he exclaimed. "I knew you would play the part of a soldier." He clapped me on the back, obviously relieved. "I trust you will be able to give a good account of yourself—and provide a good account of your labors in the morning!" He laughed in parting.

The subterfuge was easy to accomplish. By the time for the ceremony, darkness had fallen; the Harlech torchbearers had orders to stay at a discrete distance from me. A great crowd gathered around the purification lodge, and many entered to wish the Colonel well. I merely sat to one side unnoticed. When the well-wishers left, we switched clothing. My face was blackened and I was wrapped in a robe. When I emerged from the lodge, I kept my head down and did as I had been instructed. I wore a headdress of bull's horns, and hardly needed to conceal my face at all. I was escorted to the lodge by an honor guard of Benjamites. Inside the lodge, I stripped, washed the pigment from my face, and waited, shivering. The night was already cold and moving towards frost. Anticipation and dread raised gooseflesh on my arms. The night was perfectly clear, so that even the quarter moon cast a pale, unearthly light outside the tent. I listened to the sounds of drums and alien voices raised in song.

No one will believe what transpired that night, so I will omit telling it—except to say that I had ample reason to be grateful to Miriam Lander for teaching me about women and to anticipate the things that please them. And I may add that, from the behavior of my Kuhlan partners, I estimated that Zachariah ben Harlech had incurred the greatest displeasure of the Grandmothers. But how odd it seemed that my first contact with this loathsome people was of an intimate and carnal nature. In the darkness, the women were clean, sweet-smelling, and seductive. They adorned themselves with a musk unfamiliar to me but no doubt attractive to Kuhlans. Their personal odor reminded me of the smell of new lambs, with a faint admixture of some wilder, ranker scent.

Towards dawn, Amasa came and scratched at the tent flap, saying quietly that Zechariah must be arrayed for battle soon. My last companion parted from me with a show of reluctance but with great dignity. There was nothing of wantonness about her, or about any of them. This was a sacred thing, clearly, and the experience left me feeling very strange. Colonel Harlech would be rested for the combat to come, and I rejoiced in that. But what if, I could not help wondering, I had started a new life in one of the women? *My blood in a Kuhlan child?* It was unthinkable.

V

Colonel Harlech was part of the group that came to prepare the contestant for battle in the twilight; we easily exchanged places out of site of our hosts. He embraced me and expressed his gratitude before turning to the grimmer task before him. I felt that by my willingness to assist him, I had entered into a special relationship with him and joined with his closest associates, who also knew about the ruse. No doubt Colonel Harlech was a brave man, but he clearly did not relish this thing before him.

The day dawned cloudless and bright; the lake shone like a sheet of mica. The clamor of great formations of geese sounded overhead, and their flights filled the sky from horizon to horizon. I had heard them in the night, and their calls had evoked in me strange thoughts of distances and times beyond imagining.

Captain Amasa took me aside. "Are you—did everything go well?"

"As planned," I said. I did not want to discuss it. Miriam Lander was very vivid in my mind this morning.

"Let's get something to eat, then," he said. "The ceremonies will go on for some time." We breakfasted on more beef, this time thoroughly smoked and more to my liking. Amasa explained what would transpire this morning. "Colonel Harlech will offer the offended kinsmen presents and ask the warrior lodges to intercede. He's a cautious man, and he'll use many arguments that are *almost* apologies: he was young, he'll say; the quarrel is ten years old; he has tried to make amends in the past; he was only defending his father. All true, by the way. At the end, he will have made the other party look bad in the eyes of the Grandmothers. That's the battle. He will have won it."

"That's all? They argue their case before the old women—the Grandmothers?"

"Oh, no. There is still the matter of the combat. He still has to kill the man!"

"Oh."

"Yes, but then he *can*, you see. And without repercussions. That's the point. Before they fight, the women will make both sides pledge that the feud ends here, with the death of one or both of the antagonists in a fair fight. They will have a special ceremony to that effect. The women hate these affairs of honor, you see. They tolerate them, but to the women it is all male foolishness. To be involved in a feud lowers one in their esteem—sometimes fatally. The Colonel will make it abundantly clear that he is all for reconciliation. At that point, he'll say, as if it just occurred to him, that perhaps the Sage Grouse People do not see the present threat of the Kr or understand the value of the Harlech as allies against these enemies of the People."

"I see. So he saves his strongest argument for last."

"The Colonel is careful about everything he does before the People, because it affects all of us. They are very strict, the Grandmothers. The trade, the relationship with Benjamin, all of it, rests on very thin ice. He has to get through this ordeal in a way that restores him in the good graces of the Mothers, or we are all dead men."

"So, you are saying that. . . "I paused, choosing my words carefully, "that in spite of other considerations, Colonel Harlech is Benjamite at heart?"

Captain Amasa gave me an undecipherable look. "It's hard to say what he is at heart. Whatever he is," Amasa added, "I'd trust him with my life."

I pondered all I that I had seen and heard as we breakfasted. Finally, I remarked to Amasa: "I didn't realize the relationship was so precarious. Tell me, why did the Colonel ask me, of all people, to stand in for him last night if the relationship—if the standing of the Harlech with the People – is so fragile?"

Captain Amasa glanced at me and adjusted a spit above the fire before he answered:

"You were the only one," he said quietly, "who didn't know the risks."

The afternoon brought the Kuhlan warriors out in all their finery, strutting in feathers and paint and metal ornaments. I saw a man in a mantle made of the green headskins and feathers of mallard drakes, iridescent in the sunlight. Others wore necklaces and vests of kanz, no doubt plundered from slaughtered Israelites, so that one heard the soft rasp and jingle of coins when they moved. Here and there were mature women in the crowd, in simple dresses of white linen or buckskin. Behind the crowd of warriors stood a circle of younger women, handsome, attractive creatures, who made a point of focusing their attention elsewhere than the ring and did not return the admiring glances of the men. Their collective disapproval was manifest in their postures and averted gazes. I must admit the Kuhlans are a handsome people, uncommonly so. These were very fine physical specimens. Even in their outlandish costumes, they had a kind of grace and dignity.

After a time, an elderly man led a bull into the ring. He was dressed in buckskin without any of the ostentatious decoration of the younger males, and he wore a slash of white paint across his cheeks and nose. The bull was a magnificent animal, white with roan spots, and it carried a huge pair of horns. The old man led it merely by a rope around its neck, walking around the outside of the circle. The bull carried itself serenely, its long horns moving up and down with each stride like scythes bobbing on the shoulders of harvesters. In spite of its size and formidable appearance, it appeared as docile as a calf, and I wondered if it had been drugged. Four men of robust middle age, similarly dressed, approached and made speeches to the bull, which I was not able to hear, and then one of them nicked the artery in the bull's neck and caught the blood in a basin. Then another produced an axe and, with one deft blow, cleaved the bull at the base of the neck where it merges with the shoulders, so that the bull dropped to the earth with scarcely a quiver. There was a great shout from the crowd, and the men rushed forward to dip their hands in its blood, which they rubbed on their faces. Afterwards the bull was butchered and its meat distributed. The offal and leg bones were burned in a fire, and the head and hide placed on a tripod about ten feet high.

A broad circle thirty yards across had been cleared in the sky road just in front of the sacrifice. This, apparently, was the fighting ground, and it had been swept down to the original paved surface of the Ancients. The severed head of the bull faced the place of combat. In a few moments, Zachariah and his opponent stepped out of the crowd from opposite sides of the circle and bowed to each other and to the crowd. Each of the fighters held a lance and a round shield of bull's hide. An axe, the Kuhlan weapon of choice, was slung down the back of each combatant, and both had been marked on the forehead with bull's blood. There was no strutting or posturing or any sign of hostility between them. Both appeared grave and calm, and the audience was equally serious. It was a fine display of decorum. The Kuhlans apparently took their ceremonies seriously, and I had to concede that they had a style of their own.

At a signal, they two began to circle and feint at each other with their lances. Both were skillful fighters. Zachariah was the younger and more agile of the two; his opponent appeared to have the advantage of experience. The crowd followed their movements intently.

"If it comes to the axe, neither is likely to survive," Amasa said in my ear.

Their movements were quick and graceful, almost like a dance. For some moments I lost sight of the fatal nature of the contest, admiring their prowess. Then Zachariah feinted hard at the man and then retreated; the man followed quickly and Zachariah riposted and caught him off balance. Seeming to strike at his face, Zachariah turned his lance downward and slashed his opponent's knee as he dodged backwards. Zachariah then quickly backed out of reach. Blood flowed copiously from the wound.

The advantage was now all on Zachariah's side, but instead of becoming bolder, he grew more cautious, circling and feinting, all the while avoiding a close encounter and an exchange of lance-thrusts. His opponent limped noticeably and moved less and less, trying to conserve his strength. After an interminable series of feints and passes, Zachariah suddenly swooped in with a serious thrust, and the crowed inhaled audibly when he struck home. He had stabbed his opponent in the thigh, inflicting a serious wound; arterial blood pumped from the gash. The man stood immobilized. The crowd was silent. The outcome of the combat had become clear to all.

Zachariah made a show of reluctance to finish the man. He backed away and stood motionless at the edge of the circle, as if waiting for someone to intervene. Loss of blood weakened his opponent minute by minute, so he risked nothing by his show of compassion. I wondered what was in his heart. He seemed to be waiting for a signal, either to end the combat with this drawing of blood or to finish it with the man's death.

The man made a limping rush at Zachariah, but the Colonel evaded him easily. His opponent stood panting and dejected, barely able to hold his wounded leg under him. The whites of his eyes showed through his grimace.

The mob of plumed and painted warriors suddenly shouted and stamped and showed great agitation, although with a mixture of emotions I could not read. Then the crowd parted and revealed an elderly woman, seated on the ground some twenty paces from the circle, near-sightedly focused on her loom. It was an old crone with one blind eye whom I had seen earlier, limping about. I had paid no attention to her. She seemed to be paying no attention to the scene around her either, least of all to the combat of Zachariah and his opponent. In fact, she would not look up from her work to observe this bloody business. Still, Zachariah waited, watching for a sign from her. Finally, he seemed to understand her indifference as instruction to proceed to the grim conclusion of the combat. The crowd understood it too, as did Zachariah's opponent. The old woman's disapproval meant no mercy.

So this is one of the Grandmothers, I thought.

Zachariah did as he was instructed. I expected to hear shrieks and cries from the women, but instead there were only deep-voiced utterances from the men, whether of approbation or dismay I could not tell. The women kept silent and turned away.

VI

"It was necessary, Colonel. You had no alternative. He deserved to die." Major Moriah was a man of so few words that he hardly knew how to cheer his commander.

Colonel Harlech looked more like a man who had suffered a great loss than one who had saved his own life and won glory. "The women give life," he commented bitterly. "And take it away. It is their right. Still, it is an ugly thing. I cannot see how anything will prosper out of this."

I had thought Zachariah's victory would be an occasion for rejoicing—or relief, at least. But it was neither. The Colonel had spent several hours after the combat in purification and in council with the People—probably with the Grandmothers. By the look of things, the talks had not proceeded well. Colonel Harlech had only a few moments to spend with us, and he was direct: "It settles nothing after all," he said, his eyes cast down. "Fortunately for us, the Kr are intruding onto the territory of the Antelope Band, and the People's attention will soon turn to them. I'll stay with the Council and try to convince the Grandmothers of our usefulness in this coming war. Major Moriah and a bodyguard will remain with me; Captain Amasa will take the rest of the legion to the Palouse. You'll encamp there," he said to Amasa, "keeping apart from the People and maintaining the usual precautions through the full moon. I'll join you there when I know more. In the meantime, send word to the fleet to prepare for action."

"What about the Guard?" Moriah asked. "We can be of use. Or do the People regard us so lightly. . .?

"I'll do my best to have us included," he said, "but there is no precedent for it. The People have never sought allies; they have never needed any."

This war may be different, I thought to myself. The Kr are not the people they used to be.

We moved our camp quickly, Captain Amasa being anxious to get us out of harm's way in case any Kuhlans wished to avenge the death of Zachariah's opponent. I sensed that Colonel Harlech might wish in this moment to be identified wholly with his mother's race rather than with Israel—if only for his men's sake. I considered that it must be a cruel fate to be seen as a half-breed. Among the Kuhlans, apparently, Colonel Harlech was sometimes perceived as one of themselves, and sometimes as an outsider, an Israelite. I suspected he often encountered the same ambivalence among ourselves. I recalled with shame my first view of him as a mixed blood, and I felt great sympathy for his need to try to bridge in his own being these two hostile and mutually unintelligible worlds.

We traveled quickly to the southeast, moving through high plains and then into rolling hills and finally into a wild, barren land of basalt crags and canyons of layered rock. When we reached the valley of the Palouse River, there was good grass for our horses and large herds of wild cattle nearby. We had no sooner pitched our camp than an autumn storm settled in, and we had several days of cold rain and wind.

A large party of Kuhlans had followed close behind us and pitched camp a mile upstream of us—to avoid, Amasa explained, the contamination of our presence. Anticipating trouble, Captain Amasa maintained the strictest camp discipline, but in fact the Kuhlans seemed oblivious to us and to thoughts of revenge. They were now entirely preoccupied with the impending war against the Kr. The prospect of bloodshed had, I suppose, put them in high spirits. But in a short time, we were visiting back and forth and trading for small items, or answering challenges to race our horses against theirs. It got about that several officers, including myself, had recent experience fighting the Kr, and we were invited to their camp to share our knowledge and to discuss the thousand details of the soldier's trade. I soon found I could follow most of the conversations, though I did not find it easy to speak their language.

The Kuhlan camp was, according to Amasa, not a war party, but a typical camp with an ordinary mix of ages and sexes. Curiously, there were only a dozen or so females of middle age and no young women among them – nor, as Amasa pointed out to me, were there any Grandmothers. The women present were merely of middling rank, in his estimation.

"A dozen middle-aged women among two hundred males? And you say this is typical?"

Amasa replied that it was and pointed out that there were no children below the age of seven or eight, and no girls among the children.

"Why are there no young women in camp?" I asked.

"It is the People's way," he said.

"How strange! These women are all my mother's age—or older!"

"Don't underestimate their power, nonetheless," Captain Amasa warned me. "Even though these are not Grandmothers, you'll notice that the warriors defer to them."

"How is it that a handful of women exercise such authority?" I asked. "Are there no men among them?"

"They are men, all right," he said. "I don't understand it myself, but the women exercise control. These women are called Sisters, and they are like elders—and they also function as spies, observing and reporting everything that the men do. Rather like the Eyes of Israel, I imagine."

"And the warriors put up with it? I can't believe it."

"Believe it," he said.

I was curious about the customs of the Kuhans, so I listened and watched and asked what I hoped were discrete questions. I learned that the Kuhlans recognized several stages of life rather formally, in that they assigned names to them and marked the passage of individuals from stage to stage with elaborate ceremonies. I could never get the stages exactly in mind, for they had several names for each, the earliest being nestling, although they called their young by many generic names. The male children stay with their mothers until about age seven or upwards, after which they come to live in the men's camps. At that point they are called, depending on their dispositions or other subtleties I could not fathom, "bear cub" or "wolf cub" or "quail chick" or "bull calf." These appellations seemed significant to the Kuhlans, both adults and young, but no one was anxious to explain their meanings to me, so I never learned more.

The strangest part of their customs, to my mind, was the absence of any clear paternal relations between adults and young. If any man of our band was father to any of the boys – which certainly must have been the case – they made no special recognition of their own blood, but acted in a general way as father to them all. It was not a matter of their being aloof or inattentive – in fact, all the men seemed paternally disposed toward all the boys. We had a dozen or more boy-children, aged seven to twelve, among us in our small pastoral camp, and all the grown men acted as fathers – or doting uncles, as it were – to all of them.

I must except the youths among them from this general pattern. Those just coming into the early signs of manhood – from fourteen up to eighteen or nineteen, I would estimate – showed no paternal or even friendly interest in the children and took no role in instructing them. They kept to themselves and had little to do with either the men or the younger boys. The latter they viewed with undisguised disdain, and if a "cub" was bold enough to address them, they often responded with very rough treatment. The adults regarded these exchanges with a strange passivity, clucking their tongues in disapproval at the most outrageous brutality, but never in my observation, at least, intervening.

The youths in this turbulent age group had a generic name too – which translates roughly as "bachelor wolves." That is, young male wolves that have wandered away or been driven from their family groups and have not yet formed their own packs. From their shameless and arrogant way of taking pleasure with each other, I thought they might be better called catamites.

I questioned Amasa again about the virtual absence of women in the camp, and he replied it was the Kuhlan custom. "The women are sacred," he said. "They carry sacred knowledge and responsibilities."

"You mean the men revere them as the bearers of new life."

"Yes, but there is much more. The women are keepers of the Sacred Fire; they knit up the Circle of the tribes." I sensed he was repeating phrases he had heard but whose full meaning he had not appreciated. Or at least he did not communicate their meaning to me. "The women know how to read," he added emphatically, as if to compel my understanding. "They are Guardians of the law. "

"Not the Law of St. Supplicee!" I exclaimed, suddenly keenly interested.

"No. Well, perhaps. There are many similarities. Many echoes of the Law of St. Supplicee in their law," he replied. "But I am certainly no expert in regard to the People's law."

Indeed, as a Benjamite, a member of the apostate tribe, Captain Amasa was not likely to be an expert in the Law of St. Supplicee either. But this was a subject that interested me greatly, and I determined to pursue it at the first opportunity. Shortly, however, the moon waxed nearly to fullness, and I had other matters to attend to and to try to understand. More Kuhlans arrived, mixed groups like our neighbors, and several all-male war parties. Visits between the two camps and all forms of contact abruptly ceased. We withdrew to our small hilltop and kept entirely within our perimeter. Immediately uneasiness, not to say fear, took hold of our Israelite encampment.

VII

Captain Amasa woke me as soon as the body was discovered. We had the men turn out for roll call and held them in formation. There was nothing to do but wait till full light.

As soon as we could see well, I paced off the perimeter of our compound, ignoring the commotion around me. Our camp boundary was marked by small cairns of stone at intervals; sage brush and other shrubs and even tufts of grass had been carefully removed for several feet on either side of the line. The ground had then been brushed smooth. Captain Amasa confirmed that the Kuhlans had pledged that no one would cross our perimeter to harm us during the period of the full moon. Even so, the Benjamites had taken great pains to mark the boundary clearly. It could not be mistaken, even at night, in the light of a full moon.

The grass was wet with dew, the ground damp and perfect for tracking. It was clear that the Kuhlans had not crossed the perimeter. There was no trace of a human footprint all along the boundary.

"I told you," Amasa said. "No one has crossed the perimeter."

"So it would seem," I said. "The next most obvious explanation, then, is that the killer is still inside the camp." The company was drawn up in formation, and we stood out of earshot of the nearest sentry. Nevertheless, I spoke my next question in his ear: "Is it possible that one of your own men is the murderer? Did the victim have enemies? Did he quarrel with anyone lately?" Amasa shook his head.

"Is there anyone among you who is acting strangely, who may be slipping into madness?"

"Well," he replied, "that might describe the lot of us. But no, no one is showing signs of the kind of madness that would produce this sort of mayhem. I told you, I have considered all of these things. And more."

"What else? What other information do you have? Something is bothering you."

"It is the position of the victim."

"What do you mean?" I thought I knew, but I wanted to hear it.

"His tent was pitched in almost the exact center of camp. There was another soldier inside with him. Lying beside him!" Amasa's eyes watered with emotion.

"And this other man, he heard nothing?"

"Nothing. Nothing at all!"

"This is uncanny," I said.

"Yes," he replied. "Yes!" He seemed shaken, but determined to suppress his feelings. "This is what is meant by a Kuhlan moon!" he exclaimed. "I think I've seen more than enough of them!" He left me at the camp boundary while he addressed the troops and set them about their tasks.

The previous night, under a full moon, with sentries posted and a double watch, some unknown enemy had crept in among us unseen, had selected a victim and deftly cut his throat, making no noise, not even waking the man sleeping beside the victim. It was an act of perfect malevolence, performed in such a way as to say to each of us, *it could have been you; you were helpless to prevent it.*

Still, even though I was as baffled as he was, I was troubled that Captain Amasa seemed so unnerved by these events. The other officers had gathered at a respectful distance from us, obviously seeking an answer or some reassurance from us. A similar crowd of Kuhlan warriors was forming outside the perimeter, but in quite another mood. Their derision and the delight they took in our misery were obvious. I was surprised. We had enjoyed two weeks of peaceful relations with them, camped together in this valley. *Between Kuhlans and Israel, I reflected bitterly, there can be no peace. Fire and water cannot mix.*

I suggested to Amasa that we search the whole perimeter again, not because I expected to find anything, but because it would give us something to do while we pondered this mystery.

The men were anxious; as officers, we needed to appear calm and purposeful. We scrutinized every foot of the boundary. The cleared area was almost entirely bare of disturbance. A few small animals had left their tracks in it, and several large Kuhlan dogs had visited us, oblivious of the boundary. "Your men brushed the ground with sage brooms after setting up the perimeter?" I asked.

"Thoroughly," Amasa replied. "They know the People. And they know about the full moon!"

"Are you a superstitious man, Captain?" I asked, kneeling by a set of tracks left by a huge dog. The prints were wolf-sized. Captain Amasa, like most Benjamites I had talked to, seemed to half-believe the stories about Kuhlans turning into wolves. I wondered if a man could cross the boundary, sweep his footsteps with a sage broom behind him, and then coax a dog across the disturbed area, the better to hide it. Amasa knelt beside me and scrutinized the prints closely. There was no answer here.

"Yes, I am," he said finally.

Even if overly impressed by these savages, Amasa was honest. My eyes wandered to two dogs which had come into our camp looking for scraps. One was a large wolf-like creature with a yellowish coat—a war dog; a formidable-looking and ill-dispositioned brute. The other was a long-haired shepherd dog, non-descript and harmless. They were scavenging. The Esdralon Guards had dug an offal pit near the latrines, as customary, and we regularly tossed the bones and scraps of our mess into it. It was visited frequently by dogs from the Kuhlan camps in our vicinity.

In spite of myself, I thought of all the stories I had heard from childhood upward of the supernatural prowess of the Kuhlans and their power to inflict harm. Many in Israel believed them capable of shape-shifting, especially during a full moon, which was their customary time to attack us. I had been taught to reject such superstitions, but here was a situation that had no obvious explanation.

As my eyes followed their movements, one of the dogs stiffened and his hair rose on his back. The other, less bold, but reacting to the same scent or sound, recoiled visibly and assumed a cringing, submissive posture. Their attention was focused on the offal pit.

"Look," I said, seizing Amasa's arm. "The dogs! I think they've found our intruder!"

I seized a spear from one of the tripods and charged the offal pit. This filthy stratagem and the bloody, treacherous act employed to carry it out filled me with rage. I shouted my war cry and a blasphemous challenge in Kuhlan.

Out of the pit a figure emerged, throwing back a reeking hide under which he had hidden. He was young and muscular, of about my stature, but filthy with offal and blood. He was armed only with a dagger; his naked body was painted entirely black. He leapt at me headlong, screaming, hardly feinting as he rushed me. I thrust with the spear and caught him in the chest, holding him off as he slashed at me. The blade struck his sternum, but he nearly bowled me over backward, so fiercely did he lunge at me. I twisted the haft with all my strength, throwing him to the ground with the leverage of the blade. Even so, he lunged upward at me with the knife, impaling himself further, as if numb to pain. His blue eyes were fierce and unfocused, glazed over like a frozen brook.

See me! I hissed at him through clenched teeth. I leaned forward with all my weight, driving the spear through him and into the ground. His arms flailed desperately, the blade of his knife slashing just short of me and then falling back. I leaned harder, shifting my weight. His eyes bulged out at me, focused to a point far beyond me. They blazed with fierce intensity for a moment and then went out like a snuffed torch.

"There's your intruder," I said panting as Amasa came up, wide-eyed, beside me.

"You've killed him!" he said, seeming astonished.

"Of course I killed him!"

"Do you think that was wise?" he said, indicating with a jerk of his head the large and suddenly quiet throng of Kuhlans just outside our perimeter.

VIII

Captain Amasa brought the Kuhlan dignitary to the door of the sweat lodge and then ducked inside. Amasa was sweating almost as much as I, and was highly agitated. "Captain," he whispered, "this man is a Golden Eye, the Eye of an Eagle; he—whatever you do, tell him the truth! Men of his stature have power; they see things, and see through things. Don't try to withhold information or deceive him." I grasped that he wanted me to treat the man with the respect appropriate to his station. Rather than awed by the prospect of being interrogated, I was very much annoyed by Captain Amasa's deference to our enemy.

"What in the name of St. Supplicee is a Golden Eye?" I asked.

"Not so loud. It's a rank, but it's more than that. It is an exalted status."

"Like a General of the Host?"

"No, he would far outrank a General of the Host!"

"I see," I said, trying to calm Amasa's agitation. He explained he would act as translator and seated himself across from me. As I was in the midst of a purifying ritual when Amasa had interrupted me, I saw fit to resume it. It was not becoming, I thought, for an Israelite officer to show so much deference to an enemy, whatever his rank. Captain Amasa had been in the Kuhlan lands too long. Meanwhile, the Kuhlan dignitary was brought in and seated himself quietly. I continued to meditate for some time, ignoring him, while Amasa fidgeted nearby.

The Kuhlan, who was of middle age, sat quietly, his hands folded on his belly. There was nothing prepossessing or pretentious about him. He had a powerful frame, but his muscles were shrunken with age, and he had acquired a paunch. I was reminded vividly of the account I had read in Jonas Harlech's journal of his first encounter with a Kuhlan chief during a negotiation also conducted in a sweat lodge. This man was similarly sure of himself in a quiet way; there was something almost humble in his patience. Or a great arrogance. The Golden Eye waited silently for me to conclude and raise my eyes, at which point he took a small vessel and poured water on the stones. I perceived that the customs of our two peoples were alike in regard to sweat lodges and meditation; with the hiss of steam he created a space in which we could talk.

"This is Pierson Angier, Leader of the People, who holds authority here," Amasa began. "He wishes to ask you some questions. As I mentioned before, I will translate his questions and your replies." He repeated this information in Kuhlan.

"You killed a young man today," Pierson Angier began. "His name was William Willow." I understood enough Kuhlan to follow him.

"Yes," I replied without waiting for Amasa's translation. Pierson Angier looked questioningly at Amasa, who seemed beside himself. He gave me a look that showed he was aghast at my presumption. I decided to wait thereafter for his translation.

The Kuhlan chief asked me to describe what had happened, and I did so briefly and perhaps a little boldly. I wanted it clear that I was responsible for the man's death and that I would stand by the consequences. He seemed not to notice my scruples in this regard.

"How did he die?" he asked.

I started to say *just as I told you*, but Amasa caught my eye. "He wants," he whispered, "to know the details of the young man's death."

I was puzzled by the question, but I replied as best I could, holding the man's gaze in my own to gauge if I understood him aright and was supplying the information he wanted. He nodded several times, but his face was otherwise expressionless.

"He wants to know if the young man, who was in his care, died a good death," Amasa added.

Amasa's comment baffled me. What could be good about the death of a murderous lunatic who had covered himself in filth and then died in an ecstasy of blood lust? He died! He died fighting, to be sure. But in the pursuit of some perverse object against us, and in defiance of an agreement between our peoples.

"He wants you to tell him more," Amasa prompted me. "He senses you do not know the customs."

That was certainly the case! Nevertheless, I sifted my recollections carefully and said, "The young man's eyes were strange. I do not know if he saw me."

This information elicited a response; it spoke, apparently, to what the man wanted to know. It showed in his face; his muscles tightened and he held himself erect as he followed up his question. "William Willow," he said accusingly, "was a bachelor. His preparation was not complete."

Amasa leaned forward to explain the significance of what he had said. "'Bachelor' means he was not yet a man. He was outside the community, still outside the Circle, you see." *I did not see, and my expression must have showed it.* "He was not ready," Amasa added. "Pierson Angier means to say you took advantage, that you violated the young bachelor's privileged status."

"That's absurd!" I exclaimed heatedly, and Amasa paled. I doubted that I understood a fraction of what Amasa was trying to impart to me. But what I could grasp seemed preposterous. *Sacred status? Bachelors? What nonsense!* I looked at Pierson Angier and said forcefully that I was soldier whose duty was to look after my men. This young Willow, whatever his status, had crept into our camp—in violation of an agreement between my people and his – and had moreover violated one of our comrade's throats with a knife! "Bachelor or not, he killed one of our men. There was no question of his guilt. When discovered, he had the man's blood upon him. What's more, he attacked me."

I could sense a blaze burning behind the Kuhlan's eyes. "William Willow had a knife only," he said sternly, "and you had a spear."

I raised my hands. There had been no time for formalities or for selecting weapons—even had I been inclined to do such a thing. "This was not about honor!" I declared. "I found a killer in our midst, and I used the first weapon that came to hand." *You kill a rat with a stick, I thought to myself.*

The man spoke in a low voice, but I felt the menace in his tone. Amasa translated cautiously: "Pierson Angier says that William Willow was unconsecrated; the moon madness was upon him."

Of that statement I could make no meaning at all, but I sensed that some obscure but potentially fatal issue was at stake. The Golden Eye of the Eagle stared at me accusingly. Amasa warned me under his breath to be very careful how I replied. "The People are indulgent with the bachelors," he whispered; "they understand that during the full moon they can fall under its spell. In that condition, they are. . . ," he searched for a word, "*exempt* from all punishment. Remember, this young man was in the Golden Eye's care."

Strange customs! I thought. We sat silently for a time while I tried to sort out these baffling ways. It seemed obvious to me that the Golden Eye had failed in his care, and I would not scruple to tell him so. But first I inquired of Amasa: "I know nothing of this moon madness. What is he talking about?" He could not easily explain it in whispered asides, but he informed me that the young men go into trances and perform strange deeds while they are under the spell of their wolf-soul.

"Wolf-soul!" I exclaimed. Once again I thought of the stories of Kuhlan man-wolves who preyed upon Israel. Was this, then, the origin of all the shape-shifter tales?

"The wolf is the guardian spirit of this phase of their lives," Amasa explained. "They commune with it or confront that aspect of it which is within themselves. They go into trances, have fits, lapse into comas. Murder each other."

I shivered. "And the full moon brings it on?" *A Kuhlan moon! I thought.* "How long are they affected thus? And is this a young man's burden, or do they suffer this affliction all their lives?"

"It affects the young men, but only for the three days of the full moon, as they calculate it. The night of the moon, plus the day before and the day after. Then the trances and other signs abate."

"Hah!" I exclaimed, suddenly realizing the facts of our case: "then this Willow boy may not claim the excuse of moon madness! Remember," I recalled to Amasa, "we found no tracks across our perimeter." Amasa conveyed my words to the Kuhlan, while watching me apprehensively. "We set up the boundary *before* the three days of the full moon. And we were promised it would be kept inviolate. In the absence of tracks across the perimeter, we must conclude that this William Willow had to have come into our camp *before* the full moon in order to hide himself in our offal pit. And he did so, one must assume, while in his senses. If so, he was not a 'bachelor' in the grip of 'moon madness,' he was an intruder and a killer. The fact that he came in and hid himself and waited before he struck establishes malice. He killed in cold blood, deliberately." I stopped, realizing that though I had made a case for premeditated murder under Israelite law, such distinctions were likely wasted on this savage.

"Good point," Pierson Angier said, crossing his arms and nodding solemnly.

Amasa looked at me as if I had just walked across hot coals and come out miraculously unscathed.

I was much relieved myself, sensing I had passed a test. But my interrogation had only begun.

"Why are you not familiar with the customs?" the Kuhlan asked. He had recognized the differences between the Benjamites and myself. I feared the consequences of speaking the truth, but I knew better than to deceive him. I explained that I was only recently arrived in his land.

"Why? Who gave you leave to come to our land?"

Two questions and I had already put my head onto the block. Reluctantly, I explained I was not a Benjamite; "I am an Asherite," I said. "I came as an exile. I came because I had to."

He wanted to know why I had been exiled; whom had I offended and how? I put him off with a brief answer. I said I had come seeking Zachariah ben Harlech.

Why? He wanted to know.

Pierson Angier would have made a superb intelligence officer; he grilled me expertly and followed up instinctively into every area I particularly did not wish to discuss. He was as relentless an interrogator as Nisan Lot. Their techniques were much the same; even the principles of law and logic seemed similar. He let me spin out a few strands of web and then he deftly connected them into a pattern. "Why would you presume you could make peace between the factions in your country?" he asked at one point. He was quite well informed about the affairs of Israel.

I explained I was the son of Tephlin Glanz, a powerful man in Israel and chief architect of the war against the Harlech. I told him I had a commission from my father and one from the Council of Apostles that gave me an importance beyond my own merits or years or status in Israel.

"But if you sought peace with the Harlech people, you would have subverted your father's will. Explain, please."

Nothing would suffice but to tell him the story – the *entire* story—of my life. I had at times to rediscover my own motives and intentions in events. He drew it all out of me patiently, bit by bit. Pierson Angier remained as stoic as a block of wood through our long conversation, but Amasa was openly enthralled by the tale. I did not know what conclusions the Kuhlan was drawing about me—nor what Amasa was thinking, for that matter. I struggled merely to tell an unembellished version of my life in response to his questions.

Soon we found ourselves conversing openly and unreservedly. I withheld nothing that was asked of me. Eventually we came to the stories about the so-called Sword of Israel, and I described the tales and the expectations that had dogged me. In response, he noted pointedly that I had no sword.

Abashed, I had to explain the uncertain validity of the stories. He was patient hearing the details of our religious differences. Eventually, he returned like a badger to the issue of my exile, and I found myself explaining my relationship with Miriam Lander and the circumstances by which Nathan Lander had relieved me of my sword. Captain Amasa shook his head at the tale.

"You people tear each other to pieces," Pierson Angier declared when I finished. "You have no need of us." He brushed off his hands and rose. "Soon you'll be eating each other alive!"

With that our interview was over and he took his leave. Amasa and I found ourselves outside the lodge, stiff from long inactivity and shivering in a pale new dawn. We had talked through the night. A large crowd of Kuhlans had waited patiently for the Golden Eye to finish interrogating me, and they greeted him with a great show of respect.

"There is no crime here; nothing to answer for," Pierson Angier announced. "Let us honor the dead." The crowd parted for him and followed him back to the Kuhlan encampment.

Amasa and I regarded each other. I was relieved but exhausted. I wanted desperately to sleep.

"That is an amazing story," Amasa said. "Your life, I mean."

"If it had been up to me, it would have been a far simpler tale to tell."

I felt I had passed a test of the most fateful sort, but I had no clear idea on what grounds I had escaped condemnation. The only ready explanation was that the Kuhlans held to the same law as Israel—which could not be. The more I saw of the Kuhlans the less I understood them. "Why on earth," I demanded wearily, "does Zachariah ben Harlech consort with these savages?"

"Because the Kuhlans are free," Amasa replied unhesitatingly. "They are the freest people on earth. And the wisest."

Chapter 11: Valley of the Shadow

I

Within a week of this detestable crime, the People turned their backs on us and made a decision to deal with the Kr—and to do so immediately. Such a campaign was at variance with their customs. Because of the severity of the climate and the lack of fodder for their horses, they avoid campaigning after November. In ordinary times, once the fall rains begin, they remain inactive till spring. But these were not ordinary times, apparently. Colonel Harlech reported that he had never seen the People so agitated. Their decision for immediate war reflected both their anger and their estimation of the threat posed by the Kr.

There was a flurry of excitement among us when the Esdralon Guards were invited to accompany the attacking force. The Benjamite fleet was to serve in the campaign by ferrying the People's warriors across the Snake. After the incident with William Willow, I had a deep aversion to serving with the Kuhlans or doing anything to assist them. It was an insult to all of us that we were regarded so lightly, but I was reluctant to help them, even to prove ourselves. It offended me even more that Israelite soldiers should so crave the approval of these savages.

My mind and heart and will, however, were as tangled together as a handful of wool. I could sort nothing out, nor draw one thing from another. Eventually, the excitement of the preparations proved contagious and drew me in. I decided it was better to have a task and to be in motion. Action simplified and focused my thoughts. I was a part of something again, and not an outsider. To speak truly, I did not want to think. I wished to put my griefs behind me, especially my memories of Justin and Michal-Rebekah and my mother. I wanted to worry no more about being the champion of the old Israel against the Messiahists. And without quite forgiving her, I wanted to put my feelings for Miriam Lander aside as well. Thus, I took up arms and put on the black face of war. It was not exactly peace of mind to go to war, but it sufficed. *It is why war is such a temptation to men.*

We crossed the icy waters of the Snake in a frame boat with only a thin-stretched bull's hide between ourselves and destruction. It occurred to me that there is an energy in things—a force like the current beneath us – that grinds the very mountains to powder, and against which a life, perhaps all life, has not a feather's weight of significance. I felt that I could reach out and touch the Way itself, if I chose. But I had no desire to. Instead, for reasons I chose not to examine, I too was caught up in events and carried along, powerless to resist.

It must be that same energy moving the waters that drives a long, weary column of men and horses slogging through mud, steaming under a pounding rain, all their efforts bent toward a single purpose, their eyes on a single destination. The destination substituting, I suspect, for the meaning of the effort.

"Why are we doing this?" I asked Captain Amasa.

"The People protect their nest; it is their first principle."

"No! Damn it!" I found myself cursing him savagely. "No! I don't care why the Kuhlans are doing this. I want to know why *we* are!"

He looked at me stupidly.

"The Kuhlans killed our man; they slit his throat in our camp," I fumed. "And now we ride along side them."

"The Kr are our enemies too," Amasa said. He seemed even less anxious than I to reflect on things, so I let him be. The column moved forward relentlessly.

When the rain stopped it was easier going. The Kuhlan force of over a thousand warriors left us behind as they moved rapidly to attack an encampment of the Kr that had been located on the Tucannon. The Esdralon Guards were ordered to bring up the rear with the horse herd. Major Moriah was furious at the slight, and, for so taciturn a man, he delivered a spectacular series of curses against the People for their arrogance.

Colonel Harlech kept his own counsel, except to remark, "The People had done better to go out before the rains. Now it's too late to burn the prairie. What would have been easy then will be difficult now, and things possible then will be impossible. This is not like them."

I too took note of what was characteristic and uncharacteristic of the People. I learned that their famous mobility derived from their custom of taking three horses for each rider when they went on a raid. The extra horses meant that anyone seeing the marks of their passing would greatly exaggerate their numbers. I laid these observations up in my mind, determined that Israel should learn of them.

Colonel Harlech kept a strict march discipline. We had only one mount apiece, so we moved deliberately, careful not to over-tax them. The Hills of Moab roll in great swells toward the southeast, like waves at sea. Our scouts approached the tops of each of these ridges warily. In crossing them, a horseman was immediately exposed, silhouetted on the horizon, and his presence announced for miles around as clearly if a bell had been rung by his passing. Accordingly, our scouts dismounted near the brow of the ridge, and one crept forward while the other held the horses. The main body waited while the trooper on post scanned the horizon. After a time, the scout would wave an arm, and the Guards passed over the summit quickly, to reduce the time of exposure.

It was a time-honored practice, but with all this caution, I feared that we were going to fall behind even the horse drove, and thus miss the fighting entirely. I had no opportunity to observe how the Kuhlans moved in the face of the enemy, but I imagined them flowing swiftly and irresistibly, like a mighty stream. As we moved forward, we encountered dozens of their worn-out and discarded mounts. The Kuhlans used their animals cruelly, sacrificing them to obtain the speed that was their hallmark. Given our position in the rear with the boys and old men deemed unfit for combat, I concluded that this insight into Kuhlan mobility would be all that I would learn from our expedition. As usual, I was wrong.

The fourth day of our expedition dawned gray and overcast and threatening snow. We had yet to see a single enemy. As we were fixing breakfast, however, word came that the Kuhlans were engaged. We saw the signal smoke and hurried forward. By mid morning we were at the scene, with the horse herd trailing behind us. The People had struck the enemy camp, which was spread along the Tucannon valley, a narrow, winding defile with a level floor and abundant grass and timber. It looked as though the People had swept into the east end of the encampment and driven the Kr before them.

Colonel Harlech held the Guards in reserve on the rim of the valley and sent me forward with a patrol. As we descended the steep sides of the valley, I found the miasmic stench of the Kr in my nostrils once again and experienced the same mixture of revulsion and fear I had felt at Elion. Our patrol quickly surveyed the battlefield, while the horse-drovers searched for their wounded and fired the crude huts of the enemy. The initial slaughter had been one-sided, the People having achieved surprise, but here and there we found a few of the People dead and wounded.

We found no Kr alive; this was the People's way of making war. *Not that any Israelite had the slightest inclination to spare these enemies either.* I learned also that the People do not retrieve their hopelessly injured. There is no place in Kuhlan life for weakness or cripples. The irreparably injured are expected to commit suicide if able, or if not, their comrades assist them with a quick death. The elder warriors assumed that grim duty, choosing whom to dispatch and whom to assist off the field. The injured warriors whom I saw undergo this selection process exhibited the profoundest courage.

Of the Kr bodies lying scattered within the first few hundred yards, all were young men, warriors, in their familiar ragged woolens. We saw no family groups and no women. I was puzzled by their absence, but we were obliged to hurry onward. Soon we met the People's warriors drifting back – the lightly wounded who were out of the fighting. They were not cheerful as men usually are who have driven their enemies before them. I heard one of them remark with evident dismay, "This camp must extend for miles!"

I sent a messenger to Colonel Harlech saying that the battle was still in progress and its outcome possibly in doubt; the People had attacked a very large encampment without proper reconnaissance. *This is the price of their speed. I suspected that they still did not know how large a force they had engaged.*

Colonel Harlech brought the Guards forward as soon as he received my message. When I saw the troops in motion, I hurried our patrol down the narrow valley. We rode on through burning huts and scattered debris and were greeted by appalling sights at every turn. Resistance had stiffened as the attack rolled up the valley. Men and horses, Kuhlan and Kr together, littered the ground. I was not prepared, however, for the sight that greeted us as we rounded a horseshoe bend. The whole host of the People were drawn up in front of us. The People were hardly cowering, but they were not advancing either. They seemed to be gathering themselves and simultaneously trying to spread a ragged line across the floor of the valley. I sensed an unaccustomed uncertainty pervading their host. The valley of the Tucannon was nearly as steep-sided as a trough at this point; nevertheless, I found a vantage point and had a look at what lay to the front.

About a thousand yards ahead the valley was black with Kr. A solid mass of horsemen filled the valley from edge to edge; I could scarcely begin to estimate their numbers.

Even more ominous to me, however, was their silence. The Kr did not scream and hurl defiance or exercise themselves in any of the fantastic gestures peculiar to savages. But they were clearly unafraid; their stillness expressed a mixture of confidence, ill will, and menace. They seemed as little moved by the presence of their ancient foe, the People, as they had been unalarmed by our forces at Elion. The sight of them was unsettling for me; it must have been a shock to the People.

The two forces had momentarily separated themselves and were catching their breaths. The smoke and fog that obscured the valley earlier had gradually lifted, so the two sides had a good look at each other. *The People are in for it,* I thought, recalling our own rough handling by the Kr. The People were simply overmatched in numbers. The Kr in sight seemed too many to count. I wondered anxiously if there were additional hordes of Kr above us, beyond the canyon rim, moving toward our rear. We could see no more of that than if we had been in a box. *This could be bad, very bad, I thought, because this time we have no walled fortress, no Esdralon, to which we can retreat, as we had had at Elion, but rather an unfordable river at our back.*

Rams horns blew from the host of the Kr, and immediately the mass stirred to life and made for us, slowly at first and then breaking into a canter. In return, the People raised their war cry and advanced. The two sides closed at full gallop, sending up a ferocious din. The collision of the two forces was a massive swirl of violence, spilling horses and men like pent-up, raging waters.

With the Guards patrol, I plunged into the fighting along side the Kuhlans. I had the sensation of being swept up in a mighty flood and tossed this way and that. The warfare of savages is all confusion, all a swirl of motion and noise. In the close confines of the valley, we were often so crowded we could not maneuver at all, and at other times the fight would open up, and we had space to breathe and to catch glimpses of the larger action. I witnessed acts of individual prowess without parallel. Surely there cannot be a more formidable fighting man in the world than one of the People's seasoned warriors, war axe in hand, cutting swathes through his enemies. It was the very image of all that Israel held in dread—the fury of the Kuhlans! How strange it was to be fighting along side these men rather than against them!

The battle closed in on us again, and in the crush of horses and men, I lost all sight of the battle beyond a dozen feet from where I struggled. It was all I could do to keep my seat, to thrust and parry and slash. My lance was soon broken in the press, and I bent my Guards sword into useless iron. Seeking a better weapon, I swooped down and picked up an axe from a fallen Kuhlan. It was not the weapon my Hazorite sword had been, but I liked its heft in my hand and the destruction it wrought if swung properly. We fought stubbornly, in groups of five or six, supporting each other fiercely. I marveled how the Kuhlans could keep a fluid cohesion among themselves without the discipline of our formations.

Nevertheless, as a group, we were pressed backward. The Kr were relentless; anyone who became separated from his comrades was immediately unhorsed and trampled. We plunged our horses into our foes and slashed and thrust and hammered savagely, but we were slowly crowded together. If was as if some invisible force was squeezing us into a narrow confine. Belatedly I realized that this compression could only mean we were surrounded and being assailed from all sides. As the thought occurred to me, I noted that many fighters around me were casting anxious glances over their shoulders.

By a stroke of good fortune, above us on the valley rim, Colonel Harlech's Esdralon Guards were at that moment descending to our aid. The Guards made a reckless charge, cutting obliquely down the slope of the canyon and taking the forward elements of the Kr in the flank. The weight of their formation crushed the horsemen in their front and sent a portion of the Kr reeling away, trampling each other in their haste. The Guards thrust forward into their midst and then, on command, separated and reformed as if on parade. They had created about fifty yards of space in the midst of the melee. It was the finest act of disciplined behavior I had ever witnessed.

Thus reprieved, the People used the opportunity to exert themselves and quickly slaughtered the Kr who had got into their flanks and rear. The two sides then recoiled, panting. The task for us now, however, was to extricate ourselves. Colonel Harlech's bold charge had given us the separation we needed, and when the Kr pursued us, he repeated the maneuver, and broke the leading mass again with another gallant charge. I thrilled to see the Kr fleeing in panic.

They rallied stubbornly, however, and pressed us hard, with great ardor but without tight military organization. Again, the stout discipline of Israel's cavalry, fighting and wheeling and regrouping steadily in formation, kept them at bay as we withdrew up the valley. I felt a fierce pride at the Harlech performance. No less than Major Moriah, I resented the People's disdain of us. We were showing our mettle today, no doubt about that.

Unbelievably, the Kr did not break off the engagement after these bloody setbacks. Instead, they attacked again and again, fiercely, and clung like badgers to our host. I had never heard of undisciplined savages sustaining combat so tenaciously. Then, in mid afternoon, the Kr gave us another surprise. Apparently enraged at the prospect of our escape, they roused themselves for a supreme effort and flung themselves irresistibly at our depleted forces, which were by now exhausted. Even the Guard formations were in tatters. This time, the sheer weight of their numbers overwhelmed us at all points and broke us to pieces. After so much courage and tenacity, we were shattered in a moment. The supple cohesion of the Kuhlans disappeared as suddenly as the more rigid discipline of Israel. It was not terror that swept over us, but dismay. We fled abjectly, routed and humbled, each man for himself. Terror followed soon after.

I had a horse killed under me and was glad enough of remounting another in the confusion that I rode like a fury, unmindful of either comrades or foes, or even of my direction, so anxious was I to put space between myself and my pursuers.

So it went until early dark. If there were acts of heroism and self-sacrifice after we gave way, if soldiers remembered their discipline as horses stumbled or gave out, if there was defiance when groups were cut off and overtaken, I took no note of it. I flogged my horse until it died under me, and I spilled forward almost senseless, failing to leap clear. Others, less panicked or less overcome with exhaustion than I, pried my leg out from under the dead animal and lifted me onto another mount, and so I fled onward in the darkness.

II

When dawn came and I awoke from drowsing in the saddle, I discovered that my companions were Kuhlans rather than Benjamites. They seemed as surprised as I. I could not even be certain if these were the men who had saved me, or if my horse had carried me in the darkness and confusion into some other group. The night had been the stuff of nightmares; I could believe anything about it. We were all too exhausted to care. There was nothing to do but make the best of it. We fled onward, pausing frequently to rest our horses. None of our mounts was wounded or lame, but they were thoroughly spent, as we were. We seemed also to be entirely alone, which made the Kuhlans uneasy. They were not sure where their comrades were, nor the Kr. And they didn't like being without fresh horses.

There were five of us. I recognized the leader of our group as a man named Riik, whom I had seen at the camp on the Palouse. After some discussion, which I had difficulty following because of my exhaustion and my imperfect mastery of their language, he turned us south and upwards into the Blue Mountains. I assumed he chose this course because our pursuers would expect us to flee back toward the Kuhlan heartlands. As we traveled, the weather turned bitter cold and it began to snow. We all cursed our luck, for we would be easy to track. And with visibility curtailed, we could easily stumble into an ambush. My injured leg ached, and I found I could not raise my right arm. I clung to the saddle, knowing I would be abandoned if I so much as fell behind. My horse sought the company of his fellows, so I dozed again as I rode.

By late afternoon we reached the foothills and the ragged edge of a forest. If my companions felt relief at this, I did not. I felt instead the overwhelming menace of the forest. Israelites are strangers to the wilderness. It is not our home, and we do not relish excursions into it. The mountains that surround Israel are the abode of ticks in the summer and wild beasts and dreadful cold in winter. As we plunged into the dark woods, I was immediately disoriented, just as I had been on the journey to Naphtali. And I was afraid. Who knew what lay hidden in its recesses? But it was more than fear that I felt. I had lost my weapons and all my gear not actually attached to my body. I felt a twinge of compassion for Rehab Gill, as he lay in our camp above Cashmere. He had been so broken in spirit by his days and nights in prison that he feared his manhood had departed from him. I knew now what he had felt.

As we climbed, heavy snow began to fall, blotting out the trail and confining our vision to a few yards in any direction. Soon the footing was too treacherous to proceed, and we had to seek shelter. For my part, I was not eager to go higher into the mountains, where men lose themselves and perish even in less hostile seasons. My hands and feet were painfully stiff; I was beginning to fear frostbite. I was gripped moreover by a nameless dread. I had campaigned in winter before; I had led a patrol through the Lost Horse Hills to Lagash in cold weather, but it was nothing like this. This cold seemed capable of crushing the life out of us, man and beast alike.

When we moved off the trail, I found that because of the stiffness of my injured leg I could not dismount. To my surprise, I felt rough hands pushing me back into the saddle and the reins taken from me. One of the Kuhlans led my horse through the snow. We struggled to the lee side of a steep ridge in a mixed grove of cedar and fir. The wind had come up, and it tore at the tops of the trees and sent gusts of snow in our faces. It was cold beyond anything I had ever felt, and getting colder. My face ached and I could barely feel my feet. My knee still throbbed, but the pain, in these circumstances, was reassuring. We had gone only a hundred yards or so off the slippery trail when Riik turned aside into a grove of giant cedars whose branches almost touched the ground. It was dark and cave-like under the boughs, a natural shelter from wind and snow.

Inside, a giant windfall had reared its massive roots up out of the ground. Earth and clay still clung to the roots. The trunk, which was wider than I was tall, formed a solid wall on one side of our enclosure. The lowest branches of the surrounding trees formed a roof over our heads and reached almost to the ground around us. The wind howled outside, but it was still within. Though exhausted, we explored this natural enclosure eagerly, marveling at the shelter it offered. There was space enough for a dozen men, bare of snow. The ground was covered with a carpet of needles several inches deep; it was dry and soft. I almost wept with relief. If we could start a fire here, we would live.

The others helped me down and tied the horses between the standing cedars, where they were as protected as in a stable. The wind gusting in the treetops nevertheless made the horses fret. It was the cold, however, that I feared. I could stand by supporting my weight on one leg. My other leg was sore, but I had broken no bones. The Kuhlans seemed to feel the danger as much as I. In a moment they had selected the most sheltered spot by the root wall of the giant fallen cedar and started to build a fire. Each of them in turn bent over a pile of twigs and dry needles, striking their flint fire-makers. When it came my turn, I fumbled awkwardly with the tools. The cold drew the skill from my fingers so that I struck them together clumsily. The sparks died in the frigid air. I blew on my hands and rubbed them together. St. *Supplicee* I repeated to myself like a charm. I was the only one who had steel as well as flint; it was up to me. I struck the two together again, and this time the spark flew into the dry moss.

"Again!" Riik said. I held the steel exactly as before and struck again. A thin wisp of smoke rose from the moss.

"Again!"

A small flame caught and flared. No one breathed. I fanned it carefully. Then I placed a dry twig on the moss, and another, bending quickly to blow on the pile when the flame flickered out. I leaned close to the ground and blew steadily; my breath was a cloud of ice. The fibers glowed again and ignited. Riik added more moss and twigs, and one caught and added to the tiny blaze. I could hear my companions release their breath and inhale deeply. We would live.

"The Kr will find us," one of them said.

"If we don't make a fire, we die," Riik said.

"But the Kr will see it."

"Good!" Riik said in his deep voice. He was standing at the edge of our shelter. "I hope the Kr are out there, stalking us," he said. "Because very soon they will be dead men. Look," he said, urinating by the side of the entrance to our shelter like a dog marking his territory. His urine steamed in the snow for a moment. *And then it was ice.* It had frozen almost as soon as it hit the ground. I drew a sharp breath. Israel does not know cold like this.

They worked as quickly as they could with war axes, chopping dead branches from the windfall, frantic to get back to the fire and yet fearful of injuring themselves. We piled the wood high and rejoiced at the leaping flames and the heat. As well as we could in the descending gloom, we searched for masses of snow in the boughs above us that could slump down and extinguish our fire. We knew we would not be able to start another.

"More wood, build it higher," Riik said. We built a huge bonfire for the sake of the horses, which were suffering as we were. Riik and the rest spoke gently to them and rubbed their backs. They unsaddled them, arranging our saddles around the fire, but leaving the blankets on the horses' backs for warmth. We had nothing to feed them. One horse was shivering and rolling its eyes; I wondered if it would make it through the night. Riik, no doubt thinking the same, watched it intently, rubbing its nose and muzzle and making the queer clucking sounds that Kuhlans use with horses. In spite of their cruelty, the People are good with horses. I watched as Riik adjusted the saddle blanket and groomed her mane. He talked to her gently as he worked.

"If only we had some fodder," Riik said.

Instead of replying, I collapsed into a deep sleep.

I have no idea how long I was unconscious, but when I awoke, Riik was fussing with the floor of our enclosure while the other three tended the fire. The soil was sandy and dry under the layer of needles, and he had chipped a large hole in the ground. I thought it useless work as we had nothing to cook, until I saw them arranging our saddles around the hole. Riik motioned me to join them, and I saw the point of their labors. They had made a large blaze – too large to sit by comfortably; the cold pierced us from the back even when our fronts were scorching. The Kuhlans had heated stones to place in the hole, and they were arranging their gear so they could sit around it with their feet warmed by the stones. I roused myself and joined them warily, favoring my leg and wondering why I had not had my brains knocked out as I slept. Instead, the group of us bundled up like old beggars and crowded around the edge of the hole with our feet dangling into it, our backs propped against our saddles, and mutually savored the warmth. It was ingenious and quite comfortable.

There were five of us, thrown together by the fortunes of war, and now cheered and warmed by the same fire's glow. In the stress of the moment, they had forgotten I was an outsider of the mud people and therefore unclean to them. We introduced ourselves, awkwardly. I knew Riik by sight and reputation from our camp on the Palouse. He was one of the Black Willow People. Riik introduced the others with a nod in their direction: Makhey, Quarry, Woad. I had not seen any of the latter before; they belonged to the Antelope People, the band whose territory lay on the south side of the Snake. I knew enough of their language to explain that I was from the north of Israel, not a Benjamite. They nodded, but were not much interested in distinctions among Israelites.

Riik asked me about my leg and I said it was all right; it would mend. I was ashamed that I had shown weakness before them, but I was more exhausted than I had ever been in my life. It felt good to sit by the fire and not move. My arm was cramped at the shoulder, but I did not seem injured otherwise. By gestures and broken sentences, I got them to melt snow in my canteen and we shared it around. I put hunks of pemmican out of my pouch on the rock nearest the fire to thaw, one for each of us, and after watching me carefully while it heated, they each took up a piece and chewed it ravenously, licking the grease from their fingers. The fat was good medicine against the cold. Riik had strips of beef jerky in a small pouch over his shoulder. None of the others had even emergency rations; they had left their packs behind prior to the battle. *They always expect to win, I thought.*

Knowing the Kuhlan disdain toward all outsiders, I felt uneasy. But for the moment at least, the Kuhlans behaved just as Israelites would have in similar circumstances – in fact, just as my Asherite companions had done on our reconnaissance into Lagash. They were quiet, practical, and comradely. Oddly, I felt very much at home with them. Following Riik's lead, they each tore a portion of dried beef and placed it on a stone near me. For hereditary enemies, we seemed to be getting on well.

Night had long since fallen, but no one was anxious to sleep. Not while visions of the slaughter still moved at the backs of our eyes. Riik and Makhey began to tell stories of other campaigns and other cold spells. As he spoke, the wind kept the grove in constant movement.

"How are you called?" Makhey said to me at the close of one of his tales. I inferred he meant, what was my rank?

"I am a captain," I replied in the best Kuhlan I could manage. I had my insignia in a leather pouch, so I fished out my captain's bars and passed them around. The word captain meant nothing to them, so I tried to explain. When I said a captain commands a hundred men, they snorted in disbelief. Kuhlans are much less numerous than Israelites; they thought I was claiming an exaggerated status for myself. "If he commands foot soldiers," I explained. "A captain commands fewer horsemen – only fifty horsemen."

They were polite but skeptical. "How is it that a man so young could command so many?" Riik asked.

I explained that I had been trained up to fight since childhood. They nodded, but of course, I realized, so had they all. Only in Israel were a select few prepared for warfare and the bulk of the population trained for other tasks. Among the Kuhlans, everyone was a warrior. From what I had seen on the Tucannon, I imagined that Kuhlans began training for war in infancy. "I was also fortunate to have shone in battle against the Kr," I explained. I showed them my medal for valor, shaped in the form of a Kr shield with a Transmitter painted on it.

"What acts did you perform?" Riik asked.

"I rescued my brother, who was wounded," I said. "And I killed eight men. For this, I received this medal." I did not know the Kuhlan words, but they understood rewards for valor.

They nodded respectfully. Eight men they could understand, but I could see they did not think it a remarkable feat. *We are the People, their manner said.*

I might have resented their presumption of superiority, but Riik commented, "You fought well yesterday. I saw it." The others nodded. "I had not thought an Israelite could swing an axe," he added. The others broke into broad grins.

I was pleased at their praise, but at the same time I blushed crimson with shame. At some point in the battle, my arm had become numb and the war axe had slipped from my hand. I had fled the battlefield weaponless and terrified.

As if reading my mind, Riik said, "We all ran from the Kr." The others nodded. *There was comradeship, then, in defeat and humiliation as well as in great deeds. I had never spent a stranger night, never found myself on a stranger errand than on this expedition with the People.*

To reciprocate, I asked them about their own ranks and what they meant, which prompted a discussion among themselves, most of which I could not follow. Finally, Makhey pointed at Riik and said, "He is a sow grizzly."

I had to suppress a smile.

"I am also a five husbandman," Riik added solemnly. When I asked him to explain, he said he had added five souls to the People. I eventually understood that he had sired five children.

"How many sons?" I asked. "How many daughters?"

He seemed puzzled by my question. He looked at the others.

"He does not know," Quarry said. "It does not matter. Woad and I," he added, "hope to become husbandmen when we return."

After a little explanation, I understood that to be a five husbandman was to be credited with five conceptions. The Kuhlans, as I had observed before, understand paternity only in a very general sense. And I realized that the two youngest men were eager to achieve that status because Kuhlan women reward valor with sexual favors. They wanted to know how many children I had conceived, how many women I had lain with.

"Two," I replied. I thought it best to omit mentioning my Kuhlan partners of the harvest ceremony.

"Two women, or two children conceived?" they asked.

"Two women," I said, wishing to change the subject. "Some weeks ago, I talked with a man named Pierson Angier. He seemed to be of high rank, but I do not know your customs. What does it mean to be a Golden Eye of the Eagle?"

I gathered from their comments that Angier was indeed an exalted personage. They spoke of him with awe. He was both an Eagle and the Eye of an Eagle. This was a special status, but I could make no sense of the distinction. Angier had some other high-sounding titles as well. It occurred to me that their ranks referred to authority in different situations, as in peace and war and other circumstances important to them but which eluded me.

"The greatest chiefs, the Talons and the Eyes," Makhey was explaining, trying to find simple words that I could understand, "come back to the People."

"Come back?" I queried, uncertain of his meaning.

He was patient, and I finally understood the gist of his words: *those who are most resourceful and who demonstrate the highest wisdom come back after death.* "They are born again to the People," he explained.

This seemed to me perfectly absurd, but I nodded politely.

"But those who die outside the Circle," Makhey added, "must live again as wolves."

I was so startled at this notion that I blurted out "Wolves! Why would a man descend to a brute life?" *In spite of my contempt for their superstition, I felt a great uneasiness at this recurring identification of Kuhlans with wolves.*

Makhey seemed puzzled by my question. "It is a life to be desired," he said. "A wolf lives by his own cunning, and every day he pits his strength and will against his foes. He lives by the chase, and he has his companions and his mate. It is a life! Why would a young bachelor not love it? Many live out countless lives as wolves. Countless!" He made a gesture with his arms.

"They are not alone, as bachelors are," Woad explained.

"They grow in wisdom," Riik said, "and then come back to the People."

"So," I said, trying to make sense of all this, "it is a lonely life the bachelors have?"

"One to be forgotten," Riik said. "It is best not spoken of."

"*Look*," Makhey said, gesturing at the entrance. There was a pair of eyes, glowing like coals, watching us from the darkness. Then another pair. My hair rose instantly off my scalp.

"Wolves," he said admiringly. "Our brothers thrive even in this cold. It brings them out, stirs up their blood."

Suddenly a wolf howled behind us and so close at hand it might have come from inside my ear. I flinched and felt a stark animal fear take hold of my guts and raise the hair on my skin until it stood stiff and upright all over my body. Again the wolf wail came out of the darkness, keener than the wind itself. In spite of the warmth and the firelight, I shivered. "Are they satisfied, these men who hunger to live again as wolves?" I asked. "Do they experience their desires? Learn what they want to know?"

"Who can say?"

Makhey seemed suddenly troubled. He turned away from me and looked at the darkness beyond our circle of light.

"William Willow was a bachelor wolf," Riik explained. "Makhey is thinking that this may be his spirit." He gestured toward the darkness. I realized instantly what he meant: Willow was the man I had killed inside our compound.

"Ah," I said, feeling a sudden dread.

"I think that this is so also," Riik confirmed. There was no threat in his voice, but I felt I was suddenly on very precarious footing with them. The wolves were skulking outside the fire's glow, but their eyes were visible when they turned toward us. I counted seven pairs of eyes, some moving restlessly, but several, in the forefront, fixed and silent, were focused upon us. The horses snorted in fear, pulling at their tethers and stamping.

"This Willow—if he is the man I think he is," I ventured to say, "crept into our camp to kill my comrades. I thought we were safe there, under the People's protection. We had assurances. It seemed to me madness for him to murder one of my companions as he did. So when I found him, I killed him. I did not understand your customs. I still do not."

"We know the story," Riik said. "There was no fault. Pierson Angier sought it out and declared it. It was Willow's fate."

I was relieved at his view of the matter, but felt that I was not out of the woods, as the saying goes. "So, does he come here troubled?" I asked. "Is his spirit angry?"

"No," Riik said thoughtfully. "But this must be strange to him. His new life is strange to him, and we are strange to him. And yet familiar. I sense he is puzzled. He cannot understand what he feels now." As he spoke one of the beasts whined. I felt my hair stand on end again. The horses snorted and stamped.

"So, you believe that someone whose spirit inhabits an animal does not remember his life as a man?"

"How could he? And yet, that life is within him; it must shape him. It gives him the life he has. Somehow it must be with him. That is why Willow is puzzled."

"Do the women believe these things also? That bachelors have other lives as animals?"

He shrugged. "Who knows what the women believe?" His manner said that this was not a topic he was willing to explore.

I rose and limped to the edge of our shelter and looked out at the shining pairs of eyes. Not believing, but at this moment not wholly disbelieving either, I stood motionless at the entrance. My own feelings were unsettled. I wanted somehow to show myself to these creatures, to see if recognition could pass between us, whether as slayer and slain, or merely as man and beast. I felt myself at a strange threshold and longed to see if I could cross it. At the entrance, I felt the warmth of the fire on my back and a stellar cold on my face. Beyond our circle of firelight was perfect blackness. I waited for my eyes to adjust. Except for the pairs of eyes, whose lids seemed to open onto an inner blaze, I could see nothing. I stared into nothingness.

Then, just beyond the entrance, another pair of eyes raised up and moved deliberately towards me. It stopped, we stared. *I wonder what is in its mind at this moment?* I searched my own mind for some responsive chord, for something in myself that mirrored whatever glowed in those eyes. Half a spear-throw apart we gazed at one another. One of the other wolves let out a long, deep-throated howl. This one, however, kept his gaze fixed upon me silently. It did not startle or blink; nor did I. *Mutual recognition,* I thought. *Or was he gazing at meat not yet taken?*

So I could claim no understanding had passed between us. The other wolf howled again, breaking my trance. Still, it occurred to me that these wolves might be giving voice to *something*—expressing whatever in them found harmony with this abyssal weather. I pondered what the heart knowledge of these beasts might be, and whether it too connected with the Way. Odd to think the lives of these beasts might open a passage to the Way.

If the Way was speaking to us in their voices, what was it saying?

I waited, shivering, our eyes locked together. Nothing was communicated to me across the darkness. The voice, when it came, was from deep inside myself: *we are of this cold and darkness; it is our bone and blood; we carry fire in our eyes and hearts and brains. Nothing appalls us.*

I blinked, my eyes watering, and averted my gaze. I returned to my seat by the fire. If my companions noticed my emotion, they made no sign of it.

"We'll stand five watches tonight," Riik announced. "It will be a long night, and you'll be tempted to sleep. Do not! The wolves will make a try for the horses sometime in the night. If we lose a horse, we lose the man. Stay alert." He meant that if the wolves took a horse, the man on watch would pay for it.

On my watch, I fed the fire carefully, and then, still sleepy, limped to the entrance to see if the pack still waited outside. To my surprise, I saw no eyes blazing like arrogant stars in the darkness. I pulled a brand from the fire and walked around the shelter. The horses were calm, their eyes shining with reflected light. I stepped out of the entrance. The wind had died. We were alone. I tossed the brand into the snow where it hissed and went out. I looked upward and saw a sky bathed in pale light. It was very cold, and though my breath froze on my beard, the air felt perfectly dry. I could smell the cold. A few stars shone through breaks in the timber. A Kuhlan moon was rising above the cedars.

The next day Riik was cheerful about the doings of our wolf-companions. "They must have followed our trail up into the mountains because of Willow; he was drawn to us. But the valleys below are full of spoil for them. They'll be feasting on battle scraps and growing fat, while we freeze our asses up here."

I found little cause for cheer in our situation. I doubted in souls that could migrate from humans to animals and back again, and I also disbelieved in our chances of surviving if the weather did not break soon. We spent the day quietly, feeding the fire and tending the horses. We melted snow for them and fussed with them constantly, to keep their minds from their hunger. We napped and cut wood and mended our gear and tended to our weapons, going through the hundred small tasks soldiers use to keep themselves occupied. I had some concern about the rumored sexual habits of the Kuhlans, but they were comradely and cheerful and as stoic as the best Israelites. If they indulged themselves in any way, they were discrete.

On the third day, the weather was still too cold to travel. Riik sniffed the air and spat and then examined all the horses minutely. We knew what he was about; Quarry's horse was trembling, its nose almost touching the ground. Quarry occupied himself with the fire as Riik gently led the horse outside. He slaughtered it expertly, and I helped him butcher it. We cut strips of meat and made five separate piles on pieces of hide. We tied the corners before they could freeze. These parcels would be our rations till we got back to safety. Then we roasted a great deal of meat and feasted like savages. There was no sign of wolves, and only a few crows came to peck at the carcass.

That night the wind blew again, and we were cheerful, as it was a sign the weather was breaking. In the morning, we rubbed grease on our faces and lips and fastened rawhide leggings around our ankles. It was still cold, well below freezing, but within the limits that man and beast could endure.

The way down the trail was treacherous and we had to lead the horses single file. I found I could walk well enough, though I limped. Several times one of us or a horse slipped and took a spill in the snow, but it was deep enough to cushion our falls and we escaped injury. By noon the snow was crunchy underfoot; a thaw was setting in.

We had five men and only four horses, and we began to think about the Kr. We would be helpless if discovered. Coming to a promontory with a broad view of the land below us, we paused to argue over the route we should take. All but Riik wanted to veer sharply northeast, toward the villages of the Antelope People. Riik demurred silently for a while. Then he explained: "The villages are gone."

It took a moment to comprehend all that he meant: the Kr would have followed up their victory and penetrated the heartland of the Antelope People. It might be that the People had escaped, but they could not be where they usually camped and still live. The scope of the disaster sank into us slowly; Kuhlans were not used to defeat. Riik was a Black Willow and so less directly affected by the tragedy, but he had a clear head and good insight in any event. Kuhlans, I decided, are not elevated to leadership without cause. Riik estimated that the main body of the Kr would be northeast of us. With that realization, the reality of the defeat we had suffered came back to us. We had suppressed the memory of our humiliation while the cold threatened to overwhelm us. Now it was fresh again.

"If that is the case, I recommend we go straight north," I said. "We can intersect the Snake in its third reach. My people"—*by which I meant the Benjamites*—"will have boats on the river, and they can ferry us to safety."

We lost another horse the first day, and we endured a night of sleet and freezing rain huddled together in a thicket. The morning after, we stumbled upon a site where a portion of our forces had been cornered and cut to pieces. Magpies without number and ravens flew up as we approached. Wolves quarreled over the carcasses. I counted seventy-eight dead, but, given the state of the corpses, that was an estimate at best. Whether individual bodies were Kr or Benjamite or Kuhlan was anybody's guess. There were many dead horses as well. We saw many appalling things – exposed rib cages and empty eye sockets, jaws severed and licked clean. I saw the arm of a man dangling from a bitch wolf's muzzle as it trotted out of our path, the hand trailing on the ground. My companions seemed as dismayed as I, and they made no praise of their wolf brothers for a while.

"Should we do something?" I asked Riik. "Conduct a ceremony for the dead?"

He shook his head. "A man should leave no trace," he replied. "Not even a footprint." The others nodded. It was apparently part of their code, a male principle of life, to recognize the transitory nature of existence—and to exult in it, not lament it. I did not understand the nuances of their feelings, but that night they sang several of their strange Kuhlan songs, using rich bass harmonies that we do not have in Israel. I knew they were grieving for their comrades.

We endured these hardships and arrived, after two more days of travel, at the canyon of the Snake. There we were able to signal a passing patrol vessel and so were saved to fight another day.

III

Ceremonies for the fallen and cremations of the dead, as more wounded succumbed to their injuries, filled the days and nights with smoke and lamentation. The People were familiar with grief and confronted it with dignity. Nevertheless, I learned to dread the peculiar, haunting harmonies of their songs to honor the fallen. They burned sage and hemp and other aromatic herbs for incense, and the scent of their grieving was bitter in the nostrils.

In the aftermath of their humiliation, the People gathered at the junction of the Snake and Clearwater, their traditional wintering site, to bind up their wounds and take stock of the situation. We Israelites followed along, equally subdued and nursing our wounds and mourning our own dead. Colonel Harlech had taken three hundred men into the battle and lost half of them. The Kuhlans had suffered proportionately, and they had lost a village of the Antelope People besides. It was difficult to estimate the effects of all this on them. The despised Kr had not merely surprised them with their strength; they had nearly annihilated the largest force the People had put in the field for generations.

We Israelites held our own ceremonies and grieved in our own way. For ourselves, it was not so much the defeat itself that was hard to assimilate, but rather its implications for our prospects. The Benjamites had been stranded far from home for over a year, and many began to lose hope that they would ever see Israel again.

The enemy, in the meantime, showed themselves boldly on the ridges above the Snake. Judging by the smoke of their campfires, the Kr were present in strength a few miles west of the junction, on the south side of the river. The People's patrols, moreover, were unable to cross over and penetrate the screen of enemy horsemen. In fact, very few patrols sent over to the south side came back at all. This turn of events was wholly beyond the capacity of the Kuhlans to absorb. The People had never abandoned any territory before, and they were accustomed to seeing their foes cringe in terror.

As I recovered, I took an interest in emerging events, which were unprecedented in Kuhlan history. I was determined to glean as much knowledge of Kuhlan weaknesses as possible, for future reference. The legend of Kuhlan invincibility had been broken, and right before my eyes. If I could survive and return to Israel with the tale, the value of this knowledge would more than compensate for my pain in acquiring it.

But I was not the only one seeking knowledge. Colonel Harlech came to visit me frequently as I recovered, to learn as much as possible from my experience of the fighting at the Tucannon. He questioned me also about the battles at Elion and Beersheba Wells, in which I had participated the year before. I came to realize that both the Harlech and the People had arrived at the same conclusion as I: the Kr had found a leader and were now both unpredictable and infinitely more formidable than ever before.

On several occasions, the Colonel took me to councils and to sweat lodges where the recent defeat was minutely reviewed and analyzed. The insights of the People's war leaders were remarkably candid. The People knew they had been over-confident. What to do now, however, eluded them. It was hotly asserted that the losses must be avenged immediately, lest the Kr be emboldened; it was counter-asserted that winter was not the time. The People avoided fighting in the winter for good reason, because the horses were weak, and because as many warriors died of exposure as from enemy action. But the cold, it was asserted, was equally hard on the enemy, so what was gained by waiting? The point was to avenge the loss; the point was to strike before the enemy grew even stronger; the point was to husband the strength of the People so that the nation would survive. The People were divided and did not know what to do.

I sat in the midst of these discussions, and I was able to walk freely and without escort the length and breadth of an encampment that spread for miles along the bench above the junction of the Snake and Clearwater Rivers. Riik and the others who had been snowbound with me had befriended me, and they were my surety and sponsors wherever I went. To my amazement, I was no longer an outsider—either among the Benjamites or the People. To the latter, I was the Israelite who had fought with the People and who fought *like* one of the People. It was as if I had passed some initiation rite and held rank among them.

By these means, I obtained a much closer view of Kuhlan society, and the curiosity that those glimpses aroused drew me back to health faster than any unguent or salve. The women of the People, including the Grandmothers of all the bands, were close at hand. I heard them speak and exhort the warriors and evoke their own strange powers. I listened avidly. Though I continued to marvel that this warlike society could be ruled by women, I no longer underestimated them or doubted their sagacity. I was struck also by their strict adherence to their law, which in many of its features indeed resembled the Law of St. Supplicee. Their obsession with cleanliness was very like our own, as was their dread of contamination. Except in regard to the status of the sexes, I saw many likenesses.

But the Law was not the heart of their life. I had come to see that Kuhlan society was the most sex-obsessed of any that ever existed. The very principle and foundation of female rule was sex—or rather the withholding of sexual favors and parceling them out, so to speak, as rewards. This realization came to me in discussion with Colonel Harlech, who had spent his earliest years in the Kuhlan lands and had been raised according to their customs prior to receiving an Israelite education. Hearing Zachariah ben Harlech describe his childhood revealed to me that the Kuhlan way of rearing their male children was fundamental to the whole society. While with his mother, Zachariah had been showered with affection and had all of his needs instantly gratified. In this entirely female circle, all attention had been bent to serving his whims and desires; he had been coddled and spoiled and bathed in affection by all the people significant to him. Zachariah admitted when pressed that nothing in life since then had quite come up to the mark. Male children, he explained, remain with their mothers in the women's camp until seven years of age, and then they are separated from this blissful existence and turned over to the men to be trained as warriors.

It was fiendishly clever when you considered it: to experience that impressionable period of infancy and early childhood in a soft female embrace and to be reared thereafter by men, taught a severe warrior code, and held to the harshest standards—while always longing to return to the warm bosom of the mother. It was that feeling, that need, that made these formidable men docile and obedient to the women. "I see that your women exploit the principle of nostalgia," I observed to Zachariah. "You all remember your time with your mothers as the best time, and you long for that lost treasure your whole life."

"And your childhood was different from this?" he asked.

"Don't you see, the women manipulate this longing for lost happiness in order to rule you. It is the basis of their control. They give you glimpses of it, make promises to return you to that bliss, to that suckling's paradise."

The Colonel did not dispute my point, though he regarded me quizzically.

I had fewer insights into the ways the women were educated. Women's lives seemed based on the principles of restraint, responsibility, and discipline. The values associated with being female had to do with permanence, with the life of the community across many generations. Hence, the dominance of their perspective.

It appeared that the principle of men's lives, notwithstanding their lesser status, was self-indulgence, passion, and excess. Gradually I realized that this was no contradiction. To be male was to be associated with the transitory and the peripheral. Men *could* indulge themselves in many ways, not because they were privileged, but because they were less iessential to the life of the community. Women formed the center and men the circumference of the Circle. Values and actions appropriate for males were inappropriate for women, and vice versa. I never had the system perfectly in mind in all its details, but I felt confident I had the gist of it. I saw Riik soon after our return and ventured to ask him what exactly the People worship in the moon.

"You are mistaken," he replied. "We worship nothing. We despise all superstition."

His protests notwithstanding, the People seemed to have an elaborate mythology based on the moon. Its shapes and cycles provided, as near as I could tell, an image of change coupled with the idea of continuity. That was the chief spiritual meaning derived from the moon's sacred cycle. The People discerned in the figure of the moon permanence in the midst of flux, or perhaps flux as a feature of permanence, and they elevated that insight into a principle of life. The circle, also imaged by the moon in its full phase, represented perfection, wholeness, and maturity—and the whole life of the community. The other phases bespoke change, a continual waxing or waning, like the changes of a man's life. How they also derived the period of wolf-like madness from the phase of the full moon eluded me. The new moon was associated with mystery and dread and with secrets of their lore that I never penetrated.

"Kuhlan marriage is a sham, is it not?" I demanded of Zachariah in one of our conversations. "It is just a temporary liaison to reward a warrior for obedience. And after a short time, both may form similar liaisons with others, and this goes on, serially, for life."

"Only with the Grandmothers' permission," Zachariah replied. His mild acquiescence in these customs baffled and irritated me. I could not imagine why a man of his intelligence was not repulsed by them.

"Nothing the People think or do seems to please you, Captain," he remarked.

"I can never forget what I learned as a child," I said. "The People crossed the river in my great-grandfather's day. My great-grandfather and great-grandmother, and all their servants save one, were butchered at Tirzah, our stronghold, and all our buildings and possessions were put to the torch. You are correct, Colonel; they cannot please me!"

Colonel Harlech listened thoughtfully to what I had to say and then remarked: "The question you should ask yourself is not why the People cross the Jordan and attack Israel, but why they *do not*. If you can understand that, you will understand a great deal!"

Abruptly, he left me to contemplate his riddle.

IV

"The People," Colonel Harlech announced at a staff meeting of the Esdralon Guards, "are eager for a showdown with the Kr. And that immediately."

"Is that wise?" Major Moriah voiced the question that many of us felt. It was late December. We had had two weeks of bitter cold and snow.

"They see no other option but to have the test of strength right here – before spring. The young men are itching to fight—as one would expect. But even the wisest heads among the war leaders are talking of putting their whole male population across the river within a few weeks."

Major Moriah voiced the obvious objection. "That would be stupid," he said. "A reckless plan! This is not what the People do best." He meant that staging stand-up battles was not the strong point of Kuhlan warfare. The People excelled at small unit tactics, slash and burn, hit and run. Man for man, the People were, in our estimation as well as their own, the most formidable warriors on earth. Their mass attack on the Tucannon, however, had impressed no one, certainly not the Kr. Even the People acknowledged that the discipline of the Esdralon Guards had saved them from annihilation.

"It's too risky," Captain Amasa said. "The Kr will be able to observe our crossing. They'll know everything about our strength, and we'll know nothing about theirs. They will retain the initiative and fight only if they have the advantage."

"True. And we know neither the strength of the Kr nor their dispositions," Major Moriah added.

The People had been unable to scout into the interior to find where the Kr strength lay. With that uncertainty alone, they were at a terrible disadvantage. And Amasa was right; the Kr would see us deploying before them and then make their decisions based on full knowledge of our strength. I could imagine the People throwing a force across the Snake only to see the Kr retreat and avoid battle. Indeed, the Kr would do well to lure our combined forces inland, away from the juncture, and then flank or assail us with overwhelming numbers, just as they had on the Tucannon. I pointed this out to the others.

Colonel Harlech nodded. "This is all very uncharacteristic of the People. They've been unsettled by their defeat. Even the elders are lining up in favor of a quick response. I fear their passions are leading them."

"They want revenge," Moriah said.

"And they fear to leave the territory of the Antelope band in the hands of the Kr even for a season," Colonel Harlech said. "They are ashamed to have abandoned it.

"Nonsense!" Moriah said. "Whoever wins in the long run will own the land."

"That is my thought also," Colonel Harlech said frowning. "The Grandmothers have not yet spoken."

We mulled over our estimates of Kr strength and intentions, as we had many times before. "In the absence of direct observation," I remarked, "the land can sometimes reveal the enemy's dispositions."

"So?" the Colonel said. "What are you suggesting?"

I pointed to a map. "We fought the Kr here, north of Elion, in May. We saw only warrior camps, just like those we encountered last month on the Tucannon. No large flocks and herds of the savages were present at either place—though I must assume that, had we penetrated clear to Elion, we would have found them. The Kr probably fielded five thousand warriors against Israel, and at least as many against the People. That gives us an estimate of their strength. But where is their sustenance?" I tapped the map. "Where are the flocks of the Kr? Where are their families? The Kr do not live on grass."

Colonel Harlech came up beside me and scrutinized the map. "I see your point. In this weather, they would be sheltering in valleys with abundant grazing. They were around Elion, you say, in late spring? Then they would need fresh grass to winter on. We fought them here, on the Tucannon, a hundred and twenty miles to the northeast." He moved his finger across the map. "Their flocks and herds have to be here, then, on the lower Tucannon, the Touchet, or in the Walla Walla valley. Perhaps in all three places. I see what you are driving at."

"The People have your fleet which can transport them across the Snake at any point they choose. Why smash our heads against the Kr here, near the junction, where they are waiting for us? The People could just as easily cross the Snake at some point far in their rear and fall on their flocks and herds."

"And destroy their sustenance," Amasa said.

"*That's* what the People do best!" Moriah added, exulting. "Destroy the nests! This strategy is made for them. When they see what *they* must do, we will have the task of ferrying them over the Snake again. I begin to think we will make ourselves valuable to them at last."

The discussion of these possibilities rose to a clamor, but Colonel Harlech remained silent, pulling his beard and frowning. I was proud of my strategy and afraid the Colonel had detected some flaw in it. At last he held up his hand, and said to me, "Come."

"What's wrong?" I asked.

"Nothing is wrong," he said. "We're going to see the Grandmothers."

By one of the greatest ironies of my life, then, it was my plan that was chosen by the People to work their revenge upon the newly formidable Kr. It was a strange birthday present as well, for I passed my twenty-first birthday in a smoky lodge of Israel's ancient foes, working out the details of their salvation. There were many matters to work out, problems to solve, supplies and equipment to gather. We had to discover some means of slipping the fleet down-river past the Kr without arousing their attention, and we had to arrange a precise rendezvous of warrior horsemen with a Benjamite fleet. We decided—I say *we* because I was admitted thereafter into the highest councils of the People, with Grandmothers and Eagles and all—to stage a large raid directly across the Snake a hundred miles east of the junction of the Clearwater.

There were other matters of logistics that appeared insuperable. The Benjamites were ragged and ill equipped for a winter campaign. The People themselves, habitually opposed to winter campaigns, were short of items of gear and articles of clothing that the fall trade with the Harlech normally supplied.

I had another bright idea that nearly cost me the friendship of Colonel Harlech. "This is easy to solve," I said, full of enthusiasm for my plan. "We'll persuade the People to drive a sizeable herd of cattle down to Old Pasco, trade them to the Judeans, and have Tephlin Glanz outfit our expedition for us!" This seemed wonderfully simple to me. "I could arrange a truce so we can trade, and perhaps arrange also for Judah to attack the Kr in their front at the same time we strike them here!"

"I am sure you could, Captain Glanz." The slow and calculating manner in which Colonel Harlech replied filled my veins with ice and told me I had blundered badly. The Colonel turned a hard, penetrating gaze on me and said nothing further. I saw that this idea thrown out thoughtlessly by me had instantly cost me his trust.

Captain Amasa came to my rescue with an explanation: "The Colonel, you see, cannot give up the basis of Harlech wealth in exchange for an advantage in this campaign—even a significant one. That's what the war with Judah is about, preserving our trade with the People."

By this point I was perversely enamored with my plan. "But the Harlech have already *lost* that monopoly in battle. Is that fact invisible to everyone? Tephlin Glanz's forces occupy your homeland. You are stranded here and can conduct trade with no one."

"But it is we who have the relationship with the People; with that, we can eventually rebuild the trade."

"Ah," I said, "I see you base your hopes on the chance that the Messiahists will conquer Judah. Well, they may. But then you will have a much more powerful foe than my father's faction to contend with. The victors will rule a united, even if a subdued Israel. Do you think the Messiahists—or whoever wins the civil war – will be less interested than my father in this trade with the uncovenanted peoples?"

"No," he conceded. "I suppose not. I had thought no further than Tephlin Glanz's fall. But that event, as you suggest, might not be the simple blessing it has seemed to me."

"Far from it! The whole of Israel shares this secret now. Whoever wins the religious war will insist on a share of the Kuhlan trade."

"But you can see how the Colonel cannot throw away the advantage he has in the monopoly. It is, in a sense, his heritage, as well as the foundation of Harlech prosperity."

"My dear Amasa," I countered, "the monopoly is dead. The rest of Israel will share in the trade with the People and with the Kr, or there will be no trade at all. That water is out of the jar—and the jar is smashed." Amasa regarded me stubbornly so I added: "My concern is that if we do not repel the Kr and chase them back over their wretched mountains, there will be no Israel in a few years."

"But the monopoly is the chief issue of the war," he insisted.

"All the more reason to make it the foundation of a peace."

V

Colonel Harlech eventually acquiesced in my plan. The logic of the situation was both stark and compelling. The Kr had to be expelled or there would be no Israelites to quarrel among themselves over trade advantages. Moreover, I reflected, if the Kr continued to wax in strength and found a way to cross great rivers, there would soon be no proud and disdainful People on the plateau of Moses. Therefore, the Kr had to be crushed – annihilated if possible – before they grew too numerous. The winter campaign that I had proposed appeared to offer the best chance of delivering a lethal blow to the enemy with the forces at hand. Moreover, it appeared to involve fewer risks to the People and to Benjamin than any other course of action. But to launch that attack, we needed to refit. Accordingly, I wrote a note to Simon ben Gurion.

Sir,

I have as you know been delayed by unforeseen events in carrying out my mission in Naphtali. In the meantime, conditions have arisen where I could make it possible for Judah to trade directly with the Kuhlans, and to do so immediately. And, if a truce can be struck, to trade with that portion of Benjamin now exiled in the Kuhlan lands. These matters are urgent and require immediate attention, as they pertain to the joint struggle against the Kr, our common enemy.

Captain Jonathan Amasa, the bearer of this note, is authorized. . . etc...

I handed it to Colonel Harlech, who was still far from warm in his attitude toward me. "Here," I said, "this is the gist of what must be said. Re-write it in your own hand, and I'll sign."

"Why?" he asked.

"So you will know there is no coded message in what I send."

"I had thought you would go in person to negotiate this."

"No. Captain Amasa or any officer you trust can do it as well or better than I. I have no wish to see Glanz or Ben Gurion; nor do I wish to be seen as their instrument by anyone here. It is not for them that I do this."

"But for Israel," he said, smiling faintly.

"I warned you when we met that I was no renegade."

We crossed the Snake again in the coldest spell of January, preferring dry cold or even snow to soaking rain, which kills men and horses alike. The Esdralon Guards formed a small column, perhaps two hundred and fifty men – half of the survivors of the Legion. Our combined force traveled very fast this time, and we found the flocks and villages of the Kr where we expected them. We fell on them by surprise and gave no quarter. We killed men and women and children alike, and then tried vainly to set fire to the prairie, to slay their flocks and destroy their means of subsistence.

The main body of Kr warriors hurried from the east to rescue their families and flocks, but the fleet had in the meantime brought another thousand fighters over the Snake. The People's signaling system allowed us to unite our forces, and we ambushed a large body of them before they had located our strength. After that, the Kr came at us ferociously but in a disorganized, piecemeal fashion, never managing to concentrate their forces. Still, it was touch and go; the Kr were determined and formidable. We fought a series of vicious battles with them on and around the lower Tucannon. The Second Battle of the Tucannon, as we Israelites called these several encounters, was collectively the largest conflict in which the Kuhlans had been engaged for generations. In none of the fighting, however, did the Kr exhibit anything like the resolution or intelligence of my first two encounters with them. Thus, even with fewer numbers than they, we beat them handily.

"I think their leader must be dead," I remarked to Colonel Harlech after a hard-fought victory.

"If so, then all this may have been worthwhile," he replied.

After their defeat, the Kr scattered, and the fighting disintegrated into small pursuits and counter-pursuits, ambushes and pitiless slaughter. The People took no prisoners and spared nothing belonging to the enemy. I saw sights I could scarcely credit as belonging to human nature: heroism and selfless sacrifice and acts of unbelievable cruelty. The events of this campaign demolished my previous sense of the boundaries of human will and capacities, but gave me a vivid experience of its depths. I understood that we could take no captives. I knew what revenge was. I had, in fact, motives of my own for revenge. But it seemed that my comrades, Benjamite and Kuhlan alike, had reached a place where fear had become a more potent motive than vengeance. Unfortunately for themselves, the Kr had inspired a terror in us that no amount of blood could slake or appease. The campaign schooled me in the kind of war two nations wage when survival is at stake. It was not that I was moved to compassion by what I saw. It was the thought that these sights were a premonition of things to come in Israel.

But perhaps I was moved in ways I cannot analyze. In any case, a month into the campaign, I suddenly had had enough. The Kr were broken, their flocks and herds destroyed, their little ones dashed against the stones. I gathered my small contingent of Esdralon Guards about me, along with a few of the People—Riik among them—who had accompanied me, and announced that I was retiring from the field.

"There is still much to be done," Riik protested. "No Kr must be left alive north of the Blue Mountains, or we will have all this to do over again."

"You will have to do it without me."

He lowered his eyes and held his hands in the air, saying nothing, for the People respect the decisions of free men.

"Why is it that the People torment the women and the little ones?" I asked Riik. "Why not just destroy them quickly? Why torture them and desecrate their bodies?"

"To discourage the souls of our enemies," he explained. "We have no wish for enemies such as these to return and plague us. Especially these! We leave them in dread of encountering the People again, in this life or another." Riik was a thoughtful man; he saw I was not satisfied with his answer. "In a way, it is a mercy," he explained. "One death, however hard, is better than many deaths. Does it trouble you much?"

"Not as much as what we do."

Riik and I talked briefly of my reasons before we parted, and he did not rebuke me. "You conceived of the victory and made it possible," Riik said in parting. "It is for others to wring the last drop of blood from it. Go in peace."

The Second Battle of the Tucannon was a great victory, one that would be talked about in the lodges of the People for generations. If Judah had exerted itself as agreed in Engedi, then the threat of the Kr was likely extinguished for a generation. That was something, to be sure. The People called the battle the Stinking Meadows because of the carcasses of slaughtered men and animals that were its aftermath. It seemed to me a better name than ours for what we had done. Of the Esdralon Guards who had fought, many came away crippled in mind or body. No one escaped unscathed. I had a slash across my thigh and bruises and cuts on my arms and left shoulder and lost three horses under me. None of my wounds was deep, however, and they say that young men heal quickly. The mind and memory, however, take longer to mend, and the scar tissue there is easily torn and attaches unpredictably to other things, so that for a time, to move in one's mind is painful. One prefers, therefore, not to move or think at all.

The Guards camp at the confluence of the Snake and Clearwater had been converted into a hospital, and help was needed tending the wounded. Captain Amasa and I found a role in organizing the relatively able-bodied to care for the sick and wounded, and we proved reasonably efficient at it. Surprisingly, a number of severely wounded warriors of the People had been allowed to survive and brought back across the river, and they also sought our assistance – surgery and other forms of medicine not being a high art among them. *Let him who is to die, die quickly* was their usual view. But after their extraordinary losses in the war, the People seemed a little less ruthless with their own kind. "They are saving the maimed young men for breeding purposes," Amasa remarked as he applied a poultice to a festering wound. "The People waste nothing."

"How wise of them," I said.

Chapter 12: Dark, But Comely

I

Scarcely a week after our return to the Kuhlan shore, three events of significance in my life occurred in rapid succession. It was as if separate stones had dropped into a pond, and the disturbance of their impacts roiled through me over and over, as ripples mingle and connect and interfere with each other. Their circles widen and return, widen and return, and still I await the return of quietude.

First was the rescue of a Benjamite woman, wrested from her captors by a troop of Guardsmen. She had been taken by the Kr two years previously from a village below Esdralon and forced to serve and be a wife to them. Proud of his prize, the officer who delivered her to the hospital gave a dramatic account of her rescue: "I might have ridden her down myself—I swear, dressed like a Kr, she looked just like one. But I saw her swing a war club against one of their men. Her own man, as it turned out. She screamed *Benjamite!* at me, and I veered aside. In a moment, we had run down the rest of them, and I had difficulty restraining my men. But here she is. No doubt she has a story to tell."

The woman had not spoken to tell that story in three days. She was emaciated and deeply distraught; her rescuers had thought her demented. Captain Amasa took her under his care and cleaned her up. For several days more she huddled quietly in his tent, rocking and keening, so that we, too, feared her wits were shattered. But in a few more days, she was up and about, tending the wounded.

The second event was the discovery of a encampment in which a half-dozen of the enemy lay dead but unmarked in and around their filthy shelters. Curious, two warriors of the People dismounted and actually examined the bodies—as a preliminary, I suppose, to their usual desecrations. To their surprise, they found rashes covering the bodies like a smear of tar, visible even days after death when the bodies were swollen and black. No doubt their own fatigue and the numbing effects of recent events had put their caution to sleep. But in this way, from a single mistake, the fever spread to the People and then to Benjamin as well.

It spread quickly. Within a week, dozens of our men had contracted the disease. The Grandmothers immediately isolated our forces on the south side of the Snake and forbade their return until the epidemic had run its course. Military operations ceased, and our troops and the warriors of the People withdrew and went into camps near the river, where they could be supplied. In the meantime, the Kr seemed to have vanished. Our men, Kuhlan and Benjamite alike, kept a careful distance from one another and from those who ferried goods over to them. But it was too late. The fever swept through our combined forces like fire through dry brush.

Several women of the People who were expert in healing went over to care for the men. They immediately sent back a message: *Typhus.* I had not heard of the disease, but the Kuhlans knew it and understood that it was spread by body lice and fleas. We set about the most rigorous cleaning of our bodies and clothing and fumigating the tents and blankets and gear. We burned everything that could not be cleaned.

We felt pity for our comrades who were stranded on the other side of the river, but there was nothing to be done about them. It was imperative that the typhus not spread. Boats plied the river back and forth with supplies and messages, which the boatmen left on the shore. All contact was strictly prohibited. The Kr could have risen up and destroyed us at this point, but they seemed to be similarly ravaged by the disease and offered us no threat. I presume they must have melted away, just as our ranks melted and died in their fetid camps.

It was a relief to me to have the hospital camp to absorb my attention. I went about my tasks grateful for the distraction. Eventually, I learned a number of minor surgical procedures and techniques for stanching blood. As I learned more and observed how much common sense and skill can alleviate suffering, I began to respect this calling even above a warrior's craft.

Carmina—the Benjamite woman who had been rescued from the Kr—proved to have remarkable gifts in this regard, and in ways that defy explanation. As soon as she awoke from her trance and began to recover from her injuries, she threw herself into serving her rescuers, as she called us, with a touching devotion. Fragile though she was, she drove herself unsparingly. Perhaps it was merely seeing a woman of our own nation that made the soldiers respond to her ministrations with such enthusiasm. But Carmina had extraordinary powers to soothe and to lift their spirits and to heal that I cannot explain. On more than one occasion, I have seen her staunch the flow of blood in a man who was unconscious and unaware of her presence.

One day when I saw her leaning on a tent pole, pale and perspiring, I rebuked her mildly. "You cannot carry on this way," I said. "You overreach your strength. If you continue, you will be back on a litter with the wounded and be no help to us at all."

"Never!" she retorted with surprising vehemence. "I will never be a burden to these men, these heroes. I will kill myself first."

"I meant only that you make yourself less effective by not conserving your strength." I found it difficult to converse with her; she seemed always to place too much significance on my words.

"Serve them I will," she said. "Even if it kills me. Nothing is too good for them!"

Then there was Vitoria, the third event. *How can I begin to explain Vitoria?*

Vitoria was full of contradictions. She was as tall as myself and athletic. I have tried her strength, both seriously and in play, and found that she had the quickness and leverage of a male opponent. And yet she was the most beautiful woman I ever met. Her hands and wrists had fine long bones, and her skin had the delicacy and softness of a noblewoman. Fleet of foot, a fair shot with a bow, and a superb horsewoman, she seemed, in her barbarian regalia, the very image of the Moon goddess which the Kuhlans revere. In repose, resting her weight on one leg, her hip and pelvis at a relaxed and graceful angle, she was a figure for a sculptor. This pose, which emphasized her long legs and female hips, is deeply etched in my memory.

Vitoria was all that and more, and I never detected any hardness of character in her – at least not until the end. Aquiline in feature, with a proud erect face and the alert eyes of a hawk, she was, on further acquaintance, possessed of the most penetrating blue eyes that I have ever seen. Her eyes changed mysteriously with her mood and with the light. They were never still, and they missed nothing. Her hair was honey-colored with lighter golden streaks. For a time, I was content to gaze wordlessly at her, losing myself in her. She was beautiful as a goddess. And as wise.

No, it is I who am full of contradictions, not Vitoria. Vitoria was what she was, unchanging, to the end.

But how shall I begin to explain her?

Perhaps I should blame my friend Amasa for the care he devoted to the Benjamite woman. The pains he took in nursing this unfortunate creature worked insidiously on me, rekindling a desire for the ordinary decencies of life that were otherwise foreign to this place. Without his example, I believe I might have descended to a purely brute existence. But Amasa's display of patience and compassion made me remember myself as a man.

Early in March, Colonel Harlech decided that he must join the portion of his command quarantined on the south side of the Snake. It was a courageous but possibly suicidal decision. "It's the inactivity in camp that kills a man," Colonel Harlech said to me over my protests. I disapproved of the risk he was taking because he could not, by his own sacrifice, diminish the threat to his men. "I'll go over and stir up the men. Get them out soldiering again, chasing down any Kr who may still be about. This fever will pass in no time." The fever had felled a quarter of the Guards who had been campaigning south of the Snake. We both knew it would not pass away quickly. His eyes were tired and expressionless as he spoke, and it was clear that he entertained no illusions about his prospects.

Moved by a sudden curiosity, I asked, "Is it your Israelite training or your up-bringing by the People that makes you sacrifice yourself this way?"

"I'll let you worry about that, Captain," he said. "In the meantime, in my absence, I want you to share authority with Captain Amasa. Informally, I mean. Amasa is a good officer and an even better man, but he is not ready for independent command. Not in these circumstances. You understand?"

I was pleased at his confidence in me. It seemed that the Colonel and I had regained something of our former footing of trust and confidence. "Captain Amasa is my friend," I said. "We work well together."

"See that you do."

A few days later, however, Jonathan Amasa confronted me as I stepped from the main hospital tent; his face was flushed and contorted and he appeared more angry than I had ever seen him. "So, you keep always aloof from us," he said accusingly. "In every act, you find a way to mark your differences from us, from ordinary men. You vaunt your sacred calling, as you would have us believe."

"What are you talking about?" I asked. I had been this man's comrade and companion in nearly every conceivable way for the past six months.

"But in *this* thing you err—you overstep. And your arrogance has brought pain to someone dear to me."

"What do you mean?" I rejoined. I asked myself *whom have I injured?* But I could think of nothing that could explain his anger.

"Carmina, of course!" he exclaimed. "As if you didn't know. I hope for our friendship's sake that you honor a vow, and this aversion is not just disdain." He acted as if my behavior had taken him past the limits he could bear.

"*What are you talking about?*" I came within a hair's breadth of actually seizing him by the shoulders and shaking him.

"Carmina," he said again, stubbornly, as if that were sufficient explanation. Then with great indignation, "*Carmina!*"

"Ah, Carmina," I said, feigning understanding to buy some time. I needed to draw him out, but carefully. I had never seen him so agitated, not even when the demented Kuhlan youth had crept into our camp and murdered one of our men. It crossed my mind again that my friend had been in the Kuhlan lands too long. I had sensed that his sympathies were engaged with the rescued Benjamite woman, but other feelings had obviously become attached to her as well. Busy with other duties, I had not noticed. "Perhaps we misunderstand one another," I said. "I have, to my knowledge, treated her always with respect."

"You know what I mean," he said, avoiding my glance. "You *know*!"

"No, my friend, I do not." Feeling a sudden alarm for his sanity, I drew him aside, mindful of the glances already fixing upon us. "Walk apart and tell me of this thing. It pains me if I have heedlessly given offense." Amasa followed, still agitated but, if I read him correctly, he was already partly mollified. Much of the aggression had flowed out of him. *Soft words turn away wrath.*

"Is it true, then, that you have taken a vow?"

"What kind of vow?" His question threw me into a turmoil, as I recalled Justin and Rehab Gill's suspicions about me.

"Of celibacy!" he retorted, as if he could scarcely bear my obtuseness.

"Ah-h," I replied non-committally. I began to fear I understood his sense of grievance. I knew little about the Benjamite woman, except that she had suffered greatly. Her husband and family had been killed in the raid in which she had been captured. The Kr had kept her for some time and abused her with their peculiar skill. I imagined she must have suffered unspeakable things at their hands. I had heard the story that, as she was being rescued, she had killed the man who used her as a concubine. When she first came to us, she had been entirely broken in spirit, as one who would likely wither and die if she did not take her own life first. But that had passed.

"She believes you hold her in contempt," Amasa said, "and as she regards you so highly, she can scarcely bear your scorn. I left her weeping just now."

"St. Supplicee!" I exclaimed, appalled at his words. "She mistakes me entirely." I praised Amasa for his care of her and for his concern for her welfare. I saw what was bothering him. A strange scruple, perhaps, but we were in the Kuhlan lands, a place like no other on earth. "Carmina is a gifted healer," I said. "And recently, as she has recovered her spirits, she has made herself a comfort to the men, generously, thinking nothing of herself." He nodded vigorously. "You object that I have not—gone with her – not responded to her, as others have?"

He nodded again, but now he seemed embarrassed, as if he had acquired another perspective on his grievance. "We are all a year away from Esdralon," he said. "We have had no women. Carmina has been a comrade. . . ."

"Carmina is truly a comrade," I said. "There is none among us more devoted. She is a soldier, like ourselves. Trust me that I make no judgment of her. What she does is a kindness. I see that."

We walked a while in silence and then Amasa seized my arm. "When she was a captive and had a child in her belly, a Kr child, Carmina made up her mind to die rather than bear an enemy of Israel. She pierced her own womb, intending to kill herself. She ended the pregnancy, but lived – and now she is barren. The Kr would have killed her had they suspected any of this. Because of it, she feels useless as a woman, except for this one thing. She insisted that she be of service to us; she begged to be of service." His expression begged me to understand.

What times we live in! I had not heard this part of her story. I put a hand on his shoulder. "Carmina has suffered more than any of us. It is good she can find herself again by being useful. But this is here, my friend, in the Kuhlan lands. This is not Israel. I suppose I have been mindful of the time when we return."

He pulled up abruptly and stared at me. I suspected that, until this moment, he had lost the ability to imagine returning to Israel.

"Israel may not understand what is clear to us here – how this does not touch her honor, but is her honor. She recovers her dignity by being a comrade to us. We know she is not a comfort woman. But at home. . . ."

We stood a while in the twilight. "Forgive me," he said at last. "I have been a fool."

"You have been her friend," I said. "You nursed her back to health and now you protect her."

The next day Amasa appeared as excited as the day before, but this time in a joyful mood. "Carmina has agreed to be my wife!" he exclaimed. "We want you to marry us. Today!"

"Marry!" I exclaimed. "You cannot – *I* cannot do this." My objections were out before I had time to think. I had spoken before I had even formulated a reason for objecting. Nevertheless, I counseled delay; I told him he must wait, that they must have a period of reflection and preparation before taking such a step. "This is not done on a whim," I admonished him. "Marriage is. . . . " I saw instantly that he was angry and hurt again. This time I did reach out and seize him by the shoulders. I thought quickly through my objections, surprised at the emotions I found there. Finally, I had the presence of mind to exclaim, "My friend, it is not for your sake that I ask you to wait."

Amasa puzzled a moment and then was instantly mollified. I had not impugned his beloved's honor, but had rather sought to protect it. He was happy again. He embraced me. "You are concerned I will change? I see. I tell you I will not; I am determined to do this. How long a wait?

I suggested the usual three months, but he would not hear of it. "Never!" he said. "We have waited too long already!"

"You will want your commander's permission," I said. "You dare not marry without the commander's blessing."

"I am in charge here," Amasa said, with unusual force. "As commander, I give myself permission. I ask only for your blessing as a friend. Marry us!"

There was no way I could resist him; he was determined. "Give us time, then," I said, "to organize a proper celebration. Your comrades will insist. *I* insist! How will we find gifts for the pair of you overnight?"

"I care nothing for gifts. Marry us *now*!"

"Not until we can set you up properly as a household. We are Israelites, after all!"

He was finally persuaded to see reason, and we set a day a week hence.

II

Amasa's comrades in the Guards constructed an arbor of apple branches and boughs of fir for the ceremony. The branches were not yet leafed out or in bloom, but were becoming tinged with green as the buds swelled. We wove such other greenery as we could find into the arbor and decorated the camp as best we could. Green is the color of life and fertility and especially of brides; no wedding is complete without it. We arranged a bench under the arbor for the couple and one for myself, to preside over the ceremony. Israelite weddings are informal affairs and consist mostly of harangues to the bride and groom about the responsibilities they are about to assume. The couple merely speak their vows, and the crowd sitting or standing about the arbor witness it. It was simple. All I had to do was compose an appropriate speech.

In the midst of these preparations, however, we were interrupted by a delegation from the People. It was unusual to be visited at all by the People, who ordinarily kept as aloof from us as if we inhabited separate worlds. Odder still, this group was comprised of both men and women. An elderly woman, obviously a Sister, greeted us imperiously. She carried a staff entwined with reeds. After a few prefatory remarks she announced: "No couple may join together unless the man be a husbandman." Our soldiers gathered close around, unable to understand her words but disturbed by her tone. I too recoiled at this intrusion, for I was not ready to allow Kuhlans to interfere in any of our affairs. But I saw Riik in the crowd grinning broadly and nodding, as if to say, *this is a good thing, be patient.* Then I saw Woad and Quarry and others who had befriended me. I held up my hand and translated the words of the Sister. The crowd of Israelites grew silent. Without further ceremony, the woman seated herself on the ground and demanded that Amasa be brought before her. I conveyed her request, and Amasa came forward, looking embarrassed and apprehensive. The woman motioned him to seat himself before her, which he did. Then a young woman, tall, with golden hair and a regal manner, took me also by the hand and led me out and indicated that I, too, was to sit before the elder, the Sister, as I presumed her to be.

"My name is Vitoria," she said softly.

My name is Vitoria.

Her beauty was stunning to behold, her eyes like blue gemstones or the sky itself. Her scent, as she leaned close to me, reminded me of the harvest ceremony where I had impersonated Zachariah ben Harlech. It set my heart pounding.

"We have come to honor you and your comrade," Vitoria announced. "You are to be elevated to the rank of husbandmen. Listen attentively to the Sister and speak her words to your comrades as the People wish to acknowledge your achievements." She said much else of a surprisingly complimentary nature, but I could scarcely attend to what she said.

I was enthralled and found it easy to do just as she asked. I seated myself on the ground beside Amasa and waited to hear what the Sister would say, but I could scarcely remove my eyes from this golden-haired goddess. The old woman began to address us very much in the mode of an Israelite marriage ceremony—she had a great deal to say about the duty and responsibilities of our status. Occasionally she paused or seemed to wander. I supposed that her heart must not be in the ceremony, seeing that we were foreigners. Perhaps much of their usual liturgy could not be applied to us. Some fragments of what she said, however, were familiar, as I suppose the wisdom of all peoples in these matters is much the same. Although she made some remarks about Amasa and myself, she spoke on and on, it seemed to me, of the honor and respect due to women. She praised Amasa for his respect for the woman Carmina and for his compassion. I was described as a war chief and a father to my own kind. It seemed odd to be designated a father when I was younger than all the sergeants and officers in the Guards. It was odder still to be praised by one of the women of the People! I feared that these rough soldiers would grow restive and offend her, but the novelty of the situation kept them attentive. I had not realized that the People observed us so closely.

At the end, Vitoria took both our hands and raised us up. "Rejoice," she said, "for the People have marked you as husbandmen, as men who have distinguished yourselves in peace and war. The People honor your new status." We stood and accepted their applause. Our own people kept a puzzled silence. I hardly knew how to accept a compliment from one of their women myself. Vitoria was obviously one of the young Mothers, one of those whose sexual favors are, quite literally, to die for. Before I could speak, Amasa and I were led through the crowd of Kuhlans to receive their congratulations, which seemed genuine enough. We did not know how to behave. I wished mightily that Colonel Harlech were present to interpret the significance of these ceremonies for us.

At that moment, Riik approached me, followed by the handful of Kuhlan warriors in the delegation. "This is from the war leaders," Riik announced. They presented me with a double-edged war axe of polished iron. He himself had been elevated to that rank after the last campaign; I knew this gift was his doing. "For the complete warrior," he said, raising my arm in the air and brandishing the axe in the other, "a weapon fit for his hand." It was a magnificent weapon, balanced and sweet to heft and maneuver.

This time the whole crowd, Kuhlan and Israelite alike, voiced its approval. After a brief ceremony, Riik took white paint and drew a slash across my cheeks and nose. I recognized it as the distinguishing symbol of the war leader—a mark of rank. I felt enormous pride in this decoration. It was an honor from peers—and peers who, in my estimation, were the most distinguished a warrior could have.

I was moved by the gift and the honor it entailed, and my heart swelled with pride. As the implications of Riik's actions sank into me, I inferred that I had been singled out in a way equivalent to winning the Order of St. Gideon in Israel. A high honor indeed! And I had won it even though a despised foreigner. Thus, I had been doubly acknowledged by these proud and haughty people on a single day. "Convey my thanks to the leaders," I stammered in reply. I began to express more of my feelings, but the Sister interrupted me in mid-sentence.

"Let the bride be brought forth and the wedding proceed," she announced. The Sister had the voice and the manner of a drill sergeant and was obeyed by all without question. Riik met my gaze and smiled and nodded. *Enough said*, his manner implied. I nodded my gratitude to him and to the other warriors.

When the bride appeared, surrounded by a crowd of young Kuhlan women, a hush fell over the crowd. Carmina was wearing a fresh robe of white linen, as expected, but instead of wearing a crown of greenery, she was bedecked with precious jewels, silver and gold. While Amasa and I were being elevated to the rank of husbandmen, Carmina had been dressed in incredible splendor. Amasa's eyes were wide as saucers. I thought of the poverty of our own gifts to the couple. All of us Guardsmen were of course destitute; we survived here on the People's charity. The People had apparently bestowed upon Carmina an incredible dowry – albeit of a kind of wealth meaningless to them, as they used no currency. This, too, was remarkable homage to us. But at the same time, I recoiled at the sight of jewelry and precious metals, which they could only have acquired as loot from our slaughtered countrymen.

Carmina had the look of a frightened bird as I took her hand and led her to the arbor. "Wear these jewels in good health and fortune," I whispered. "Better this use, for your dowry, than for any other imaginable."

With the couple seated under the arbor, I began my speech. I had had several talks with Amasa and his bride and knew they planned to adopt orphans and to assist others impoverished by the war. Accordingly, I made these plans known to the audience and thanked our Kuhlan hosts as graciously as I could for providing means for the couple to do good. The wealth bestowed by the People, I emphasized, would save lives and dry many tears. From there I launched into the traditional admonitions on the duties of marriage and parenthood, ending with all the adages I could bring to mind: "The parents' heart should incline unto the children; children should respect and love their parents. This is the beginning of wisdom. Brother and sister, do not be weary of doing what is right."

Jonathan Amasa and Carmina listened patiently, nodding, their eyes shining like children expecting a treat. When I asked, somewhat fearfully, if anyone present had knowledge that would prevent this marriage from proceeding, there was a moment of silence and then a shout of "No! No! Let the marriage proceed." Carmina looked bashfully at Amasa as the crowd roared its approval.

After I finished, the couple said their vows to each other, stressing their bonds of friendship and promising to uphold and support each other in all things. Then I rose and tied Amasa's tunic and Carmina's skirt in a knot. When I turned to present the couple, knotted together both symbolically and in fact, there were many tears running down dark, bearded faces. There was another roar of applause. Amasa was beloved by the men, and Carmina's suffering, as well as her efforts on their behalf, had touched them all.

The Guards had a few musical instruments, so afterwards we sang the traditional wedding songs. It had been months since we had heard Israelite music. Without wine and our own women, however, we hardly knew how to celebrate. Some of the men performed a rough parody of the dances of our country, but everything about the ceremony evoked painful memories of our homeland. The songs especially made my heart ache for Israel. I sought a glimpse of the young Kuhlan woman who had assisted at the ceremony, but she had disappeared. Then, in the midst of the congratulations of the Guards, who clustered about me marveling at Riik's gift of a war axe, I heard a voice in my ear: "When you have had your fill of the celebration, I would speak with you." I turned and saw Vitoria, looking composed and serious. She smiled very formally and departed. My comrades raised their eyebrows and signaled in the usual soldiers' ways their admiration for her beauty and their astonishment that any of her attention should be bestowed upon me.

I lingered at the celebration longer than I intended and then walked some distance along the banks of a stream that flowed by our camp and into the Snake. I was looking for the young woman. I had no idea what to expect and no knowledge of why she wished to speak with me, but I had a great deal of curiosity. It was nearly dusk and turning cool when I found her. To my surprise, she was waiting for me. She motioned for me to accompany her, and we walked silently by the bank. I was struck again by how tall and elegant she seemed in her robe of white linen. Her strides were as long as my own, and I felt an awkwardness, almost a shyness, in her presence. *What in the world does one say to a Kuhlan priestess?* I asked myself. What can she want with me? I realized that, prior to today, I had not spoken directly to a Kuhlan woman in the six months I had been an exile in their land.

Vitoria seemed entirely composed, as if she had no need for speech and perhaps did not desire it. We followed the stream along a canyon whose narrow floor held cultivated fields. Some of the ground had already been plowed and planted. I assumed that the Benjamites had grown their own food here the previous year and were preparing a second crop. *Or—the thought suddenly occurred to me – did the People practice agriculture as well?* We maintained our silence until we came upon a stone bridge and a water mill with a large wheel. I was so surprised at the sight of such a structure in the wilderness that I muttered, almost to myself, "Remarkable! The Harlech have built themselves a mill even here."

"Even *here*?" she said. Her voice was low but not necessarily gentle. "The mill belongs to the People. We built it long ago."

I looked again and saw moss on the stones. "And the fields round about. . . ?"

"They belong to the People also."

This was a new thing. Not just the wretched inhabitants of Moses Town but the People themselves practiced husbandry. As far as I was aware, no one in Israel suspected it.

"At the ceremony today," she asked suddenly; "at the wedding, did you mean what you said?"

I hardly knew how to answer her. I had delivered a conventional homily on marriage as Israel understood and valued it. "Part of what I said is traditional wisdom," I replied. "But Amasa is my friend, and I know he feels very tenderly toward Carmina, though they have known each other only a short time. But yes, I meant what I said to them. I meant all of it."

"And you believe this marriage will last their life-times, as they vowed?"

"Yes," I replied unhesitatingly. "At first, when Amasa mentioned the marriage, I had doubts, and I discouraged my friend from taking this step. I feared the unusual circumstances of their coming together here, in the war, and far from home. . . ."

"I understand," she said. "Still, your customs are very strange."

"Amasa is a gentle soul, and he will not forsake her. And Carmina, I think, is a fine match for him. They will do much good and be good for each other."

"I understand the woman is infertile. What can marriage mean in such circumstances?"

"Why, it can mean anything and everything!" I said. "They love each other. Benjamin is full of orphans. They will raise a numerous brood."

"These orphans, as you call them, are strangest of all to think of. There could be no such children, no orphans, in our land unless all of the People—*all* of the adults—were dead. Do you understand? There are no orphans among us; all children are equally sons and daughters of the People."

With the barrier to speech removed, I found myself asking her many questions. I especially wanted to know of the law that the People followed, of its origins and principles. Vitoria explained that they traced their rules of life to an ancient teacher—a woman. From what she said, I gathered that the People revered this female teacher much as we honored St. Supplicee. She also confirmed my impression that the People practiced many of the same customs that Israel thought peculiar to itself. I was intrigued by her explanations, and my curiosity was aroused to know even more.

"The People abide by very strict reproductive laws," she said, "and many of our customs derive from them."

"As do ours!" I exclaimed. Reproduction was in fact the foundation stone of Israel's Law. I questioned her eagerly, wanting to know more of their marriage customs and why they raised their children as they did.

"The People raise their children deliberately," she replied, pausing to engage my questions and gazing full at me with her serious blue eyes. *Involuntarily, I thought of the unblinking wolf gaze I had encountered in the Blue Mountains.* "The People are free; therefore, we prepare our children for a life of freedom." She paused, searching for words. "We understand that life is motion; it is always changing, always becoming. Death is the absence of motion, the end of growth. Therefore we think of life at every phase as a journey."

I listened politely but I was unable to connect these exalted principles with the cunning manipulation of male children that I had recently come to understand. "So young boys journey from their mothers to the warrior camps, and from there. . . ?"

"The journey does not end with puberty or the age at which young men become warriors. It never ends, till death. To cease to explore and grow is to die. That is our nature."

I was amazed at how closely this view of life accorded with our own—with our own endless quest for knowledge of the Way. I almost expected her to fall into our vocabulary of growth and heightened awareness, but she spoke in her own way of these things.

"Therefore," she continued, "we embrace it as a duty to encourage our children to fulfill their natures. This duty persists, for all of us, throughout life. As spouses, as leaders of the People, no less than as parents, we assist our fellow beings on their journeys. Neither adults nor even the aged may relinquish the journey." She stopped and looked at me with her clear blue eyes. "The moon either waxes or it wanes."

I did not fully comprehend her, but her comment about the moon reminded me of the young bachelor who intruded into our camp to do murder, and I must have bristled.

"The young bachelors," she said, as if reading my mood, "are only young males arrived at a complex and difficult stage of the journey. They still think and feel as children, though they have acquired the bodies and many of the powers of men. In them the moon is full, but they have no knowledge, and therefore no restraint."

"I should say no restraint!"

"Understand that we do not impose restraint upon them from without. Instead, we let them explore this state, this full moon within a new moon, which is strange to them. Old to humankind, but new to them. We encourage it."

"What do you mean?" I asked.

"The young men have feelings of desire, for example. This is natural, so we do not attempt to constrain them. They are free to indulge their feelings and to follow where they lead. *Wherever* they lead." She gave me a long, interrogating glance. "If they lead into dark places, it is better that they should know—and that the People should know—before they are older and assume responsibilities."

I felt this Vitoria, this strange, cool inhabitant of another world, was reaching out to me, trying to explain the incident that had befallen us on the Palouse. She wanted me to understand. I was strangely moved by that realization, but at the same time I found myself resisting everything she said.

"All their previous lives as children," she continued, "they are helpless to act. They experience feelings of envy and resentment and hatred – feelings of all kinds, in fact. Suddenly, in this phase of their lives, they acquire the power to act on such feelings. They are given opportunities to do so. No one prevents them."

I thought instantly of the madness associated with the full moon, the Kuhlan moon in Israel's folklore—and of all the generations of atrocities. *Unfortunate! I thought to myself. Young men passing through a difficult stage!*

"Young bachelors," she continued, "naturally desire to form attachments as well. Attachments of all kinds. They feel intense desire and sentiments of longing. We give them the freedom to do all these things—as long as they perform them outside the Circle."

"Why?" I asked incredulously. I could think of nothing more dangerous than to give free rein to the passions of youth.

"So they will become familiar with these impulses and come to know which is stronger and which is truly satisfying. Thereby, in action, they come to know themselves."

But at what cost? I asked myself.

"They come to know themselves, and the People come to know them also. We cannot know these things of people in advance, or in general. Each person is different. Therefore, we allow our young men freedom to act, and we observe them carefully. That is one of the responsibilities of the Sisters.

"Forgive me, but this sounds to me like a recipe for disaster."

"Some of the young men go to strange extremes, it's true. Some attach themselves to undesirable things. . . ."

"How 'undesirable'?" I interrupted. "In what sense?"

"Undesirable from the point of view of the totality of the life of the People. That is our single measure of all things. If they remain attached to undesirable things, they remain outside of the Circle. Most return of their own choosing, however, and when they return, they come back with knowledge. Understand: there are no unplumbed depths, no secret desires or frustrated impulses in a leader of the People. Our men have explored those depths, tasted those desires, experienced what they wanted to experience, and they know the value as well as the cost of the things that stir them deeply. They have never had to pretend that they were not stirred or drawn to them." We walked for several minutes before she spoke again: "It is not easy to say what is the right choice for a young man. We follow the law, but we do not live by simple rules. Our law is a set of precepts. We do not turn it into a snare for ourselves so that we choke on it."

I marveled, noting again the similarities of Kuhlan law with the precepts of St. Supplicee. "And the women? Is their education similar?"

She hesitated. "We women also lead lives of self-exploration, but we are under discipline in ways that men are not. In ways that men cannot understand. We bear responsibility." She said this with a mingled pride and humility that impressed me deeply.

We walked again in silence for a time. My skin was prickling with excitement, though whether from the insights I was deriving from her conversation or merely from proximity to her beauty, I could not well say. "I believe I begin to understand," I said. "But what do you mean, if they make the wrong choices, these young bachelors will remain outside the Circle?"

She ignored my question and recited an adage familiar to me: "If there is darkness in your heart, our teacher says, it is far better for you and for the world to acknowledge it than to keep it hidden."

I stopped in my tracks as I recognized the saying. *She was speaking the very words of St. Supplicee!*

When I returned to camp, equally bemused and exalted, I needed to talk to someone and sort through my thoughts. Jonathan Amasa was my only trusted friend among the Benjamites; I sought him out even though it was his wedding night.

"You must be an idiot," he said when I told him of our conversation. "You have just been made a husbandman, and you talk to her of the Law of St. Supplicee? I see you *are* a fanatic! I thought you must be. She was offering to be your consort!"

"That cannot be," I said. Nevertheless, I reviewed our whole conversation rapidly in my mind.

"Well, I only wish Colonel Harlech were here to explain it to you. You might believe him!"

"She is very beautiful," Carmina said. She sat close to her new husband, leaning against him with her hand protectively on his knee. "I don't know if I have ever seen a woman who is her equal."

"That she is," Amasa agreed. "Very beautiful indeed!"

What Amasa was saying intrigued me. I had distinguished myself, as she had herself said to me, among the People. I had acquired the status of a war leader among them, and they had approved of my presiding at the marriage of Amasa and Carmina. It might just be true that she wished to be my consort. I wondered suddenly if I could make up the time I had lost.

Amasa rose and put his hand on my shoulder. "She's beautiful, all right. But, my friend, be careful."

"Do you think I am in danger?" I was beginning to feel proud and whole for the first time in months.

"Their racial prid," Amasa said. "The People have racial pride like a disease."

III

We climbed the canyon to an isolated spot. The glades around us were just leafing out, and dark stands of fir towered above us, which made me uneasy because of ticks. We stopped among a grove of wild plum in full-scented, fragrant bloom. The grass beneath us was green and tender, and when we dismounted the horses began to crop it eagerly. I had not felt desire for months, since the beginning of my exile. What I felt was not desire, exactly, but I found myself trembling with anticipation. I felt certain that Vitoria's interest in me was a mark of favor, and I began to half-believe Amasa's assertion that she intended to be my consort. But at the same time, I could not imagine it. Vitoria was as cool and distant as a planet that showed itself briefly in the evening sky, shone like a diamond for a time, and then withdrew. Moreover, Vitoria was Kuhlan and I Israelite. Even though these differences remained unspoken, I could not imagine a way to bridge the hereditary enmity between us. Nor could I think of anything to say to her. We walked amid the newly sprouted grass and inhaled the scents of early spring, but neither of us spoke. I might as well have been tongue-tied.

"I have heard," she said, turning to face me, "that you are adept in the martial arts, especially in the ancient art you call the Mano. I wish to see a demonstration." She slapped the reins of her bridle against her leg imperiously. Her gaze, when she turned it on me, was anything but alluring.

"Is that why you brought me here?" I asked, incredulous.

To my amazement she peeled off her outer garments and stood before me in a linen wrap that barely covered her breasts and a smaller garment, also of linen, around her hips.

"The Mano is not a game," I said. "I cannot show you."

"I understand what it is. I too have been trained as a warrior. I insist you give me a demonstration."

Her manner angered me, but I explained as patiently as I could that the discipline does not admit of casual demonstrations. It was, in fact, a secret art that I was honor-bound to protect. As I spoke she stepped close to me and stared boldly into my eyes. "I'm sorry," I began, and hardly had the words left my mouth than she struck me a hard blow with the flat of her hand.

She stepped back quickly and assumed a fighting position. The left side of my face was on fire, my ear ringing. My blood rose; she was challenging me as if she were a man. "You will give me a demonstration," she said as she began circling me,

I raised my hands, feigning mirth and said, "Surely you cannot—"

She attacked again with amazing speed. Instinctively, I parried the blow of her right hand with my left, but she delivered a solid kick to my belly. I let out a loud grunt and doubled over. She lashed out with an open-handed blow to my head, behind the right ear, and then retreated as before. My horse raised its head and looked at us and then resumed grazing.

I felt consternation and surprise and not a little fear. She had been trained all right! St. Supplicee only knew what tricks these Kuhlans might have! "Sorry," I said, as casually as I could while bent over in pain. "I cannot."

When I straightened up and faced her, I saw she had stripped off her upper garment, exposing her breasts. She was panting a little, and her breasts rose and fell with her breath. Her skin, where her clothing had covered it, was as white as alabaster. Her breasts were perfectly formed, and her nipples, instead of brown, were a delicate rose color. They stood erect, the longest and tenderest-looking nipples I had ever seen. They might have been rose buds on a field of snow.

"So you have never seen breasts before?" She said, sneering at me. "I thought I was contending with a man."

She attacked again but I avoided her, moving now in concert with her. She was quick and agile, and she concealed her intentions well. I knew better than to take her lightly. I made a half-serious counter-attack and she danced away. I noted how she moved—just as quick as many a male opponent I have faced, and far more agile. Men typically betray their right or left-handedness as they move. She had the fluid grace of a cat, and she showed me nothing but her beauty.

"Let me remove my tunic," I said.

"Do it," she replied, keeping her distance. I hurriedly stripped off my tunic and hurled it as far away as possible. The cool air brushed my skin, stimulating me. But my blood was up. I had to decide what to do. I had no intention of hurting her *or* giving her the demonstration of the Mano that she demanded. On the other hand, I had no intention either of letting her beat me to pieces, which she seemed fully capable of doing.

"If you condescend to me again," she declared, "I'll crush your skull like an egg!"

She made another feinting pass at me, and when I grasped at her body she spun away. Then, standing off a few yards from me, she flung her last garment off, as if to deny me the advantage of seizing it. She stood naked before me, arrogant and lovely. Her manner said she was stripped for action, not love, but I felt myself powerfully aroused, involuntarily engorging with blood against my will. Desire mingled with anger in a way I had never experienced. It was as if this appetite whetted the hot resentment in my blood, and anger increased my desire. It was an exquisite and troubling sensation, and while I remained wary of her power, I was far from immune to it.

"Take a good look," she taunted me. "It may be the last thing you ever see." She stood with her hands on her hips, her legs apart, and shook her breasts at me in disdain. I marveled that the small triangle of hair on her pelvis was scarcely darker than the hair of her head. And then, as if goaded by my prying gaze, she launched a silent, swift attack at me. She struck with blurring speed, feinting with her hands as well as jabbing and slashing at me, intending – as I had expected – to deliver a series of powerful kicks.

I responded wholly according to my training, unconsciously blocking and dodging what I could. I took only one of her kicks, which landed squarely on my chest and nearly cracked my rib cage. But her follow-up kick I parried, and I managed to seize her ankle while she was off balance, sending her sailing into the air. She hit the ground solidly on her back, stunned, and I was on her like a panther. She was helpless for a moment, and I pinned her to the ground before she could recover. Unfortunately, I had no idea what to do next. Though angry and stinging with pain from her blows, I had no wish to harm her. I wanted—no, I *needed*, for my own protection – to control her, to put an end to this foolish contest. But I doubted I could hold her, lithe and supple as she was, just by main strength.

As I rolled on top of her, struggling to pin her arms, the contact of our bodies was delicious to me. At the same time I feared a sudden knee in the groin when she recovered herself. Accordingly, I forced her legs apart with mine and pressed them down violently. I held her wrists flat against the ground and shouted into her ear, "You must stop this! You must stop!"

She opened her eyes only inches away from mine, and we gazed at each other, panting. The fierce light in her eyes had abated and there was something else in them. Something I could not read. At first I thought she had been knocked senseless for a moment. But she seemed alert – though no longer struggling against me. She was fully conscious, gazing up at me unafraid. I on the other hand was gripped by fear that she was luring me to relax, playing a Kuhlan trick that would put my heart and genitals as trophies on her saddle horn. I embraced her savagely again, exerting my full strength and will, futilely trying to render her helpless without harming her. Her bare legs slipped easily from under my knees and encircled me.

"That's better," she said, her voice barely a whisper.

"Better?" I said.

"Yes," she whispered. She raised her head and brushed her lips against mine. Her lips came away bloody. She had scored twice on my nose and mouth.

"Ah," she said, her voice a sigh. "Much better." I felt her hips and pelvis move ever so slightly against me as she held me in her undecipherable gaze.

If I relax my grip, I thought, she will drive one of those long-nailed thumbs into my brain. *Nevertheless, I was so fully aroused that I was mad to have her, desperate to plunge inside her. I could tell she felt me, was caressing me with her body. I gripped both of her slender wrists in one hand and seized her throat with the other. I felt her strong pulse under my fingers. Her arms were limp and unresisting, but I knew her strength and quickness.*

"Stop this!" I said.

She raised her head, pressing her throat against my hand, which suddenly had no force to restrain her, and she brushed her lips against my mouth again, lingering, with her eyes close to mine. She touched my smarting lips with the tip of her tongue, caressing them. Tasting my blood. Then she kissed me fully and intimately, searching my mouth.

If this is a trick, I thought, *I am a dead man.*

Afterwards, we lay in the spring sunshine, the breeze raising goose bumps on my naked skin. My mind was in a turmoil. I was afraid to speak, uncertain whether I had forced a Kuhlan priestess or been seduced by her. She lay with her eyes shut, her face turned away from me, but her fingers lightly caressed the small of my back. They moved slowly up my spine and then onto my neck and hair. My hair was long and uncut; she took a fistful in her hand and gently pulled. I kissed her neck, and she pressed her fingers into my back and gently accommodated her body to mine.

So, I thought with relief, it was lovemaking after all, and not a fatal crime I have just committed. Am committing.

It was a relief also that Vitoria was so matter-of-fact when we rose from our bed of grass. I still could not think of a word to say to her. "There may be many prying eyes," she remarked, frowning. "Nevertheless, we must be purified."

I helped her make a small enclosure of branches and we made a fire and heated stones in it. She led me to a nearby brook and we both bathed in it, in water hardly warmer than ice. She lathered my body with a soap-like root she took from her saddlebag, and I waited, shivering while she did the same to herself. She was hurried but purposeful, unmindful of me. She had an unconscious grace, like a wild creature that does not know it is being observed. After we were both thoroughly and intimately lathered, she took a small basin and dipped water over us to rinse away the soap. It was all I could do not to flinch from the cold. The steam of the sweat lodge afterwards was very welcome. Vitoria was pensive and silent, and though I suspected she prayed or meditated silently, following some ritual of her people, I could not begin to fathom her mood. I relaxed by degrees in the familiar clouds of steam and thought my own thoughts.

We rode back to the camp, and when it was time to part, she said simply, "I will come for you tomorrow."

IV

When morning came and Vitoria appeared, I could hardly believe I was awake and not dreaming. Her golden hair was aglow in the light, and her grace and beauty past imagining. She rode a tall, spirited bay mare and she was carrying a bundle. "Here," she said. "Put these on. It will be safer." It was clothing – buckskin and fur decorated in the Kuhlan manner. I looked at my own clothing of good Israelite wool, which I had clung to in spite of Amasa's urgings that I try to blend in. They were clean but ragged. I would look like a beggar in Israel. But the clothes were my own; they said who I was.

"These clothes will disguise who you are," Vitoria added, seeing me balk at her gift.

She had a way of both swelling me up and letting me down in very short order. I had been congratulating myself for her interest in me, seeing our relationship as the epitome of the honors I had received from the People. I assumed I must be the only Israelite so singled out and distinguished by the People – as a peer among their warriors and a husbandman to one of the women. When I was exiled to the Kuhlan lands and awoke swordless on their shore, I had felt totally stripped of worth, a disgrace to myself and those close to me. Having betrayed my calling and my teachers and having let all my responsibilities fall to the ground, I had felt myself a pariah. Somehow, in the intervening months, I had managed to redeem myself, to become accepted by former enemies, the Harlech, and even by Israel's eternal enemies, the Kuhlans. And I had, as Vitoria and the Sister themselves had acknowledged, distinguished myself among them, both in battle and in strategy. It was my plan of action against the Kr that the People had adopted. As much as anyone, I could claim to have brought about the favorable outcome of the war against the Kr and thus to have averted a great calamity for Israel. That the victory over the Kr had also meant salvation for the People was equally true, if not my particular intent.

Vitoria interrupted this chain of thought to tell me that she would inspect our hospital while I changed into her Kuhlan garb. "I am told your people's skill in healing greatly exceeds ours. If your people are allowed to stay in our land, I will be one of those who observes and studies your medicine."

If your people are allowed to stay. . . . I caught the full implications of her words; Zachariah was right to fear the Kuhlans' intentions.

Vitoria took her time. Amasa and Carmina were almost obsequious in showing her about, and the visit attracted the rapt attention of our patients. When she emerged, I was waiting on my horse, dressed in full Kuhlan regalia, the double-headed war axe resting across my saddle horn.

"Josiah," Amasa observed appreciatively and with his own style of humor; "you look every inch a warrior of the People!"

Vitoria did not seem to appreciate Amasa's jest. She mounted wordlessly, wheeled about, and kicked her mare in the ribs. I could do nothing but follow in her wake.

Vitoria seemed to have two styles—one as a peer and fellow, a warrior like myself on serious business, and the other as a lover. She was impressive at both, but I never understood how she moved from one to the other. There was no visible transition. While not as abrupt as our first coupling had been, our passage to lovemaking remained a mystery to me for its suddenness and the absence of preliminaries. Our embraces were always initiated by her. She was generous with her favors, but much of the time I felt myself more a baffled observer than her lover. We met daily for more than a week, always at a different site, and Vitoria went to elaborate lengths to ensure we were not followed or observed. I attributed this care to modesty, even though she seemed perfectly forthright and uninhibited when it came down to it. She seemed determined, in fact, as Miriam had once been, to discover my limits each day and press beyond them. I thought of Miriam often and saw her through the glass of this new relationship; somehow those memories had grown accessible again and less painful. But there was nothing playful or seductive about Vitoria. And there was something else, something missing.

"Why can't we spend the nights together?" I complained one afternoon after our lovemaking. The sun was warm on my face, and I desired very much to take a nap and recover my ardor.

"I cannot just visit you openly and spend the night," she said, somewhat crossly.

"Why not?"

"Too many among the People object to this relationship. The full moon is a week away, and we are in danger enough as it is."

"We are in danger?" I could scarcely believe the idyll I had been living had involved us in danger. "From whom? *Why?* Are you not a Mother of the People and empowered to enter into relationships as you choose?"

"Anyone might resent what we do," she said, screening her eyes. "And then there are the bachelors."

I grimaced at the thought. *Bachelors!*

"I have a plan," she said. "It is important that we spend the next week together, full moon or not. I'll bring a lodge and supplies tomorrow, and extra horses, and we can meet and get away from here. We'll spend a week or more away, through the full moon and after. Then you'll have your nights with me."

"I'll need to get leave from my duties," I said.

"Get it, then," she said. She gave me directions to meet her a day's ride from the camp.

Following Vitoria's directions, I met her in a wilderness of basalt canyons where the Palouse River drops over a considerable falls into a gorge several miles above its juncture with Snake.

"This is sacred land," Vitoria explained. "I thought we might be safer here. The young men are fearful of sacred things. I doubt that they will follow us here."

I asked her why the area was sacred, but she had little to say. She pointed out some rock formations and small steep-sided mesas where the People exposed their most honored dead. The People do not practice burial, and cremation is not always convenient, so they practice sky burial, exposing the dead on platforms. The rugged rock formations hereabouts no doubt provided many natural platforms where the dead would be out of reach of predators.

We traveled south from the falls to where the canyon opened out a bit and set up our camp. Vitoria had two pack animals and a wealth of goods, it seemed to me, for such a short journey. We set up a large cone-shaped lodge of tanned cow skin such as the People use. It is an ingenious design, snug and warm when closed, but capable of admitting light and air in mild weather. Its shape deflects all but the most powerful winds, and smoke can escape through the top of the tent, if a fire is needed in cold weather.

She made a soft bed of rugs and robes of hide. When I returned from tending the horses, she was naked as the day she was born. She took me by the hand and drew me inside the lodge and embraced me. "I think this will do," she said, entwining her limbs with mine. She had scattered aromatic herbs, and our bed was scented with sage and musk and flowers.

Afterwards, in the dusk, I made a meal for her from my army rations—flat bread and beans and lentils. "It might do with seasoning," she said. "The bread is good. It has texture and flavor."

Vitoria had little sense of humor and there was no playfulness about her, but I never heard her say a false thing. We made love again after the fire had died down to embers. Then we lay under warm covers like two spoons in a drawer, and I reveled in this time we could share together. I kissed her where her neck and shoulder joined, savoring the warm scent of her body. The curve from her thigh and bare hip to her narrow waist was a marvel to me and a perfect rest for my hand. "This is good," I said, kissing her again and feeling her hair against my cheek. "Nice texture, good flavor."

"Yes," she whispered. "Very good."

"I have work to do here as well as serve you," Vitoria declared the next morning. "There are a multitude of plants to be harvested. You can hunt and supplement our food supplies while I gather and dry plants."

We spent several days scouring the fields and canyons and even patches of woods, in defiance of ticks, for the plants she wanted. I was impressed by her knowledge. She knew the name of every weed and flower and shrub and where they grew and when they bloomed and seeded out. We searched dry hillsides and rocky slopes and the damp nooks and crannies around springs and under cliffs. Some plants were gathered several times a year, she said, to exploit different properties. She described the variety of uses of most of the plants she collected, but some she left unexplained. Some she gathered intact and whole, and from others she took only the flower or leaves or roots.

"What is this plant for?" I asked. We had plucked it from the edge of a wood.

She hesitated a moment before she replied. "It depends. A little administered daily will bring blood to the cheeks of a sickly man or woman. It restores energy and circulation and increases the strength of the pulse. A large dose and the heart races madly for a time and then stops."

"I see."

The times Vitoria hunted with me were sheer delight. She was an excellent rider and a good shot with a bow. She delighted in coursing after wild cattle or deer or elk, although we never took any meat. The animals were too large for our use without waste, which she would not allow. But the chase was exhilarating. She had a wonderful eye for the health and condition of animals, and she explained to me that the People do not herd their cattle, but merely cull them periodically to strengthen the breed. I learned that the Kuhlans practiced a similar selection on their newborn children—one far stricter than Israel's. They applied the same principle to the husbandry of their land and animals that they used with themselves.

The pastures in this part of the Kuhlan lands were rich and well watered, and the grass was festooned with flowers of many kinds. It seemed a paradise. We rode through a landscape of soft green hills, feminine in shape and contour. The wind played over the new grass, making it roil and shimmer like waves in a lake. I was reminded of a rich, green velvet cloth raised and crumpled into hills. I felt a pang of envy.

"The People could put ten thousand cattle on this range," I remarked. "It seems a shame to let it go to waste this way."

"Yes, they could," she said dismissively, "and soon ruin it. The People have learned to control their greed and to live within what the land yields. That is the secret of our greatness." She looked rather down her nose at me, as if to imply that *this is precisely what separates your people from mine.* Later, as if to soften the criticism, she added: "The land is actually very fragile and unforgiving. In this season, it looks richer than it is, because the rains have not yet ceased. But in a month or two, in the dry season, these same pastures can support very few animals. Too many cattle would strip the land bare very quickly, and then it would wash away. All waste is wrong, but to ruin the earth is the worst folly of all."

I thought of how Israel habitually squeezed the last possible blade of grass or kernel of grain out of its land, and yet was often in want.

We traveled far afield, up on the plateau, seeking flowers and roots that Vitoria needed for her collection. When it rained and we had to seek shelter, or when we paused for rest or for a meal, Vitoria would often turn to me as if she had just discovered my presence. Her serious look would gradually fade, to be replaced by another of unfeigned but unflirtatious desire, and I would find myself in her embrace with no more preliminaries than those of the innocent beasts of the field. She gave herself to love making with an abandon that I would have attributed to a lioness or a bitch wolf—and with such fierce passion that I knew if she but turned and snapped at me, I would wear the mark for a lifetime. Afterwards, her brows would slowly knit with concentration, and she would become as before and we would continue our work.

Returning to our camp one late afternoon, I unsaddled the horses, hobbled them, and let them drink. It was hot; we were thoroughly sweated and thirsty. I was glancing about for the packhorses, thinking they must have strayed, when I heard an exclamation from Vitoria. I turned and saw her frozen, just in front of the lodge flap, her body bent forward, as if about to enter the tent. My first thought was a snake. "What is it?" I shouted, running to help.

She waived me away. She turned her face a moment and I saw the disgust on her face.

"Is there a snake in the tent?" I cried, panting as I came up to her. The canyon was thick with rattlesnakes. I had remarked our first day here that these basalt cliffs seemed to be sacred to rattlesnakes as well as to the People, and she had been characteristically unamused.

"Yes, there is a *snake*!" she said. Vitoria opened the lodge flap and a huge rattler slithered out, buzzing, and immediately coiled up at her feet, threatening her. She took the tip of her bow and hurled it into the brush without a glance at it.

At that moment I was assailed by the odor in the tent.

"Stay back," she said. "I'll take care of it." She unfastened some tent ropes and raised the sides of the lodge. A smaller rattlesnake crawled out the side of the tent and made off into the grass. The odor was sickening.

We had had a human intruder. Someone who had urinated over the inside of our tent and defecated in the center of our bed. I searched the surrounding terrain for signs of visitors, notching an arrow in my bow. I examined the ground for footprints while Vitoria dragged our bedding out of the tent. There were two sets of footprints in the dust outside our lodge-flap.

"They have destroyed all my work," she said quietly. "All of it."

"Who? Who would have done this?"

She didn't answer. I helped pile the bedding outside the tent. The intruders had fouled the tent itself as well. I started to build a fire to consume what had been desecrated.

"Don't," she said, putting a hand on my arm. "We'll have to leave it. Let's see if anything can be saved."

"It was the young bachelors, wasn't it?" I demanded. "Young boys playing at being wolf souls!"

She said nothing, intent on her ugly task. I started off to find the other horses. "No, don't go," she said. "Stay with me. They could be anywhere. There could be many of them."

"There were only two who came to the tent," I said.

"There could be others. There must be. They are waiting to ambush us. We must have ridden past them on the way in. They obviously wanted us to see what they had done before they struck. Now that we have seen it, they will kill us."

"Kill *us*? Kill *you*? You mean to say *you* are in danger from them too! How can this be? I thought only I was in danger."

"They can. They will. It happens sometimes. As I said, they are outside the Circle.

They can do anything."

"We'll see about that," I said, throwing the saddle back on my horse.

"Wait, no. You can't."

"Can't? *Can't*, you say? Are you worried about their safety or mine?" I demanded.

"You have killed our young men before," she said dully.

I stared at her. Incomprehension choked me into silence.

"I have a duty here," she said, seeming almost distracted with pain. "It is difficult. I do my best. But you must do as I say. We must elude them; we *must*!"

Vitoria seemed so upset that I consented – reluctantly – to follow her lead. I salvaged my extra clothing, which had been under a pillow. We saved one of the robes and my cooking gear. We had no tent, no extra clothing, none of Vitoria's dried plant material. It was getting on toward dusk. Vitoria urged me to hurry, to flee from these would-be murderers before they came looking for us. We headed down the canyon toward the Snake and then turned westward. She had reasoned out what she thought our intruders intended to do and where they would expect us to go, and so we did the opposite.

On our way down the canyon, I found the packhorses. Our intruders had slit the tendons in their hind legs and left them for us to find. They were in a bad way, so I destroyed them quickly, and we hurried on in the twilight.

V

At moonrise, we tried to climb out of the breaks, but our horses were exhausted and the canyon too steep. We hobbled them on a bench to let them graze and huddled together under our single robe. The wind coming up the canyon had an unpleasant edge even in this season. I held Vitoria tenderly all night, knowing that she was unsettled, not just by the danger, but by the dilemma the situation presented. I did not pretend to know what rules of conduct constrained and troubled her, and I did not care. I was determined to save her life and honor if it were possible to do so.

When dawn came, we fled westward, trying to put as much distance between ourselves and our enemies as possible. In our rest periods for the horses' sake, Vitoria tried to explain how it was with the young men of the People. I sensed that she wanted me to understand and share her view of our situation. The three days of the full moon were beginning that very night, she explained, clearly alarmed at the prospect. *I thought of Amasa's dread of the Kuhlan moon and marveled that she seemed to share it.* She repeated much of what she had said to me the day I met her. Then she carried her explanation into unfamiliar territory. "Many young bachelors," she said, "unfortunately do horrible things, things that are condemned in your law and our own."

Now we come to the truth! I thought to myself.

"But thereby, you see, they confront the darkness and the misshapen things in themselves. They discover what they are capable of doing and purge themselves of what is unhealthy. That is why they must do these things apart from us, while they are separate."

I urged her to explain.

"Outside the Circle there is no law; the law does not apply. Do you understand?"

I did not. I looked at her impatiently.

"Whatever happens in this phase of their lives does not count; they can come back into the Circle clean and chastened, and their past actions are washed away and forgotten."

She was not being particularly coherent, but I recalled from my interrogation by Pierson Angier that the bachelors were immune from punishment. "So they go free, unpunished, no matter what?" I said. *"Why?"*

"It is then, and only then, that the young can truly and unreservedly embrace the law. They do this freely and of their own accord, you understand? Some of these men who have explored their own darkness in this way become our most valued leaders."

In another mood I might have been curious about what she was saying—and puzzled about where the implications led. But in the circumstances, I was impatient at her words. We were in danger; she was herself in danger. *I wanted to act.* "Do you mean," I demanded, "that these malevolent man-children could kill and rape and mutilate *you*—as well as me – and then be welcomed back into the tribe at some future date? You can't be serious! And you want me to spare their precious lives so they can kill us tomorrow, if they happen to catch us unaware?

"Does it seem strange to you that young men would long to savage as much of the world as they can grasp? Does this not accord with your own experience as a man and a soldier?"

I waved her question away. My blood was up or I might have listened more closely.

"Not all of the young men are this way. Others, in fact, are born gentle and remain that way through all stages of their journey. They too are greatly valued by the People."

Suddenly the piousness of her words and manner provoked me, and I blurted out:

"The young bachelors I observed were a shameless lot of maricons." I was instantly sorry I had mocked her, but she did not change expression.

"You do not have such behavior in your country?" she asked mildly.

"Of course we do."

"The bachelors are by definition not yet husbandmen; they are not yet eligible for truly satisfying contact with the young Mothers of the People. They are essentially alone. If they are lonely, they may practice their desires with the Sisters who are past child bearing. Or they may use each other for pleasure. It does not matter. If they go to the Sisters, they begin to learn the lore of the People. They begin to learn how to behave with consorts, when they will have earned the privilege, and—"

"And if they remain fixed in their attachments to each other?"

"It happens thus many times." She paused, reflecting. "It is difficult, however, for such a one to enter into the Circle."

You mean the women do not tolerate men who cannot be controlled by women, I thought to myself.

"It happens more often that young bachelors attach themselves to the Sisters in undesirable ways than fix their desires upon other men," She added. "Still, for most of them, either kind of attachment is only a stage. Usually they outgrow it."

"And some of your most valued leaders come from among them?" My comment was sarcastic, but I was feeling a needle-sharp memory of Miriam Lander, who, while a beautiful woman, was also a matron of thirty-seven. I knew something of the lonely ache for a woman that mingled desire with a child's need for affection.

"Yes, you mock me," she said calmly, "but it is true. The bachelor life is lonely and uncertain. And their passions are strong. If we were to set any restraints on their desires, they would feel compelled to break them."

The Law is not mocked, I said to myself.

"Still, we do not hold such youths in contempt. They are often capable of the most selfless devotion to the People later on. Therefore we value them and wait for them to journey on to the next phase of life. The People are patient."

I kept to myself the thought that the People's patience in this regard seemed to me the most sinister thing about them.

The land through which we fled was a rugged jumble of hills, outcroppings of basalt, and eroded canyons. Late in the afternoon, we concealed ourselves in a hollow and let the horses graze. We took turns napping, in preparation for staying awake all night. The full moon was already visible in the late afternoon sky, gigantic above the eastern horizon. It would shine like a beacon during the night.

"When is the greatest danger?" I asked. "When the moon is visible, or after it sets?"

"At both times," she replied. Her eyes had a sunken, strained look I had never seen before.

Vitoria and I shared a cold meal of bread and jerky. It was the last of our food supplies. Since a fire was out of the question, we bundled up in our robe again at nightfall and set ourselves to wait out the darkness. Vitoria shivered in my arms, and I was certain it was not from the cold. I was visited by a similar dread. Strangely enough, I had lived and campaigned in the Kuhlan lands for months, and I had never, at least after my first day or two in their midst, felt the instinctive dread that Israelites have for the People. *Until now.* In the bright moonlight, I felt like a hunted animal. There were moments that night when, if I had not labored to control my breathing, I would have fled in a mindless panic.

In the dregs of the night, shortly after the moon had set, and the landscape turned pitch black, Vitoria turned to me and buried her face in my neck. In a moment I felt her hand groping for me. "Take me," she said in my ear. "*Please.*"

At Vitoria's urging we traveled only a short time the next day, intending to hide and watch during the day, and keep on the move during the moonlit night, when we would be hard to see from a distance. I killed a bull calf, and we stopped to roast it to satisfy our hunger. Vitoria took the hide, which was spotted and therefore sacred to the People, and pegged it out and scraped it while the meat cooked. "They will see our smoke," she said, not looking up. "But it makes no difference. Our young men are unequaled trackers."

We ate hurriedly and then packed up the rest of the meat and fled further westward. In the afternoon, Vitoria found the kind of cover she sought—a small, well-concealed ravine underneath a stony knoll. There was grass for the horses in the ravine, and we could lie on the top of the knoll and watch the countryside, which was more open and less rugged than the area where we had spent the night. It was a good defensive position. There was no easy way to approach unseen, and we had an unobstructed view of the countryside. We would be hard to track through this dry and rocky country, the tracking skills of the Kuhlans notwithstanding.

"This is good cover," I said. "It gives confidence."

She gave me a harried look and took a swallow of water. "They can find us," she said.

We lay flat on our bellies for several hours, scanning not only our back trail but observing every point of the compass. We were careful to stay low to the ground and not reveal our silhouettes as the sun set behind us.

We waited until the moon was high in the sky and the landscape bathed in pale, unearthly light, and then we saddled the horses and fled westward again. At dawn, I recognized that the hills in front of us, floating like clouds above the haze, were in Israel. We were approaching the Great Jordan. It gave me an indescribable feeling to recognize the landmarks of my country from the Kuhlan lands. There were the ridges, including the Pyramid, north and west of Hebron, that separated Judah from the other tribal territories. The land on the Kuhlan side descends toward the confluence of the Jordan and the Snake. The haze along the horizon was, I realized, smoke from Hebron and surrounding towns. I was elated, but I wondered what Vitoria felt. To her, these features, blue with distance, were not safety and home, but an alien land.

Long before we could see the Jordan, we guided ourselves by the huge pilings that reared above the river. Great bridges had once spanned the Jordan River here, and the ruins of the nearest was like a gigantic monument to the Ancients. Tall shafts of stone and metal and concrete towered above the river. Countless years of floods and river ice had done nothing to diminish them. The abutments on both sides of the river were still visible, though the spans between them had long since collapsed.

"The works of the Ancients always amaze me," I said as we rested on a low hill overlooking the river. Our horses seemed nearly played out, and I wondered what Vitoria was up to. If we were still being pursued, we could easily be trapped against the river. I was certain she did not contemplate Israel as a place of refuge in any circumstances whatsoever. I looked over at her, wondering what she had in mind, but she was gazing straight ahead, past the ruined pilings, at Israel.

"The Ancients had a great deal of power," Vitoria replied gravely, "but they used it to no very intelligent purpose. Our teacher, Cecilia Pleece, saw that. But of course she was a woman."

"So your law-giver was. . . Cecilia. . . ?" *The name teased my ear.*

"Cecilia Pleece. She lived in the time of the Dissolution, and she saw what was happening and left us a legacy of wisdom that has preserved us."

"She sounds like a very great teacher. Our own tradition. . . ."

"I know all about your tradition!" Vitoria replied in a tone that forestalled further conversation.

From our vantage point, we could see a green strip of cultivated lands along the river—the fields of Old Pasco, the famous enterprise of my father, Tephlin Glanz. "Those fields yonder belong to my father," I ventured to say, gesturing in their direction. "I'm told that they formed the basis of his wealth and power."

"Those are the People's lands," she replied shortly. "Not your father's." Then she exclaimed, "What arrogance is this?"

It was her turn to point, and as I followed her arm I saw a group of horsemen ascending from the valley toward us. Even at this distance, I recognized them as Israelites. An Israelite patrol, on the Kuhlan side of the river. What in the world was going on?

We watched them come nearer. We were in their line of sight and they were obviously making for us. Nevertheless, we stayed firmly in place. Vitoria, I surmised, would flee from an unknown handful of her countrymen but was not willing to give ground to a dozen Israelites. "Since when do your countrymen intrude into our territory so boldly?" she demanded, as if I were responsible for the patrol.

"Never, to my knowledge," I said. And then I recalled the trade that had occurred in mid-winter at this spot. *The trade that I had arranged.* Perhaps I *was* responsible. "I doubt that they have friendly intentions," I warned. *They were getting close.* But almost as I spoke, the horsemen pulled up abruptly. They seemed startled; they sawed their horses to a halt and gestured in our direction.

"It's not us they see now," Vitoria said, turning in her saddle and shading her eyes to look above and behind us. "Look! There on the ridge."

I saw three horsemen silhouetted on the ridge above us. It was our pursuers. We were trapped between them and the Israelite patrol. "There are only three of them," I said. "Let's take our chances that way."

"No!" she exclaimed.

The Israelite patrol had stopped. I reasoned that with five Kuhlans in sight, they might be wondering how many more lay concealed and waiting for them.

There was a outcropping to the north of us that would hide us from view from above. If the Israelites were fearful of pursuing us, and if the Kuhlan youths who had been chasing us remained preoccupied with the Israelite patrol, we might, I thought, slip away undetected beneath it, and then circle around behind the Kuhlans. I estimated we had about one chance in twenty of succeeding – but I preferred three opponents to a dozen. When I pointed out this course to her, Vitoria immediately agreed to try it. "The moon is waning," she said. "Soon we will be safe."

As night fell, it appeared that we had eluded both groups of pursuers. Finding no one on our back trail, we slept that night by a little mud-hole of a spring with a few cattails around it. We were exhausted, bodies and minds alike. We had not seen the bachelors since our one glimpse of them on the ridge above us. Vitoria was confident that our ordeal with them was over. Though the moon was still bright enough to light our surroundings that night, she assured me that the period of the moon madness had passed. Accordingly, as soon as we had satisfied our thirst, we feel asleep, heedless of danger. During the night, however, she nudged me awake and caressed me. She brushed her lips against my ear and face and then kneaded me in her hands like dough. "I need you," she said. "I need you to be inside me, if it is possible."

Groggy as I was, I responded to her. I held her in my arms and kissed her and slid my hand into her garment to fondle her breasts. She tightened her hold on me and panted for breath, returning my kisses with ever greater intensity. Strange to say, in this state of exhaustion, both of us unwashed and hungry and tormented by fear, a passion swept over us and possessed us. As I penetrated her body, it was as if the shuttle of my days and nights ceased and held still, and it was I who was transfixed. For that single moment, my senses thrilled like a lyre when every string is touched and singing at the same time. Afterwards we both lay perfectly still.

I must have slept like the dead, for the sun was an hour high when I awoke. But I felt instantly alert; I had heard something, sensed something out of place. I touched Vitoria and glanced quickly around, trying to focus my eyes. I had searched a quick half-circle when my eyes fell on the source of the sounds. A few yards off from us, a human figure was standing facing us, haloed by the rising sun.

I bolted upright, shouting a warning to Vitoria. I rose instantly, forcing all my senses awake and trying to absorb the situation. Vitoria sat up and, perceiving the situation faster than I, suddenly screamed, "No!" and seized my legs from behind, almost tackling me. I had my Kuhlan war axe raised to defend us. "No!" she screamed again. "Don't even think of it!"

It took a moment to realize her words were directed at me rather than at our intruder; in the meantime, I had made out the figure of the young man before us: he was tall and slender and wore a mask of deer hide with two spike antlers rising from his head. His face was entirely concealed. Then I noticed he was unarmed, and instead of threatening us, he had uncovered himself and was flaunting himself at us, fondling himself shamelessly. As Vitoria interposed her naked body between him and myself, I saw him ejaculate in her direction.

Ignoring the young man, Vitoria gripped the axe with both her hands and repeated fiercely in my face, *"No!"* I was dumbfounded, but the sense of threat in the situation had somehow flowed out of me. When she felt my grip relax she turned and gave the young bachelor-wolf before us a tongue lashing such as I had never heard. In a moment, two companions dressed in wolf headdresses and wolf hides rose out of the brush nearby. Their masks made them seem formidable, but I noted their arms and bodies were slender and their limbs had not yet filled out. They laughed and smirked at Vitoria, showed her their bare bottoms defiantly, and then trotted off into the brush.

When I found my voice, I said, incredulously, "We fled for three days from these children?"

"Don't underestimate them," she said. "If they had caught us, they would have killed us."

"Not likely!" I said.

"Oh, yes," she said. "Or you would have killed them. Either outcome would have been equally unfortunate."

VI

"But if they do not move on? If the young bachelors remain fixed in these destructive ways, these moon-urges, as you call them, what then?"

I tried to speak of these things with Vitoria for several days as we journeyed back to the heartland of the People, but she would have none of it. Late the fourth day, she found a large camp of the People as if she had a map in her head by which she could plot their every movement.

I asked her again as we entered the encampment, but she dismissed me as if she had long ago wearied of the conversation. We parted company immediately, as she had female rituals and duties to attend to. I would have been at a serious loss as an outsider, had not Riik and several of my warrior friends happened to be in the same camp. I was seething with anger and bafflement and was glad to have someone to complain to. Riik took me outside the village and constructed a sweat lodge. He heard my story as we purified ourselves.

"It happens so sometimes," he said. "But there may be a remedy. The People have a way."

I gave my assent to anything that he cared to try that could bring harm to these young men or satisfaction to myself.

Several of his friends joined us at the lodge outside of camp, and Riik had me tell my story to these warriors, who voiced their disapproval of the young men with fierce grunts and exclamations. I bathed and sweated myself again in the lodge. Riik in the meantime took every article of my clothing and burned it in the fire. Then he and a friend washed everything else I possessed, including the Kuhlan war axe, with fresh water. They washed my bow and lance and dagger, my bridle and saddle. Then they gave me fresh clothing but had me put on only a loincloth of deerskin.

"Now I have to teach you a song," Riik said, solemnly throwing dried hemp into the fire. The song was a simple chant that I had heard many times in the campaign against the Kr. It mostly consisted of shouted, rhythmic lines, and it had a choral refrain:

Mother of darkness hear my cry!
Cleanse the poison from my blood,
Lift the darkness from my eyes!

The smoke was acrid and stung my nostrils. We composed a few shouted lines detailing my complaint against the young men. It seemed ludicrous to me, but Riik was patient and got me to sing a few lines and a chorus. The song was in the bass range, and, strangely, it seemed to express perfectly my feelings of frustration and rage. I appreciated the comradeship of Riik and the other men, so I persisted in the ritual.

"This is not the ritual itself," Riik explained, "but a preparation. Tell us of your feats of arms." He had me recite – to what I felt was unfeigned approval – all the actions of my military career in which I might be thought to have distinguished myself. As I spoke, Riik drew the same white line across my face that he had painted there on the day of Amasa's wedding. It reminded me that I held the rank of war leader among the People.

How many battles had I been in, Riik asked. He drew seven black circles on my chest. Wounds? He painted six blood-red slashes on my left arm. How many men had I slain? He drew twenty-three black lines across my right arm, from shoulder to wrist. The other warriors muttered their approval; this was something.

"How was that figure drawn on the shield your people gave you?" Riik asked. He was referring to the Transmitter on my decoration for valor. I was moved that he had recalled this detail. He had me paint a Transmitter on a fresh shield of bull's hide, while he and his friends copied the same symbols on the flank of a white stallion—adding six red slashes for wounds across its face, seven black circles for battles on its chest, and twenty-three black lines on the its forelegs for the men I had slain in battle.

"This is a good horse," Riik said. "Well trained. You can guide him with your knees. Hold the shield and the war axe this way, and guide the horse thus." They looked me over thoroughly. I felt intoxicated with the combination of the smoke and their approval.

"Now you are ready to speak to the People. The song will speak for you."

They walked beside me to the village, giving me instructions. My sense of the absurdity of what I was doing vanished amidst their assurance and comradeship. My horse began to dance as soon as I broke into song; my friends joined in on the chorus:

Mother of darkness hear my cry!
Cleanse the poison from my blood,
Lift the darkness from my eyes!

Figures emerged from their lodges immediately but stood watching respectfully. I saw several gangly youths in a cluster, and my anger blazed up. I brandished the axe at them with murderous intent, and they stepped back, abashed. Riik stayed at my side as we made a circuit of the village. As we returned to our starting point, many of the People joined in my song. I felt exhilarated; my skin prickled. The chorus rose up from the entire village, which had taken my wrongs as their own.

Then I saw a thin figure emerge from a lodge and my blood rose like fire up a pine; he wore the deerskin mask with the spike antlers. He stood before me defiantly, but before I could move to strike him down, Riik had leapt in front of me and thrown his hands in the air. My horse danced and reared, and it was all I could do to keep my seat. Riik and his companions had kept the song going, and a drum somewhere had taken up the rhythm. I rejoined them, feeling a wonderful sense of freedom that my own darkness, my own rage, was in the voices of the village and in the song. I saw how it was all intended to work, how it gathered the People into a Circle and affirmed their solidarity, even as it singled out a wrongdoer. This was not an individual matter, a personal cause for revenge; this was an offense against the People themselves.

Thus, I was not even astonished to see an old woman, very stooped and frail, and assisted by a robust woman of middle age, emerge from a near-by lodge. She approached the masked youth and in a quick, decisive, bird-like gesture, tore the mask from his head. With a little help from the younger woman, she ground her foot on the mask. "You have no face here," she said to the young man. "No face among the People."

The young man fled out of the village, followed soon after by his two companions. I watched them disappear, feeling a rich satisfaction that was better than vengeance.

I completed my second circuit of the village, my song still on everyone's lips, and drew up before a lodge where Vitoria stood. She was dressed in fresh bleached buckskin, and her long golden hair was washed and combed and pulled up in a roll behind. She was gazing at me and smiling, and while I could not read everything in her look, I knew it contained a larger measure of approval than I had ever seen. When I halted, she drew near, looking up at me, admiringly it seemed, and put her hand on my leg. She was the image, I thought, of a virtuous daughter of the People, approving what they approved in all things.

"Come," she said softly. "The lodge is ready." There was more invitation in her eyes than I had ever seen before. The drum throbbed like my own heart.

Inside the lodge, however, she surprised me again. "You have asked me what happens to young men who do not give up their destructive ways," she said. Her eyes were gleaming as she spoke.

"Yes," I replied. *"Yes?"*

To my astonishment, she drew a finger across her throat. She made this gesture delicately, almost provocatively, her nail pressing lightly against her skin. "If they do not grow," she murmured, "and if they become a burden to the People, they lose their right to live."

For a few short weeks, Vitoria and I stayed together, apart from the world, and I forgot that the transition from companion to lover had ever been awkward for us.

Light was streaming into the lodge when I awoke. I was groggy with lovemaking; I had overslept. Vitoria had already risen. I could hear a soft rustle of movement outside the lodge. I wrapped a blanket around my shoulders and ducked through the lodge door.

The sight of Vitoria drew me up short. She was facing the sun, with her face and hair aflame with the morning light. She wore a rapt expression, as if she were greeting the day with some ecstatic ritual. She seemed calm but intense, and hardly aware of the external world. Though naked, she seemed as oblivious to the morning chill as she was to my presence. She held her body in a graceful pose, her weight on her left leg with her hips and pelvis both relaxed and composed, as if for action. The posture was athletic and feminine and displayed the curves of her lovely body. Though I knew each separate feature of her intimately, I had seldom viewed her so fully, nor drunk so deeply of her beauty. The sight of her took my breath away.

Pensive, she touched her belly lightly, and with the other hand she held her breast. My heart melted with desire at the sight, and I ached again with longing for her. As I watched, she moved her hand to her other breast, touching herself delicately. She looked down at her breasts and then cupped them in each of her hands, as if weighing and measuring their firmness. She turned part way toward me, but without seeing me, as if her gaze was focused on some inward event of great significance. Finally she raised her eyes and acknowledged me: "I am with child," she said. "The signs are faint but unmistakable."

She walked past me and entered the lodge as if she were no longer aware of my presence. I had not yet absorbed the full import of her words before she reemerged, wearing a linen robe. She looked at me without any expression on her face.

"I am with child," she said again. "I have done my work, and you have done yours."

She had a small bundle in her hands, which she held out to me. It was my clothes.

"Go in peace," she said.

VII

Having no other place to go, I returned to the Benjamite encampment. I found that the plague of typhus had abated, and Colonel Harlech had pulled the remnant of the Guards back across the Snake. Captain Amasa was establishing a separate camp for those still recovering from the fever. It was not known how contagious these unfortunates might be, but it was thought best to take as few risks as possible. There had been new cases among the People on the north side of the river. Their villages were scattering, both to avoid the contagion and to find grazing for the horses. I could not even feign interest in these events.

"My friend," Zachariah said to me in a private moment, when we had pitched the new camp. "I understand you have recently had experience of our customs."

I nodded. I had no desire to speak of it.

"The People reward valor like no other nation," he said. "But the end of one's favored status comes swiftly. I know this myself," he added. "I have not gone with one of the Mothers of the People for years."

He seemed to want to comfort me. I did not know how to reply to him.

"Also," he said, "I have a wife in Israel."

I considered this revelation of his, realizing that Zechariah ben Harlech must be one of the loneliest men on earth. *It is better to be head of a family in Israel, I thought, than to be the greatest hero and husbandman among the People.*

"You can, if you wish, request another consort," he said. "The Grandmothers will select one for you. I took the trouble to ask."

"No, thank you!" I replied.

"I understand. But I was thinking in part of Vitoria. If there were another child like hers born soon after, it would be easier."

"Easier how? I don't follow you." Since parting with Vitoria, I had dwelt entirely on my own grief. Surely much of my pain was vanity. The child she would bear had not fully entered my imagination. "So, do you believe she is pregnant then? We spent so little time together."

"You had six weeks or better!" Zachariah declared. "Vitoria showed you great honor. Consider the circumstances, my friend. It may even be that conception took place immediately. I imagine she may well have prolonged your time together. The People are not sentimental about love, as we are, but they experience feelings of attachment too. She honored you." He waited while I digested his words and then added: "And yes, the women know these things. If she thinks she is pregnant, it means that she is."

I considered his words and asked, "But what did you mean, it would be easier if there were another child born soon after Vitoria's?

"Why, your child, Captain. Another child of yours. Then Vitoria's child would not be the only one."

"The only one what?"

He hesitated. "The only one with dark skin."

I was seized with a sudden, violent rage and I might have struck out and done the Colonel harm, had I not realized that I was hearing these words from a man who had himself been, in his time, the only dark-skinned child among the People.

"So, they despise us so much?" I was recalling Amasa's comment about the People's racial pride.

"They nurse their ancient feelings about us, yes. Perhaps no more than we do about them. Still, it is an ugly thing."

"So, you are telling me that you – you and your mother – have both suffered because of your race?"

"I imagine it was especially difficult for her. I was a child, ignorant of these things. And my mother played her role well, caring for me and assuring me that I was adored like any other child of the People. I am grateful to her for that. Believe me."

"Yet. . . ?"

"Yet after I was sent to the warriors—and later, to Israel – it became more difficult for her. We have grown apart of late. She has other sons, born of the People, and it is easier for her to be close to them."

His mother was one of the People, one of the very women—perhaps even one of the Sisters—whom we saw daily. And yet I had never seen an acknowledgement of kinship or love or even of casual interest pass between any of the women and Zechariah. *I felt a sudden bond of kinship with the man. We had more in common than I had imagined. We talked for a long time, and I put aside any reservations I had about him.*

While sympathetic to me, Zachariah was preoccupied with the fate of the Harlech within the Kuhlan lands. All the signs suggested that the People were turning against them and their special relationship. He feared that the trade with the People was about to be lost, and that the decision that had allowed his own birth had been, or was about to be, revoked. "It's possible that the People may reject us," he said, "and end the trade covenant with Benjamin." *I wondered if his mother's coldness was a signal of those intentions.* "The trade will not end, I think, but the People will seek other partners."

"And to think," I exclaimed, full of remorse, " I am the one who arranged for them to trade directly with Judah!"

"You intended only good. You had only the war with the Kr in mind. I know that."

"Why would the People turn against the Harlech? You have just given them valuable assistance in the war against the Kr. You Benjamites have shed your blood abundantly with and for them!"

He shrugged. "Perhaps because of that. The People do not like to feel beholden to anyone. Perhaps they feel themselves becoming dependent on us and on the trade – or perhaps they merely feel too deeply engaged with us. I do not always understand their motives. But they guard their independence fiercely."

"But you—you are not a foreigner to them. You—"

Colonel Harlech shook his head, closing off that discussion. We talked about the People's view of themselves and their possible motives, but I felt he had grown suddenly evasive on this topic.

In the midst of these heavy matters, my own preoccupation remained Vitoria and my parting from her. Eventually it occurred to me to ask him the obvious question: "If the People despise us as mud people, why did they make me a husbandman and send Vitoria to me?" *Another question that I could never speak also lay in my heart: How could she leave me, cast me aside, so easily?* The fact that she had not even chosen me of her own will was just gnawing into my consciousness. Even so, I was unprepared for his answer.

"But I thought you knew," Zachariah said, as if explaining the obvious to a child. "You told Pierson Angier yourself that you had had the mountain fever as a child and survived it. The People have little immunity to it; Vitoria's own child died of it. The People want that immunity."

I felt a sharp constriction in my chest. *It was no achievement of mine, no sacrifice or act of valor or even my distinction as author of the plan that had defeated the Kr. It was an accident of blood, my capacity to resist the fever that had led Vitoria to my bed.* I thought of her left breast, where the pigment had bleached a little on one nipple, and I recalled my own observation at the time that she must have nursed a child. More vividly than ever before, I saw her in my mind's eye, and I saw, for the first time, the child we had conceived.

Then a thought like an arrow out of the dark: have I conceived a child who will lead the Kuhlans against Israel?

When I could bring myself to speak again, I felt compelled to ask one more question of Zechariah: "You told me once that I would understand a great deal if I could learn why the People do not always come over against Israel. And why they withhold their raids."

"Yes, I remember."

"I feel very urgently that I must know," I said. "This riddle torments me. Especially now."

"I see how it might, my friend, but knowledge is often pain. Do you feel up to speaking to the Grandmothers?"

The old crone with the blind eye was seated in front of a lodge, working as ever at her loom. All the while we spoke, her hands never ceased moving nimbly at her task.

Faster than a weaver's shuttle are my nights and days.

"You have come to complain about the woman," she said sourly. "I have no time for foolishness."

"No," I replied. "Vitoria is a daughter of the People. I have no complaint." I clasped my hands together and said, with the best heart I could muster, "My thanks to the Mothers."

"Well, then?" She cast her ugly, sighted eye at me, but it was her dead white eye that seemed to catch and hold my gaze.

"I have a question. Why do the People cross over the river and slaughter my people? Why do you choose to be a plague to Israel?"

She turned to her loom with a scowl, as if the question surprised but did not interest her. "Israel," she said. "Israel? You still call yourselves *Israel*?" She laughed, a harsh, discordant cackle.

"I must know," I said. "And also why you leave us alone."

"You mud people," she sneered in her raven's voice, "dare to call us Kuhlans, after the times that you harried us from the valley and hunted us in the ravines and hills of our plateau. *You* call us Kuhlans even now, even after you have gone with one of our daughters and conceived by her!"

She was very angry, and of course she was correct. I still used the term, though until this moment I had been ignorant of its origins.

"You are an arrogant and a stiff-necked people; you are presumptuous and full of pride, and yet you cannot restrain yourselves. You breed like rabbits and eat up your own country, so that you must look for other lands to settle in. And you keep slaves – our kinsmen – as slaves!"

A host of objections to her characterization of my people formed on my tongue, but I waited to hear what more she would say.

"You are not law-abiders," she added, much to my surprise. "You never have been. You are children, you are animals lacking reason; you only play at life. And you call yourself *Israel*! You have no more right to call yourself Israel than that heap of cow shit yonder." She spat. "You mud people are incapable of managing your own affairs. You always have been. You always will be. So we manage them for you."

I caught in her ancient rasping voice a word I had heard my second day in the Kuhlan lands – *"manishmah"*—the word that the inhabitants of Moses Town had uttered with such dread.

"So," I struggled for several moments to find my voice; "so, then, you *presume* to manage us? What gives you the right?

"Yes, we *presume*, young man. We *presume*! What gives shit the right to stand on two feet and presume to speak to *me*, to question what the People do? When you overrun your own country and threaten ours by your sheer numbers, yes, we manage you, we cull you like our cattle herds in the fall. And with far less compassion and regret, young man! Far less regret!"

Since that time, that moment, I have often thought of what I might have replied to her, as she glared at me, toothless and half-blind – yet triumphant and scornful and as dismissive of me as if I had been dung on the road. I have thought of many words I might have spoken, each of them filled to suffocation with rage and hatred and exasperation, speaking for all the generations of my people snuffed out of existence by Kuhlan arrogance. If I could have clenched all my anger into a curse – or into a fist and smashed it into her face, it might have—not sufficed, to be sure—but *helped* somewhat to relieve my heart. I could have compassed the extermination of her whole people in an instant and laughed afterwards. It was in my heart to do so. My heart was dark and my blood poisoned for a long time.

My mood was not lightened when Colonel Harlech came to me with the news that the trade relationship between Benjamin and the People was indeed broken; his men, the Guards, all the Benjamites in the Kuhlan lands, would have to leave at once. The Grandmothers had reached a decision.

"But the timing!" I cried. "Why now? What does it mean?"

"I think they were waiting for Vitoria to finish with you."

This new burden gnawed at my heart. I tried to see some escape from this dilemma. "Is this the end of the trade, then? I can't imagine the People just giving up the goods they are used to having."

"The trade will go on in all likelihood, but it will be dominated by Judah—by Tephlin Glanz." Zacheriah said this without irony or rancor. It was a fact; he was a realist. "The People thought they received better value from Judah at the mid-winter exchange," he explained.

I cringed inwardly. *I had done this thing to him.* "Good value this once, perhaps!" I exclaimed. "But if Tephlin Glanz gets a monopoly, the rates of exchange will surely alter."

"True. But he won't get one. The Grandmothers are not stupid. They have promised some crumbs of the trade to us, and I understand there are already some contacts to the north." He shrugged. "I think the People want multiple trading partners. They feel confident that they can manipulate Israel without becoming dependent on any single source – or becoming friendly with their new partners. I think all this contact we have had lately has threatened their purity, as they imagine it."

St. Supplicee! I said to myself, with a dozen different emotions.

"But that's not why I came to you," the Colonel said soberly. "The People will hold another great council at Moses Lake at the time of the summer solstice. When the council is over, we must be gone from their lands."

"But we have sick and wounded. How can we—"

"What's worse, we have no homeland to return to. No place to go. Therefore, it will mean surrender. I have been reluctant to think of that, naturally. But I come to you now to ask if you could negotiate terms for us with your father."

"St. Supplicee!" I exclaimed again. "No!" I said. "*Never!* You must *never* yield to Tephlin Glanz!" My mind raced a moment. "I have a better idea," I exclaimed. "We are not without options. Not if the Kuhlans will let us be until the solstice and then allow us to leave on our own terms. But first, tell me where the source of recovered metal lies in the Kuhlan lands."

"The *People*, the *People's* lands," he corrected me. "Why, that would be Old Spokane, in the ruins there. I suppose there is a great deal of metal yet to recover. Why do you ask?"

I explained to him what I had seen at Meribah on my trip up the Jordan: Benjamites chained in a slave coffle, bound for the Glanz metal recovery mines. "They mentioned 'further Lebanon,' where even the Harlech could not find them. Would that be Old Spokane?"

"I assume so, yes." Colonel Harlech knew that Benjamites had been forcibly removed from Esdralon, but he had not known they had been taken as slaves. While he was appalled at the news, his mind was very busy, adding things together. "Old Spokane can be reached by water transport," he said, drawing a map for me in the dirt. "The Spokane River is a tributary of the Jordan. It lies in Sage Grouse territory." He looked at me. We both had arrived that instant at a new understanding of the Sage Grouse People's opposition to continuing the trade with the Harlech. I told him the names of the Benjamite slaves I had written down and memorized that night at Meribah. He shut his eyes and listened.

"Well," he said when I had finished, "I think we should fetch them along when we leave the People's lands, don't you?"

I nodded.

"I think we can manage a raid while the People are in council at Moses Lake, and then make a dash across the Jordan. Where is it that you intend for us to cross? Where would you take us?"

"Dan," I said, my mind churning with the possibilities.

The end of an epoch had come for Benjamin and for the bold and brilliant Harlech clan. I thought of Jonas ben Harlech's journal and the events that had brought the current era into being. "We are one people" he had acknowledged to the Kuhlan negotiator of his day. *We are one people.* But we have always failed to act as one people, or to acknowledge our common bonds.

"We are one people," I had said to the one-eyed Grandmother in parting, acknowledging our bond not as a thing of value, but as a curse. I said this while clasping my hands together in the posture of grateful reverence, but I was saying in my heart, *you are the worst of what we are, and more. And if the People come across the Jordan to manage us, they will leave their bones in Israel!*

As we made our preparations to depart from the Kuhlan lands, I could not quiet the tumult in my heart. I could no more meditate than I could fly. It was truly as if I had been poisoned. This one-eyed, baleful hag and all her kind I would have gleefully crushed to a pulp or swept into oblivion behind me. I could have cheerfully obliterated all traces of their existence with a consuming fire. I longed, in fact, to set their world aflame and to scatter the ashes with my boot.

If the People come over against Israel again, I imagined myself shouting at the old crone, we will manure our fields with your flesh!

But then I would think of Riik, my warrior friend who had given me the trophy axe and initiated me as a war leader, and who had sat beside me in a sweat lodge, stolidly painting my deeds on my body as he taught me the song of darkness. At other times, I would imagine my son, tall and fair and serious like his mother. *My son, leading the People across the Jordan. That single thought plunged me again into the depths of the river.*

I sat in the sweat lodge alone, seeking to mark this passage in my life, searching for balance and harmony with the changes, but feeling as if I were in fact falling through space. *Israel's only salvation was the Law.* I knew that in every fiber of my being. My people must learn to restrain themselves and become stern and disciplined, as the Kuhlans are stern and disciplined. I knew also that because *I* realized this – understood it in my bones and flesh beyond all others now alive – it had become my task to teach them. Unfortunately, it was a task for which I was uniquely unworthy.

But if I could perform it, it might keep my son on the Kuhlan side of the Jordan.

Book Four: Shall the Sword Devour Forever?

Chapter 13: Sun, Stand Still

I

Standing again on the soil of my homeland, I felt nostalgia strong enough to unstring my limbs—and then a wild relief, like a lost child finding its mother at last, after hope was gone. But I did not embrace the sacred soil of Israel either to rejoice or to weep. I was reassuming burdens temporarily cast aside. I had not come home to peace, but to exchange one form of warfare for another. The task I resumed when I emerged again, wet and dripping from the Jordan, would engage all my energies and resolve.

Colonel Zachariah ben Harlech looked at me, wanting an explanation. *I borrowed his glass and scanned the ridgeline. The sun was bright enough to dazzle. Sweat trickled down my forehead and into my eyes as I searched for explanations, for it was I who had led us into danger. There were several hundred mounted men arrayed on the ridge opposite us. The whole slope seemed in agitated motion "These are clansmen, not the Danite Legion," I said. "Wait! Yes, there is one cohort of the Legion in the center."*

"Why should Dan be on a war footing?" Colonel Harlech demanded. "And why arrayed against us?"

"Perhaps they take us for Kuhlans," I said. "But we must find out why they are mustered for war in a hurry."

I spurred my horse down the steep slope ahead of our formation. The Colonel shouted orders behind me, holding his men in check. A sudden unexplained movement could launch the two forces down into the valley at each other. Thirty yards ahead of our line, I wheeled my horse in a tight circle – the signal for a parley. Colonel Harlech plunged down the slippery incline and sawed up beside me, swearing. Above us, I heard the familiar cadences of the cavalry drill. He had ordered Moriah to draw the men up in parade formation and separate them into clear military formations. The shouted commands would not carry across the valley, but the sight of our formations would. The Colonel was attempting to announce our identity as Israelites, hoping this would give the Danites pause.

The Danites, however, did not reciprocate by sending a horseman out to make the circle announcing that the parley was accepted. Apparently, they were spoiling for a fight. The Colonel frowned and nudged his horse forward. We descended to the valley floor and reined in at the edge of a small stream that bisected the valley, respecting the visual boundary between the two forces. The Colonel rose in his stirrups and saluted in the general direction of the Danite colors. Then we waited.

The forward edge of the bench obscured our view of the ridge top. We heard galloping hooves, and then a trio of horsemen rose up on the bench above us. "Who are you?" a voice shouted at us.

Colonel Harlech turned in the saddle toward me, as if furious: "Damn it!" he cried, in a voice loud enough to carry, but as if not deigning to answer them. "Is there no courtesy in Israel! We asked for a parley!" With studied casualness, the Colonel dismounted and gave his horse rein to drink from the stream.

The officer who had hailed us maneuvered his horse down the ridge to where we waited. "My commander says you trespass on Danite territory. Surrender or die!"

"Is Dan so eager to savage its neighbors?" the Colonel shouted back. "Captain," he said, turning to me, but in a voice loud enough to carry, "I suppose we'll have to send you off to see about this. Tag along with this man and see if you can get an explanation." He planted his feet wide apart with both hands on his hips. "I'll rely upon your diplomacy."

I saluted him, understanding both the stage manner and the instructions he was giving me. "With your permission, Captain," I said to the Danite officer. I guided my mount across the stream and up the bank where the Danite cavalry waited. "This is not the kind of reception one expects in Dan," I said when we had joined the others. "Whom do you take us for?"

My escort said nothing, his teeth fiercely clenched on his helmet strap. Two of the troopers fell in alongside me as though escorting a prisoner. One of them, however, seemed less intense than his captain. "Your man – the Colonel down there," he began, "his speech is strange. Is he Ephraimite? Or Manassite?"

"Silence!" the Captain ordered.

"Neither," I replied, ignoring the Captain. "He is, as you no doubt inferred, a southerner. And one of the most famous men in Israel."

"*Silence!*" the Captain ordered again, and this time his manner said he was not to be trifled with.

As we approached the circle of officers a great shout went up, and I was deluged with threats and curses. Fierce Danite tribesmen shook their weapons at me. I was relieved to see one cohort only of the Danite Legion, calculating that we might have a chance against clan levies, outnumbered though we were. Then I recognized the commander of the force arrayed against us as Captain Ethan Boz, son of the Apostle Caleb Boz—only now, his insignia revealed, it was *Major* Boz.

"Major, this man has come up to discuss surrender terms."

"Major Boz," I saluted him. "We meet again." When I removed my headgear, I saw that he recognized me, though he worked at maintaining a stern, expressionless face. *Very grim, these Danites.* I looked about; I could not even guess at the cause of the hostility surrounding me. "Apparently, not even your father's statecraft could keep Dan aloof from war," I remarked.

Young Boz was not inclined to be conciliatory: "State your business—and be quick about it," he snapped.

"Forgive our ignorance, Major. As you can see by our clothes, we have been absent from Israel for some time." I still wore the buckskin and leather clothing that Riik had given me. I had a Guards helmet, but my clothing and equipment were otherwise Kuhlan in origin. "My companions yonder are Benjamites. They are the remnant of the Esdralon Guards – and exiles now, like myself, and seeking refuge. So far as we are aware, Benjamin and Dan are not at war."

"Benjamites!" Major Boz exclaimed suspiciously. "What in the name of St. Supplicee are Benjamites doing on Danite land?"

"We have spent an exile in the Kuhlan lands, they as well as I. But this force you see has survived and has returned to Israel in the only way open to them."

"You have no business here. *You,* I mean. My father explicitly outlawed you and signed a warrant for your death."

"Indeed, I remember! And I remember when Israel had laws and justice!" I was tempted to say more, but thought it best to concentrate on the Benjamites. "My friends have been cast out by the Kuhlans. Judah occupies their homeland, and they could go nowhere but here." Many of the clan leaders crowded around, and I saw they were interested in the story I had to tell. I explained that we had crossed the Jordan above Chinnereth two days ago and sought asylum.

"And yourself? What are *you* doing back on Danite soil?"

"That need not concern us now. I speak as a delegate of these men of Benjamin."

"Well, then, what are their terms for surrender?" he demanded.

The fool chooses to persist. "No terms, Major. The Esdralon Guards do not surrender. If you choose to make enemies out of would-be friends, you will be remembered as one who throws away gold."

There was a murmur from the clan chiefs who had formed a circle around us. *A fool throws away gold, the adage went.* They knew I had insulted him. Major Boz demanded to know if there were Kuhlans behind us.

"They expelled us from their lands, but they do not pursue us." *Already, I was using my special knowledge of the Kuhlans.*

The Danite Guards officers remained sullen and suspicious, but to the clan chiefs we had become objects of curiosity rather than threats. Major Boz, however, continued to press the issue of a Kuhlan invasion and demanded to know whether they might follow us across the Jordan.

"The Kuhlans cross the river when they choose," I said sharply. "They do as they like. But they will not come because of us."

"In any case, do you imagine that anyone may trespass on Danite land?"

"We had no choice. Behind us, we have women and children and many crippled by war. These Benjamites seek safe passage through your lands to theirs. Or if that is not possible, they seek suppliant status." I paused, feeling a flood of memories rush back to me, and with it a cold anger. "Suppliant status," I said to Boz, "as I was once a suppliant in Dan." This time I could tell he was aware of the treachery of his father. I chose the moment to announce: "Our commander is Zachariah ben Harlech, Colonel and Apostle-to-be in Benjamin."

A murmur went through the group.

"I see that Colonel Harlech's fame reaches even unto Dan," I said. "Justly so. With your permission, Major, I will introduce you."

"No! Wait!" he said. "You have no permission here!"

Few things, I reflected, are more dangerous than a fool with strict orders. "Gentlemen," I said, trying to disarm their hostility, "it appears that our difficulties have driven us here at an unpropitious time, but we know nothing of your troubles, or even of recent events of the war." Judging that everyone but Boz understood our plight, I added: "Understand that necessity drives us, and we cannot turn back. We come in peace, but we are not helpless. We will shed our blood to defend our women and children. Make no mistake! If Dan chooses to dishonor itself, we will make this a day that your people will recall with grief as well as shame."

Boz hesitated, glancing at his officers and the clan chiefs. "Dan honors the customs," he said reluctantly.

While waiting for Colonel Harlech to come up, I explained that my companions had fought against Israel's enemies, the Kr, and thus averted a threat to the nation. I thought it best that we be thought formidable, but I only guess what else might enhance our cause. The Danites studied me carefully in the hot sun, and I studied them in return.

"Ah, Major," Colonel Harlech said coming up the ridge. He saluted with perfect aplomb, smiling. "We meet at last." After Colonel Harlech had introduced himself around, he asked: "What calamity has brought Dan out in arms?"

Dan's clan chiefs were bursting with grievances. Dan had been raided, they complained; camps had been burned, wells destroyed, women and children slaughtered. We inquired who had done these things, but the Danites did not know. "Whether Kuhlans, or yourselves, or other Israelites pretending to be savages, no one can tell," one of the chieftains replied. "They leave no witnesses alive."

This was indeed strange. I wondered whether it was Manasseh who was their enemy, or Hanford's successors in Naphtali. I could think of no other likely suspects for these crimes.

"Who would have a motive to harm you?" Colonel Harlech asked. "Who holds Dan so lightly that they wish you as enemies? I assure you," he said with a laugh, "my men and I have enemies enough! Come inspect our gear. If you find Danite possessions among us, you can avenge yourselves. We crossed the Jordan but two days ago, above Chinnereth. The stronghold is in our hands, by the way, but it is a poor prize. Come, examine our horses. See if any belong to Dan. Do you imagine," he added shrewdly, "you would have seen more than our rumps if we had Danite horses?"

The Colonel's manner, more than his answers, seemed to satisfy the suspicious tribesmen. The danger subsided as quickly as water is poured from a vessel. Even though they were incensed by the recent incursions that left behind no witnesses, the Danites were hospitable people. It was only Major Boz's determination not to fall short of his father's instructions that kept us on the edge of hostility. There were a number of Sevfolk of Jerub's clan among the host; some of them recognized me, and we were soon on a friendlier terms.

As we considered these events, Colonel Harlech began to draw the obvious conclusions. "These raiders are not Kuhlans," he pointed out, "and they are not ourselves. So whom does that leave as possibilities? Are the Northern Lights Guards out to stir up trouble?"

"Not likely," one of the officers said. "Relations with Naphtali have been correct of late, if not friendly."

"The Northern Lights Guards have kept to their stronghold in Jezreel," another explained. "We hear they have difficulties of their own in the north, on the Okanogan. I doubt it is they who have made these raids into Dan. They have no reason to trouble us."

That made sense. After Hanford Glanz's death, the new leaders of Naphtali would be preoccupied with consolidating their position. So that left Manasseh. Colonel Harlech politely suggested as much.

"Manasseh has no motive to harm us," Major Boz said. "My father has cultivated the Messiahists very carefully – especially this past year." *I suspected that he was cultivating them with the money I had deposited in Danite banks.* He frowned, as if thinking the same thought.

Our interrogation turned by degrees into a conversation, and soon the clan chiefs were inviting Benjamites to share a meal around their campfires. Major Boz announced that he would send a messenger to Hazor for instructions about how to treat the Esdralon Guards. Turning to me, he said, "It is you who concern me. My father has published a warrant for your death."

I scoffed. "Your father should pretend more respect for the Law. Nisan Lot took a deposition clearing me of guilt in the Valdez affair months ago. Surely this is known everywhere."

Boz made a gesture that told me that Nisan Lot was not popular with the Apostle's clan. "It is the death of Brother Ignacio that is at issue. That, and your interference in Dan's internal affairs—particularly our relations with the Messiahists."

"There are many in Dan," I said, indicating the clan levies around us, "who take the same view of Ignacio as I. And of Messiahists generally. Before you arrest me for Ignacio's death, perhaps you should see if they are behind these raids into Dan."

I heard rough murmurs of assent to my last statement. Major Boz kept his own counsel, apparently familiar with the views of his eastern tribesmen.

"Tell me candidly, Danite," Colonel Harlech interjected, "is it safe for me to bring our women and children into your lands?" Major Boz obviously did not catch his drift, so Colonel Harlech explained: "When Hanford Glanz's successors in Naphtali hear of the mischief we did in Chinnereth, they are likely to make demands on you if you harbor us. What will you say to them?"

The young man scowled deeply, visibly needing instructions before he replied.

"We have no desire to entangle Dan in our misfortunes," Colonel Harlech warned. "But we will protect our women and children."

Seeing Boz's confusion, the clan chieftains took up this issue among themselves. They agreed that our presence, especially our seizing of Chinnereth, would offend Naphtali – a prospect they rather enjoyed. But they were not at war with Naphtali and had no desire to be. "Naphtali may well mount an expedition to re-take the portage," one of them suggested.

"That is no concern of ours," another remarked.

"And it is no concern of Naphtali whom Danites admit as suppliants," one of the elders declared. There was general agreement on this point. "So I say, by all means," the eldest of the chieftains said, "bring your people inland, where they will be safe."

Major Boz was willing to follow their lead: "Your women and children will be under my protection, whatever my father wills about this son of Tephlin Glanz."

Colonel Harlech bowed in acknowledgement. "I understand," the Colonel said boldly to Major Boz, "that there is a difficulty over an amount of money between the Captain here and your father, the Apostle."

"Two hundred thousand kanz of funds entrusted to me for my mission!" I exclaimed. "And money which, I suspect, the Apostle Boz has appropriated for his own use, confident that I was dead. Yes, if that is the case, then we have a problem. And you can all understand Boz's motive in outlawing a creditor who is owed such a sum. It is well said, *who is more suspicious than the evil-doer?*"

The sum of money involved sent another murmur through the group. Major Boz flushed crimson, perhaps as much from shame as anger. "My father bought time from his creditors in New Jerusalem," he declared, "and he used it to put Dan on a war footing."

His answer confirmed my fears. The Apostle had stripped me of the money entrusted to me for my mission. "I have regretted my own father's actions every day of my life," I said to him, aware of the many ironies in the situation. "But your father took my money and my assistance and then sought my death. Do not pretend that he does justice!"

"I was just thinking," Colonel Harlech interrupted, anxious to defuse the situation, "of the supplies you signed for at Chinnereth. All that rigmarole about the seal of Tephlin Glanz and bills of credit, and it turns out you wrote a bogus bill of exchange. That is, if it is true that the Apostle of Dan has seized all your assets. It appears that you have robbed the new rulers of Naphtali blind—even as you were robbed by the Apostle of Dan." The clan chiefs appreciated this humor at the Apostle's expense. Colonel Harlech gave an account of our seizure of Chinnereth, making a tale of it. "To think," he added, speaking in my direction, "that Josiah wrote a false draft to the murderers of his brother! There may be justice after all."

"Justice in Dan?" I retorted. "I doubt it!" There was much laughter and slapping of quirts. It appeared that we were establishing ourselves as comrades and allies. Major Boz, however, remained sullen and aloof. I had taken his measure already, and unless I was badly mistaken, most of the clan chiefs and his own officers already shared my estimate of the man.

When I stood to make my plea, which is the suppliant's right, my words were more a challenge than a plea. In the Kuhlan lands I had endured both hardship and humiliation, and I had returned scarred and angry and impatient. If the Apostle Boz chose to step in my way, I warned, he did so at his own risk. I accused the Apostle of theft and fraud and conspiracy to murder, and I reminded my hearers that though the Law had fallen asleep in Dan, it was far from dead. "If there is justice in Dan, let the Apostle tear up his warrant and honor his debt to me. If not, let the consequences fall on his head!"

I heard many cries of "bwen, bwen," and a fierce thumping of quirts. Major Boz kept his eyes on the ground, but Colonel Harlech looked at me searchingly, his eyes narrowing with questions he did not ask.

For myself, the most pressing question of returning to Israel had been whether I would be killed on the spot or taken into custody. That issue resolved—or at least held in abeyance – another question emerged: *Who, then, were the raiders?* We sat under an awning with the clan chiefs discussing the possibilities. We helped ourselves out of a bowl of lamb and lentils and beans in a savory sauce. I began to feel at home again.

The elder who invited us to bring our children to safety appeared to be well informed. "Nisan Lot" he said, nodding to me—"the Captain may remember the Mayor of Hazor? The Mayor fears that some faction of churchmen, perhaps those prophesying the Judgment, have come up against us."

"Why would they break the peace?" Colonel Harlech asked. "What motive would the Messiahists have to antagonize Dan? Surely they would not start a second war with Dan while they are engaged in the south?"

"Manasseh has embraced a strange fanaticism of late," the old man said. "There are many who claim that with the millennium, we will see the third appearance of the Savior."

"Yes," another said, "and the saying is, the whole of Israel must be in the fold and under Messiahist rule for the Judgment Day to come."

"All of Israel under Messiahist control?" I asked. "So the Third Coming is conditional?" They confirmed that it was. *Very convenient, I thought.*

"But what of the war with Judah?" the Colonel asked.

"A month ago at Gibeah, the Messiahists won a victory. They chased the Judeans down the river."

My heart rose into my throat. I pleaded for more details.

"The Messiahists did not destroy the Judeans," the old man explained, "but they pressed them hard." General Pasco had been relieved and Ahaz put in his place.

Colonel Harlech saw the implications instantly. "If all this is true, Major Boz, then I am anxious for Dan." He took a map out of his battered case and unrolled it for us. "See here, if Judah is temporarily weakened and disorganized by this defeat, then a portion of the Messiahist force is freed to do mischief. Have you heard anything of a follow-up—or of pursuit and subsequent battles in Judah? Anything? Nothing! Well, then, suppose the Messiahists raid here in the eastern part of your lands, where there are only flocks and shepherds. Why would they intrude here?"

Young Boz was silent. The clan chiefs looked at each other and back at us.

"There are, begging your pardon, no targets of strategic interest here," Colonel Harlech said. "Therefore, the attacks may be a ruse, intended to draw your cavalry away from the heartland of Dan." He looked around the group. "How much of the Danite cavalry is deployed here?"

Too much! Boz's pained expression revealed. There were frowns and mutterings from the group. It was obvious that if the recent raids marked the beginning of hostilities with the Messiahists, the real threat to Dan lay in the Yakima valley, along the road to Hazor. That would be the invasion route. Boz flushed angrily, clenching his teeth, and refused to speak. The Apostle's son was a slow thinker, more anxious to deny us information than to enlist us as allies.

Colonel Harlech drew the obvious conclusion for him: "Perhaps the Messiahists intend to crush Dan with one quick blow in order to secure their rear. Then they could concentrate their forces against Judah and finish the war."

"Then they would have all of Israel in their power," an elder said, "and the Judgment Day could come. The Messiahists," he added solemnly, "say that this time they are determined they will not be left behind." His comment caused a stir in the group.

Judgment Day, I thought. *The idea is a curse!*

Boz excused himself and went to consult with his officers. The clan chiefs continued in anxious debate over the possibilities ripening out of our line of sight. Within the hour, Major Boz left in haste with his troop of the Danite Legion, riding westward. His departure gave me pause for reflection. I had been but three days on Israelite soil, and already I was immersed again in its politics and quarrels and the struggle to define its future. My nine months in the Kuhlan lands already seemed like a distant memory.

II

We brought up our women and invalids, abandoning Chinnereth behind us, and pitched our camp with the Sevfolk. We had many soldiers ill or recovering from wounds. Of Esdralon Guards fit for duty, we had barely 300 of the original legion. A remnant merely, though every one of them was a seasoned veteran.

Amidst the lively trading and story telling that ensued, my old acquaintance, Jerub, Sheriff of the Sevfolk, sought me out. "Well, Asherite!" he said, "you intrude onto Danite soil again. What is it you intend to do this time?"

I bowed and introduced him to Colonel Harlech.

"This young man is trouble," Jerub said of me. "But you are welcome among the Sevfolk, Colonel. Your fame carries even here. And Jezreel"—he exclaimed, turning back to me. "What about Jezreel?"

"Just as I told you, Jezreel belongs to Dan. As soon as I rule Naphtali, it shall be so."

"Good, good! The boy has a memory! Make sure you hold onto it!" he exclaimed. Then he added slyly: "I hear you forget things." He turned to the Colonel, pleased to have tweaked me a little. "The first time I saw him," Jerub announced, "he drank so much his eyes crossed and he fell down flat on the ground. I suppose he remembers nothing of that! I thought he was the biggest fool I ever saw. So young, and yet so foolish. It takes most men years to become so accomplished. Now he returns, a friend of one of the famous men of Israel."

Colonel Harlech bowed, acknowledging the compliment.

"But he arrives dressed like a beggar – and still needing assistance. That much fits what we saw before."

A group of Sevfolk tribesmen shared a laugh at my expense with Colonel Harlech. Jerub was a jovial host, but his recollection of those events made me uneasy; I glanced around looking for his daughter.

"Tell me," Jerub said, pressing his attention on the Colonel, "is this young Glanz a sage – one of the great men, like the Dolorites of the past? Or is he a fool, as dangerous to himself as others? The Apostle Boz meant to drown him in the Jordan, and Nathan Lander tried to feed him to the Kuhlans, yet here he is again, bobbing up like a submerged log."

"Well," the Colonel answered, smiling, "sage I don't know about. But he is a warrior. Ask the Kuhlans," he said, falling into Israelite usage. "The Kuhlans honored him above all other men among us. You see the war axe and shield they gave him," he added, gesturing toward me. "He is a chief, a war leader, among them. That quiver of spotted calf skin is the gift of a priestess – one of the Mothers."

I was dandling a baby, awkwardly, hoping it wouldn't make a mess of my clothes. I flinched at his mention of Vitoria's gift to me, but Colonel Harlech's revelation about my status among the Kuhlans excited murmurs among the Danites.

"A chief among our enemies," Jerub said, rubbing his chin and regarding me skeptically. "That is something, to be sure. But what?"

Suddenly, a young woman whom I recognized as my partner of a year before stepped out of the crowd. She had a baby only a few months of age in her arms. *I counted the months in my head.*

"The women remember your presents," Jerub said pointedly. I looked at the infant in his daughter's arms.

"More than any other gift, the Sevfolk will remember the return of Jezreel to Dan," I replied as coolly as I could.

"Good!" Jerub exclaimed. "Remember that!"

"Tamar?" I asked softly. She nodded. She seemed to stare at me very intently and at the baby I held, a squirming one-year old.

"Here, hold mine," she said.

I took the child from her gingerly as the talk proceeded around us. It was a brown, dark-haired baby of about three months. I observed it with care, thinking: *the timing is right*. But its face and features, hands and feet, were like those of a thousand other Israelite infants. I felt no instinctive bond, no rush of paternal feelings.

"This is my husband," Tamar said, interrupting my reverie. She introduced me to a square-shouldered man of medium height. I felt relief sweep over me. I smiled and handed the child back to her. We made conversation while Jerub and the Colonel approached the business at hand. I offered the conventional compliments on their child, but my own thoughts were on a child yet to be born in the Kuhlan lands. *That child would be fair-skinned and blue-eyed and wild, and, if he ever set foot on Israelite soil, would come as an enemy.*

Though Jerub and the Colonel appeared to get on well, we were forced to haggle. "You can't expect us to wait to see what Caleb Boz will decide to do," the Colonel declared, turning the conversation to the business at hand.

Jerub agreed heartily that Boz was a treacherous swine, but could not see how that fact obliged him to offer us any trade concessions.

"We must rearm and remount the Legion," Zachariah said. "Our equipment is worn out—and besides, the women and other civilians we brought back with us are destitute." Colonel Harlech explained that Benjamites had been taken as slaves out of Esdralon and shipped north to Glanz's metal recovery mines. We had freed these victims of the war and brought them back with us.

"Yes, very sad," Jerub agreed, pulling at his beard. "I've seen them myself. Seen the coffles at Jezreel. I knew they were Benjamites." He turned and looked me over seriously. "How is it, Colonel, that you can be friends with the son of such a man, the son of Tephlin Glanz?"

"You may well wonder," Zachariah said. "But in his heart, Josiah is no more the son of that man than I am."

"We need clothes, good Israelite clothes," I said, willing to change the subject. "And weapons and horses. Food, blankets, tents. All of it."

"Good!" Jerub replied. "Excellent! Just show us what you have to trade."

"I have the better part of 200,000 kanz, as you well know. We can pay—just as soon as your outlaw Apostle restores my funds."

"Yes," Jerub said, rubbing his hands. "We'll trust him to do that. And we will trade, *then*. But then or now, we will want cash."

Colonel Harlech threw up his hands.

Jerub, however, was not through with me. "How is it," he asked, his shrewd eyes only inches from me, "that you still carry your father's commission?

"In my life," I replied, "there is one instance only where we have agreed, and that is that *I* should rule Naphtali."

I accompanied Colonel Harlech as he returned to our camp. A good deal of trade was going forward anyway. The Sevfolk were fascinated by our Kuhlan gear and gladly traded good Israelite products for our ragged things.

In the afternoon, I withdrew a space and built a sweat lodge and a small canopy outside it. I needed to purify myself and meditate. Afterwards, I sat in the shade of the canopy, wrapped in my own thoughts. I had much to think about: Justin and Michal-Rebekkah, as always. Miriam and Nathan Lander and the tangled mess I had left behind with them. Vitoria intruded into my thoughts as well, but I put her memory aside to concentrate on my many flaws of character. Also troubling to me was the bizarre relationship between the Kuhlans and Israel that I had discovered before leaving the People's land. Concerning the latter, I would have preferred simple enmity, however bitter, between our two nations. But the actual nature of our relationship—a presumptuous kind of responsibility exercised by the Kuhlans on our behalf—made me ashamed and furious. To be culled periodically, allegedly for our own good, was to strip us of our dignity. We were no more than cattle to them. Still, I could not but acknowledge the truth of their disparaging view of us. We did not truly heed the Reproduction Laws, and we used our lands up greedily. And in the matter of the Reproduction Laws, I had myself exhibited as much unwisdom as anyone. Strict adherence to the Law alone could save us from the People's depredations. The Law and a wise spirit of self-restraint. But what could I say to my people about self-restraint?

And yet I must speak what I knew. *Power is a sacred trust*, St. Supplicee says, and the knowledge I had was clearly a form of power. I possessed it in trust, and therefore I had to use it on behalf of my people; I had to share that knowledge and lead where I could see the path and others could not. But it was a heavy burden to carry, and I felt keenly my own unworthiness.

As for the situation in Dan, I had been relieved to hear that the College survived and had become a stronghold for Old Believers, and that Burgos and Brother Peter and Rehab Gill still lived. I longed to send them a message and visit Hazor myself, but if I set foot inside the walls, I was likely to be hanged. Dan, I learned, was sharply divided between Old Believers and those who favored an accommodation with the Messiahists. Of actual Messiahists, there seemed to be few in Dan, but there were many who feared the churchmen and preferred to put them off with soft words. The Apostle and his circle were for accommodation. Much of the rest of Dan rejected the claims of the churchmen and were wary of their intentions; the Council itself was split. Meanwhile, the eastern clans were increasingly rebellious.

The Mayor of Hazor, Nisan Lot, had had a falling out with the Apostle, who believed him to be too partial to Old Believers. It was also reported that the Apostle was ailing—that he had grown even frailer than he was unpopular. This was not unwelcome news, for I saw the Mayor as the most likely successor to Boz. In that event, I surmised, Dan would follow a path more congenial to my purposes.

At sunset I was roused from meditation by visitors. Groups of Old Believers from Dan had come to trade and to gawk, and they gathered about me, some out of curiosity and some, apparently, to pay me homage. I wondered what I must do, what further folly and disgrace I must fall into, to discourage the hopes of people like these. I wanted to cry out, *You waste your time here!* But I kept silent. They were respectful, almost timid, as they tried to converse with me.

"Are you the one we wait for?" one of them ventured to ask. "Are you the Sword?"

I returned their greetings, but disabused them of this hope, saying, "I have no sword; it was taken from me. I lost my way. I lost my sword." The crowd seemed to search my face as if to delve beneath the surface of my simplest utterance. I repeated many times that my sword had been taken from me – and with justice. My audience, however, did not shrink from me for these failures I confessed. Instead, I felt their warmth and approval. Their generosity moved me deeply. I reached out and touched the hands of those nearest to me, and felt them reach out to me in return. "My sword was taken from me," I said. "I was not worthy of the least part of the task."

For more than a year, I had reflected on my preparation at the Refuge, realizing that I was in all likelihood a project of Ebenezer's that had gone astray. Still, the "Sword of Israel" had never been mentioned there, not once. I had never heard the term until I arrived in Dan. But if Ebenezer had imagined I could assume such a role, he was wrong. *I was not the Sword of Israel.*

Nevertheless, I suspected that Josephus and Ebenezer had trained me with that end, or one like it, in mind. They had raised me on tales of Dedicated Ones and Dolorites from the past. These stories had resonated powerfully in me—and still resonated powerfully. Had my Masters seen that? *Of course they had.* Had my Masters hypnotized me to act as their proxy? Seeing my eagerness to serve, had they made a monster of me, a creature with no will of its own? No, I could not believe that. I had been just a strange, lonely boy left on their doorstep. A boy with odd mental quirks and bouts of amnesia—and some potentials, apparently, that they recognized and nurtured. Perhaps what I chiefly possessed had been a desire to please. I had striven to please them with all my heart. Thus, the stories of ancient heroism and sacrifice had taken root in my heart, like a seed in a well-prepared soil. Perhaps it was my own wishes that had fathered the perception that the ancient tales pertained to me. *Dolorite. Sword of Israel.*

I looked and saw the crowd gazing at me expectantly. When had they gathered? And so many? "Are you the one we wait for?" they implored me in the gathering dusk. I raised my hands to acknowledge them. As I moved about, I felt the crowd stir. It was like a breeze moving through trees. As I grasped their hands, I felt their strength flowing into me, and I was filled with gratitude and then with elation. New comers had brought torches, and the hillside around me was soon ablaze with lights. I was still light-headed from my long meditation, but gradually I seemed to see things in a new and luminous perspective, like the deep clarity of the evening sky: *I was not the Sword of Israel. Of that I was certain.* The Sword of Israel was only a name, a forlorn hope dreamed up by desperate old men. But this passion, this energy that animated the crowd, as they touched me and communicated it to me, was real. Quite real! Here also was a power that could grind the mountains to powder. I was not its creator, but I might, I thought, become its vessel and transmitter. *I had a sudden memory of Nathan and Miriam Lander, and I recalled Lander's suggestion that there would be a fourth party in the war – the party of the Old Believers, led by me.*

I reached out for the hands of those nearest me in the crowd and said to each of them, "Trust in the Law. Abide in the Law. Take its precepts to heart and let them guide you." *We can keep the Kuhlans from our land if we do.* "Keep the Law" was the whole of my message. To skeptics, I said, "I never knew its worth until I had to live apart from it in the Kuhlan lands. The Law is food and drink. We are nothing without it. We are no better than cattle – no more than wild beasts. But if we keep the Law, the Law will keep us. If we walk in its light, our lives will reflect that light. Then, though our lives are lost, they are not flung away like broken clay or cast like straw into the fire."

I said many other things that came to me unbidden. The wind seemed to pick up as I spoke. I felt an energy move in me. As this mood took hold of me, I repeated the same words about losing my sword, but with a different heart, and as I spoke, I sensed the change in them too. My chest seemed to open and expand with each breath, each inhalation, until I thought I could float above the crowd. I felt an exaltation rise in me such as I had never experienced in my life. Still the crowd closed upon me, seeking assurances; its pressure was an irresistible force. "It is not me that you seek, it is the Law," I insisted. They waited dumbly, patiently. Finally, I consented.

"As long as I have strength," I cried, "I will not let your hopes fall to the ground. But you must abide in the Law!"

A cry arose from many throats as I stepped back under the canopy; the sound was like a rush of wind and like the bellowing of bulls. I spoke with the crowd through the night, and when dawn came I was exhausted and sweating like an athlete after a race.

Zachariah greeted me when I returned to camp. I could tell by his expression that he had been present and had witnessed the events of the night before. I encountered something felt his gaze searching me.

"Remarkable," he said. "Quite remarkable! These tales. . . ." He paused, as if he did not know how to speak his thoughts.

"I thought I had left these tales behind forever when I crossed the Jordan," I said.

"Apparently not!"

"The tales are not true," I assured him. "But I understand them differently now."

III

"The Danites," Colonel Harlech said briskly to the officers gathered under his tent, "are in for it! The question now is, what's to be done?"

As we had anticipated, Manasseh had launched an invasion into Dan within a week of our arrival. It was aimed directly at Hazor. On their way north, the Messiahists had overrun my homeland, Asher. I had not expected otherwise, as Asher could not be left unsubdued on their lines of communication. We gathered round a map, and I pointed out the strategic points. "Hazor must be cut off already. The Danite cavalry are no doubt massing somewhere east of Hazor, maybe here or here." The Messiahists' goal, apparently, was to prevent the countryside from rallying to Hazor's defense. The churchmen were seeking a quick deathblow.

We were less able to envision what Dan would do in response. The Sevfolk seemed to be stunned by the news of invasion. Jerub was sulking in his tent rather than preparing for action, and no one seemed to have an idea of what to do. We could only wonder whether the Apostle's government had fallen into a similar panic.

"The Messiahists have achieved surprise," Colonel Harlech observed. "The government of Dan seems paralyzed. In the meantime, Josiah, the Sevfolk here seem to be waiting for you to perform a miracle. What is it that you intend to do?"

I was in no mood for joking. I imagined the Messiahist cavalry was already deploying eastward from Hazor, feeling for the counter stroke they must surely expect. To isolate Hazor, they must spread themselves thin—thus making themselves vulnerable. The Danite cavalry was a formidable weapon, and if someone had sense enough to use it properly, it might save the day. I wanted with every fiber of my being to be part of the counter stroke. My heart was racing at the prospect. I had, however, only a handful of men who had declared themselves for me, and no idea of how to use them. If Hazor fell, the College and all that pertained to it would be destroyed. With the city isolated, I could not even contact Burgos and Gill.

"Let me make a suggestion," the Colonel said, leaning over the map. "The Messiahist infantry must come up the Yakima canyon, correct? And must be supplied by this route?"

"Yes. Here is the Refuge where I was educated. Right in their path! It's not a refuge now but a point on the enemy's lines of communication. It pains me to think of the danger to my old Masters and colleagues there. The Brothers are their oldest and bitterest enemies, the Messiahists are pitiless"

"Well, then," the Colonel said, "I think we must find out what is happening and lend whatever assistance we can. If we happen to cut the enemy's communications at the same time, well, that is an added benefit."

"This is not your quarrel, Colonel," I replied, my heart pounding. "The Esdralon Guards have endured a great deal. You must preserve the remnant."

"Remnant!" he snorted. "The Esdralon Guards are the most formidable cavalry in existence, and they go where I tell them to. We are at war with Israel, so the Messiahists are my enemies, no less than your father's miserable cabal!"

"I thought you planned to seek an accommodation with Manasseh."

"Do you actually believe I could trust them? No, Josiah, I despise both sides of your civil war, and I do not intend to be beholden to either of them. I will not be remembered as one who bent the knee to either faction." To my surprise, the Colonel put his hand on my shoulder and added: "I do intend, however, to be remembered as the friend of the Sword of Israel."

Following Colonel Harlech's decision, we swung into action. Jerub grudgingly consented to outfit and remount us on good horses. Some two-dozen of his people insisted on coming with us and attached themselves to me. We left that night, swinging due south and then southwest in an arc that avoided enemy patrols. Our Danite volunteers led us across territory they knew well, so we moved efficiently, changing horses like Kuhlans. By dawn, we were nearing the bare ridge that marked the northern border of Ephraimite territory, and there we turned west across arid, broken country toward the Yakima. We arrived at the canyon of the Yakima by noon; an hour later we were at the Refuge.

A large supply train was strung out along the canyon floor. We struck it like a hawk strikes a quail chick. I took no notice of the fighting, but instead searched with a sinking heart through the smoking ruins of the Refuge. The Messiahists had wreaked a terrible vengeance on my teachers. The Refuge was no more. All the buildings where I had lived and gone to school, the barracks and classrooms, the shops and hospice – even the library of Ancient works – were pillaged and burned. Many of the stone buildings had collapsed inward as the rafters burned, so that I scarcely recognized the place. Smoke still rose from the rubble. There were also many dead scattered about the site, blackened by the sun. All wore the wool surplice of the Brotherhood. From the number and positions of their bodies, it was apparent that the Brothers had been massacred.

I searched for my friends and Masters, but found no one I recognized. I retained some faint hope that Josephus and Ebenezer had escaped by concealing themselves in the caverns deep in the canyon wall. I knew the library had secret chambers and passages, even though I had never seen them. But the Messiahists had known of these hiding places, apparently, or discovered them during the destruction. The library had been pillaged and burned, its passages closed off by collapsing walls. Bodies were strewn throughout, and no doubt others were buried in the rubble. *Amid these events,* I reflected, *Josephus and Ebenezer would not have tried to conceal themselves.*

After surveying the carnage, I concluded that my Masters most probably lay in a group of bodies that had been given special treatment by the Messiahists. A half dozen charred corpses hung together from crosses near the entry to the Refuge, burned past recognition. The fires beneath them had been fueled by books from the library. I searched through the ashes, but there was nothing to salvage. The Refuge had owned the largest collection of books from the Ancients anywhere in Israel. I wondered at this fury against books and knowledge; it made no sense to me.

"Moriah!" I shouted. "Do you imagine you can persuade your men to take some prisoners?" The Esdralon Guards, coarsened by their experience of war among the Kuhlans, were slaughtering the wagoners and their guards. I rescued a handful of prisoners and put them to work building a pyre for the dead. We pulled intact timbers out of the ruins and gathered other wooden debris from the wreckage. Some of my Benjamite comrades helped me gather and stack the bodies. After the pyre was lit, I paused and indulged my feelings a little.

To save them—and perhaps to save others as well – I sent the prisoners scurrying southward with a personal message from me: "Let the Messiahists keep the rules of war in Asher or beware the consequences!" At that moment, I could not resist the bitter jest that welled up in me: "And beware the Sword of Israel!"

As I performed the tasks of cremation, Colonel Harlech stood by patiently, his helmet cradled in his arm. The sun was hotter than I ever remember it; my throat was parched and I was blinded by sweat. Moisture trickled down my cheeks and dripped from my beard.

"We have captured wagons filled with grain and other supplies," Colonel Harlech said, gently interrupting my reverie. "What do you suggest we do with them?" He deferred to me on my own territory, and in the grip of emotions that he knew well enough himself. He was a man of unfailing courtesy.

"We will need the grain," I said. "There is a trail out of the canyon along a creek bed that runs northeast. Have the Sevfolk take the train as far as they can and then hide the wagons in the desert. They can unhitch the mules and pack out the grain. Every kernel will be precious this year."

My new Sevfolk followers leapt at the opportunity to separate themselves from us. They had not seen war conducted as the Esdralon Guards conducted it. And having seen it, they wanted no part of us. Only a handful of the men who had chosen to follow me remained after the wagons departed.

Colonel Harlech held a council of war to consider our next move. The prisoners had given us all the information they had or could invent. Selah was under siege, and the rest of Asher lay under the heels of the churchmen. Reinforcements and supplies were coming north daily. North of us, in Dan, at least three legions of the enemy were encamped before Hazor. The enemy's cavalry was ransacking Dan and preventing Dan's tribal levies from interfering with the assault on Hazor. We surmised that the enemy hoped to defeat Dan's cavalry before they launched their assault, but even now, their infantry were preparing to storm the city. Our task was to interfere with these plans as far as possible. But we had to act quickly.

There was a trail out of the canyon through the wilderness of Zoar that would place us in the rear of the invading host north of us. This was my home country; I knew it both by day and by night. I led our small column into the desert country west of the Yakima, angling northward toward Dan. We crossed Manastash Ridge, the boundary of Danite territory, at dusk. From there, we could see the campfires of the enemy spread out below us, in a half circle around Hazor. The enemy had gathered a huge herd of stolen livestock near the gap in preparation to drive them south. Under a full moon—by a nice irony a Kuhlan moon – we attacked the rear guard and stampeded the cattle and horses. We burned the camps of our enemies and spread terror and havoc. I felt a strange exhilaration campaigning as if I were a Kuhlan. We took our fill of destruction and slaked our thirst in the Yakima. Then we regrouped and filed off to the northwest.

The next day we forded the Yakima in its upper canyon and scooped up some Messiahist raiding parties who were pillaging the countryside northwest of Hazor. The Messiahists were expecting little resistance in this quarter, and they were certainly not expecting us. After the briefest encounter, those who could fled in panic. They were Ephraimites, tribal levies – not much sport for Esdralon Guards. The folk of Dan that we saw along the way also fled at the sight of us. Of course we looked like Kuhlans to them, and I suppose we acted like Kuhlans as well.

Shortly after noon, we made contact with units of the Danite cavalry north of Hazor, and after some preliminary misunderstanding, we identified ourselves as friends. Our troops caused a stir when we arrived at the headquarters of the Danite forces. In command was a Colonel Enoch Malachi, younger brother of the general whom I detested so thoroughly. Though he greeted us skeptically, this younger Malachi appeared to recognize our value as allies. After he inspected the troops, he warmed to us quickly, and I noted that he seemed a very different man than his brother. We rested our horses and ate a meal from their mess—our first cooked food in two days. The summer heat was terrific, and both horses and men were suffering from its effects.

We learned that a series of skirmishes had been fought east of Hazor, though neither side had gained an advantage. That morning, however, the Messiahist cavalry had withdrawn to their camps. It appeared that something had happened to shake their confidence. When Danite troopers told us of the rumors of Kuhlan raiders, Colonel Harlech threw back his head and laughed. "Now I understand these tales of Kuhlans fighting on our side," Malachi declared. "That story may be worth a legion to us."

The next day, the Messiahist infantry made an attempt to storm the walls of Hazor, but failed. Colonel Malachi bided his time, watching the enemy and drawing in additional levies of horsemen. All the clans were aroused, and as they came in, our camp buzzed like an angry beehive. The enemy cavalry remained inactive, apparently held in reserve to protect their infantry. At nightfall, scouts reported that the Messiahist were evacuating their camps and had begun to file back through the gap and down the canyon of the Yakima. Colonel Malachi immediately sent a force to probe and harry the enemy in the darkness, and at dawn he blew the trumpet through all the camps and gathered his entire force, which he threw against the retreating enemy. We joined in the attack and took their trains. The Messiahists fought stubbornly and with considerable skill, and their cavalry kept us from cutting the column into pieces or blocking its way south. To our dismay, the garrison of Hazor stayed safely behind its walls and did not join in our attack or even in the pursuit. Had the moment been seized, we might have smashed the whole force of the enemy. For whatever reasons, however, the Apostle Boz did not seize it. In spite of our efforts, then, the Messiahists got most of their army away.

We took a hundred prisoners in a sharp encounter near the Wayfarers' Refuge and then pursued the Messiahists into Asher, slashing at their rear. Colonel Malachi pressed home his attacks with reckless courage. He took a wound in the fighting just above Selah and was carried off. Without his leadership, our pursuit tapered off, and the enemy withdrew through the Lion Gates of Manasseh. We then retired to the southern edge of the wilderness of Zoar, awaiting events.

Dan had won a victory over the Messiahists, but not a decisive one. I took a long look at my homeland from an arid ridge in Zoar. Columns of smoke rose from horizon to horizon. I laid up this image in my mind and then returned to the Refuge to finish the task of putting our dead to rest.

Colonel Harlech assisted me in the rites I had omitted previously. I searched for survivors and books valuable to preserve, but there was little to salvage. This early portion of my life had been as completely obliterated as if it had never existed. I could not be sure that the bodies I had cremated earlier had included Ebenezer and Josephus. Everything tended to confirm the likelihood of their deaths, but I could not know for certain. So until every body had been consumed in the fire, I could not rest from my obligations.

At the end, Zechariah put his hand on my shoulder and said, "You have done the part of a brother, without fault. Let your heart find some peace in that."

"This is Israel's loss, not mine alone. The library, the learning. . . "

"What was done here cannot be undone. Josiah," he said, waiting until he had my full attention, "you will not find what you are searching for here."

I was filled with nervous energy, but I had, I realized with his words, run out of useful things to do.

Zechariah seemed to understand my fruitless searching. "My friend," he said, "come along. You know what you must do."

In truth, I was far from knowing what I must do.

"You can do nothing for your Masters—and for the moment, nothing for Asher."

"I could! I could do much! If that coward Boz would attack—"

"He will not. You know he will not. So for the time being, you can do nothing for your people. The Messiahists are too strong there. In time, perhaps an opportunity will arise."

I exhaled a deep breath. The Colonel was clear-sighted.

"It is known in Hazor that the Esdralon Guards played a role in Dan's victory. It will be better known, once the story of our attack on the Messiahist rear guard is spread about. Dan is saved for the time being, and you were instrumental in its salvation. This is an opportunity for you."

"Caleb Boz will do nothing," I protested. "He will let this slip through his fingers."

"Yes," Zechariah agreed, "but everyone knows that the victory is not complete because of the Apostle. So you must go back to Hazor and gather your followers and follow up your victory. The Messiahist party within Dan is no doubt crippled, and you must see that it does not recover."

"How can I? The Apostle has a warrant for my death."

He smiled. "We will see just how much power his writ carries. Caleb Boz will have to trample the Esdralon Guards to enforce it."

I gripped his hand, searching for words to thank him.

"Come," he said, "I'm curious to see what you can accomplish. It almost restores myits to imagine it."

IV

The Esdralon Guards made a memorable entrance into Hazor. We were known; news of our exploits had preceded us, and the astonished soldiers at the gate stood aside and allowed us to enter. Our horses' hooves clattered on the cobblestones, and the whole populace came out to stare at us. *Kuhlans!* I heard many people gasp as we passed. I thought of my leave-taking of the city nine months earlier, and the contrast was deeply pleasing.

The Council of Elders was in session in the House of Assembly. I dismounted and entered the crowded hall, flanked by Colonel Harlech and Major Moriah, all of us savagely attired. A group of nobles who were delivering a petition to the Council paused and immediately yielded the floor. A silence settled over the hall. The Apostle Boz gave me a look from his high seat that could have pulverized stone, but he remained motionless. I saw that his left arm hung limp at his side. When he spoke, his speech was slurred and his body shook with a slight tremor. He was outraged, he said, that I had come into his presence – I who had spilled blood in the streets of Hazor!

"Indeed, I have returned," I replied, "and I have not come to ask your pardon. It is true that I am responsible for the death of Brother Ignacio, but I had no role in any citizen's death." I recognized General Malachi and Nisan Lot and the others, along with some new faces. Their expressions were interesting to behold, but I spoke to Boz alone: "Your policy of conciliation with the Messiahists has failed. They betrayed you, as recent events have shown." I heard mutters of approval from the crowd. "However, because of the engines I built for your walls, the streets and houses of Hazor are still intact—still Danite – and not cinders under the feet of the churchmen. Surely everyone sees this—except perhaps the Apostle of Dan." The hall erupted at my words. I turned to the crowd. "Will you allow the Apostle Boz to placate the Messiahists even now? How is it that he still grieves over the death of their agent here in Hazor? A spy who came to stir up strife among you?"

Cries of "No! No! Death to the Messiahists!" filled the hall.

When the hall subsided, I spoke my demands: "I say to the Apostle of Dan, withdraw your warrant, acknowledge my innocence in the Valdez affair, and return my money, and I who gave Dan the war machines to protect its walls will be its faithful ally." There was applause and angry voices directed at the Apostle. When the noise subsided, I said that I would wait upon the judgment of the Council, and left. In my last glimpse of the Apostle, Boz's face was distorted with rage; he looked as if he could die of anger.

If I had expected a similar triumphal entry into the College of Hazor, I was disappointed. Colonel Harlech, Moriah, Amasa and I were admitted at the ancient gate, which had fallen into even worse repair than when I had seen it last. The courtyard was crowded with people of all ages—refugees from the Messiahists. A multitude was camped within the compound. Many were strangers; some appeared destitute and near starving. Still others, the wounded from the recent fighting, were lying on pallets in bloody bandages. Brother Peter emerged from the main building. He looked care-worn and thinner than I remembered. "So, it is you," he said without enthusiasm. "The stories we heard are true." He wiped his hands on an apron and gave my companions and me a slight bow.

I found Burgos ladling soup out of a huge pot. He did not look up to greet me, but continued with his task. I felt shame to be met on such terms where I had expected warmth. "What times we've had since you left, my lord," Burgos said to me. "Too bad you missed it. What was it you said to me? Sometimes one must wait? Well, we have waited all right. We have waited for *you*!"

I saw that they had endured hard times because of me—and that Burgos laid all their difficulties at my door. I inquired after several people who had joined us a year ago and learned that most were gone. My old bodyguard had dwindled to a dozen men.

"Mostly we care for refugees," he said. "There is no lack of them. Your funds have disappeared, but we have donors. The College feeds several hundred people, and we offer shelter to all who flee the Messiahists."

"Donors? Who assists us?"

"Chiefly Nisan Lot, the man who sent you to the Kuhlan lands, my lord. Aside from that, he has been generous. Perhaps he was generous in that as well."

"So, he seeks the support of the Old Believers?"

"He wants to see you, I know that. He asked me to tell you as soon as you returned."

I inquired about Gill—whether he had recovered from his wounds. To my surprise, Burgos told me that Gill was in prison, along with other Messiahists, including his father and his entire family.

"But why?"

"You didn't mention that Gill is a Messiahist. He brought his family here from Hebron—his parents and his wife and children. He made no secret of his beliefs, nor did they; and when the invasion came, Malachi came and arrested him."

"Gill is Messiahist, yes, but not a traitor. Not a Third Comer who supports the churchman. He belongs to a different sect." I thought a moment. "We must get him out."

"You'll have to speak to General Malachi about that. He's the one who has swept up all the Messiahists since the invasion. He is a boar in a flower bed; he tears up the ground."

Nisan Lot came out to the Guards camp the next evening. The evening was warm and still. I lit lamps so we could see well enough to converse. When Lot seated himself heavily on the piled rugs, he seemed weary. "When I saw you last, many months ago," he said, coming straight to the point, "I spoke of a possible alliance."

I recalled the circumstances of our last meeting vividly. "You said you wanted me off the board for a while," I replied, "but in six months or a year, you speculated that I might become a useful ally."

"I spoke better than I knew, "he said. "I am no longer Mayor of Hazor. The Apostle deposed me a month ago and has assumed that post himself."

This was a surprise. "What does Boz think he is doing?" I asked. "He has no policy."

"The Apostle stalls for time. He thinks if he waits long enough, the things that have happened will not have happened, and everything will be the way it was."

"He seems ill; he looks as if he cannot last the summer."

Lot shrugged.

"So you have come here to talk about the succession," I said, watching his reactions.

Nisan Lot made a noise like a laugh. "I can hardly aim so high. I have, at the moment, nothing in my hand." He pulled back the sleeves of his robe and looked at his empty palms. We were both reminded of my first, disastrous speech before Dan's Council of Elders. He was telling me that fortune had reversed our roles, and he was now in the position of the suppliant. "No," Lot said, "I come on a more personal matter. Not that the succession is far from my thoughts—nor should it be from yours. But first, there is the matter of Miriam Lander."

I winced inwardly. "Why speak to me of Miriam Lander?"

"Because she is dear to me."

His answer touched a nerve, seared me like a hot coal. *I had not expected this.* Without any drama or special inflection of his voice, he had told me volumes about what had transpired while I was in the Kuhlan lands.

"I came because she is dear to me," he continued, "and because her service is valuable to Dan. But chiefly I came because you have cause to nourish a grievance toward her." He looked at his hands. "Also," he said, "she asked me to come."

I offered him a basin in which to wash, grimly pleased that my own hands betrayed no tremor. "What do you want from me?"

"She wants to see you."

"*She* wants to see me?" Remembering her with sudden vividness, I forced myself to recall the terms on which we had parted. "Why?" I asked.

"She wants to save her husband's life."

"Orderly!" I called, stepping out of the tent. "Bring our guest some wine and something to eat." To Lot I said, "I must hear from you what has transpired in Dan in the past nine months and also the news of the rest of Israel." *I needed time to think and to understand what this man was telling me, asking of me. We would share a meal, and then I would consider what he had to say.*

We talked into the night. "The Apostle refused to see the Messiahist invasion coming and so did nothing to prepare for it," Lot complained. "Except to build those machines of yours." He gave an account of the Apostle clumsily playing one faction against another, oppressing the Old Believers in Dan so as to curry favor with the Messiahists. Lot had an immense store of knowledge of the conflicts in Dan and the alignments of factions and clans within it. Knowing it was he who had funneled money to the College in my absence, I believed him. His story accorded well with his behavior when he came to take my deposition in the Valdez affair. Whether he acted from motives of policy or from conviction, he had preserved the College as a refuge for Old Believers. I acknowledged to myself that I owed him a debt.

"I made it my business to reconcile all parties in Dan," Lot said. "To the Apostle, this made me suspect." Boz had stripped him of his office as the tensions between factions grew.

"Does he believe he can placate the Messiahists?" I asked.

"Apparently he does. But in the end, Boz violated everyone's trust, and then the invasion came anyway. Since then, the affairs of Dan have been in chaos. In March, the Apostle suffered a stroke, as you saw. Since then, as you noted, Dan has had no policy."

I mentioned that my associate, Rehab Gill, had been imprisoned along with his family – and that his arrest was both unjust and foolish.

"I am aware of it," Lot replied. "The arrest was not the Apostle's doing; it was General Malachi." Lot explained that over a hundred people, most of them harmless citizens, had been arrested since the invasion. "We have no prison to hold them all."

I secured Lot's promise to assist me in securing Gill's release. As we talked further, the former Mayor and I managed to find common ground on several issues important to us both. Soon, in spite of misgivings, I found myself beginning to regard Miriam Lander's new lover as an ally. Then, just as I was about to broach the subject of an alliance, he revealed that the Apostle Boz had recently sent emissaries to New Jerusalem to seek peace.

"Peace emissaries!" I exclaimed, rising from my seat. "The fool throws away the victory! If he runs after the Messiahists now, when the dust has not settled from the fighting, they will know they have nothing to fear from us. Why should they make concessions if we sue for peace?"

"That is my view as well," Lot said. "Unfortunately, the Apostle's stubbornness is well known, and now he is half-paralyzed and more than half blind. Worse, he listens only to General Malachi. And since Malachi senses opposition against his master, he grows ambitious himself. As you know, the General is an imbecile—and thus, if anything, would be a worse master than Boz."

"So, the Apostle Boz courts the Messiahists, while General Malachi imprisons them. And you, meanwhile, try to reconcile all factions. This means, I believe, that there is no government in Dan."

"No government worth speaking of," he admitted.

When we had finished our meal, I asked: "Are you also anxious to save Miriam Lander's husband?"

"If it pleases her," he said evenly. Lot, I saw, would not change his speech to please me now that the power was on my side. He wanted me to know that his relationship with Miriam Lander was not merely one of convenience or exigency. He cared for her. "Lander himself," he added cautiously, "is not without usefulness in the larger scheme of things."

I kept my thoughts on that subject to myself.

"There is this consideration also," he added, "though I hesitate to speak it. Your sword could be returned publicly, with an acknowledgement of wrongdoing. With an apology." He put his hands in his sleeves, folding his arms across his chest. "All this could be accomplished with any amount of drama you wish."

"As to these personal matters, as you call them," I said, rising to signal the end of our meeting, "they need not detain us. You and I have more important things to consider. True, I want the sword returned. And I need assistance in quashing the warrant against me and getting my money back. As to the rest, I will do whatever you wish, as a favor. We can arrange a day mutually convenient to us, and this event you describe—the return of my sword – can take place then. In your presence."

"Until then," he said, gripping my hand.

The former Mayor had given me a shrewd account of the situation in Dan and where he stood and what he wanted. It remained for me to decide whether I could forego my vengeance against a man who had humbled me before all Israel and then conspired to kill me. I weighed the threat Lander posed if alive against the advantages of having him dead. *What, I asked myself, would others think if I spared Lander's life?* I doubted that Lander retained much power to harm me. He was not powerful of and by himself, but a bird who must perch in another man's lattice. Taking vengeance would only draw attention to those flaws of character that had turned him against me. *Compassion, our Teacher says, never rusts, and mercy shines forever.* I had to rebuke myself to be ever mindful of my larger purpose and to hold tight to the precepts of St. Supplicee. I had to seek harmony in all things, for I had been entrusted with much.

Still, the prospect of revenge was sweet. *I had the taste of it in my mouth.*

V

As the Apostle Boz persisted in appeasing the Messiahists, his policy not only aided the enemy but put Judah at risk as well as Dan. As I looked about for something to do to counter his policy, Ephraim beckoned. The Messiahists had laid a heavy hand on the Sevfolk lands. Though Boz had forbidden provocative actions, the Sevfolk kept up an angry clamor to avenge the raids on their territory. Those raids, we knew, had been launched from Ephraim. Thus, a punitive raid would serve my purposes as well as theirs. Eager to send a message to the Apostle, the eastern clans elected me to lead the raid.

Colonel Harlech also brightened considerably at the prospect of complicating Boz's negotiations. The idea appealed to him so much that he offered a troop of Guards to accompany us. Then, at the last moment, the Colonel asked to accompany the raid as an observer. It seemed a strange request, but since the Guards were his command, I had no reason to refuse him.

We swept into the dry eastern portion of Ephraim unopposed, destroying several small settlements and taking over two hundred civilians of all ages prisoner. By day's end, long files of captives and livestock raised a cloud of dust that mingled with the smoke of burning crops and farmsteads. In ordinary warfare, we would never touch the non-combatant population. But the Messiahists had set ugly precedents in their invasions of Dan and Asher, and now their allies in Ephraim were paying for it. The Law permits retaliation in kind, but only after a warning and a demand that the opponent desist from the unlawful action. I was conscious that we were bending, if not breaking, the precepts set down by St. Supplicee. Moreover, as I looked over the prisoners, I saw hardly an able-bodied man of military age the entire length of the dejected, weeping column.

"Are there no soldiers among our captives?" I inquired of the clan chiefs. A group of elders had joined me on a promontory to scan the horizon and to take stock of our situation. Of pursuit there was no sign—no dust raised by an enemy column hurrying toward us. We had struck Ephraim when it was helpless to resist. Several of the clan chiefs advocated a sweep clear to Shiloh, the Ephraimite capital. They were elated, imagining the wealth of livestock they could run off. I thought instead of the miles of desert our prisoners would have to cross on foot. There were many elderly and children and women carrying in their bellies or with babes in arms.

The Ephraimites had an unusually large number of infants and children among them, confirming the rumor that the Messiahists had abandoned the Reproduction Law. Skeptics claimed that they disdained the Law purposefully, aiming to increase their own numbers in order to overwhelm Israel. Whatever their reasons, this flouting of Israel's fundamental law had borne spectacular fruit in only a few years. Bitterly, I recalled the Kuhlan's disdain of us and our unrestrained breeding—and of the inevitable poverty and famine our recklessness brought.

I had just announced my intention to release the prisoners when we were joined on the ridge by Colonel Harlech and a squad of Guards cavalrymen. "You've taken revenge enough," I was saying to the elders. "Behold the destruction behind us. You have taken triple the wealth you lost in June. Call in your young men."

The chiefs protested vehemently. Their blood was up, and the prospect of plunder beckoned.

"Josiah," Colonel Harlech interrupted. "I must report something to you. We've ridden practically to the gate of Shiloh. There are no troops in Ephraim. Just a handful of militia."

"I don't wonder," I replied. "Because of Boz's dithering, the Messiahists fear nothing from us and have concentrated their troops against Judah. Judah is paying the price of Boz's delusions."

Meanwhile, the Sevfolk tribesmen raised a clamor against me because of my order, so that I had to pause and assert my authority. I reminded the chiefs that I had been elected to command this expedition, and I had issued a command. "Set the prisoners free," I said, "and we will return home with what we have."

When they demanded my reasons, I pointed out that the old and very young would not make it half way to Dan, and it was unlawful to cause the deaths of so many helpless ones. Though the elders still protested, I ordered the procession to halt. When it did not, I cantered to the head of the column of prisoners and repeated my orders. One young warrior who held a weeping Ephraimite girl across his saddle chose to defy me. When he refused my direct order, I knocked him off his horse with the butt of his own lance. His horse reared and the young girl sprawled on the ground. After I had disarmed and subdued him, I turned him over to his own clan chief for punishment. "Is this the way you teach discipline in Dan?" I demanded of the elders. Shamed by this display, they acquiesced in my commands.

"Ride apart with me a moment," Colonel Harlech said. Zachariah seemed possessed by an excitement I had not seen before, and that had nothing to do with the incident he had just witnessed. I knew before he spoke that he had decided to return to Lagash.

"It would be suicide," I protested, "to take the Legion through the heart of enemy territory!"

"Suicide to take the legion, yes. But an acceptable risk for a handful of men." He quickly outlined his plan. The country was empty of troops. Messiahist forces were engaged in the south against Judah. "If I can get as far south as Wapato, or near there undetected, we can cut across the desert to Lagash."

"But even if Manasseh is deserted, you risk the ticks in the wilderness!"

"Risk is a soldier's lot. Josiah, I *am* a soldier, not a sacrifice for the larger good of Israel. I never aspired to be a Dedicated One or a Dolorite. I have served Benjamin for many years, and I believe I can recognize its interests. But what constitutes the greater good of Israel remains a mystery to me." He raised a hand to silence my objections. "I know we differ on this subject. It is enough that I want to see my home again, and that the way is open. I long to see my wife and son and to know if my father lives. I have a plan," he added, "and a disguise. I'll go as a Messiahist priest escorted by Ephraimite militia men. We have a plausible story to tell. We are fleeing Ephraim with news of your barbarity!"

When I did not respond to his levity, he added soberly: "We have a good chance. We have a chance."

"The three of you, perhaps. But what of the Esdralon Guards?"

"I'm leaving the legion in your charge. The Guards are the best men in the world—"

"Surely, you cannot be serious!"

"You will take care how you use them," he continued calmly, "the same as I would. And you, my friend, have a use for them unique to yourself. Yes, I see what you are and what you are poised to do. I see also that you have been raised up for a great task—albeit not the one for which your Masters prepared you. They may, as some claim, have trained you as an assassin, but I take the view of the People, who elevated you to a war leader. Indeed, that is what you are, a leader—and of a special sort. I have observed much of the process myself, not that I understand it all. But I saw what you did to drive the Kr from the People's lands, and I saw your role in repelling the Messiahists from Dan and the esteem in which you are held by many here. Moreover," he added, "it is in your power to care for the Esdralon Guards, and it is no longer in mine."

He smiled, suddenly jovial, "Admittedly, you cannot succeed as a mere captain. Therefore, from this moment forward, Josiah, your rank is Colonel. I would raise you to a generalship if I had the power, but I do not. Accept my congratulations! Let this be your first step toward high command!" He shook my hand warmly. "I do this," he added, "partly out of consideration for Major Moriah's feelings, not just for yours. Can either of us imagine Moriah would obey a mere captain? You'll have trouble enough with him as it is."

That seemed likely enough.

"This will come as no surprise to Moriah. I have planned this course for some time, which is why I was eager to come along on this expedition. I thought it might be possible to make a dash for home if we found the way open. I would of course prefer to take all my people with me, soldiers and civilians and invalids alike, but that would be an unacceptable risk—suicide, I believe you said."

"Your whole plan sounds like suicide to me."

"For men such as we, my friend, it will be a light-hearted errand. I have hesitated only because of my concern for the Guards. But with you in command, I can be confident they are in good hands. They will understand that I am of greater use to Benjamin in Lagash than in Dan, while the Guards will be of great service here. They know, at any rate, that I cannot take them there."

When I seemed doubtful, he took hold of my horse's bridle and leaned toward me. "There is a condition. Major Moriah will obey you only so long as he feels the interests of Benjamin are being served. If you endanger the Guard without commensurate benefit to Benjamin, he is absolved of his allegiance to you. It was his condition, but I consented to it. This is a strange arrangement, I grant you, but the circumstances are unprecedented."

"So, you are determined to do this?"

"I am. And I know that you will care for the men with the same zeal as I, and probably more skill. But now, I have a journey to begin."

We embraced, and I held him at arm's length for a long moment. His last words to me were spoken in the language of the People: "A man should leave no trace, not even a footprint." Whether at this moment he was Kuhlan or Israelite, I knew he was a friend from whom I could scarcely bear to part. As Zachariah and his two companions disappeared from view, I thought of the leave-taking that fate had denied Justin and me.

I gathered the elders and men of Ephraim who were prisoners and spoke to them. "Behold, I hold Ephraim in my hand. I have taken you hostage as surety for the people of Asher and to deter your leaders from further outrages. But seeing your plight has reminded me of the Law. Therefore, I release you, and you may return to your homes in peace. But tell your leaders to stop their depredations in Asher. Tell them to obey the laws of war, or there will be consequences. *Tell them!*"

No one thought to contradict me, and the Ephraimites seemed pleased to depart from us. We returned to the Sevfolk lands with our booty.

VI

It remained to settle my quarrel with Nathan Lander. *Never despise a poor relation, a weak enemy, or a small wound,* the adage goes. *Unattended, they will surely fester.*

On the day appointed for the return of my sword, I had a canopy erected on a hillside and gathered the Guardsmen around me. I had accepted Nissan Lot's view that the reconciliation must be as public as possible, to clear the air and clarify all the relationships involved. Vendettas, he pointed out, were always a matter of public concern. Many of the Sevfolk and the other eastern clans had come to watch; the hillsides were dark with their horses. We waited as the procession wended its way across the plain. First came the adherents of the College, led by Brother Peter and Manuel Burgos, who had become an important figure among the Old Believers. They paid me homage as their chieftain and patriarch, after the customs. Next came Nisan Lot, the former Mayor of Hazor and member of the Council of Elders. With him were three members of the Council—a sign of Lot's alliance-building—and their several retinues. They paid me formal respect, but not homage, in token of my status as one of the powers in Dan. Last came Miriam and Nathan Lander with their retainers. As the Landers came before the canopy, they knelt and touched their foreheads to the ground. Their role in the ceremony was to acknowledge my authority as a condition of reconciling. Lot had arranged it all, with a nice flair for the dramatic. As I gazed at Miriam's slim body, kneeling before me, my blood sang in my ears and time seemed to race backwards. What ceremony could possibly give expression to my feelings in such a moment?

Miriam had sense enough to remain perfectly still, but Nathan—always the less astute of the two – rose to his knees and began to speak – whether to apologize or to justify himself I do not know, because I cut him off sharply and bade him be silent. The crowd was suddenly still as well, recalling, as I was, my rights under the Law. In truth, the sight of him filled me with rage. I did not intend to suffer a word from him, either in explanation or regret. "Did you really believe," I demanded under my breath, "that it was your part to choose the Sword of Israel?"

Lander inclined his head, avoiding my eyes.

"The sword!" I demanded, returning to our script. Miriam, without looking up, motioned with her arm, and an underling came forward with a bundle wrapped in precious cloth. At my signal, Captain Amasa stepped forward and took it and unwrapped it.

"It is the sword, Colonel," he said, laying it upon my knees.

I removed it slowly from its scabbard, examining every inch of it. Seeing its beauty flawless and intact, I rose and held the sword above my head. A roar went up from the Guards and spread through the crowd. All the while, the Landers knelt motionless. Nathan's eyes seemed focused on some interior scene and not on the one before him. I wondered if he was seeing our camp on the Kuhlan shore where I had lain drugged and helpless before him while he held my sword in his hand. *Is he regretting he didn't take my head off? Or feeling the skin of his own neck itch and crawl?* I stepped toward him, the naked sword in my right hand. Through Nisan Lot, I had informed the Landers what they must do; I had not told them what I would do. I thought for a moment how it would feel to avenge myself on him where he knelt. But I did as I had planned, and took Miriam by the hand. She lifted her face to me with anxious questions in her eyes.

"What Nathan Lander did," I declared to the assembled throng, holding the sword above my head, "he meant for evil. But fate has turned the evil away. What he meant for evil has turned to good."

There was another great cheer. I knew that my escape from the Kuhlan lands and the honors bestowed on me by our enemies were taken as nothing short of miraculous by the populace. Indeed, the Kuhlan honors were a greater source of prestige for me than the sword had ever been. At this moment, I wore the white slash of paint on my face that signified my rank as a war leader among the People. It stood between the crowd and me like a mask, and what they saw was a dreaded Kuhlan chieftain whose power was miraculously enlisted on their behalf. When I could be heard again, I declared: "What was intended against me, I do not forget. Nevertheless," I said, drawing Miriam to her feet, "I forgive these offenses and I forgo my revenge."

I looked about; Miriam's eyes were locked onto my face. Others looked startled or thoughtful, according to whether their expectations had been dashed or fulfilled. Nisan Lot, whose gaze had been riveted on Miriam's perfect rump, which had been raised up throughout the ceremony by her kneeling posture, was now searching my face intently, sizing me up as a rival. As I confronted the crowd, the first small spatterings of applause turned into a storm of cheers. *The people are puzzled, I thought, but they do not disapprove.*

Brother Peter conducted an elaborate purification ceremony to mark the putting aside of a blood feud. As planned, the ceremonies turned into a feast of celebration. I had a good deal to celebrate; my sword had been returned, and I had established myself on a new footing. I was filled with energy. Lot and I used the time to work out an agreement with the Landers, giving me a lease on their estate. We needed a place of our own, secure and private, and far from the public gaze. More importantly, Lot and I informed the Landers that they would give no further intelligence to the Apostle Boz. From now on, they were to serve our purposes, not his. I also gave Nathan powerful incentives to recover from Boz the funds entrusted to me by Tephlin Glanz. I kept aloof from Miriam, not wanting to rekindle any of my own feelings nor to jeopardize my alliance with Nisan Lot.

From Lot and his allies on the Council of Elders I learned that a new situation had emerged in Dan. The Old Believers were organized, and they now formed a powerful faction opposed to the Apostle. To that extent, they supported Nisan Lot and his emerging alliance in the Council. The eastern clans were in virtual rebellion and would shed blood rather than submit to Caleb Boz. By small, careful steps, we planned to remove Boz from his seat.

"If we can get two more members of the Council to side with us," one of the members said, "we can overthrow the Apostle."

"Get them," I said.

"That won't be easy," Lot cautioned. "And I don't intend to overturn the government; I mean only to guide it. The last thing I want is bloodshed."

"With Malachi controlling the Danite legion, bloodshed is what you are likely to have," I said. We spoke at length of contingencies, and I asked after the health of the younger brother of General Malachi, who had commanded the Danite cavalry.

"He lives," Lot replied. "He may survive. I hope he does. He is capable of seeing reason, where his brother is not. As to his wound, the dice are in the air."

"What is next, then?" I asked, as we were ready to part.

Lot hesitated, as if unsure of my response. "We must reach out to the Messiahists in Dan and to their sympathizers," he said. "We must put an end to their suffering."

"Do it, then," I replied. "If it will ensure the votes of two more Council members."

We parted on good terms, full of plans and expectations. With one part of my mind, I was fascinated with Nisan Lot's maneuvers, but even so, I had the sense that his policy was calculation rather than care, and that his caution was grounded in self-interest rather than in a sense of responsibility to the people. Lot was one of the cleverest men I had ever met, but he knew nothing of St. Supplicee. He had no understanding that power was a sacred trust and must be exercised on behalf of the people. Lot would make a formidable leader, but not necessarily a good one.

At the same time—and inexplicably – I had begun to feel a tide rising—whether in events or in my blood I could not well say. But what was coming seemed suddenly clear. As the millennium approached, the Messiahists would grow desperate and would redouble their efforts to bring all of Israel under their control. Their desperation would lend them strength, and they would appear more and more formidable, even invincible. But the tactics they would employ in their haste would cause enmity. Every success would build resentment. As they grew stronger, so would resistance against them. It would hollow out their strength, even as it expanded; the stronger they seemed, the emptier they would become. What was needed was a bastion in the north – a hard, unyielding center of resistance. Then, whatever happened to Judah, if that bastion held firm, all the Messiahists' pretensions would eventually dash against it and break. I longed for quiet and a time to meditate to see if I could put myself in harmony with these developments.

In a few days, I returned to Hazor and spoke in the market, choosing the very place the priest Ignacio had stood. It was my first occasion to speak for myself and not as an agent of others. The gist of my speech affirmed an ancient principle of Law. "It is not expedient," I admitted, "for Old Believers to allow Messiahists among us, since the Messiahists have made themselves our enemies. Nevertheless, we *must* allow them to worship unmolested. Freedom is the heart of the Law. Messiahist freedom it is a necessary condition of our own. We cannot be creatures of the Law without championing the freedom of all. And under the Law, belief alone cannot warrant any interference."

I announced further that I embraced all Messiahists who did not support the pretenders in New Jerusalem, and I accepted them as co-religionists. I reminded my listeners that we were all under the Law, and that our submission to the Law subsumed all other issues of belief. I then made a brief argument about the nature of the Messiahist government we faced as an enemy. I was much influenced in these views by Nisan Lot, who was as careful of the powers he was about to assume as a hen with its chick. The church government in New Jerusalem had usurped the legitimate government of Manasseh and maintained itself by force. Because they had excluded and persecuted non-believers, they were not a legal government. They had trampled the laws of peace as well as the laws of war. These evil principles, I begged both the people and the government of Dan not to embrace.

Most of Dan, including my own followers, had expected me to take a very hard line against the Messiahists. No one could accuse me of being their friend, and in fact my feelings ran very hard against them. Accordingly, what I said surprised many. But to restore Israel, I had to define my cause in positive terms rather than as opposition to a religious faction. In addition to making a plea for the release of Rehab Gill and other imprisoned Messiahists, I was laying the foundation for the war I intended to wage. The character of a war dictates the nature of the peace that follows. Therefore, for Israel's sake, I had to move deliberately, carefully. Ironically, it was Nathan Lander who had put the idea of a fourth party in the war in my head: the party of the Sword of Israel against the Messiahists.

Not everyone approved of my speech. Manuel Burgos upbraided me afterward at the College, saying "What madness are you committing this time?"

"*Lord*," I said sharply. "'What madness are you committing this time, *lord'!*" His eyes narrowed, and I added: "You should be used to my madness by now."

"Yes, truly, I should be, my lord," he replied, making a mock-humble face. But I thought his eyes appraised me shrewdly nonetheless, as if he felt a kind of relief after long uncertainty. I knew that Burgos could not easily forgive me for putting aside, as he saw it, the burden of the nation. But he had no alternative to supporting me. Nevertheless, he felt compelled to add: "Your mad whims are a grief to me. It makes me wonder if I am really the sad one, the Dolorite."

"You are right to judge me harshly," I admitted to Burgos in a private moment. "But the power that brought me back here and placed me at the head of the Old Believers is not my own. It does not derive from me. And it seems unaffected by my shortcomings. There are larger forces involved here, quite beyond me."

"Larger forces!" he scoffed. "You sound just like a woman. Never believe," he declared solemnly, "that your power is not affected by your many shortcomings! My *lord*," he added prudently.

"On the contrary," I replied, anxious to have the last word, "I think it must be just as Master Israel Zhen-Gwo has written – that understanding is not necessary."

But in fact, Burgos' words had unsettled me. I no longer knew what I thought.

Nevertheless, things were in motion. A week later, Nisan Lot introduced, as he had promised, a resolution in the Council to release all the Messiahists prisoners who had committed no overt act against the safety of Dan. The motion carried, six votes against four, over the opposition of the Apostle. Lot had obtained his majority in the Council.

VII

Following Lot's victory in the Council, Rehab Gill and his family were among those released from prison. "This is absurd," I said to Gill when he presented himself at the College. "I have better things to do than to keep rescuing you from prison!"

"On the contrary," he said, "it seems to be one of your few harmless pastimes – and one uniquely useful to myself." We embraced and he introduced me to his family. "This is my father, Haman Gill. And my wife, Johanna." His son and daughter were named Elihu and Leah. Then he took me aside and asked seriously: "What forms of disaster and destruction have you let loose since I saw you?"

"Only yourself, Gill," I said. I assured him I was relieved to see his family safe in Dan – "though perhaps as much for my sake as for theirs." He understood my jest and gave me a crooked smile. Gill, I noted, retained a limp from his adventures in Naphtali. I explained the circumstances of his release and my desire to use his talents in my enterprise, as Miriam had called it. "Oddly," I said, "though I have accepted you as a friend and ally, we have never discussed your beliefs and how they affect your allegiances. I want your services in the struggle ahead, but many among the Old Believers wonder at your loyalty."

"Let them distrust me," Gill replied sharply. "I am a Messiahist; I wait for the Savior."

"Yes, yes, I know that," I said. "But you are not with the churchmen; you do not believe in the Third Coming and the end of the world."

"But I do. I *do* wait for the Savior."

"St. Supplicee!" I exclaimed.

"My family worships the Child," Gill said. "As I do." When I stared at him open-mouthed, he added, "You should consult my father about our beliefs. He knows the doctrines better than I, and he is strict in his adherence."

I had expected Gill to be difficult, and he was. So was his father. The elder Gill was tall and lean like his son and had the same crinkled black hair and dark skin. And like his son, he was belligerent. "It is against the Law to punish a man for his beliefs," he declared angrily, as if I had been the cause of his imprisonment rather than his release. The elder Gill's account of their beliefs was little better than his son's and largely opaque to anyone not a co-religionist: "In all things, we follow the Child," he declared, as if this alone sufficed to define his views.

I pressed him for an explanation of what he and his co-religionists might mean by the term *God*. "Do you imagine an actual person – a spirit – from whom the world's laws and energies emanate? And do you imagine the world operates by this spirit's whims?" *I wondered if these followers of the Child also believed that a few words uttered earnestly – or a splash of cock's blood – could turn the natural laws aside.* "Or do you merely personify by the term 'God' all the forces and laws of nature?"

The old man seemed uncertain what to reply, so Gill interrupted: "Israel Zhen-Gwo himself personifies the Way. You quoted him to me yourself in Meribah. 'Cleave the stone, I am there. Seek me in the heart of the fire'."

"Yes, I know what Israel Zhen-Gwo says, and I think I know what he means. What do *you* mean?"

"Our beliefs are no different, "Gill declared, which seemed to me no satisfactory answer at all. The elder Gill recounted their creation story. Apparently, they conceived of their god in terms of their narratives about him and entertained only the vaguest ideas about his nature.

"None of us can speak wisely of creation," I observed, citing the adage of St. Supplicee.

"What about the Messiah, the child whom you worship?"

"He came into the world to save it," the elder Gill replied.

"Save the world? Does the world seem *saved* to you?"

"That is why He must return," the elder Gill declared.

"We believe," Rehab Gill added, sensing my dissatisfaction, "that the world is born anew each day."

"Are you deliberately speaking nonsense?" I demanded. "The world today is the same world as yesterday, rolled forward in time. Do you deny its continuity?"

"No, of course not," Gill said. "It is a manner of speaking. We believe in a universe that renews itself. That is the foundation of our belief—and of our understanding of the Way. The story we tell of the Christ Child is about the world becoming new again. The Child embodies its renewal. If you place yourself in harmony with the Way, you renew yourself."

I looked to his father for confirmation, and he nodded.

"We believe, moreover," Gill continued, "that each child born is potentially a savior of that new world."

I asked if he believed that each individual born existed in a new world, and he said, "Yes, in a sense. But that also is a manner of speaking."

"Ah, another manner of speaking!" I began to understand Gill's exasperating habits of mind; they were rooted in his religious training.

Haman Gill explained that with each man's death a world ends. "For each man who dies, it is the end of time. For that individual, it is Judgment Day. In each man's life – or at least in a reasonably good individual's life, the whole scheme of redemption is played out."

"Redemption?"

"Yes. In an evil life, the process is aborted. For the evil doer," Gill explained, "redemption is rejected. In such a life, none of the potentials for good are realized, but are lost forever. That is what we mean by being lost or damned. To fail to realize one's own goodness, one's own best potentials, is to be lost. One loses oneself. Or saves oneself. Thus, one may speak of redemption."

"In a sense?" I asked ironically. They nodded vigorously. *Seriously.* I groaned inwardly. *What can they possibly mean by 'savior'? I asked myself. If the world was perpetually being saved, why does it go on as it does?* I inquired whether they believed in an actual soul and in life after death. To my surprise, they shrugged. I had expected that all Messiahists embraced those beliefs. Third Comers expected to be lifted bodily into the sky, naked as nestlings, on the last day.

"Who knows?" the elder Gill replied. "We do not waste time on useless questions. But only a fool says in his heart, there is no God!"

"For us," Rehab Gill added, "questions about another world or another life seem not very practical. We are concerned with this world and our lives in it."

In this single sentiment, at least, they seemed Old Believers. Their creed, however, seemed highly individualistic to me. Dangerously so. Aside from the vagueness of their doctrines, I saw little concept of the community of men, or of Israel, in what they professed. I sensed also that the stories of creation and the birth of the Savior that they cherished were allegories of the nature of the world, as they conceived of it. We talked for a while about various aspects of their beliefs and their connections with the Way—most of which, I thought, were expressions of wishful thinking.

"So, you wish to believe that the foundation of the world is love—the creator's love for His creation? And that love is a fundamental aspect of natural law?"

"Exactly!" the elder Gill replied. "*The* fundamental aspect." His son nodded.

"There is much that contradicts your view."

"True, so we admit," Haman Gill said. "But we who follow the Child hold that this principle is worthy of belief. Our faith rests upon the evidence of things not seen, to be sure, but also upon the substance of things hoped for."

Formulas again, I thought. There are many things worthy of belief, but very few true things. I heaved a sigh, doubting that I would learn anything of value from Gill and his father. "Do you believe," I asked, pressing them one last time, "that the whole world—the world that all of us inhabit together—will come to an end on December 31st of next year?"

"Of course not!" the elder Gill retorted. "That is superstition. That is Bishop Bon's great pretense and fraud, and the means by which he tries to foist his evil rule on Israel!"

"So you oppose him? And oppose the rule of the churchmen?"

"Of course! His perversion of our doctrine is offensive to us. Such literalism is destruction, pure and simple. It is hateful."

"But what you profess sounds very different from Israel's tradition of seeking to grow in understanding of the Way."

"Not so much, really," the elder Gill said.

"It is a different perspective than you acquired at the Refuge," Gill admitted. "However, what you believe accords with our beliefs, though we use different terms and have different emphases."

"So we believe," Haman Gill said solemnly. "And so did the Council of Apostles at the time of the Religious Settlement, when they affirmed that we are all of one faith."

"But with different emphases," his son added.

"In a sense," I acknowledged wryly.

I left no wiser than I came, but I was content for the time. Anyone who was not against us was with us.

Nisan Lot moved with great skill to consolidate his power in Dan. Once he had a dependable majority in the Council, he withdrew Dan's emissaries to the Messiahists – "to give them fresh instructions." He released all those who had been imprisoned because of their beliefs, thus becoming the champion of harmless Messiahists without offending those who followed St. Supplicee. By mid August, he had himself reinstated as Mayor of Hazor, and shortly after, he announced that the Apostle was retiring from public life until his health mended. Seeing which way the wind was blowing, General Malachi approached Lot privately and pledged his support—in return for keeping his post.

"The Apostle's retirement is permanent," Lot explained to me. "Caleb Boz can scarcely live beyond the new year; his health is failing rapidly. During the Apostle's retirement, the Mayor of Hazor becomes the effective head of the Council, so I have taken over the executive functions of the government. I have the power I need, and I have it legitimately."

"You are a fool if you trust General Malachi," I warned.

"Malachi still commands the army, but I command the army's purse strings," he replied. "It is not a question of trust, in any case. It is a matter of configuring the powers that exist and finding a balance that permits action."

I disliked his decision to retain Malachi, but I was interested in his reasons. Mayor Lot moved carefully, deliberately, like a cat stalking its prey.

"Why don't you just dismiss the Apostle and hold an election?" I asked, seeing he was content to rule informally. Lot now controlled seven of the nine positions remaining on the Council. His allies were bound to him by solemn oaths. I assumed he would soon move to oust his two remaining opponents.

"We shall hold elections for members of the Council," he explained, "but not for the Apostleship. I do not want another Apostle elected." Although the former Apostle was disgraced and ill, the Mayor feared that ancient attachments to the Boz clan could put his son, Major Ethan Boz, in the Apostleship. "The landed electors are hidebound, "he explained. "They live by their traditions, and it is not yet clear enough to everyone what a fool this young Boz is."

He had a point. Nisan Lot's support was concentrated in the city of Hazor, while the electors were chiefly landed nobles in the countryside. As a merchant and not a Name in Israel, Lot was not eligible for the Apostleship. So he was wise to be cautious. In time, the old families might come round, but in the meantime, he would have to tread carefully.

"The Apostleship is dead," I prodded him. "Why not make a new start?"

"True, it is dead," he admitted. "But its memory lives on. Never underestimate the power of a dead thing that is remembered." Lot preferred gradual change to any sudden break with tradition. "This is not the moment," he said. "The people are unsettled, and when they are afraid, they can commit surprising things."

I acknowledged his point. On the other hand, fundamental changes were in progress, whatever he felt about them. But Lot wanted neither to excite the people nor to commit Dan to any long-term arrangements such as a new Apostle. It was the man he was. He would see what was possible as time unfolded. Lot even preferred to retain members of the opposing faction on the Council. "No sense closing out our opponents," he explained. "If they retain some role in the affairs of the government, they will not grow desperate."

"Even so," I warned him, "you must eventually change the form of government in Dan. The Apostleship is gone, and you must put an end to the privileges of the landed class and extend the vote to all citizens."

"In due time, perhaps," he replied.

Until its internal dissention was quelled, Dan would be helpless to move against the Messiahists. The reunification of Dan was therefore of first concern, though it lay entirely in Nisan Lot's hands. Lot was a shrewd ally; I left Dan and its troubles to him and concentrated on my own plans, which involved Naphtali.

A general truce prevailed with the churchmen. When negotiations with the Messiahists resumed, I sent Rehab Gill to New Jerusalem. It created a sensation that a Messiahist could represent the ferocious Sword of Israel, as I was taken to be. This time we made demands. Gill asked for the release of all Asherites imprisoned in the recent war in exchange for the prisoners we had taken, and he was to insist on the removal of Messiahist troops from Asher and demand reparations. Short of obtaining these things, he was to press for as much freedom as possible for my countrymen and to seek the status of a neutral city for Selah, the capital of Asher. At intervals, when negotiations broke down, I influenced the Sevfolk to raid Ephraim.

I did not entirely trust Gill. But if he was a double agent, I made certain he could put at risk no essential interests of mine. And if he served the church in secret, the Messiahists would surely allow him concessions to prove his value to me. Thus, whatever his allegiances, he could help my suffering countrymen.

VIII

My eyes remained fixed on the north, on Naphtali. I threw myself into the work of preparation single-mindedly. My experiences in the Kuhlan lands had given me a strange kind of fame. Recruits came to us and supporters opened their purses for our cause. Many people came only to stare, but even among those, some joined us. Refugee nobles from Asher and elsewhere sought us out, and I soon had a small cavalry force, who schooled themselves under Major Moriah and the Esdralon Guards. Meanwhile, I had written to Ahaz requesting instructors to teach my new recruits the infantry drill and tactics of the First Apostles. From mid-August, then, I had an infantry force in the making, and Burgos labored to find the arms and armor to equip them. We could manufacture everything we needed except arms, which were scarce and very dear in Dan. Burgos was my Chief of Commissary, and he spent his time between Lander's estate and Hazor, feeding and outfitting our new recruits and laying up stores. We gathered grain and arms and cloth and all things needful for war about us, while the refugees at the College and the Benjamites we had rescued labored day and night.

By the time frost came, I was ready. I had three very green cohorts of infantry and another three in training. "All I need is fifty men from the Esdralon Guards," I told Moriah, "and I seek only volunteers."

Major Moriah shook his head. "Your plan is madness. Your men are only half trained and you have barely the skeleton of a legion—while General Huerta has the largest legion in Israel."

"Yes," I acknowledged, "but their strength is divided among several garrisons. We will pick them off separately, one by one, before they can concentrate against us. Therefore I need take only the portion of the Legion that is adequately trained and equipped."

I had reasonably good information about my enemy. The bulk of the Northern Lights Guards were in the Okanogan valley, ninety miles to the north of Hammoth-Wenatchee, where they were said to have their hands full with hostile Canadians. Jezreel, on the coast of Dan, held a garrison of 300, but it could be immobilized by the Sevfolk without their actually engaging in hostilities. The target of my attack was the Wenatchee valley and the capital, Hammoth-Wenatchee. The city had a garrison of about 400 men. But with the frost, many of these troops would be dispersed, overseeing woodcutting parties in the forest. I intended to take my newly trained cohorts over the mountain road that Burgos and I had traveled the year before. We would break in the back door of Naphtali by surprise and seize Cashmere. Then I would push rapidly on to Hammoth-Wenatchee and take the city.

"You have three cohorts, a handful of cavalry, and a body guard," Moriah scoffed. "The garrison of Hammoth-Wenatchee alone will outnumber you."

"That's why I'm asking for fifty volunteers from the Esdralon Guards," I said. "With fifty such men, I can overpower any force the Northern Lights can raise against me."

Moriah scowled, believing my compliment just, but my plan dubious.

"Consider this," I said, "with any prospect of success, the population of Naphtali will rise up against General Huerta and his rule."

"And you *count* on this?" Moriah was offended at my recklessness.

"Who would fight to protect Huerta who is not coerced to do so?"

"Never underestimate the power of coercion," Moriah warned.

I took his point. Nevertheless, I was convinced I could take Cashmere quickly and then move on Hammoth-Wenatchee before the force deployed in the Okanogan valley could move against us. Once in motion, I had approximately six days in which to maneuver and attack the separate garrisons. Admittedly, I was cutting the odds pretty close.

Moriah pointed out that any small setback could defeat the whole enterprise. *He was correct, I had to admit.* But in the end, Moriah assented and was the first of the Guards to volunteer. He demanded, however, that we take the entire Esdralon Guards Legion rather than a handful of volunteers. I was pleased to have him. Though arrogant, he possessed genuine skills and a peculiar zeal as a soldier.

I ordered Captain Amasa to assemble a force of Sevfolk and other shepherd clansmen on the hills above Jezreel by the second week of October. "Your job is to keep the garrison penned up in the Vantage until you hear from me. Use the untrained cohorts for the demonstration. The Sevfolk will assist you. To succeed, you must appear formidable and capable of interfering in any move the garrison may make. But don't initiate hostilities if you can avoid it. Commit no overt act of war until it is clear that this scheme of mine will work. Your main problem will be restraining the Sevfolk."

Amasa nodded. He would not fail me.

Each of us knew our roles in the plan and was prepared to perform it. It was true that Colonel Sepulvida's veteran cohorts on the Canadian border cast a long shadow over my plans, but I was confident that I could deal with that problem when the time came.

I completed my preparations for war with the ceremony of commissioning my new legion, which I named, in honor of our first objective, the Great Jordan Guards. Our uniform colors were gray with blue trim, in token of the omen I had received on the Yakima. Our standard was a heron opening its wings for flight against a golden field, representing Asher. I assembled my men in their new finery, received their oaths, and distributed the colors to each cohort. I had six cohorts in all, good men and eager, but only half were trained enough to commit to battle. We feasted solemnly, and the next day, under a clear autumn sky, I set in motion my plan to seize Naphtali.

In the event, we ran immediately into difficulties. An early snowstorm caught our column in the mountain passes. We were delayed four days, but struggled on through the drifts and cold. We had to leave our wagons and most of the supplies on the pass. More importantly, the delay meant my schedule was disrupted. Amasa would therefore move against Jezreel before I was ready to descend into the Wenatchee valley. Huerta would thus be forewarned that some move against him was in progress. The snow also immobilized the woodcutters of Naphtali, however, and we scooped up twenty or so on our way into the valley.

Moriah was impatient at these delays and rebuked me for wasting time on prisoners. As we expected, Nahum of Cashmere, the chief landed noble of the upper valley, rose in rebellion against Huerta at our approach. Nahum brought out over a hundred kinsmen and supporters and announced himself as my ally. I welcomed him warily and armed his men from the stores we had brought with us over the mountains.

The snow persisted through the first day of our descent into the valley. I deployed my forces and our newfound allies around the walls of Cashmere. It was a sorry place, as I remembered. I was anxious to attack the city before nightfall, but our ballistas and ladders had lagged behind. Until we had assured every chance of success, I was reluctant to commit green troops to an assault. Accordingly, I led my cavalry east to secure the bridges over the Wenatchee and reconnoiter beyond. I wanted to look over the terrain myself and guard against surprises.

Surprise, however, always comes from the direction least expected. We found no sign of the enemy downstream, but when we returned to Cashmere, I found the men of Naphtali making a loud commotion around their fires, under the very walls of the city. When I came near, I realized it was the prisoners we had taken in the woods who were hanging over the flames.

"Moriah! Captain Jared! Eli! In the name of St. Supplicee," I exclaimed, "who is responsible for this?" I charged through the group, my horsemen scattering Nahum's men. I cut down a bound and still living victim from the poles over the fire, and dashed the fire with my boot. My troopers quickly followed suit and we saved three men, though they were badly burned. We rescued others, bound and waiting their turn. Half a dozen men hung motionless from spits.

I held in my arms a young man of mixed blood, mostly white, whom I had rescued from the fire. He was whimpering incoherently. His reddish hair and scalp had been singed by the fires. Large, wet flakes of snow descended into my face as I simultaneously searched for restraint and envisioned the disrepute into which we had just fallen. The reputation of the Herons, my new Great Jordan Guardsmen, was already stained by the scorched flesh of these prisoners. "Who is responsible for this?" I demanded. "Speak *now*!"

Moriah stood silent, and my new captains muttered that this was Naphtali and "this was *their* country and *their* countrymen." I glared at Moriah, thinking that, as the ranking officer on the scene, he was responsible for this outrage. Just as I was about to hold him to account, a young man of Naphtali stepped forward and said, "I am responsible." He seemed proud of his crime and haughty, as if daring me to resent it.

"Is this true?" I looked to Moriah and then to Nahum, who had come forward on horseback, surrounded by a group of his retainers. Moriah nodded, and Nahum squinted at me with hostile eyes.

"Your own words condemn you," I said, and I ran the young man through where he stood.

There was a great commotion at my action, and the two groups, my troopers and Nahum's men, rushed at each other and came to blows. As things worked out, it would have been better to have finished what we started at this moment, but Moriah and his staff leapt to separate us before much blood was shed. As it was, half a dozen figures lay in the snow. Moriah hurried me aside, which I resented greatly, but he indicated he wished to speak to me urgently.

"Major, we are not Kuhlans!" I declared to him. "You must get that through your head! Torture is unlawful, and the Herons *exist* to embody the Law."

"Striking that young man was not the Law!" he snarled at me.

"He condemned himself. His own words condemned him. And you stood witness." The stupidity of this act was almost as blatant as its cruelty: to abuse prisoners in full sight of a walled city we had yet to assault! "Have you taken leave of your senses?" I demanded.

"That young man was the nephew of Nahum of Cashmere," Moriah replied.

Nahum's men stormed out of our encampment. They headed east, over the bridges toward Hammoth-Wenatchee. I was glad to see them go, but Moriah warned me of the mischief they could cause in the lower valley. At his urging, I dispatched a party of horsemen after them. If Nahum planned to change sides and was hurrying down the valley to alert the garrison against us, I could do nothing about it. But I needed to prevent the enemy from sweeping over the bridge at us in the midst of our assault on Cashmere.

Many of my own troopers were scattered through the countryside requisitioning horses and wagons to haul the reassembled ballistas and catapults—work our Naphtali allies should have been doing. My infantry were still assembling assault ladders before the walls of Cashmere. I expected we would carry it in our first rush, but time was passing.

Anxious, I took another look down river, overtaking my patrol. I had no sooner joined them when I heard a great uproar and panicked shouts of "Cavalry!" I saw men running and then a mob tumbling out of the fog, and then horsemen rising in their stirrups to slash at fugitives. "Cavalry!" they cried. "We are lost!"

"Stay together!" I cried, galloping toward the melee. It was Nathan's men, and they had been attacked by Northern Lights Guardsmen. "Use your pikes! Stay together. Move into the orchards!" It was no use. I watched Nahum's recruits dissolve into a mob of terrified fugitives. I was forced to flee back to Cashmere, barely escaping capture myself.

I found the first cohort of my new Guards formed up not two hundred yards from the bridge, their front facing toward this new danger. They presented a solid mass of bristling pikes with archers behind them. The mounted men who had pursued me reined in abruptly as my infantry moved forward. Seeing a handful of the Esdralon Guards cavalry forming up nearby, I shouted to Major Moriah, "Secure the bridge!" Then I hurried on to bring up another cohort of the Herons. Cashmere would have to wait. I feared we would be taken in detail if the Northern Lights Guards came across the bridge in strength.

As I hurried back with the rest of our force, the First Cohort had already pushed forward nearly to the bridge to prevent just such a maneuver as I feared, and a sharp fight was in progress. I breathed easier. Major Moriah and Captain Jared had seen exactly what to do. Many of the enemy cavalry on our side of the bridge had already been unhorsed or scattered. I saw Moriah rallying the men; his troopers were collecting the riderless horses.

"Damn his evil, blundering soul!" Moriah complained as I approached. "Gill assured us that the Northern Lights Cavalry would be in Lebanon."

"These troops aren't regular cavalry," I noted, quickly surveying the field. "They are not armed for it. Look, they lack bowmen and lancers. This must be part of the garrison of Hammoth-Wenatchee playing at being cavalrymen. They came out to slash at civilians with borrowed swords, and now they are having second thoughts."

At my command, the Second Cohort swept forward and cleared the bridge, crossed it, and formed again on the far side. The Northern Lights Guards left half a dozen bodies on the bridge, including a wounded officer. I sent our few Asherite and Benjamite horsemen forward in pursuit.

"We need intelligence," I shouted to Moriah. "Can you persuade your renegades to take prisoners?" He waved at me and spurred his horse away.

I dismounted to question the captured officer, a Northern Lights Guards Lieutenant. I chased away the Benjamites who were rifling through his clothing. "Begone!" I shouted. "Savages!" To the Lieutenant, who had a nasty wound in his thigh, I said, "Tell me how many soldiers are in Hammoth-Wenatchee. Are all the garrison as eager as you?"

"Who wants to know?" he demanded, still defiant.

I told him who I was. "What is the force that opposes us?" I demanded, gesturing down river. "How many troops? Who commands them?"

He sneered at me. "I wouldn't know."

"Stand when you talk to the Colonel!" One of our sergeants seized him, dragged him to his feet, and cuffed him vigorously.

I repeated my questions and received the same reply. Seeing his defiance, the sergeant drew his sword, but I waved him off. "Treat him gently. Get him to one of the cottages over yonder and see that his wounds are dressed. If he lives, he retains his commission in the Guards. I need officers like him."

The Lieutenant gazed at me in astonishment. I thought it likely that he would live. I wanted to use the Northern Lights Guard, not destroy them. I doubted I would find many officers with this man's zeal.

There were no longer sounds of combat coming from our front; our men had pushed forward beyond earshot. I remounted and ordered the column forward, with the Esdralon Guards in the lead. I doubted that there was a unit in Naphtali willing to challenge these fierce Benjamites, now that their identity was known. We saw as we moved forward that the scratch force of men raised by Nahum of Cashmere had been scattered and massacred.

"Green wood," Major Moriah spat, leaning from his saddle. "You can't make a fire with green wood."

"This may be a blessing in disguise, Colonel," Captain Jared said. "If Nahum is dead, the Northern Lights Guards have rid you of a rival. I think all your charm will not reconcile Nahum to his nephew's death today."

But Nahum of Cashmere was not among the dead. We found him at the edge of a wood with a guard of retainers who had survived his ill-timed foray. I asked him tersely if he and his men could demonstrate outside the walls of Cashmere and keep the garrison inside. He assented grudgingly, seeming somewhat shaken by his first experience of war. I returned his salute, thinking, *Just one useful thing out of you, and then we will have our reckoning.*

I hurried my forces toward the capital city. Major Moriah and the other officers objected that I was leaving both an enemy force and a treacherous ally across our lines of communication, but I dismissed their protests. I had no choice. "If we don't take Hammoth-Wenatchee immediately," I reminded Moriah, "our whole enterprise will fail."

As dusk fell, our scouts picked up a handful of prisoners, and they confirmed that the garrison of Hammoth-Wenatchee was barely 300 strong. The best troops and the regular cavalry were still on the Okanogan, several days to the north, and the portion of the garrison that had ventured out to meet us had fled in panic. I conferred briefly with my officers and set our small column in motion again. The men moved spiritedly and in good order. Large flakes of snow were falling, but they were melting as they landed. I took it as a good sign. The new cohorts had performed well, and I congratulated myself on their training and discipline. They were nothing like the Esdralon Guards, of course, but there was no more hardened or determined fighting force in the world than the remnant of the Esdralon Guards. And no group, I was beginning to find, harder to restrain.

As we approached the city, more men of Naphtali seemed to materialize out of the brush and small hamlets, swelling our forces and confirming my hopes about their resentment of their overlords. Our invasion had raised the countryside against Hanford's successors. Things were looking well. I was gathering about me the nucleus of a legion. With time and luck, I could shape this core of men into a formidable weapon. In the meantime, Naphtali was rising—and not under the leadership of Nahum of Cashmere.

We arrived at the city walls after nightfall, our way lit by homesteads burning along the road. An orange glow rose above the city walls. Inside, a riot seemed in progress; sounds of disorder and panic rose with the flames. Looking at the walls, I felt a moment of dread – and regret that I had assumed I could take such a place within a day of reaching it. Hammoth-Wenatchee was a formidable city, well positioned for defense and ringed by high ramparts. Standing at the foot of its outer wall, I had the bitter realization that this confidence was foolishness on my part. Moriah had been right.

I disposed the men in camps outside the city, waiting for the assault engines, which I expected to be up by morning. I anticipated desperate fighting in the morning. I ordered my exhausted soldiers to prepare defenses against a sortie, while the civilians who had joined us made fires and cooked a meal.

News of our coming had preceded us, however, and before long a delegation from the city came out to treat with us, bearing torches and led by a major of the Northern Lights Guards. They brought news that General Huerta had fled in haste with most of the garrison and that the outer walls were undefended. It was barely midnight, then, in the glare of many fires that I accepted the surrender of Hammoth-Wenatchee.

Chapter 14: A Mighty Fortress

I

Naphtali had fallen into my hands like ripe fruit. After so much anticipation, it had come into my possession almost too easily. "Enjoy it, Colonel," Moriah advised. "It will be the last easy thing you ever do. Now you must rule it." Burgos, who tended to nourish grudges, had a poor opinion of Naphtali from our previous visit. "This place is a madhouse, my lord. I say we give it back."

I had no intention of giving it back. I would rule Naphtali or die trying. We disarmed the remnants of the garrison and sent them back to their barracks. Clemency here would prevent resistance in the future. The disorder in the city was harder to quell. Reprisals were being carried out against the wealthier citizens, especially those who had cooperated with Huerta or my brother Hanford. I dispatched troops to restore order and stop the reprisals within the walls. We could do nothing for the moment, however, about the violence raging outside the city.

Moriah accompanied me as we inspected the citadel by torchlight. Hammoth-Wenatchee had an outer wall that encompassed the city and an inner wall, which enclosed the civic buildings and barracks. Within this inner city, the citadel rose four stories tall. While the city was not large, its defensive works were impressive. I marveled that General Huerta had fled at our approach; I doubted that with our force we could have taken it against even token resistance. Fires glowed around the city. Major Moriah was right; my plan had been reckless.

"So you knew all along," he remarked gruffly. "You knew from the first that your reputation, your fame, would inspire this fear. General Huerta was defeated as soon as he learned of our approach. He fled with his tail between his legs when he heard that the Sword of Israel was descending upon him!"

I of course had had no idea Huerta would flee at our approach, but I was reluctant to admit to Moriah that I had been as foolhardy as he thought.

"What I am not able to decide," Moriah added, "is whether you are in fact this figure, this Sword of Israel – or one of the Dolorites of old."

"I have given much thought to that question myself," I replied, "and I am at peace about it."

"Maybe you are," he sniffed, "but *I* do not know!"

"I am at peace about that, too."

Moriah was right, however; Naphtali would prove more difficult to rule than to conquer.

We found Solomon Glass cowering in his quarters. I ordered him held under close guard and sealed all the records pertaining to company finances. I would wait for Gill's arrival to interrogate him thoroughly. In the meantime, I wanted to give Glass opportunity to consider who his new master was.

I slept a few hours in the quarters that General Huerta had just abandoned, and then, at first light, I roused an escort of Harlech cavalrymen. We saddled fresh horses and headed south down the river road to Jezreel. I left Moriah in command of the city, still putting out fires and arresting looters. I was confident that he would hold on to the place like a mastiff with a bone.

The river road to Jezreel was little more than a path in some stretches, and where it fronted cliffs, we would have been helpless against an assault from the river. But no boats appeared on the water; no one barred our way. Our attack seemed to have paralyzed our enemies. We rode hard, not sparing our horses, and by evening we arrived in Jezreel.

An encampment of my untrained men plus large numbers of Danite tribesmen was spread over the hills above the town. The Northern Lights colors still flew over the Vantage. Captain Amasa had followed his orders faithfully. Though both sides were on a war footing, no overt act had as yet been committed. I found Amasa and Nisan Lot conferring with the Sevfolk clan leaders, and Amasa reported that all was in readiness for the next phase of my campaign. I thanked him and announced to Jerub: "Once we are successful here, Jezreel belongs to Dan." The Sevfolk broke into loud celebration, and I hoped the garrison of the Vantage could hear their fierce enthusiasm. "If it comes to an assault," I added to the Sevfolk clan chiefs, "and Dan sheds its blood in the attack, then I impose no conditions. But if the garrison surrenders first, then the troops belong to me. You will take possession of the Vantage and all it contains, but the troops are under my protection, and you must forego all revenge."

When they agreed to my terms, I signaled for a parley. I sent a message to the enemy commander—the same Major Gutierrez who had tried to capture me in the citadel the year before – announcing that Hammoth-Wenatchee was in my hands and that its garrison had acknowledged me as its commander. I promised Gutierrez that I would protect him and that his unit would continue to serve under me. "If you refuse to surrender," I wrote, "I have assault weapons on hand, and I intend to move immediately on your fortress. If it comes to a sack, you will know best what scores the Sevfolk have to settle." I enclosed copies of my orders from the Council of Apostles and from Tephlin Glanz, on the small chance he would be impressed by lawful authority. I demanded an answer within the hour.

While waiting for a reply, I hurried the assault weapons into place. I had no ready means of taking the Vantage, but I had learned the value of a convincing bluff. I had at hand only a few Benjamite veterans, whom I would not risk in a frontal assault on a fortress, and three untrained cohorts of my new legion, the Herons, who were not yet ready for such a use. There were also the Sevfolk and their allies—another 300 formidable men and warriors, but none of them trained for this kind of business. If it came down to it and my bluff failed, I could do little more than say to Jerub, "If you want Jezreel, you must take it yourselves."

I confided these things to Nisan Lot, who seemed afterwards to watch my preparations with renewed interest. I placed my three cohorts and the Benjamite cavalry on level ground opposite the main gate. "In case they sally against us," I explained to Lot. "But that would be too much to ask."

With the spectators from the shepherd clans of Dan clustered round about, we looked like a formidable host. In addition, I had real weapons, the catapults and ballistas, that were not an element of bluff. When the deadline passed, I ordered an immediate barrage. We lofted heavy stones and burning material over the walls, and soon there were flames rising inside the fortress. I positioned other engines facing the main gate, in case the Northern Lights Guards came out against us.

At dusk, I called a brief halt to the hail of missiles and had another conference with Jerub. I told him bluntly that my men would stand at arms all night, to guard against a sally from the Vantage, but it was up to the Sevfolk to scale the walls and capture the fortress in the morning. He snorted at the prospect. "The attack must come at dawn," I added. "Pick your men and have them ready at first light."

Jerub sulked off without answering. As I conferred with Nisan Lot and my officers, the Sefvolk began to settle old scores with townspeople of Jezreel. New people, outlanders who had settled in the town after Hanford seized it, were resented by the Danites. The Sevfolk had chosen this moment to vent their frustrations on the populace. In the twilight, flames began to break out in the lower town, and we heard terrified cries and sounds of violence.

"Is it possible to do something?" I said to the Mayor. This was Danite territory, and I had no authority over the Sevfolk. Nevertheless, I was mindful of the Law. I had unwittingly put many innocent people in peril of Sevfolk vengeance.

"We will wait for now," Lot replied. "It is best we wait."

After an hour Mayor Lot went down and talked with the clan leaders and got them to spare the foreigners who remained alive. When most of the warriors were under control, we formed a column of wretched civilians and surrounded them with a guard of Benjamites, and marched them up to the front gate of the Vantage. While this was the only way I could reasonably protect the prisoners, it was also a challenge to the garrison to come out and rescue them – and an implied threat as well. The civilians had become hostages. Our captives spent a dazed, fearful night on the ground. I spent the hours uneasily myself, regretting this use of the innocent. My purpose was to save lives, but the tactic was brutal. In spite of my best efforts, I dozed fitfully and then, overcome by fatigue, I fell asleep on the ground.

In the morning, a flag of truce appeared on the wall. Captain Amasa went forward to parley, and a sack was thrown down to him from the wall. When he returned, carrying the sack gingerly by one ear, he wore a strange expression on his face.

"It's the head of Major Gutierrez," he said. "The garrison respectfully ask what terms you will offer now."

I gave them easy terms. They retained their colors and marched out of the fortress with honor intact. They stacked arms outside the gate, the officers retaining their swords. I promised the expelled civilians protection and re-settlement in Naphtali and the soldiers continued service under my command. We escorted the garrison northward, back to Hammoth-Wenatchee. I commandeered boats for the civilians and for those too injured to walk. We left the Sevfolk to celebrate the triumph.

Before departing, I took Mayor Lot aside and told him I expected freedom of access to the port of Jezreel, without tariffs, perpetually. He agreed readily, pleased to have Danite territory returned at no cost to himself. "There is still the matter of Chinnereth," I said. "The portage down to Judah is critical to the river trade. I intend to dispatch a portion of my legion to take it. In the interests of permanent peace between our two peoples, I propose that Dan and Naphtali hold that portage jointly, sharing the costs and the revenues equally."

Chinnereth had never been a part of Dan; possession of the fortress and portage would bring Dan into the commerce of the Great Jordan as never before. My offer surprised him, but I knew Lot could not refuse such an opportunity. He considered for a moment, stroking his beard, and then took my hand, seeming well pleased with the bargain. We agreed to work out the details later. In the meantime, Lot offered to lead the expedition to Chinnereth himself, seeming elated at the prospect. I was glad to delegate that task to another and keep my own forces intact. In sharing control of Chinnereth I was offering a valuable concession to Dan. Since it was a highly strategic possession of the Northern Lights Enterprises, I was also aware that Ben Gurion would not bear its loss gracefully. I had more immediate concerns, however. I needed to concentrate my forces in Hammoth-Wenatchee before Huerta and Sepulvida could turn on me. At the moment, therefore, Chinnereth was a distraction. And the thought was in my mind that, in the long run, if my father came up the Jordan against me, he would, by these arrangements, have to come through a portage held by Dan. In a sense, I had invited Nisan Lot to step into a snare and bind himself to me in a defensive alliance. Such an alliance would be the foundation stone of my policy.

Lot would make a valuable ally, to be sure. But I had seen another and darker side of the Mayor the previous night, and I took that lesson to heart. I had understood what he was about in refusing to quell the riot immediately, and I had acquiesced. Thus, I had also had a glimpse of another side of my own character and had that lesson to absorb as well.

To hold Naphtali, I had to eliminate the Northern Lights Guards. I had taken two of its strongholds and perhaps 400 men. More than two thirds of the legion remained at large and were now concentrated on the Okanogan, where General Huerta had fled. Though Huerta was formidable, I estimated that Colonel Sepulvida was the more dangerous of my opponents. He had a reputation as a soldier, and he led troops who were battle-hardened. According to the best information I could gather, my enemies had eight to ten cohorts with which to contest my possession of the north. If I could link my forces at Jezreel with those at Hammoth-Wenatchee before the enemy could react, I would have something like equal numbers. I counted, of course, on the enemy remaining ignorant of how unprepared most of my men were.

Exhausted as I was, I had to make haste. As we hurried our captives and our forces back up the river road, we saw boats on the water keeping watch on us. I feared that Huerta and Sepulvida would attack before we could concentrate my troops in Naphtali. Whoever was watching our march, however, withdrew before us, and we arrived in Hammoth-Wenatchee without incident.

Major Moriah greeted us in the citadel with his usual stolid demeanor, but he expressed surprise at our easy victory. "The head of Major Gutierrez –and that without a fight! That is something!" he conceded.

"And Jezreel fell into his hands as well," Burgos added, "though a moment later, he gave it away."

Moriah gave me a sour look and reminded us that Sepulvida's cavalry were probing the Rocky Reach portage and there was a fleet on the river. We rode out to see to the defenses. The portage, hemmed in by steep canyon walls, seemed as defensible as any on the Jordan. Moriah had put one of my cohorts into the stronghold. It was a strong position. I would not relish the task of assaulting it myself. We saw horsemen a mile off and water striders on the river. Neither seemed eager to engage us. I found a soldier who knew the flag codes and asked him to signal the enemy.

"What message shall I send, sir?" the soldier asked.

"To Colonel Sepulvida," I said. "Tell him to bring me the head of General Huerta."

Shortly thereafter both boats and cavalry retired from before us, so I returned to the city.

II

I had a fierce energy in those days and nights and a will equal to the task before me. I drove myself like one possessed, surviving on little sleep and less food, and thriving on difficulty rather than nourishment. It was good that I did; there was much to do. The people of Naphtali, particularly the nobles, proved a vengeful, intractable lot. A clandestine war burned among them like a buried fire, occasionally flaring into open violence in the countryside. The nobles had had much to resent from Hanford and his successors, who had oppressed them sorely, but they seemed motivated as much by envy as by real grievances. It was their neighbors they assaulted, not me. I put an end to their ambushes and murders within the city and harried them in the countryside. I kept martial law in effect and administered summary punishment to a few of the more arrogant. As soon as a degree of calm was restored, I appointed a judge, a native of Naphtali and a son of an established lineage, before whom they could bring their grievances.

"What a people!" Moriah complained. "Half want to slaughter the others, and all of them clamor to be informers!"

I sent for Gill, who was still negotiating with the Messiahists in New Jerusalem. I needed him to establish my intelligence network. I had the bare foundations of a system that Lander had laid, but I wanted my own separate eyes and ears. Until Gill arrived, I would be blind and deaf to what transpired in Naphtali. I also summoned Captain Amasa, who had remained in charge of our activities in Dan. It was time to concentrate our operations as well as our forces, and I wanted a gentler hand than Moriah's resting upon this city I had captured. With Amasa in charge of the city, Moriah could turn his full attention to the army.

I ordered scouts northward to watch the enemy and to make contact with Colonel Sepulvida. My message to him was no subtler than the one I had signaled to the fleet: to live, Sepulvida must deliver General Huerta into my hands. Huerta, it was known everywhere, had murdered my brother and his family. There could be no reconciliation between us inside or outside of the Law, and there was no point in pretending otherwise. Major Gutierrez had also been part of the conspiracy that had overthrown Hanford, and Gutierrez was now dead. Sepulvida had not been present at the murders, but I had no doubt of his complicity in them. Sepulvida had good reason to believe that I would be relentless in the matter, but he could only speculate about what I knew of his role in it. I was deliberately inviting him to believe that I thought him innocent.

As weather permitted, I observed the training of the Herons outside the walls of the capital. We cleared and leveled a parade ground, and my young soldiers struggled with the intricacies of the infantry drill. The noble-born cavalry performed under the stern eye of Moriah, and there was much rivalry among them as well as emulation of the veteran Benjamites. But my eyes were on the infantry as they progressed in their discipline. On a hunch, I invited our prisoners to exercise with us and thus put them under the scrutiny of my drill instructors, who had the capacity to grade and cull them. No sooner had the Northern Lights Guards shown themselves out of the barracks, however, than citizens of Naphtali began to rush forward with complaints and indictments for crimes committed under Hanford and Huerta's rule. As a champion of the Law, I could not but permit these charges, even though I suspected that Nahum of Cashmere was somehow behind them all. Soon most of the officers and many of the soldiers were languishing in the great dungeon of the citadel.

With Burgos, I inspected the several warehouses of the Northern Lights Enterprises.

We found immense stores of grain and beans, dried fruit, wine and brandy. Naphtali was a treasure house. If we could find shipping enough to move these goods, we could allay fears of famine in Judah this winter. Inside a walled compound by the river, we found wealth beyond imagining—stores of recovered metal and an arsenal full of weapons and armor. "Here is enough good metal to equip a legion," Burgos exclaimed, admiring a heap of iron ingots.

"Two legions!" I replied. This store of metal was doubtless the product of the recovery operations at Old Spokane—an enterprise that Zachariah ben Harlech and I had smashed in our raid to free the Benjamite slaves. Both Hanford and Huerta had apparently been hording metal for years. I would put it all to good use.

Burgos discovered a large sack in a corner; its weight was apparent as he dragged it into the light. "St. Supplicee!" he exclaimed. He tipped the sack, spilling its contents. Large, double-bladed axe heads of the type preferred by Kuhlans tumbled onto the floor. I stooped and picked one up. Its heft and sharp iron edges were exactly like my own war axe, the gift of Riik and the warriors of the Black Willow People. Burgos whistled in astonishment. When I asked for his thoughts, he replied: "I'd say we have an explanation, my lord. I believe we now know the price of metal recovery in Old Spokane!"

The sight of these weapons made a number of connections in my mind—connections that I should have made long before. *My father and Hanford Glanz had sold iron weapons to the Kuhlans.* The Harlech had not, and it was that scruple that had cost them their trade agreement with the People. I was relieved to know that I had not been the sole cause of Zachariah's losses in this regard, but this discovery constituted yet another grievance with my father. That cup was almost full.

As I attempted to form a government in Naphtali, I chafed at my lack of knowledge of the territory I had conquered. There were decent maps and a census in the archives. Naphtali held nearly 3,000 households, of whom approximately 200 families qualified as noble. Nahum's power rested on the landed class, especially the nobles of the upper valley, who lived remote from the city and from commerce. Although landed traditions did not run deep in this new land, the pretensions of the class seemed well established. In response, the merchants had allied themselves with Hanford, and their views and money dominated the capital city, which boasted nearly 4,000 inhabitants.

I looked for other clues of what Naphtali held for me. Unfortunately, the information in the archives was over a decade old. Hanford had kept the census only to tax the inhabitants. There was no registry of births and no record of licenses to bear children; my brother had let the Reproduction Laws entirely lapse. I marveled that anyone could so misconstrue the functions of government as to use them merely to oppress. The new merchant tyrants were a plague to Israel, not its deliverers. I intended to establish a different kind of rule, neither of landed arrogance nor of merchant greed. Meanwhile, I needed to match the information gleaned from reports and ledgers with what I observed with my own eyes. At the first opportunity, I embarked on a tour of inspection.

Though isolated from the rest of Israel, Naphtali engages in a vital trade with the northern reaches of the Jordan and funnels those products down to Judah. The land itself was a rich garden. Within sight of the capital, ruined walls and towers from Ancient times rose amid well-kept fields and strongholds. Four miles above the city, the Wenatchee River emptied into the Jordan. The inhabited part of the Wenatchee valley was a narrow, winding canyon scarcely more than a mile wide and twenty miles deep. The valley was a rugged jumble of benches and cliffs cut by the river, but it held some of the best land in Naphtali. A great variety of crops grew there. Cashmere, the second city of Naphtali, lay some twelve miles up river. A few miles above the town, forest-covered mountains shouldered against the river, and men could go there only after the frosts.

Northwest of the Jordan, there was additional cultivated land on the shore of a great lake called Chelan, but for the time being it was in the hands of my enemies. Directly north of Hammoth-Wenatchee, the mountains came down to the river's edge. I was able to reconnoiter as far north as the Rocky Reach portage, but the enemy had pickets within a few miles of the stronghold. I let them alone. I wanted to consolidate my power before opening the next phase of the conflict.

As part of my tour of inspection, I took a column of men up the valley to Cashmere and accepted its surrender. Nahum and his followers had been besieging it ineffectually for two weeks and had managed to terrify its small garrison but not to harm them. I had only to promise them the same terms I offered the garrison of Jezreel, plus safe conduct to Hammoth-Wenatchee, and they complied eagerly.

Nahum, the chief landed noble of the upper valley, had used the siege as an excuse to begin reconstituting the Naphtali Guards, the old tribal legion that had existed before Hanford usurped power and built his own armed forces. Nathan had gathered over 200 men, who were moderately well equipped but untrained. Seeing them arrayed around the city, Moriah warned, "You can tolerate only one legion in Naphtali, Colonel. If you come to it now, you will be quit of it later."

"It must be later," I replied. My concern at the moment was that portion of the Northern Lights Guards still under Sepulvida's control, and I was reluctant to start a civil conflict in Naphtali. Before I moved against Nahum, I meant to detach the nobles from their loyalty to him. Accordingly, I thanked Nahum and his men for their services and ordered them to disperse to their homes. They protested. Nahum was indignant and used intemperate language. For a moment, it looked as if the confrontation was at hand. I was not unhappy at the prospect if hostilities were initiated by him. I summoned a herald to state my demands again: Nahum and his men must disperse to their homes or take the consequences.

Nahum sat motionless for a time on his huge buckskin, wrapped in furs like a bear, and glared at us, but eventually he complied. Afterwards we made a sweep through the estates in the region and picked up another half a dozen soldiers of the Northern Lights Guards held prisoner there. Others, we suspected, had been done away with, perhaps in the same cruel manner as the prisoners burned at Cashmere. No one was talking. The upper valley was a hostile land, but there was nothing to be done about it for the moment. We gathered nearly 50 slaves from the valley and took them back with us. I saw to it that the owners were fairly compensated, but I would accept no argument about it. Slavery was dead in Naphtali.

As we descended the valley, the rain stopped and the sun broke through the clouds. Towering peaks of slate and deep blue rose immediately behind the valley's steep shoulders; even now they were beginning to acquire a light snow pack. I recalled how the sight of them had filled me with dread on my first journey to Naphtali and how an early storm had caught us in the passes on my second. The valley was bright with autumn colors and its inhabitants were gleaning its last produce before winter set in. Though picturesque, the prospect made me melancholy. The valley's rugged terrain suggested its possibilities for defense. Who would not fight to hold such a bountiful place?

Returning to the Great Jordan, I stopped at the stronghold of the former Apostle of Naphtali, Isaac Peshatin. The Apostle Peshatin had died of a fever shortly before Hanford's death, and it was said that he had been entirely Hanford's creature. Having played no role in the government during Hanford's rule, Peshatin had virtually allowed the Apostleship to lapse, and General Huerta had of course not permitted the election of a successor. I was not unhappy that the former Apostle had disgraced the office, for I was toying with the prospect of starting a new form of government in Naphtali. As the Apostleship tended to run in families, I was curious to meet this family and learn whether they would help or hinder my plans.

The stronghold of the Peshatins was a modest great house with a walled enclosure. An orchard, still in leaf but damaged by the recent ice storm, straggled right up to the walls. The whole estate looked poorly planned and badly kept; the main gate was broken off its hinges. Leaving our escort on the road, Captain Jared and I knocked and were admitted to the stronghold. We introduced ourselves to the widow of the Apostle and to her household. The widow, the Senyora Ollala Peshatin, was a tall woman of middle age who seemed somewhat alarmed to see us. Nevertheless, she served us bitter tea and bread and deigned to converse with us – albeit in a guarded, disdainful manner. She spoke of the troubles that had plagued her family and reported that an elder son of the family had died in Hanford's time, shortly before his father. She spoke also of a daughter, but the girl was not presented to us. As I took in the household and its formidable but somewhat unpleasant female head, it seemed to me that the Peshatins had indeed fallen on hard times.

When I inquired about the daughter, intending only polite curiosity, the Senyora Peshatin bristled, and her hospitality grew several degrees cooler. "The girl is not—she is not presentable," she declared. "My daughter suffered greatly in the recent disorders. Dreadfully! She was—they forced her to—" She paused, placing a hand on her throat, as if she had barely escaped heaving up some awful revelation. Then, to my astonishment, she blurted out what had stuck in her throat: "My daughter was violated!" She stopped before she blamed the disorders on my invasion. Captain Jared and I sat stiff with embarrassment at this revelation.

We expressed our condolences and quickly took our leave. Afterwards I discussed the incident with Captain Jared, who was the son of a good Asherite family situated not far from Tirzah. "How strange for a mother to reveal such a thing about her daughter," I remarked. I was still puzzled at her behavior. I thought of Tirzah and of how far my own family had fallen from its days of greatness. But this was extraordinary.

"It's more than strange," Captain Jared replied. "And something else; I sensed great hostility toward you."

"She may well blame me for her daughter's misfortune."

He shook his head. "I think it is more likely a message to you. If the daughter is of marriageable age, the mother was saying—saying as emphatically as possible—that she is ineligible to marry you. Or you her, perhaps."

I flushed, thinking of my dubious parentage, which would be an offense to established families connected to the Apostleship. Then I thought again and considered other motives that the Senyora Peshatin might have for discouraging any possible attention to her daughter. Perhaps it was only the mystery surrounding the family, but I found myself very curious about this daughter of the Peshatin clan. "All these questions begin to whet my interest," I remarked to Jared. "I begin to think I would like to meet this daughter of the Apostle."

III

What drove me relentlessly was my need to acquire legitimate power in Naphtali rather than to hold it merely by force. My aim was to turn this territory into a bastion against the Messiahists—and, if necessary, against Tephlin Glanz himself. To do so, I had to free myself of dependence upon Glanz and win the support of the citizenry. I held the land by right of conquest and by a commission from Tephlin Glanz – a commission that was beginning to seem illegitimate even in my own eyes. Moreover, conquest makes few friends, even when an evil ruler is deposed by it. To build the bastion I desired, I had to reconstruct the country on new lines, and do it quickly.

Rehab Gill arrived from New Jerusalem in the first week of November, seeming exhausted from his travels and not altogether well. As soon as he had refreshed himself, I took him to the citadel and showed him the sights of the city from its battlements. He remarked on the size and construction of the fortress as he limped across the parapet beside me, holding his cloak tight against the wind. "I find the citadel a bit more comfortable than my accommodations in the dungeon," he announced wryly. "Less drafty." We retired to my quarters to discuss events. I inquired about his health and his family and then asked after my own family in Asher, and whether he had heard anything of the Vashons and their fates.

"Nothing, my lord," he said, easing his feet up on a stool. "There has been no word." Then, to fill the silence, he demanded to hear of our recent campaign. I gave him a brief account of our sweep down the valley and of Huerta's flight.

"Huerta lost the game when he abandoned this fortress," Gill observed. "And then he waited too long to counter-attack. Now, even with untried troops, you would be difficult to expel from Hammoth-Wenatchee." When I agreed with his estimate, he added, "What I find amazing is that you seized two fortified cities with so little fighting."

"Surprise is a potent weapon," I said. "I doubt that Huerta was even aware of me as an enemy till we burst into the valley."

"True," he said. "Nevertheless, I believe this campaign is surely one for the Academy."

"Not quite yet." I reminded him that Huerta and Sepulvida still had the better part of a legion a few days to the north.

"Sepulvida is not so likely to run," he mused. Then, changing the subject in his unpredictable way, Gill declared, "Your reputation rises in the south like a storm cloud, Colonel; it rises like a column of smoke. You cannot imagine the combination of fear and awe and loathing in which you are held in Manasseh. You quite dominated the negotiations, even while absent. What is the old saying? You are become a sign to the nations! The Messiahists blame you for their failure in Dan, and now you have surprised Naphtali and taken it for your own. They are not pleased; in fact, I think they are quite alarmed."

When I asked about the progress of the negotiations, Gill explained that they had reached a stalemate. "Meanwhile," he informed me, "the two sides have devastated each other's territory so thoroughly that there is scarcely a blade of grass between Hebron and New Jerusalem. The destruction is beyond anything imagined since the Kuhlan war. And now the churchmen drive all unbelievers from Manasseh and Ephraim. As they continue to cleanse the Holy Land, as they call it, Judah and Dan are filling up with refugees. Truly, it is beyond all shame."

"So famine will visit Israel this winter." As I considered these prospects, I thought suddenly of Judah and its new possessions in Engedi and of my father's fields and gardens across the river in Old Pasco. Those places were out of reach of Messiahist cavalry. I could, moreover, send stores to Judah from Naphtali. Perhaps the advantage had swung at last to Judah.

"Famine, yes," Gill said, as if anticipating my thoughts, "but opportunity as well. In fact," he added, brimming with secret knowledge, "it is because of the impending famine that I have, in a sense, saved your people Asher!"

"What have you done?" I demanded, fearing he had committed some foolish act he was trying to disguise by this claim.

Gill insisted that he had truly managed to save Asher. "Though they went to great pains to disguise it, the Messiahists' food stocks are nearly exhausted. Both sides have done their best to destroy the sustenance of the other, but your father's lands on the Kuhlan side of the Jordan are safe from destruction—quite beyond the reach of the Messiahists. Meanwhile," he added, "according to reports, your father is now conducting a thriving trade with both the Kuhlans and the Kr."

My father thrives on carrion, I thought to myself. *But unlike a vulture, he also kills.*

"How does any of this affect my people in Asher?" I asked.

"Ah, you see, the Messiahists need a sanctuary too, where they can grow next year's food. Thanks to my diplomacy, Asher will be that sanctuary."

"Gill," I protested angrily, "you compromise me entirely. If I protect my people in this way, in the short run, it will prolong the war. If the Messiahists are now weakened to the point of collapse, to supply them will save them from defeat."

"Perhaps they are not so near collapse," he replied coolly. "The Messiahists have means; they have granaries inside their strongholds, and they are ruthless, God knows. In any case, the Messiahists can survive the winter – and your Asherite kinsmen cannot. Asher has been sheared like a lamb. If someone does not provision them, your people will starve. There is no long run for them." When I objected, he added, "Understand, if Asher is not willing to become the granary of the Messiahists, the churchmen will simply take the land and make it so. Then where will your people be?"

I muttered complaints, but I saw his point. In exchange for a truce, my people would remain on their land and survive. The Messiahists would supply them through the winter.

"The Messiahists," Gill said, "know that if they expel Asher from their lands, you will retaliate and destroy every ear of corn that grows on Asherite territory. But they know that if your people are allowed to stay on their land, you will not. They know you will respect the truce. Very clever of them, I must say. And since the Messiahists can manage no other way than by this arrangement, I believe they, too, will abide by its terms." Gill was very pleased with his cleverness. When I thought through all the circumstances, I could see no other course myself.

"What about Nisan Lot? Is he a party to this agreement?"

"The Mayor is practical in all things. He sees the need—and he sees the advantages as well. Dan could use a breathing spell, as far as that goes."

I nodded, finding his account of things plausible.

"I have the document here," Gill said. "It needs your signature."

I examined it and altered several details. I insisted on the release of imprisoned Asherites and other Old Believers and demanded that they be allowed to settle in Asher. Asher would become a neutral state in the war and a refuge for its victims. Gill muttered in his turn, but in the end he promised to negotiate the changes.

Solomon Glass was not happy to see Gill; he squinted at the worn parchment and then at us with red-rimmed, near-sighted eyes. Gill gave him a menacing look. "So, you two have met before?" I asked mockingly. I had waited for Gill's arrival to interrogate Glass, who was both the Treasurer of the Northern Lights Enterprises and, I suspected, Glanz's chief agent in Naphtali. I asked him to interpret the document I had carried with me on my mission to Naphtali.

"These," Glass acknowledged with evident distaste, as if examining the parchment for vermin, "are the numbers of bank accounts. The first entry represents an account held locally, at the branch of a banking house owned by the Enterprises."

Gill and I exchanged glances. I asked Glass what he knew of the purpose of my mission to Naphtali the year before, and if he understood the relation of these funds to that mission.

Glass made no effort to deny his role in Glanz's network. "You were given a draft for 200,000 kanz and, unbeknownst to yourself, the seal of Tephlin Glanz. I believe the seal was to be hidden in a decoration of some kind. A small statue. You were to present these tokens to me and draw that money from the local bank and deposit it in this account. The money was designated for your mission."

"For what purposes?"

"A portion of it," he said, "was to pay for the assassination of Hanford Glanz."

"And then what?"

"My instructions extended no further than that."

"He's lying," Gill said.

I pressed on. "Who were Hanford's assassins?"

"General Huerta and some of his associates."

"And you could name these other associates?"

"He knows his own name, at least!" Gill said scornfully.

Glass ran his tongue over his lips and said. "I can name them all." None of the names he gave surprised me, however. Aside from Huerta, most were in custody or already dead. *Very safe. He had omitted Sepulvida's name.*

"And the other numbers on this document, are they accounts also?"

He squinted again at the parchment. "I don't recognize them or understand their significance. I am unable to help you."

Gill prompted him. "The first three digits are the codes of banking houses, aren't they? You have just revealed that JAL is the code for the local house here in Hammoth-Wenatchee. The other two prefixes are probably banks in Hazor and New Jerusalem, places into which Glanz and Ben Gurion could not easily reach. These are secret accounts used by Hanford to squirrel away the treasure that he looted from the company."

Solomon Glass shook his head, denying Gill's interpretation of the document, but I trusted Gill's intuition in these matters.

"You will have to work with Captain Gill," I reminded Glass when I grew tired of his evasions. "My advice to you is to try to get on better terms with him. He has, as is well known, an ugly disposition—and I must say, his temper was not improved by his imprisonment here in Naphtali. In fact, if I were you, I would do my best to please him, since I am giving him unlimited power to conduct this investigation – along with, of course, unlimited powers of interrogation."

Glass's throat bobbed as he swallowed. *Glass would, I suspected, have cause to remember the bastinado delivered to Gill's feet the year before.*

"You will need to give Captain Gill something daily," I said, "just to keep him happy. We can start with the secret accounts of Huerta and the other conspirators. And then your own accounts, when you have become accustomed to divulging secrets."

"Excellency, I merely followed your father's orders. Not a hair more nor less."

"Perhaps you did, but at this moment I do not know that. You should think of ways you can corroborate your story. Short of that, you should find ways to impress Captain Gill."

"Why am I under suspicion?"

"You survived when Hanford was murdered," Gill said, "which can only mean that you served Huerta to his satisfaction."

"If you would only contact General Ben Gurion," he said. "I obeyed his commands. . . ."

Gill seemed amused. "Do you believe Ben Gurion's praise would commend you to us? Do you believe Ben Gurion would still bestow it? I suggest you consider the probability that you have outlived any use General Ben Gurion might have for you. And then consider where that leaves you."

"Your fate now depends upon your making yourself useful to me," I said. "And pleasing to Captain Gill."

Solomon Glass squinted at these possibilities as if he were reading fine print. "I have records, ample records," he said, running his tongue over his lips. "Although they are in code." He meant he had intelligence files on the citizens of Naphtali.

"Those would be useless to me," I said, dismissing his offer. "I intend to establish a representative government in Naphtali with a council speaking for the people."

"I can tell you," he said, "who in Naphtali are Messiahists."

IV

Afterwards, I admitted to Gill that these arrangements made me uneasy.

"I should say you're uneasy!" he declared, watching me pace the room. "What is it then?" He raised an eyebrow and waited, like a scholar with a slow pupil.

"Thanks to you, I have just entered into an agreement with the Messiahists that will put their soldiers in the field next summer. For the first time, I have given my father an actual grievance. I have expected my commission to be revoked at any time—even without giving Glanz or Ben Gurion a provocation."

"Of actual grievances your father has never had a need," Gill observed. "Besides, Asher would have become Manasseh's granary whether you agreed to it or not. They need crop land out of range of your father's cavalry or they will starve. You did only what you had to do."

"Lives will be lost in Judah because of it, nonetheless. A chance of victory will slip away."

"Regarding these things the dice are in the air. All you have done is to see reason in this matter and make an agreement that will allow Asher to survive. The arrangement is temporary, until you can prepare a sanctuary for your people here in Naphtali.

I was pleased that Gill saw my ultimate purposes so clearly. I reflected that the fact I had saved Asher would be remembered longer than that I had fed Manasseh for a season.

"Do you remember our conversation as we fled north from Chinnereth?" I asked Gill. *As I spoke, I recalled the oppressive heat and the taste of the foul-smelling water from our water skins.*

"Of course," Gill said. "We talked about Glanz and Ben Gurion's intentions behind that preposterous mission of yours." He paused and looked hard at me. "Remarkably, now that I think about it, I see you have actually succeeded in carrying out their orders."

"Yes, I have. But having done what they asked of me, I'm sure I must remain—what was your phrase? – a troublesome entry in their ledger. They will revoke my commission at the earliest possible date. Or they will eliminate me." As Gill considered my estimate of the situation, I asked: "What do you think of my chances of preventing them from assassinating me?"

"Slim," he admitted. "None, if they are determined."

"And neither of us doubts that they are determined. Or will be, once they understand what I am about. So I have very limited time in which to act. I must, in whatever time I have, establish a government here and turn Naphtali into a stronghold against the Messiahists—and, if necessary, against Tephlin Glanz."

Gill whistled. "Why not set yourself to some task that would truly annoy your father!"

"The war in the south gives me a free hand here. In alliance with Dan I can succeed. If I do, Israel will not die."

"Ah, the temptation of saving Israel!" Gill exclaimed. He seemed always incensed by my larger purposes, and he was visibly upset at this one. He demanded to know what I had in mind to do, and I briefly sketched it for him. He cut me off sarcastically, even contemptuously. "I don't need another lesson in your foolish whims!" he declared. "But consider that you have only half a legion to fight all of Israel! The nation must have twenty-five thousand men under arms. Do you imagine you can defeat them all?"

"More than twenty-five thousand if you count militia."

He threw up his hands. "Don't forget that to succeed, you must make these Naphtali renegades work together and accept you as their master – neither of which they seem much inclined to do."

"Perhaps I can do those things and more. The forces contending in Israel are evenly balanced. A small weight placed on the scale could tip the balance."

He groaned. As I did not need Gill's approval, I changed the subject to a task concerning which he was well equipped to assist me. "What do you think *they* will do next? What would Glanz and Ben Gurion want from this victory of mine?"

"They want control of Naphtali, obviously—which you will obviously not relinquish to them. Short of that, they will want profits and metal and grain for Judah. They want Naphtali's help with the war."

"I have already set aside grain and metal and cloth. I am sending them soldiers too."

"Soldiers?"

"Yes. As I identify the poorest prospects among the Northern Lights Guards, I send them down to Judah. I intend to integrate the best men into my own forces."

"Good," he said. "Very good. Even clever. In the meantime, we will take precautions. We'll double your bodyguard, and I'll take a hand in training them. You'll wear armor at all times when you go about in public. And that will not be often. Yes," he said, "we can take precautions. But you cannot expect to defeat all Israel!"

Still less, I thought, can I expect to escape the assassin forever.

At Gill's urging, I sent an account of my doings to General Simon ben Gurion. No doubt Ben Gurion and my father had their own sources of information about me, but my purpose was not to inform, but to appear compliant to their will. I needed time to consolidate my position and prepare my next move. I wanted to postpone the inevitable day when they revoked my authority or removed me from among the living.

> To General Simon ben Gurion:
>
> *This is to inform you that I have taken possession of Naphtali and the Northern Lights Enterprises. With the assistance of Captain Gill, I am conducting an audit of the company and will inform you more fully as the situation clarifies itself. As you no doubt anticipated, there is considerable confusion in the affairs of the company, and there have been losses, owing both to Hanford Glanz's tenure as agent, and more recently, to the actions of his successors. Those usurpers and their chief lieutenants are, with two exceptions, either dead or in chains and in transit to Judah, where you may deal with them as you see fit. Nevertheless, a full account of the state of the company and the actions of its representatives lies beyond my power at the moment.*
>
> *To this extent have I fulfilled my charge. Much, obviously, remains to be done. In the meantime, Naphtali's resources can play a role in alleviating the present distress of Judah. [I listed the men and goods I was sending to Hebron.] That the company's situation here is precarious is already known to you; of the long-standing and grievous causes of it, you were aware when you commissioned me for this task. Misuse of company power has created deep resentments here. Only time and a bold and unconventional use of the powers vested in the agent on the scene can hope to restore stability. I intend to use my power to those ends, expecting at the last to stand before you to make a full accounting.*

"Good," Gill said. "It reads well. Reasonably well. You seem obedient; you serve their interests; you play for time. Thus, it will meet their expectations." He perused the note again, commenting on its astuteness. "Mind war," he declared, "perhaps you finally grasp it!"

He glanced over my letter again and frowned: "But if you read this carefully, with only a little knowledge of your character, it sounds like a threat."

V

I set Gill to work with Solomon Glass to survey of all the property of the company, its real estate in Naphtali, and the lists of accounts in banks. I wanted an exact tally of the capital goods and all commodities that passed through the Northern Lights Enterprises. Burgos and I had already made an inventory of the contents of the warehouses. I was driven by a powerful sense of urgency; I had to move quickly.

I invited fifty eminent men to Hammoth-Wenatchee to begin drafting plans for a council and civil government. I invited landed nobles and merchants alike, making no distinction of birth, but seeking instead men of property and substance from both the city and countryside. I intended to abolish the distinction between the landed and other classes and to draw forth the best energies of both groups in the service of Naphtali. I expected to bring about the very changes that I had encouraged Nisan Lot to make in Dan. In the event, however, only a dozen Naphtali merchants appeared, along with three nobles from the countryside near the capital. The latter stood about scowling visibly, while the merchants whispered among themselves, hiding their hands in their long sleeves.

I walked through the plaza by the House of Assembly with Burgos, inspecting the spits on which sheep and cattle were roasting. I had anticipated a celebration at the prospect of civil government being restored and had prepared a feast. As usual, Burgos was pleased to rebuke me for my naiveté. "The landed nobles are afraid," he chided me. "They are not certain whether you invited them here to be entertained or to be murdered. But they do know that if they cooperate with you, Nahum of Cashmere will burn their estates."

"I need to do something about Nahum."

"Truly, my lord! The merchants are willing enough, but they fear Nahum too—to say nothing of Huerta and Sepulvida. After all, they cannot trust that you will be here next year to protect them."

So, they needed some signs of legitimacy before they would show their hands. Our interests coincided, in this at least. Therefore, legitimacy they would have!

I had had high hopes for the proceedings, but the reluctance of the delegates to appear was troubling. As in my first effort at diplomacy in Dan, I had failed to prepare carefully and thus had failed. I intended to persevere nevertheless. The day was cold but clear and bright; the people were out and doing business; a market was in progress in the plaza. A small crowd had gathered, and some musicians struck up a lively tune. I was busy with last-minute questions from the kitchen staff when suddenly I heard my name cried out as if it were an obscenity. I turned to see a disheveled, angry man a few paces off, who was trembling with rage and glaring at me.

"You bloody man! You beast out of Hell!" he cried, his face red and distorted, his eyes wide. "The blood of your brothers is on your head. Murderer! The blood of two brothers, evil and good, are on your hands, and you are a bloody man!"

I was turning to Captain Amasa for an explanation when I was struck a powerful blow in the chest that instantly knocked the breath from me. Stunned, I fell backward over benches and onto a table, which collapsed under me. I must have fainted, for my next moments were filled with tumult and confusion of which I could make no sense. One of my bodyguards was bending over me, pinching and slapping my face and shouting. His face was contorted and tears ran down his cheeks.

"Enough!" I said, and the effort of speaking caused a great pain in my chest. I felt a constriction so tight that I could scarcely breathe. Then, dimly, I perceived the shaft of an arrow protruding from my chest. I felt a thrill of horror. Then I must have lost consciousness again.

When I was next aware, someone was cutting away my armor. "Don't," I protested and pushed at his hands, and someone said, "It's all right, the arrow did not penetrate far; it has come away. We can take his armor from the back." In a short time, I had my wits about me. Like the Kr arrow that had felled me in Engedi, this one had spent its force against my armor. I had a shallow puncture wound and a huge bruise on my chest. It hurt to breathe.

"The rib is broken," the surgeon said prodding me.

No doubt! I would have cried out, but I could not get breath enough. There seemed to be something wrong, something not visible about the wound.

"Stand back; can't you see he cannot breathe!" It was Carmina. She thrust herself into the group and scattered them like quail. Then she gently pulled my clothes aside and examined my wound. Amasa was by her side. I felt her cool hands on my throat, taking my pulse, and then she touched me lightly on my chest, her fingers exploring the area around the wound and then the wound itself. I had no impulse to flinch; the pain was registering somewhere in my mind, but not urgently.

"The bleeding stops!" someone said.

"This is nothing," she said. "He bleeds inside. This rib is cracked, and the head of the arrow causes bleeding here, where we cannot see it. This is the danger so near his heart." I felt her running her hands over my torso; then she lifted my head. I tried to look at her but my eyes rolled of their own accord. "Josiah," she said as she closed my eyes, "you must use your discipline and meditate. You must lie beside a cool spring and be perfectly still." I felt her hand on my forehead. Her touch was soft and cool. "The water of the spring is cold and it has the power to heal, to cleanse you of this blood." I felt a cold liquid spilling on my chest, just at the point of the wound and then spreading out from it, like an expanding pool. It cooled my flesh wherever it touched. "Your blood withdraws from the wound, from the bruise beneath. I am with you, your friend Jonathan Amasa is with you; you can feel the blood withdraw. It is withdrawing now. Everything is fine now, and you can relax." She held my hand in hers and my chest felt cool and light and I found I could breathe much easier. I must have dozed off. *I dreamed of Justin Apollo and his crushed breastbone after the fight with the Kr. We rode side by side, each on a travois, jolting through a sea of grass. My brother turned to look at me and his face was calm, as if to say, you see, this is not so difficult.*

My officers had gathered round and waited as Amasa and Carmina gently raised me and put pillows behind my back. Carmina waved away all who offered to help. I was in my quarters in the barracks; it was night. "My lord," Burgos said, touching my hand to his forehead. Each of my captains did the same, kneeling in turn before me. They were solemn and quiet. I took a little wine from Carmina, and it raised my spirits. "Speak," I said. "It was a close call, to be sure, but only a close call. What do we know of the attackers?"

Gill described how I had been struck just as I turned to speak to Amasa. The first assassin had climbed on a cart across the plaza and had hit me from close range. Due to the angle created when I turned to Amasa, my armor had absorbed most of the blow; a straight-on shot would have killed me. As it happened, I had been knocked backward by the blow—another factor that had saved my life. A second arrow, from the roof of a nearby building, had whizzed past my head as I fell and struck one of the musicians. A third assassin, brandishing a dagger, had burst out of the crowd as I fell. My bodyguard had made short work of him. The bowman on the cart had been chased and killed. The assassin on the roof had escaped. He was apparently a stranger to Naphtali, as were the two assailants who had died.

"So, you have no one who can lead us to the authors of this attack?" *I wondered which of my enemies was more likely to be responsible: Nahum, General Huerta, the Messiahists, or my own father.*

"We have the man who denounced you," Burgos said.

"That man is plainly a fool and no assassin. I cannot believe he knew of the attempt, even if he was used as a decoy."

"That seems to be the case," Gill said. "It is consistent with what he revealed under interrogation."

I had a sudden mental vision at the thought of Gill's methods of interrogation. "Bring the man here," I ordered.

"He may be able to tell us something about the conspiracy," Gill said, sensing my disapproval. "His wife is outside."

"He can tell us nothing but the lies the Messiahists have been telling about me. Nevertheless, have them both brought to me."

Gill was not a gentle inquisitor. The man who had denounced me required considerable cleaning up; he appeared before me bandaged and still terrified. The man's wife stood beside him trembling uncontrollably. I had them sit at the table and ordered food brought for them, while Carmina fed me spoonfuls of broth. Amasa spoke for me, intuiting that I wanted the man treated well, but disabused of the falsehoods he had heard of me. Amasa explained that I had had no role in the deaths of either of my brothers. "It was his brother Justin's arrest that sparked the rising against the churchmen in the south. If you seek an explanation of the enmity between Josiah of Asher and the church," he concluded, "look no further than what the churchmen did to his brother." The wife nodded vigorously to everything Amasa said while her husband sat bewildered. I suspected that both would repeat the stories told of me tonight with the same uncritical enthusiasm with which the husband had shouted Messiahist lies about me.

In the morning, I learned that the notables who had answered my invitation had also been detained. I ordered them released and brought to me. They entered, exhibiting varying degrees of rage or anxiety, according to their natures. "Gentlemen," I greeted them, "it was the zeal of my friends that made you our guests in the citadel. Whatever recompense to your dignity is within my power, I will provide. Please, sit, and we will speak a little of our intended business before I let you go." I explained to these ruffled dignitaries that I meant to create a government in Naphtali that would include and represent all classes, not just the merchants and not just the landed nobles either. I intended to seek their counsel in conducting a census, selecting a slate of electors, and planning for elections. I mentioned also that I feared that the Northern Lights Enterprises had become oppressive to the people. I sought their advice on how to reform the company and make it serve the community. They listened sullenly and departed.

"They'll be back," Gill said cheerfully. "I've been studying Solomon Glass's records on these model citizens. We know who was Hanford's man, who is Huerta's, and who managed to be both. Glass has collected some very interesting information."

"So what do you think?"

"I think there was no one here who did not deserve to be thrown into prison!"

We laughed. "So, there begins to be justice in Naphtali, if only by accident. What else?"

"Nothing else," he said. "What I'd really like to know is who among these specimens is Tephlin Glanz's man."

"Yes, and who is Nahum's man – and who serves the churchmen in New Jerusalem. That would be good to know. You have work to do, Captain Gill."

VI

As I recovered from my wound, I busied myself with whatever work lay close at hand. There was the drill of the legion to observe and officers and men to commend or correct. My habits of meditation had been taken up by the officers and some of the men, so I had eager students to teach the old disciplines. I selected a group to whom I could entrust the secrets of the Mano and began to impart its concepts.

Among my informal council of friends, the question of how to establish my legitimacy in Naphtali was hotly debated. I had created the Great Jordan Guards with my father's funds and used the legion to accomplish my mission in Naphtali. But now I had further uses for it in mind – uses that Tephlin Glanz would hardly approve. As my body mended, I mulled over how I might achieve independence from Glanz and Ben Gurion. Meanwhile, my friends' attention had focused on the daughter of the former Apostle, whose name, we learned, was Judith Peshatin.

"I am not at all certain if I want the Apostleship to continue," I protested, "let alone become an Apostle myself."

"You cannot rule by martial law forever," Moriah warned. "Sooner or later, the people will clamor for the old government. When they do, they will demand an Apostle to lead them."

"And whoever marries the daughter of the last Apostle will be a claimant to that office," Burgos warned. "Resistance will naturally form around this person, whoever he is. It is a danger. Judith Peshatin is a danger. But you have, my lord, the power to clamp a lid on that pot before it simmers over." I thought his metaphor worked against his point, but I grasped his meaning.

"If you marry the Apostle's daughter," Gill added, "you will forestall any danger from that quarter. And you can then decide at leisure what form of government to establish in Naphtali and whether the office of the Apostle will live on."

As reluctant as I was to enter into marriage on such terms, I was persuaded by Gill's logic. There were larger considerations than my happiness at stake. Gill took the initial negotiations upon himself, and he proved successful beyond my expectations. The formidable matron of the family, the Senyora Peshatin, had done a turn-about in her views of me and appeared to welcome the alliance. I was invited to the stronghold of the Peshatins as soon as I was well enough to ride.

In the event, I found the girl pretty enough. No doubt she was a beauty by Israel's standards; she had even features and full lips and exhibited that early ripeness so admired in our young women. I would have guessed her age as near my own, though her mother informed me she was barely fourteen. I carried on a polite conversation with the matron of the house and drank a toast to our proposed connection, while the bride-to-be sat silently to one side. Judith Peshatin's feelings about the proposed betrothal proved hard to read. She seemed more indifferent about the matter than I expected of a young girl meeting a potential husband for the first time. When the mother left us for an hour or two to get acquainted—a liberty rarely granted by Israelite mothers—I found it difficult to converse with her. She evinced no curiosity about me and responded in monosyllables to my inquiries about her own life.

Israelite girls of good family are raised almost in seclusion, so I thought it natural that she had little to say. I would have expected, however, that in my uniform and red sash and gold cord of Asher I cut rather a dashing figure before one who had seen so little of the world. There was, to be sure, the tragedy of her violation—whatever it had amounted to –

which had taken place during our invasion. While I did not expect her to refer to such events, which were no doubt horrific to her, neither did I detect any shadow of that misfortune in her behavior. If anything, her manner seemed to express a mild complacency, as if she did not require to be entertained and was not moved to entertain me. I tried to overcome her reserve, if reserve it was, and in her mother's absence she soon became talkative and even flirtatious. Before taking my leave, I took her in a light embrace and kissed her. She accepted these liberties willingly, and I had the feeling I might easily have taken more, though she seemed not to welcome them with any enthusiasm.

I left disappointed, but rebuked myself for these feelings. It was not fair to compare this girl to Miriam Lander—whom I had remembered continually during our interview. Miriam was a woman of intelligence and passion, skilled in managing business affairs as well as men, and she was accomplished in the art of love. I thought it possible that in preparing me for marriage, Miriam had actually spoiled me for it. I would find no shrewd political intellect, no sense of a peer or teacher or companion in Judith Peshatin. I reflected that her parents had likely neglected her education, rearing her in this rough and isolated spot without much forethought of her future. But there was something else about her, too; something missing. I doubted that we would ever be companionable or intimate.

Captain Jared, who had accompanied me on this errand, took a more cheerful view of the girl, remarking on her beauty and ample figure. "There's woman enough there to lie on comfortably at night," he assured me as we departed.

"I want more than a pillow," I said. I thought of Vitoria with her fair hair and eyes, serious even when she abandoned herself to love making, and knew that I would not quench my desire in the embrace of this pretty cipher.

Back at Hammoth-Wenatchee, Gill and Burgos were enthusiastic for the match – Gill because it solved, as he saw it, the problem of legitimacy both for myself and the government I was trying to establish. Burgos no doubt favored the match because he sensed there was nothing in Judith Peshatin capable of distracting me from my larger mission. Jonathan Amasa and Carmina reserved their judgment, asking me a few questions but offering no advice. In the end, I consented reluctantly to a betrothal, but left the date of the wedding unspecified. This arrangement would preclude other matches being sought with the girl, and hence, would discourage potential rivals. But postponing the wedding would give Judith time to mature and educate herself and would also forestall a moment I dreaded. *Given time, I thought, something might intervene.* Though I had consented to it, I was vaguely angry at the situation. I felt I would have to sacrifice my life before it was well started.

In the meantime I continued my talks with the chief merchants of Naphtali. They liked the idea of the Law as it related to social order and protection of property, but they wanted nothing to do with constraints on their own behavior or their opportunities to trade. Some of them already held estates under leases from Hanford, but none had adopted the noble class's martial ethos. "Surely you understand," I chided them, "that no one can hold the land who is not willing to defend it! What you desire is against nature itself – power without responsibility." I made it clear that to end the divisions between landed nobles and themselves, they must take up the burden of defending the community. "That means your sons must bear arms and must be willing to sacrifice their lives for the community. Otherwise, how can they claim a voice in its affairs?"

When I spoke of my hopes to fuse the interests of the landed class with the merchants, they remained skeptical. *How?* they wanted to know.

"I will give those nobles who want it a stake in the company," I explained. "I'll see they have shares of stock and ownership in shops and mills and shipping. And I will put merchants and tradesmen in the legion and give you land that you must defend. I will make your interests and theirs identical." Taking the old census information, I had them estimate the worth of the holdings of those who held noble status. They arrived quickly at a minimum figure. "Not a paltry sum, to be sure," I acknowledged. "But how many of you are worth as much or more? Having such means," I demanded, "are you content to remain barred from active citizenship?"

When they saw I was serious about eliciting their views and protecting their interests, their numbers at my informal meetings grew, and they began to speak and argue and assert themselves. Moreover, ships belonging to Naphtali or to the Northern Lights Enterprises began to appear almost miraculously in the harbor. However, try as I might, I could never obtain a favorable hearing for the Reproduction Laws. Eventually I realized that most of these men of Naphtali had fled from Israel and its constraints and did not wish to live under the Law again. Nor were they anxious to conduct a new census, since they inferred—correctly—that a census could only be a preliminary to re-instituting the Law. Naphtali was, to be sure, a newly settled place, but it was also an outlaw society. I began to suspect that they had tolerated Hanford because he had been essentially one of themselves.

VII

I was entertaining a group of nobles when word came that a delegation of Canadians had arrived and wished to speak with me. I hurried to the citadel, for I knew that Rehab Gill would have them arrested in an instant. It was his way with all strangers these days.

"Gill," I said, bursting into his headquarters, "these men are a delegation; they are protected under the law of envoys." I knew almost nothing of this people, other than their reputation as light-skinned barbarians who spoke the language of the Kuhlans but were somewhat less intractable. These Canadians might be backward and rude, but if their people were threatening the Northern Lights Guards in the Okanogan valley, I was interested in what they had to say.

The Canadians in question were huge men, dressed in bearskins and fur boots. I greeted them courteously in their own language, making a show of anger at Gill to assuage their injured dignity and to separate Gill's treatment of them from my own. The Canadian delegation had waited on the Kuhlan side of the Jordan just across from Hammoth-Wenatchee, signaling to passing boats until an Israelite captain had had the courage to pick them up and carry them across. I was curious to know what Canadians were doing on Kuhlan lands, and on what terms they had relations with our foe. But first I needed to hear what they could tell me of the Okanogan valley. I invited them to eat with my officers. The mess offered no very luxurious fare, but it was a hearty soldiers' meal, and they ate in company with some of the most famous soldiers in Israel.

After they had satisfied themselves, I led them into the former private quarters of Hanford—a place not much used by me, out of deference to my brother and his family, who had been murdered there. I asked Captain Amasa and Carmina to accompany us, Carmina to act as hostess and Amasa, who could speak a little of their language, to converse with them alongside me. My guests seemed even less used to such sumptuous surroundings than I was; they professed themselves impressed and pleased with our hospitality.

"I am Laban MaGowan," the chief man among them announced after the formalities. He explained that he was head of his clan and the elected leader of numerous other groups that he recited and of which I had never heard. He was a big man, a good four inches taller than myself and still powerful-looking in middle age. His brown beard was streaked with gray.

"If you come seeking peace," I said, "you are welcome here."

"Not necessarily seeking peace," the man replied boldly.

"Do you know to whom you speak?" Amasa demanded.

"Aye," MaGowan said, looking at me. "I well know. In Moses Town I heard of you; they talk of little else. The Israelite who is a war leader among the People and the companion of Vitoria, a Mother of the Black Willow People."

"I am Josiah Glanz ben Haggadah," I said. "I hold this land by a commission from the Council of Apostles as well as by force. You are welcome here as my guest-friends, and I will listen to what you have to say."

Laban MaGowan took his time preparing as a way of telling me it was important, and then he spoke with conviction. "Understand that I am no fool and that we are not come as suppliants or beggars. I seek justice for my people. Peace may be desirable," he declared, "but it is not always possible. Those who look for peace without justice are already conquered. That is not—thanks be to God—our situation. But whether we have war or peace with you Israelites, it is justice I demand!" As his companions growled their assent, the Canadian chieftain recited a long list of grievances his people had suffered at our hands. They had been evicted from their lands and abused by the Israelite garrison, they had been cheated by our merchants, and even when there was peace, crimes against them went unpunished by Israelite authorities. The wrongs he spoke of seemed fresh and raw.

"Why do you speak to me of these things?" I said, refilling his wine cup. I wanted to know how far he was aware of events in Naphtali, and if he knew that the army there was not under my control. On the other hand, I had no desire to reveal Israelite weaknesses to outsiders. It was dawning on me, however, that in Naphtali's conflict there was a third party—these Canadians—and one to which I had hitherto given no consideration.

"It may be that you approve of these acts against my people," Laban said. "But I came here hoping you do not. I came also to warn you that my people are at the end of their patience. Nearly all the clans are for war now, and they see this moment when their enemies are divided as an opportunity."

"So, you know of the divisions between the garrison in the Okanogan and myself."

"Of course. Every child knows that there is war among the Israelites, and that Huerta and Sepulvida are your enemies."

"Good. Then you must know also that I had no part in these crimes that you allege. Indeed, I had no knowledge of them."

He acknowledged my point, but warned me that a general war was in the making between his people and Israel. Israel had been very insolent of late, he claimed, and the old boundary between his people and ours had been violated and a new one imposed 20 miles to the north. This recent annexation was intolerable. His people would not accept such treatment; hardship and starvation would result if they submitted. He also described an ongoing migration of his people from the east, from beyond the forests. "We are no longer as weak as we have been in the past," he declared. "It would be foolish to despise us."

"How can your people travel through the forest?" Amasa asked.

"We have learned to travel in the snow," he replied. "It is difficult, but it can be done. Necessity drives my people here."

I heard this news with dread, wondering what it might mean for Israel. "With these provocations and with the opinions of your people tending toward war," I asked, "do you still hope to avoid it?"

"If possible," he said, and his companions nodded in agreement. "I would avoid it if I can. *If* my people can obtain justice and resettle the lands they formerly occupied, and can live there unmolested, I am for peace." I indicated that I had noted his conditions. "I came here also because I wanted to know the new ruler of Naphtali, to see whether we will be friends or enemies. Your fame has reached my country. In either case, peace or war, as God unfolds these events, it is better that we know one another."

I weighed his words carefully. The Canadians could be useful allies in disposing of Huerta and Sepulvida and thus freeing my hands for whatever needed doing in the south. But I was ignorant of his land and people, and I knew nothing of this migration of which he spoke—nor of the lands from which such people could come. I needed to remove the danger to my rear, certainly, but without creating a greater threat in the long term. Cooperation might be possible; it might even offer a solution to my problem with Huerta and Sepulvida, but I expected an alliance to be costly. I leaned back to listen; the Canadian still had much to complain of, and he spoke earnestly and without art. Carmina brought us more wine. I was mentally calculating his likely asking price for cooperation when Laban suddenly leaned forward and spoke in a low, almost conspiratorial voice:

"My wish is that our peoples may become one."

His words chimed like a bell in my mind. Jonas ben Harlech had spoken similar words to the Kuhlans of his day: We are one people, he had said. "My wish is that our peoples may become one." Jonas ben Harlech had built an empire on a similar insight.

"Indeed," I said, rising to shake hands with them all, "you may have hit on the perfect solution. I thank you for coming, but I must say good evening to you for now. I invite you to rest here tonight and enjoy our hospitality. In the morning we will speak further. And whatever the outcome of our discussions, be it peace or war, you will remain my guest-friends, and I will protect your coming in and going out."

I cut short our evening talk because I was ignorant of the claims the Canadians had made. I sent for Gill and roused Solomon Glass, and we poured over maps and reports and the archives of the company. There was a history in the documents of contacts several generations old, and I needed to absorb it before we talked further. Glass knew a good deal, and though I resented having to use his knowledge, use it I did.

"This is the boundary that the Canadians described," I said, comparing several maps. "Apparently, the company or the Northern Lights Guards have intruded above here for a considerable distance."

Glass confirmed my observations. Sepulvida had campaigned in the Okanogan the year before, ostensibly to punish outlaws among the Canadians, but in fact to expel them from lands that they occupied. With a little prodding, Glass informed us that Colonel Sepulvida was the most ambitious man in Israel; his hunger for lands and estates was a jest in Naphtali. A man of no family, Sepulvida longed to be part of the landed class—to become, in fact, the richest noble of all. Hanford Glanz had known this of him and exploited his greed to unleash a war against the Canadians. Most of the disputed land wrested in recent years from the Canadians was held in title by Sepulvida himself. His claims were hardly legal; the deeds had only the power and standing afforded by the cohorts of the Northern Lights Guards that he commanded. Nevertheless, Sepulvida laid claim to more land than any man in Israel. I determined to find a way to turn this knowledge into a snare.

We resumed our conversations with the Canadians amidst the winter celebration, the Feast of the Three Kings, which I had restored to its ancient prominence. The feast was held in the market place, and tables for more exalted persons were set up in the main plaza. I wanted to show myself generous to the poorer members of the community, who had suffered from the changes of power. There was much to do in preparation, but I relinquished my duties to subordinates and spent the morning in discussion with the Canadians. I had taken an interest in their chief, Laban MaGowan. He seemed candid as well as intelligent, and, though I assumed him capable of any device necessary to preserve his people, his preference seemed to be for plain words, bluntly spoken. A man bold enough to speak his mind openly could make a good friend.

When I asked him why he believed our people could live together in peace, he answered that his people lived rough and hard lives in a severe climate. Canadians, he lamented, had lost the arts of civilization. He admired Israel as much for what it had preserved as for what it had created. Many of his countrymen expressed contempt for Israel's airs of superiority, its arrogance, and effeminacy. "But this is envy," he declared. "Many in Israel live soft, as my countrymen claim, but that soft living is exactly what our people desire, if they would admit it. Warmth and comfort and a life beyond mere surviving."

I hardly knew how to answer him. Israelites had difficulty living peacefully with one another, let alone with strangers. I asked him how people as different as ourselves would go about becoming one. I mentioned the barriers of language and customs—

"And color," he interjected. "You Israelites are proud as Lucifer of who you are, and you keep people who look like me as slaves."

I asked him about his own people's views, and he admitted that their racial pride was little different from our own. "But you and I," he said, "we speak each other's language, and I do not detect in you the scorn for light skin that I have encountered in others."

"True," I admitted. "No one who carries the war axe of the People can hold your race in contempt. But I do not think the differences between our peoples can be easily overcome."

"Still, it is something to know that it can be!" He knew, apparently, that I had had a Kuhlan consort and conceived a child by her.

I felt the issues that pitted Israelites against each other too keenly to admit of much hope of bridging the differences between his people and mine, and I recalled that my own knowledge had been acquired very painfully. "Even more than its race," I warned, "Israel cherishes its identity. Among us, the slightest differences of opinion can have fatal consequences. Therefore, any arrangement your people and mine might come to could only rest on the foundation of the Law of St. Supplicee. There is no other possibility. The Law is the foundation of my people's life."

Laban looked at me skeptically, as if to say he had seen very little of the Law of St. Supplicee in his dealings with Israelites.

"Naphtali is a lawless land, I admit. But I mean to establish the Law here as a basis of a new society – a just society – and I will establish it as far north as Israelite power extends and as far south as my right arm can carry it. The citizens of Naphtali may not like it, but I intend to hold them to it nonetheless."

He listened attentively, occasionally asking shrewd questions that told me he understood far more than he spoke. He asked me why I suffered the provocations of Nahum of Cashmere when it was in my power to crush him. I wondered at his sources of information, but I replied only that Nahum was allied with the landed nobles, whom I intended to convert to my cause. "At the moment," I explained, "I cannot reach him without giving them offense. I must find a way to separate him and his cause from the landed warriors, who will be valuable in the Naphtali I will build hereafter."

"Is it possible you overestimate the value of these nobles?" Laban asked. "Or the extent to which they are amenable to your cause?"

I was taken aback by his question, for it was becoming plain to me that of all the citizens of Naphtali, the nobles most resisted my rule. Indeed, I had almost despaired of making a peaceful settlement with them. But it alarmed me that this stranger could see so much. He was well informed about the precariousness of my position in Naphtali and knew of the assassination attempt against me. He was also aware of the civil war between the Third Comers and Old Believers in Israel—a conflict that had subsided during the truce, but could well break out again at any moment. I was thinking to myself that this man is dangerous—too dangerous to have as an enemy. Consequently, I was surprised when Laban spoke to me of his daughter. He was very circumspect and came at the subject by elaborate indirection, but I sensed his drift immediately.

"I am recently betrothed," I said in answer. I explained the circumstances of this arrangement, and he nodded.

"This was no idea of mine," he said, "though I approve it. It was my daughter's thought. Our women are free," he explained, "and my daughter is wholly free in this matter. She bestows herself where she chooses. Any husband she takes must please her and they must reach an agreement between themselves. However," he added, "it is because you are who you are and possess the fame you do, that I have my daughter's consent in this. But in this and in all things, she is the faithful daughter of her people, no less than the Mothers of the Black Willow People."

I did not much appreciate his reference to Vitoria. Nevertheless, I expressed my regret that I could not oblige her.

The Canadians sat beside me at the culminating ceremonies of the Feast of the Three Kings, and I considered Laban's proposals as I presided over the dinner. Specially honored today were the guild of fishermen, who had achieved a rare success. They had caught a giant sturgeon, a monster of a fish with a long ugly head and of such size that it had to be hauled from the Jordan by a team of horses. Sturgeon was the traditional food of the winter feast, but it was rare to have a specimen so large. The Canadians gaped in astonishment as a dozen servants brought the fish out on platters and reassembled it on a long table. The flesh of the sturgeon was white and flavorful and almost as firm as beef. It made a delicious soup, and even its eggs—served in unappetizing black globs on bread—were regarded locally as a delicacy.

As the feast progressed I explained the meaning of the customs to our guests. At one point Laban interrupted me and said, "It is not the Three Kings, but the Christ child who is honored. Your people have forgotten—or denied – many things."

We managed to converse for a while during the quiet moments of the ceremonies, but soon he and his companions were too far into their cups to conduct business. I made it known at the close of the feast that I was negotiating with the Canadians and looking toward an end to hostilities in the north.

When the Canadians were ready to depart, I assured Laban that it might be in our power to curb the ambitions of Sepulvida in a peaceful way. As we sought to find such a course of action, I would seek his assistance and he could seek mine. The great obstacle in all this, we both understood, was the lack of easy means to communicate with each other. We parted friends, but I sensed he was disappointed.

VIII

Not long after the Canadians departed, the head of General Amarante Huerta arrived in a sack, along with an ingenuous and exculpating letter from Colonel Sepulvida. Sepulvida had had no role, his letter explained, in the murder of Hanford Glanz. He had cooperated with the conspirators after the fact only out of loyalty to the Northern Lights and to Israel, in order to protect its investments and the Israelite settlements in further Lebanon. The Canadians were hostile and treacherous, he claimed, and it was all he could do to keep them in check and defend the company's holdings. It was that emergency alone that had kept him from appearing in person to report to me. With General Huerta having met his deserved fate, however, and the barriers to communication between us now removed, he looked forward humbly to hearing my wishes.

"This Sepulvida is a treacherous son of a bitch," Burgos declared. "He deserves to die a thousand deaths."

"True," I said. "Undoubtedly true."

"What do you plan to do?"

"Promote him."

Burgos muttered and swore, but I had little choice. I did not yet see how to remove Sepulvida and his thousand men from my rear. Although my own force was growing and I could now meet him in the field on equal terms, the expenditure of lives needed to defeat him seemed prohibitive. I had not formed the Great Jordan Guards to fight my brother's successors and their armed thieves. The problem was, however, that until they were dealt with, I would have no freedom of action against the Messiahists. Furthermore, I had no trustworthy eyes or ears in his camp. Being no better informed, we were forced to speculate about the causes of the falling out between Colonel Sepulvida and General Huerta and the timing of it.

"I'll wager it was the merchants returning with their ships to Hammoth-Wenatchee that precipitated Huerta's murder," Gill said. "When the merchant captains accepted your control of Naphtali, Sepulvida knew the game was up. It meant that you are the master here."

Moriah suggested it was the threat of a Canadian war. "He cannot have supplies enough to carry him through the winter. He needs your assistance to survive."

"Perhaps," I said. "News that I was negotiating with the Canadians must have been a factor. The threat of a Canadian war also touches Sepulvida's fondest hopes. I expect he may even try to enlist my help against them to protect his lands. If he does, I will have an opening."

The situation in the north was largely beyond our power to analyze, let alone control. It hung, rather, like a boulder poised to fall on our heads out of the darkness. If war came, it would be the wrong war in the wrong place and at the wrong time. In addition, the Canadians represented a new and largely unknown factor. Laban himself had freely expressed his doubts that he could hold his countrymen in check until I brought Sepulvida and his army under control. It would be convenient for me, of course, if the aroused Canadians simply disposed of Sepulvida by themselves. But if the Canadians commenced a general war, where would they stop? Once war began, Laban would likely lose what little influence he had among his own people, and if they overwhelmed Sepulvida and continued south, I would be compelled to fight them.

With Naphtali not yet secure, I had little relish for a stand-up battle with either the Northern Lights Guards or the Canadians. My own forces were far from being in a state of readiness. If I took my Great Jordan Guards Legion out of Naphtali at this point, I could easily lose my base of operations, my bastion. It would surely be so. But it was not my purpose, I reminded my counselors, to lead the Herons to meaningless graves in the north, but to put them to better use in the south. I wanted a resolution of the issues in the north expressly so I could move against the Messiahists.

Accordingly, I sent Sepulvida a flattering letter addressed to the "*General* in Command of detached portions of the Northern Lights Guards." Ignoring the state of hostilities that existed between his forces and mine, I recommended a way by which his ambitions to hold the lands he had conquered from the Canadians could be realized.

> *"The MaGowan clan, among others of the southern tribes of Canadians, present a rival claim to these contested lands on our boarder. If you can resolve your claims and theirs in peace, you will have done Israel a great service and saved many lives. Given the troubled state of affairs in Israel, a man wise enough to avoid war would win the approval of the nation."*

However repugnant Sepulvida might find dealing with the Canadians, I suspected he would leap at an opportunity to ingratiate himself with me and win the esteem of Israel. I relied on Sepulvida's ambition to retain the lands he had seized to carry this stratagem through. If peace could be restored with the Canadians, I would soon be able to detach portions of the Northern Lights Guards from him and send them down to Judah. In this case at least, time was on my side. His present force could not support itself in the Okanogan valley indefinitely. It was a matter of months, I calculated, before Sepulvida would exhaust his own supplies and have to make overtures to me. When Sepulvida was sufficiently weakened, I would deal with him.

"How can you presume to raise this scoundrel to a generalship," Burgos demanded, "when you are only a colonel yourself?"

"I doubt that General Sepulvida will be much concerned with legalities," I said. "After all, a commission is a commission." *Justin had said that very thing to me once.*

I confess I did not think much about the fate of Laban MaGowan's daughter, even as I was planning to make a bride and then a widow of her.

Not long after, Gill asked for a private interview. The request itself filled me with curiosity, as we had fallen into the habit of discussing all things openly among ourselves—Gill, myself, Moriah, Burgos, and Amasa—and often Carmina as well. I put aside my papers and asked an orderly to bring tea. When we were alone, Gill came immediately to the point. "You have been much abused, my friend, much abused! And your closest associates, myself included, have led you astray. Our advice was folly. Your betrothed, Judith Peshatin, has betrayed you."

"Ah," I said. *I had scarcely thought of Judith Peshatin in the weeks since our betrothal.*

"She has a lover," Gill said.

"You are certain of this?"

"When I met with the Senyora Peshatin to make the arrangements, I took the trouble to employ one of the servants as an informer. A precaution merely." In spite of the gravity of the situation, he smiled at his own cleverness. "There is more," Gill said. "Your betrothed has not only taken a lover, but is with child by him."

Gill seemed far more exercised by this news than I. True, a betrothal gone sour in this way was one of the transgressions that most excited Israel. Under the circumstances, it was a killing offense, and the Law provided the severest penalties for it. But my feelings had not been engaged in this arrangement. I reminded Gill of my motives and he seemed relieved. I found myself feeling a measure of relief as well. I had dreaded the marriage.

"What's to be done then?" Gill asked.

"That remains to be seen. You did well to speak of this thing privately—for which I thank you. But I need a woman's view of the matter. I want Carmina to hear this tale. Then we'll decide what's to be done."

Within the hour, Carmina and Amasa were closeted with us and heard all the details of the Peshatin family's double-dealing. Amasa was incensed, particularly at the collusion of the mother. Somehow I was not surprised and felt a growing relief that I could thus avoid a connection with her.

Gill was alert to the event's other implications: "This betrothal was not popular with the citizens of Naphtali, especially the landed class. It turns out that they have strong proprietary views of the Apostle's family and lineage. I erred in recommending this alliance to you. But note that the young man, her lover, is a member of the noble class—and distant kin of Nahum of Cashmere."

I was not surprised by this news either. I expected that these events were intended to embarrass me and defeat my plans to create a government in Naphtali. I asked Gill if the relationship had preceded our betrothal or occurred afterwards.

"Before *and* after. I believe the servant can confirm that."

So, the mother's role in a conspiracy seemed almost certain. She had told us a tale of her daughter's desecration when, in fact, she had been covering up her daughter's behavior. Later—for who knows what motive—she had entered into a fraudulent marriage agreement with me. The simplest explanation for all of it, I thought, is Nahum of Cashmere.

"The mother's duplicity will have its effect on people's view of this scandal," Amasa said. "If the mother knew and made the agreement after the fact, it will tarnish her name and not yours." Amasa meant, but did not say, that to be spurned by my betrothed would subject me to general contempt and ridicule. This twist on the story would direct some attention to the perfidy of the mother.

I turned to Carmina, who had been silent through our discussion, and asked her what she thought.

"I think you are well out of it," she said.

Gill already had men in place to apprehend the young couple as they met tonight. Always mindful of evidence and appearances, Gill had planned to arrest the two together.

"Arrest the mother too," I said, "and all the household staff." *Fear will turn them into willing witnesses.*

The arrest of the young couple and the Senyora Peshatin occasioned much public excitement—not of protest, but rather unfocused passion and indignation. Perhaps because it is strict in sexual matters, Israel revels in gossip and scandal. Ugly slogans scrawled on walls and scuffles in the market revealed how unpopular had been this match between the Apostle's family and myself. Apparently, I was not destined to be the Apostle of Naphtali. I put that hope aside without regret and turned my energies to creating a new form of government.

But what had happened was a cause of shame too, and Gill was assiduous in spreading the details of the liaison and the mother's role in it, precisely to influence the public view of these events. With martial law still in effect, I was able to guide the legal proceedings. I kept all three prisoners separated, especially the mother from her daughter, and arranged a hearing for the mother alone on the day prior to the trial. The Senyora Peshatin was first indignant and then furious and finally reduced to abject pleading as the charges against her and her daughter and the evidence to support them were laid out for her, detail by detail. The judge I had appointed was a paragon of severity. When he announced that the court would seek her death on the morrow, the Senyora Peshatin was visibly shaken. At that point, I asked the court permission to speak with the defendant privately. I told her that although she and her daughter and her daughter's lover all deserved to die, I would be content with another outcome. She glared at me through tears, with hatred and calculation struggling in her face.

"It is unnecessary that anyone die," I said. "There was wrong done here, but there may also be a remedy. The value of the betrothal to me was the connection it established with the heir of Naphtali's former Apostle. That connection and the value it held are now destroyed; the contract is a dead loss to me. But it is a loss I will forgive if the advantage cannot be assumed by another."

"What do you mean?" she asked.

"Consider that your daughter shamed your family, not me. Disinherit her, sever her connection with the office and lineage of the Apostle, and her lover has robbed me of her person only, and that is a loss I shall bear cheerfully. What I will not tolerate is for this crime to raise up a rival to me in Naphtali. Disinherit her, and I will ask the court to dismiss all charges. You can save your daughter's life and your own—and even the life of the young man. Repudiate her, and I will provide a dowry for her and safe passage to Judah for the couple. And you shall live."

The Senyora Peshatin heard this in silence. She glanced around the court, looking for support and solace, but I had arranged that she would find none. When the judge reminded her that the evidence was sufficient to exact the death of her daughter, her daughter's lover, and herself, she was not slow to accept my bargain. The young couple was married in prison before the day was out and were on a ship bound for Judah next morning. The Senyora Peshatin retired to her estate in disgrace, and the citizens of Naphtali were treated to the spectacle of a young and powerful man willing to forego revenge for a sexual slight. Such an event was rare enough in Israel to occasion wonder and disbelief.

Compassion never rusts, our Teacher says, and mercy shines forever. In fact, I was filled with relief, believing with Carmina that I was well out of the relationship. "This whole episode is an unexpected blessing," I acknowledged to my inner circle of friends. "The Peshatins have taken themselves off the board, as Nisan Lot would say, and the party of Nahum of Cashmere derives no good of this scheme, but sprawls in the mud. I could not have contrived a better way to extricate myself from a hateful union and at the same time remove the threat of a rival Apostle."

My friends congratulated me warily, scarcely able to believe that my pride was not stung by this insult.

"I left my pride in the Kuhlan lands," I said. *It was true. I seemed to have no emotions left for this disappointment—if disappointment it was.* "Whatever the Peshatin family intended, they have given me freedom. I begin, in fact, to be curious about this daughter of Laban MaGowan, this woman of Canada. Perhaps I—"

"My lord," Gill interrupted, "I neglected to tell you. The daughter of Laban MaGowan—her name, I have learned, is Odessa—has just married. Odessa MaGowan has taken General Sepulvida as her husband. They were married two days ago. In the excitement—"

I held up my hand to silence him. I had been about to toast my good fortune, but I set my wine on the table. *Odessa,* I said to myself, feeling the syllables on my tongue. *A bad marriage for you – and new threat from Sepulvida.*

My friends and I looked at one another in consternation.

Have I, I asked myself, created the very monster I sought to avoid?

Chapter 15: Whither Thou Goest

I

I had created a monster all right, but not in the shape I had imagined.

Gill and I were at breakfast early next morning when a messenger reported a commotion down at the harbor. Refugees from the north were arriving, bringing news that fighting had broken out on the Okanogan. Israelites were fleeing for their lives. Gill and I hurried to the docks and met dozens of terrified civilians disembarking from all manner of boats and rafts. Many huddled in blankets, having fled without their clothes. Soldiers, some of them bearing wounds, were scattered through the crowd. "The Canadians!" they cried, still panicked. The Canadians had attacked up and down the valley. Many civilians had been massacred and several settlements burned; the Fort itself was under attack. The northern frontier was in flames, they claimed, though they could give no coherent account of it.

In spite of Laban's warnings, the timing of this Canadian uprising took me by surprise. I dispatched several fast boats northwards to gather intelligence. I assembled my officers at headquarters to try to make sense of the news, which continued to come in hourly. Soon all the bells in the city began to toll the alarm, and anxious crowds gathered in the plaza. At midday we had more news from Chelan. When Sepulvida's forces pulled back from the Chelan area, we had moved quietly into the vacated space. Our troops there dispatched messages that confirmed a rising was in progress and that refugees fleeing from the Okanogan valley had reached Chelan in large numbers. So far, no hostile forces had penetrated the Lake District.

"I thought the marriage of Laban MaGowan's daughter with General Sepulvida meant a resolution of the problems in the north," Amasa said.

"So did we all," Gill replied. "Laban must have deceived us."

"I can scarcely believe that Laban acted treacherously," I said. "I heard him speak of his daughter; he cannot have sacrificed her in this way."

"So you think not?" Burgos said. "And I suppose you think the Messiahists have a monopoly on treachery? I say he used her as bait to lull the Israelite garrison—"

"I think something must have happened; something must have gone wrong."

"That may be," Gill admitted. "Or the other clan leaders may simply have pushed Laban aside."

We sifted our meager information, hoping in vain for clarifying news. "In any case," I said, "we must defend Chelan. If the Canadians penetrate so far south, it will mean war whatever Laban MaGowan intends. But we need our forces there immediately. Major Moriah, you must take the Esdralon Guards north immediately and block any attempt to invade Naphtali."

Moriah reared back in protest. "You can't mean to risk *my* cavalry against an enemy of unknown strength! This is a fool's errand! I refuse it!" Moriah was often provocative, but he surpassed himself in this moment.

"I respect your concern for your men," I said. "Therefore, take the Asherite cavalry along with your Benjamites."

Moriah refused to be mollified. "You said yourself that this is the wrong war at the wrong time. It is doubly so for Benjamin. We have no stake in this quarrel."

Gill and Burgos were incensed at his insubordination, forgetting the conditional nature of Moriah's service under me. Zachariah ben Harlech had foreseen a moment like this, and he had given full latitude of decision to his lieutenant. No doubt Moriah had chafed under my command for some time. Nonetheless, I made an appeal to his sense of honor: "Major, this war has chosen us—chosen Israel. Our land is threatened with invasion. I ask you to stand with us for Israel's sake, just as I would stand by Benjamin if it were invaded."

"But you would send my cavalry to fight in a box!" Moriah objected.

"True, you could easily be hemmed in around Chelan—in which case you must take your men inside the fortifications and wait for us. I will be coming behind you with all the power I can muster. There will be fast ships on the river guarding your flank and denying that route to the Canadians. You will succeed if you act boldly."

I consulted Burgos and Amasa about supplies and shipping and dispatched orders to the legion to prepare itself. "We can have the Great Jordan Guards and a fleet full of supplies off Chelan in four days," Burgos announced. Amasa concurred. We turned to Moriah.

"You must be in Chelan in two days at the latest," I said. "There is grain and forage there; we will bring additional supplies up the river when we come."

Moriah consented grudgingly. "My troops are too few for the job," he declared. "I'll take the Asherite horse as well as my own men." He glared around the room and then focused on me. "Be sure you don't dally coming up the Jordan!"

"You should clap him in irons," Gill hissed when Moriah had gone. "Damnable arrogance! He *refuses,* he says! *Don't dally coming up the Jordan*! Damn his insolence!"

"He is our best soldier," I replied. "Once he is in motion, Moriah will not tarry."

Major Moriah took his cavalry up the Jordan as ordered, moving rapidly. Instead of withdrawing inside Chelan's citadel when he encountered a raiding party of Canadians, Moriah ran over them with great slaughter and then pursued and cornered their leader and took him prisoner. When I arrived with the infantry on the 1st day of March, backed by a fleet of supply ships, Moriah had the immediate situation in hand. He had patched together an account of the rising from refugees' tales.

Fighting had broken out the very night of Sepulvida's wedding with Odessa MaGowan. The outbreak had come unexpectedly, and as a result, it was said, of an insult to the daughter of the Canadian chieftain. Within a day, the whole frontier was on fire, and a portion of the Okanogan garrison sent to quell the violence was ambushed and destroyed. The Canadians were wild with rage, and their numbers, as well as their strength in combat, had surprised the army. Reports put at least 2,000 warriors outside the walls of Fort Okanogan, plus more south of the river. The Okanogan valley was lost to us if but half of this news was true.

"Sepulvida lost at least a cohort, maybe more, in the ambush," Moriah added, briefing me on the situation. "He hasn't ventured out from behind his fortress walls since. There is a small garrison at Chilliwick twenty miles up the Okanogan. It is surrounded and cut off, if it has not already fallen. There is another garrison at Pateros on the Methow River, eight miles below Fort Okanogan. They are in communication with Sepulvida and with me, by boat on the Jordan, but the Canadians are everywhere in between on land, and between us and the valley." Moriah reported this with a kind of grim satisfaction, as if the difficulty of the situation only confirmed his reluctance to take part in it. "I have a captain of the Northern Lights Guards with a message from Sepulvida waiting to report," he added. "It would be a pleasure to put him on the rack."

"I would be obliged, Major, if you merely hear what he has to say and leave him for my interrogation." I hated to deny Moriah his pleasure, but I had to tread carefully with Sepulvida. "I'll want to question your prisoners too, but first I need rest," I said. I was nearly frozen from the trip up the Jordan. We had faced a headwind most of the way; it had taken my best energies to arrive at the moment I had promised. My wound was not yet healed, and it made itself felt in the cold. Leaving Moriah in charge, I stretched out with my staff and bodyguard by the huge fireplace. Chelan's citadel was rudely built, but it was warmer and more comfortable than a water strider.

The Canadian prisoners were brought in while the Northern Lights captain was giving his report. They were big, fine-looking men, though badly knocked about. Except for one young man, whom I took immediately to be their leader, they looked cowed and fearful. Moriah was so little conciliatory to his friends that I myself dreaded the thought of falling into his hands. An orderly brought a kettle of stew and hot bread and ladled out portions to us casually, no doubt mistaking me in my old, ragged surplice for a common soldier. None of us wore visible insignia, and we were sprawled in a very unsoldier-like manner by the fire. Seeing us fed, the leader of the Canadians complained loudly, demanding food, but the orderly only snarled at him and moved on. Moriah darted a threatening look in the prisoner's direction. Not wanting to see him mistreated, I gathered up the bread we had been issued and distributed it to the prisoners. Both Moriah and the Canadian glared at me; the rest of the prisoners seemed happy enough to have a crust to chew on. I sat down and listened to Sepulvida's man. Moriah was pressing him on the causes of the outbreak, and the man was obviously flustered, trying to conceal what he knew. A child could see he was protecting Sepulvida.

"That lying bastard!" one of the Canadians exclaimed in his own language. "He knows very well what happened!" The young man whom I had identified as their leader nodded grimly.

I listened unobtrusively to both conversations, the officer's report and the prisoners' commentary on it. The Canadians' dialect was very similar to Kuhlan speech. They had no reason to suspect that any of us understood their language.

"Your sister will be grieved by Orden's death," one of the prisoners said.

"No more than by yours! No more than by my own!" the young man added bitterly. "We were fools to listen to him. As if Orden could impress her now! He had done better to honor my sister when they were sweethearts than to try to avenge her now. This will cut her to the heart, knowing that we lost our lives for her sake."

"But what they did to Odessa! Surely – " *I pricked up my ears at the name of Laban's daughter.*

"My father warned me not to carry the war out of the Okanogan valley. This is no land of ours; our people have never lived here."

"Orden has paid for his error," another said.

"And we are about to pay for ours," the young man exclaimed in a low voice. "When they finish with this captain of Sepulvida's, they will turn their attention to us."

"Who would have thought the mud people could have soldiers here so quickly!"

"This Glanz or Haggadah, whichever he is, is a devil out of Hell. And Moriah there is his chief demon. They say he is from the southern-most part of Israel."

"Aye, would he had stayed there! Why come all this way just to hang us on a gibbet!"

"We will be lucky if that's all he does to us." The young man seemed overcome for a moment; a spasm shook his body. "I can't think what they'll do to our people now that they have cause—as well as the means—to do it. I overheard our guard say that the whole legion of the Devil is mustering here. It was a trap for us."

"Do you mean that the insult to Odessa was deliberate? That this Haggadah, this Sword of the mud people, planned it all?"

"My father said he turned down the offer of marriage with Odessa—and then he wrote suggesting that Sepulvida take her. If it was not a deliberate ploy, it was an insult. Poor Odessa; she meant only good for the people."

"But your father trusted him."

"Yes, and see what it brought him!"

I had heard enough by this point. I rose and said to Moriah, "I'll take over now."

Sepulvida's own messenger confirmed the general outlines of the story I had gleaned from the prisoner I knew to be Shaiym MaGowan, eldest son of Laban MaGowan. I had a scribe take down the officer's account as I questioned him. He was reluctant to say anything to harm his master, but I pressed him hard on what happened to Odessa. "We'll have a full inquiry when we reach Fort Okanogan," I warned. "If I find that you lied to me, you will suffer for it."

I then had the young Canadian brought before me. "Did you understand what this man said?" I asked in his own tongue.

He flinched slightly, surprised that I could speak his language. He was trying to recall what he had said in my hearing, but he took pains to show me nothing.

"You have an opportunity to amend this man's story," I said. "I expect you to tell me the truth about what happened to your sister. Consider that you are under oath to whatever is sacred to you. I expect no less from the son of Laban MaGowan."

He glared at me, his nostrils flaring.

"I am Josiah Glanz ben Haggadah," I said. "I will ask you questions, and this man will write down what you say in our language." When I had his bonds removed, he hardly deigned to rub his wrists to restore circulation. He was handsome and proud, and his anger looked as if it would take many lifetimes to subside. I asked the questions and translated his answers, and the scribe recorded everything.

It was as I feared. Sepulvida had gone through the marriage ceremony, but then on the wedding night, he had rejected the bride. She was not a virgin, he had declared. For this provocation, he had beaten her, and when she resisted, he had slashed her face with a knife. Finally, he had raped her and sent her, scorned and mutilated, back to her father. Not to be outdone, Colonel Malek, his chief of staff, had raped and beaten his own bride, virgin or not, before turning her out of the city. As MaGowan's son told it, many others had participated in this humiliation of his sister and his cousin. As far as the brother was concerned, *all* Israelites had participated in it. It was an insult no people on earth could endure.

A crowd of officers and men had gathered around us in the great hall to listen. I meditated silently upon what had happened for a time, and then I spoke to the young MaGowan in his language and then repeated it in my own, for the scribe to take down. "This has been shame for me to hear. General Sepulvida and Colonel Malek have caused this war. What they did would constitute a provocation to any nation that respects itself. Therefore, under the Law, we cannot hold these men accountable for the blood that has been shed." To Shaiym MaGowan I added: "I absolve you of blood guilt in this matter, and your companions as well, and I assume the obligation myself, as the commander of these offending officers."

He made no sign that he had heard me.

"Chance has made you our prisoners," I said. "It may be that because of it we can begin to set things right. I will return you to your people—that I promise. In turn, you must inform your people that Sepulvida acted without my consent or knowledge and expressly against my wishes. If your father consents, I shall seek an alliance with him against them, but they shall in any case be brought to justice."

There was much murmuring as I translated my remarks for the scribe. Shaiym MaGowan remained impassive as stone.

"I ask that you stay with us a while until I can find this man, this Sepulvida and his creature Malek, and hold them to an accounting. I want you to report to your father what you see."

He glared at me a long time but finally, almost imperceptibly, inclined his head.

II

I summoned General Sepulvida to report to me at the stronghold Pateros, situated at the confluence of the Methow river and the Jordan, eight miles southeast of the Fort. He demurred with excuse after excuse, as I expected he would. Meanwhile, the Canadian host hovered in our front, ready to prevent our juncture with Sepulvida's men. I could not move to Sepulvida's assistance without dividing my forces, which would be foolhardy in the extreme. I could transport the infantry by boat, but I had no way to ship the cavalry at the same time. To buy time, I sent one of the Canadian prisoners to Laban, saying that I had his son and would return him safely, as soon as I had disposed of the criminals who had offended his daughter. What message the man also carried from Shaiym MaGowan I cannot say and do not care.

After two days of waiting, I demanded that Sepulvida appear before me to give an account of events and the dispositions of the enemy. As my forces would be exposed to attack as they moved along the bank of the Jordan to Fort Okanogan, he had to accept my request to meet with me as reasonable and dictated by military necessity. His own position was untenable in the long run, and he could not dismiss the possibility that I had come upriver merely to join forces with him against the Canadians. I had already decided what must be done. His party would come by boat. I had seats and tables arranged by the small landing of the stronghold, and I gave my bodyguard and the Esdralon Guards their instructions while we awaited his arrival.

It was nearly noon when his flotilla appeared. The day was clear and cold, with a brisk wind blowing off the Jordan. I ordered places set on the tables as their ships approached. Cattle were roasting visibly on large spits. This was duplicity on my part, but I wanted to avoid general bloodshed. To this end, I intended to lull Sepulvida's suspicions and encourage a sense of security. Major Moriah and his staff stepped forward and greeted the party as they disembarked. Sepulvida had brought an extensive bodyguard—nearly a cohort of armed retainers. Moriah handled the formalities well; he was known by reputation throughout Israel and was therefore a useful focus of attention. I remained seated in the background, the better to observe and to choose my moment.

Sepulvida was a tall man, not yet forty, with a long face and a widow's peak. He looked as morose and taciturn as Moriah himself. It would have been interesting to watch them further in each other's presence—two famous men with dangerous tempers. Major Moriah brought General Sepulvida before me and spoke in a low voice, but I had fallen into a trance-like state. Something in Sepulvida's bearing or face—perhaps it was his confidence as he saluted—put me in mind of Senesh Velco, my enemy at the Academy, and that long-ago scene came rushing back to me, obliterating all else. I rose slowly and approached him, saw his eyes narrow as he appraised me—just as Senesh Velco's eyes had searched me and probed me contemptuously in that fatal moment.

Bastard! He had flung at me suddenly. *Son of a whore! Son of a Glanz whore!*

I said nothing and caught nothing of what Moriah was saying. If Sepulvida spoke to me, I could not hear it above the roar in my ears. I glanced at his men at arms and gestured slowly toward the tables laden with food, my hand seeming to move through a medium denser than water. And then I half turned away, also slowly, as if distracted. . . .

It is the oldest move in the art, the turn to the left. It conceals the reach for the sword hilt, and then, when the body pivots quickly back to the right, it imparts momentum to the blow. Performed correctly, the move concentrates the entire weight and strength and will of the attacker in the edge of the descending blade, which moves so swiftly that it is scarcely visible to the victim. . . .

"Your mother" . . .

Sepulvida was wearing armor. Ordinary swords would have failed to penetrate his thick neck protection, though the force of the blow might have sufficed to break his neck. My Hazorite sword bit deep and true.

I saw Senesh Velco's body collapse almost in two from the blow, observing the scene in my mind's eye for the first time since the event itself. His life's blood spurted from him in a brief fountain – five, six, seven jets – as he lay in a widening pool of his own blood. I had not known a body could hold so much blood.

I came to myself in an instant. Putting a foot on Sepulvida's chest, I wrenched my sword free. It had penetrated armor and flesh down to his sternum.

"Which one is Colonel Malek?" I demanded. "Place him under arrest."

I conducted the trial of Colonel Malek on the spot. I wanted these acts of justice performed as publicly as possible. I would have preferred more formal proceedings, but time was of the essence. The Canadians watched silently as the scribe took everything down. When I beheaded Malek myself at the conclusion of the trial, it was so the Canadians would understand that I had made a personal accounting with these two – which was necessary, I believed, if I was to regain any standing with the elder MaGowan.

"Tell your father what you saw here and take him the heads of the men who violated the women of your household. Tell him that I cannot undo the hurt that was done, but that I will make whatever amends can be made. Then send one of these young men to us again, or come yourself, and tell us when your father consents to meet with me. I wish to end the shedding of innocent blood between our peoples. Your father is wise; he will know what must be done. Hurry!"

III

I decided that the best way to enter the fortress and seize control of the garrison was to do so before its officers had a chance to plan a response. I took two hundred men, half Esdralon Guards and half from my own legion, so they could share the risks equally. It was necessary to humor them; both units had become intolerable on the subject of their honor and precedence. The common soldiers of the garrison seemed glad to see a relieving force. I arrested the deputy commander and convened a court martial without delay. A few heads rolled in the plaza before sundown, and the Northern Lights Guards were thus brought under control.

The next morning I sent a flag of truce to the Canadians requesting an end to hostilities. I emptied the dungeon of Canadian captives in a show of good will, but there was no response from the other side. Delay and uncertainty constitute the special curse of dealing with barbarian peoples, who have no chain of command. There was nothing to do but wait until their chieftains made up their minds what to do. The same day, at Pateros, Moriah scattered a small force of the enemy who crossed the river and tried to reach his rear. I decided to wait three days for a response to my peace overture and then, if I had no positive sign from them, to attack the Canadians in my front. Every moment spent on this crisis was a distraction from my main purpose.

The issue was almost settled the following night when our sentries detected the Canadians moving their field works closer to the north gate of the fortress. I could not accept such a violation of the truce passively. At first light, two cohorts stormed out of the gate and overran their positions. In thick mist, they broke into the trenches and took a number of prisoners. They would have gone on, but I held them back, not able to see how the main force of Canadians was reacting. After an hour, the mist dispersed, and I saw the whole enemy host arrayed in my front. Immediately, I ordered the drums and trumpets to sound and deployed nearly the whole garrison, plus my own cohorts, in front of the gate.

"Is this wise?" Captain Jared asked. "Are you—sir, are you certain that this is the best course?"

"If they mean to have war, we can finish it here. It will save us trouble in the long run." When he looked at me questioningly, I exclaimed, *"I have no time for this!"*

At the last moment, the Canadians made the sign for a parley.

I took with me only Won Morales, the youth I had saved from the fire at Cashmere and who had since become a member of my bodyguard, and Elihu of Benjamin, a grizzled veteran of the Esdralon Guards who could speak Kuhlan. Elihu would serve as my orderly, if need be, while also serving as a useful pair of ears. Morales, though badly scarred on face and scalp, was visibly of the same race as the Canadians. He was fanatically loyal to me; I was confident that any potential assassin would have to come through or over him. I left my sword in the keeping of Captain Jared and with instructions to award it, in the event of my death, to the bravest of the soldiers who were learning the disciplines of the Old Believers. I took my Kuhlan war axe instead, and for insignia I wore only the white slash of a war leader across my face. The Canadians were distant kin of the People and so, I presumed, understood their customs.

When we passed through the Canadian lines and met their delegation, I issued them a warning: "Major Moriah commands in my absence. If we do not return by noon tomorrow, you will explain it to his lances." I suspected that however little the Canadians knew about Israel in general, they had already learned something about Moriah.

We entered a lane formed by their warriors and passed down their gauntlet. We were taunted and insulted and spat upon. It is the nature of barbarians to be undisciplined and insolent, and I was proud that my two companions took no notice of their threats and jeers. The Canadian camp was a disgraceful clump of tents and lodges and brush huts of the flimsiest kind. I remarked to Elihu that, given the state of the camp, we could likely expect a plague to break out among our foes, and so we would not have to kill them all ourselves. Though stout of heart, he seemed cowed by the ferocity of the Canadians.

The council met under a dirty cloth pavilion. I asked for Laban, but they put me off with evasive answers. He was in Omak Town, they said, consoling his daughter for the wrongs committed against her by Israel. I listened while the chief men of the Canadians rehearsed their long list of grievances. I said nothing until, finally exasperated beyond reason, I told Morales, who did not even speak their language, to explain to them that these deeds had not been performed under my orders; that I had no responsibility for them and repudiated them. Morales had a stammer when nervous, so his reply stretched the capacities of their interpreter to the utmost.

I was smoldering with a rage that I could hardly account for. One chieftain, bolder and more insolent than the rest, berated me for the insult done to Odessa MaGowan and her cousin. I nodded at Morales and he described the punishments that Sepulvida had received, emphasizing that all those who had had a role in Odessa's humiliation had already paid with their lives. This seemed to impress many among the Canadians, but not my particular tormentor. His face was twisted with anger, and he sprayed me with saliva as he denounced my attack on their fortifications that morning. He threatened my life and demanded that Israelites abandon all of Naphtali north of Chelan.

In spite of my training, I succumbed entirely to the rage directed at me. "Tell this man," I said to Morales, "that he is an insolent swine and I would love to choke the life out of him." Morales was aghast and said nothing; my voice, however, had carried and enough Canadians understood our language that it grew suddenly quiet. The man who threatened me evidently knew our speech—or read my manner—because he stepped quickly back out of reach. I pulled myself up, mindful of the People's customs in dealing with affronts and longing for a complaint song to ease my heart of the violence that raged in it. I leaned forward, both my hands on the haft of the war axe I carried. It was the posture of a complainant—and among the People it demanded attention. The Canadians understood and waited.

Battle fever welled up in me, and it was all I could do to stand still. "There are no issues between our peoples," I said, searching for words that would calm the storm in me, "that we cannot resolve peacefully, now that Sepulvida is dead. Sepulvida has paid for his crimes, and the troops that he commanded now answer to me. There are no obstacles to peace except those you place in the way. I have come to learn what restitution can be made to Laban MaGowan and his daughter. Whatever is in my power and is just and right to do, I will do. But I will not endure to be insulted."

I was dizzy as I spoke these words. When my opponent still glowered threateningly, I burst all restrains: "Both our peoples long for a blood-letting," I said. "It may be that we must indulge these feelings. Perhaps then, when we have taken our fill of slaughter, the survivors may wish to talk. I am content to have it so. I would prefer peace, but I will accept battle, no quarter asked or given. However, nothing would satisfy me like single combat *now* with this buffoon who calls himself a chieftain. I will fight on behalf of Israel – and he can fight for any who claim him. This fool, who has insulted and threatened me from my first moment among you, even though I came in good faith under a flag of truce!" I glowered back at him, ready to throttle him. Elihu put a hand on my arm, but my blood was singing in my ears. "Did you think you could daunt me with your bluster? Did you imagine I would cast away my people's interests because you threatened me? I choose the double-headed war axe; select whatever weapon you wish and clear a space for the combat. I will endure no more of this."

As it happened, cooler heads among the Canadians prevailed, and my tormentor was pulled back into the crowd and silenced. We had some desultory talks that afternoon, but I remember none of it.

Laban and his son Shaiym arrived the next day, accompanied by a large group of kin and retainers. I looked for his daughter, expecting she might be among the women who hung in the background, but I saw no one who seemed likely to be her. The presence of the women was a good sign in itself, however; it meant that the Canadians intended to talk peace in earnest. Laban looked sober and downcast and did not embrace me or offer a hand to shake. I expressed my condolences for what had happened to his daughter.

"Who would have thought this great misfortune would come upon us so quickly," I said. "If we had only had more time to plan together—"

"It was I who acted hastily," Laban said, and his words caught in his throat. "The fault is mine."

"You could not know." I searched for words to console him, assuring him that I, who was Sepulvida's mortal enemy, had not realized the man was so entirely without honor. "Those who are truly to blame have suffered for it," I reminded him. "Let us put our minds to salvaging what we can." To that suggestion Laban appeared to assent, though reluctantly. We seated ourselves under a pavilion with half a dozen Canadian chieftains and his son, whom I was glad to see again.

"Is it true," Laban asked me after the preliminaries had been completed, "that you challenged Angus Fawqwar to single combat yesterday?"

I admitted I had made a challenge to a person unknown to me. "It was foolish, but I was angry beyond measure at the violation of the truce, and the man provoked me."

"It was Fawqwar who pushed the trenches forward, so you challened the right man," Laban replied. "He is the spokesman for the war party among us."

"Now he is spokesman for the women who pulled him back from danger," one of the chieftains remarked, bringing smiles from the others. A group of women had interposed themselves between him and myself and thus saved him from my wrath. The Canadians, I noted, allow their women a very large role in their affairs—a much larger role than Israel thinks proper.

With Laban presiding, we struggled toward a peace accord. To end the hostilities, I asked that the Canadians withdraw their forces northward to the nearer disputed borderline. We would work out later where the permanent boundary should lie. Neither side would seek indemnities. On their part, they demanded that we abandon Chilliwack and Fort Okanogan, which I refused to do.

After a day of talks, I asked to speak to Laban privately concerning my personal debt to him. "Do you retain your wish that our peoples may become one?" I asked. He searched my face for a time and then nodded. "I share this hope – though it will not be easy to achieve, especially now. Let me show you something concerning the boundary of ten years ago and the boundary after Sepulvida's campaign. Understand, however, that I will consent to either border, as you wish." I displayed a map showing all of Sepulvida's land claims colored brightly; they nearly filled the contested zone.

"What's this?" Laban demanded.

"All this land belongs to your daughter, as the widow of General Sepulvida. This is the land he claimed, and she is his heir. In Israelite law, in the absence of children, the wife inherits." As he mulled this over silently, I added: "However, she inherits only if this territory remains under Israelite law. Your daughter could hold or dispose of the land as she sees fit, according to your customs."

"I must ask," Laban said, "what purpose you have in showing me this?"

"The disputed land could be a borderland where we can learn to live together. I am proposing that the land remain Israelite territory, under Israelite law and customs. Its seat of government would be at Chilliwack, and both Canadians and Israelites would share in it. They would have to learn to work together, with your family owning most of the land, free to enrich whomever they choose."

Laban hesitated for some time, turning over this proposition in his mind. "It is a wise plan," he said at last. "It would be a step in joining our peoples together. But your proposal also separates myself and my clan from the rest of my people. This, as you know, would involve a great risk—and it would threaten to divide my people."

I bowed slightly, acknowledging his astuteness. We understood each other.

IV

"You have received bad news?" Laban inquired of me the next day.

"Indeed, I am unlucky in war as well as in love." In the midst of these negotiations, I had received messages from Amasa and Gill. In my absence—and in the absence of most of the legion—Nahum of Cashmere had raised an army and burst out of the Wenatchee valley. On March 8, the date of Amasa's letter, Nahum's forces were approaching Hammoth-Wenatchee, plundering the countryside and punishing those who had cooperated with me. In Amasa's view, the city could be held with the forces on hand, but he recommended I return immediately and crush the rebellion.

I received Amasa's message on March 11th. Gill's letter had been sent the day before Amasa's, on the 7th, but the courier carrying news of the rising had overtaken Gill's. "I have unraveled the mystery of your assassination attempt," Gill wrote. "It was a Messiahist plot, hatched in New Jerusalem." This news only confirmed my own suspicions. Tephlin Glanz could employ assassins aplenty, and so could Nahum, but few hirelings of either man would be disposed to commit suicide in order to accomplish their mission. And the foolish man who distracted my attention at the moment of the attack had been pumped full of Messiahist lies. A Messiahist conspiracy is what I had thought all along.

Gill's letter gave an account of his efforts to gather evidence that would solve the mystery. He had watched who had had contact with the man who had denounced me, and then watched those who had contact with the others. Gradually he had identified a network of people and then a place where they met—to worship, as it turned out. One of my assailants was a priest recently sent from Manasseh. Gill promised quick action against the conspiracy: "I'll have the whole lot in custody before you return," he wrote. "One thing only has surprised me," his note concluded. "In Naphtali, it is the landed class who practice the objectionable forms of the Messiahist faith, not the merchants and craftsmen. But more of that when you return. I intend to move against the conspirators immediately."

The last bit of news gave me pause. Had Gill's arrest of the Messiahist cell included people close to Nahum of Cashmere? Had the arrests precipitated the rising?

I made no attempt to hide these troubles from Laban and the other chieftains. "I need some time to attend to urgent business," I announced. "I must beg your leave to interrupt our discussions."

Moriah had kept the rising secret, but the news would travel north within a day or two of the courier. I convened a council of my officers. "How many troops will you need to subdue Nahum?" I asked Moriah. "You may have your pick of the units."

"So, you intend to stay *here,* meddling in this dunghill?" Moriah disapproved of my expending any energies on the far north of Israel.

"If I leave without an agreement, while the blood is not yet dry on our Canadian frontier, we will lose control of the northern reaches of the Jordan. Laban has been discredited by what happened to his daughter. But as long as I am here to bolster his views and offer rewards for making peace, their peace party may prevail."

Moriah was scornful of any peace with barbarians that was purchased with gold or lands. "Let them feel the edge of your sword," he said, "and then they will whimper for peace!"

"I scarcely have sword enough to go around for all my enemies at the moment! Surely peace with some of them would be a good thing." I reminded him that the Canadians had proven stronger than we anticipated. "In the meantime, we have two crises, and I cannot be two places at once."

"Beware," he warned, "they will see your weakness as soon as our troops depart. You cannot hide it."

"True, this is not the time I would have chosen to show weakness to the Canadians. But Nahum picked the moment, and he did so with great skill. We must deal with what is."

Moriah grumbled his assent. "Nahum's rebels cannot be very formidable, whatever their numbers. I'll take the cavalry and as much infantry as we have shipping for."

"Speed, Moriah," I urged him. "Speed is everything."

He saluted. "We can be at Hammoth-Wenatchee in three days. I'll make this Nahum skip to a different tune."

When I returned to the negotiations, I informed the Canadians that I had troubles at home and had dispatched part of my forces to deal with them. After hearing this news, they were noticeably slower in arriving at agreements, and in the afternoon, several of the hostile chieftains grew bolder in pressing their demands. It was clear that the talks would go nowhere until they had seen what advantages could be wrung from my difficulties.

Morales and Elihu and I pitched our tent in their midst, and Elihu cooked our evening meal. Captain Jared would be uneasy while we were away from the fort, but I intended to signal my lack of fear to the Canadians. Nevertheless, I was relieved when Laban MaGowan joined us after dusk had fallen. He was curious about the nature of my troubles, and I told him frankly that they involved Nahum of Cashmere.

"I thought so," he said. "Many of the clans chiefs believe they have you at a disadvantage," he continued. "But I told them that Moriah will scatter your enemies like chaff, and then you will be stronger than ever."

We talked a while of my plans for Naphtali and then I spoke what had lain in the back of my mind for some time: "I have a desire to meet your daughter, if she is well enough and willing. Since our talks appear to be moving slowly, I thought there might be an occasion for us to become acquainted."

To my surprise, Laban was not enthusiastic. "She has seen you already," he explained. "She has been in your presence. Her mind has changed a good deal, you understand—in light of events."

"When? When was I in the presence of your daughter?"

"Women take things to heart," he said, "and then there is—"

"She was in my presence *when*?—and why did she not make herself known to me?"

"It was when you first came to talk peace, after the fighting before the gate of Okanogan."

I summoned my memory of those events. After my outburst at the Canadian chieftain, a group of women had interceded and pulled him away just as our confrontation had been about to break into violence. I searched my recollection for details.

"I was in Omak Town," Laban said, "disgusted at the war—and, to speak the truth, angry that I was no longer listened to. Nevertheless, Odessa wanted to see you, and so she came back to Okanogan, in spite of her wounds and humiliation."

Had wanted to see me. His manner and his putting his daughter's wish in the past tense alarmed me. "So, she was disappointed?"

He spread his hands. "Young women, you know. It is hard to live up to their expectations." *And well she might be disappointed.* I had been in the grip of an unaccountable mood, a fury almost, and I had spoken to her people through my bodyguard, a private soldier who did not even know their language. She had seen the arrogance of that—and then she had seen me challenge this chieftain, this Angus Fawqwar, as I learned his name to be, to single combat. I had a reputation as a fighter, and no doubt this challenge to an older man had seemed like bullying. *Had* been bullying. I was suddenly ashamed, feeling the justice of her view of me.

"I owe a debt to your daughter," I said. "Perhaps you can speak to her on my behalf."

He shrugged. "With women, nothing is certain, so I suppose anything may be possible."

V

When I heard that Odessa had consented to see me, I ransacked the fortress for furs and cloth and jewelry and other items suitable for gifts—of which there were considerable stores. I had them packed on wagons and carts and set off for Omak Town, the seat of Laban's clan. A late winter rain descended upon us immediately. The oxen and the carts sank into the mud, and we were all exhausted and miserable before we were half way there. I had asked Laban to provide an escort of Canadians, and he sent his son and a group of warriors to accompany us. I was grateful for the chance to become better acquainted, because I knew already what I had to do.

My time for maneuvering was running out; the glass was nearly empty. A settlement had to be reached here in the north that freed my hands before the summer campaigning season. This was the year of the millennium, and the Messiahists would surely break out in all their fury upon the rest of Israel the moment it suited them. In the short run, I was confident that Amasa, Gill, and Moriah could deal with any crisis that Nahum could raise in Naphtali, but I resented the need to delegate solution of that problem to others. So far the exercise of power had taught me more about the constraints of acting than about freedom of action. Necessity was a hard teacher. I had resented having to enter into a betrothal with the Peshatin woman—partly because she did not please me, but also, as I reflected on it, because she represented benefits I would not likely live to reap. A poor bargain, to trade whatever portion of happiness I might look to have in life for an eventual Apostleship of Naphtali! I had hoped that the marriage to the Apostle's daughter would reconcile the citizens of Naphtali to my rule, but that had proved a false hope. Naphtali was indeed difficult to rule; I had not yet found the key to that puzzle. But a marriage that would achieve peace and forge an alliance with the Canadians immediately – that was no small consideration in the scheme of things. More than the devotion of Naphtali's citizens, *I needed a free hand in the south.* Thus, necessity drove me on.

Given my need for haste, the slow progress of our small caravan was torture to me. Irritable though I was, I determined to use the time and learn what I could about the MaGowans and my escort, Shaiym MaGowan. This young Canadian seemed to have courage and a sense of honor. Curious how Odessa had formed an opinion of me, I ventured to ask him what reputation I had among his people.

"You have two reputations," he replied; "one spread by your enemies and the other the account your followers give about you." Without prompting, he added: 'Your enemies describe you as a fiend out of Hell, an enemy of all religion, and the cruelest monster imaginable. You are said to wallow in blood and to savor the taking of life." He gave me a sidelong glance. "And worse, much worse!"

"I suppose my friends describe me much the same way," I replied. "What aspect of my behavior offended your sister most?"

He made no attempt to spare my feelings: "She said you are as arrogant as one of the People, but more savage."

"Savage?"

"Yes, you came dressed in old furs and ragged woolens and carrying a war axe, as if seeking to insult us in as many ways as possible. You threatened one of our leaders with the axe. And earlier, you had sent the heads of Sepulvida and his henchman to us, as if our people would not be able to accept my plain account of their deaths." Canadians, he explained, are reverent of the dead and do not display body parts as trophies.

"If you had spoken to me of your customs. . . "

"I told her that. I warned her to be cautious of making judgments based on such matters. I mentioned that I had failed to notice you at first at Chelan, so it is possible that you are more than you seem. And I told her that, in my observation at least, you keep your word."

"Ah, something to build on, at least."

The next day, after a long, wet march, we arrived at Omak Town. The settlement was an unimpressive sprawl of log huts, unpainted and without order or regularity. Public and private spaces were mingled indistinguishably and seemed equally shabby. No welcoming party greeted us. Instead, the sullen inhabitants of Omak Town came out of their hovels to glare and utter curses and threats. With a heavy heart, I knocked at the largest building, which was the seat of government as well as the residence of the MaGowans. I felt much as I had when I arrived at Moses Town in the Kuhlan lands—a sick sensation of despair mingled with distaste and repugnance. *Is this, then, all there will be for me?*

My knock produced several of the male kin of the MaGowans, who greeted and then insulted and nearly assaulted me. They disputed my claim to Laban's protection and declared that they despised my gifts for his daughter. Not even Shaiym's presence and my escort of Canadian warriors could overcome their hostility. Then they ripped back the canvas covers on the wagons and broke into excited conversation, after which they turned on me angrily. "You call these gifts!" one of them shouted at me. "We have seen these before! Did you come to insult our cousin yet again?"

Seeing the contents of the wagons, Shaiym too was caught up in their indignation. "These are Odessa's wedding gifts!" he cried. "Do you mean to heap burning coals on her wounds?"

I had, I realized – my heart suddenly a lump of tallow – unwittingly brought Odessa MaGowan the gifts Sepulvida had given at her wedding. "How could I know that some items among these goods had been her wedding gifts?" I exclaimed. I protested feebly, realizing that this was a circumstance in which good intentions counted for nothing. "If these things are her property, then I merely return what is hers. As for the rest, they are offerings of respect. Ask your sister to accept them in the spirit in which they were offered – or spurn them as she wishes."

There was nothing else to say or do. We took ourselves out of the angry hive of Canadians to a hill outside of town. I ordered a camp pitched, but I was thoroughly dismayed and ready to make whatever escape was possible. To turn tail, however, was to invite these barbarians to slaughter us, so I determined to put the best face on things I could and await Laban's arrival. Elihu and Morales did not say that I had made a fool of myself and probably destroyed all hopes for a peace with these people. They did not dare speak it, but we all knew it. "Bad luck" was all Elihu said. Knowing a little of Canadians, I predicted that they would work themselves into a frenzy and come after us at nightfall. We waited, considering our slim array of options.

Instead of a drunken mob, however, we saw on orderly procession wind its way up the hill just before dusk. The group approached under a standard of ermine tails fastened to a crossed bar, which I recognized as the insignia of the MaGowan clan. Leading the procession was a tall figure, unmistakably feminine even in the furs and trousers the Canadians habitually wore. Her head and face were wrapped in a shawl of fine wool with only her eyes showing. Before she spoke, I knew it was Odessa MaGowan. I greeted her formally and apologized for the mistake I had made.

These things aroused my kindred, not me." she replied. "I care nothing for mistakes, nor for gifts."

In the dim light I could see that her face was bandaged. The shawl only partly concealed the thick wrappings below her eyes. Her eyes were large and wide-set and intelligent. They were good eyes. Above all they were alert and expressive, though profoundly sad. "Regarding all things pertaining to my wedding," she said, "I am past anger. Therefore, I grant you your good intentions and thank you for them." Her words were polite and formal, a speech such as a man might make, or a chieftain, and they put us on a plane as equals. But her manner said, *What have I to do with gifts of cloth and gold; my face and heart and prospects are marred indelibly.*

I took her hand. "Lady Odessa, I hope you and I may become better acquainted." I sought words to express my condolences—and my shame – that her injuries had been inflicted by one of my countrymen, but I found myself nearly speechless. I faltered in the midst of the adage that wrongs could not be undone; I stopped, bewildered.

"I believe that wrongs can be undone," she replied. "And I came to undo the discourtesy my household showed you earlier today. I invite you and your men to be guests of the MaGowans, poor though our hospitality has shown itself today. It would please me if you would enter under our roof and enjoy shelter and food with us. It is pleasing to God to make amends, and He enjoins us always to forgive. Therefore, I ask that you come with us and accept my apologies. Tomorrow my father will arrive, and you can continue your discussions on behalf of our two peoples."

The Laban household was spacious, but dark and windowless. It had stone chimneys at each end of a long, narrow, rectangular hall. Cloth curtains could be drawn to partition spaces off for private use, but the appearance of the whole indicated its chief use was as a hall of assembly, suitable for public occasions. Tables of uniform size were scattered about, constructed so that they could be assembled into one long board for formal purposes. The mantle and tables and roof beams were all carved in fantastic figures and designs. I inferred that the Canadians had no very elaborate private life. Though crude in its material aspects, their life was a public one.

Servants gave us seats by the fireplace in front of the blaze and we refreshed ourselves with mugs of native beer and slivers of spiced, dried beef. Shaiym MaGowan served as host, looking strained and embarrassed as he introduced us to the same kindred who had driven us away in the morning. Clearly, the word of the chieftain's daughter counted for something in this household.

Odessa reappeared wearing the typical costume of her sex and station—an embroidered wool tunic and leather pants. A shawl of fine blue wool was arranged around her neck and shoulders, revealing part of her hair and the shape of her face. The bandages on her cheeks marred but did not entirely conceal her features. Her nose was a little too prominent by Israelite standards of beauty, but it was an interesting face, a face with character. I longed to see it unbandaged and unmarked, and again I lamented Sepulvida's treatment of her in my heart.

She was accompanied by a girl of about eleven years of age, whom she introduced as her sister Matild. The girl was tall and somewhat gangly, but wore the promise of remarkable beauty—and she bore an obvious resemblance to Shaiym. I looked from brother to younger sister, trying to guess the details of Odessa's features. Seeing her beside her older sister, I recalled the lament from the old love song, *"My little sister has no breasts."* Odessa had an impressive womanly figure, and her stature gave her a kind of dignity, like a woman of the People. Her little sister's time would clearly come.

Matild left us to stand by her elder brother's knee. She leaned on his shoulder with an arm curled fondly around his neck. Odessa seated herself beside me and gave me her exclusive attention. I gazed at her long enough to create some self-consciousness on her part, which I attempted to relieve by averting my eyes and engaging her in small talk. Still, her curiosity matched my own. In the midst of these others, I perceived that she and I could speak privately. I inquired after her life, and she told me that her mother was dead and that she had five brothers and sisters, only two of whom—Shaiym and Matild – still lived. I noted with approval the mutual affection of the family. But at the same time, I recoiled inwardly at her people's reproductive practices—their reckless excess, in my view. However, I said only, "You remind me of your father. You seem to have his good sense and discretion."

She would not consent to be flattered and turned the conversation to the civil war in Israel and my role in it. Odessa asked me about my troubles in Naphtali, careful not to pry into state affairs but allowing me to speak of things close to my heart—and, I suspect, to show me she had a man's understanding of these things. "It has made me wonder," she said, "to hear that one so young as you, someone no older than myself, could acquire such a reputation as you have. I have been very curious to meet you."

"I know I have disappointed you," I said. I apologized for my behavior in the encounter she had witnessed and fumbled for an explanation. In truth, however, I did not know myself why I had acted with so little wisdom or self-restraint. Certainly, my Masters had taught me better. In her company, I could not, of course, admit that everything pertaining to the Canadians was merely a distraction for me, a diversion from my real task, or acknowledge that I was desperate to free myself to deal with the Messiahists. She must have thought me inarticulate or stupid when I ended my stumbling account.

"My father told me you had a mission to perform on behalf of your people. He said you are revered by your countrymen in a remarkable way, and I would understand nothing about you if I failed to grasp that."

"Surely you must be equally set apart from the women of your own country. I'm told you have suitors among your countrymen, and yet you have determined to devote yourself to cementing an alliance between our two peoples. That is truly remarkable." I felt myself walking a fine line here, wanting to acknowledge the situation that had brought me here, but in such a way as to avoid giving offense.

She did not flinch at my reference to her misfortunes. "Either in alliance or in a closer union, I believe our peoples could achieve greatness. I have thought it worth the effort to bring such a union about—especially as I saw things drifting toward war. Not all of my people approve of my course. In fact, only my father has had the vision to acknowledge how much there is to admire in Israel. Though I am not blind to your country's faults, I too am an admirer—even though I have had recent painful experience of your prejudices."

It was my turn to be abashed. "To our shame and everlasting regret, my lady." I told her how much I admired her courage, and how it reflected honor on her people.

"On the contrary, you cannot have formed a high opinion of us these past few days. I saw at Fort Okanogan that you scorned us. Perhaps you are correct in your estimation, but I assure you my people can be very tenacious when aroused." I attempted to deny these feelings, but she continued. "We are a free people, but we often wear our freedom like clumsy boots. I know we must appear mired in our primitive ways and bad habits. And it may be that we are exactly what we appear to be." Seeing me reluctant to comment, she added, "Would you like to know how Israel appears to us?"

"I would be grateful if you would spare me an account of that," I assured her. "I believe I have acquired some knowledge of Canadian views in the past few days."

To my surprise, she smiled. She had full, well-formed lips and an expressive mouth. Then her brows knitted thoughtfully, as if she hesitated to ask her next question. "My father said that you told him you were unlucky in love as well as war. What did you mean?"

I described my betrothal to Judith Peshatin and its abrupt end. She expressed her condolences, her eyes moving alertly. "Please, lady, no sympathy," I said. "I am glad of it. There was no attachment on my part; it was purely an affair of state." I did not say, *just like your marriage to Sepulvida.* But I had a sense that many things were passing between us unsaid.

She held my gaze as if exploring every nuance of meaning and emotion in my face and words. I spent an intense, though pleasant hour in conversation with her, and then she and her sister excused themselves.

"I wish you success tomorrow in your discussions with my father," Odessa said in parting.

As they entered the family's private partition, I overheard Matild remark, "How strange he seems! His speech sounds just like one of the People, but he is as brown as an otter."

VI

We took breakfast with the family in the morning, as Laban was late in arriving. I found the company of Odessa and her sister interesting and even charming as we compared stories of our childhoods. Matild had lost her mother at the same age that I had lost mine, and I felt a strong empathy for the child. Odessa seemed more reserved than the night before, though it may have been the fresh bandage masking her features that conveyed an impression of distance. But when I suggested a ride to see the land hereabouts, she replied quickly that it would be best not to leave the house. "We should wait for my father," she said.

Laban arrived at mid-day, with a long face and weary step. I was alarmed at his grimness.

"We have much to discuss," I said in greeting.

He shook his head. "I fear it's too late." He took me aside. "The southern clans want war," he said without preamble. "They are mad for it. Worse, Fawqwar and the others are determined to kill you while you are apart from your troops. I don't know that I can prevent it. I don't believe I can prevent it."

Elihu and Morales were instantly alert, their hands on their sword hilts. Many angry retorts came to my own mind, but it is the curse of unorganized societies that the honor of one leader is often undercut by the actions of others. An Israelite who held authority would die before allowing harm to come to anyone who had been invited under his roof—let along an envoy under a flag of truce. However, with no power to enforce decisions, barbarian peoples necessarily seem capricious and unprincipled.

I thought quickly through the consequences that would come of my assassination. "I want to marry your daughter," I said.

Laban looked at me uncomprehending.

"Yes, and I want to do it immediately. It may save her. Possibly Matild as well."

"What are you talking about? You cannot pacify the clans with a gesture now!"

I waved his misguided concern away. "I'm thinking of *my* people—and of what will follow."

Shaiym MaGowan had joined us; evidently, he knew what was afoot. "What do you mean – *what will follow?*" he demanded.

"My countrymen put great store in flags of truce. By Law, my person and the men who accompanied me are inviolate. It is the usage of all civilized peoples." Laban and his son looked at me, as if to say, *What does that matter to us?* "Moreover," I said, "there is the special regard in which I am held by my soldiers."

"You pick a strange time to speak of marriage," Laban said, still uncomprehending.

"I'm speaking of a *reckoning*!" I exclaimed, furious at their obtuseness. "I'm speaking of vengeance. My legion will exact a terrible retribution. But if Odessa is my wife and that can be made known to them, she may be spared—though she and Matild and the women of your household must flee immediately and as far away as possible. As for the males of your household and all your other kindred, there is no point in fleeing. My people will hunt you down or bribe your own people to slay you. The law of envoys is sacred—and my legion is not like other forces in Israel. In my absence and for this cause. . . ."

"We are quite capable of defending ourselves!" Shaiym retorted.

"*Are you*?" I replied. "You met a handful of Moriah's cavalry in Chelan. Did you learn nothing from that experience?"

"In defense of our own soil, we. . ."

"You fools!" I cried, hurling obscenities at them. "This is no time to bristle and strut and boast of your manhood. A disaster is in the making, and you worry about defending your land! Do you think my men will care a straw about your land? When they come here—and they *will* come – they will be seeking your blood, not your land! They will make a desert of this place and for a hundred miles northward, and everything named MaGowan will be trampled and obliterated! You will die, all of you, men, women, and children. Israel's revenge code is strict—and my men will exceed its demands a hundred fold, I promise you!" I subsided, breathless, and as angry as I have ever been.

Odessa and Matild had joined us unnoticed. Matild tearfully sought her father's hand. Odessa stood, arms crossed, and looked at us. "You men must find a better way," she said.

By dusk, Laban and his kin had found a better way. They returned, winded and a little bloody, with Fawqwar and three other clan chiefs bound and sputtering. With them came a troop of women and children. Laban had taken them all hostage.

"You are clever as the Devil, Israelite," Laban flung at me. He seemed well fortified with drink. "See, I have let loose a vendetta among my people, and you haven't yet made a single concession! But you have already divided us and set us at each other's throats! If you are going to negotiate a settlement with me, then, by God, this is the time!"

I was more than ready, but first I insisted that he give his blessing to the marriage of Odessa and me.

"Uh, well, I don't know about that." Laban seemed confused, as if he had forgotten this factor in our negotiations. He looked to his daughter for guidance, and – though I saw no change in her countenance – she must have signaled her assent. "All right then," he said gruffly, "but you'll have to please *her*. It is her decision after all."

I had spent the day with Odessa and her sister, feeling virtually under siege in the MaGowan household and anticipating at any moment an intrusion that could mean the deaths of all of us. Through it all, she had remained calm and composed—almost serene—as she waited to see what fate had in store. I concluded I would be getting a warrior and counselor as well as a wife, if I could persuade her to accept me. I took her hand with genuine enthusiasm. "Whether it be peace or war, Odessa MaGowan, I want you to be my wife. It may be that we will have very little time together—and we may pay for what we are attempting here with our lives. But I see we have the same mind and the same heart on many things. I ask you to be my wife."

She held my gaze for a long time, until she had satisfied herself that she had weighed and measured everything there was to be seen there. Then she replied simply, "I consent." She squeezed my hand before releasing it. Matild rushed to embrace her, and the two withdrew to the family quarters.

"Tomorrow, then," Laban said. "First thing in the morning."

A considerably softened man, one who no doubt remembered himself as a father, sat down to work out the peace with me. He arranged his prisoners around the hall, so they could witness our discussion, but he gagged Fawqwar and gave stern instructions to his son to keep him quiet and attentive. Laban demanded that Israel—it was clear he meant *me* – recognize a new entity, a Canadian state, independent and sovereign and equal to the states of Israel, but allied with Naphtali. Its government would be at Omak Town, and it would be a *Canadian* state.

"Under Israelite Law."

Laban had reason to believe I would not budge on this issue. "Yes, yes, under Israelite law," he conceded. "But under a law imposed in stages and administered by Canadians, as we grow accustomed to your ways."

He reminded me of the peoples to the east who were moving our way. The Canadian state, he declared, would serve as a buffer protecting Israel. And Israel would extend its protection and commerce to the new state in return. Through it, Israelite customs and laws would spread north and eastward along the trade routes.

"Boundaries?"

He was vague as to the northern boundary, which was no concern of mine. On the south, he insisted on the old boundary, before Sepulvida's aggression – the line that lay only a few miles north of Fort Okanogan. At the same time, he insisted that all the land Sepulvida had claimed now belonged to his daughter. I agreed to his point so readily he became suspicious, casting about for an explanation, even turning at last to his bound prisoners.

"What does Israel get in return?" one of them prompted.

"Yes!" Laban said, turning to me. "What does Israel get in return?"

"The property is Odessa's under Israelite Law," I answered. "If you insist on her ownership, the Law necessarily comes with it, to validate and uphold her claim." *A state under Israelite Law, I thought to myself, is an Israelite state.*

"Why, Israel gets peace, you fools!" Laban exclaimed. "Peace and an ally, instead of war. And wealth for both sides. Come, let me show you something." He motioned to me and lurched out the door. Shaiym accompanied us, bearing a torch. He took me to long shed adjacent to his house, which proved to be a warehouse full of costly furs—marten, mink, and beaver in bales and prime pelts of lynx, fox, bear, and wolf, and more besides.

"The Okanogan valley is the natural route for the trade," Laban said, seeming suddenly sober. "If Sepulvida had had brains enough to see it, he would have understood that we could be much more valuable as partners than as slaves."

I was impressed by the richness of his stores and the potential scale of the trade. Obtaining it would be a good thing for Israel—and a valuable card to have in reserve with Ben Gurion and Tephlin Glanz. Even more important was the opportunity to extend Israel's civilization and influence. But I also foresaw that in a decade or two, the Canadians might be strong enough to push down to the Jordan. If they could seize Fort Okanogan, they could interrupt our communications with Old Spokane and take control of metal recovery there. It was clear to me also that the Jordan was the true strategic route for this trade, not the Okanogan, but Israel had never been able to exploit it. Acting together, we might be able to. All in all, this was a large and attractive and very dangerous package that Laban was offering me. *Opportunities and problems,* our Teacher saw, *come bundled together,* and he taught us to be wary. But he also taught us not to flinch from what life brings.

"I cannot abandon my countrymen at Chilliwack," I said. "Make provision for their safety and autonomy if they are to be included in your state."

Laban thrust his face close to mine. In the glare of the torch I could see his bulging eyes and inhale his sour breath. He knew I would assent to his proposal if I assured him of this one thing. "Israelite!" he exclaimed, "I will adopt them as my kinsmen! I will guard them like my own chicks and ducklings. Whoever harms a hair on their head or steals a nail from Chilliwack will answer to me!"

"Then I will establish a college there and a school, so writing and the Law and our history can be studied. Chilliwack will become the light of your new state."

When we reentered his quarters, I announced that we were agreed. There was much rejoicing. Laban crushed me in his grip and danced around the room.

"This is peace with justice and endless benefits for my people!" Laban exclaimed. "These fools," he said, giving one of his hostages a kick, "resent Israel and envy what they would give their eye teeth to possess. They hate Israel because it is foreign. But I have made it our ally, and in this role Israel will become our teacher and benfactor."

The women of the household appeared and a boisterous celebration began. In his enthusiasm, Laban untied his hostages, even the gagged and still seething Fawqwar, and all but he embraced Laban. Fawqwar still protested bitterly. "Don't you see," he sputtered angily. "This man wants to marry your daughter! It is a trap."

"Yes, he does," Laban replied complacently. "So be careful what you say about my son-in-law."

"But don't you see, under Israelite Law, the wife's property is controlled by her husband. He's tricking you!"

The group burst out laughing at his fears, hostages and MaGowan clan alike. I was quick to assure Laban that Canadian custom would prevail. The property was Odessa's to dispose of as she saw fit.

In the wee hours of the night I found myself singing songs I did not know and downing mugs of beer with men who in the morning had been plotting to kill me.

VII

The next morning my head ached and my tongue felt like one of the pelts in Laban's warehouse. I made myself as presentable as possible and steeled myself to endure whatever ceremonies the Canadians used for marriage. Nothing had prepared me for the reality. I was so intent upon settling the details of my agreement with Laban that I failed to notice a white-robed priest standing at the end of the hall until the singing began and the ceremony was under way. My heart sank and then seemed to disintegrate. How had I not *realized* that the Canadians embraced some version of the Messiahist faith? I wanted to flee, to hide myself under the mountains or in the depths of the Jordan. Only the mysterious dread of social embarrassment – more powerful even than my detestation of Messiahist priests – kept me rooted in place.

Odessa appeared dressed in her native finery, but veiled – I presume in deference to her still-bandaged face – and took her place beside me. She was composed and modest; I was rigid as a block of stone, sweating and panting like one in agony. I scarcely attended to the words of the ritual, which spoke a good deal about their god and his alleged ownership of marriage. I had to be prompted once to reply to a question and I stumbled in speaking all the vows. The ceremony was mercifully short; if it had lasted a moment longer, my clenched leg muscles would have pitched me forward in a faint.

Afterwards, I could not think of a thing to say to those who offered me their congratulations. Through it all, my face burned like a hot coal, and my hands were clammy. Fortunately, an elderly aunt of the bride coached me through my role in the wedding feast. Laban busied himself mending relations with the clans, and soon nearly all the guests were in their cups. After a round of ribald songs, Odessa and I were led to the private quarters in the rear of the hall. As we entered the chamber, I realized I had not spoken a sentence to my bride nor touched her since the ceremony began. A group of richly dressed young women accompanied us into the quarters, making a fuss about removing her veil and undoing the brooches that held her hair. Odessa sat passively on the bed, her eyes averted. It occurred to me that her wedding to Sepulvida had taken place not quite a month earlier. I wondered what she was thinking. She dismissed a woman who had undone a clasp on her blouse.

"What?" I replied irritably to a half-heard question behind me. Odessa's younger sister, I realized belatedly, had been asking me what I believed about the afterlife.

"I am an Old Believer!" I replied, more emphatically than I intended. "We do not believe in an afterlife." Strange to say, our religious differences were in fact paramount in my mind at that moment.

"But what happens to your soul?" Matild insisted. She reminded me of a pretty bird perched on a slender branch. Nevertheless, I was glad to have the distraction of her conversation to vent some of my feelings. Odessa signaled to the maids of honor that their work was done. I sat down beside her on the bed, trying to compose a brief answer to Matild. Harsh words on this subject were crowding to get out, but I repressed them. "We do not believe in souls, either," I explained. "We believe our lives and our selves are part of the world, integral to it, and part of the energies that play in it forever. So when we die, we are simply re-integrated into that ceaseless play of forces. We cease – to be separate."

"I don't understand," Matild said frowning. "Without the prospect of Heaven, what meaning can life have?"

"That is a mystery only to Messiahists," I said. "We believe that our lives have value even if our actions are not written in the heavens. Lives acquire significance from the way we live them, not from some imagined future life. And not from some alleged other world."

"How awful, how empty of hope!" the younger sister exclaimed. Along with her dismay at hearing my beliefs, Matild was enjoying being part of a grown-up conversation. I sensed that Odessa was both interested and uncomfortable with the discussion.

"We do not see life as devoid of hope," I said. "And in any case, it is reality. We accustom our minds to it."

"But not to wake up in Heaven, full of light and joy, that would be dreadful!"

"I imagine if one were to wake up in one's own senses and with one's sense of self intact and everything else transformed or absent, it would be very sad. Terrifying, perhaps. But chiefly sad."

"Why?" Matild asked, her eyes wide. "I don't understand."

"To be separated from all that engaged and held one in place and gave meaning to one's existence, to one's pain and struggle in this life, that would be sad. One would grieve a long time in your Heaven, I imagine."

"But you would be reunited with all those who had died. And you would be united with God."

What in the world can that mean? I wondered. I thought of my mother. To see her again – that would be something. Incongruously, I thought of Rehab Gill and his father. "How do you conceive of this god of yours?" I asked, wondering if I could get a better answer from a child than from my Chief of Intelligence. "Do you think of him as a person? A force of nature?"

"I think of him as a princely spirit – a perfect gentleman," Matild said somewhat primly. I felt certain that Odessa wanted the conversation to end, for she reached out and put her hand on my arm. "Yes," her younger sister added, with the confidence that only children possess, "I think of God as one who shows unfailing courtesy to the souls of the departed. In His house there are many mansions. That is a saying of ours. We believe that He is hospitable to all who come to Him."

"Someone like your father, then?"

"Yes, our Father in Heaven."

Odessa had kept silent during this whole exchange; she looked at me now with her serious gray eyes and kept silent still. Laban, however, had apparently heard part of the conversation through the partition, for he burst in, his face red with drink and not altogether pleased. "Foolishness!" he cried. "You girls speak of sacred things! You know nothing! This man is wise in such things. In his own country, he is revered. And you quack to him of things you know nothing of. Geese! He will think I have raised a flock of geese for daughters! Begone!" He shooed Matild out of our quarters. "You two still talking?" he said gruffly. "I would have thought you'd sent her out long ago. Talks more than her mother did, what a child!"

"Matild is good company. We are content," I assured him. I took Odessa's hand in mine, and it was the first time I had touched her as my wife. I was determined that in our first night together she would experience nothing to remind her of the brutality of her first wedding night. She blushed deeply behind her bandaged cheeks and looked away.

Before I discovered her religion, in spite of the differences between our peoples, I had been eager for this marriage. Odessa seemed eminently sensible, with the same incisive mind and directness as her father. She had devoted herself unselfishly to her people—to their improvement, as she saw it—and had faced the consequences of her choices with unflinching resolve. She had grace and courage and a sense of honor. Moreover, it had not escaped me that she was also, by the standards of her people, or by any standard whatever, very attractive—at least she had been before Sepulvida slashed her face. She had hair almost as thick and luxurious as Miriam's, but light brown in color and finer in texture. She was slightly taller than I, with long legs and a lean body that stooped ever so slightly as she stood beside me in the ceremony, as if she regretted being taller than her husband. These few items represented, I reflected, nearly the extent of my knowledge of her. As I studied her downcast face and heavy lashes, it occurred to me how little I knew this woman I had just married.

Marriage, the old jest in Israel goes, *makes strange bedfellows.*

VIII

The day after my wedding, I was invited along on a hunting party into the mountains. The MaGowans and their many kinsmen made up most of the party, though there were several minor chieftains and their retainers. They treated my invitation to accompany them as a signal honor, so I reciprocated. I inferred that this ritual was another way of solidifying the arrangements, both familial and political, that Laban and I had just entered into. The distraction was also a relief, as I found I had little to say to the stranger who had become my wife, and time hung heavily upon my hands. I needed to be in Naphtali.

The snow was deep in the hills, and we wore "snowshoes," the clumsy webbed contrivances Canadians use to travel in winter. They probably serve well enough when one gets the hang of them, but I was blistered and weary after a few hours. When the dogs struck up the chase, my father-in-law and his immediate family hung back, and I saw that this was a courtesy to their poorer kin. Honors were meted out carefully by the Canadians; the humble were not despised. I saw that it was a good custom—and one that saved me exertions I was glad to spare.

By nightfall, when we caught up with the hunters, I was pleased to find the camp already pitched. There were tents and a roaring fire and dressed meat hanging from trees. We feasted on wild flesh, our faces lit by the blazing fires, and threw the bones and entrails to the dogs. Afterwards, the Canadians sang their hunting songs—wild and sad and wistful melodies that reminded me of nights around Kuhlan campfires. As always, the Canadians had a good deal to drink and grew quarrelsome before they fell asleep, curling up in their robes in the snow like their sled dogs.

Laban MaGowan and his son Shaiym and I shared a bottle of good Israelite brandy by our fire. As the camp quieted and the fire died down, I sensed that Laban wished to broach a topic with me but was, at the same time, reluctant to do so. Firelight sparred with the edges of the dark, but the shadows gradually closed in around us.

"Honored father," I said, for this was the manner in which he was addressed by his people, "I hope we always speak our minds with one another."

"Yes," he said. "Good. We need to speak freely—and often. Our peoples know too little of each other. Ignorance, God knows, breeds misunderstanding." He mused for a time and then spoke what was troubling him. "My daughter Odessa is young and knows little of the world. That is why, I tell myself, that her heart is torn." He frowned, as if searching for the right words. "You must be plain with her and teach her what to expect and what to do. You must not keep her in the dark. She is quick to learn, I promise you."

Odessa wounded? I had had no inkling of it. "How so?" I asked in alarm. "If I have offended her, tell me how!"

"Women set great store on their wedding nights," he said. "Odessa's first wedding was not one to cherish, as you know. And now I understand she has cause for more disappointment—"

"It was for this very reason," I exclaimed, feeling baffled and dismayed, "and knowing how fresh her memories are, that I treated her with the greatest respect. I thought—I was *certain* – we understood each other."

"Perhaps it is our customs, the differences in our peoples' ways, that are at fault here. My daughter is a woman of sense, but in some things, perhaps, she is a girl." Laban explained with some delicacy that among his people a marriage is supposed to be consummated immediately. Failure to do so was an affront to the bride, as it suggested disappointment or reluctance in the groom—or incapacity. Either of which was cause for grief.

"It was none of these things, I assure you. It was, on the contrary, my concern for her and – " I paused, almost in despair. "You are right, our peoples have different ways. And Israel's ways are strict. Sometimes I think we revel in how severe we can be."

"It was not her scars that displeased you? Not the absence of virginity?" Shaiym asked me this very earnestly. He knew I had overheard him say that before she married Sepulvida, Odessa had had a lover from among her people. *Sepulvida's fury was in my own mind and, I suspected, in theirs as well.*

"We also value chastity in women," Laban said, "but we do not make a fetish of it."

"Put your mind at ease about that," I said. It was difficult to explain in a few words our Reproduction Laws as they applied to second marriages. "In my country, the legitimacy of a child—proof that the child is the seed of the husband—is important. No, it is *everything*!" I could have added that my own birth had been under a cloud, and I had suffered for it all my life. And for that reason alone, many of the best Israelite families would reject me as a suitor.

"Speak plainly," Laban said, seeing me hesitate. "We are all men here and have understanding."

"When a woman remarries, she does so only after three months have passed. Or she lives apart from her new husband three months before they have intercourse. This is proof to the community that she does not come into the marriage pregnant by another, and that any child she bears is her husband's."

"Why all this fuss? A child is a child, thanks be to God!"

"Its parentage is important to the community," I replied. "In my country, permission must be obtained to bear a child. Therefore, particularly in families of stature and influence, legitimacy is important. No, it is *fundamental*. This is, in fact, much of what marriage means to us. And where the on-going life of the family is at stake, the desires of the couple – or of the bride – are necessarily subordinate."

"So, this is how a husband behaves in your country if the woman has been married before?"

"Yes. If three months have not yet passed before they marry, the husband must abstain. It is the Law."

"Three months," Laban said, weighing all that I had said.

"In my country, the wife's honor is at stake in the waiting. Odessa's honor, when she lives among my people. And also the status of our child, if we were to have one immediately."

"God grant it!" My father-in-law said.

"God grant it," his son echoed.

"Aside from these questions of the Law, it was out of deference for her recent injuries, the wounds that are not yet healed on her body – still less, I imagine, in her heart – that I was willing to forgo the husband's right, as Israel thinks of it. I would have waited, in any case, for her sake, until we knew each other better. Until she was ready and could choose the moment."

"These are strange reasons," Laban said. "Yet they seem to me good ones. You were careful, after your own customs, of my daughter's honor, and you acted for the sake of her children to come. Shaiym," he said to his son, "your sister should know of these reasons. Her husband is not displeased with her."

He nodded.

"Will you go tonight then?"

"Gladly," he said, rising and gathering his gear. I saw the depths of Odessa's pain in the concern father and brother felt for her.

I sat by the embers, regretting that I had given my young bride cause for distress – but at the same time dreading a future in which such misunderstandings would be my daily bread. "Tell your sister," I said in Shaiym's ear as he strapped on his snowshoes, "tell

Odessa that it is very difficult, the waiting. Tell her that three months seem like an eternity to me."

He looked up and, for the first time, my brother-in-law smiled at me. Then he disappeared into the darkness.

It was dusk of the next day before our party returned to Omak Town. I saw Odessa waiting, standing by herself on a hill overlooking the town, bundled in furs. I turned aside from the party and greeted her. The coldness of her hand told me she had been waiting for some time.

"My lady Odessa, we must learn each other's customs, or we will never know each other's hearts." I apologized at length and explained Israel's customs and the reasons for them. I knew her brother had already described our marriage laws to her, but I wanted her to know that my intentions had been respectful. "I had no one to tell me about the ways of your people—no one to prepare me for what you would expect. How can our peoples become one unless you and I understand one another?"

"I understand now," she said.

As we walked back to the town together, I encouraged her always to speak openly to me, as I had encouraged her father, so that we could avoid such misunderstandings.

"My father says that Israelites treat their wives like servants," she said. "That will be difficult for me, but I will accept it. But I want you to know it is because I choose to accept it, not because I feel I must. I do this willingly for you."

"Odessa, I will never treat you like a servant."

"My father says that you will, and he is wise about many things. I believe you are sincere, and if you do treat me as a servant, it will not be because you intend a slight, but because custom and usage are strong in any country, particularly in these matters."

I stopped in the path and thanked her for this sentiment. I took her in my arms for the first time and embraced her gently. She held her still-bandaged face away from mine, but I unloosed her scarf so I could bury my face in her hair. The warm scent of her was strange to me but good. I held her tightly for a long moment and drank her in and savored it.

The next morning I left for Naphtali.

IX

I returned to find that, in my absence, a massacre had taken place. Two massacres, rather – one of which had been committed by my enemies, Nahum and his disaffected nobles from the valley, and one by my friends.

Nahum had risen like a whirlwind, bringing fire and sword down the valley upon all who had cooperated with me. Those who could, fled to the safety of Hammoth-Wenatchee. For five days Nahum's landed nobles wreaked their pent-up fury, stored from the decade of Hanford's rule and from Huerta's and my own, on the defenseless countryside. Then they pitched their tents outside the walls of the city and demanded its surrender. At that point, I speculated, the more astute among them realized they were doomed to failure. They had no means to take the citadel against a determined, competent defender—which Amasa certainly was. Their reprisals had solidified support for us among the citizenry. Thus, there was no one to let them into the city—except a small Messiahist conspiracy that Gill had already ferreted out and crushed.

By the time Moriah arrived, many of Nahum's followers had begun to disperse quietly back to their homes, realizing their cause was hopeless. Those who stayed by Nahum's side were run down mercilessly by Moriah's veteran cavalry. I saw the heaped bodies of the slain before the walls of Hammoth-Wenatchee and in a bend of the river where a fleeing group had been cut off and slaughtered. The road to Cashmere was littered with more dead. Moriah had sent his cavalry into the high valley and arrested the families of the rebels. Cashmere was a prison, its walls filled to bursting with prisoners.

"Do we make war against the families of our enemies?" I asked Amasa after I had seen the cringing survivors of the rebellion.

He begged me to talk to Captain Gill and Major Moriah before deciding their fates. Accordingly, I assembled my counselors, including several of the leading merchants, to assess the situation and decide what to do. Burgos was adamant that I not squander with misplaced clemency what had been won with so much difficulty. "The landed nobles will oppose any form of government you would establish here," he pointed out, "and they have made themselves despised by all the other classes. If you exterminated them and their families, you would be applauded in the city, I can tell you that!" The merchants did not disagree with him. Amasa gave me a vivid account of the rising and the outrages that had been committed.

"They rose against us, yes," I acknowledged, "but I have not yet established a legitimate government. There are no grounds in the Law for proceeding against them as traitors. No doubt from their own point of view, they are patriots."

"Surely you don't intend to allow their point of view to prevail!" Moriah exclaimed. "We've won a victory. Don't throw it away!"

"The rebels are Messiahists," Amasa said quietly. "If you leave their families on the land with their property intact, you are sowing yourself a crop of trouble."

"What do you say, Gill? These people are your co-religionists?"

Gill was silent. He seemed embarrassed – either by his co-religionists or by his own failure to anticipate the rising.

"These are the people who conspired to kill you," Burgos added. "Besides, there can be no reconciliation with the churchmen."

I looked to Gill again for confirmation. It was he who had discovered the conspiracy against me among the Messiahists in Naphtali.

"What about the Edict of Tolerance you gave in Hazor last year?" Gill demanded. I was surprised by the question, wondering where his thinking led. "If you move against the Messiahists because of their faith, you will contradict –"

"He moves against them because of their *actions*!" Burgos declared. "Because of treason, because of conspiracy! Because of murder!" Burgos was as exercised as I had ever seen him.

I had no intention of throwing anything away, but I had a larger end in mind. "Let me see the list of Messiahists that Solomon Glass prepared and that Gill has confirmed" I said, "and then see who among the prisoners is on that list."

The leaders of the rising, including Nahum of Cashmere, were put to death. I sentenced all others who had been involved in the rebellion to an exile of ten years and confiscated their lands, on the authority of martial law, which I still exercised. The worst rebels I exiled to Old Spokane and reopened the metal recovery operation that Zachariah ben Harlech had destroyed when we left the Kuhlan lands. I saw the irony of that, but was not troubled by it. The others I sent to the unsettled shores of Lake Chelan. Sadly, the wives and children and elderly relatives of the rebels were forced to accompany their sons and husbands and fathers into exile. I had no authority under martial law to break up the homestead of a noble family, but I was confident that the government I would institute in Naphtali would ratify my actions.

Confiscation of rebel wealth gave me control of an immense amount of property. In addition, I had the resources recovered from Hanford's secret accounts as well as those of Huerta and his henchmen. Solomon Glass had proven very helpful in ferreting out this information and recovering these ill-gotten gains. There was also the accumulated wealth held in company warehouses, besides much land already owned by the company. Thus, I had at my disposal more wealth than anyone in Israel, with the possible exception of my father and Bishop Bon. With these resources in hand, I had the means to enforce my will.

The secret of using wealth to advantage, I discovered, is to give a good portion of it away—selectively, of course, and for good reason – while retaining enough to tempt others into compliance. Accordingly, I distributed estates and lands to loyal Old Believers, especially to men who had distinguished themselves in battle, but also to prominent refugees who now flocked to Naphtali. I sold some of the land at bargain prices to members of the merchant class. To end the distinction between merchants and landed nobles, I distributed Northern Lights shares to soldiers and sold them at a discount to farmers and tradesmen and the handful of nobles who had not been exiled. From the groups made wealthy by these distributions, I created a Council of 300, a new body of electors for Naphtali—and made certain that a third of them were my officers and men and another third reliable Old Believers. I invested in improvements in the city, strengthened the citadel, and repaired bridges and canals. I needed a fleet, and I employed a good portion of Naphtali to build one. Soon there were no unemployed paupers in Naphtali.

With these measures in place, I found the task of reconstituting the civil government suddenly become easy. When the Council of Elders was elected, *behold,* I was elected not only an Elder, but Chief Elder and Speaker of the Council. I did not have to manipulate these outcomes behind the scenes; my plans went forward, as the adage says, as if on wheels. The questionable legality of my property distributions made all men who had benefited from them my brothers, eager to assist me and sustain me in power.

The first act of the Council was to abolish protected property in land, so that the noble homestead could be relinquished, bought and sold, like any other property. By this act, the landed nobles ceased to exist in Naphtali. In this, as in all instances, I struggled to persuade rather than coerce. We had lively debate and argument in the Council, especially on the question whether the population should be subject to military conscription, like the nobles. The Elders balked until I agreed to establish a separate legion, which I accomplished by resurrecting the Naphtali Legion, which Nahum had thought to lead.

Regarding the census and the re-imposition of the Reproduction Laws, I would not yield the principle, but accepted a compromise that was less onerous to them and allowed them time to accustom themselves to the Law's discipline. We agreed to a preliminary census for tax purposes, and I insisted that they establish elders in each district empowered to take the census and establish lineages. When it was protested that Naphtali's population was still in flux, I made provision that each district establish its lineages as the land became filled. But in ten years time, all of Naphtali would be counted, and thereafter the population would be fixed and all births licensed and authorized.

Prompted by Amasa, the Council of Elders raised me to the rank of General of the Host. Three legions now answered to my command, in addition to the remnant of the Esdralon Guards. In the midst of these successes, I wrote Ben Gurion an innocuous version of my plans for the future and sent him soldiers I had culled – to batten off his stores rather than mine. I said little else of the new order that prevailed in Naphtali. In the south, the truce of hunger, as it was called, still prevailed.

X

Thus, it was in the midst of success—even of triumph—that the essential harmony I enjoyed with my closest associates was lost. It is ever thus, our Teacher warns us; it is the nature of the world we inhabit. Nevertheless, the event came as a shock to me.

"You must desist immediately!" I exclaimed. I was furious at this breach of my edicts—and not least because Rehab Gill had chosen to speak on behalf of the miscreants. Before me stood representatives of the Messiahists who had remained in Naphtali after the purge. They had pledged their loyalty, but shortly after were reported conducting blood sacrifice in secret. "Sacrifice," I declared emphatically, "is an abomination and I will not permit it!"

"My lord," Gill said, "they are merely slaying with reverence. Slaying with reverence, equally with prayers and meditation, is permitted by the Law. They do not sacrifice."

"What is the difference? How could anyone tell one from another, if the accused were disposed to deceive?"

"The difference lies only in the intent, my lord, that is true. And intent, I grant you, is not easy to determine. Fortunately, their defense does not rest on such tenuous grounds as their own characterizations of intent, but on the very heart of the Law itself, which you affirmed in Hazor in your Edict of Tolerance. Belief alone, you declared, cannot warrant any legal action by the state. So, even supposing their intent *was* to sacrifice, the Law cannot move against them. Sacrifice is worship; it is not treason or murder or conspiracy, but merely worship—and is therefore protected by the Law of St. Supplicee."

Gill rested his case—rather smugly, I thought. The accused looked at him with unconcealed admiration. I gave them a stern warning and released them. From Gill, however, I demanded answers. "Gill, you and your family do not conduct blood sacrifice. Tell me this is true."

"It is true. We are not so gullible. We hold that blood sacrifice is superstition. It has nothing to do with the Messiah we wait for or the world He will redeem."

I was becoming oppressed by the varieties of Messiahists and their differences. I wondered what it would be like being married to one. "Do you imagine," I asked Gill, "that you can alter natural law or reverse causation with a little splash of blood on the ground? Do you think you can forestall the future with an earnest supplication—or a verbal formula of any kind?"

"Of course not. But I see you do not respect our beliefs."

"What is there to respect? The great mass of your co-religionists accept things a child would reject as fantasy! How can it be that you are so unmanly, so naïve. Wishes do not alter reality. If that is the case, as I take it to be, then it follows that our first duty is to get a firm grasp of reality, abide by it, and then refine and expand our understanding every day of our lives." Gill tried to defend the efficacy of prayer and ceremonial slayings, which he distinguished from sacrifices and claimed as forms of meditation, but I cut him off. "You have a mind; you see clearly. You are capable of reason. How can you entertain such notions?"

"There are many aspects of reality," Gill maintained stubbornly, "all of them elusive."

"Elusive, yes, I grant you. But this is not a child's world of magic and pretending."

"I wish merely to live in a world better than this one," Gill said. "I wish only that."

"There is no world better than this one! *This* is the only world there is! If we want to improve it, we have to live *in* it and act in it—according to our understanding of its terms. All else is delusion and wasted effort. How can you hope to change the world by *wishing* for a better one?"

"How can you change it without such a wish?"

"Ah, you fence with words again."

"No fencing," he said. "No play on words, General, I assure you. On these matters, I put my trust in the Lord."

Fortunately, with the responsibilities of rule came privileges. In anticipation of Odessa's arrival, I ordered an apartment furnished in the citadel, two floors above headquarters. It was large and light and secure, and I had little doubt that my wife could make it comfortable, once she had grown accustomed to our ways and fashions. While distributing lands to my followers, I had taken the estate of General Huerta, which was well watered and convenient to the city. Its buildings were most like a stronghold of any estate in Naphtali; it had a walled enclosure and great house and ample quarters for a bodyguard. The house and outbuildings had been sacked and partly destroyed during the disturbances. I rode out frequently to view the progress of the repairs.

My new estate lay adjacent to Captain Amasa's, and I liked nothing better than to visit him after a hard day's work. Amasa and Carmina employed many of their injured and disabled countrymen about their estate. Their plans to adopt war orphans had been postponed until they could return to Benjamite territory, but I suspected they had begun to think of Naphtali as home. Amasa was immensely popular as my stand-in Speaker of the Council of Elders. I was considering relinquishing that post to him, knowing it would be in good hands. More important, despite her earlier conviction that she was infertile, Carmina was carrying a child again.

They greeted me warmly and invited me to enjoy their library while they continued in the fields. The disturbances had so delayed planting that much of the army was assigned to these tasks. I expected food to be in very short supply in the coming year, and so had taken steps to assure that Naphtali would become Israel's granary. New ground was being broken everywhere. I walked out to see how the planting was going, savoring the scent of the newly ploughed fields. I saw a field planted in potatoes and watched the cattle amble single file back to the barn to be milked and then joined my hosts in their great house.

Amasa and I sampled one of the beers of his cellar, lately the property of a rebellious noble, and talked of the prospects of war and peace and crops. Dusk came very gently to this land, as the great bare ridges to the west cut off our view of the sunset. Carmina came in and lighted the lamp, her figure showing the first traces of her condition.

"Beautiful!" her husband said, beaming at her.

"Yes, it is a beautiful night," she said.

"A beautiful prospect of a good crop, I believe he meant!"

Amasa grinned and rose to embrace her. I took delight in their affection and their prospects for a child. If anyone deserved a good life, it was they. At the same time I envied them the intimacy they shared. It reminded me that I was a married man too, but in a marriage of a different sort. We gradually fell to talking about it. Carmina worked at a small handloom as we talked. She was weaving a blanket for her child.

"The Canadians will take some getting used to," I said. "They seem as unsteady as water."

"But at least they lack that awful seriousness of the People," Amasa said. "I expect you have had your fill of that."

"Yes, such deadly earnest!" Carmina agreed. "I could go a life time and never miss it." *I was reminded vividly of Vitoria, and not all the recollection was pain.*

"Still, there are events and memories there that I would not relinquish," Amasa admitted. We seldom spoke of the Kuhlan lands and our experiences there. It was as if all that had happened in another life.

"I saw very little of any kind of seriousness or discipline among the Canadians," I said, "even when their purpose was evil." I retold the story of the drunken reconciliation of the quarreling factions of Canadians the night before my wedding. "Can you imagine me sharing a drink and singing sentimental songs with Bishop Bon or Brother Bulavar scarcely an hour after our differences were settled?"

"Hardly!" Amasa said. "For that matter, I find it difficult to imagine us ever settling our differences with the Messiahists." He frowned. "I suppose Israel has its own deadly earnestness about its quarrels. Once at odds, we do not reconcile easily."

"We are the least forgiving people on earth," Carmina said. "And that is why we are continually at war."

Carmina was earnest enough in this belief that her husband seemed eager to change the subject. He asked me to tell them more about Odessa. I described her as before, exhausting all of my meager knowledge of her, but finding it pleasant to revisit the subject in company with friends I trusted. "Odessa has a kind of composure – and serenity—that reminds me of the People," I said. "But Odessa is not proud. There is a reserve and sadness about her, but no arrogance."

"I don't wonder she is sad!" Carmina said.

I thought of Odessa's slashed face and the mortification she had endured. Selfishly, I wished her beauty could be unimpaired. I had never really seen her face, though I had a strong impression of her looks.

"Burgos is pleased at the marriage," Amasa observed. "I heard him say so several times."

"I imagine he must be pleased to trade my future for peace with the Canadians."

"He thinks always of the Messiahists," Amasa said. "But he thinks of you as well."

"I fear for *her*," Carmina said. "I don't envy her the prospect of coming to live among us. Besides being unforgiving, Israel is—"

"A nation of judges," I said ruefully. I tried to imagine how it would be for her, knowing but little of our language and wearing the complexion of a slave – and with her face mutilated as well. Learning to live among our proud and unforgiving people would not be easy. "She will be lonely," I said. "We must help her find her way."

They readily agreed to do so. I drank more than I was used to, but found my anxieties about Odessa undiminished. Our marriage would surely make her a target of harsh censure, but I did not know what to do about it. "Sometimes I fear it is we who are a peculiar people," I said, thinking of Israel's fierce exclusiveness. "We justify ourselves by the Law, but somehow we have never caught its spirit. In fact, these citizens of Naphtali pride themselves more on their resistance to the Law than their obedience to it."

"Damned stubborn malcontents!" Amasa offered. He was tired and losing interest in the conversation.

"True, they have resisted us tenaciously," I said. "Or at least they have until now. Recently they are become like lambs, agreeing to everything we ask. Your husband," I said to Carmina, "will be known as the most effective Speaker in generations. The merchants crowd around to take sugar from his hand."

"Well, it is no wonder. We do much good here."

"It is not the *good* we do," I rejoined. "They love us because I have exterminated the landed nobles!"

Jonathan Amasa, tired from his labors, was a poor audience for my insights. Carmina, however, looked up from her work and said sharply, "*Abolish*, not exterminate. You *abolished* the nobles. And doing it gave you the bastion you needed. That Israel needed. It was the price of protecting the nation."

She was right. I had sacrificed the nobles consciously, knowing it would achieve my purpose.

"Now it's up to you to use what you have built wisely." Carmina gave me an encouraging smile and resumed work on her child's blanket.

Book Five:
End of Days

Chapter 16: Make Haste My Beloved

I

Predictably, Burgos was alarmed by my plans. "June the twenty-second, my lord General, and not a day earlier!"

"Nonsense," I said. "Odessa married Sepulvida in February. Three months will have passed on the 28th of May. I'm going up and collect my bride on that day. There is no need to wait three months from our wedding date."

Perhaps rightly suspicious of any sign of enthusiasm in me, Burgos raised objection after objection. In truth, I was eager to go. It was a mixture of curiosity about Odessa and about the married state—plus, I must admit, simple desire on my part. Something about Odessa, some aspect of our meager acquaintance, had reawakened longings in me that had been buried for months. Such feelings had burned fiercely in me for short periods previously, first with Miriam and then with Vitoria. These relationships had both ended abruptly, and the awakenings had afterwards caused me intense suffering, as these fires had of necessity to be banked down and smothered. In the challenge of capturing and then ruling Naphtali, I had found some relief. Indifference to my own desires had eventually become habitual, and I was, at times, even grateful to be free of this distraction while I turned Naphtali into a rock of resistance. But the bastion was now built, and my thoughts turned to other things.

There was another element in my impatience. We expected the Messiahists to launch their campaign to bring Israel under their control sometime during the summer. The precise timing of their offensive was unknown, but we expected it would come after they had gathered enough of the harvest to carry them through the winter. Consequently, we were watching the ripening wheat and barley very carefully in Asher. We estimated that at the earliest, the enemy attack would come in August, after the grain harvest was well under way. These prospects did not leave much time to devote to my personal life.

"With you and Gill and Amasa attending to business here in Naphtali," I said, tweaking Burgos a little, "I could easily take an extended honeymoon."

"Not so, my lord!" Burgos exclaimed. "That would be imprudent—or worse!"

I assured him I was joking and reminded him that my marriage was for state purposes. He did not seem wholly reassured. We all knew the truce of hunger would not last.

Odessa was to meet me at Pateros, as I wanted to spare her a second experience of Okanogan. I sent many gifts and messages and invited her to bring along as many friends and relatives as she liked, since I anticipated her first months among us would not be easy. I took a small escort and arrived a day early to ensure that all was in readiness. This proved to be a mistake, as I grew nervous as a caged lynx waiting for her.

The day of her arrival passed with agonizing slowness, and it was dusk before a small party of horsemen appeared at the gate of the fortress. I was certain something had gone wrong. Forgetful of all ceremony, I rushed to the courtyard to hear the news and found myself standing before Odessa herself, who was mounted on a spirited bay mare. Her mare danced skittishly at my approach, and its rider, too, seemed to draw back in alarm. Seeing her control her mount expertly, I marked down another piece of knowledge about this mysterious person who had become my wife. Odessa wore a veil of white gauze like a scarf, but I recognized her instantly. I greeted her and reached up and took her by the waist to help her dismount, feeling in her body's tenseness her mingled dread and anticipation. As she stood before me, I gently unwound the veil and saw the still livid scars on each cheek. On the left cheek, the scar had puckered slightly where it crossed her cheekbone. Our eyes found each other and I mumbled, "Welcome," and kissed her lightly on the lips. She smiled fleetingly, and I relaxed and remembered myself.

"Honored father," I said addressing Laban, "forgive my neglect of ceremony. You are welcome here. Welcome, brother!" I said to Shaiym. I greeted them all and was introduced to their party by Laban. At a distance, I had taken them to be warriors, but the group included women, friends and kin of Odessa. Laban seemed pleased at my attention to his daughter. I inquired after Matild and learned that she was at home in good health. I took them all in to dinner, relieved that Odessa had come at last.

Odessa sat at my left at dinner, but was reserved and spoke only in monosyllables. Playing host and translator to the party, I could address only brief private remarks to her in the midst of the general conversation. "I am very pleased to see you," I assured her several times. I noticed she kept the gauze scarf as close about her face as possible. "Be more comfortable, my lady," I said, hoping to reassure her. In truth, her scars were quite visible. While they marred, they could not efface her beauty. She had fine, handsome features, beautiful eyes and lips and strong cheekbones. "I'm pleased you brought your friends and family," I repeated, possibly for the third time during a break in the conversation. I was at a loss for what else to say. At the end of the meal, I whispered, "I'm anxious for us to talk privately, Odessa," and she nodded without speaking or meeting my eyes.

Either she has changed her mind about me, I decided, or she is very nervous. Oddly, I felt grateful that Miriam Lander had prepared me for the peculiar ordeals of marriage. I was more than a little anxious myself. Wedding nights are fraught with tension as well as significance, and our own moment—so long delayed – seemed to carry particularly heavy burdens. It seemed far more natural to me to move by gradual stages from a general relationship to sexual consummation. In Israelite marriage, however, one moves from an abrupt consummation to acquaintance and then to whatever relationship will emerge—a procedure that seemed to me exactly backwards. And of course in this order of things that initial embrace assumes enormous significance—which was the cause, I sensed, of our mutual anxieties. Male lore on the subject of nuptial consummations seemed to me ludicrous, being chiefly concerned with establishing one's authority or, even more foolishly, overawing the bride. I hoped for her sake that female lore on the subject was more sensible.

In the event, when we had finally bade goodnight to our party and retired to the bedroom, I was chiefly anxious for Odessa. Mortified by her scars as well as by the events by which she acquired them, Odessa had to try to seem desirable and even alluring to me, and yet, in view of her history, not *too* experienced in love and above all neither wanton nor indifferent. If her wedding night with Sepulvida weighed on my mind, it must, I thought, loom like a glacier in hers. It was impossible not to imagine it. I particularly dreaded reenacting the stage when Sepulvida had discovered her absence of virginity. The mechanics of intercourse being what they were, however, I could scarcely hope to avoid it.

I sat on the bed beside her, taking care to manifest no signs of haste, and inquired about her family and her life since we parted. I rambled on about the events in Naphtali that had kept me occupied since our last meeting and described the preparations I had made for our wedding night—the costly draperies and rugs, the flowers and scented herbs arranged around the room. Color came and went from her face as we talked. She undid her blouse slowly, eyes averted, as I talked of these inconsequential things and tried to seem casual. *Should I speak of my previous experience with Miriam and Vitoria, to distract from hers, I wondered? Should I shower this relative stranger with endearments or passionate vows? Neither course seemed appropriate.*

In a swift, decisive gesture Odessa slipped her open blouse backward and then pulled the sleeves off behind her back. The movement revealed her full breasts and lovely skin; her neck, as she held her face in profile and partly averted from me, was long and graceful.

Beautiful, I said to myself.

She rose off the bed, half-naked and very visible in the glow of the candles. She put her hands on the belt at her waist and then paused. "Is the light necessary?" Odessa was wise. In the darkness, everything went more smoothly. We lost our self-consciousness and learned, by stages, to explore each other, cautiously at first and then eagerly, and things proceeded to a consummation that even Laban might have approved. We did not relinquish our embrace until we had reached a second, in which I felt far more confident that I was giving as well as receiving pleasure. Then we truly relaxed and lay in each other's arms and talked of the events that had brought us to this night and of our hopes for the future. I went to sleep well contented, with my wife's head resting on my arm. In the gray light of dawn we both awoke and reached for one another.

The following day's activities passed in a blur of inattention, as both of us were eager for a return of night and our privacy together. This time, Odessa was not shy of the light, and in the warm candle glow she let me have full sight of her beauty. I was surprised by her loveliness. She possessed a graceful and voluptuous figure largely concealed by her Canadian mode of dress. Besides the long neck and full breasts I had glimpsed the previous night, I found she had a delightfully sculpted belly and lovely female hips above her long legs. She was well muscled from vigorous activity as a child, but feminine and refined. Best of all, Odessa possessed a delicate, almost jewel-like perfection in her most intimate details that fascinated and aroused me.

Her curiosity about me was as great as mine of her, and she examined me in turn with a tender thoroughness, showering me with kisses and planting her lips on all my scars and imperfections, as if to heal and simultaneously take possession of them. She was particularly solicitous of my recently healed chest wound, lamenting both the harm that was done and the greater harm that was intended. "So near your heart!" she exclaimed softly. "It is a miracle I have this time with you."

With undisguised and, I believe, unfeigned enthusiasm, she explored me minutely, not just with her eyes but by touch and taste and scent. "Talk to me," she pleaded, taking me in her mouth. "Let me hear your voice." I responded with all the endearments and words of encouragement I knew, until I was almost delirious with pleasure.

"You two seem to be getting along," Laban commented as we took a light meal in a meadow above Pateros. I had taken our party on a ride to explore the neighborhood of this northern outpost. The ridge gave us a fine view of the Jordan and its canyon.

"Yes, we are," I said. "In fact, I can scarcely believe it. We get along perfectly."

"Good. It's well that you do. As you will learn," her father warned, "Odessa has opinions. I hope you two get along half as well when you get to the talking stage."

"I am content if we take some time getting to that stage." Laban and Shaiym smiled back at me, and I found myself laughing easily with them. "All this feels very strange," I said. "Very good, but unfamiliar."

Odessa's friends asked if we would share our joke, and I replied, "No joke, ladies. I was just describing how pleased I am to find myself married to the best of women. Surely the singers will make songs of us when they hear of our happiness!"

"The singers had better not hear too much about our happiness!" Odessa said sternly.

As the party moved on, admiring the sights, I kissed her on the cheek and said, "You delight me."

We spent the better part of a week getting to know one another and becoming acquainted with each other's friends. I had brought Major Jared along with several of the younger officers, all of them handsome and courteous, and they made a favorable impression. Odessa decided to bring only her brother and two of her friends to Naphtali, confident that she would be comfortable in her new circumstances. Laban also seemed content with the prospects for his daughter's happiness and talked to me endlessly of his plans to make over his capital, Omak Town. I promised to send him architects as soon as we returned to Hammoth-Wenatchee.

Our party set sail for Naphtali in one of the larger merchant carracks—a richly ornamented vessel that boasted two compartments below decks. Odessa's female friends occupied one and Odessa and I the other. The weather was pleasant and the scenery fine, but I was unused to idleness and the light banter appropriate to our long days under the ship's bright awning. Fortunately, Odessa seemed to feel the same as I, and whenever conversation lagged or she sensed I was bored, she would squeeze my hand and lead the way to our compartment. Odessa was forthright and earnest about her desires, and she never failed to leave me astonished and breathless.

Once, returning to the deck after an afternoon of love making, her friends teased us, asking if we had felt the sudden storm that had set the boat to rocking. "And not a cloud was in the sky when it struck!"

Odessa returned their jests with a smile. "Indeed, I did feel it," she admitted when they pressed the joke. "And I hope we shall have another like it soon." Our companions had taken to raising a bright-colored banner on the mast each time we retired below deck, and the whistles and cheers we heard from the soldiers on the other boats signaled that the banner was being lowered at the end of our embraces.

We anchored each night in sheltered places—once in the lee of an island. The night was warm, so Odessa and I came out on deck to catch a breeze. Her brother Shaiym and Major Jared had the watch, so we chatted with them and gazed at the star road wheeling overhead. The four of us were becoming friends. Watch fires in the fleet encircled us protectively, but also served to remind me of the war waiting for me. As my thoughts turned to the coming campaign, Shaiym suddenly slipped off his outer garments and dropped over the side. Alarmed, I leapt for the rail, but Odessa restrained me. "Don't you swim?" she asked.

"Never willingly!" I replied. *This is the Jordan, I thought. No one chances the Jordan who does not have to.*

"It's cold," Shaiym said, sputtering, "but it's not deep here. Look, it's barely up to my chin."

Major Jared could not resist the challenge and was overboard in a moment. The noise of their splashing brought Odessa's friends up on deck, and they too seemed eager to try the water. They looked to Odessa as if for permission, and then dropped the nightclothes in which they had bundled themselves. Clad in flimsy undergarments barely consistent with modesty, they stood at the bow and laughed at the antics of Jared and Shaiym. "Are you going in?" they asked, but did not wait for a reply.

"*Are* we going in?" Odessa asked.

The memory of my first plunge into the depths of the Jordan was vivid in my mind – so vivid it made me shiver. Odessa leaned forward and gave me a long kiss, and I shivered again, of a different cause. "Yes," I said, feeling my hair stand on end and my heart pound.

"Let's try the water."

We shed our clothes and jumped in together. The water was a shock, and I had a moment of terror. Finding the channel bottom under my feet, I moved determinedly toward the island until I could stand comfortably with my neck out of water. Odessa, who was apparently an experienced swimmer, never let go of me. So strange were the myriad sensations I felt that I was hardly aware of the others, who were splashing in the shallows nearer the island.

As I savored the novelty of being in the water intentionally, Odessa snuggled close against me. In the cold current of the Jordan, I felt the warmth of her breasts and legs pressing against me, as if she were trying to mold her body to mine. She twined her arms around my neck and kissed me lightly on the lips. She looked at me in the moonlight and then gave me a long, deep kiss and encircled me with one thigh and then the other, straddling me at the waist. We balanced thus in the water, my hands cupping her buttocks and rocking her against me as I tasted her endless kisses. She pressed herself harder against me, searching me with her tongue and breasts and pelvis. The sensations aroused such desire in me that I parted her flimsy undergarments as if they were paper. Her desire was a match for my own. Without taking her arms from my neck or drawing away from our kiss, she found me swiftly, surely, with her body. I rocked her slowly in the current, savoring the exquisite friction of her upon me, and then we began to move more and more fiercely. Encompassed in the Jordan and entwined almost weightlessly in each other, I felt as if we might both dissolve and melt into each other's bodies. My release came with a shudder from deep within me.

"Shhhh," she said, touching my lips with her wet fingers. Apparently I had cried out. She kissed me lightly until the others had gone back to their play and ignored us. "You weren't thinking how I was going to get back on the boat, were you, darling?"

It took us a while to find her undergarment, and by then I was cold. Back on deck, we wrapped ourselves in blankets and warmed ourselves by a fire. My heart was too full to speak much. I noted that Shaiym and Jared seemed to have gotten themselves sweethearts.

In the middle of the night I found myself sitting up in bed, panting. Odessa, who had been awakened by my abrupt movement, sat up beside me. "I nearly drowned in the Jordan once," I said, trying to explain. "That moment came back to me." She rubbed the back of my neck and coaxed me to tell the story. She listened patiently, and afterwards I was glad to fall asleep in her arms.

II

After five leisurely days on the Jordan, we hauled in sight of Hammoth-Wenatchee. On the docks and the stairway was a crowd of people, women and children, people of all ages, weeping and distraught, being herded by angry, impatient soldiers. As we approached, we could see shackles on the men, and I understood what was happening. I saw a young wife and an old woman pleading with one of my soldiers. A small boy held tight to his mother's hand. The soldier was not listening.

"Not the welcome to Naphtali that I had envisioned for you," I said to Odessa. I signaled the captain of the vessel to pull off; we would disembark at a later and more propitious time. "These are the people who rose against me, the nobles of Naphtali," I said. "They are being sent into exile."

"And their families?"

"Yes, their families too. They are bound for the metal recovery mines in Old Spokane."

"And they—they are all Messiahists?"

Her question caused me acute discomfort. "Their crime was rebellion," I insisted. "In many cases, they have committed murder."

Odessa assured me that she had not asked the question to rebuke me. "My father told me about the rising—and how you would have to deal with the rebels harshly. He said the rising was a conspiracy by nobles who were also Messiahists, as you call them."

"Their exile is temporary, but, to be candid, it is harsh enough. We are engaged in a larger war, and it is that necessity that drives me."

"I would like to know more about the religious disputes in your country," she said.

We have arrived at the talking stage, I noted to myself.

We delayed our arrival by a day, until the exiles could be shipped northwards. The heat of our anchorage, plus the sights that Odessa had unfortunately seen, considerably depressed our spirits. That night we lay side by side but discretely apart. Images of the deportation troubled my sleep, and Odessa put her hand on my arm to comfort me. "I am your most devoted follower," she whispered. "They should not have conspired to murder you. I have no pity for them."

In the morning we encountered a proper welcome, with the docks cleared and swept and a military band playing a lively tune. We disembarked and were greeted by Captain Amasa, Warden of the Citadel, and his wife Carmina, followed by all the dignitaries of Naphtali. From the city wall, we watched my Great Jordan Herons and the reconstituted Northern Lights Guards pass in review. When the cavalry passed, I heard Shaiym say to his sister as he pointed at the Esdralon Guards, "Those are the soldiers who captured us—the ragged ones. And there is the Devil himself – Moriah!"

At the banquet in her honor that evening, Odessa rose and thanked the assembled guests in our own language. I realized with pleasure that she had been practicing for such an event for some time. Her accent was charming and she made a favorable impression. We spent our first night in the apartment in the citadel, and early next morning we rode out to see the estate I had taken as my own. Some of the outbuildings were still being repaired, but the barley and wheat were up and the irrigated crops were coming along. The estate offered several fine views of the countryside and of picturesque ruins from Ancient times. We had orchards well away from the house and a fine vineyard with several varieties of grapes. Huerta's former estate also had a small formal garden with roses and peonies and other flowers unfamiliar to me, and an herb garden near the kitchen. Odessa expressed her delight with these features, which were almost unknown in her country, and I saw them afresh through her eyes. There was much to do in furnishing a home, and I left it to her and Carmina to decide what should be done.

I had much business to attend to and scarcely saw Odessa over the next few days. She met me in the hall as I returned, late in the evening, and greeted me with a wifely kiss on the cheek. "No doubt you chafe here by yourself," I said, "because I have so little time to be with you."

"Not at all," she said. "I have many things to do at the moment myself." I noted she held a copy of the *Sayings of St. Supplicee* at her side. "If, however, *after* I have proven capable of assisting you and you still exclude me from serious business, that will be another matter. But I begin to see the responsibilities you carry. I will help if you let me."

Israelite wives do not ordinarily assist in their husbands' affairs, but I had learned something of expectations and how easily they are disappointed. I inspected the changes she had made in the house and admired the bouquets of flowers she had arranged. She learned very quickly—large things as well as small. We sat down to a meal of her own making, without servants to wait on us. Canadian fare is very simple compared to Israel's, but my own taste in food was not elaborate. I enjoyed her first attempt immensely. Afterwards we bathed together.

"I believe this will be my favorite Israelite custom," she said smiling.

We dined frequently with Amasa and Carmina and with guests of their inviting, and Odessa absorbed very quickly the nuances of Israelite social customs. She enjoyed our highly spiced dishes and was eager to learn what herbs released which flavors and how my favorite dishes were made. At the same time, she made rapid progress in our language. Like Carmina, Odessa took part in all topics of conversation, without any sense of male privileges or Israelite rules of propriety. I asked my friends not to correct her in this, saying it was better for Israel to adopt her ways rather than impose ours on her. Somehow, in her father's rugged land, Odessa had acquired an education and was able to speak sensibly on a wide variety of topics.

Opinion of Odessa among the general public seemed to be favorable. She was credited with bringing an end to the Canadian war, and her efforts to learn our customs won favor. Thus, though foreign, she was an attractive novelty. Within my circle of friends, Odessa was received with enthusiasm. Carmina was at first well disposed toward her merely because of what she had suffered, but on further acquaintance the two became friends on their own terms. Burgos was a little alarmed at Odessa's beauty, but in a short time he was smitten by her, as were all my male friends.

I took Odessa unannounced to the first meeting of my council of friends, now augmented by several members of Naphtali's Council of Elders. The group assisted me in staying abreast of intelligence and forming policy, so I had included as many points of view as I could identify. We met at Amasa's, where Carmina would be present. I introduced Odessa as a person knowledgeable of Canadian matters. After some initial reluctance and embarrassment, the conversation proceeded as usual. Odessa, in fact, was quite well informed about her father's situation and spoke articulately, with Amasa translating for her.

One of the merchants complimented me on solving the Canadian problem with this clever marriage, not realizing the subtle offense to Odessa. Carmina flushed angrily. I quickly answered that it was clever indeed, for I had combined an interest of state with my own desires. "Odessa is a loyal daughter of her people in this," I added, "for she seeks their interest. But she also shares with me a vision of a future in which our peoples will be one. Our union is an emblem of that future." Not everyone was enthusiastic about this vision of the future, but those who were not prudently held their tongues.

Afterwards Odessa shared with me what she had observed of the group. "The members from Naphtali are still in awe of you and your friends. They say little and try to reveal even less. Your friends worship you, except perhaps for Gill. Moriah is not your friend. As for the others, I sense that their loyalty is absolute. However, they feel free to disagree with you and challenge you. This is a good thing, but I don't quite understand how it can be."

"You notice a great deal!"

"In what exactly does your authority consist?" she asked. "They all acknowledge it. If I understood that, I could understand many other things."

"I don't know. I believe it must derive from my association with you." We laughed and embraced, and Odessa suggested it was time for a bath together.

III

Matild came to visit us in July, the season when cherries ripen. Laban had forbidden her to come earlier for reasons of state. With one daughter married to a foreigner, he had determined to reserve Matild for a Canadian husband. He feared that too much early exposure to Israel would turn her head away from her own people. Matild had missed her sister, however, and was persistent in her pleading. "Like water dripping on a stone!" Laban declared when he delivered her to us. We held a banquet in his honor, and Odessa, dressed elegantly in Israelite clothing, presided confidently as hostess. Laban was pleased and wistful and grew more garrulous as the banquet proceeded. Matild was all eyes and questions and enthusiasm for her sister.

"I thought women in your country are free to marry whomever they please," I said privately to Odessa. "How is that your father is making wedding plans for your sister?"

"My father is not the most tractable of men," she said. "We have a saying that it is best for the daughter and the father to agree on a match; it makes for peace in the family."

It was a time of plenty in Israel, but also of danger because of the ticks. We feasted on bright scarlet and golden and black-purple cherries as they came into season, each with its own intoxicating aroma and taste. We suffered cramps in our bellies for our excesses, too, but everyone seemed to think the feast of cherries worth the pain. It was high summer and life was good. Our servants pressed the juice for wine, which, given a quick fermentation, was Israel's traditional drink at the Feast of the In-Gathering. We boiled the pulp for jams and jellies. Sugar was very dear this season, as most of it came up-river from the beet fields of Judah. Our Canadian guests were impressed by the bounty on our tables. The gardens of Naphtali yield a great variety of foods and, this year at least, yielded them abundantly.

Matild was much taken with the sights and events of Naphtali, and I suspected her father was justified in fearing that she would acquire tastes that her homeland could not satisfy. In between the several harvests, there were feasts and celebrations, including traditional dramas enacted on the riverbank. I learned from my guests that I had neglected the music of my county, which was on display nightly both in the city and at private gatherings in the countryside. Matild quickly grew enamored with our songs and gave us no peace until I purchased a guitar for her and hired a musician to give her lessons.

One evening, the young man who gave her lessons brought some friends and gave us a concert. Moved by the rhythms and melodies of Israel, Odessa and her Canadian friends put on a display of their own people's mode of dancing—at least as women danced with each other. Israel's dances tend to be formal affairs, with male and female partners and much symmetrical and swirling movement. To be sure, Israelite women manage to flirt and men succeed in displaying their physiques, but our customs seemed tame and rigid compared to their free, unconstrained movements. The dancers faced each other in a small circle and moved as their feelings led them. Their rhythmic movements seemed expressive of women's lives and women's knowledge, deeply held. Matild danced with them and seemed precocious in these things as well as others. I felt jealous of their knowledge of themselves and of the cycles of earth singing through them.

In our quiet moments, Matild often expressed a youthful curiosity about religious matters in Israel. I inferred from her interest that our beliefs were a frequent topic of conversation in her father's house. Her questions related chiefly to our views of the afterlife, and since Old Believers have no expectation of such a thing, my answers always disappointed her. Once, however, she asked a question that stung me: "How can Israel call itself free when you can't have babies without permission?"

I mumbled something about the Reproduction Laws being an acknowledgement of necessity, but Matild was not satisfied. That evening Odessa resumed the discussion in the privacy of our bedroom. "You are very patient with my sister," she said. "Her curiosity is genuine, I'm sure, but Matild has a good deal to learn about tact."

When I assured her that I took no offense, she added, "If you don't mind, there are some questions I have been wanting to ask you as well. You can tell me at any time if I too need a lesson in tact. I have been reading your St. Supplicee," she said, "and I see much to ponder in his sayings. But I see nothing that would explain the bitterness of Israel's religious conflicts—especially your enmity with the group you call the Messiahists. How does your faith differ from that of your enemies? And how did this conflict come about?"

Odessa had no doubt perceived the similarities between her own beliefs and the Messiahists' and wanted to know if our hostility would extend to her faith. I explained that the chief issue that divided us was the Messiahist claim of supernatural revelation; in my view, all our difficulties proceeded from that pretense. In our philosophy, the truth of any claim had to be self-evident to all or it was not accepted. Among the Messiahists, however, individuals claimed to hear whispers of a god that others could not see, yet their word was taken as binding on *all* others, not just their co-religionists. I thought this very offensive—and even more dangerous. "Supposing their god does exist," I said, "how could one distinguish a genuine revelation from a lie told by someone conniving to get power? Or from the ravings of a madman?" For these reasons, I argued, Messiahist claims constituted a dangerous form of aggression—and a presumption deeply resented by non-believers. "If their god wishes to reveal his will to the world," I added, "why doesn't he do it publicly, in some unambiguous way? As it is, every claimed revelation empowers some new individual or group of clergy, and it always means strife for the nation."

"I understand your objections," Odessa conceded. "I see the possibilities of fraud and error at the heart of their faith, and I understand that their claims to revelation and absolute truth could be seen as threats." She hesitated as if weighing her next words carefully. "In our faith," she added, "we believe the revelations came once and for all in the distant past—in Ancient times, actually, when the Messiah lived on earth as a man. That is, revelation came to us in a public way. And because we accept that revelation as final, we do not credit any who claim revelations after that."

"That would protect you from the most unstable and unscrupulous people in your midst," I said. "But how do you know the Messiah actually taught the things you believe? Or that his teachings have not been distorted by others between his time and ours?" Canadians in recent times often learned to read and write from us, but they were not historically a literate people. "How could you know the truth of these matters without an unbroken written record?"

"I can't answer you," she said thoughtfully, "except to admit that you may be right."

Hearing Odessa's views was reassuring. I had feared that differences of opinion on this subject might divide us, but she seemed reasonable and open to other perspectives. I was beginning to feel immensely relieved, but Odessa was not done with her questions.

"I begin to think I understand the view of the world implicit in your faith—in the sayings of St. Supplicee," she said. "That is, I understand the world described in it. But what eludes me is what your faith offers the believer. Holding these beliefs, what do you have that you would not have without them?"

I was taken aback by her question. This was a criticism of our faith commonly leveled by the Messiahists. Odessa had come to it quickly. Either she had been prompted—but no. I began to see she had mind like Gill's, unfettered by the assumptions with which I had been raised. I replied that in the first place, we were not 'believers,' strictly speaking. "We accept nothing that cannot be proved or is not self-evident. Our creed thus grounds us solidly in reality, not illusions. What could be more valuable than that? It frees us from superstition to act in the world as it is. That is true freedom. That is why we Old Believers boast that we are free."

"Your Teacher is wise," she said. "But I believe that people need to believe in the essential benevolence of the world, and to feel that they can invoke powers able to protect them. A mother who sends her son to war says a prayer for his safety, as does a wife whose husband must leave her. We cry out in childbirth for God's assistance with a safe delivery, and even soldiers pray, facing death on the battlefield. This seems to me natural—or, at the very worst, harmless. For myself, when I pray, I acknowledge that I am small and nearly powerless and that there are powers that can harm or assist me. Even if I do not summon any of them on my behalf, I at least focus my own. And if God is present with me, does it matter whether I am weak or strong—or live or die?"

Odessa went to the heart of things; in addition to trying to understand the views of Old Believers, she was seeking a middle ground between us. Prayer was objectionable to us only because of the false belief it engendered that the course of events can change because of individual wishes. As she described it, prayer sounded much like meditation. I struggled to describe our view of meditation to her, but it is difficult to explain our traditions to outsiders. "Through meditation," I said, "we train our minds as an athlete develops his body. It allows us to avoid false hope and to deal with what is. Admittedly, deep meditation allows one to escape from pain for a time, but our Teacher insists that it is our duty to return and face things as they are."

"Seek your courage in yourself; find salvation in the world," Odessa said, aptly quoting St. Supplicee. "This seems to me a very admirable sentiment. But it also seems to imply that each of us is entirely alone in the world."

"You would have been Ebenezer's favorite pupil," I said, marveling at her. Her insights impressed me even more than her knowledge of the *Sayings*. This was no ordinary woman I had married. "If you were a boy and had attended the Refuge with us, Ebenezer would never have noticed me at all!"

"If I had been a boy? Husband, I have never wanted to be a boy – or a man. Let me teach you something about what it means to be a woman." She gave me a look that put aside all thought of sayings and doctrines for a time.

I was glad to exchange this discussion for her embrace, but Odessa had asked me a question I could not answer: how had such fatal discord arisen among our religious factions?

IV

"Is it war, then?" Odessa asked, all color drained from her face. She held the bed covers loosely about her. One breast was uncovered and her long hair was in disarray from sleep.

"Not yet," I said, re-reading the dispatches from Nisan Lot and Brother Peter. "Nevertheless, I am needed in Hazor. I'll have to leave immediately." I assured her that this errand was about a book that had been found, a relic of the Ancients, and involved no danger. I promised to return soon. I hurried south with the taste of her still in my mouth and her question ringing in my ears. *Why had Israel's religious quarrels turned into bloodshed? Why could we not accept our differences and live in peace?*

I took the huge but fragile codex in my hands. The cover was yellow and brittle and obviously of great antiquity. "Do you believe it is authentic?" I asked. "Can this be the actual Holy Book of the Ancients?" I looked around the solemn assembly for answers, but saw only troubled looks and doubt.

Brother Peter attempted to summon up an appearance of sagacity, but I realized he had no knowledge whatever of the religion of the Ancients. The book had been made known to us by an ignorant shepherd, a ragged, beggarly fellow who kept his flocks in the hills west of the Wayfarer's Refuge. He claimed he had found it in the ruins of the Refuge, but we had no means of verifying his story. I turned to Gill, whose religion claimed to trace its roots to the Dissolution and before.

"Many of the stories are familiar to us," he acknowledged, "in outline, if not in all details. It's possible it is authentic. I wouldn't stake my life on it."

I agreed with his estimate, though I had had only a day to peruse the book. "Somehow, this book – these stories and fragments of things – are not how I pictured them."

"Nor I," Gill said. "Some of these tales are tedious and impossible, and many long passages are—I don't know what. It contains an implausible mixture of things—*many* things. I don't know what to make of it."

That was the problem. There was no discernable unity in the book, no principle of selection that I could fathom in the materials. I had expected any relic of the Ancients to have something of the grand rationality of their roads and buildings, some mind-expanding abstraction such as was embodied in the very geometry of the Temples of Destruction. "It's as if something is missing," I said. I had also expected a holy book from the Ancients to be filled with the strange signs and symbols I had seen at the Refuge – signs that appeared to represent another language altogether, perhaps one not altogether human. Josephus claimed that this language, which none could unlock today, was the secret of the Ancients' power. This "Bible," as it was titled, had no trace of such language, and parts of it were disconcertingly similar to the texts of the Messiahists.

Gill read a section from the first book and noted that all the names were familiar to Israelite usage.

"It is a genuine book of the Ancients," I acknowledged; "I have no doubt of that. It is very old, and it has the mechanical writing we read about. No hand could trace so small a script – or so uniform. However, even if we concede that this is a book from the Ancients, we still cannot be sure what status it had or know precisely what meaning it held for them." That left the question of what to do with the book. I suggested that we establish an endowment at the College to ensure the study of this relic of the Ancients. The rest of the Council remained skeptical, and Brother Peter protested that the book should be destroyed. I reminded the group that news of the find was already abroad; it would only do us harm to hide it now. "We can establish a center here in Hazor and invite scholars from all over Israel to come and study the book. Brother Peter can supervise them at the College. Perhaps in time they may unlock its meaning for us."

"Each scholar will have a different view of its meaning," Burgos objected, "and out of each opinion a new school or sect will emerge to annoy us and disturb the peace!"

"And the Messiahists?" Brother Peter objected. "Shall we allow Messiahists to come and spy out our land and deceive us?" Nisan Lot and some members of Dan's Council appeared to share his concern.

"You think they do not deceive us now?" I said. "Do you believe they need additional eyes in Dan?"

"But the war. How can we—"

"How can we know the book is authentic and not a trick of the Messiahists?" Burgos asked. It was the question that troubled all of us.

"Let the scholars decide," I said.

Brother Peter pulled a long face. I suspected he was fearful of this project and was seeking excuses to avoid it. "Some say this is a dangerous book we have found, Excellency. A *very* dangerous book! If our ancestors went to such lengths to hide and suppress it," he warned, "no doubt they had good reason."

"Perhaps." I winced at his admission that Old Believers had hidden this book—whatever it was. *My people had lied to the world – lied to themselves – about the Ancients.* "This Bible may well be dangerous," I acknowledged, "but since it has come to light, we must see that the world has a chance to examine it. It is past time, in my view."

"And the Messiahists? You would willingly strengthen their hand against us?" Brother Peter was relentlessly opposed; I resolved to find another for the task of preserving and studying the book.

"Having examined it briefly," I said, "I would expect that some of the Messiahists' claims will be vindicated, and some not. It's possible that they may find the book more troublesome than we do." In truth, I suspected that openness in the matter would involve the least risk to our cause, but I did not intend to trust merely to luck. As the meeting adjourned, I suggested privately to Lot that he arrest the shepherd who had found the book. "We need to know exactly where it came from," I warned, "and learn if there are any more surprises lurking out there."

Miriam Lander smiled becomingly at me. She was dressed in rich fabrics in shades of scarlet and green and set off at her throat and wrists by silver and turquoise. Her eyes and hair shone with a luster brighter than her jewelry. She was gorgeously attired, alluring, and standing alone with me in the council chamber. "You look. . . older somehow," she said, examining me closely.

"Indeed, I suppose I am," I replied. She, on the contrary, seemed remarkably unchanged, as if time could not affect her. But I had experienced more in the Kuhlan lands than most men see in a lifetime. No doubt I must seem different to her. But she had seen me when I had first returned from exile. What was she getting at?

"I miss the boyish quality you used to have," Miriam said, her eyes warm and intriguing. She approached close enough that I was encompassed in the familiar scent of her perfume. "I expected marriage to soften you, Zaiyah," she added, affecting a frown. "Instead, you are lean and hard and—"

"I am here on a serious errand," I said. I was not anxious to offend her, but I had no intention of allowing her to re-establish our relationship on any sort of intimate basis. "I expected the Council of Elders to be here."

She stepped back from me as if scalded. "The Council was delayed. Nisan – the

Mayor himself – sent me ahead to meet with you."

"If he sent you, he must have had a purpose in mind."

As we regarded one another, her face, with her dark kohl-lined eyes and full red lips, hardened slowly into a mask. In it, I saw the undisputed head of Dan's intelligence. In spite of my knowledge of her, it was a revelation to me.

"You intend to challenge our policy," she said sharply. "You want Dan to adopt your own aggressive stance against the Messiahists, and that we will not do. Dan will defend itself at its own border, at the Manastash ridge. That is our decision and the terms on which our alliance must rest."

"And the Mayor asked you to tell me that?"

"He wanted to forewarn you, to avoid an unpleasant scene before the Council. I trust you will not embarrass yourself."

So those were the terms on which our relationship now stood. "I thank you for the warning," I said, "but I will speak what I have to say and let whoever is embarrassed be embarrassed. Sometimes it is the office of a friend to speak the truth." She sniffed at my words and her eyebrows rose like hunting hawks, challenging me. The Council came in shortly and Miriam Lander and I took seats opposite one another, not quite strangers but certainly not friends any longer. Love dies. *The world is a flame fed by human hearts.* Nisan Lot brought the Council to order.

"Friends," I said, "I am here because I have learned of your war policy, and I hope to persuade you to adopt a better one." When General Malachi objected, I silenced him with a question: "If *I* know about your policy, do you imagine that the Messiahists *do not*?" The General scowled and cast his eyes around the room, wondering how I had learned of the secret deliberations of Dan's Council.

"Dan plans to remain passively on defense in the coming campaign. You will stand behind your ridge and defy the Messiahists, but you will not venture out to strike them." I paused, but no one disputed my summary of their policy. "This is folly! If you announce in advance you will not cross the Manastash ridge, you give away an enormous advantage. Your policy is a gift to the enemy." I reminded them that Bishop Bon had claimed that the Third Coming was imminent—but only if Israel had submitted to the church by the end of the year. "Does anyone doubt that the Messiahists will attack the areas of Israel not under their control? When that day comes, their zeal will encompass all of us. Whether they strike south in their initial attack, or northward into Dan, they must conquer all of Israel for the Judgment to come. That is what they believe, and the churchmen have a reputation of acting on their beliefs. If your policy prevails, you may succeed in deflecting the first blow toward Judah. But if Judah falls, as seems likely, the second blow will be aimed at Dan. Then where will you turn for help? You plan to sacrifice Asher as well as Judah, but I promise you, if you stand by and let Asher perish, then you must expect consequences from me as well as from our enemies. Understand, I will assist my countrymen any way I can – at any cost to this alliance!"

"What would you have us do?" The question was not from General Malachi, but from a new member of the Council.

"Uncertainty is better than a poor plan that your enemy knows. At the least postpone the decision of how you will respond till the time comes. Then the Messiahists will not be able to predict your actions. But if they know you will not come out of your valley fortress, they will turn all of their strength against the south. Can you not see this yourselves?"

I left uncertain whether I had made any impression at all, but I was determined to resist their view; Dan's policy was not only craven but probably suicidal as well.

The next day Nissan Lot took me aside. "I think you have the decision from the Council that you sought," he said ruefully. "The Council members are entirely uncertain and have no plan at all!"

"Good," I said. "I wonder how long it will be before the Messiahists know of it."

"You are not very complimentary to our intelligence service, and it is noted in some quarters."

"Good!" I thought to myself.

Lot invited me to share some wine, and soon we were on easier terms. "I expected you to make a different argument before the Council," he said. "It makes me curious why you did not play a certain card in our game last night."

"You mean the Sevfolk?" Since I returned Jezreel to the Sevfolk, this clan, formerly the poorest of Dan, had a new source of wealth, and they had tied themselves closely to the river trade. In addition, they had attached themselves to me personally, as if I were a good luck charm. The Mayor was evidently not sure of their allegiance.

"The Sevfolk are giddy with success right now," I said. "In time, they will remember their kin and where their real interests lie." His expression told me he was not so certain. "The cornerstone of my policy is my alliance with Dan," I assured him. "As long as you are forthright with me, you may depend on it remaining my first consideration."

Lot relaxed visibly, and we clinked goblets and toasted each other's health. "I asked," he said, "because you do not seem yourself lately. Since you came to Dan, you seem troubled. Even deeply troubled." He took a sip from his cup. "I have heard your recent marriage is a happy one." He was fishing for an explanation.

"It is," I assured him. "I am unhappy to be apart from her."

"And I sense that between you and Miriam Lander there is"—he paused, looking for a discrete word—"closure."

I nodded.

"So, may I intrude into your private thoughts? Allies should know—"

"It is the Bible," I admitted. "The Holy Book of the Ancients."

"You are troubled by this book? Why? It is a book belonging to the past; it means nothing to us."

"It means a great deal. If it is truly the lost Holy Book of the Ancients, hidden all this time in the library of the Wayfarers Refuge, then it means the Messiahists tell the truth about one thing, at least. The Ancients' religion was suppressed after the Dissolution. And it was suppressed by Old Believers, by *our* forebears and co-religionists."

"So, then?"

"I am dismayed that the Messiahists are correct about anything!"

"Because you fear they may be correct in other things?"

"Yes. *Other* things. Not all things. I am certain of that."

"But what else? I saw you blanch yesterday when you held the book."

"It was the maps I looked at. Did you see the maps?"

"Not really. I glanced at them. They are of unknown places."

"They are maps of *Israel*!" I exclaimed. *"Israel!* Only it is not Israel that is portrayed. The names—some of them – are the same. But the land, the configuration of mountains and rivers, are nothing like our land."

"The land can change in a thousand years," he said. "Names and cities move about. We live among ruins." Lot crossed his arms, hiding his hands in his long sleeves. He was a not a man to be moved by religious questions.

"Nothing could change so much as this," I explained as calmly as I could. "On these maps, there is a sea to the west, not a mountain range." I searched for a way to convey to him what I saw, for I had not put my thoughts into words before. "*That* Israel, the Israel of the Ancients' Holy Book, is not our land, I tell you."

He stared at me uncomprehending, until I was almost frantic to make him understand.

"We are not – *that* Israel. We are—*I don't know what we are!* It's clear from the maps that the Israel of the Ancients was another place, another people. We are not *Israel*!"

V

I returned from Dan burdened with this knowledge and longing, beyond all things, to see Odessa. I hurried through some business at Headquarters and rode hard to the estate. I threw the horse's reins to a servant and strode into the house eager for the sight of her. The house was empty. I searched the garden and grounds and was heading toward the outbuildings when I realized her bodyguard was absent. "Elihu! Morales!" I cried, seized with a sudden dread. Elihu and half a dozen of our guards appeared from the barracks, looking shamefaced. "Where is Odessa?" I demanded, fearing some disaster.

"She is—she is not here, my lord General."

"Not here? You mean to say she has *gone*? *Where* has she gone, and *why*?" They were chagrined and fearful of my anger, but I sensed no grief or horror in their reluctance to speak. I tried to modify my tone to get an explanation out of them. "Elihu, you are chief of the guard. Tell me what happened and be quick about it."

"My lord General," he said, "I told her it would not do, that it was not done, but she would have her own way. She commanded us –"

"Morales, tell me what happened."

"She left, my lord, with a group of her countrymen. Canadians, about a dozen of them. They left four days ago."

It was the impropriety of Odessa's behavior that throttled them into silence. They were indignant for my sake, but dreaded to speak a word of criticism of her before me. "Was her brother with her?" I asked. Hearing an affirmative answer, I said, "Well, then, there is nothing to worry about. She merely exchanged one group of guards for another. You men have not been derelict." They were visibly relieved at my words. I had them stand at ease. "You were right to obey her. She is a free woman, here among us of her own will, and we are still learning each other's ways." *I wondered if Elihu had really had the nerve to tell Odessa that Israelite wives do not go galloping off on their own with a group of men. I had my doubts that he had.*

I spent an uneasy day supervising work on the estate and then rode back to Hammoth-Wenatchee in the evening. Not wanting to spend a night alone in either of our beds, I spent most of the night catching up on reports and correspondence. In the morning, a messenger came from the estate, saying that Odessa had returned. I sent a brief reply and bathed and rode to the estate at a deliberate pace, rebuking myself at every step. The faith and reputation of the Old Believers had just been undermined by the discovery of the Ancient's Holy Book, and I was in a sulk because of my foreign wife's impropriety!

But it was not the impropriety that bothered me. No point in pretending it was.

Odessa was all smiles and warmth when she greeted me. She looked particularly splendid in her Canadian blouse and leather trousers, and my stomach churned to see her so lovely. We kissed, formally. For the life of me, I could not but be reserved and cold, although I willed myself to be otherwise. She noticed my manner, but made no mention of it. "We were just about to have breakfast," she announced.

Shaiym rose to greet me and I did a better job of affecting cheerfulness with him. Our bodyguards were sulking worse than I, so I dismissed them, wanting to have some privacy. While I ate my eggs and toasted bread and conversed with her brother, Odessa stood behind my chair like a good Israelite wife of days gone by. I wondered at this charade, as Odessa did not admire the customs of Israel as they related to women and marriage. For his part, Shaiym seemed distracted; he pushed his food around the plate but ate little.

"While you were in Dan," Shaiym said, "I took a party of our friends north, to the place where Orden Macuntur and the others died." Both of us remembered the circumstances of his friends' deaths. A shadow of that knowledge passed over his face, but only a shadow. "I wanted to say farewell and attend to the rites. It was time. You were engaged with your duties, so I asked Odessa to come along. She was – " he hesitated and then plunged onward," – they were old friends too, Macuntur and her."

"Yes," Odessa said, "I wanted to come. It was time I said good-by."

"You still miss him, then?" *I could have bitten my tongue off for asking that question. But the thought of Messiahist rites and the bleached bones of her lover had brought my stomach into my throat.*

"He was a friend to me from childhood upwards—and much more for a time, as you know. But all that ended before his death, and before I met you."

I turned to Shaiym and asked about the journey and his health and a dozen trivial matters, glad to have a plain male face to look at and things to say to him and ask about. I described briefly the business that had taken me to Dan—the discovery of the Ancients' Holy Book and the embarrassment it would cause Old Believers. As I tried to describe the uncertain status of the book, my voice trailed off into silence.

"Husband," Odessa said, putting her hands on my shoulders, "I am content. We have different customs, you and I, and often it is hard to read the meaning of each other's actions. I find I have shocked Elihu and our bodyguard—and disappointed you. But understand that I am content; I miss no one."

"Truly, your customs are a mystery," her brother said, anxious to take her part. "I hardly know how to eat in company, your manners are so formal. I'm half afraid to—"

I turned to Odessa and took her hand. Her eyes widened in surprise as I pulled her down on my lap. "Perhaps we Israelites could learn new ways," I said. I kissed her and offered her a bite of bread and egg. She looked at me quizzically while I wiped her lips with my napkin. "Our customs are a barrier," I admitted. "They are like the languages we both must learn to speak. We often stumble and make mistakes, however well we intend. But I'll tell you a stranger thing: you and I have been together two months, and yet when I was away from you for only a few days, I could hardly form a sensible thought on any subject other than yourself. I spent the time miserably unhappy and longing to see you. When I returned and you were gone, I was desolate. I was overwhelmed with anxiety—even grief. And now here you are, sitting on my lap."

"Yes, husband. Here I am." She curled her arm around my neck and pressed her forehead against mine. *As I held her, I thought how little one moment was like another, and how fragile are the threads that hold the moments of a life together.*

I did my best to put aside my fears and learn to know and appreciate this woman I had married. Odessa shared many of her memories and childhood hopes with me. She described how she had visited Israelite settlements with her father as a child and acquired a vision of a more ordered and civilized life than her own people had attained. Her father had hired a tutor from whom she had acquired the rudiments of our history and language. Though her tutor was not proficient in our tongue, she had learned to read it perfectly and had an extensive vocabulary, even though her circumstances had given her little opportunity to speak it. The turbulence of Canadian politics and perpetual fighting among the clans kept the family on the move and often in want. The MaGowans' struggle to control Omak Town and to become preeminent in the fur trade had involved a good deal of bloodshed. In the last clan war, she had lost her mother and an elder brother.

"Ah – the loss of your mother – that must have been hard!" I felt keenly the inadequacy of my words; I hoped she would intuit all that I meant.

"Yes, it was," she replied. "My mother's death was needless—absolutely needless! And so unutterably cruel. It did nothing to advance the cause of the murderers, and in fact my father hunted them down in the end. So her death was meaningless – as was the revenge exacted for it. You men and your wars! But I knew as a child what agonies my mother had suffered. I imagined them very thoroughly. So I know that in my day and night with Sepulvida, I experienced the merest hint of what she suffered." She paused as if remembering, and I was amazed at the serenity in her face. "For that, among many other reasons," she added, "I have often been drawn to the People's ways, and I admire their wisdom in leaving matters of war and peace in the hands of women. But I also find their customs repugnant. Compassion is not much honored among them, though it is central to our faith—and fundamental to my own life."

I had also sensed something deeply alien in the People's ways; perhaps Odessa had just articulated it. But I was not yet anxious to have a conversation about the Kuhlans with her.

"After my mother's death," she continued, "I resolved to spend my life trying to lift my people above such brutality. To find a better way. I looked to Israel for alternatives."

"Israel has had its great days of peace and order," I said. "But sadly, the Israel of our day is no shining example." *I had spoken of "Israel" without thinking. Certain habits of mind run deep – none deeper than one's sense of self.* "We must disappoint you badly."

"True," she said, "Israel has disappointed me—particularly during the years that Sepulvida preyed on us. For a time, I lost hope that things could ever change for the better."

I inferred—though she was silent on the subject – that this period was when Orden Macuntur had entered her life.

"It was foolish of me to marry Sepulvida knowing what I knew of him – even to try to save my people from war. Very foolish! You may sense in that decision some of my desperation to break out of the familiar prospects of my life." As I marveled at the distance from which she could view her most painful disappointments, she suddenly smiled. "Be assured I am not disappointed by the *second* Israelite I married!"

At the moment I could hardly think of myself as an Israelite or endure the name—knowing that the same mendacity that I despised in Messiahist doctrine lay at the heart of my own tradition. *Israel is not Israel, I acknowledged bitterly to myself. Still, there was no point in inflicting this burden on Odessa.*

"I deeply regret the disappointment I must have caused you," I said. "I see now that when your father told you I was betrothed to someone else, the news must have dashed your hopes for your people." *There was more to say, but I could not speak it.*

"True, I was discouraged. And not just for my people's sake. But I determined not to grieve for someone I had never met." She looked at me brightly, as if all this was ancient history. "Yet I did grieve. I needed badly to throw myself into some project or cause. And that is when Sepulvida's marriage offer arrived."

"Odessa, I'm sorry for that. The timing of my betrothal was a disaster in every way – and one of my life's most unhappy chances!" *But it was not just chance that kept us apart. To serve my own ends, I had been willing to position Supulvida on the board so that he might take her like a pawn; I thought nothing of making a bride of her while intending to make her a widow soon after.* "If only I had known you sooner," I said lamely.

"No one is to blame," she said, "and eventually it all worked out." She ran her fingers through my hair. "My darling Josiah," she said seriously, "I have loved you for a long time. Do you know that? From before I ever met you. But you had no inkling that I existed."

I kissed her scarred cheek and inhaled the scent of her hair. "Odessa, you have carried an ideal of a man who was the solution to your people's problems—and a figure of your dreams. Those are powerful emotions, and I respect them, but let's not speak of love."

"Why not speak of love?" she insisted gently. "I have loved you forever, Josiah ben Haggadah."

What kind of man could live up to the ideals of a woman like her, I asked myself. I knew I could not! These hopes had sustained her through times that lacked any hint of fulfillment or other solace, particularly in the period after her mother died. I dreaded to be measured by them. "Odessa," I said, "I am not the solution to your people's problems any more than I am the savior of Israel."

She patted my arm affectionately and did not dispute my point. "I think I am able to distinguish between those hopes of mine and the man I married," she said.

"Well you may say," I replied, "but your brother told me what a fool you thought I was the first time you saw me. And the stories circulating about me portrayed me as a monster."

"True," she said smiling. "But all the stories about you fascinated me, good or bad. I was drawn to you regardless. I suppose the worst accounts lent you an aura of danger. Do you doubt that women find that attractive? I felt a sense of kinship with you, too – with the person I glimpsed behind the stories. Your determination to serve your people shone in all of them—and even in your exile from Israel, you cast the shadow of a man fated to do great things. Oh yes, try to deny it!" She teased me gently about some of the stories and then added: "I understand why your enemies revile you, but you are not the least part a monster, my love."

I kissed her again, far less certain than she what I was and was not. "Yours is a loyal wife's view, I'm afraid. Stories tend to cast a rose-colored glow over things. The truth has a way of disappointing."

"In fact, the stories about you contained hints of a certain irresistible quality," she insisted playfully. "Your attachments to lost or improbable causes—or to *women* who could only mean trouble for you – recur in all the tales. Yes, that quality fairly intoxicated me long before I knew you. Josiah, you must accept that you are a deeply romantic figure, one that appeals irresistibly to women. To this woman, at least!"

"But you see now that I am not this figure, but just an ordinary man."

"Do I?"

Touched by her generous spirit, I shared with Odessa many of the experiences of my own life, so that our time together flew by—I must say very happily. It's not that we were perfectly candid. Both of us withheld some aspects of our pasts, and we respected each other's reticences. But each unfolding confidence deepened the bond of trust between us. What most amazed me in Odessa was her unfeigned desire to know me and assist and sustain me in every way possible. The knowledge that this woman, this wife-stranger of mine, for reasons mysterious to me, seemed eager to support me unreservedly moved me deeply. That her feelings seemed also to mirror exactly my own for her seemed nothing short of miraculous. We seemed very much alike; so much so that I could scarcely credit the degree of similarity. But truth to say, in the midst of bliss I rebuked myself many times for naivete. No point, I told myself, in building expectations that are bound to be disappointed. And I chided myself for desiring the unreserved commitment that only a mother can give a child. *You are not a child, I reminded myself, and your mother is lost, and you will not find her here or anywhere. Marriage is another thing altogether, and it comes always with reservations.*

Nevertheless, the serene days and nights of August went by like the blurred movement of a shuttle, so rapidly that I dreaded every sunrise and each little parting it brought. September came, and with it preparations for the Feast of the In-Gathering. I renewed the tradition of fall games in connection with the feast, largely to please Odessa and to show her the high minded and noble side of our nation. Young men threw themselves into the games and won glory for themselves, while distinguished elderly men awarded the prizes and extolled the value of excellence in all things. Our best efforts, they recited, lead on to knowledge of the Way. It was a new experience for me to remain a spectator, but I found a pleasure in watching and appreciating the achievements of others that I had not known before.

We lit the fires under the Harvest Men and the music and dancing proceeded joyously in the firelight. Odessa clapped her hands and exclaimed, "Oh, I wish Matild could see this!" Later she asked me, "Why aren't there women's events in the games? I don't believe your St. Supplicee excludes us from the pursuit of excellence."

"Good point," I admitted, wondering if I dared tamper with the traditions for her sake.

"What is it, darling?" Odessa asked me as the games concluded. She sensed that, in the midst of joy, I also played unwilling host to an assortment of other feelings. She pressed me for an explanation, but I had only the unsettling sensation that my life was pouring out like sand through an hourglass. I woke again in the night, wondering what was troubling me. When I saw Amasa the next day, I saw the same strained look in his eyes. He gave me the answer to my question before I asked it.

"It cannot be much longer, my friend," he declared. "It must be any day now."

Chapter 17: Sow the Wind

I

"So this is it!" I said, crushing the dispatch in my fist. My comrades understood the news as well as I. I searched their faces, but saw only resolution. I was grateful that word had come in this public way, in the midst of business at Headquarters. I could deal with it more easily as a public crisis. "Apparently," I announced, "Bishop Bon has claimed so often that Israel will be in the Messiahist fold by year's end that he has come to believe his own lie. But we will make him eat his words!"

The churchmen had waited to strike until after the Feast of the In-Gathering and then had overrun my defenseless homeland, their granary – the better, I presumed, to seize the harvest. They had occupied Asher with home guards only, which meant that the disposition of the hard core of their forces, and thus their larger intentions, remained concealed. Would they strike north at Dan, or move to crush Judah in the opening phase of their campaign?

"So, it begins," Burgos remarked grimly. "Given its timing, the chronicles will likely remember this as the War of the In-Gathering."

"Let's just hope they don't call it Judgment Day!" Gill remarked. I would have liked to know the thoughts behind his comment, but Gill stared gloomily at the table and said nothing further.

My comrades and I each had a task to perform and we parted soon after. I had long dreaded this moment. Still, my first thought was gratitude that the Messiahists had delayed so long, giving me extra time with Odessa.

I took a painful leave of Odessa, grateful for her understanding of events and my role in them. She and I yoked together easily and with ever increasing affection. For her sake, I left the Northern Lights Guards in Naphtali as a reserve—just in case restive Canadian clans chose this moment to rise against Laban. In any event, my Herons were far better trained and quicker on the march. I put the Great Jordan and Esdralon Guards in motion and quickly deployed my thousand infantry and four hundred cavalry into Dan.

As soon as we arrived in Hazor, however, the speed and sureness of our movements faltered. Dan's Council remained uncertain what to do. As I feared, most of the Elders had no stomach to venture south of the Manastash Ridge. General Malachi championed this purely defensive posture with great passion and conviction. I kept my composure as best I could, but it pained me to have to wait passively while the enemy despoiled my homeland. Refugees reported that the Messiahists had identified which of my countrymen were Old Believers, and these families were subjected to murder and rapine and novel forms of torture in addition to losing their crops. I pressed for an immediate offensive with a unified command under my leadership. The latter might be an irritant to Danite pride, but it was essential for victory.

"This could be a trap, you know," Nisan Lot warned. "The Messiahists have not yet committed their strength, so they may intend to lure you within striking range of their main forces."

This was not a far-fetched idea. My units were formidable but small, and Asher was practically the doorstep of Manasseh. Lot's reasoning compelled me to wait until we had a clearer picture. *He who defends everything defends nothing.* Meanwhile, my countrymen suffered agonies.

Without consulting Lot, I stirred up the Sevfolk to raid Ephraim. They brought back little information, and nothing to suggest that the Messiahist campaign was predicated on my actions. All the evidence suggested that the timing and direction of their campaign were governed solely by the approach of Judgment Day. To them, one opponent was like another. Finally, in the first week of October, we had word from Judah that the main Messiahist army – seven legions and their regular cavalry – had taken the field against them. All the most feared units had been identified. Their plan had come clear: the first strike would be southward.

To my dismay, the Council of Dan appeared relieved at this news and remained indisposed to act. I made an angry plea that we coordinate our efforts with Judah and not leave them in the lurch. "Don't expect the Messiahists to spare you because they have made Judah their first target!" I warned them. "Dan's turn will come." I again proposed an immediate attack and a unified command. The Danites, however, held stubbornly to their course. At last, Nisan Lot, who had a fair head for strategy, agreed to a reconnaissance in strength into Asher – but at the price of a divided command. The Danite forces would cooperate with me, but serve under their own commanders. I consented to these arrangements with deep misgivings and met with Malachi and Ethan Boz to patch together a plan. "We can't delay," I warned them. "Like it or not, we are in the Jordan. Things are in motion and they will carry us along."

Our plan called for a coordinated move, with the army of Dan and my forces marching together to strike the Messiahists in Asher. The Danites characterized our effort as a feint, to draw troops away from Judah, but I had more serious intentions. If we could surprise and drive the enemy out of my homeland, it would not only relieve Asher, it could disrupt the enemy's whole campaign. If we had but a single success, the Messiahists would have to divert forces from Judah to deal with us, and that might easily bring about a stalemate that could last into the new year.

My legion took the Ancients' double road up on the plateau, a route devoid of water and exposed to enemy cavalry, while the Danite infantry took the canyon road. I gladly traded the greater risk in order to avoid seeing the Wayfarers' Refuge. Ethan Boz, now Colonel and commander of the Danite cavalry, preceded us, throwing a protective screen across our front. We emerged from the desert to find that Boz's cavalry had abandoned their screening role and were raiding Asher, leaving a path of destruction of their own. In my estimation, these actions succeeded only in announcing our presence while exhausting the Danites' horses. In the morning, our patrols found regular units of enemy cavalry on the plain just above Selah. Young Boz had heart enough for one indecisive skirmish, but lost his aggressiveness very rapidly. Had I held overall command, I would have sacked him instantly.

While waiting for Malachi to arrive, I found a good defensive position where the canyon road comes out of the arroyo onto the plain of Selah. The Yakima canyon mouth was narrow enough to prevent horsemen from getting into our rear. I selected a stronghold with stone corrals and set my men working to make it defensible. Refugees came into our lines or passed through on the way up to Hazor, and many joined us. We put them to work building barriers and digging ditches while we sent out patrols to secure information. The news they brought back made my men savage to close with the enemy.

The Danite infantry arrived the following day. It had taken General Malachi three days to cover the distance we had crossed in a day and a half. Rather than join forces with us, he put his legion into camp a mile above us in the canyon. When I met with him and his officers to hear an explanation, I learned that having come this far, General Malachi had determined to wait and receive the enemy's attack. *In this piece of idiocy, I recognized the author of Dan's defensive policy.* We had thrown away surprise, Boz had worn out his command, and the Messiahists had reinforced their forces in Asher. Now Malachi's dispositions invited the enemy to attack and defeat us separately.

"Why would the enemy care if you hide up the canyon?" I taunted him. "What harm can you do them here? In the meantime, they turn Asher into a desert." I had intended only to mock the commander and his lieutenant Boz, but I went on to deliver a tongue-lashing such as I expect they had never heard before. I told them I had served with incompetent officers, but I had seen nothing like the stupidity exhibited by the pair of them. All the things that made coalitions odious were present in themselves. If they persisted in this cowardly plan, I promised I would myself attack their camp with all the forces at my disposal. "Choose now," I said. "If your men are not marching south at dawn tomorrow, expect us to march north at you!"

II

At dawn, the Danite Legion marched south, thus sparing me the need to make good my threat. We held a brief and very surly conference as they came abreast of our camp. Stung by my words, General Malachi demanded the place of honor in the advance. "Very well," I said. "Put your legion in the front. But if you tarry, the Herons will tread on your heels."

We had not gone a mile when we fell to quarreling again, this time over the route. Malachi was proceeding down the east bank of the Yakima, and this course, if continued, would keep the river between us and Selah. We needed to cross the river immediately at an undefended ford, to avoid having to fight our way across at some point nearer the capital. General Malachi found reason to see things differently. Colonel Boz came up and backed his chief, and Moriah had some harsh things to say on my behalf. The rancor among ourselves was thus hardly distinguishable from our feelings for the enemy. I was almost relieved to hear that the enemy was coming out to meet us—a large force of infantry and cavalry was reported approaching rapidly on the *west* side of the Yakima.

"Perhaps," I taunted him, "the General would prefer to await the enemy's arrival before we cross the river!"

Our column had scarcely completed the crossing when the enemy's cavalry appeared on our front. We formed a line of battle where the plain opens up above Selah, ancient seat of the Apostles of Asher. The first brigade of my legion formed the left with our flank on the Yakima and the catapults behind the line and the Esdralon Guards cavalry held in reserve. The new Danite infantry had formed up on our right, about 800 strong, with the Danite Horse Guards on the right, guarding our exposed flank. Their standard, a golden lion on a red field, was planted behind the infantry, where General Malachi placed himself and his staff. Colonel Boz had also quarreled with the General in the meantime and had taken himself off with the Danite cavalry.

I walked out before the lines to inspect my legion, anxious to bring my second brigade up quickly. Our heron standard snapped in the wind. Some of my men had painted images of Transmitters, the menacing stick figures from Ancient times, on their capes and shields. I had acquiesced to this extent in my soldiers' preference for this bizarre emblem, but had refused permission to paint these figures on the cohort standards. As I watched, the Messiahist army formed itself in our front, perhaps a thousand yards distant. They appeared to be of equal strength with us. I was relieved that the standard of the Second Apostles was nowhere to be seen. At least I did not have to concern myself with Mac Dogol and my old comrades.

After the preliminaries, the drums sounded and the enemy moved toward us at a deliberate pace. I felt a flicker of anxiety, thinking that General Malachi was untried at this sort of thing, as were his men – and that Boz was headstrong and foolish. It would be vital to coordinate with both of them as the battle developed. But it would be difficult when they had separated themselves and we were all in a temper. Thus, the evils of divided command and coalitions.

I sought out General Malachi to request that he move his command further to the right, to make room for my other brigade to deploy. My second brigade would form the center of our line. To my astonishment, the General would not speak to me. He stared straight at the advancing enemy, looking stolid and determined, but giving no instructions to his officers. I insisted, declaring that only my first brigade had room to deploy in a line; the second was still in column behind it. If we did not extend our combined line quickly, it would be outreached on the right and overwhelmed. In response, General Malachi snapped,

"I know of no such command. And it is madness, sir, to maneuver in the face of the enemy!"

I was thunder-struck. The Messiahists were but seven hundred yards distant and coming on. "General," I insisted, "we need room to fight. Just have your legion face right and quick-time to the flank. My men will fill in the center in an instant. You must do this, sir, or we will be outflanked."

"I will not, Captain," he replied. "I command here."

Captain! He had chosen this moment to insult my youth and rank and probably my origins as well. The General's ancient pride of place—a status that rested on no record of achievement that I was aware of—was more important to him than our chances of victory. I was suddenly glad I had abolished the landed class in Naphtali.

About halfway to our line, the enemy cavalry swung out from behind their formation to make a broad sweep around our flank. I wheeled my horse around and dashed back to my command, shouting for the wagons to close up as much as possible. I ordered the second brigade to form a square behind them; they could move instantly into the center gap as soon as the Danites gave us room. Out of the corner of my eye, I saw Colonel Boz put his Danite cavalry in motion to counter this familiar flanking move. But then the Messiahist horse swept far out to our left, forded the river and kept moving toward the Ancients' road, as if to strike our lines of communications rather than our rear. The Danite cavalry wheeled after them, and I held my breath. Boz could let them go and we would win the day here in an instant. If their cavalry took themselves off the field, we could overwhelm their infantry very quickly. But instead of understanding the flanking move as an opportunity, Boz saw only its threat. With a sinking heart, I watched the Danites flog their horses in pursuit, abandoning us on the field. Silently, I cursed Ethan Boz for a fool.

As they moved toward us, a great cloud of dust rose above the host of the enemy. For a moment I thought of General Bosheth on the field in Engedi, when the onslaught by the Kr had overwhelmed his understanding. I had certainly not envisioned the battle thus, and I began to feel a kind of tightness in my head and shortness of breath. I resolved to get a firm grasp of all the factors that existed on the field. With the Yakima on our left, we had some protection for our flank. My men were trained and wore armor – the best to be had anywhere – and their ranks stood solid, shield to shield. They would take a toll on the enemy as they closed with us. I moved along the rear of the first brigade line. There was no time now for maneuver or for moving the second brigade up along side them. We would have to repel the first assault and then gain some space.

Dust enveloped us as the armies closed with one another. As I anticipated, the enemy's light missiles did us little damage, and we pounded them with catapulted stones and arrows as they approached, causing much confusion in their ranks. Their first javelin throw was ragged and disorganized, much of it falling short. Our return throw created havoc. Even before the shock of collision, the enemy were wavering and seemed ready to break. Apparently these were recent levies, unschooled in discipline and effective infantry tactics. I was confident we could beat them.

Our second pike throw, coming with a redoubled avalanche of stone missiles, jolted the enemy backward. It was clear that they had no will to close with us, and I turned to communicate this opportunity to General Malachi and to call for an advance all along the line. To my astonishment, I saw the Danite infantry starting to give ground, slipping backward, and the enemy pressing past our flank boldly in what seemed to be great numbers. As I watched, a great shout went up from the Messiahist forces. A thick dust cloud, moving slowly at first and then rapidly, like water past a failed dike, signaled the collapse of the Danite Legion. In a moment, a rout was in progress.

My own troops were holding firm under the onslaught, keeping ranks and standing by the colors. Desperately, I looked around for something to halt or reverse this disaster. Major Moriah had positioned his Benjamite horsemen to the rear of the second brigade. As the elated Manasseh and Ephraimite infantry swept past us, I shouted and gestured at Moriah to retire across the river, but the distance and noise were too great. *Act like you're fleeing, I meant to convey to him, and then turn and take the enemy in the rear.* Moriah, however, was already moving his men out of harm's way. The cavalry were fording the river. At the sight, the Messiahists emitted a howl of triumph. I watched our horsemen emerge on the far bank and move on out of arrow range.

To my dismay, however, they kept moving south and away from the battle. They moved deliberately at a trot, the ranks forming again as they passed out of my line of sight. *What was Moriah doing? Were the Benjamites abandoning us as young Boz had?* My brigade officers crowded around for an explanation, but I had none. Again, I experienced the sick sensation I had felt when surrounded by the Kr at Elion. I seized the captain on our extreme right and shouted, "Form your men on the First Cohort. Stay dressed to the right; don't open any gaps!" I then aligned the next cohort with the same instructions, and so with the others. It was a maneuver not practiced on the drill ground, but the captains saw what had to be done, and the men performed it admirably. There was no panic, only a kind of dismayed surprise like my own. Everything had been going forward; victory seemed assured – and then this disaster. They were looking to me to fix the problem.

At my command, the second brigade changed formation from square to line and moved quickly into place alongside the first brigade. I had bent our first brigade backwards to parallel the river. I ordered the catapults moved over to the center. As the Messiahist army flowed on past, the racket raised by their triumphant shouts was deafening. As the dust and noise diminished, it became clear that the battle had broken in two. The Messiahist army, like ours, was organized in two wings, and one of them had struck, routed, and then pursued the Danites, and was now well past our flank and moving rapidly away from us. The second wing still threatened us, though half-heartedly. The forces in our own front seemed wary of closing with us and had actually separated a bit. Our lines now ran parallel to the river, and the enemy was positioned to force us into the Yakima. Several of their units began to cluster on our right flank as if about to launch themselves against us and cut off our line of retreat.

I watched this transpire as if from a great height, until it seemed that my brain would burst through my skull. "This is intolerable!" I exclaimed. "Intolerable! They think they are going to have their way with us, these fanatics." My staff stood by expectantly. I signaled for the drummer to beat the advance. The drums began to rattle defiance. "Herons!" I cried. "answer their curses with your swords! *Forward!"* The bugles took up the call and the captains blew their shrill whistles. My line surged forward like unleashed wolfhounds.

It chanced that at the same moment I signaled our lines to advance, the enemy launched his own thrust at our right flank. The unexpected effect of this meeting engagement was that our left overwhelmed their opponents immediately, while the enemy massed on our right put up a stiffer fight. Thus, the lines swung around on that pivot of resistance, so that we soon found ourselves facing north and the Messiahists south. The enemy, seeing themselves caught between us and the confused melee in their rear, quickly lost heart. In a moment, they began to flee in disorder. We followed hard, our officers striving mightily to keep our own units in hand, until, after a pursuit of three miles, we came upon both wings of their army, now hopelessly mingled and confused and penned up in front of the field fortifications we had left in the morning. Malachi's troops had fled straight into our earthworks and were fighting for their lives. The enemy had been about to launch a determined assault against them when the soldiers who had fled from us burst upon their rear, spreading panic. Messiahist officers were now desperately trying to reverse front and face us with an organized line.

I halted the Legion and dressed our lines while the men caught their breath. The Herons kept an ominous silence. It was clear that there was not much fight left in our opponents; a general bleeding away of the enemy's strength was visible on both flanks. Even as I ordered the advance, the Messiahists began to cast their weapons on the ground and hurl their standards into the dust in front of them.

"Unbelievable, sir!" one of my officers cried. "If we had cavalry, we could bag the whole lot of them!"

Where *are* our cavalry? I asked myself. And where are *theirs?*

Seeing that the situation was hopeless, the enemy commander rode forward and offered up his sword.

"If Boz and his cavalry were here where we need them," I reminded my jubilant officers, "we could be in New Jerusalem tonight." But they were not. Moriah's horsemen had also disappeared southward, apparently on some errand of his own. Knowing what opportunities were being wasted because our cavalry was absent, I could not share the elation of my men. At least our Danites allies were shame-faced and repentant. I left them to disarm and guard the prisoners.

Having sent several messengers after Moriah and received no word, I gathered up every horse I could find and pushed a patrol forward toward Selah. I was desperate to retrieve Moriah's cavalry and discover what enemy forces remained between us and New Jerusalem. The main body of Messiahist cavalry could still descend on us without warning and reverse our victory in a moment.

A mile south of the battlefield, I found one of my messengers near a heap of slaughtered Ephraimites. None of our dead lay among them and there were no wounded of either side. I demanded an explanation, but he seemed puzzled and wary. "P-p-prisoners," the messenger stuttered. "Moriah p-put them to death." When he saw my face he quickly added, "As you ordered, sir."

"By St. Supplicee," I cried. "I ordered no such thing! Even in war, the Law governs!" But even as I spoke I experienced a sinking sensation. I had given this messenger instructions in great haste; I struggled to recall my exact words. "Soldier, I said to tell Major Moriah not to bother taking prisoners – by which I meant *let them go*, and come back to protect the infantry! I told you to tell Moriah to return to us immediately!" The messenger stared at me. I wanted to seize this simpleton and shake some sense into him, but I restrained myself.

I found Moriah within the hour, and he was proud and disdainful and refused to admit any error on his part. "You know Boz is unreliable!" I said angrily. "After he left us on the field, the Messiahist cavalry could have reappeared at any moment and slaughtered us! Could you not see the mistake? Could you not understand where your troops were needed?"

He had planned to take the enemy in the rear, Moriah replied haughtily; he had intended to come upon them by surprise. Our victory had come so quickly the battle was over before he had gotten into position. He had thought it best thereafter to scout southward and prevent surprise from that quarter.

"Moriah, could you not see that the enemy was broken? What were you thinking? The chance to destroy the enemy completely was in our hands. Had you been where you should, we could have captured two legions on the field intact! Think of it! The door to New Jerusalem is torn off its hinges; all of Manasseh lies open to us! If I had Boz's cavalry now as well as yours, we could burst through the Lion Gate and overrun Manassah. We could force the enemy to disengage from Judah to deal with us; we might even destroy another portion of their forces before they regain their balance. Don't you see! This is not just a battle; this is the *war* you have thrown away!"

"You overreach yourself," Moriah retorted. "You forget that we serve Benjamin, first and last. My orders from Colonel Harlech were to serve *with* you, not under you. I agreed to cooperate to the extent that it served Harlech interests – and to use my judgment when to separate from you. In my judgment, that time is now."

"If you desert us now," I exclaimed, astonished at his perverse obstinacy, "you will do inconceivable harm! This is the *war!* This is Benjamin's war as well as mine. We hold the end of all this suffering in our hands! If you desert now you throw away the victory!"

"Don't prattle to me of desertion. Our service here is over."

"This is *worse* than desertion! It is treason! Are you blind?"

Moriah replied icily that he could see as clearly as I.

"You see nothing!" I exclaimed. "What kind of fool would believe that I'd issue an order to kill prisoners! I have won a great victory today, and because of your bloody-mindedness, my name will stink all over Israel. And now you intend to desert me!" I resolved to sack him in spite of the conditional nature of his allegiance to me.

"You are the fool," Moriah replied haughtily. "In a civil war there is only one law. Spare an enemy and he will stick a knife in your back at the first opportunity."

Friends will often do the same, I noted to myself. "Major," I exclaimed, wholly beside myself, "take your Benjamites back to camp and await my orders." He started to protest, angry as a rattlesnake, but I shouted, "You are *relieved*!"

Moriah drew himself up and informed me that the Esdralon Guards were, from this moment forward, no longer under my command.

"Go, then. *Go!* Get out of my sight! If you cross my path again you are a dead man." I would have said more, but my sword leapt from its sheath, ready to speak for me. Moriah looked from my face to my hand and back again and took himself out of my way.

In the glare of a burning stronghold, I assembled the men of the Esdralon Guards who were about to desert my cause. I spurred my horse back and forth in front of them, shaking with fury and for a time unable to speak. The men sat motionless in their ranks, dressed in every kind of outlandish attire – more savage looking than Kuhlans, they seemed to me. *Burgos remarked once that the Esdralon Guards would wear anything but a uniform.* My heart changed as I looked upon them. We had been through hardships and triumphs beyond counting; together we had accomplished unbelievable things. There were no soldiers like them anywhere; so few, yet so formidable. The Guards would be spoken of in cities and sung in lonely shepherds' camps all over Israel for generations to come. Future ages would marvel at their prowess.

Repressing all else I wished to say, I acknowledged that Moriah was taking them back to Lagash without my blessing or consent – taking them out of the campaign at the moment they were needed most. I felt that each of these veteran troopers understood the nature of the situation—that this was the crisis of the war, with victory won but thrown away by this act of Moriah's. Everyone saw this but Moriah, and even Moriah understood it in his heart, blinded though he was by pride and resentment. I stood in my stirrups and looked up and down their ragged ranks before I continued. "You know that Zachariah ben Harlech was my friend. For his sake I will honor the agreement under which you served with me. But any who wish to remain and continue in my service are welcome. I thank you all regardless. You have served with great steadfastness and valor; you are incomparable soldiers. I honor you all from my heart." I saluted them and received the tribute of their bare drawn sabers and a cheer.

About forty men backed out of the formation and followed me. Moriah fumed and swore and looked black at me, but there was nothing he could do. Old comrade or not, I would have killed him had he raised a hand.

III

My parting with the Esdralon Guards was interrupted by loud cries from one of our scouting parties. A patrol came racing back, their horses in a lather, and they were shouting incoherently. "Your mother!" I heard, when I could make out the words. "We've found your mother!"

My mother? My mother is dead. My mind raced about for a moment like a headless chicken.

"We've found her! Your mother lives! Come quickly!" The soldiers were Asherites. These men knew me, knew my family. *It could be true!* My heart leapt. I hurried after them and met a crowd of refugees coming down the road from the Wenas Valley. One of the officers led me to a ragged, elderly couple resting by the roadside.. Immediately I recognized Abigail, the elderly servant of our household. She was sitting by a thin, aged man. Seeing her, I was caught up in such a violent storm of feeling that I cannot describe. I dismounted and embraced her, sweeping her up in a single motion.

"Abigail, can it be? They say that my mother lives!"

My old nursemaid had grown frail and apparently could no longer see well, for she recoiled from me. Before I could reassure her, her companion reached out and laid a rough hand on my arm – a cracked, weather-stained hand that I recognized instantly as a slave's. "Back, don't touch me!" I cried, sweeping his arm away and turning furiously to confront him. I froze with my arm in the air. The face was strange and familiar at the same time, as faces sometimes are in dreams. His rough, red features seemed hewn out of sandstone, and he had sunken rather than fleshy cheeks. Instead of bright auburn hair, his was bleached an impossible carrot color. Unsightly flecks of pigment marked his face and arms. I stepped back aghast, trying to take him in, trying to make what I saw square with memory.

"Lukash!" I exclaimed.

"The same, Master. It is Lukash!" He embraced me like a huge bear, weeping great tears. "It is Lukash, Master Josiah. Lukash!" The familiar smell of him brought tears to my eyes as well.

"Zaiyah! Master!" Abigail threw her arms around me. "Can it be? Can it truly be?" She stepped back and looked at me with rheumy eyes. "Master Josiah," she cried, evidently bewildered, "you are so tall!"

It was then I noticed that one of the rag bundles on the roadside moved almost imperceptibly. I saw it as a hunter's eye picks up the slightest motion at the periphery of vision. Without looking directly, I noted that the bundle was an old woman, a frail huddle of bird-bones beside a ragged pack, indifferent to all around her. Lukash and Abigail still embraced me and cried with joy as I cast about, seeking a glimpse of my mother. But somehow my gaze, like a ball on a tether, swung back to the figure on the ground. The old woman did not turn her face up to me, but I could see a forehead framed by strands of white hair.

"Mother?"

All the doors and shutters of my mind slammed shut in an instant. I felt a vague sense of embarrassment. *This was impossible. This is not my mother!* This was one of a thousand hungry and helpless old women on the roads of Israel these days, marked for death, a burden to themselves and to their families. A used-up, useless old woman beyond all help or hope. My *grandmother* had never seemed so old.

"Mother."

Abigail stooped and whispered in the old woman's ear, gently raising her. Lukash bent to help, his back clumsy with age.

"Oh Master Zaiyah," Abigail said in a tremulous voice, "bless the sight of you, we have had hard times of late. But we served her faithfully, Lukash and I and some of the others, and saved her life and all, poor soul. But she is – your mother – dear, is not herself."

I stood rooted to the ground.

"Look, Mistress!" Abigail said gently, speaking to the old woman as if to a child. "Look, it is your son, Josiah, come to save you."

It was my Mother! But it was not! Could not be!

The old crone gazed at me, frowning. Abigail and Lukash lifted her so that she stood upright, precariously. The top of her head did not reach my chin. *This is impossible, I thought. My mother was tall.*

Her lips moved soundlessly. Then her eyes widened and the old woman cried out in a voice of startling strength and intensity. In a motion swifter than thought, she embraced me. Seizing my face in her bony hands she kissed me full on the mouth. "Emanuel!" she cried. "Emanuel!"

"No, Mistress Rachel! No!" Abigail and Lukash had to restrain her. "No, you silly goose," Abigail murmured gently. "Not E-man-u-el!" She enunciated each syllable carefully, patting her all the while. I felt a horror I could not dispel seep into my flesh and unstring my limbs. The old woman's claws were not easily detached from around my neck.

"Emanuel!" the old crone cried softly, still clasping at my chest. *"Emanuel!"*

"No, Mistress," Abigail said firmly. "Not Emanuel, but Josiah. This is Josiah. Your son. Hush, hush. Your son Josiah has come to save you at last."

The old woman raised a crooked hand to her face. "Josiah?" she said, in a voice tender but bewildered. "My son Josiah?" It was a voice achingly familiar, yet altered beyond imagining. As she looked up at me, I glimpsed a fleeting expression of clarity and remembrance.

"Emanuel!" she cried fiercely, burying her face in my chest and weeping bitter tears. "Emanuel, my dearest love," she cried over and over, speaking the name as if it were a prayer.

It comforted my mother to be near me, so I sat under a pavilion with her near our makeshift fort while Abigail and Lukash told the sad tale of her exile and privation. Dusk was coming on, and a chill with it. They wrapped themselves in ragged blankets as if in luxury, while I listened dully. My thoughts and emotions seemed to have migrated to a distant place, strange to me, shrouded in darkness and swept by savage winds. The joy Lukash and Abigail expressed at seeing me was, I suspected, exaggerated for my benefit, to make up for my mother's disappointment. She refused to recognize me as her son – or to recognize me at all. I could not be certain why. Perhaps I bore a Glanz taint in her mind and therefore seemed to her the author of all the misery and destruction around us. Or maybe I reminded her of the desolation she had suffered in her own life. Most likely, she just preferred to believe herself in the presence of her lover after so many years. She sat humbly, silently, drinking me in with her eyes as I listened to Abigail and Lukash recount the lost years.

"It's true, Master, you are the image of him," Abigail said, speaking to Lukash and me simultaneously. "Is he not the very image of him – your father?"

My father?

"It's no wonder, really, that your mother takes on so," Abigail said. "Her griefs and the life she's lived, they've turned her wits. I've no doubt she'll see things more clearly in a while, but you must have patience, Master Zaiyah. Patience!" She patted me as if I were still the child she had raised. "It was the diet, poor soul. She had to endure on so little. So little! They starved her, your uncle and them. She lost her teeth, and it was a torment for her, she was so vain of her smile. Then in the spring, the mountain fever – Her hair fell out and grew in white."

I looked to Lukash and back to Abigail. "You said I was the image of my father."

"That you are, child!"

"Yes, Master. His likeness, head to toe."

"Lord, child!" Abigail exclaimed softly. Her dim eyes seemed to search everywhere but my face. "Can it be – can it be you never knew? Never realized?"

"No, I. . . *never!* Not until this moment."

"Oh my dear Master Zaiyah!" she said, putting her hand to her mouth. "Your father, bless his memory" – she seized my arm as if to press the truth of what she said into my flesh—"was Emanuel."

Emanuel. . . ?

"Emanuel Vashon, elder brother of Elkiah Vashon. Dead these dozen years or more."

Her words sank down in me, searching for a place to rest, to settle and engage my understanding. They say that after an earthquake a man may not get his feet again for hours. As I sat on the ground, the earth and sky spun away from me. As I groped for one stable, unmoving point in the world, a sudden, vivid remembrance burst in my mind: Major Vashon's personal ensign, a heron stretched out in flight, was snapping on the pennant pole when his troop rode into camp under the storm clouds in Engedi. Father and son swung down from their mounts looking like twins, like versions of each other at different times of life. *And both of them, in hindsight, looking very much like me. . . .*

At last I understood why. Elkiah Vashon had called me kinsman when we grew acquainted. I am in fact his nephew, son of his dead brother. And cousin to Erech.

I sped through a hundred memories, grasping for details. My brother Justin—*who, I realized with a sharp pang, was not my brother* – must have noticed that resemblance as I saluted Major Vashon and embraced Erech. Justin had surely realized something that day that he did not speak. It must have been the close family likeness. Strange! How much had he realized at that moment on the windy plain of Engedi? And how many others saw and understood? *While I had not.*

Even Senesh Velco at the Academy knew, and knowing had cost him his life. *"Bastard!" Senesh Velco had flung at me. "Son of a Haggadah whore!"* My sword descended diagonally through his body, from his collar bone to his short ribs. His body fell like split kindling, and his life gushed from him like a fountain. I could remember it all and see it fresh in my mind as if it were still happening. Sadly for him, I had not realized that he was paying me a compliment. *My father was Emanuel Vashon. Not Tephlin Glanz.*

"How was it," I ventured to ask, "that Emanuel Vashon came to die?" I could not yet bring myself to call this man my father, though my lips and tongue formed the word in my mouth. The answer beckoned to me from the recesses of memory, but I could not coax it forth.

"No one knows, Master," Abigail said. "Except that Emanuel was murdered and his body left on the road to New Jerusalem. Tephlin Glanz – we always assumed it must be him. You were just seven at the time."

Yes, of course. So Glanz knew – had known all along. He had killed my father. He had arranged with his characteristic malice and calculation to have my father murdered. I ransacked my childhood memories, searching for the time when Glanz had left my mother. I had no memory of the event, just the vague knowledge that he had left before my birth. Glanz had abandoned his young, noble, and very pregnant bride, leaving her alone on her father's estate in Asher. It was a family story. But what had been the cause? *Had he known then that his wife was in love with another man? Had he realized that I was the seed of another man's loins?* If Glanz knew my mother was in love with Emanuel Vashon or simply discovered that she had had a lover, he must have turned his back on her, waiting, knowing the truth for years, ignoring the offense but not forgetting it. Putting his rights as a husband in escrow, as it were, but waiting patiently to take his revenge. But then something else must have happened. It would have been in my seventh year.

Of course. The relationship, long put aside, between my mother and Emanuel Vashon had been renewed. Embers grown almost cold and dead had burst into flame again. Some word of it had reached Glanz in Hebron, and he had moved swiftly to exact his vengeance. My father had been killed on the road not far from his estate by some unknown assassin—doubtlessly some hireling of Tephlin Glanz. And then his minion within our family, my uncle Brandon, had arranged for my mother's exile – her social death. In my grief over my mother's disappearance, I had not been aware of this other loss—the death of a man who was, to me, a mere neighbor. I searched to find some prescience of the bond between us in my past, some glimmer of recognition between father and son. In truth, I could scarcely remember the man.

Emanuel Vashon. . . .

Even as I dismissed his memory, I recalled strong hands lifting me and tossing me in the air. He caught me easily in his huge arms and set me down beside my mother, whose leg I immediately encircled with my arm. There was a crowd around us, and the Straw Man was burning. It was the Feast of the In-Gathering. Firelight gleamed in everyone's eyes.

For a time I felt an indescribable relief. Tephlin Glanz was not my father and therefore neither a monster in my blood nor an image of my fate. He was a stranger—a bad man, perhaps, but a stranger, whose cruel and unfathomable ways were no longer my intimate burden. Glanz had lived his life—and lived yet—and he had swooped perilously close to me and to those close to me. But he was separate from me, from us, unentangled in my destiny. He was a person, I assured myself, of no real consequence.

Nevertheless, I cast about for some understanding of this man, this enemy who had been rendered suddenly a stranger to me by Abigail's revelation. For her infidelity, Glanz had exacted the spirit if not the letter of the Law from my mother. Jealous, he had killed her lover, and my uncle Brandon had done the rest.

But no, to attribute normal human passions to such a man seemed implausible somehow. Perhaps Glanz's motive had not even been revenge. Perhaps instead of revenge, he meant to recover the full value of his investment – whatever it had been – that he paid my Grandfather for my mother's hand. To get what he paid for, in some coin of his own making.

But what had Glanz needed from the marriage that required the death of my father and a lifetime of deprivation for my mother? His motives were beyond my power to fathom.

Abigail sat by me patiently. As I thought about it, it seemed likely that my uncle had been the one to carry the news of the renewed relationship to Glanz, the better to curry favor with him. Perhaps he had done more. *Perhaps he had been the go-between—or even the assassin!*

"So," I said to Abigail, "it was my uncle Brandon who served Tephlin Glanz and brought this evil on my mother."

"Your uncle Brandon thought to save the property in the family," Abigail said. "I'll say that much in his behalf. Your grandfather had put everything at risk with his foolishness. But Brandon was a cruel and callous man. He cared nothing for your mother, nothing!"

"He will pay for that," I vowed.

"Too late, Master," Lukash said. "Your uncle has paid, to be sure, but not for that crime. Bishop Bon broke his body on the rack in Selah. It was last year, during the invasion."

Ah! I thought bitterly, *it is my misfortune that the Messiahists are so thorough!* It would not have been good to be the agent of Tephlin Glanz when their forces swept through Asher. I felt no elation at my uncle's death, but rather a sense of having been cheated. I knew now that Brandon ben Haggadah had arranged my father's death as surely as if he had done the murder with his own hand and before my eyes. I was certain of that. And then he had arranged for my mother's exile. *And now he was beyond my reach.*

And Tephlin Glanz—was he beyond my reach? I would never know what he had wanted and connived to bring about. *If I knew what it was, I would willingly die to take it from him.*

The last streak of red sky faded behind the mountains; darkness was falling. For the first time in my life, I felt a pang of regret that there would be no Judgment Day, no symmetry of rewards and desserts for Glanz – or for my uncle. Or for any of us.

IV

I awoke startled, the sun in my eyes. *I had the answer! It had come to me in a dream. He had wanted me.* Tephlin Glanz had wanted *me!* That's what Glanz had wanted so badly that he killed my father and left my mother to be tortured into madness by her long exile. *He had wanted a son of noble blood, a child of his loins, his flesh, to serve his ambitions, to project his will into the future and thus cheat death itself even after it had claimed him.* And instead my mother and her lover had cheated *him* of his noble heir, thereby snatching away his scheme of immortality.

Nevertheless, Glanz had acknowledged me as his son, knowing I was not. *I believed I understood why.* Glanz had wanted *me*. Or rather someone like me, a son eligible for all the offices and honors that Israel could bestow, but obedient to his will. A child who would carry Glanz's purposes forward in time, beyond his own life, extending his dead hand and undying malice into the future. To this end, he had watched me, toyed with me, seeing me educated and turned into an instrument by others, while he persisted in his testing and manipulation, curious whether he could capture and control me. He was determined to know if he could make me into *his* instrument. It must have teased his imagination to find if he might transform me, in spite of my alien blood and education, into a monstrous creature of his own pride – or contempt, or fury against life, or whatever it was that moved him. I pictured myself in his imagination as a stiff, metallic creature, devoid of will or flesh and fashioned exclusively for his purposes, striding into the future, bent on destruction.

He had succeeded in part, I had to acknowledge: Tephlin Glanz had indeed had a role in creating me. He had planted in me a determination to kill him at the first opportunity.

The sun was two hours high. I had been in a meditative trance—or a trance, at any rate—all night. I stretched my limbs and tried to rise, but I was stiff and numb. I had sat for many hours in the posture of meditation. My officers clustered about me, looking apprehensive. They had not dared disturb me, though there was much urgent work to be done. That realization brought shame, for this was no time for indulging personal feelings. There was a commotion from the canyon behind us, where the prisoners were. *My mother and Abigail and Lukash! I remembered in a flash.* "Where is my mother?" I demanded.

"Your mother is resting, my lord General. A doctor is attending to her. She is very weak, sir. The servant woman is making her a broth. What she needs is meat and greens, but we have none. She had some gruel last night."

I was dizzy with confusion. *Where was the Messiahist cavalry?* I should have had patrols out toward the Lion Gate and in our rear. "Where is the Danite cavalry?"

"My lord General, there is trouble with the Danite Legion, sir—and trouble with the prisoners."

I pulled myself together and hurried toward the canyon, not waiting to hear what the trouble was. The prisoners had been penned up between the Danite Legion and ourselves, hemmed in by the steep walls of the canyon. Loud cries and wailing and an occasional scream sounded from that direction. *How had I remained oblivious to all this?*

A delegation of Danite officers met me on the way. One was General Malachi's son Rueben, a Colonel in the militia, and they bore a soldier on a litter. It was a Danite soldier. He was dead. They put the litter on the ground and turned him over, so I could see his back. The flesh had been laid off his bones.

"Your officers killed him!" Rueben Malachi exclaimed furiously. "They put him to death for pissing in the Yakima!"

I stared, uncomprehending, at the body. Ten lashes were the prescribed sentence for breaches of discipline jeopardizing the army. Urinating in the Yakima above our camp, I reasoned laboriously, was no doubt a fine insult to us, but fouling the water could destroy the health of the entire command. So, my troops had caught the man and given him the regulation ten lashes—but ten lashes of such savage force they had ripped the life out of him. I tried to sound firm and reasonable, but in truth the canyon walls seemed to rise up as if they would swallow me. "This punishment was harsh, admittedly," I said, looking for some ground to stand on, "but it falls within the limits prescribed by Law. As to the procedure of his court martial, there will be time enough to inquire into it at the close of the campaign. In the meantime, you must keep your command under better discipline."

Hearing my answer, the younger Malachi gave a great cry and seized me by the throat. The power of his lunge threatened to bear me over backwards, but I slipped from his grasp and delivered an open-handed blow that caught him in the throat. It was all reflex, a product of my training. Malachi sprawled on his backside, holding his throat and looking astonished. For myself, I was shocked by his attack, a capital offense in the military code. I stood over him, casting about for some explanation of this extraordinary behavior when one of my angry bodyguards looped the reins of his bridle around Malachi's neck as if to choke him and then slapped the horse. Malachi was sitting dazed on the ground with a hand to his throat. The horse reared and jerked backward in fright, threatening to pull his head off.

"St. Supplicee, enough!" I cried, seizing the reins. "Restrain yourselves!" In a moment I was able to control the horse and free Malachi. When I untangled the reins from his neck, Malachi seemed not to be breathing. I put my ear to his mouth and then raised him off the ground by his belt. He groaned and tried to speak. He was breathing, but my blow had damaged his voice box. Two of his fingers had been caught in the loop around his neck; otherwise, his neck would surely have snapped. His fellow officers knelt to assist him.

I rebuked my guard and sent him away under arrest. "What were you thinking?" I demanded. I was alarmed at these events. My men had no more respect for Danites than they had for the enemy. Apparently, I had set them a poor example. "Gentlemen," I said to the Danite officers, "get your officer back to camp. We have enemies enough without turning on each other. We'll see about this other case, but not now."

More shocking sights greeted me around the first bend of the canyon, where the prisoners were herded together. A group of Asherite civilians appeared to be holding some sort of rump trial. Better than a hundred prisoners were bound and lying or kneeling on the ground, and men were moving among them, giving them very rough treatment. Then I perceived the nature of that treatment.

'Halt!" I cried. "Stop this butchery! This is unlawful!"

An officer was slashing wildly at the bound captives; he appeared out of his head. Prisoners shrieked and groaned where they lay, stabbed and slashed and, in one case, disemboweled. I seized a lance and made for him, and he quickly came to his senses and retreated. "Have you all gone mad?" I demanded. I confronted a group of elders from my tribe; they had indeed convened a court and were handing out summary punishments to officers and prisoners who wore either a red cap or cockade. "You have no authority; this land is under martial law," I exclaimed. "In the name of St. Supplicee, cease immediately!"

They protested my interference angrily, determined to exact their revenge. One of them declared the red caps were worn as badges announcing that the wearers were willing to accept martyrdom for their faith. "The Messiahists slaughtered us, murdered our families, and took all our possessions. It they die subduing us, they are promised immediate entrance into Heaven. That is the reward, they claim, of holy war!"

"This is not war," another exclaimed, "but murder sanctioned by superstition, and so we are bound by no laws! And, by St. Supplicee, we are *willing* to inflict martyrdom on them!" Almost choking with rage, he described the newly proclaimed doctrine that those who had taken the oath of martyrdom were absolved of all sins—could not in fact commit sins! The Law was miraculously rescinded for them.

"What are we doing?" I exclaimed, my head spinning at this news. "Have we all lost our senses? *We* are not Messiahists!" was all I could think to say. I brought up a cohort of the Herons and arrested the lot of them, my own government, reminding them sternly of the Law. Nearly fifty of Messiahist prisoners were sprawled on the ground in various positions of agony, bloodied in what I can only imagine had been some form of frenzied interrogation. I ordered the rest of the bound prisoners cut loose and returned to the larger pen. They dragged their wounded comrades with them.

A quick inspection showed that the prisoners had not received food or water or medical care. I organized details to fetch water from the Yakima and blistered the hide of the Danite officer who had not fed or cared for his charges. "Either find some food for these wretches or you will join them in the pen," I warned. Within an hour we had stretched pavilions for shade and sorted the wounded into the three usual groups. We had little to share, and our surgeons were still busy with our own wounded. I encouraged the prisoners to assist each other and to follow the regulations governing hygiene. We gave them what comfort we could. Civilians had plundered their wagons and packs, and we had no blankets or tents to share with them. The night would be a misery to them, especially the wounded.

I looked over this horde of helpless and very discouraged men, feeling to a degree helpless and discouraged myself. I had a herald cry out an inquiry for me – whether there were any among them who were kin to the Velcos. No one volunteered until I swore an oath that I meant only to do mercy. "I have a blood debt to the family, and it may be I can do someone a kindness today." One man stepped forward. He was a junior officer and wore a red cockade, and so would surely have reaped his martyr's reward had I not happened upon the court in progress. He was a cousin of Senesh Velco and knew the story of his death. "Come with me," I said. "I have neglected my debt too long."

With a little order restored, I gathered my officers and sifted through reports and fresh intelligence. We had annihilated the forces in our front, though they had consisted only of hastily raised militia units with a stiffening of veterans. There was still no word from Colonel Boz and his cavalry. Major Moriah had also deserted us, taking the bulk of my own horsemen and leaving me scarcely a hundred Asherite cavalry. I had barely enough men to mount patrols in all directions. Thus, with no idea whether the Messiahist cavalry was still somewhere in our rear or about to descend upon us, we were pinned to our fortified camp as surely as if we were besieged. We took stock of our supplies, of the civilian refugees who kept pouring into our camp, and counted the casualties.

"We've not much food," Burgos reported. "We can barely feed ourselves. We'll have to send the refugees who can travel on north to Dan. There is no help here." *That would be a cruel journey with no food. Dan was two days march for a healthy soldier.*

"What about your mother, sir? And her servants?"

I had not let myself revisit the fact of my mother's presence or her condition. I shut my eyes against the images summoned up by his question. Suppressing a shudder, I ordered that my mother and her servants be treated equally with the other refugees who were not able to journey on to Dan.

We waited to see what the Messiahists would do. Toward late afternoon, cloudy, colder weather settled in. Feeling I had to be out and seeing things for myself, I took a patrol toward Selah. We arrived under its walls at dusk and found bonfires burning at the base of the bench on which the fortress stood. "Who are these people impaled on stakes?" I demanded. The flames lighting the area were funeral pyres, but there were many dead scattered about who had not been collected and given rites.

"They must be Old Believers, my lord General. People who offended the Messiahists."

We ran into a picket line outside the city and took a few prisoners. I had difficulty restraining my men. I sent the prisoners into the city with a message. "Tell your people that the Messengers are at the gate." *I had spoken unawares describing my men as Messengers, but my troops instantly voiced their approval of this characterization of the legion.* "Warn them to cease their destruction and their persecution of Old Believers immediately. I will leave a corridor open tonight, so all who cleave to the Messiahists can leave the city. Leave they must; let them make no mistake about it. Tomorrow, whoever and whatever is left in the city that pertains to the Messiahists will be destroyed."

We rode on nearly to the border of Manasseh, where I released the prisoner who was kinsman of the Velcos. When I removed his blindfold, he recoiled visibly at the sights around us. "The war has grown savage enough for the most zealous of your brethren," I said to him. "Perhaps some of them have had an early taste of the Judgment today." He was very nervous and evidently in no mood to appreciate my humor. "No doubt you have seen more than is prudent for me to reveal about our forces, but I promised myself to make restitution for the death of Senesh Velco. You are that restitution." *As far as I was concerned, we were quits.* "Go quickly to your masters. Say that I have a thousand prisoners and very little food or medical care for them. You saw how my aggrieved countrymen longed to destroy you, and you know the reasons for it. Tell your masters I will treat your comrades as the Law requires, so as far as circumstances permit. But make it clear that if I have to choose between feeding my own forces or my enemies, things will not go well for your comrades. You Messiahists have set the tone for this war; now you see what it has become."

I asked him if there was anything he needed to have clarified. He shook his head, looking resolutely at the ground.

"Go, then. We will be here tomorrow if your masters wish to treat with us. Equally if they come to contend with us."

He sprinted for the Lion Gate as if pursued by demons.

V

Shaiym MaGowan had ridden down from Hazor over night, braving the dangers of night travel and the hostile forces in our rear. *I was surprised I could still draw such inferences.* It baffled me that after such exertions I could not find sleep. Yet two days after the battle, my mind was a dog that would not cease barking. I had not slept; I had yet to lie down. "Welcome," I greeted him. "Tell me my lady your sister is safe and well!"

"She is, and she sends her affection."

Shaiym MaGowan had already gotten an account of the battle from those he met on the road. I had no energy to repeat it. "You should not have come," I said. "Things have not gone well here."

"You have won a great victory!" he exclaimed. "A triumph! In any case, I thought my place was by your side, in the place of danger." He expressed his regret for having missed the battle.

"There will be danger enough for all before we are through," I said. "Tell me, is Odessa well? When did you last have word from her?"

"She is well. I saw her yesterday in Hazor."

Hazor? I had left Odessa in Naphtali.

"She will ride down today. I thought it best to warn you."

"She must not! There are enemy cavalry north of us!"

"I spoke with Colonel Boz on the way here," Shaiym assured me. "His command is encamped just below the Manastash ridge. The Messiahists horsemen have been defeated also and are drifting back west of here. They are whipped dogs—and no danger to Canadians! Odessa has an escort of our people," he added, as if that allayed the whole issue of danger.

"I specifically asked Odessa to stay in Naphtali, out of harm's way. We could have lost the day here."

He shrugged. "You were warned that she had opinions."

We walked together as I inspected the camp. I showed him the horde of prisoners we had taken and the pile of red caps and cockades we had taken from the dead.

"Do you know Odessa so little by now?" he asked. "Canadian women are not notably docile, and I believe my sister is as little docile as any female among us."

"Your sister should not take such risks on my behalf," I said. "But she is welcome here – welcome with all my heart." I did not lie, but somehow I dreaded to see Odessa in this waste of shame.

We came to the encampment of refugees, a group hardly less wretched than the Messiahist prisoners. I found the tent where my mother lodged, noting it was supplied with blankets and some items of food. I introduced my brother-in-law to my mother while Abigail and Lukash watched sympathetically. My mother stared at Shaiym but did not acknowledge him. I explained to him that Asher had been gutted and boned and its carcass scattered. I had nothing to feed the refugees, and there was no way this land could feed its inhabitants, let alone sustain a campaigning army. "In all candor," I admitted to Shaiym as we left, "I have not felt so sick at heart but once in my life. As you see, I have found my mother—and have lost her a second time."

"I heard the story from your officers." He was too tactful to try to commiserate with me.

We rode out to see the battlefield. The dead were being interred in mass graves in the absence of wood enough for cremation. My ragged, vengeance-minded countrymen had stripped their slain enemies of clothing and valuables and desecrated their bodies. Their behavior reminded me of the People's fury against the Kr. I understood their actions, but I was ashamed – especially to have my brother-in-law see it. At the same time I marveled at how prophetic those experiences in the Kuhlan lands had been of things to come in Israel. "The best and the worst of Israel contended here," I said. "I am grateful you did not see it."

"I heard it was a miracle—an unheard of triumph!" Shaiym declared, trying to cheer me. "The Messiahists are saying you are a rebel angel. I don't wonder! Two legions destroyed on the field and your own forces still intact! They say there has never been such a victory."

"Intact, you say? A victory? My best troops, the Esdralon Guards, have just deserted me. My ally, General Malachi, sulks in his tent, and yesterday we came near to blows with the Danites over the laxness of their discipline. Malachi's son actually tried to choke me for my impudence in pointing it out to them. And then I had to arrest what is left of the government of my own country because they were murdering prisoners without a hint of legality. I have never heard of such a victory—and given its nature, perhaps it is well that I lack the means to follow it up."

"General Malachi is dead," Shaiym said. "I heard the story from his officers. Last night, after midnight, he fell on his sword."

"I didn't know," I said. *It softened my view of him a little to hear that Malachi had felt his disgrace keenly enough to act on it.*

We found a banner of black cloth planted on one of the trench graves. I presumed it was a sign of mourning until I approached nearer. On it was an image of a Transmitter, a Messenger of the Ancients—placed there perhaps to commemorate the lawlessness into which both sides had descended in this war. Or perhaps it proclaimed the triumph of things that no one had wished for, but which we had somehow summoned nonetheless.

With Shaiyam and a handful of cavalry, I again ventured south to Selah and found that the Messiahists had fled the city. The destruction they had wrought defied belief. My countrymen were at work avenging themselves upon those who had cooperated with the invaders. I put a stop to it and rebuked them, feeling again disgusted and sick at heart. They informed us that a delegation of Messiahists waited under a flag of truce at the Lion Gate.

"Hypocrites!" Major Jared said. "They recognize the rules of war only when it suits them!"

"See what they want," I commanded. One of my officers galloped forward and planted a banner within haling distance of the enemy. It was not my heron standard, however. It was the black flag of the Messengers. *Let it be then, I thought to myself. We are who we are. Who we have become.*

I recognized the huge torso and bulging shoulders, even though he was in military dress rather than clerical robes. It was Bulavar, now in the uniform of a General. His helmet and breastplate shone in the sun; his cape fluttered in the wind. The Messiahist delegation stood under their banners waiting for us.

"Cousin!" Bulavar called out in his deep melodious voice, gesturing at the banner my officer had planted. "You show your true colors at last! I would not have recognized you." "But of course your sword! Vanity, Josiah! Was it vanity that led you down this path of destruction? You've changed, you see, darkened in the service of evil, as—"

"I am not your cousin, Bulavar. Between us there is no relation whatsoever. But to the point: I have one thousand of your men prisoners, and I cannot—"

"The stripe across your face—is that the mark of the Devil? Is that the sign he gave you when you bowed down and signed away your soul? I never thought to look on your face again, never! Not after you blazed your wicked path through Esdralon's citadel and the church's sacred clergy! You fooled me with your look of innocence; no doubt you have fooled many beside myself! They say your guile has led a multitude to destruction." He made a great show of revulsion and added: "I recall only too well your soft and studious looks!"

I reminded Bulavar that I had come to treat on behalf of the prisoners I had taken, but he burst out violently: "The Church of God does not bargain with heretics—even in a good cause."

"Heresy is it? Is that what this is about! So heresy it must be!" *His words recalled to me his blanket condemnation of failure at my earlier interrogation.* "Therefore it must be heretics that I have in my prisoner cages! For from what can failure spring?" I taunted him. "From what but lack of faith in Zion's cause? Hence, I have a thousand defeated heretics whom I cannot feed. They wear the uniform of your cause and bleat for deliverance. Give me a hundred wagons of food, and I will redeem them to you on the usual terms – or exchange them for an equal number of our people rotting in your dungeons."

"Treat with you, you son of infamy!" You chopped my Rodrig to pieces! How long had you practiced to dissemble! If I had but known then, when you stood in my grasp—"

"Blame your god for that," I retorted. "Where was the gift of prophecy then? A revelation would have been timely for Zion's cause, would it not? Just a whisper in your ear to beware—that I would surely be your enemy because of what you had done to Justin! Why didn't your god speak to you, Bulavar? Why *didn't* he warn you? Such a simple thing for omnipotence! Perhaps *he* was angry because you had just murdered my brother! Perhaps your god recoils at murder and loathes your bloody sacrifices!"

"Your brother was a fool," Bulavar said. "He reaped what he had sown."

"Enough!" I cried, a white-hot fury blazing up in me. "Not a word! If you say another word about my brother, I will tear the heart out of you where you stand, flag of truce be damned!"

Bulavar glowered at me. "It is ever thus, the filth of heresy. I see your lips move but only filth drops from your mouth. So it is with the impure, who speak only to blaspheme!" Bulavar drew himself up, his voice low and menacing. "There will be no exchange!" he announced. "There will be no compromise. Do you think the Church of God goes to war on a lark? Do you think we play games, that we will falter on the path? The Church makes no bargains with evil, Josiah! It makes no covenants with death! That you will learn, my son, you will learn to your sorrow! This war, this very war you set in motion, is no game at all, I say, but a bitter struggle to the death. Understand me: *to the death!"*

I stood silently, taking in his decision and what it meant. "Just as you say, then," I said, "so let it be," and led my delegation off. On a sudden whim, however, I turned and shouted, "See you in Hell, Bulavar! You carry the stink of it with you now." To my surprise, I saw him blanch and quail. He stood speechless, his mouth slack and open. His companions drew visibly back from him.

VI

As soon as I saw Odessa, threading her way through the masses of wounded and the refugees who had come into our fortifications, I remembered how filthy I was. Just as I had not slept, neither had I bathed since the battle. I was repulsively unclean. Shaiym greeted her in his usual way, but I could not. Miraculously, she saw my distress and understood. We retired to my tent and Odessa warmed a basin of water and had me strip so she could bathe me with a small cloth. There was no soap. Shaiym stood guard outside the tent so not even my staff could interrupt. Odessa had part of the ritual by heart and spoke the words of purification as she scrubbed and then dried me with a clean cloth. Afterwards, she undressed and lay down with me in my soldier's bed. Though she cherished me patiently, I could no more embrace her than I could fly. I apologized and tried to describe to her all the events that had transpired here in Asher. I must have fallen asleep instantly.

Around midnight I rose and dressed and read the dispatches. My staff was waiting with other business. Scouting reports were coming in, and I read a long, accusing letter from the Council of Dan. I gave instructions for the infantry to break camp at dawn and return to Hazor. The cavalry would remain in place to screen our movement. "The refugees must fend for themselves and make their way as best they can," I said to my staff. "We'll take as many wounded in the wagons as we can. Officers must make the selections."

I found a writing pad and scratched out a condemnation of the Messiahist government. They had usurped the previous legitimate government, imprisoned or slain all those who opposed them or held other beliefs, and were now conducting warfare without regard to the laws of war or humane constraints. Therefore, I declared them outlaws and apostates, and called on all loyal men to hurl them from their seats. I offered rewards for the heads of the Primate, Bishop Bon, and his henchman Bulavar. I ordered the document posted in Selah and read aloud. "After that, the cavalry must oversee the evacuation of Selah. It is indefensible with the forces we have."

"I'll see about your mother," Captain Jared said.

"See about my wife. Take them up together."

"I will, sir!"

I commanded my staff to release the elders of Asher and bring them to me immediately. Lastly, I ordered Captain Eli to separate the Martyrs and the officers from the other prisoners. Bulavar had declared this a war to the death; *war to the death he would get.*

In the morning, I spoke to the prisoners – all those who remained after the officers and red capped Martyrs had been bound and led away. I repeated what Bulavar had said to me, that there would be no ransom for them, no exchange, and no constraints on the way the war was to be conducted. "Your Bishop abandoned you to your fate, declaring that this is a war to the death. He has, in effect, laid you under sentence of death because you failed. I ask you now whether, with this knowledge, any of you wish to renounce your allegiance to the churchmen and join with us." I gave them an hour to decide.

More than a hundred men stepped forward and we accepted them. To the rest, I said, "You have made your choice. I will be kinder to you than your own Bishop, but your lot will not be easy. You will be held captive until the war ends or your government agrees to an exchange. Any who seek to escape or resist or conspire to harm us will be treated harshly, I promise you. Otherwise we will not seek your lives. It may be that you will survive this ordeal and return to your homes in peace."

"What about our officers and the Martyrs?" a prisoner called out.

"What about them?" I replied.

Ninety-seven men, the remaining officers of the two legions engaged against us, and all who were identified by their red caps or cockades as members of the Order of Martyrs, had been bound and led up the Yakima and into a side canyon shortly after dawn. There the remnants of Asher's government waited to carry out the sentence of death I had passed upon them in the middle of the night. The surviving Elders of Asher and such citizens as had the strength for it laid them under axes and under hoes and under harrows of iron.

VII

Officers of three Messiahist legions had stood with Bulavar under the flag of truce—proof that we had disrupted their campaign in Judah. That much was good, but I knew I could not hold Asher with the forces at hand. Selah lay so close to New Jerusalem that its garrison would be hostage to the Messiahists rather than deter their aggressions. While my cavalry covered the withdrawal, I paid a visit to Tirzah, which was only a blackened ruin; likewise the estate of the Vashons, my father's people. I found no sign that any members of my own household or the family of Elkiah Vashon had survived the devastation. My mother and her servants had escaped the general massacre because of the remoteness of the shepherd's cottage where she had lived in exile. My childhood and the history of my family were thoroughly erased. Smoke rose from a hundred strongholds similarly despoiled.

Some Asherites who favored the Messiahists or feared the Third Coming elected to stay and join our enemies, and they were not treated kindly by their countrymen. And so the murders and depredations continued as the two populations separated themselves, one sad, terrified column fleeing north and another to the south. The roads were littered with their abandoned possessions and their unburied dead, and wherever the two groups met on the road, there was more bloodshed. Every kind of cruelty found expression in these days, and anguished cries without number went up to the life-giving sky. As a community, Asher now existed only in scattered groups in exile and in memory.

I redeployed the Great Jordan Guards above the Manastash Gap, guarding the entrance to Dan, with my horsemen watching the approaches through the Wilderness of Zoar. I set up headquarters in an abandoned stronghold just inside the Gap. There, Odessa and her brother, my mother and her two servants, and a handful of Odessa's Canadian friends settled in with my headquarters staff. These arrangements were hardly satisfactory, but they had to suffice for the moment. I wanted to be near Odessa, and it was necessary to keep my mother close by. Her journey to Dan had been hard on her, and she remained withdrawn and disoriented. I was not in the best of shape myself. Returning from the debacle in Asher, I slept for nearly twenty hours. When I awoke and bathed and purified myself, I sought Odessa's arms. After this strong medicine, I felt better, although for a time I felt neither fully awake nor dreaming. There was a pervasive air of unreality about my days and nights. I spent my days in the saddle inspecting and briefing and seeing to the thousand details of command, and at night I took my dinners in my mother's presence.

"You must return to Naphtali," I said to Odessa. "You'll be safer there. I don't know if we can hold off the Messiahists if they come up against us."

Odessa regarded me silently. My mother continued to eat as if all this had nothing to do with her.

"Mother needs to travel on to Naphtali where she will be safe. You could accompany her to Hammoth-Wenatchee."

"Your mother is too weak to travel," Odessa said. "One place is like another to her now, and one person like another. If you insist on her leaving, Brother Peter would be as good company as myself. My place is with you."

I took heart from her loyalty, for I was as little willing to part with Odessa as she with me. We lay each night in each other's arms, sometimes without speaking and often innocently as children, when the day's events had driven my manhood to cover. Once I returned to find Odessa waiting on my mother like a servant and being scolded like one. I was shocked to see this petulance in my mother; I wondered if it was an aspect of her present infirmity or a trait of character I had not detected as a child.

"You need never speak harshly to your mother on my account," Odessa assured me.

"She treats you like a servant! You are my wife—and the daughter of a chieftain! She will treat you accordingly. *I winced to think how Odessa's light skin defined her as a slave to my mother. I wondered how many other Israelites made the same association.*

"It is no great matter how she treats me," Odessa said. "I serve her because she is your mother. I choose to do it."

Once in safety, my mother's old servants, Abigail and Lukash, relaxed and put down their heavy burden. Abigail was increasingly absent-minded, and Lukash quickly resumed the vices of his youth and was often drunk. I had freed both of them, and for Lukash especially, the absence of external restraint after a lifetime in bondage proved demoralizing. It occurred to me that he needed a good whipping, but I could not bring myself to give him one, however repugnant his behavior. And it was unlawful to whip a citizen who was not a soldier.

Besides persisting in her delusion that I was Emanuel Vashon, my mother exhibited many exasperating habits. "What is this cloth that she takes such pains with?" I complained to Odessa. "She never leaves off weaving and unraveling it, and never makes any progress. I don't remember my mother being so particular."

"I thought you knew," Odessa said. "She says it's for the baby."

Her words wrung my heart. I tried to maintain my composure by pretending to complain: "Very well, very well, then. She—my mother – is not the way she was."

"Perhaps," Odessa said, "your mother is living over the important events in her life, trying to get them right."

"There's an idea!" I said, my eyes, in spite of my efforts, filling with tears. "Amen to that!"

Odessa's presence, no less than my mother's, was a new and unfamiliar factor in my thinking. Somehow, even when we married, I had not made provision in my mind for a long future together. My plans had revolved around the war and my imagination had stretched no further. But I now had, as the saying goes, a wagon load of things to think about—a wife and a demented mother to care for, as well as a war to fight. It complicated matters that Odessa was Canadian and Messiahist, and that she kept an entourage of Canadians, including her brother Shaiym and several of his friends, with her always. A woman of restless energy, she maintained her freewheeling foreign ways among us, riding about and dropping in on me unexpectedly at some far-flung outpost. I admired her for her independence, but the Canadians aroused suspicion among the troops.

To prosecute the war, Dan acceded to my request that we establish a joint War Council. Rehab Gill, Burgos and I spoke for Naphtali. In reporting on the campaign in Asher, I said very little about Boz and Malachi and their incompetence. It was more important to envision what to do next than to assign blame. The Danites, however, were uninterested in hearing me on any subject and unwilling to take action on mine or any other information. They clung to their single idea of defending Dan at its southern border and would listen to nothing else; they cared only for themselves. "We cannot feed all these refugees coming up from Asher!" they complained. "Dan is a poor country."

"It is a poor country indeed," Burgos retorted, "that cannot defend itself and has not sense enough to reconcile its only ally!"

I was dismayed by their shortsightedness. "With the forces now on your frontier," I warned, "the churchmen have the means to destroy you. Only if they hold to their plan to conquer Judah first can we expect a breathing space." In view of our sorry performance as a coalition, I pressed again for a unified command and a rapid build-up of our forces. The Danite cavalry were much disorganized by the recent campaign, and the infantry was a shambles. Moreover, Dan's landed nobles were not pleased with Lot's government, and they were even less happy with my policies toward their kindred in Naphtali. Thus, in spite of our success, the situation was altogether cloudy and unpredictable.

October slipped away, and no invasion came. Except for complaints, we had little news out of Judah. Their accusations confirmed that the Messiahists had reverted to their plan of crushing Judah before turning their attention to us. A letter from Ben Gurion relieved me of command of the Northern Lights Guards. I read the document before the Council and then burned it, to general laughter and applause. It was my public declaration of independence from these former masters. In this fashion and by no merit or effort of our own, we had our breathing space and I established myself as an independent power. But it seemed to me that we wasted the time in argument and dissention without adopting any effective measures. By failing to follow up our victory, we lost the initiative and were forced to await our enemy's next move.

Fearing the disaffection of the landed class in Dan, Nisan Lot was reluctant to take any action they opposed. The Mayor was cautious by nature, and his Council had only the vaguest idea of how to conduct the war. I was surprised, therefore, when Lot announced his acquiescence in my views. He was prepared, he said, to offer me overall command of military forces in Dan. When I expressed my thanks, he regarded me coolly. "Understand," he said, "the price of a unified command will not be cheap." Lot spoke at some length in high-sounding generalities before coming to the point: the price of a unified command was the elimination of Colonel Rueben Malachi.

If Lot expected me to balk at his condition he was disappointed. The Malachi clan and their allies were a genuine threat; their fangs must be pulled. From Lot's point of view, preferably by someone other than himself, but I did not shrink from the task. Striking a superior officer was an offense punishable by death, and Rueben Malachi had made himself eligible for that penalty in Asher. I had not pressed charges at the time, but in fact I was not willing to serve with such a man or endure another act of insubordination. I was determined there would be no repetition of our first disastrous effort with Dan.

Accordingly, I gave the necessary orders and took a small escort to the house of Colonel Enoch Malachi, the former commander of Dan's cavalry and uncle of the man who had struck me. With the elder Malachi's suicide, this younger brother Enoch had become head of the clan. I owed him an explanation.

A female servant opened the door to my knock and shrank back, her hand over her mouth. I managed to extract from her that her master was on the portico. The Colonel lay under blankets in the shade of an awning. His face was gray, and he grew paler at the sight of me. "I come in peace," I said, "though my business is not of a pleasant nature." He gestured toward a chair and I took it and pulled it by the divan where he lay. "I bring bad news," I said, searching for a place to start. "Your nephew, Rueben Malachi, faces a military court even as we speak. You know the offense." I suspected he knew the certain outcome as well. There was a commotion outside; his neighbors had no doubt carried the news that my escort and ensign stood outside the door of Enoch Malachi. His kin and retainers would be swarming like angry hornets to protect him.

"It was deemed necessary that he face charges," I continued. I despised this dressing of harsh truth in velvet, yet I flinched at the plain words of the matter. *"Do not say murder!" I had exclaimed to Burgos in a similar situation.* Nevertheless, murder it was.

There were sounds on the stairs. Several of Malachi's relatives and Major Jared burst through the door onto the portico. When they saw us seated and engaged in conversation, they clustered close around us anxiously and waited to hear.

"As High General of Naphtali, Dan and Asher," I announced, "I came to pay respect to the greatest soldier in Dan." I recounted briefly his deeds in the campaign that drove the

Messiahists out of Dan and added that I would welcome his counsel. "This, however, is a very different matter, and one I regret to lay before you." I put the warrant for his nephew's death on the divan beside him.

"What's this?" he demanded, taking up the document. He read it slowly and glanced at his kinsmen, his eyes blazing.

"Dan's Council has been reluctant to take action against the noble clans, even though your opposition has weakened the war effort," I said. "You will understand by these events that the Council is putting aside that reluctance." It was a message from Lot – partly conciliatory, and partly a threat. I was only the messenger at this point, but I could, my presence said, become more than that if necessary. *It was time for the landed nobles to end their opposition.*

"For myself," I added, "I shall take no part in the internal affairs of Dan except as they affect the war. However, where opposition affects our ability to wage war, I shall have no reluctance to act."

I stayed long enough to speak a few words to his kinsmen. Malachi's people were grim but quiet and subdued. There was nothing personal here; I had come on the business of the state. Their kinsman's death was the business of the state as well. None of us mentioned the word *vendetta.* We skirted the topic as if it were a corpse laid out for the rites, and when I left I knew it was understood between us – there would be no vendetta. It was, in a way, a triumph of policy. I thought of Justin all the way back to headquarters. *Base triumphs, our Teacher says, become unhealing wounds.*

"It is done," I reported to Lot. "Colonel Rueben Malachi was sentenced to death. The sentence has been carried out."

"Please, General, not so grim," the Mayor said. He was in a cheerful mood. "It's not so crass a transaction as all that. Colonel Malachi deserved to die. By his death and his father's suicide, the disgrace to Danite arms at the Gates of Asher has been set to rights. A rough sort of justice, to be sure, but the rank and file will understand. We will see that they do. Ultimately, it will improve discipline. In the meantime, Reuben Malachi and his father are off the board." He smiled and winked. "An added benefit, I must admit."

I took my leave. The war had taken its toll on all of us. We had all become more ruthless, more disposed to take the quickest way to our goals – which, we were convinced, were not trivial matters. What we fought for was worth dying for, and hence, it followed inevitably, worth killing for. Admittedly, the quickest path frequently led over mounds of dead.

I was formally invested with the powers of High General of Dan and Asher and Naphtali and the attendant so-called honors in a ceremony in the Hall of Assembly. Remembering how I had confronted the Apostle Boz in this very chamber only two years before, I marveled at the way fortunes rise and fall. And seeing my light-skinned foreign wife in the audience seated beside my mother, who was busy with her handloom and oblivious to the ceremony, I felt my head swim with the improbability of it all.

At Lot's invitation, I established the military headquarters of the Northern Alliance in the Citadel of Hazor, in the former palace of the Apostle. I suspected that the Mayor feared the opprobrium that still attached to the place after Boz's ouster, and so avoided it himself. The location gave me easy access to Nisan Lot and the new Council. My staff and extended family moved into this dark, maze-like structure, and I found rooms with light and fresh air on an upper floor for my headquarters.

I wasted no time in sacking Colonel Ethan Boz and replacing him with a junior officer, Jubal ben Eretz, who had managed to rally the Danites and wrest a victory from the debacle Boz had set in motion in Asher. This gave me an able cavalry commander but did not mollify the landed nobles. The infantry legion was still demoralized, and I saw no one with the skill and energy to lead it. For the short term, I loaned them some of my junior officers to teach them the drill and put some starch into them. As soon as I could find a leader for the infantry, I intended to go on the offensive and relieve Judah.

All that was needed was to delay a Messiahist victory until after the new year.

VIII

The moon cast a ghostly light into the room. Perhaps it was a noise, or only the strain of remaining alert for the assailant who would come to claim my life that had roused me and taken me to the window. I glanced out at the dimly lit landscape, shivering. Any glimpse of the full moon was enough to make me uneasy. It summoned up memories of the Kuhlan lands, and with it a vague sense of dread and the conviction that someone was stalking me. I felt my skin prickle and the hair rose off of my arms.

Involuntarily, I turned, catching a flicker of motion in the corner of my eye. *I was being stalked!* In the instant between my first awareness of a presence in the room and my recognition of who it was, I shouted *"Odessa!"* and crouched in a battle stance. Odessa sat upright in bed, her knees raised and the covers pulled to her chin. She seemed to take in the scene instantly, moments before it resolved into meaning for me.

It was my mother!

She stood in the center of the room in her nightclothes, her hair awry, pointing a finger at me. "Liar!" she cried in a shrill voice. "Liar! I knew you were lying! I knew you were sleeping with this light-haired whore! Just like your grandfather! Whore!" she screamed, turning her fury on Odessa.

I stood fixed in place by the window and then, realizing I was naked, dived under the covers. Strange to say, I was so unsettled by my mother's wrath that it took me a moment to understand what she had said. Two of my bodyguards burst into the room with lanterns, and I motioned them to stand by. Odessa remained composed and took my hand under the blanket. "She said your grandfather slept with his slaves," she whispered. "That means she recognizes who you are!"

My mother was standing at the foot of the bed shrilly condemning me for these imagined transgressions and berating Odessa for her wicked presumption. As soon as my heart subsided enough for me to speak, I said, "Mother, you are mistaken. I have told you before, this woman is my wife. This is Odessa, and while she cares for you out of the kindness of her heart, she is not a slave and never has been. She is a daughter of a chieftain and—" My voice trailed off. My mother's eyes were fiercer than any beast or bird of prey I had ever seen.

"You say your father slept with his slaves?" Odessa said. Her voice was calm and matter of fact in tone. "So his name would be Samuel? Is that right?"

"Samuel, yes! Of course it is his name!" my mother cried. She grasped her hair with both hands as if she was about to tear out fists full of it and sank slowly to the floor. "He *still does*!" she wept. I had never witnessed such anguish.

Odessa slipped into a robe and knelt to comfort her; I did the same. We talked with the old woman and rubbed her wrists and ankles, while I reassured her that I was not sleeping with my slaves—that I had, in fact, abolished slavery in Naphtali and would do so in Asher as well. Odessa was my wife, I was Josiah, Samuel was Samuel and had been dead now a dozen years. By the time we got my mother back to her own room and safely in bed, I was no more confident of these things than she had been.

"Your mother is recovering," Odessa said, slipping back under the covers. "She knows a few things."

Later that night I awoke again, as disquieted as before. I sat up in bed, rubbing my eyes. Odessa lay beside me breathing gently. This time it had been a dream that had shaken me from sleep. I had dreamed of the Kuhlan lands, and I had seen Vitoria. The dream took me to the moment when Vitoria realized she was with child and knew she held our son – the first stirrings of his life – in her womb. I saw Vitoria naked again in the morning light and felt the same ache as I had in the event and relived the pain of her loss.

Afterwards, I saw a boy of seven or eight years sitting with his back to me. He had his mother's hair – golden and fine, catching the light like carded wool on a spindle. The bones and musculature were hers, too, and his pose reminded me of the way Vitoria leaned sideways from the waist. Then he turned and I saw his face. *The boy was mine all right!* I saw the same startled, unhappy recognition in his eyes that he must have seen in mine.

As I sat alone in the darkness, sweating and anxious and deeply unhappy, I searched my mind for what, beyond these mute images, this dream vision had to teach me. Unwittingly, I reached for Odessa, running my hand over her belly as she slept. Feeling the warmth of her flesh I wondered if she had conceived – if she, too, had caught the future and wound it like a spool in her womb.

Sons! One of my sons belonged to the People, and if I got another on Odessa, he would grow up to be a Messiahist. *Enemies both, ranged against me in the future!* I did not deceive myself that a long life lay before me, a life in Tirzah or Naphtali under my own vines, with children and grandchildren at my feet. I needed no dream to tell me that. Instead, the dream had shown me how the future unravels what we weave with our hands and will and energy. If Odessa bore me a son, I would not live to rear him. He would grow up in the faith of her people and live in a world defined by his mother. He would not know my people or the Law. The dream had showed me how it would unfold. All my efforts to be the hard, resisting rock of the Old Believers would come to nothing. I had, by my own efforts, raised up counter-forces—sons! – who would unmake everything I had ever done.

Victory and defeat are equally illusions, our Teacher says. And who are these creatures, these women, who bear us in their wombs and comfort us as men and infants, and in the end devour us?

Odessa stirred and put her hand over mine. She looked at me through half-closed lids and smiled sleepily, mistaking my mood. "Do you want me?" she murmured.

"*No!* I cannot! Not in this moment." I slipped quickly out of bed, then turned and looked at her. I was reluctant to leave. I owed her some explanation.

"What is it?" she asked, fully awake.

"I have to go," I stammered. Then I realized what I had said and was ashamed. "I'll be back," I promised, not knowing what else to say.

She sat up and took my hand. "Tell me," she said.

"I cannot well say—I cannot say at all." I hesitated, not wanting to leave her without an explanation, but powerless to provide one. "One does not live," I said haltingly, "in just a single moment of time. Right now I am beset by—I am visited by other moments. Rest now. This will pass." I wandered the maze of halls and corridors of the palace till dawn, as distraught as my mother had been.

A week later, I ordered the Danite cavalry to raid into Ephraim toward Shiloh, to take prisoners so we could obtain a view of what ordinary Messiahists were thinking. I wanted to know whether they had the will to sustain the war or were growing weary of it. To my astonishment, Jubal ben Eretz, newly made a Colonel at my urging, refused my order. I commanded his immediate arrest and sent my own men to carry it out. This brought the Mayor of Hazor running over to my headquarters. "Something I neglected to tell you," Nisan Lot said, puffing and throwing himself heavily into a chair. "The details, as it were, of our contract."

"What are you talking about?"

"The Council thought it prudent to limit your powers as High General of the combined forces of Dan and Naphtali. Danite forces operating south of our border retain a certain amount of discretionary power." He coughed and tugged at his sleeves. "Colonel Eretz acted properly under these arrangements," he assured me. "In his judgment, your proposed raid was provocative. That is my judgment as well. It's all written right here." He tapped the document in his hand, all the while watching me apprehensively.

"And you didn't show me this document—or hint of its existence?"

He was, he claimed, bending to the influence of the landed nobles. The Council was committed to a defensive policy, and he feared I was not. The hereditary class did not trust me or like his government; hence, he had been forced to make this concession. This act of self-assertion by Jubal ben Eretz would, moreover, be deeply satisfying to them. He offered more in the same vein, and I saw he expected an outburst from me and was surprised that I stood quietly. I was seething inside, but I made no show of it. I had already decided that I would accept no explanation or amends for this betrayal.

"The more you string out your reasons for this decision," I interrupted, "the less convincing you sound. In fact, I can readily imagine an account of what was said, and who said it, that is much closer to the truth." *For the first time in our relationship, I felt that Nisan Lot had lied to me.* "Listen to me, Lot," I warned. "You have been misled. One does not cut the hamstrings of one's horse before going into battle and call it wisdom. This is what you have done. And this catering to the nobles, coaxing them to remain loyal – this is a very dangerous game you play."

Nisan Lot had no idea how dangerous was the game he played. He had urged me on several occasions to bring down more troops into Dan, to bolster its defense. I resolved to do just that—to send immediately to Amasa and summon the most battle-ready cohorts still training in Naphtali, but for my own purposes, not his. That would give me a force that Lot could hardly hope to reckon with. If Lot and his Council gave me another such surprise as I had just had, they would have cause to regret it. In any conflict, I reflected, the army eventually makes its will known. That was a lesson that Lot was coming very near to learning.

Partly to mollify me, I suspect, Lot called a meeting of the Joint Council to sort out the conditions of my commission. The meeting did not go well; Rehab Gill and Burgos excoriated him and the Danite Council. I said little, intending to await the arrival of reinforcements before I made my feelings known.

Afterwards, Lot showed me to his private chambers. "I have something to show you," he said. "Something of great interest." He was obviously trying to conciliate me. He explained that my suggestion to arrest the shepherd who found the Ancients' Holy Book had paid off.

"Eventually," he boasted, "the man admitted he had made another discovery, which he hid in a cave near where he tends his flocks—and which I now have to show you. He claims it has more importance than the Ancients' Bible. I have kept its existence a secret until you could see it." Lot no doubt thought to humor me in this while making a concession of no significance to himself.

The Mayor unwrapped a package in which lay an ancient corroded box made of velvet-covered wood and rusted metal. He removed the lid and revealed a manuscript inside. It was thin and insignificant looking—yet its importance was proclaimed by the special care given to hide but simultaneously preserve it. The box, he explained, had been discovered in a secret chamber deep inside the rock at the Wayfarer's Refuge. The chamber itself was a mystery, hidden inside the Library of the Ancients, but apart from the other secret rooms. The wall had been sealed off ages ago, but the heat of the fire and the work of the elements since the destruction of the Refuge had opened a crack that revealed its presence. Alert for plunder, the shepherd had broken in and looted its contents.

There were but a few pages, badly stained and brittle—and so old they were actually crumbling into dust and mingling with the remains of the padded material on which they had lain, time out of mind. I sniffed. The box and manuscript had a musty, unpleasant odor of tarnish and decay.

"This relic may be worthless," Lot admitted. "The pages are faded and the words nearly illegible. But you know the language of the Governors. I thought you could make something out of it if anyone can."

I lifted the manuscript carefully out of the box. The water damage seemed to me recent, perhaps since the Refuge was destroyed. The pages stuck together. Moisture had fused them together so that I could not examine them without causing harm; even the gentlest handling tore them. I noted the distinctive mechanical script of the Ancients. This was an authentic relic, apparently a letter. It was addressed to a "*Charles*" but the last name was illegible. I could make out a few words and phrases on the top page, but the damage had proceeded too far for coherence. In the middle of the first paragraph, I read part of a sentence: *". . . situation is deteriorating and will continue to, unless we take. . ."*

This fragment was followed by two other legible phrases: *"assess the radiation danger. . ."* and *"identify which isotopes. . . ."* The letter used an arcane vocabulary; I was not familiar with some of the words.

The second paragraph began: *"I have taken upon myself the task of setting down a few practical rules. . . ."* Because of water stains, only one other line was readable: *". . . terrible health hazards for an indefinite time. The D.O.E. has refused. . . ."* A few practical rules? And what was a "D.O.E"? I could not begin to make sense of it.

The bottom of the second page had a short section in a different, more personal tone: *"Honest to God, Charles, I would like to throttle every preacher I can get my hands on! The tension between the Hispanic population and the. . ."*

I carefully pried up the page to see how the sentence continued on the next, but they were stuck together at the top. I pulled gently and the page tore. I muttered in frustration and continued to translate the legible parts of the text, finding the better part of an intact paragraph farther on: *"I have given orders to arrest the worst offenders among the clergy. You can imagine my distaste at this, but this crisis is without precedent to my knowledge. Incredibly, we have several congregations actually plotting to increase tensions and encourage conflict. They say that by doing so they are serving the will of God and bringing about the Judgment! Can you fathom such a faith? They believe they will be yanked up naked into Heaven when Jesus comes! And of course our local problems only mirror what's happening nationally and internationally. I cannot imagine that people of intelligence and good will are actually stoking the fires and increasing the tensions with China and the Middle East because they are convinced that the end of the world is imminent. You would think the stakes of a nuclear war. . . ."*

Again, the arcane vocabulary and what appeared to be place names baffled me. I scanned the page for other readable sections and turned it over. Near the middle of the last page I could see a signature, too blurred to read, and—

I dropped the ancient manuscript like a hot coal.

Alarmed, Lot exclaimed, "What's wrong? What is it?"

I let loose a string of obscenities and every curse and imprecation I knew and ended with a groan. Under the signature, still legible and written in the Ancient's mechanical script, was a name: "*Cecilia Pleece.*"

Cecilia Pleece!

"What's wrong?" Lot demanded. "What does it say?"

Cecilia Pleece! I could not delude myself; I could hear the ancient name mispronounced in our language. "C. Plee-ce." But I could never, even should I live a thousand years, be able to compass what this name on this document meant or express all that it revealed was wrong. I suddenly remembered Vitoria revealing to me the name of the teacher of her People and her contemptuous dismissal of our traditions.

Perhaps, I thought to myself, we had earned that contempt.

"You're right," I said finally to Nisan Lot, knowing I could hardly hope to dissemble my utter dismay, but feeling simultaneously brazen and empty. "This document is of no significance whatever." I thrust it into the candle where it curled rapidly and then burst into flame. I dropped the burning letter on the floor and, when it had been consumed, ground the ashes into a black smudge with my boot. "It is illegible—the whole document—just as you feared. I'll take the box with me, if you don't mind." Lot stared at me as if I had gone mad.

I puzzled for a long time after whether Lot had any inkling of the significance of this ancient letter from Cecilia Pleece – or had lied to me about that as well. I concluded at last that he was genuinely ignorant of the contents of the manuscript, and that the secret was mine to keep or divulge as I chose. A small matter, considered in the balance with other things, but I was grateful for any consolation.

Chapter 18: Bars of Iron and Bronze

I

I came in late from the field morose and exhausted and bearing news I would rather have been flayed than speak. Odessa helped strip off my armor and scrubbed me with a cloth and heated the stones and poured water over them. But on this night, there was no relief in purification. I found neither peace nor clarity in the enveloping steam. Instead, clothed and sitting on my bed afterwards, I felt perfectly desolate. "Odessa," I said, feeling a compulsion to speak but not knowing where to begin, "how was it that our lives came to be knitted together?"

She instantly abandoned her usual cheerful manner and sat beside me.

"I look for a reason, a pattern in the play of will and accident and necessity." I paused, searching for a different track; this one seemed to lead nowhere. "When we talked before of how we came together, you said you had followed the stories about me and formed an idea of my character. But you admitted the stories were often distorted."

"The picture I formed was accurate in small ways as in large," she said. "I have not been disappointed."

"Never?" I said sharply. I could not bear to hear love talk or flattery. *Before I knew her, I had been perfectly willing to sacrifice her to my "enterprise."* "If you heard stories about me, " I said, "you must have known that I had a woman from among the People."

"Yes, Vitoria, a Mother of the Black Willow People, and a beauty famous even among a people known for their graces. Sometimes I wonder if you still think of her."

I looked at her as if to say, *Why would I not? Just as you remember your lover.* "Vitoria conceived a child by me, and that was the end of the relationship. You know the customs of the People. At the time I did not. But no matter; that is not my point." *I was not certain what my point was.* "There was another woman, a married woman of my own people. A relationship of the kind we had was absolutely forbidden, but we—somehow it happened. It is an old story."

"You mean Miriam Lander, wife of Nathan Lander, and a woman also famous in her own right."

It was a relief that Odessa knew at least the thread of my life story. "Husbands, I suppose, if they talk about such matters, trivialize the other relationships or speak of flaws in the women." Unconsciously Odessa reached a hand to her cheek. "I'm sure these two women had flaws enough," I said.

"What are you trying to tell me, husband?"

I had never had so much difficulty sorting through my thoughts. *What was it I wanted to say about these women?* "There were moments with each, " I said, "which, if I had had the power, I would have extended forever. No – I don't believe in forever. But I would have extended these times, these feelings, as long as I could. I don't know if I am making myself clear. I suppose I did live in these moments as long as I could, though one's power to extend any experience is absurdly small."

"I have had many such moments with you," Odessa said.

That was the truth. She had given me incomparable moments. "You are yourself a gift," I said. "Every moment. It's rather that – " I stopped again, feeling myself reach through cobwebs for something I could not grasp.

"Go on," she urged.

"There came a point with each when I discovered that these women were strangers. I realized I knew no more about them, really, than a perfect stranger one collides with in the market – or even an enemy one strikes from afar. In fact, we *were* strangers. They are strangers to me now. I'm sure it is the same for them."

"So this troubles you."

"Yes." I exhaled a great breath of air. It was a relief to speak of these things, and a greater one to sense that Odessa intuited something of what I was not able to speak. Thankfully, she had had a life of her own and had had her own precious moments that had come and gone and left only questions in her heart.

"You speak of losses—and drastic changes," she said. "Why would they *not* trouble you? Especially now. You have just found your mother, whom you believed lost, but she is nothing like the memory you cherished of her. You had a moment of hope, and then, just as suddenly, it was gone. And you were left with this stranger. I can scarcely imagine the pain it must be to know that your mother is in fact lost forever."

"Mother is not quite a stranger. But it would be easier—"

"Easy? It cannot be easy to face what your mother's condition means. No doubt because of what has happened to her, you wonder if *you* are the person you thought you were. Perhaps you feel a stranger to yourself—a stranger to your own heart." She regarded me steadily for a moment. "Husband, I deeply regret your losses, and I honor the pain your struggles cost you—and all the costs of your resistance to those who attempted to define your life or take it from you. But I believe that these struggles have given you your life—given it its form and substance. And given me the man you are as husband."

As always, she seemed aware of much she did not speak. And was generous beyond imagining.

"I sense you are in danger here," she said softly. "Something has shattered—you have had a surprise—a shock of some kind – that has made your life come loose from its moorings."

I mumbled something incoherent, still caught up in my own thoughts.

"I had such a moment myself the night of my—the night I spent with Sepulvida – a feeling of utter confusion and loss of balance, when all things lifted out of their accustomed places." She suddenly touched my arm, as if reassuring herself of my presence. "I felt as if I were floating. I did not really feel the pain. The sensation of coming loose from my life was worse than the pain."

She pressed both hands against her temples. "I see," she said, "and now you wonder about your wife."

I protested, but she raised a finger to my lips. "Don't flatter. It flatters me enough that you broach this subject with me. You wonder if you can trust me. You wonder if you can trust anything. Or have knowledge of another person—or certainty of any kind. When the world spins off its axis, where and what is the foundation stone?" We sat silently on the bed for a long time.

"These are hard questions you raise," she said at last. "Your St. Supplicee acknowledges that there are many barriers to knowledge. He is wise. Perhaps they are insurmountable."

"Odessa, don't speak to me of St. Supplicee! *Never* speak to me of St. Supplicee!" I leapt to my feet and blurted out the discovery of the letter of Cecilia Pleece and how it made a travesty of the wisdom of the Old Believers. *"There is no St. Supplicee!* The real St. Supplicee was a woman!"

She seemed unimpressed by my revelation, which I had kept from her until this moment. I described what I had learned of the real "St. Supplicee," the woman of the Ancients whose letter I had read.

"So, your St. Supplicee is a woman named Cecilia Pleece. Then why not admit that whoever wrote the *Sayings* was wise? Can you not learn something from a woman, from this woman of the Ancients?"

I was too depressed to answer.

"Will you learn a lesson from me?" she persisted. "A woman you love but sometimes wonder if she, too, can be an enemy?" Her voice was calm but serious, as if she were dressing a wound or tending a fever. She took my hand and kissed the palm and pressed it to her throat, where I felt the pulse beating. With the other hand, she opened her blouse and moved my hand to her heart.

"Each of us is mysterious – to ourselves as well as others. Nevertheless, husband, understand that there is nothing about me that doesn't want to be known by you." She unbuttoned her blouse and then, still using one hand, released the belt that held her skirt in place. The cloth rustled to the floor. "Here is a heart that loves you and a woman's body that knows you and yearns for you when you are absent." She moved my hand to her breast, and the nipple rose at my touch. "This is a woman who longs to be known by you, and to know you in return. A woman who is not and never will be your enemy." She moved my hand down her belly to her pelvic ridge, with its soft, clipped, curly hair. I hesitated a moment outside of the warm female den of her body, and then traced the line of her parted lips, feeling its moisture welcome me.

Our lovemaking was not so much an interruption of our conversation as a long, sweet exclamation point. She was telling me that her love was an invitation to know her, unreservedly. Her embrace was a pledge that she would never be my enemy. Afterwards, Odessa raised herself on one elbow and touched me gently, but I was not asleep. "It's true," she said, "there may be barriers we can never cross. But let's see how far we can travel together. Let's take our time and savor the journey – every moment of the journey."

I crushed her in my arms and covered her with kisses. We lingered in this moment as long as we could. Even in the midst of our embrace, I realized that Odessa had deflected a question she could not answer. The question was there, even if neither of us knew how to answer it. Afterwards, I slept—and dreamed of standing in a boat that moved steadily away from the shore where she stood.

I arose before dawn, hoping not to wake her, but she was up and had my breakfast waiting by the time I dressed. She had not bothered to make herself beautiful. Her hair was tousled from sleep and love making, and she was still sleepy. I thought I had never seen anything so endearing.

"That was a strange mood I brought to bed last night."

She brought eggs to the table and leaned over and kissed me. The mood had not quite left me. "I expect most men engage such questions silently over a lifetime," I began, "and let experience answer their doubts. In my case—"

Odessa knelt by me. "What is it? *You must tell me* what has happened!"

I gathered myself, feeling the world rise like a flood lapping at my house. "Judah has been defeated. Their army ran from the Messiahists. By all accounts it is a disaster." I told her what I had learned, of how Messiahist officers in the Judean army—*Messiahists presumably of the harmless variety*—had betrayed the garrison and let the enemy into their position. "These traitors were all secretly Third Comers! They hid their real allegiance until the last and then they—"

"This news is what prompted your questions last night."

"When I heard of the disaster, I felt—I don't think I have ever felt so empty of anything but pain. The war is lost; nothing seems solid any more. My life. Israel. Oddly, hearing this news, I suddenly missed my brother. It was not his memory that grieved me, but the realization that I had *not* missed him recently. In the midst of things of late, my sense of him has diminished—as if I have forgotten him. Justin was my whole family once. I grew up alone and got used to it, and then I found a brother. Everything was different for a while. Since he died, it is as if I have no family—though that is not the case, obviously. I have my mother—and I've learned that Elkiah Vashon is actually my uncle, and Erech my cousin. So—"

"Let me be your family, Zaiyah," Odessa said. "As I am your wife and friend and lover, let me be your mother and sister and brother too." She kissed me and held me for a long moment. Then she lowered her eyes and gazed at my hands as if they held some awful secret. "This news means you will be leaving."

"I must. Judah is collapsing, and I can get no decision out of these Danites. I'm through with them! I'm taking the Herons out of Dan and down to Judah by the Jordan route. The Danites can look out for themselves." *It was easier for me to think of the military situation than confront the parting it entailed. To think of the prospects for my own life and Odessa's was intolerable.* "I can have the legion in Judah in a week. We will take the Messiahists by surprise. If so, I may be able to reverse this disaster." As I spoke, I glanced at Odessa, but I could sooner read the surface of a lake. "You'll have to take my mother to Naphtali," I said. I had not wanted to tell her any of this; I had postponed the news until the last possible moment.

Odessa did not weep or protest. To my surprise, she pulled the table away from me. "Shhhhh!" she whispered as the table legs grated across the floor. "We don't want to wake the servants."

She stood in front of me in her linen robe, brushing her hair out of her face. Then she slowly lifted her robe and gathered it above her hips with both hands. She wore nothing underneath. I gazed at her bare legs and hips and the dark triangle of hair as if I were seeing them for the first time.

I put my hands on her hips, intending to restrain her, but she raised her gown further so I could hold her bare waist. "Odessa," I protested, "Darling, I can't. There is no time."

She opened her gown and slipped it off her shoulders, and then settled on my lap facing me, curling her legs around me. "Here," she said, cupping her breasts in her hands and raising first one and then the other to my lips. "We don't live in one moment only," she whispered. "Remember this one. Take it with you and live in it whenever you can. I will be living in it too, wherever I am."

II

I wrote Odessa from Jezreel. At a loss for words, I closed after a brief paragraph, needing to take up my next task. In truth, my mind had changed in the months I had known her. I felt compelled to finish out the war till the millennium came, but in my deepest heart, I hated anything that took me from our life together. I wondered again at the events that had thrust me into this role of champion of the Old Believers, and I felt for the first time not only ill suited for it, but reluctant to serve. I no longer believed in myself or in the wisdom of Clement and Israel Zhen-Gwo and the so-called St. Supplicee. I no longer believed in my mission. The only future I could imagine was our private one.

Still, the war did not evaporate because I wanted nothing more to do with it.

I would have paid dearly for real freedom of action, but I could only flex my muscles a little against my bonds. My path was fixed whether I liked it or not, and, at the moment, I seemed to be descending round and round in a funnel. Stubbornly, I searched for ways I could act and choose and make decisions within the constraints of my circumstances. *At least I had broken decisively with Dan.* I took some satisfaction in that.

Nisan Lot had been incredulous at my news. He had glanced around the Council and then back at me. "You're taking your legion out of Dan?" he exclaimed. "What will we do if the Messiahists attack?"

Burgos answered for me: "Defend Dan at the Manastash ridge!"

"I must urge you to reconsider," Lot said.

"My cohorts are already moving; the first should be arriving in Jezreel as we speak."

"I agree with the Mayor that you should reconsider," Gill interjected. "In my view, the obstacles the enemy must overcome to defeat both Dan and Naphtali before the millennium are insurmountable—*if* we keep our forces intact and united. But if you take your legions into Judah we may lose everything."

"However that may be," I replied, "I will not stand by and leave Judah to its fate. You can thank yourselves that the time to create a united force in Dan and Asher and Naphtali has come and gone. That opportunity has been frittered away by jealousy and short sightedness, squandered through selfishness and fear. And now that the crisis of the war is at hand, don't expect me to sacrifice Judah for a moment's safety. As for the consequences for Dan, they are your affair. You have clung stubbornly to your policy of isolation; cling to it still."

Though my officers chided me for it, I wrote Odessa again at Chinnereth, as our boats and supplies were being passed through the portage. I was gripped by a somber mood as I confronted what lay ahead. There were many things I needed to say and arrangements for her and for my mother that needed to be made if some accident befell me. And we had had disturbing news.

> *My dearest Odessa,*
>
> *Word has come up river that the Messiahists have made much capital of our discovery of the Ancients' Holy Book. They claim it confirms their faith and validates their every practice. They say that blood sacrifice especially is sanctioned by this Book, along with many other things that are abhorrent to common sense. They say the Book confirms their expectation of the Judgment Day.*

It seems that Brother Peter was right and I was wrong; we should have destroyed the Bible immediately. I have grievously weakened our cause by making this discovery public. How could I, after the life I have lived, believe that the truth must necessarily emerge from the jostle of the world? I flattered myself that I had put aside childish ways, but I see I have not. Still, the Messiahists might have made even wilder claims had we destroyed the Ancients' Holy Book. Perhaps in time, the Book will constrain them. Or perhaps it is all one, whatever I do or have done, or whatever their Book says.

My beloved Odessa, you came to us trusting in the idea of Israel, and in me, but I fear you have come to us just at the moment when all is failing. It is necessary that I go forward to salvage what I can of the nation, but every moment I am apart from you is pain, and I desire nothing so much as to return to you in peace.

From where I stood at the harbor of Meribah, I could see smoke rising from the sanctuary and signs of violence along the main path. Much of Captain Eli's cohort was employed in holding back a horde of pilgrims who had come to Meribah for healing, but had been treated instead to a massacre. Captain Eli stood before me grimacing in shame.

"Captain," I said sternly, "I did not give you the post of honor in our advance in order for you to blacken the name of the legion and bring our cause into disrepute!"

"They resisted, my lord General," he said. "It was unexpected. I failed to see it coming." He was deeply chagrined, but his face hardened as he described how it had happened. "These Messiahist priests reviled us and tried to prevent us from taking the livestock. And then the pilgrims came to their aid and began to stone us."

Once the violence had started, his men had gotten quickly out of hand. It was all as plain as if I witnessed it happening. *Stones and clubs, I thought!* Captain Eli's soldiers could have disposed of this rabble with their spear butts. And the priests! I could not imagine a real threat from a thousand of them.

"They cursed us and called us messengers of Satan," Captain Eli added. "They threatened us with the Judgment, if you can believe it!" He dismissed the idea with a curl of his lip. "Messiahist dogs! We put an end to their barking!"

My staff and I walked over the ground to survey the damage. The sanctuary at Meribah had been despoiled, its centuries-old treasury looted, and the priesthood nearly annihilated. As I examined the heaps of gold and jewels and chests of kanz that the priesthood had beguiled or extorted from their victims over the years, I could not but wonder at the magnitude of their ill-gotten wealth. Besides confiscating the sanctuary's treasure, Captain Eli's men had seized livestock enough to feed the legion for several weeks. All these resources were now available for our purposes. With this treasure, I could purchase supplies and compliance and assistance of various kinds almost indefinitely. All these things would be needed in the struggle to come.

I looked around the site, wondering what to do next. I had a sense that events were moving of themselves and that the final stages of the conflict were taking shape quite apart from my intentions. I surveyed the crowd of angry but frightened pilgrims, clinging to these Messiahists lies and pretensions as to floating debris after a shipwreck. The sight suddenly filled me with loathing. I remembered Israel Zhen-Gwo's warning: *"Beware the god-clamorers who speak of things they know not. Fight against the lies of those who claim to hear the voices. Their delusions bring locusts to the fields and owls into our farmsteads;*

they know nothing of divine things."

I turned to Captain Eli, who was still fearful of the disgrace he was about to suffer. For the first time, I saw him for what he was: a leaf in a current, a particle of a mighty flood. It had been no order of his that had set these events in motion; his men had encountered the enemy and had acted on their own. It occurred to me that the legion I had brought into being had discovered a mind of its own. The Herons were created to destroy the tyranny suffocating our country, and they had proven not just willing, but eager to do so. While not the Sword myself, perhaps I had unwittingly forged the Sword of Israel.

"Since the job is begun," I said, "let us make thorough work of it."

Captain Eli straightened his back and saluted me, while Gill looked at me in amazement and began to protest vehemently.

"This is not the Law!" he exclaimed. "This is—"

"Their guilt is obvious. A trial would be a formality, a waste of time. I have no time."

"What guilt? Guilty of what?

"Blood sacrifice, fraud, deceiving the people. False promises. Murder. The list goes on. We saw their work when we came up the Jordan—how they garroted those who came to be healed. This priesthood has long been a cancer upon the body of Israel. It's time it was removed." Gill continued to rail at me, but I felt a serenity into which he could not intrude. "If we leave them alive," I observed, hoping to end his litany of complaints, "these priests will spread damaging lies about us. We will not suffer it."

"What will they say, my lord General? That we are a lawless gang of fanatics, only partly under discipline? That we are thieves and murderers? That we looted the treasury of one of the most sacred sites of Israel and massacred its priests? Well?"

"That's exactly what they'll say, and more."

"And if you exterminate the priesthood of Meribah—what will the people say then?"

"They will say what they please, but they will know we are in earnest."

"This is a mistake," Gill warned, wagging a finger at me in his insolent way. "A fatal mistake!"

It frustrated me that I could not make Gill see the moment and its significance. "Blood offerings and the whole host of Messiahist superstitions are finished in Israel. People will know that too."

Gill turned his back on me and gestured vaguely at the crowd of pilgrims, who were bleating plaintively for the lives of those who had habitually sheared and slaughtered them.

"Gill, you have eyes; use them! This is not just the crisis of the war, but the culmination of our long struggle against superstition! If we don't put an end to these things, this moment could be our own Dissolution. Besides," I said, "this is justice."

"Justice? *Justice!* Beware," he exclaimed, "that you do not become what you fight against!"

"Beware," I said, turning on him angrily, "that *you* do not become what I fight against!"

I gave orders that the priests be dispatched and that the soldiers who had started the work must finish it, as punishment for exceeding my orders. Afterwards, the priests were all cremated with due ceremony and not—as was their practice with destitute pilgrims – cast like driftwood into the Jordan. Following these rites, I had the sanctuary cleansed and purified. The soldiers doused the great slab of unhewn stone with water to remove the caked and puddled blood, and then they built a purifying fire on the altar itself and burned resins and sacred herbs. It was a long and disagreeable task to get the blood stench out of the sanctuary. Lastly, I had the altar broken into pieces and cast into the Jordan.

We beached our fleet on the shore directly east of Hebron; the legion disembarked in less than half a day. I had shipped horses enough for only a troop of cavalry, so we were virtually blind outside our encampment. Major Jared took an escort to the city to announce our arrival to the government and coordinate our movements with Judah. I intended to cooperate with the Judean forces but not serve under them, and had written as much in a letter announcing our arrival. Part of me worried whether Ben Gurion and Tephlin Glanz would accept me on those terms, but I put those thoughts aside and bent my energies to preparing the legion for action. Meanwhile, patrols scoured the countryside for horses and wagons.

Just before dusk, Major Jared and his men returned, galloping into camp in great haste and excitement. "We are denied entrance to the city!" he exclaimed. "They treated us like enemies! Enemies!"

I commanded silence and brought him into my tent. My officers quickly gathered. Even in the candlelight, their dismay was evident. Major Jared described graphically how he and his men had been turned away from Hebron's gate.

"Let me speak to them," Gill interjected. "Let me go to Hebron!" The other officers protested strenuously, and I felt a sudden unease at his request.

"And what would you say to them beyond what has already been conveyed?" I demanded. "We are here to fight the Messiahists alongside them as allies, but not as underlings. Do you have something else you want to say?"

The group received Gill's silence with icy disdain; I did not have to speak my own disapproval. Gill was not trusted by the army; I was not sure I trusted him myself. But I had no time for personal matters.

I reviewed the situation as far as we knew it. The defense of Vista Grande was not going well. That garrison was trapped; the enemy's main army had presumably penetrated to some point southeast of there and was maneuvering to bring the Judean army to battle again and finish them. That much we knew before we departed from Dan. I had brought the Great Jordan Guards Legion down to Judah in a week's time—so rapidly that in all likelihood, the Messiahists were not even aware of our absence from Dan, let alone our presence here in Judah. If we moved quickly, we could join forces and strike an unexpected blow. It was possible we could turn the tide of war now running so powerfully against Judah. And if we frustrated the timetable of the churchman, so that much of Israel was unsubdued when the Millennium came, we could bring their whole preposterous theology crashing down.

But now Judah was rejecting our proffered help.

"What are the Judeans afraid of?" Major Jared asked. "Why do they shun us?"

"They must distrust our intentions," I said. I turned over in my mind the things that had taken place since I captured Naphtali. No doubt there was much to object to from Glanz's point of view in my handling of events in Naphtali, but goods and soldiers and profits were coming down to Judah again. Could Glanz know my larger goals? That I planned to make Naphtali and the north a bastion against the Messiahists—and against himself? *I looked at Gill.* Could Glanz be aware that I finally knew the truth of my parentage and had formed certain determinations about him? *Again, in seeking an answer, I looked at Gill.*

"What was it exactly that you wished to say to Tephlin Glanz, Captain Gill? Come, I'm very curious to know."

Gill gathered himself and departed without a word.

We had few options to consider. What we needed was intelligence. I ordered a trench and barricade thrown up around the camp and I sent out patrols in all directions. Then I bade my officers good evening.

"It would be helpful if we had more cavalry, sir," Major Jared said in parting.

"Indeed!" I replied. I pulled my mantle tight against the evening chill. I needed to think this through alone. A crowd of civilians had gathered, some to protest our requisitioning their livestock and wagons, but others to see the famous Sword of Israel. I moved among them and conversed with them briefly, and then excused myself and walked along the bank of the Jordan. The night was clear, and the stars shone with icy clarity. The sky road lay directly overhead and seemed to plunge into the bed of the Jordan. To the superstitious, this would not seem a good omen. I emptied my mind of all things, silenced the memories crowding for my attention, and breathed in the cold, sweet air of autumn.

In the clarity of solitude and darkness, the thought came to me: *Somehow, I had always expected to choose the timing of my struggle with Tephlin Glanz.*

III

In the morning I re-embarked the troops and supplies. Rather than attempt reconciliation with Glanz and Ben Gurion, I had decided on a bold move. It was too late for reconcilation; they must know it as well as I.

The weather continued fair, and by dawn the following day, we were standing off the portage of Esdralon, which my men captured without difficulty. I lit a signal fire and sent patrols out. In a few hours, I saw cavalry approaching. I almost held my breath until I recognized him.

"Cousin!" I exclaimed, riding out to meet him. We dismounted and I embraced him. "I have a favor to ask of you and your father. A large and very dangerous favor."

"*Cousin*, is it?" Erech Vashon replied coolly. He looked us over suspiciously and demanded to know what we were doing in Engedi. He was lean and hard and weather beaten, and he looked every inch a soldier. "So you have learned some things in the past few years," he said to me, referring to my mode of addressing him. "Still, this looks like mischief to me. What are you up to, *cousin*?" His voice was a challenge; I saw that I had not endeared myself to him by seizing a military post for which he was responsible.

"Indeed, it is mischief," I admitted cheerfully, "and of the worst kind. You had best fetch your father, and I'll explain it to both of you. But I must warn you, time is of the essence!"

Erech saluted and was gone. I knew his father—and my uncle—still commanded the cavalry in Engedi. I could only hope the Colonel was nearby and that Erech would not delay in bringing him to me.

My luck held. At dusk a party of officers approached us rapidly on horseback. At its head was Colonel Elkiah Vashon. He greeted me formally, shook my hand, and then took me in his arms in a quick embrace. "Welcome, nephew!" he said. I could tell he dreaded what I had to say, though he remained, as always, impeccably courteous. My uncle had aged visibly; his hair was gray and his face deeply lined. "We have heard many strange things about you since we parted," he said, sizing me up. "But I must say, I am less surprised to see that you outrank me than to find you here on my doorstep, armed and uninvited! What has brought you intruding into Engedi?"

He was telling me I had put him in a difficult situation, where his honor pulled him in two directions. I explained that, with the war going disastrously for Judah, I had brought my legion down to help, but Glanz and Ben Gurion had barred my way to Hebron.

"Why would Glanz reject your assistance?"

"You must ask Glanz about that. I wrote offering an alliance, but stipulating that I would not serve as a subordinate. Glanz may be reluctant to recognize me as anything but his instrument. But too much has happened between us for me to consider serving under him. I found my mother two months ago when we fought in Asher, and so I know the story of my real parentage and my father's death."

"I see," Elkiah said, searching my face.

"In the meantime, I hold Naphtali and further Lebanon in my own right. I am High General of Dan and Naphtali and what is left of Asher, and I have my whole legion behind me."

Perhaps, as I reflected on these things, Glanz was right to fear me.

"Much indeed has happened since we parted, nephew. I long to hear the whole story, but first I must know what you intend to do *here*." My uncle's manner reminded me he had duties to perform.

"Quite simply, I need your help. I need your advice and counsel as my kinsman—and, to speak plainly, I need your cavalry. I brought only a troop of horse down from Naphtali. And, to speak even more plainly, I intend to take Esdralon."

"*Take Esdralon!*" the Colonel exploded angrily. "Have you gone mad?" Then, when he had regained control of himself, he asked warily, "What would you do with it if you had it?"

"My purpose is to wage war against the Messiahists; make no mistake about that. But to ally myself with Glanz, I may well have to coerce my way into a partnership. Possession of Engedi would make my voice heard by those who need to hear it. I also intend to give this land back to Benjamin and thereby right one of my father—one of Tephlin Glanz's—wrongs. My plan is to intervene here in the name of peace in Judah's war with Benjamin. This unjust war with Benjamin must end. I mean to end it so we can face the Messiahists united."

"So you would dictate the terms on which you cooperate with Tephlin Glanz?"

"I do not intend to let him dictate to me, Uncle. Beyond that, we'll see. But I expect coercion is the only way with him, other than surrender."

He looked at me as he thought through the implications of my words, and then his eyes blazed a moment.

"Let me be blunt," I said quickly. "I came here to ask you and Erech to violate your oaths and to risk death with me. I want you to commit treason and rebellion and join forces with me in what I admit is a desperate venture. Lastly, as I explained, I mean to take Engedi and the city of Esdralon."

"That's plain enough!" he said. "You ask only for my honor and my life!" He drew himself up in a way that put all my senses on alert. *Here is a dangerous man,* his body told me. Then the moment passed. "What do you think of this madness, Erech?" Colonel Vashon said, still aroused, but turning to his son.

"It's not completely mad," Erech said. "He would gain control of a good part of Glanz's food supply and all of his wool. It would get his attention."

Colonel Vashon slapped his quirt against his knee, looking grimly at me. "Treason and rebellion!" he exclaimed. "It's a pretty pass I've come to, then, and my country too!" He looked at his son and then at me. "But I'd be less than a man if I didn't take up arms against Tephlin Glanz when given a chance. I may be insane myself, but I'm inclined to join with you in this madness."

"And I also!" Erech added enthusiastically. Moved by the spirit of the moment, the three of us embraced. We were kin above all other considerations; we had found our way to this alliance as seedlings find a way to light. I needed no oaths or protestations from them; the Vashons were with me to the death, and I with them. We settled down to the business at hand like hardened conspirators.

"Esdralon is lightly held," my uncle said, describing the situation in Engedi. "The only obstacle between you and the city is my cavalry." He informed us he had but 300 men, mounted on horses in poor condition. "The men are reliable," he assured me, "even if they don't look like much." He described the garrison of Esdralon scornfully as a mere penal colony of the Northern Lights Enterprises. "I'm told that you actually sent part of this rabble down from Naphtalil. Ben Gurion, being no fool and able to find no better use for them, sent them on to Esdralon."

Burgos and Gill and I were amused at this characterization of Huerta's soldiers, whom I had culled from my forces and sent down to Hebron. "That we did," Burgos admitted, "though we did not intend to plague the two of you with them!"

I invited them to form a plan with us to take Esdralon and they took up the task eagerly. "The Northern Lights garrison are more an embarrassment than they are soldiers,"

Colonel Vashon said. "You could take the city with a handful of children."

"Good," I said. "Let's take it tonight, then, before Glanz and Ben Gurion have an idea of what we are up to."

"Tonight?"

"Just get us inside the gate. Tell the garrison commander that a tour of inspection is coming or that they are being called up because of the reverses in Judah. Threaten them with being sent to the front. Tell them anything," I said. "Just get me inside the gate!"

Major Vashon contrived to get a picked group of my men inside the city, and we negotiated the surrender of the citadel before the sun rose.

I inspected the citadel of Esralon, where I had launched my personal vendetta against the churchmen, and I marveled at the time that had passed and the events that had come out of it. I moved into the same Headquarters that General Boseth had held in his time, and I gazed again across the Jordan at the hills of Judah. Much had come full circle. As we shared a hasty meal in General Bosheth's old office, I told my uncle and cousin the story of how I had found my mother. "At last," I said, "I know who I am and understand our kinship. And knowing that, I doubly appreciate all your kindness to me."

My account of my mother's condition moved both of them to tears. Elkiah explained that he had thought it inappropriate to broach the subject of my parentage. He had taken it for granted that I knew the truth all along and was surprised to hear I had not. "Your mother Rachel was a beautiful woman," he said, "and your father loved her dearly. I find it hard to forgive your grandfather, Josiah, but I expect I would do many things myself to save my lands and heritage."

Very gently, I broached the news that the Vashon estate, like my own, had been destroyed by the Messiahists. "I made inquiries," I said, "but found no one in Asher who knew the fate of your family. I am sorry to bring you this news."

"There were none but servants there and renters whom I do not know," my uncle said. "My Sarah died of the fever years ago, and we have not had the means to keep up the estate ourselves. Erech and I have earned our bread as soldiers here in this waste land of savages and merchant conniving."

I expressed my regret for the loss of his wife and Erech's mother—and for having compromised their honor by turning them into rebels. But Elkiah and Erech would hear nothing of apologies.

"You saved us by this intrusion, nephew. I came down to Engedi to serve the Council of Apostles, not knowing then that Glanz ruled the Council. Surely you know I would never have served *him*! Once the war with the churchmen broke out, we were stranded here, Erech and I. Defending Israel against the Kr has been my duty, and I have accepted it. But I am happier still to take up arms against enemies who have despoiled my country. And if, in the course of time, we turn our swords against Tephlin Glanz, then I think that my life and my efforts and all my suffering here will have some meaning."

IV

I sent messages to Judah, both to its government and to General Ahaz, commander of its armies, explaining my intentions in seizing Esdralon, and I dispatched a delegation to Lagash to make contact with the Harlech. I had no immediate answer from either. A week went by and then another, and I began to worry about the silence out of Lagash.

"You've made a fine mess!" Gill rebuked me. "Your own rashness has isolated you. Holding fast in Dan was the surest way to prolong the war into the next millennium. It was reckless to bring the legion here, where the prospects are uncertain at best. In fact the outcome of the Judean war may be a foregone conclusion." He recited the advantages of defending the north—the distance, the terrain, the logistical difficulties for the enemy.

He was correct in a way, but also wrong. The Messiahists were growing bolder with each victory, and they began to seem invincible. Soon people would accept their claims merely on the prestige of their arms. But I knew their strength was hollow. A rebuke to their arrogance, even a single defeat, could snuff their false beacon light. It was therefore worth a substantial risk to give them a setback.

So I could answer Gill's objection to my putting the legion at risk in Judah, but regarding the Benjamites and their silence in response to my overtures, I was puzzled and apprehensive. Though I had parted in anger from Moriah, I had lived and fought along side Benjamites for two years. I could not think of them as anything but friends. Surely I could reach an understanding with any government in Lagash. "Does it mean nothing that I—"

"That you have good intentions?" Gill scoffed. "That you have a vision of Israel in which Benjamin plays a large and honorable role? No, I think not. Benjamin has its own vision of the future. They pursue their interests purely as they see them."

"Are they blind? Can't they see that together we can defeat the Messiahists and put an end to all this misery?"

"You are the one who is blind. For Judah and Manasseh to go on savaging each other is in Benjamin's interest. If they exhaust each other, Benjamin wins. The Harlech detest both sides—and apparently they are not interested in you and your plans. Yes, I know, you saved Jonas II Harlech from drowning, and you served honorably with Zachariah ben Harlech. But Benjamites, you must know by now, are not a grateful race."

As I listened to his rebuke, I considered what their hostility must mean. "This silence from Lagash means that Zachariah is dead. He cannot have arrived home after we parted."

"Very likely," Gill agreed. "And we don't know if Moriah and his men reached there either."

"I only hope that in Zachariah's absence the leadership of Benjamin can see reason."

"Reason!" Gill exclaimed. "I tell you that Benjamin will see its interests lie with the Messiahists. Until the Messiahists have destroyed Judah, that is, and exhausted themselves in the process. I fear that the Harlech are about to ally themselves with the churchmen to that very end. Perhaps they already have."

"Impossible!" I exclaimed, knowing that it was not impossible, but quite likely. Whatever else he was, Gill was a clever strategist.

"Let Zelaph ben Harlech be brought here," I said to Gill. "I have a letter to write."

Zelaph ben Harlech and two of his associates presented themselves before us. As one of the few remaining members of the Harlech clan of any standing in Esdralon, Zelaph had seemed suitable to serve as a figurehead of a Benjamite government. He had been cooperative thus far, and he had reason to, for I had worked diligently to improve the lot of his countrymen. At this moment, however, he seemed resentful, and I thought I detected uneasiness in his manner as well.

"It has been two weeks, and we have no word from the Apostle of Benjamin, " I began. "No word from your masters. My delegation has not been heard of. What do you know of this?"

"Nothing, my lord. I know nothing at all." Zelaph looked to Gill as if for confirmation, and then to me. "Nothing at all."

Gill leaned forward and whispered in my ear: "He's lying."

"Take down what I speak," I ordered Gill.

> *To His Excellency, General Ahaz, commander, Armies of Judah, etc.*
>
> *It is vital that you know that I pursue a single policy in relation to our common enemy, and that is to reconcile Judah with Benjamin, so that together, they and the forces I command, can act in concert against the Messiahists. Together, we could defeat the Messiahists once and for all. If we remain at odds, however, it is ourselves who will likely be defeated. The terms necessary for reconciliation with Benjamin are self-evident: restoration of all lands taken from Benjamin in the recent conflict and resumption of the trade with the uncovenanted peoples on a shared and equitable basis.*
>
> *I have lately sent a delegation to the Apostle of Benjamin, or to whatever government now exists in Lagash, to acquaint them with the proposals outlined above, seeking to end hostilities between Benjamin and Judah and to pursue joint military action against the Messiahists. But I write to inform you that my delegation to Lagash has not returned, nor have I received word of their safe arrival there. This silence out of Benjamin may mean many things, but it does not bode well for a joint effort against the Messiahists, and it is that apprehension that impels me to write.*
>
> *It may be that Benjamin will not accept an end to the present war short of the destruction of Judah. I have no privileged knowledge of their views. The present conflict has, however, been harsh enough that the Harlech may be irreconcilable. Or, more likely in my opinion, their estimate of the relative strength of the forces now contending in Israel puts yours at a disadvantage. Benjamin may believe your forces are vulnerable and that present circumstances offer an opportunity to exploit. Thus I fear they may move against you, either by themselves, or jointly with the Messiahists. Either prospect has its dangers; the latter is to be dreaded as fatal to our cause.*

I paused to let this sink into Zelaph. I could not tell if he anticipated where all this was leading. It was important that he understand, but he appeared puzzled and uneasy. I watched him as I resumed dictating:

> *I fear that unresolved differences between ourselves may not only weaken us in this crisis, but embolden others against us. Let it be known therefore that Judah has nothing to fear from the forces under my command. Moreover, I mean to make it known to Benjamin that an attack by them upon your forces will be received here as an attack upon ourselves.*

Now I had Zelaph's attention! He looked up at me, surprised and indignant.

> *I will state further for their benefit that Engedi is not a goose on a platter laid out for their taking, but will be theirs in exchange for an alliance against the Messiahists. Engedi has a price, and a high one. Benjamin must ally with us against the Messiahists, or fight to take it from us.*
>
> *I write this in hope as well as apprehension, trusting that Benjamin will commit no rash action against us, but see reason and join with us to seek an end to enmity. Yours, etc.*

Gill finished his hurried scrawl and blotted the paper. I took up the pen to sign it. Zelaph's face was dark and perspiring. He scowled fiercely, his hands clenched in his lap. I wondered what he was thinking. Obviously he had no experience in diplomacy.

"Any points that need clarification?" I asked. He gave me a murderous look but shook his head.

"Make two copies; send one to General Ahaz immediately and give the other to Zelaph here. He will know how to make its contents known in Lagash."

"You lie!" Zelaph cried and lunged at me, his right hand plunged into his tunic.

I raised my hands to ward him off and caught the blade of his dagger in my left hand. I had not seen him draw it. The blade pierced between my second and ring finger and slashed downward into my palm. The force of his body drove me backward, tipping my chair; we tumbled together onto the floor, his body on top of mine,

"Guards!" Gill shouted. "Alarm!"

My assailant screamed as Burgos stabbed him from behind. Another of my bodyguard speared him as we wrestled on the floor. Zelaph cried out, and I felt his muscles clench spasmodically.

"Careful!" Burgos shouted. "Don't harm the Master!"

I felt the room spin; Gill was cursing. "Fetch the surgeon!" he shouted. "Alert the garrison! The Master has been struck down!"

My assailant let out a sigh, spraying me with blood. I felt his body relax, and his dead weight drove the blade downward into my palm, causing excruciating pain. For a moment, I was overcome by the confusion and noise; the pain made me giddy. The guards pried his body off of mine, Burgos fiercely levering him off with his sword. I struggled upright into a sitting position, holding my hand.

"The bloody fool! Why – ?" Burgos's face was purple with rage.

The two other Benjamites were pinned against the wall, the spears of my bodyguard at their throats. Their eyes bulged with fear; one was bleeding. "Take them away!" Gill commanded.

"Take care you spare them for questioning," I said, gripping my hand.

"Morales!" Gill shouted. "Make haste!" In a softer voice, Gill asked, "Are you all right, my lord?" I found myself slumping in his arms back to the floor, dazed and overwhelmed with nausea. Gill raised my head, frowning at me. "He is in shock. Fetch the surgeon."

The knife was still thrust through my hand, and the wound was bleeding profusely. The pain was unbelievable. Zelaph must have twisted the blade as we struggled, separating or breaking some of the bones in my hand. Burgos muttered angrily as he tied a cloth around the wound. He fumbled with the knot but was unable to staunch the bleeding. The blade stuck out through the back of my hand.

"Burgos," I said, "it's only my hand. We've seen worse." He helped me onto a couch. After a while I felt my head clearing and sat up. "Question the other two to see if there was a larger conspiracy, but treat them justly. We have no evidence at this point."

Gill gestured to Burgos and said to me sternly, "You need to lie down." I obeyed and lay back on the couch. I had time, waiting for the surgeon to arrive, to consider the problem of how the knife would be removed.

When the surgeon had finished his work, we considered the evidence. "I think this Zelaph acted alone, my lord," Gill said. "The others appeared genuinely surprised when he drew his dagger." Burgos confirmed what Gill had observed of the incident.

When Zelaph's two companions were brought before me, I was relieved that neither showed any effects of their interrogation. Though my hand was throbbing, I was able to feign composure. "Your comrade was hasty and undiscerning," I began, gesturing them into silence. "He imagined I intended to betray your long-suffering country. It is important therefore that you understand my purposes fully."

"My lord, we had no role in this folly; we –"

"Yes, I know. It was necessary to inquire into the matter, but I am satisfied that what you say is true. Zelaph acted alone and without premeditation. He was a fool on all counts."

They nodded vigorously.

"It is imperative now that we move forward. Time is of the essence. I must have contact with your masters in Lagash. Benjamin and Judah must put an end to their hostilities. That is my purpose, and it has become your purpose as well."

They looked at one another and at me; one nodded slightly.

"You understand," I continued, "that I have been a friend to Benjamin. You know that I served with your countrymen in the Kuhlan lands, and that they served with me later in Naphtali and Dan and Asher. As comrades."

They nodded, still sweating.

"For these reasons and others, I desire an Israel that is whole again, and I want peace with Benjamin."

"And you want an alliance with Benjamin against the Messiahists."

"Yes," I admitted, irritated at being interrupted. *This one at least is not a fool.* "I helped Zachariah ben Harlech escape from the Kuhlan lands and saw him as far as the border of Ephraim. If he did not make his way safely to Lagash, it is not my doing."

"We understand, my lord."

"My fear is that some misfortune overtook him on the way, and that the leaders in your country do not understand what I seek or trust my intentions. I have taken Engedi back for them. My purpose has always been to return it to Benjamin and to secure justice for your countrymen. But now necessity makes me say that the price for its return is the alliance I seek."

They hesitated. They understood that Zelaph ben Harlech had been moved to rage by this determination of mine, which he had seen as a betrayal. Thus, they were careful not to show disapproval. They nodded to signal that, whether they agreed or not, they understood me fully.

"Very well then," I said. "Engedi lies in my gift. I can make amends to Benjamin without seeking the consent of Judah in the matter. I will return Engedi as soon as we reach an understanding. And that is my desire."

"So we shall say to the government of Benjamin."

"Then may good fortune speed you on your way."

"Tell them," I added emphatically as they turned to leave, "tell your masters also how you were treated in custody after your comrade plunged a knife into me." I was thinking of my delegation to Lagash. "Tell them to release my envoys and have them come to me again in peace."

"We will, my lord," they said in acknowledgement, bowing low and taking their leave.

"Do you think they will carry my message?" I asked Gill when they had gone.

"They will have a tale to tell," Gill said humorlessly, "if they do."

V

The man who presented himself before me was old and bent and had a hawk's nest of white hair. "I am Lamech," he said. "You know my clan and lineage. I received your message, the one you wish communicated to Lagash."

"So, you are the authority of the Harlech here in Esdralon. Very well!" To Gill I remarked, "At last, I meet the real government of Esdralon. The man I picked was a fool."

The old man inclined his head slightly.

"What can you tell me of the fate of my delegation?" I demanded. "Speak plainly; I have little patience at the moment."

"I fear they were not well received in Lagash," Lamech said, licking his lips. He had a cavernous mouth, partly hidden by his beard, and he had lost most of his teeth.

"Your *Excellency*!" Gill prompted.

"Are they dead?" I demanded. "Or prisoners?"

"They are hostages, Excellency." The old man stared at me with watery, unflinching eyes.

"Hostages!" Gill exclaimed. "They were envoys protected by a flag of truce!" Gill expressed my outrage for me; it freed me to weigh what I heard.

"I meant Benjamin no harm," I said. "Surely you know that, and if you know, so must your masters. Moreover, the law of envoys is known to everyone. These conventions come down to us" – *I choked on the words*—"from the past."

"Excellency, I regret that so rash an action was taken toward your envoys. What you say is true, and this breach of the Law gives me pain. The decision was made, to be sure, without the knowledge of your actions and character that we now possess. Nevertheless, it is a fact. It is done." He raised his white head and regarded me: "And it is a message."

Neither Gill nor I obliged him by asking *what message?*

"Benjamin will make no alliance with Judah," Lamech continued doggedly. "And Benjamin will make no alliance with you."

"No alliance? Are they mad?" Gill exclaimed.

"No alliance as long as Tephlin Glanz and Ben Gurion rule in Judah."

This was clever. Very clever. It was known, apparently, that I had my own scores to settle with my alleged father and his minion, Simon Ben Gurion. The Harlech were attempting to bind me to their purposes just as I was attempting to bind them to mine. But something in the situation gave me pause. *Who* was making these calculations? I felt another wave of nausea pass over me. That I was so deeply estranged from Tephlin Glanz was known only by my closest friends and confidants. "What you say implies that I am not dealing with Jonas II Harlech or his son Zachariah. Who, then, speaks for Benjamin in Lagash?"

"We know, my lord General, the story of Zachariah's departure from you in Asher," Lamech replied. "But sadly, he has never arrived in Lagash. We assume he is dead at the hands of the Messiahists or lies in their custody. And we now know—though we had not known before—that you are innocent of his blood. She knows. We have informed her of it. Nevertheless—"

"*She?* Whom do you mean?"

"– she is for hard war, war to the finish, and I do not believe she will release your hostages until you have overthrown the usurpers in Judah."

"And *she* is?" *I knew the answer before he spoke.*

"The Senyora Michal-Rebekah Harlech, Apostle of Benjamin."

I invited the old man to dine with me, the better to knit up the frayed relationship between our peoples. I did not want my men to avenge the attempt on my life, and I wanted to show them that my friendship with Benjamin had not altered. In spite of the cold, we ate on the portico of the Headquarters building, as publicly as possible. It is a persistent myth that Israelites will not betray those with whom they have just taken a meal. While I have not found this to be true, such, I hoped, would be the message of our meal together. I had no appetite, but I managed to take a few spoonfuls of oatmeal and dried fruit. The menu suited my elderly guest very well. As I ate, I mused on the events of my life that had transpired in these quarters. On the floor above, Justin had once come to the Commissary to invite me to dinner at the home he shared with Michal-Rebekah.

"You will assume charge of affairs in Esdralon," I said to Lamech. "You will command the Benjamite militia, preside over the court, distribute rations, and administer whatever else I do not retain in my own hands."

The old man nodded, eating slowly but with relish.

My staff hovered about wanting to assist me. I waved them away. "Perhaps it is better now that the masks are off," I said. "Some masks, at any rate. Perhaps if I live long enough, all masks will be removed, and we shall see face to face at last. Or is that a Messiahist conceit?" *I was thinking of Justin.* Lamech was busy with his bowl. I was talking mostly to myself, but I was beginning to see things and make connections; the past was falling into place. "You must," I told Lamech, "communicate to the Apostle of Benjamin, the Senyora Michal-Rebekah Harlech, my condolences on the death of her son."

In truth, I had been staggered by the news that Michal-Rebekah was alive – scarcely less than by the dagger Zelaph had thrust into me. My first emotion was disbelief. Michal-Rebekah alive and the Apostle of Benjamin! And also bent on hard war against Judah – and against myself? It was almost too much to take in at once.

"And Appian?" I had asked. "Is her son alive?"

Lamech had closed his eyes and let his chin decline to his chest. "Regrettably, your Excellency. . . ."

So, Appian was dead. Gentle, precocious Appian. I had wanted desperately to know how Michal-Rebekah had come to escape and how Appian had died – and to express my relief that she was alive and my sorrow for Appian's death, but the sudden release of these pent-up feelings had unmanned me, and I had wept in the old man's presence, unable to restrain myself.

In recent days, I had thought much about Justin's love for Michal-Rebekah and of my own feelings, for which I had no explanation. But as I turned these matters over in my mind in light of her present high station among the Benjamites, our relationship appeared in a new and disturbing light. Her escape, Justin's arrest, and the charges that had been leveled against him formed a pattern that I could not dismiss. In all probability, Michal-Rebekah had not merely been a member of Benjamin's intelligence network in conquered Esdralon; she had directed it. Which meant that she had either turned Justin or exploited him. *My tears had continued to fall as I realized these things, but for different reasons.*

"Have another bowl," I said to my ancient guest. "You will need your strength in the days ahead."

Lamech put his food aside and looked at me expectantly. He would be a good messenger.

"Assure the Apostle of my esteem for her."

It occurred to me that when Michal-Rebekah suddenly fled Esdralon, it would have exposed Justin. Her flight might well have precipitated his arrest and execution. That was, in fact, the most likely explanation of its timing. It was also just possible that she had deliberately contrived my brother's death – as revenge for the slaying of her husband. That, too, was possible. But I could not know for certain from any information I had now or was likely ever to have.

"Remind the Senyora that we are well known to one another, and that, in spite of all, we are not enemies. Say that we both have power in our respective lands to affect the lives of many people. If we act with foresight and wisdom, we have it in our hands to put an end to this suffering. Say to her that the release of my delegation in accordance with the Law of Envoys will signal to me that such wisdom—and such civility – is still possible in Israel. Tell her *to release my delegation.*"

Lamech blinked at me and nodded. He understood. I bade him send word with all possible speed.

Gill helped me from my chair when Lamech had taken his leave. "So it is hard war, then?" he said in my ear. "War to the finish!"

"So you heard Lamech?"

"No," he replied. "I heard *you.*"

Justin's death was a fresh pain. It had never been absent from my mind; only now that pain was aggravated by the knowledge that Bulavar had, in a sense, been right about him. Whether I napped or lay awake, enduring the pain in my hand, I played host to the same memories of Justin's arrest and my interrogation by Bulavar: *"The charge? Let me think. Sedition, perhaps? Consorting with the enemy? Adultery? Spying for the enemy! Attempting to incite Israelites to rebellion! Treason! Heresy!"*

That Justin had been turned by Michal-Rebekah and had been playing the part of a traitor was possible, but seemed unlikely. It was too simple. Justin had been converted to Michal-Rebekah's view of the war, to be sure. He had seen the war as an injustice that needed to end as quickly as possible. And the merchants had also come to see the war as a mistake, a loss that needed to be cut. It seemed likely, then, that Justin had been his father's agent – warily no doubt, duplicitously perhaps, and with what qualms and reservations one could only imagine. But on the issue of ending the war, Justin and his father had come to see eye to eye. Justin may have acted for Tephlin Glanz in any secret contacts he had with the Harlech. Or he may have led his father.

"A channel of communication, you suggest? Of course. A channel! The imagination runs riot! But channels, don't you see, run both ways. And just how much information has she passed the other way to the enemy? Ah? Can you answer me?"

At last I could see the situation as Bulavar saw it. Justin had entangled himself in the web Tephlin Glanz was weaving and in another spun by Michal-Rebekah. I wondered if he had been an agent in these matters or merely a tool. *Did it matter, finally? My clever, brilliant brother!* Justin had blundered into these webs and broken his neck in them. I would never know precisely what had brought about his arrest or know the manner of his death; only that his arrest had signaled war between the two factions. From the merchants' perspective, the Messiahists had overreached themselves; to the churchmen, Glanz's faction had failed in the crisis. Justin's arrest had in turn precipitated other events. Even the chronicles would say that.

To that extent can truth be known and spoken.

I thought of my own bloody work in the citadel of Esdralon after Justin's arrest and wondered what the chronicles would say of that. I, too, had risen up and set myself against the church and, for all I knew at the time, against the government of Israel. I could remember it all quite clearly. I had climbed the scaffolding by the fortress and entered by the top floor, and I had wreaked havoc on the Messiahist clergy there. I had never counted them in my totals of enemies slain because they were not warriors, and not all of them had been armed. There must have been a dozen of them, including two guards whom I left bleeding and lifeless as I ran amok through their quarters. I had been barely twenty at the time. Afterwards

I had set fire to the building. My actions, however wild or even mad, had merely anticipated what Tephlin Glanz and Ben Gurion had already decided to do; I forced them to act sooner than they had planned. But, as Ben Gurion had noted ironically to me, the chronicles would say that I *led* the rising, which would be characterized as a spontaneous outbreak against the tyranny of the church.

In a sense, I had. And in a sense it was. But mostly it was a lie. I had played more the role of a blind worm in a compost than the leader of a rising. But the most difficult—the most intolerable—realization I had to stomach was the thought that Bulavar was, according to his lights, acting in those events just as I was, for the greater good of Israel.

Israel! I shuddered to think of all the word entailed: truth and lies inseparable forever.

The one truth to which I clung, after all, was that Justin was truly my brother.

VI

In these familiar surroundings, I was continually burdened by a sense of my brother's presence. I saw him everywhere – at headquarters and on the street or in the small shops where we had eaten together. Once I had the courage to stand in the street and look up at the quarters where Justin had lived with Michal-Rebekah and Appian. I put a foot on the stairs but could not climb them. I tried to describe to Odessa these thoughts and the memories of Justin that events had aroused in me:

> *"I seem to have arrived by a different path at Justin's dilemma – to an overwhelming desire for peace in the midst of a war that I am compelled to fight. I find myself champion of a cause in which I no longer believe, and I am in possession of knowledge that might, in principle at least, reconcile the warring parties. But events have advanced so far that I see no way to arrest or divert them. Must we go on till we exterminate each other?"*

"Must we go on till we exterminate them?" Justin had asked a similar question years ago on the plain of Engedi.

I overwhelmed Odessa with advice – to visit her father and look after Matild and keep in close touch with Amasa, who would know of events as they transpired. I inquired after her health and asked a multitude of mundane questions. With the river traffic disrupted by the war, the mail was irregular, and I had not heard from her since leaving Jezreel. Her silence weighed heavily on my mind. Eventually I exhausted the things I could say without having said the things I most wanted to tell her. I put a period to my letter and took up the next task.

Colonel Vashon never tired of reminiscing about his brother Emanuel. "Your father was a paragon among men," Elkiah assured me over and over, as if he feared I thought badly of him. Hearing his living memories of my father, I felt as though I was myself remembering. The man gradually took shape in my imagination. On the occasion of my birthday in late December, we had a meal together to celebrate the passing of another year of my journey. Emanuel Vashon was very much in our minds.

"Your father was honorable in every way," Elkiah insisted. "I say that even though he broke the Law with your mother. Emanuel's intentions were honorable, even if frustrated by events, and he remained loyal to her all his days. He never married, you know, although there was no hope of his ever having his beloved Rachel. I liked old Samuel, in spite of his flaws, but it breaks my heart to think of what he did to that young couple."

I had often spoken to him of Odessa and I remarked that among the Canadians, women are allowed to choose their own mates. "Divorce is possible as well," I added, "and easily obtained."

My uncle was scandalized by such moral laxness. "What about legitimacy?" he protested. "Surely their lives must be chaos! I cannot imagine such a society."

I sat quietly until it came to him that my presence was proof that Israel's customs did not always assure legitimacy either. When he remembered, he was embarrassed and apologetic. Erech was tactfully trying to change the subject when a messenger broke in upon us; his face conveyed the news before he spoke. "The Messiahists have won another victory! Judah's army is routed and fleeing toward Hebron!"

We all bolted from our chairs. We inferred from his account that Ahaz had been slain in battle, and that his death was the cause of the rout. But as more details emerged we learned differently. Ahaz had been assassinated prior to the battle, and news of his death had in all likelihood prompted the attack. Demoralized by his absence, the Judeans had fled from the field. Ahaz's successor, General Hezekiah had not inspired confidence or taken the army in hand. We were afire with questions: "Who was the assassin?" my uncle demanded. "What was the motive?"

"They came from Hebron," our informants declared, "not from the Messiahist camp." They left us to draw our own conclusions. Gill was the first to propose an explanation: "Ahaz was in communication with the enemy. That's why Glanz and Ben Gurion thought it necessary to remove him."

"What are you talking about? How do you *know* General Ahaz was in communication with the enemy?"

"Because I copied the letter you dictated to him."

I felt a wave of revulsion and alarm, knowing he might be right. "But I am not the enemy—exactly. At least not till the Messiahists are disposed of."

"I'm not saying you are to blame," Gill said. "It is their everlasting suspicion that is to blame. I think the pair of them, Glanz and Ben Gurion, are about to die of their own intrigues. How fitting that would be!"

I had little time for irony; I had to intercede somehow in this catastrophe and stave it off. I immediately sent the cavalry across the Jordan at Achish, to see if we could assist the Judeans or at least ascertain what was going on. They confirmed that Vista Grande had fallen and the army was falling back toward Hebron. I ordered the infantry to march east to the portage where they could be ferried across the Jordan. The information we gleaned was sketchy but clear in its general import: the Messiahists were making a supreme effort to defeat all their foes before the new millennium arrived. Victory would bring the Kingdom of God back to earth.

"Not an easy task," Gill observed, "fighting against the Kingdom of God!"

My messages to Judah's army continued to go unanswered. I saw immediately that I could sit quietly and do nothing, or intervene in events and try to salvage them. Accordingly, I abandoned Esdralon and took the whole army across the Jordan. We encountered small groups of demoralized and straggling Judeans but failed to make contact with their main forces. Messiahist cavalry were probing everywhere; we were unable to reach the Yakima. Colonel Vashon's command worked themselves to exhaustion and suffered many casualties, but in vain.

Then, as events fell out, we found ourselves suddenly closer to the Messiahist army than to Judah's, so I had to drive my men mercilessly to prevent our being cut off and destroyed. The roads were filled with fleeing civilians, and wild tales of defeat and doom were repeated up and down the land. Even the weather turned hostile, with wind and cold and clouds full of snow. We conducted a forced march of two days through the hills of southern Judah and gathered ourselves at last on the banks of the Yakima a few miles below Hebron, near its confluence with the Jordan.

VII

Crossing the Yakima required the whole night. I ordered nearby houses and outbuildings dismantled to obtain planking for the bridge. We lit bonfires to illuminate the work and hasten the evacuation. In the glare of the flames, we must have seemed like demons to the people we had come to save. The destruction we wrought was indistinguishable from that of an invading army, but it was necessary. War is cruelty; there is no mitigating it. I had to steel myself against the cries of the inhabitants, who saw their shelter and livelihood consumed before their eyes. But I had learned to be appalled by nothing; I carried my purpose like a hot coal in my brain.

The scene around me was lit like a feverish dream of flame and leaping shadows. Messengers continually arrived and departed, and terrified refugees streamed into our lines. As the weather worsened, gusting winds threatened to tear the pontoon boats from their moorings. Sleet lashed the faces of my soldiers and the civilians who had fled to us – wretches of all ages and sexes and degrees of infirmity. Partly to control their fear, I set them to constructing a defensive barrier around our lines. The labor warmed their bodies and gave them something to do. That theirs was a forlorn hope was only too obvious. Their miserably frail obstacles would not even slow a determined enemy. A sudden assault could throw my legion and the hordes of refugees into the Yakima.

At midnight the infantry began their march across the rickety planking of the pontoon bridge. The cavalry, with the wagons and ballistas, crossed in boats. The horses were led down to the water and swam across in small groups, the riders leading them by their halters from the boats. The water was a terrible shock to them; some of them drowned or died out right and were swept away by the current. Meanwhile, I positioned my bodyguard by the moorings of the pontoon bridge on the western side of the river, ready to slash the cables if we were set upon by the enemy. Miraculously, the long hours of the night passed without an attack, and the evacuation proceeded. I crossed with the last cohort of infantry just before dawn. Because of the multitude of refugees, the crossing took much longer than I had anticipated. Fortunately, the enemy in our front remained quiet. I was grateful for the reprieve, whatever its cause.

The weather abated with the dawn. It gave me a moment to take stock of things. The infantry sprawled about their fires, preparing messes of porridge and pemmican and dry bread, and girding themselves for the exertions that lay ahead. Refugees were filtering into our camp from this side of the river as well, and the news they brought was disconcerting. Messiahist troops, both horse and foot, were already on the *east* side of the Yakima, north of Hebron. *This was a surprise.* That meant that the enemy was sweeping around Hebron to cut off all approaches to the city. The land approaches on the eastern side were being sealed, even as their main army drew near from the west. The situation was truly desperate.

As I imagined these separate forces moving across the map, I realized suddenly that the detached portion of their army on our side of the river was isolated and vulnerable. Since they were separated from their main army by more than a day's marching time, I saw that our force might be sufficient to crush these detached units. It was a matter of timing and energy. A small force thrown onto the scale at the right moment could tip the balance. If we could destroy them and then join the garrison of Hebron, we might save the day. *Victory still lay within our grasp.*

I looked around at my exhausted men. We had been on the march for two days with little sleep or nourishment. It was necessary to make some concessions to nature before we took up this task. I ordered the legion to rest for an hour and to eat a hot meal. I needed rest as well; I was finding it difficult to draw breath against the icy gusts of wind and was feverish and chilled by turns. My staff had pitched a tent for me, and I gratefully slipped inside and lay down. "One hour," I said to my orderly. "No more." Someone handed me a piece of bread but I had no appetite. I lay the bread aside and stretched out on the carpet. My hand was sensitive as a boil and throbbing.

It seemed only a moment later I was being shaken awake. Rising with great difficulty to a sitting position, I found my hand swollen and my head and body burning. Then I was seized by a sudden chill that set my teeth chattering violently. My orderly wrapped me in a blanket, and I concentrated all my energy, hoping to subdue the fever, but I could not. I felt an odd malaise permeating my entire body, and my mouth was parched. "Water," I said, scarcely recognizing my voice. Burgos came into the tent, gave me a worried look, and withdrew. Several of my staff came crowding in, and one of them offered me a flask. I found I could not hold it steady enough to drink. Someone assisted me, and I took a few swallows. The ice-cold water, however, caused a violent spasm in my belly, and I lay down again, shaking. It was painful to move, even to breathe.

"Fetch Colonel Vashon," someone said.

"Get the infantry moving on the road," I commanded, but no one seemed to hear.

In a few moments, Colonel Vashon entered the tent and knelt by me. "How are you feeling, nephew?" he asked. He held my good hand and felt my pulse.

"I'm afraid I've caught a fever." *I had not had such a fever since I was a boy.*

"Josiah, you must see about the hand," the Colonel said. He meant *you must have it amputated.*

I shook my head. I dreaded the disfigurement more than the operation itself, but there was no time at the moment, even had I so desired. I had urgent business to attend to, and thus reason to delay. The Messiahist force encircling Hebron had to be defeated today, within hours, or Hebron was lost. And the war with it. "Colonel," I said, "we must get the legion moving." I explained to him what had to be done, how the legion had to destroy the Messiahists. "Time is everything. Get the infantry on the road immediately. The cavalry can follow as soon as the horses are fed and rested a bit." *One can drive men mercilessly and they respond till their hearts give out; dumb beasts are more fragile and require rest and fodder.*

"You cannot rise by yourself, let alone ride a horse," my uncle said. "Let's take a look at the hand."

"My hand is nothing," I said. "However it looks, we must postpone the amputation. Whatever the cost. We have to find the encircling arm of the Messiahists up ahead and sever that limb, today." I roused myself from the mat. "Today! That is our single task. Otherwise, the last land route to Hebron is gone. The war –"

"I'm aware of the situation," he said shortly. "We'll see. Josiah, you have not attended to this intelligently," he added, indicating my bandaged hand. As I lay helpless, a great racket broke out outside – horses and wagons and men's voices – and nearby the high-pitched cries of a woman. The surgeon entered the crowded tent, and as he unwrapped my bandages, Elkiah continued to lecture me for my carelessness. "Never despise a small wound," he said, citing the adage: *Never despise a small wound, a weak enemy, or a poor relation.* The woman's cries broke in upon us again. I wondered what was happening, but felt a strange lassitude invade my mind. It was too great an effort to know.

"Ah!" the surgeon exclaimed as the last wrapping was removed. A sick-sweet smell of rotting flesh assailed my nostrils. I looked away, embarrassed. Fear clutched at my heart. *I had not realized it had gone so far.* This was not good, not good at all. My fear was confirmed when the others would not look at me. "The hand must come off," the surgeon mumbled. He seemed shame-faced to tell me.

"Yes," I said, "and welcome to it. But first we must crush the Messiahists."

"The arm, too, in all likelihood," he added.

His words thrilled me with fear. "Not now," I said. "I need a few hours, only a few. And I intend to have them." *I forced myself to look at my offending flesh.* "If we destroy the enemy, you can perform the operation tonight in Hebron."

The surgeon and Colonel Vashon exchanged glances. Colonel Vashon knelt at my side again; his eyes were shut and he held a cloth to his face. "Josiah, we would all follow you to the death. . . ." His voice trembled.

"Good! Then do as I say, Uncle. You see I cannot tarry here. I have no time! You must all do as I say." I had to make it clear to all that we must fall on the Messiahists while their army was divided; otherwise there was no hope of relieving Hebron. A victory in this dark hour would hearten Judah as much as it would demoralize the Messiahists. It was only two days till the new year – till the Millennium. The Messiahists were enslaved to their superstition of the world's impending end. If we could defeat them now, on the eve of the Third Coming, we might dishearten the lot of them. Abashed on the eve of their expected triumph, the Messiahist army might melt away. I meant to undermine their pretensions and topple their ludicrous theology. I explained these things as well as I could, struggling for breath.

Colonel Vashon heaved a sigh and glanced at the others. "I have already sent Erech forward with a troop of cavalry," he said. "We'll carry you in one of the forage wagons."

The surgeon re-wrapped my hand, clucking in disapproval. The cries of the woman increased in intensity, like a probe in my brain. I allowed myself to be bundled into a wagonload of hay. They made an elaborate bed with many blankets for me, but the cold penetrated my bones so that I shook like one possessed. The preparations seemed to take forever. As we rolled jolting out of camp, the family of the woman whose labor I had heard raised the red-faced newborn baby to me, as if for a blessing. I raised my good hand aloft, acknowledging their homage, but realizing in my heart that the child and I were setting forth upon opposite roads.

VIII

The Great Jordan Guards marched in a compact formation, Naphtali in the lead, then the wagons and ballistas, and Asher in the rear. The ranks were tightly closed, their lines dressed, resolution showing on every face. Ill as I was, I felt a thrill of pride. The bulk of the cavalry, however, were not yet up, and I had an urgent sense that we needed them with us *now*. I returned to my wagon, and my bodyguard propped me up on my load of hay. I was weak, but my fever had subsided. We were in familiar territory – just south of the road junction that led west to Hebron. This was the same spot where Major Jared had been turned back by Tephlin Glanz's officer a month before. The men in ranks cheered as they passed me. I waved them onward.

The roads had been filled with refugees all day, and we had pulled all males able to fight away from their families, armed them with pikes, and ordered them to fall in behind us. Most of them came willingly enough, in spite of the distress of their loved ones. That Judah was on its last legs was abundantly clear to everyone. Either we made a stand today, or we died as a nation. Up ahead the country was on fire. Such destruction had not been witnessed since the last Kuhlan war. Perhaps only I knew how thoroughly Israel was doing the work of the Kuhlans for them.

The trooper cantered to a halt, spraying frozen clods in every direction. He swung down heavily from his horse, which stood wide-legged, blowing and quivering, its muzzle flecked with foam. "Infantry ahead!" he announced. While the scout gave his report to Colonel Vashon, I scanned the horizon. Thin columns of smoke were rising in the north into a low overcast. We had scouts out in front of us, feeling for the Messiahists. The smoke told us clearly enough where the enemy had been, but not where they were *now*. I was relieved by this news of contact.

My officers clustered about the wagon. "My lord General, we have word of the enemy," Colonel Vashon reported. An infantry force of indeterminate size was about two miles in our front. Messiahist cavalry, he added, were plentiful, but apparently dispersed for plunder and destruction. They were thus not immediately available to support the infantry force.

I was elated at the news. It meant our enemies were not expecting us. If we could only close with them in the next hour or so, we would achieve tactical surprise. But our own cavalry were not up. Without them, we were vulnerable. Common sense as well as military doctrine dictated that we should stand pat.

I chewed a piece of straw, squinting at the sun, which barely glinted through the overcast. We had a few hours of daylight, but only a few. I felt my fever pounding in my head again. Always calculate what you are up against, I heard my Master Ebenezer say. I searched deep inside myself for strength and clarity of mind. "Perfect, gentlemen!" I said, assessing a situation far from perfect. "I believe we have them."

"My lord General," Major Hosea objected, "we have no knowledge of the enemy's strength, and they bar the road to Hebron."

"The enemy bars the road to nothing!" I exclaimed. "Rather, he has placed himself in our hand. And what we must do now is simply close our fist." I closed my good hand. I could see their confidence waning. They were uncertain whether my illness was clouding my judgement.

"Excellency," Colonel Vashon said, "My lord General, I suggest we wait for the cavalry to come up." *I always hated it when Elkiah used formality with me; it was his way of telling me I was wrong.*

"No time," I said. "Gentlemen, whatever the odds, we have one course and one course only. We must crush the Messiahists here and crush them *now*!"

A moment later a second trooper galloped back, bringing news that the enemy was aware of our presence and moving down the pike toward us. My officers looked apprehensive at the news. "Even better," I exclaimed. "Excellent, in fact! I had feared the enemy would escape. Colonel Vashon," I said, "come with me, and we'll look over the ground."

We had half a mile of plowed ground in front of us. The plain of Judah was level and nearly featureless. A small irrigation canal ran parallel to the road a hundred yards east of our position – a handy barrier to cavalry, but unfortunately for us, shallow and narrow. There was an orchard on our right. Immediately behind us was a large field of standing corn, picked but not yet shocked. Our flanks were in the air.

"What is this place?" I asked. One of the staff ran to inquire. "This is rare," I said to my uncle. "How often does such a chance present itself?" My uncle stared at me with raised eyebrows. "I mean the opportunity when everything one has fought against and detested from the very core of one's being places itself right in front of you, where you can strike it. Smash it! Obliterate it from the earth!"

Elkiah looked at me quizzically. "Never," he said finally.

"What do you mean?"

"I mean I never expect that to happen. It doesn't happen, Zaiyah."

My uncle seemed troubled, and I longed for a way to lift his spirits. Glancing around the terrain, I noted that the overcast had lifted a little. We could glimpse a pale sun disk, and to the south the great pylons of the Ancients' bridge across the Jordan loomed above the mist. "Look," I said. "We are being watched." The towering structures had erect ear-like points at the top and resembled giant, unearthly creatures that had sat patiently, eon after eon, like cats at a mouse hole. I was reminded of the legends of the fall of the Ancients.

"The Messiahists," I said, "claim that the Ancients were lured to destruction by evil beings—by rebel angels of some kind—and that they caused the Dissolution. Do you know those old tales?"

"Rubbish!" Elkiah snorted.

I realized that, having read the surviving letter of Cecilia Pleece, I knew more about the Dissolution than any man alive. "I know a different story," I said, "a story I believe. The Ancients were afflicted just as we are by these tales of the Judgment and the hope of supernatural intervention in the world. A group among them provoked a terrible war, believing they were doing god's work by hastening the Judgment Day, and so they destroyed themselves."

"Bah," Elkiah said. "The Ancients needed no supernatural intervention to find their way to ruin."

"How can you be so sure?"

"Look around," he said, seeming not much interested in the question. "Their ruins are everywhere—*everywhere!* Obviously, they had no restraint. No wisdom. I can't imagine them *not* destroying themselves! They were consuming the world. The Ancients destroyed themselves because of what they were. The Dissolution was an expression of their nature!"

"And us? What about us?"

The staff officer interrupted us with a report: "The canal – as well as the hamlet yonder – is called Chebar."

"Perfect! Chebar," I said. "From this day forward, Chebar will be one of the sacred places in Israel."

"We'll make it memorable, at least!"

Elkiah Vashon had once said to me that we know the value of something only when we are willing to die for it. I wanted to argue the point and contend instead that it is love that gives us the measure of things, not blood. But there was no time. I thought of Odessa and of having this conversation in her arms. But there was no point in longing for impossible things, and I had a battle to prepare.

I sent Colonel Vashon back to bring up the cavalry. Shortly after, the rest of Erech's troop came cantering in from the front, covered with mud and steaming. While he reported, I deployed the Naphtali brigade to the right of the pike. Its formation did not reach to the orchard, so I placed most of our recently pressed civilians on their right to stretch out the line. The rest I placed on the left of the pike, and to the left of the Naphtali brigade and in front of the cornfield. From even a hundred yards away, the sight of their line would blend into the corn, making it difficult to estimate our strength or the depth of our formation. I formed the wagons in a half-circle on the road behind the center of our line, as a barrier to cavalry. The Asherite brigade and the ballistas I deployed in the corn on our left, where they would be hidden from view.

I summoned the officers and explained my plan. "The civilian auxiliaries will form our extreme flanks," I said. "As the enemy approach, I will withdraw those on the left and have them form a reserve in the rear. But until the enemy is near to closing with us, I want to disguise our strength. I want our left to appear weak, so as to draw their main attack." This was a compliment to the Asherite brigade, and the officers acknowledged it. "I want them to come at us boldly, leading with their right. At the proper time, I will order the auxiliaries back, and the Asherite brigade will stand and receive their assault, breaking their lines with their missiles as they come. No one is better drilled at this than yourselves. Gentlemen, they have only to put themselves in javelin range and they are ours."

We went over the details of my plan. When they all understood what was wanted of them, I said, "One thing more – we will mask our identity until the last moment. Let them believe we are hastily raised militia, the last remnants of Judah. Keep the standards furled until my order."

The officers applauded these arrangements, but Major Jared said cautiously, "My lord General, our flanks are in the air."

"True. But with luck, Colonel Vashon will be here with the cavalry before we engage, and he will protect our flanks. Absent the cavalry, the cohorts on either flank will hold the place of honor. I will support you to the extent possible with the reserves, but the brigade leaders will have to be alert to flanking movements. The enemy's horses are scattered, either scouting or pillaging, so we may have an advantage – if we can lure them into attacking us quickly."

And if we cannot? The question lay unspoken among us.

Major Eli was scanning the enemy through a glass. "They have cavalry with them, sir. It looks like several troops."

Bad luck!

We watched the enemy deploy on both sides of the road before us, a dark mass spreading ever wider and wider, like spilled syrup. They were forming about a thousand yards in front of us. My head felt light, like a bubble rising in a vat.

"I see two standards. *Two* legions, sir."

My heart sank. "Two legions," I said, "but at half strength from hard campaigning. We nearly match them in numbers. Man for man, we are their masters." I was more worried about the cavalry. "How many pennants do you count?"

"Four," one of the captains answered.

"We have extra pikes and lances, sir," Major Jared said. "May I suggest, my lord General, that we make a barrier in the cornfield in our rear that they won't be able to see? That could add a bit of protection to our flank and rear. It could give us the edge of a moment's confusion."

"Excellent idea!" I said. "See to it immediately." *But it would be better,* I thought, *if our own cavalry came up.*

Major Jared shouted orders, and the Asherite brigade hurried to the task, building a fence of sharp stakes behind them. Gill was standing beside me, and I heard him muttering under his breath. "What is it, Gill?" I sensed his anxiety and recalled his growing reservations about our cause.

"Lord," he was saying under his breath, "let your loving kindness be upon us, who put our trust in you."

I packed him immediately off to Hebron to gather information on the situation there. He was of no use here, and I wanted the Messengers to be of a single mind. I wondered, though, in my heart of hearts, if anyone ever achieves singleness of mind in such circumstances. Or if anyone is truly obedient unto death. Obedient, yes. Soldiers obey orders and risk death in war; it is a daily occurrence. We who command willingly put ourselves and others in harm's way. But do we not always trust to luck—trust to some miraculous deliverance that will save us, perhaps alone, from the general catastrophe? I wondered if even the Dolorites of old or the proud, hot-blooded noble warriors who chained themselves to stakes in defiance of death did not believe until the last instant that some deliverance would come. *Some miracle.*

When I was a boy, I was convinced I could control the fall of the dice merely by wishing.

Brother Josephus played endlessly at dice with us. He had us calculate all the combinations possible with two six-sided dice. Of thirty-six combinations, six of them, he pointed out, added up to seven. He challenged us to avoid sevens and try to make other combinations appear in our throws. We used a small wooden box so we could not influence the fall of the dice with our hands. We tried for hours and occasionally threw for long stretches without a seven. One young boy from Issachar seemed particularly adept at making the dice fall as he chose.

"Good!" Josephus would say. "Keep it up."

Invariably, if we continued, the stretch without sevens would end, and we would roll a series with many sevens. Or only one.

"Can you by wishing or by magic deter the sevens combinations?" Brother Josephus demanded.

"Yes! Yes!" we all replied in a chorus.

"Show me then," the old man said with a twinkle in his eye. "What is the trick?"

We were all convinced we could do it. Sometimes it seemed we had. I recall one stretch of several weeks when I was twelve in which we did little else, and each of us recorded thousands of rolls of the dice, using all of our concentrated might to keep the sevens from appearing. One by one the other boys gave up. Only the boy from Issachar and I persisted, more stubborn than the rest. I refused to accept that I could not will the outcome of a throw – it seemed such a little thing, the throw of the dice and the outcome. At last I was the only holdout.

"So what are your eyes telling you?" Brother Josephus asked me with some asperity.

"I know I can do this," I replied. "I can learn the trick."

"I give up!" he exclaimed. "The boy is a lout, a lunk head, a peptide, a lepton! The densest polysaccharide of the lot!" Brother Josephus had privileged access to the library of the Ancients in the deepest recesses of the mountain, and, when he was in a temper, he used the old vocabulary as a substitute for oaths.

Eventually I conceded and admitted it to my Master.

"This is not about numbers merely, boy," he said. "It is about the Way. The combinations fall by chance – by luck, as you young photons would say! Not by will, not by magic! Remember the saying, because it's aimed at you: *Only a fool trusts to luck.* If you roll the dice once, you can get any combination; twice, you may well get the same combination – or another. But if you roll them ten thousand times, the combinations will appear very nearly in the frequencies you boys worked out. Very nearly; not exactly. That is the way of the world; that is chance. That is the Way. So what have you learned?"

I remained silent, stubbornly imagining I could influence the dice. Suddenly he slapped my face hard. I drew back in surprise, and tears welled in my eyes.

"I do this so you will understand and remember, tadpole! You cannot influence the Way by wishing!"

I rubbed my face, big tears spilling down my cheek.

"Remember that! Remember that, you young biome!" he exclaimed, and he boxed my ears again to encourage my better recall. "Remember that! Remember! The lesson is that there is no trick! You will be a leader, you will bear responsibility, and so you must understand. You cannot shape events by wishing, or by magic, or by any other means. Events," he said, wagging his finger at me, "shape themselves. They will shape you more than you shape them."

"That is the first lesson," he said, dismissing me for the day. "There is another," he added, eyeing me shrewdly.

We never got to the next lesson. But I understand the first. Events shape themselves. You roll the dice and anything may happen. There is no trick.

That is the first lesson. Perhaps the trick is not to care how the dice fall. For all I know, that may be the second lesson. If it is, it is a false lesson—or one I have never mastered. I care about the outcome a great deal. I thought of Odessa and realized that above all else, I cared about the outcome!

The enemy came on boldly, eager to engage us. "Can you make out their standards?" I asked my staff.

"Sixth Manasseh on their left, sir."

A solid, veteran outfit. I was not pleased at the news. "And on the right?"

Major Eli paused, lowered his glasses, and did not look at me.

"And on the right?"

"Second Apostles, sir."

My old legion! My heart thudded like a drumhead. So, I faced Abner Mac Dogol and my old comrades. The knowledge was a wedge driven into my chest blow by blow under a sledgehammer. I shut it out. Closed myself to it. I calmed myself by my breathing exercises. The pain subsided as I regained control of my breathing and thinking. At one time, I would rather have died than raise a hand against Abner Mac Dogol. My former commander had been like a father to me. But war changes things. It changes everything. I had not entered into this war against the Messiahists lightly. If Mac Dogol had stayed with his wretched masters in New Jerusalem out of expediency, in hopes of making a career, those were his choices and he would have to live with them. As I would with mine.

"Major!"

"Yes, sir."

"Send a man out to signal a parley."

"Sir?"

"The Second Apostles is an excellent legion, sir. My old comrades. I intend to give them a chance to surrender." This was nonsense of course. But I wanted desperately to communicate with my old commander. And buy a little time.

Major Hosea looked at me quizzically.

I smiled and said, "It will give us a little time to let the cavalry come up." My staff understood I intended only a ruse, a delay, and were relieved. Everyone understood that

Mac Dogol would never surrender. We made the signal for a parley. Astonishingly, the Messiahists honored the request. The lines stopped and an officer came out from the lines on horseback and made the reciprocal circle. Always the professional, I thought admiringly of my first commander.

I chose Major Jared to be our herald and spoke my instructions in his ear. "Give my compliments to the commander; tell him the reputation of his force is well known. Tell him that regrettably, he must either leave Judah immediately or surrender his command. And tell him. . . . No, that is enough. Go."

"Do I reveal your—or rather *our* – identity?"

"No! He'll know soon enough. Give him my compliments—the commanding officer's compliments. No names."

The parley was over in a moment. The officers cantered back to their respective lines, and soon a great hoot of derision rose up from our enemies.

The cohort and brigade commanders gathered around me to see what the parley was about. I explained my delaying tactic and gave them their final instructions: "This is Abner Mac Dogol we face. The Second Apostles Legion has a sharp edge. Beware of it. The Sixth Manasseh on our right I am not concerned about. But mind the Second Apostles! I know Mac Dogol's tactics, and he will try to hit our rear with the cavalry at the same moment his infantry collides with ours, to shock and demoralize us. He's had a look at us, and he sees that his line overlaps our own. So it's likely he'll try a double envelopment with the cavalry administering the knockout blow in our rear. Gentlemen," I warned, "Mac Dogol will not just try to chase us from the field, he will try to annihilate us. He's bold, very bold. But his boldness will offer us opportunities as well, if we are lucky."

"There's not much margin for luck, sir!" Major Hosea exclaimed. "If the enemy tries a double envelopment, sir, we have only these ragtag refugees holding our flanks. They won't stand."

"True. But it's too late to change the formation now. Look, they are coming on again. Hold your lines together. When they come within the killing zone, engage them fiercely. Act as if your lives depend upon it. Mac Dogol will have to thin his center to envelop us. Something has to give in the center. We'll need a break-through there, if you can give it to us. Keep the flanks intact as long as possible."

We were going shield to shield with the very best soldiers the Messiahists had. And we were strung out very thinly with our flanks open. I would have given anything to be able to select a different time and different ground. And a different foe.

"Mac Dogol will be surprised," I said, "when we don't go to pieces on their first slam into us. They are confident now, but we can take the heart out of them if we show resolution. This is the test we have trained for so long. Remember, we are the Herons." *I'm putting everything on one roll of the dice. They all see it.* "Break out the colors on my command only. Let them despise us till the last moment. It may give them pause to see who we are." I dismissed them smiling at this small ruse. Involuntarily, I looked over my shoulder thinking, *where are our cavalry?*

I was suddenly exhausted and needed assistance to stand. My bodyguard helped me back into the wagon and propped me up on the straw. The enemy advanced noisily, their hoots and jeers rising into a deep-throated cheer. They pounded their weapons on their shields and emitted a deafening roar. The Great Jordan Guards held to our custom and kept silent. I hoped it seemed an ominous silence to our foes. When the enemy was within two hundred yards, I ordered the auxiliaries back and the Asherites forward out of the corn. "Show your colors," I shouted. "Show them who you are!"

The Asherite brigade stepped forward in unison, to the rustle and snap of corn stalks. The lines adjusted, the standards went up, and the color-bearers shook out the cohort ensigns all along our lines. Our blue heron standard snapped in the wind; the twelve banners of the cohorts reared erect. Each had the cohort number and a Transmitter, rigid and menacing, painted white on black cloth, with blood-red pennants below. The sight made my blood pound. Our legion was known among the enemy as the "Messengers," and the Messiahists attributed all sorts of malign powers to us. My men reveled in their reputation as dark angels – a reputation I had labored to avoid, but to no avail. *At a moment like this,* I thought, *it is a good thing to be feared.*

The enemy immediately wavered and their noise subsided. I felt a fierce joy well up inside me to know that we were recognized and dreaded—and that we had by our mere presence silenced their howls of defiance. It appeared to take them a moment to absorb who it was that they were facing.

Then their lines came on again, their officers bellowing and cursing.

So be it!

I saw hundreds of red caps among their host, and a dozen black-robed priests dancing in ecstasy in front of the lines. As they leaped and contorted themselves, I was transfixed by the sheer malice of the spectacle, by their frenzied will for our destruction. Absorbed in the spectacle, I did not hear at first the responding murmur in our ranks, and then I was slow to catch its import. Gradually the sound swelled from a whisper to a growl, and then to a deep-throated roar—a tumultuous storm emanating from a thousand throats but with a single message: "No prisoners!" they cried. "No prisoners! *No prisoners!*"

The archers began their work and filled the air with missiles. I sent the catapults forward and ordered them worked with the greatest possible speed. Our missiles did damage, and their effects increased as the enemy covered the ground between us. I was intent upon the exchange of javelins that occurs just before the lines collide, at thirty paces. That sharp forward edge of collision is the deciding moment in many battles. As I watched, the enemy came into the killing zone and the drill worked to perfection. Mac Dogol's men were shaken by the first exchange; they suffered heavily, and the second exchange was more deadly.

My attention was diverted from the third and final exchange by the sounds of Messiahist cavalry swooping down upon our rear. Mac Dogol's timing was perfect. The horseman came at us in echelon, from the left, like the professionals they were. The first troop ran upon the rows of pikes in the cornfield; their leading rank impaled themselves and tumbled violently in a heap, and the remainder recoiled in surprise. The second troop, wheeling on their right flank, hurled itself straight down the pike at our rear, at the wagon barrier. My bodyguards and Erech's handful of horsemen turned to meet them. As the crews of the war machines shifted frantically about to meet this new threat, I caught a glimpse of the third troop bearing down on our right rear, upon the cohort of Naphtali Guards, who were desperately trying to change front to meet them. *I should have formed the brigades in squares,* I thought. *Too late!*

Our crews turned the catapults and cut a swath through the ranks of enemy horsemen, but Mac Dogol's cavalry pressed onward recklessly, determined to overrun us in a rush. I admired the tenaciousness of our opponents even as they drove home their assault. A cavalry officer lifted his horse over the wagon barrier in front of me, his saber flashing and eyes wide, only to spill forward over his horse's head as it lost its footing. Other horsemen followed undeterred. My bodyguard stood their ground, using their long pikes and evil-looking hooks with great skill. Both sides fought fiercely, resolutely, asking no quarter and giving none. We unhorsed a great many of their cavalry, but more came on and flowed around and through our clumps of resistance. I saw the handful of Erech's cavalry overrun and trampled by their charge, and I had a glimpse of the auxiliaries on our right fleeing into the orchard and being cut down like scythed wheat. The remainder of the pressed civilians were fleeing through our position, saucer-eyed and screaming. They entangled themselves among our fighters in their panic, running blindly, bolting like rabbits in every direction.

The battle dissolved into a perfect chaos of screaming men and the neighing and braying of terrified beasts.

"Hold your positions! Stand your ground!" I shouted, threatening a group of fugitives with my sword. I had a glimpse of dazed and terrified civilians flying past me, and then another I had not seen ran full into my chest, knocking the wind out of me and felling me to the ground. I grasped his tunic and struggled to my feet, only to be struck down by a riderless horse. The force of this glancing blow spun me loose from the earth. I had only a glimpse of the ground rising to meet me.

IX

I awoke staring at the sky, from which a few cold drops of rain were falling. I was numb, leaden in all my limbs. My injured hand felt like a gourd on a stem.

"Look, he stirs. He is alive!"

I was lifted up and carried lumpily across plowed ground, biting my lips against the pain. I had crazy glimpses of activity – men carrying fence rails and others chopping down an orchard, and all around me was a chorus of moans and wails of anguish and bloody figures sprawled on the ground. I could not place myself in this time or space. I felt a great anxiety, a terrible dread; I was haunted by a sense of something left undone or something to come that I could not name. Soldiers placed me on the ground, on a bed of straw and a blanket, and I saw a familiar face bending over me: the surgeon, Captain De Soto. The numbness was leaving me, and was replaced with a red-hot pain that emanated from the left side of my chest and down my arm .

"My lord General! Thank goodness you're alive, sir! We had lost track of you somehow. No wonder, my lord, I must say!"

"I told you he was alive. See, he lives."

"Leave us," the surgeon ordered. He was covered with blood from head to foot and he seemed about to collapse from weariness. "Bless you, sir! If you are alive," he said hoarsely, "then our victory is truly won."

"Victory? Lift me up, let me see!"

"Let me dress the hand first, sir. It's lain in the mud; it's a sight. I can't believe you are alive. Bless you, sir. Bless you!"

I pushed his hands away. The dimness of the light was oppressive, and I was afraid. *Could they not hear me? Could no one obey a simple command?* "I insist on being lifted!" I cried again. "I must see! I must know what happened!"

The surgeon called to some soldiers who pulled me to my feet and supported me. When I could not stand, they made a chair with their arms and held me up. There was a commotion around me and then I recognized Morales of my bodyguard, though he too was covered with blood and his helmet was in tatters. A small crowd gathered and I heard cheers and weeping and saw bloated, distorted faces peering at me. The ground was littered with what seemed to be sacks of wheat.

He's alive! The General lives!

Morales embraced me tearfully, crushing the scar tissue on his forehead against my cheek. The soldiers knelt before me, and the men holding me arranged my body as if I were sitting on a throne. Nevertheless, I leaned heavily against the chest of one, unable to support my head. They turned their heads away from the smell.

"Victory, sir! We have won a great victory!"

The men supporting me turned slowly in a circle, and I beheld a field of many acres strewn with corpses—more corpses than I had ever seen in my life. In a moment, I was able to orient myself by the heaps of slain. I recognized our line of battle, where it had stood to our front—a line now marked with rows of our own dead, mingled with the enemy. Mounds of enemy dead lay in their front. And beyond them, more dead, irregular clumps of dead, stretching away from our lines. There had been a pursuit.

In the orchard, flocks of crows were already gathering where the white wool garments of our Judean conscripts lay in heaps among the trees. And in our rear, also littered with dead men and dead horses and splintered wagons, the two sides lay mingled together in great confusion. The wagons and ballistas were smashed and overturned, the cornfield was beaten to the ground, and mangled bodies and dead horses lay everywhere. The ground itself was churned and rutted. Here and there sergeants went about delivering mercy blows to the wounded, and a flock of civilians was stripping and looting the dead. A heap of Messiahist red caps had been collected by the road. The field looked as though a mutual catastrophe had overwhelmed both armies. "Will someone tell me what happened?"

By bits and pieces I got an account from the survivors – I cannot call them victors. "You did it, sir! Just as at the Gate of Asher. Two battles and two enemy legions annihilated on the field in each. No one would have believed it possible!"

"Colonel Vashon brought the cavalry up just at the right time. If he had come a moment later, we would have been overwhelmed."

"Your position was overrun just before Colonel Vashon arrived," Major Jared added. "I expect you got trampled in the confusion. Everyone thought you were dead, sir. Your bodyguard fought like demons, sir. They did everything they could to drive off the Messiahists and rescue you. Not many of them left, sir."

When they showed me Erech Vashon, I did not recognize him. His body was crushed, and he had lain face down in the mud. He was much trampled, as if the fighting had passed back and forth over him several times. I had not felt such sorrow since – I was confused, trying to remember: *was it Justin's death? My parting from Vitoria? Finding my mother on the road to Selah*? The light was failing; I heard the trumpets recall our pursuing forces. I was still searching for answers in the gathering gloom when Colonel Vashon returned from the pursuit, but I did not spare myself the task of giving him the news about his son.

When I was aware again, it was dark. As I lay on a pallet, wracked with pain, alternately shivering and sweating, a troop of horsemen galloped into camp, and its officer threw down a bundle before me. "Victory, my lord!" the officer exclaimed, swinging from the saddle. In the firelight, his horse's eyes bulged and blood flecked its nostrils; it was blowing blood with each breath. The officer's face seemed familiar but I could not place him.

I had not the strength to rise from my pallet, but some young men gathered up the bundle and unwrapped it. Burgos took it up and dangled it in front of me, holding it by its long hair. "Victory!" Burgos announced, shaking the trophy in my face.

I recognized the head; it was my friend, Abner Mac Dogol. His eyes were open and not quite expressionless. The mouth was open, too, but whether in outrage or surprise I could not tell. His bald head shone in the firelight; his hair was long on the sides and back. *So, you wear your hair in the noble fashion,* I thought.

"The last resistance formed around this man, my lord General," the officer reported proudly. "We crushed them!" He seemed exhausted himself, so that he could barely describe the triumph. "A few fled – made an escape. If we had had light enough – "

"Enough!" I said, gazing at the man who had been my first commander and my friend. "All that flesh and blood are capable of you and your men have performed. Israel," I said, swallowing the word, "will be grateful."

I had Mac Dogol's head placed on the ground before me, close by my litter. The bare dome of the skull was cold to the touch, the hair matted and wet. I wanted to ask about the manner of his death—if he had had a good death, a gesture worthy of his life. But such a question would be unseemly with the suffering of my own men around me. Whether heroic or craven, painful or quick, Mac Dogol had had whatever death he would have. It was over. I wiped some clay from his face. His brow was furrowed with a faint vestige of pain or bafflement; his eyes were glazing even as I watched. That hive of hope and subtle conceptions and desire was inert as clay.

Burgos nudged me; the officer was waiting. "Well done," I forced myself to say. "See to your men. Get some rest."

It occurred to me that I had been fortunate to have many fathers, including this man, Abner Mac Dogol. Josephus and Ebenezer had been fathers to me too, patient and caring beyond all expectation. And Elkiah Vashon—who ever had a better father than Elkiah Vashon? But my real father was Emanuel—a man I scarcely knew. Even so, I was confident that my father had been a good man; everyone praised him as a paragon of the old Israel. And whatever he had felt about me, he had loved my mother. He had, I felt certain, spilled me into my mother's womb with passion and conviction. Thus, in spite of irregularities, I came of good stock – a scion of the old Israel! I laughed out loud, unembarrassed by the irony. *Israel!* At least I was not the son of Tephlin Glanz; I felt the satisfaction of that!

I motioned to Burgos and asked him to place my friend's head among the heaps of slain, to be interred with them in a mass grave or cremated, as circumstances permitted. Mac Dogol would want to lie with his comrades. *A man should leave no trace, not even a footprint, except in the hearts of his friends.*

The men close by cheered when they saw Burgos pick up the head of our enemy. "Viva Israel!" they cheered. "Long live Israel! The Messengers are invincible! The Sword of Israel is victory!"

"Israel?" I thought. "Israel does not exist!"

"What does he say?" A soldier explained behind his hand that I was delirious.

"If only he could appreciate what he has done!"

Perhaps I am delirious. How can Israel not exist, when so many have just spilled their life's blood for it?

St. Supplicee does not exist—or rather was a woman named Cecilia, and her rules were a guide for survival during the Dissolution of the Ancients' world. My people had turned her rules into a way of life, mistaking them for the law of the universe. Thereafter, we confused the Law with the path to wisdom and harmony and then made the Law into a code of holiness itself. Holiness, however, proved elusive. It fled from us, however we disciplined ourselves. We could never quite attain it, though we pursued it diligently, nor summon it, though we meditated earnestly. Holiness! We could not coerce its presence even when we constrained our neighbors as ourselves. We cupped our hands together, hoping to drink, but the water trickled through our fingers.

Our tradition, I was compelled to admit, was compounded half of error and the rest of self-deception. We had constructed our whole world by distorting an actual body of teaching. Real wisdom, perhaps, but for a moment of time. But now the conditions of existence have changed. Cecilia Pleece's rules no longer serve as a guide, but are a burden to my people.

And the sum total of our wisdom—is it not the absence of holiness in our midst? Thus, I who have lived by the code and fought to preserve it, have just seen my friend's head tossed in front of me like a sack of oats. And I admit it was my purpose to have it so.

The flames of our campfire flared and snapped and ebbed again. It was our lonely, smoldering hearts that reared up "Israel" like a fire on the horizon, our voices expressing what we desired, not what is. Our desires fed the flames, and Israel rose up like a fire, like a column of smoke. *"The world is a flame fed by desire,"* our Teacher says. But our "Teacher" was a part of the flame itself. Thus, the Law does not exist – and I am its champion. My world is smoke; Israel is burning.

In a little while Burgos roused me. "Colonel Vashon returns," he said.

"We see only what we wish to see," I muttered. Then my friend and kinsman stepped into the firelight. His body was bent and haggard. He was followed by a litter on which his son's body lay. My uncle knelt on the ground by my pallet, taking my good hand in his and staring at me wordlessly. Gazing into his eyes, I found I could neither speak nor breathe, but I managed one clear, unequivocal thought: *This is not what I wish to see!*

After a time he rose and said hoarsely, in a half-whisper: "Hitch a team to one of the forage wagons. We must get the commander to Hebron tonight."

X

In the wagon on my pallet of straw, I felt every cobble, every frozen rut under the wheels. Mercifully, I could no longer feel my hand. I tried to think, to compose my thoughts, and to put my grief behind me before it overwhelmed me. When the sleet abated and stopped, I missed the sting of icy particles in my face. We met people on the road, men and families fleeing from Hebron, and they gave confused stories of fighting inside the city.

"It must be an evil event that drives these poor wretches out into such a night," Colonel Vashon said. "What can it mean?" An orange glow of flames rose ahead where the city lay.

After a while we encountered a party with torches and a wagon, and they gave a better account of the fighting. The Palace of Ingots was in flames, they said. The House of Assembly and the central plaza were occupied by troops who had returned with Hezekiah. Looting had broken out. The soldiers were out of control, but our informants had no idea who was fighting whom, or why.

"A coup is in progress," Colonel Vashon said. "The army must have risen against Glanz and Ben Gurion and the Council. This is a piece of luck. If we just hold on, everything will work out. Every sacrifice will—will have been for a reason. Nephew," he said, shaking me, "we are in luck!"

I could not raise my head to answer him.

I was combing my pony's mane while Lukash curried his back. His mane was the color of cream and very coarse, and it combed out in long, straight streamers, like a waterfall. Bandero looked at me with his amber eyes and let me rub his nose. His face was long and bony, but his muzzle was like velvet. Suddenly a door banged in the great house, and I turned to see my mother running across the courtyard. The way she carried herself told me she was upset. I thought she was going to the coop where she kept her prized bantams, but she ran instead to the wall, to a place where it had crumbled and fallen. As we watched, she hiked up her robes in one hand and climbed over the fallen stones to the wall. Her legs were thin and girlish, like my own. Then, to my astonishment, she leaned one hand down on the wall and vaulted over, robes and all. I turned to Lukash, who put his arm on my shoulder and said, "Why don't we get Bandero a treat?" We led my pony to the storehouse and Lukash gave him a carrot. When he finished, I let him eat a handful of oats out of my hand. His lips tickled my palm.

Odessa's eyes met mine in the darkness; when I closed my eyes, I could feel her breath. She cupped her breasts in both hands and held them like an offering to me. She brushed first one and then another against my lips, and then back again. Her nipples were hard and wet. I took her breasts greedily in my mouth and reached to touch her intimate parts, and I felt their delicate flutter and contractions. "Oh, Zaiyah," she breathed in my ear, "love me!" I raised my head and saw her eyes gleaming in the half-light. We kissed, devouring each other, and she let her long, sweet-scented hair cascade over us. Then she moved onto me with swift, sweet precision. "Odessa," I cried out.

Soldiers came running. I was in a crowded courtyard with torches leaping in the fierce gusts of wind. Colonel Vashon was speaking with the soldiers, but the wind blew their voices to shreds. I felt the tread of infantry on the road. Above the clatter of hooves, Colonel Vashon shouted, "It's a coup all right. No point entering the city till things sort themselves out. Gill will find out for us. In the meantime, we'll get Josiah out of this weather. Fetch the surgeon. Maybe there is time."

Amid torches and shouting, soldiers carried me on a litter into a house and then upstairs. They were clumsy and loud and banged me against the stairwell. I made no sound. Burgos placed a candle by the bed and leaned close. "We'll make a fire, my lord, if we have to break the furniture. Can you hang on?"

My teeth were chattering, but I could still hold my tongue. *I heard my grandfather saying, "Learn the Law and obey it."* My mother's voice is nearby, singing a lullaby whose words I cannot quite make out.

From my bed I hear hooves clatter on the cobblestones, voices raised in argument; a door slammed. It was Elkiah's voice downstairs: "Gill! Gill, what is it?"

"Tell your men to stand down, Colonel."

"What on earth! Do you know who –?"

"Yes, is he upstairs?"

"You disturb us at such a time?"

"My God, is this—Erech? It is Erech. Forgive me, they look so much alike. My condolences, Colonel! My deepest condolences! My dear Elkiah I scarcely comprehend how you can bear such losses. Both your son and your nephew in one dark day."

"It is two sons I lose today."

"Ah, no heavier loss! Please, Colonel, you must sit down. My news and my mission here will be a heavy blow, and you must attend carefully to what I say."

"After what I have endured today you can hardly add to my burdens."

"I think your pain, sir, has only begun. General Hezekiah has struck a bargain."

"With the Messiahists? Impossible!"

"Not impossible. You are aware of what he did to the Council of Apostles, to Ben Gurion and their whole circle?"

"Dead? Tephlin Glanz too?"

"All of them? To no one's regret!"

"All – except perhaps for Glanz. He may have perished in the flames; no one knows for certain. But his government is gone."

"That is heartening news; it will strengthen the resistance."

"No, sadly! Hezekiah is gaining space to negotiate. To surrender."

"That cannot be!"

"Then we must stop him! This war is not lost! We've just won a victory! Josiah says if we can resist another day—just hold out until the millennium comes – we will expose their lies and their cause will collapse."

"All your efforts at Chebar are meaningless, Burgos. Meaningless! Hezekiah is through with the war. He is demoralized and the army is demoralized as well."

"I can't believe it."

"Believe it. Hebron will be offered up tomorrow. It only remains to be worked out on what terms."

"This is preposterous! The world is not ending! The day after tomorrow when things go on as before –"

"The world is ending. For the Israel we have known, it is over."

"Hezekiah has lost heart, and so all our effort, all our sacrifices, and what we believed in, come to nothing? Is that it?"

"And you – you come here now hoping to profit from it – to cooperate with the traitors?"

"Yes, Burgos, and to allow many others to profit from it – at least to the extent of surviving. Listen to me, you must think through the circumstances we are in, that Josiah is in. General Hezekiah is determined to hand over the city."

"All that strength in hand and he means to surrender?"

"Yes. And that quickly, to end the bloodshed—and to save himself, no doubt."

"What has this to do with us? The Messengers do not surrender."

"Burgos, you must understand what Hezekiah needs to salvage something out of this disaster. I believe, as you do, that the world will not end tomorrow or next week, and eventually the Primate will have to explain why things go on and the Judgment has not come. He will delay and make excuses, but eventually the fanaticism that supports him will wither. In time, things will meliorate. He may even be held to an accounting. That's why I have hope, why I am trying, as I imagine Hezekiah is, to salvage something. To buy time. To save lives."

"He wants Master Josiah, Colonel! Hezekiah wants –"

"No, Burgos! It is not so cruel if you think about it."

"I will never hand over my nephew a prisoner to –"

"I would not ask it of you. How is he?"

"He is upstairs, more dead than alive. His wound has festered; the poison has moved up his arm. He slips in and out of consciousness. I doubt if he can live the night. We had hoped that a surgeon – that the operation could be performed here tonight."

"You see. I had heard his situation is hopeless – that he cannot live even if the arm is removed. Burgos, you've seen wounds; what do you say?"

"The Master is not like other men! He survived the mountain fever, and today, by St. Supplicee, he broke the Second Apostles like a rotten stick!"

"Ah, but he *is* like other men! He told me that himself. And you, Colonel, what do you say? Could he survive the amputation?"

"Perhaps. I think he has a chance. He is – but no, the poison has reached to his armpit and past; it reaches towards his heart. There is no amputation can save him now. He might linger a while, days or hours. Josiah waited too long. He sacrificed himself."

"Enough. We agree Josiah cannot survive. Burgos, do you not see that? Your service is done. You cannot save him, though you lay down your life a thousand times."

"I would and gladly! I –"

"Enough, Burgos! We know your loyalty. That is not in question. What is in question is what happens to you and Colonel Vashon and to the legion."

"The Messengers will die resisting!"

"I'm thinking of Asher and Dan and Naphtali. Josiah's family. My family. Gentlemen, the object of war is to survive."

"I am exhausted, Gill. You must be plain."

"General Hezekiah does not need Josiah alive as a bargaining chip."

"What do you mean?"

"What's this? What's in the bottle?"

"It's a narcotic, very powerful. In small doses, it gives a powerful sense of euphoria, even joy. But too much is fatal. One drifts off. Painlessly."

"If you put a foot on the stair, Gill, you are a dead man!"

"Burgos, don't let your heart speak in this; use your head! It will be the three of us going upstairs together, or none of us. Colonel, hear me out. Here's what you must do. The Messengers must be gathered and marched to the river. You must leave your dead son and attend to it. Don't say never; that is foolishness. You must get the men away. Perhaps you can gather ships enough to take them to Naphtali. If you can, then at some point, Dan and Asher and Naphtali may be able to come to terms with the Messiahists. I mean terms better than surrender. You can manage it if anyone can. And through you, some portion of the old Israel will live on. But you must save yourself in order to save others."

"And you? What will you –?"

You have been my friend   I always expected this.

"If I come back to Hezekiah before dawn with Josiah's body to show the Primate and have in hand signed documents showing that the three northern tribes, whose authority Josiah bears, have submitted to the Primate's authority, I can buy some time. It will not mean peace but an interval, a breathing space. We can forge his signature if necessary. It would be better if we did, in fact, so you can repudiate the submission later on."

Send Odessa back to her people. Hide her as far north as she can go.

"Gill, I will die before I harm the master. You will die if you attempt it."

"Burgos, let it rest! This is painful for all of us. Elkiah, you said he is conscious sometimes."

Burgos heed my mother. Be patient with her.

"It would be better if we put it to him plainly and let him choose himself what must be done."

I will take the poison and take it gladly.

This is no one's will. It is necessity.

I will sign nothing.

immense fields of snow stretch away to the holy mountain
the holy mountain Rainier glows like a candle
glows in the cold like a clear voice singing
Emanuel
Emanuel shall come to thee
O mother come to me   O Israel

clouds of breath rise from the manger
snow slants through the lantern's glow
mother says the birth is hard because
the calf is too large
the lantern pulls my arm like a stone aching to fall
if I hold it all   as still as breath
she will come to me at last

rejoice   rejoice O Israel regoice
Emanuel
shall come   to thee   O Israel

darkness brushes my face in the snow
mother of darkness hear my cry
mother
I cannot catch
my breath

Epilogue

from the *Later Chronicles of Israel, 1029-III*

The circumstances of the death of Josiah of Asher were never established with certainty. On the last day of the millennium year of the Third Tribulation, a body identified as the famous rebel was delivered to the victorious host at the surrender of Hebron. In the Edict of Triumph issued on that day, Polymer XII accepted the surrender of Judah, declaring that all Israel had submitted to God's rule. The nation was thus prepared for the Third and Final Advent of its Savior. Sacrifices and prayers and all the worship of Israel went up like a sweet savor to Almighty God.

"Behold the heart of this bloody man!" the Primate declared to the people. "He is the enemy of God!" And the people approved his words, and partook of the sacrifice, which was the first burnt offering of the new era, of God With Us On Earth.

But as is now known, parts of Benjamin and the north of Israel had not truly bent their necks to the rule of God, but remained unreconciled, their hearts uncircumcised. That this perfidious and stubborn rebellion was the legacy of Josiah of Asher is nowhere doubted.

Though many swore that the body was indeed his, this apostate called by some the Sword of Israel, it was later claimed that it belonged to a cousin and near twin in appearance. Indeed, it was put forth by the Resisters that the Sword of Israel had substituted the corpse with one arm amputated, as a ruse to confound his enemies – the missing arm signifying that the Sword could never be wholly overcome. Some among his faction have also believed that the missing arm meant that this Servant of the Anti-Christ was not dead, nor could he be slain. Others hold that this Josiah died of his wounds, unreconciled to the Coming, and that his body was interred secretly on the field of Chebar.

Resisters claim, however, that he survived, escaping along with the infamous Messengers Legion up the Jordan. There, in Naphtali and further Lebanon, he organized opposition to God's cause, eventually disappearing into the far north where he was hidden among his wife's people. And there, it is avowed by superstitious partisans of his cause, he waits in secret still, ready to come forth at the moment of ripest opportunity.

Within a year of the Millennium Victory, Polymer XII died, though whether of the plague of fever that followed hard upon the war, or by treachery, remains unknown. Bishop Bulavar succeeded to the Primateship as Polymer XIII, but was shortly after assassinated and proved the last of the line of Primates in New Jerusalem. Thus, the millennium came and went, and Israel awaits its Savior still. The northern parts of Israel remain to this day unreconciled and apostate.

fragment of The Book of Josiah *[date uncertain]:*

"Before I formed you in the womb I knew you, and before you were born I consecrated you. I appointed you a prophet to the nation. I appointed you over the nation, to pluck up and to pull down, to destroy and to overthrow, to build and to plant." Thus did Josiah, son of Asher, all that was commanded him, and he was zealous in the Law all his days and did not depart a hair either to the right or to the left; so that the Sword of Israel was a light to his people and a terror to his enemies. In his mouth the Law was a blade, and his teachings like a burning star.

"For the time had not come," says the Lord; "My people were not ready. They wandered in darkness, drunk with their own ways. And so I sent my servant Josiah to be a light unto them, and a scourge, to prepare them for the Judgment. And he led them unto the Law again, like a flock to a clear spring, and like a doe into a clearing. And the people hearkened unto him, and followed him."

"And as for my servant Josiah, he was one of the sorrowful ones who eat their bread in sadness. He was like a suckling child who turns away from the breast, and his sorrow was Israel's strength. And out of his strength shall ever come forth sweetness, for he took upon himself the sorrows of the land, and embraced them, and he took up his burden like a man lifts up a bride over the threshold, and he carried it all his days.

And so for his sake, in the Day that comes, when they shall end their warfare, and they shall no longer hurt or destroy in all my holy mountain, then" says the Lord, "they shall remember my servant Josiah. For I am about to create a new heaven and a new earth. The former things shall not be remembered nor come to mind. Therefore be glad and rejoice forever in what I am creating, for I am about to create Jerusalem as a joy and its people as a delight. But my day was not yet come in the days of Josiah of Asher."

And there has not arisen an Apostle, nor a lawgiver, nor a prophet in Israel like Josiah of Asher, with all his power and all his great and terrible deeds, which he wrought to purify the people, and to turn them from their errors.

Blessed above sons be Asher;
let him be the favorite of his brothers,
and let him dip his foot in oil.
Your bars shall be iron and bronze;
and as your days, so shall your strength be.

About the Author

Richard Law lives in Pullman, Washington and teaches at Washington State University. Richard is married and has four grown children. His interests include American literature and culture, world history, and the history of religion. He can be reached at richardlaw43@hotmail.com

Also available from Fine Tooth Press

Fiction

Limboland by J.E. Deegan
Trickster Tales by JP Briggs
Trespass by Craig Wolf
Infinite Wonderlands by Oscar De Los Santos and David G. Mead
Border Cantos by Chuck Etheridge
Street Angel by Martha Marinara
Hardboiled Egg by Oscar De Los Santos
To Beat a Dead Horse by Bill Campbell
White River by Will Bless
The Shadow People by Esther Schrader
Pressure Points by Craig Wolf

Non-Fiction

Looking for a Face Like Mine by William H. Foster III
Breakout by Ronnie Wright
The New Goddess: Transgendered Women in the Twenty-First Century edited by Gypsey Teague
Spirits of Texas and New England by Oscar De Los Santos
Scenes from an Ordinary Life by Lou Orfanella
Reel Rebels edited by Oscar De Los Santos
When Genres Collide: Selected Essays from the 2006 Science Fiction Research Association Annual Conference, edited by Oscar De Los Santos and Thomas J. Morrissey

Poetry

Allurements and Lamentations by Lou Orfanella
The Last Miles by J.D. Scrimgeour
Composite Sketches by Lou Orfanella
Balloons Over Stockholm by James R. Scrimgeour
typical girl by Donna Kuhn

For more information about these and other titles, as well as author bios and interviews and more, visit us on the web at:

http://www.finetoothpress.com

Printed in the United States
209187BV00006B/136-144/P

9 780979 477072